CHILDREN OF THE GHETTO

THE VICTORIAN LIBRARY

CHILDREN OF THE GHETTO

A Study of a Peculiar People

ISRAEL ZANGWILL

WITH AN INTRODUCTION BY
V. D. LIPMAN

LEICESTER UNIVERSITY PRESS

1977

First published in 1892
One-volume edition published in 1893
Victorian Library edition (reprinting 1893 text)
published in 1977 by
Leicester University Press

Distributed in North America by
Humanities Press Inc., New Jersey

Introduction copyright © Leicester University Press 1977

Printed in Great Britain by
Unwin Brothers Limited, The Gresham Press
Old Woking, Surrey

ISBN 0 7185 5028 5

THE VICTORIAN LIBRARY

There is a growing demand for the classics of Victorian literature in many fields, in political and social history, architecture, topography, religion, education, and science. Hitherto this demand has been met, in the main, from the second-hand market. But the prices of second-hand books are rising sharply, and the supply of them is very uncertain. It is the object of this series, THE VICTORIAN LIBRARY, to make some of these classics available again at a reasonable cost. Since most of the volumes in it are reprinted photographically from the first edition, or another chosen because it has some special value, an accurate text is ensured. Each work carries a substantial introduction, written specially for this series by a well-known authority on the author or his subject, and a bibliographical note on the text.

The volumes necessarily vary in size. In planning the newly-set pages the designer, Arthur Lockwood, has maintained a consistent style for the principal features. The uniform design of binding and jackets provides for ready recognition of the various books in the series when shelved under different subject classifications.

Recommendations of titles for THE VICTORIAN LIBRARY and of scholars to contribute the introductions is made by a joint committee of the Board of the University Press and the Victorian Studies Centre of the University of Leicester.

INTRODUCTION

In her novel *Robert Elsmere* Mrs Humphry Ward explained that she 'wanted to show how a man of sensitive character, born for religion, comes to throw off the orthodoxies of his day and go out into the wilderness where spiritual life begins again.' Here was the germ of *Children of the Ghetto*, for it was the success of her book which led the American Jewish judge and scholar, Mayer Sulzberger (1843–1923), to think of commissioning an analogous novel in a Jewish setting – 'a Jewish Robert Elsmere' – for the Jewish Publication Society of America, which he had recently helped to found. He approached the Anglo-Jewish historian and journalist, Lucien Wolf (1857–1930), then foreign editor of the *Daily Graphic*, and asked him either to do it himself or find someone to do it. Wolf replied that there was only one man in England capable of the work, and that was Israel Zangwill.[1] Zangwill was reluctant to accept the commission: he was beginning to make his name as an English humorous writer. But, as he wrote to Sulzberger, 'I certainly intend, if I am spared, to write a Jewish novel: there is one inside me and it must come out some day. . . only I could not undertake for any amount of dollars to write a novel which would appeal exclusively to a section. . . Behind all the Jewish details there must be the human interest which will raise it into that cosmopolitan thing, a work of art.'[2] In this one can see the conflict, which continued throughout Zangwill's life,

The East End of London *c.* 1900, showing Jewish residents in proportion to the total population (adapted from Russell and Lewis *The Jew in London,* and reproduced from Lipman *Social History of the Jews in England 1850-1950*)

between his capacity to depict Jewish themes and his aspiration to be a major figure in the wider scene of English literature.

How far Israel Zangwill succeeded in the aim he set himself in *Children of the Ghetto*[3] each reader must judge for himself. The evidence on which to base a judgment is in the text of the novel itself. The object of this introduction is to help the reader to form this judgment by explaining why the Jewish situation in England around 1890 called for a novel that would have a wide appeal, and why Zangwill was the man to write it. Much of the novel is autobiographical; much of it has the character both of a documentary and a *roman à clef*, so it is necessary to outline the background of the London Jewish community of the time. This is particularly important because the novel is an authentic historical source for the social life of London Jewry in the generation in which it was written. Zangwill knew the milieu, because he was brought up in it; yet he had emerged from it sufficiently to see it in perspective. Finally, it is possible to say something of what happened to Zangwill, and his subject, after the novel appeared in 1892.

The medieval Jewish community of England had been expelled in 1290. From then until 1656, when open re-settlement was permitted by Cromwell, there had existed only a few individuals or groups of secret Jews or Marranos dissimulating their Jewish observances. From 1656 onwards the community grew by immigration. First came Jews of families originating in Spain and Portugal, though the lands from which they directly came might be Holland, the West Indies, the Canary Islands, Italy, North Africa or the Levant. These were the Sephardim. Soon too came the Ashkenazi Jews who by the early eighteenth century outnumbered the Sephardim, and progressively formed an even greater majority. They too came from Holland but also from Central Europe and, from the middle of the nineteenth century, from Eastern Europe (Russia, Prussian Poland, Russian Poland and Austrian Galicia). The differences between Ashkenazim and Sephardim were not doctrinal; they began as variations of religious ritual and pronunciation of Hebrew, and become social and even economic, the Sephardim being generally more assimilated to their surroundings and often wealthier. By 1880 there were over 60,000 Jews in England, over 40,000 in London alone. They were an increasingly middle-class community: financiers, merchants and shopkeepers, with a few professional men. They had largely adopted the social habits of their environment while conservatively holding to their traditional religious practices. Comparatively recently, they had gained full political emancipation – the right to sit in Parliament and to serve on local councils – as well as to graduate from Oxford and Cambridge, and to practise the professions.

In 1881, the assassination of the Czar Alexander II led to a series of pogroms and subsequent governmental decrees restricting the lives, livelihood and residence of the Russian Jews. The result was a massive emigration of between one and two millions to the countries of the West in the years up to 1914. Most of these people went to the United States and many others who came to Britain did so only on their way to America. Nevertheless, even in the first decade from 1881 to 1891, which is the background to *Children of the Ghetto*, some 30,000 Russo-Jewish aliens settled in Britain.[4] This number of highly noticeable immigrants was quite enough to make the 'Aliens Question' an issue in British politics.

The aliens concentrated geographically in a few areas: in East London in an area which never exceeded about two square miles (from the City to the beginning of the Mile End Road, and from Bethnal Green to Cable Street); and also in comparable areas in the inner rings of Manchester, Leeds, Liverpool and Glasgow. They were also concentrated in a narrow range of trades: tailoring, boot and shoe manufacture, and, later, and to a much smaller degree, cabinet-making. In 1901, the Census was to show 40 per cent of the gainfully employed male Russo-Poles in London to be in the tailoring trade.

This topographical and economic concentration gave rise to a number of charges against the alien immigrants. First, they were poor but industrious. They would work long hours for low wages; and therefore they caused unemployment among British workers and depressed wage levels. Second, because they worked for small masters, mainly immigrants themselves, in insanitary conditions, they were responsible for the introduction of 'sweating'. Third, they caused pressure on the limited amount of housing, which resulted in high rents and demands for 'key money' (as premiums for leases were generally known). Fourth, the immigrants were usually unhealthy or insanitary in their habits, and criminals came in with them. Fifth, they were alien in speech, manners, appearance and faith; they would undermine the Englishness of England, and destroy the peace of the English Sunday.

Select Committees of the House of Lords in 1888 and of the House of Commons in 1889 – the first of a number of such investigations – generally found against the attribution of these evils to the immigrants, although they recognized the existence of the evils themselves. The Committees found no case for restriction of immigration though such restriction was already a popular cause, especially among working-class voters. Joseph Chamberlain made the restriction of pauper immigration a plank in his social policy. Right-wing Conservatives and trade unionists, such as Ben Tillett, joined in 1891 to found an Association for Preventing the Immigration of Destitute Aliens. At their inaugural meeting, Sydney Buxton, then Liberal M.P. for Poplar (and later President of the Board of Trade) said 'we are all agreed that England ought to be preserved for Englishmen'.[5] It should be added that then, as later, the supporters of restriction insisted that they were only opposed to aliens and 'pauper aliens' at that, and not to the English Jews, whose own interests would be protected by restrictions on immigration. The dimensions to which the 'Aliens Question' subsequently grew are well-known. It is clear that even in 1891 a young Anglo-Jewish writer commissioned to write about the London ghetto would wish to demonstrate to the non-Jewish world the problems and virtues of the immigrants, their relationship to the previously established Jews of London, and their aspirations to become accepted into English society.

While Israel Zangwill presented the world of the recent Jewish immigrant in London to the English reading public, the first half of his novel – which on internal evidence must relate to just before 1880 – describes an East London Jewry in which there was only a minority of Russo-Polish immigrants, because the pogroms had not yet caused mass emigration from Russia. And he was himself the child of earlier immigrants. His father, Moses Zangwill, was born in 1836 in Ravinisek near Preili, north of Dvinsk (Dunaburg or Daugavpils) which in the nineteenth century was part of the Russian Governorate of Vitebsk, but was included in the Latvian Republic in 1918. Moses Zangwill arrived in England in 1848, married Ellen Hannah Marks, an immigrant from Poland, and settled in Plymouth. Israel, their second son, was born in 1864 during a visit by his parents to London. They later moved to Bristol. There was an older sister, Leah, and the other children were Mark, Louis and Dinah. Moses Zangwill was a pious, scholarly, unworldly character and has been identified with Moses Ansell in

Children of the Ghetto. Israel Zangwill's biographer, Joseph Leftwich, states that Israel's widow wrote to him: 'my husband told me that his father never earned more than a pound a week', and this at a period when Charles Booth put the dividing line between 'poor' and 'very poor' in London at 18–21 shillings per week (the 'poor' were those earning less than 30 shillings per week).

If Moses Zangwill was the prototype of Moses Ansell, Ellen Zangwill was a vigorous character, some of whose traits have been recognized in Malka in *Children of the Ghetto*. Malka's Zachariah Square also had its origins in Israel Zangwill's life, because it was Ebenezer Square, off Stoney Lane, where he was born, hard by the Jews' Free School. The site was later occupied by artisans' dwellings, erected in 1884. It is significant that when Esther Ansell in the novel comes back ten years later, in about 1890, she found the street 'strangely broadened. Instead of the picturesque houses rose an appalling series of artisans' dwellings, monotonous brick fronts, whose dead, dull prose, weighed upon the spirits.' When the Zangwill family left Bristol, they settled in Princes Street (later called Princelet Street).[6]

Israel Zangwill was a pupil at the Jews' Free School, which he describes in *Children of the Ghetto*, and became a pupil-teacher and later a teacher there. He took the degree of B.A. at London University, but he gave up teaching because he wrote anonymously a Jewish story of which the school authorities disapproved. Given the choice of submitting future writing to censorship or resigning, he resigned and became a journalist and author. He began with humorous stories such as *The Premier and the Painter* (1888, jointly with Louis Cowen) about an exchange of identity. He continued in this *genre* with *The Bachelors' Club* (1891) and *The Old Maids' Club* (1892), collections of humorous stories; and a mystery story, *The Big Bow Mystery* (1891).

In the Jewish field, he contributed to the *Jewish Standard* (which appears in *Children of the Ghetto* as the 'Flag of Judah'), edited by Harry S. Lewis (Raphael Leon), and published two serious short stories, later reprinted in *Ghetto Tragedies*: 'Satan Mekatrig' and 'The Diary of a Meshumad' (Jewish convert to Christianity).

In the 1880s Zangwill was a member of a group of Jewish intellectuals and professional men known as the 'Wanderers' or 'Wandering Jews', both because they met for discussion in one another's houses and because in discussion they tended to wander from the subject. Grouped around the Rumanian-born rabbinical sage, Solomon Schechter (1850–1915), who lived in London until he moved to Cambridge as Reader in Rabbinics in 1890, they included, besides Zangwill, Joseph Jacobs, the Australian-born journalist, folklorist and historian, who subsequently edited the *Jewish Encyclopaedia*; Lucien Wolf; Asher Myers, editor of the *Jewish Chronicle*; Israel Abrahams, then tutor at Jews' College, the Jewish seminary; Oswald John Simon, an amateur theologian; Herbert Bentwich, lawyer; Solomon J. Solomon, painter and later Royal Academician; and Arthur Davis, civil engineer, Hebraist and later editor of the Jewish festival prayer book. They all lived in Kilburn or St John's Wood, Zangwill himself in Cambridge Gardens, Kilburn.[7] His membership of the group formed a natural basis for Zangwill's article in the *Jewish Quarterly Review* in 1889 on 'English Judaism: A Criticism and Classification' that established him as a commentator on Jewish problems. Writing this article, like *Children of the Ghetto*, was characteristic of the dualism in Zangwill's whole life. He was already making his way as an English author; he was the friend of young authors like Jerome K. Jerome, Eden Philpotts, Barry Pain and Robert Barr[8]; he had given up the religious practices in which he had been brought up.[9] Yet he could not resist joining in a debate on Jewish problems, and in this he resembled characters in *Children of the Ghetto*, notably the adult Esther Ansell.

The article on English Judaism, commenting on previous articles by the historian Heinrich Graetz and Zangwill's mentor Solomon Schechter, is important not only because it brought Zangwill the commission for *Children of the Ghetto* but because it sets out his philosophy of Judaism which underlies the book. Zangwill insists that Judaism is a revealed religion and that revelation is embodied in the Bible, or at least the Pentateuch. The 'natural Judaism', which the Reform movement in nineteenth-century Judaism advanced, was, in his view, a form of natural religion with nothing essentially Jewish about it. Nevertheless, he somewhat grudgingly admits that 'although logically a Judaism which does not accept the Biblical account of the revelation on Sinai may seem literally *toto coelo* from traditional Judaism, yet, in so far as it is conceived as a development from the old Judaism, [it] has an hereditary right to the title.'[10] The article is pointedly written and shows a fine taste for identifying nonsense. One can understand how it must have appealed to Justice Sulzberger as being the work of a young writer, brought up in a traditional home yet able to find his way among the sophistications of contemporary controversy. Basically, Zangwill is critical of the new Jewish theologians, and while he is condescending towards the spirit of Jewish nationalism, in 1889 emerging in modern form (which he called 'old lang syne raised to a religion'), he shows an understanding sympathy for the age-long faith of the simple pious Jews: the way of life of his father, in which he was brought up. He can no longer follow its observances; but to him it is the real Judaism. It was natural therefore for him to turn with sympathy to depicting the Jewish society in the East End of London in which this way of life was to be found, and to explain and defend it not only to the non-Jewish world but also to the more assimilated English Jews. When he returned to East London to write his novel, he found the *milieu* more crowded, more Jewish, less English, even than that in which he was brought up. For Zangwill grew up, and the first half of his novel should logically be set, in East London before the mass immigration from Eastern Europe which began in 1881.

There is an ambiguity in the East London which is being described in Book I between the pre-1881 community of Zangwill's childhood and youth (in which for reasons of internal chronology Esther Ansell must also have spent her childhood) and the East End of the early 1890s when the novel was being written. Probably the answer is that the two are fused. Zangwill had from his youth noted down observations and anecdotes and his notebooks served as a basis for his subsequent 'ghetto' stories. But Zangwill also went back to the ghetto to work up his material, although, as his brother Louis wrote, it was a different ghetto from that of his boyhood.[11]

The differences, apart from personalities, were in the composition, numbers and spread of the ghetto. During the 1870s the Jewish population of London rose from 32,500 to over 40,000, of whom about 30,000 lived in East London. Apart from natural increase, the newcomers were nearly all recent immigrants from Russian Poland which had replaced Holland as the main source of immigration. Of the Jews of East London at least 30 per cent (25–30 per cent for London Jewry as a whole) were receiving at least occasional charitable relief. East London Jewry in the 1870s was clustered in the streets immediately to the east of the City with an outlying colony in Stepney Green. About 25 per cent were tailors, 25 per cent street traders, 10 per cent cigar makers, 10 per cent boot, shoe and slipper makers, and 10 per cent glaziers. 'Cigar makers with very few exceptions are all Dutchmen, tailors and shoemakers nearly all Poles and Germans.'[12] Yet the Jewish population, despite the number of immigrants, was becoming increasingly anglicised: the 'Jewish cockney' was a typical figure and East Enders, even in Book II of *Children of the Ghetto*, are far from being immigrant foreigners in every case.[13]

The new immigration from Eastern Europe which began in 1881 was to increase the Jewish population of East London to 125,000; and even by 1890 the number of Jews in East London was probably around 60,000, half in Whitechapel. At least half the Jews of East London in 1891 were immigrants of the previous decade.[14] They were strange in appearance, Yiddish-speaking, with distinctive traits in religion, in political and social organization, in culture, in occupations. A much higher proportion of them than of the Jews of the previous generation were tailors working in small workshops of the type of the Belcovitches' in *Children of the Ghetto*. Whereas tailoring had previously been merely an important part of East London Jewish economic life, it now became (with the depressed boot, shoe and slipper trade) the dominant one. The little synagogues or conventicles exemplified by the 'Sons of the Covenant' in the novel, of which there had been about 20 in the 1870s, increased to over 40 by 1890, mainly associated with a particular town or area in Eastern Europe;[15] they also provided, in effect, the benefits of a friendly society but adapted to Jewish religious requirements. The area of Jewish settlement spread eastwards through Spitalfields to Stepney and southwards into St George's-in-the-East, though the move northwards into Bethnal Green did not come till about 1900.

But our description of the background to *Children of the Ghetto* must not exclude the 'Grandchildren' in Book II. This introduces Mr Henry Goldsmith and his family and friends. Mr Goldsmith is 'financial representative' (the term in the United Synagogue for a local synagogue treasurer) of

the Kensington Synagogue, whose minister is the Rev.
Joseph Strelitski, previously met in the East End of London.
These chapters enable Zangwill to portray the opposite
extreme of the London Jewish community, for the Kensing-
ton Synagogue is no doubt based on the New West End
Synagogue. Mr Goldsmith lived in Kensington Palace
Gardens ('Millionaires' Row') as did his real-life contemporary, Samuel Montagu, who was then Warden of the New
West End Synagogue and also M.P. for Whitechapel. The
New West End was the wealthiest Jewish congregation in
London in the 1880s and 1890s, the very type of those who
patronised the Jews of the East End. The period was, however, one in which Jews increasingly settled in the suburbs
of North and North-West London, and Zangwill in his later
stories shows something of their lives, not least of the lower
middle-class community of Dalston. But in *Children of the
Ghetto* we are given the two extremes of East End and
West End.

In commenting on Zangwill's Anglo-Jewish novels and
stories, one is always tempted to identify people, places and
organizations with their real or apparent originals. Thus the
'Flag of Judah' is the *Jewish Standard*[16] on which Zangwill
worked as a journalist; the 'Holy Land League' is the proto-
Zionist Lovers of Zion;[17] the description of Jewish trade
unionists is based on the strike of some 10,000 East End
Jewish tailors in August–September 1889.[18] This documentary aspect is reinforced by the many characters based on
well-known individuals in the Jewish life of East London in
the period. Reb Shemuel is Rabbi Jacob Reinowitz (born
Poland 1818, died London 1893), a *dayan* or assessor to the
Chief Rabbi and known in East London as Reb Yankele
(diminutive of Jacob). Joseph Strelitski is Rabbi Goodman
Lipkind, who later served as a Rabbi in New York.[19]
Raphael Leon is based on Harry S. Lewis, who read Hebrew

at Cambridge, and became a resident at Toynbee Hall,
devoting himself to social work in East London and editing
the *Jewish Standard*, before moving to America.[20] Karlkammer is Nathan Löb David Zimmer (born Fürth 1831,
died London 1895), a well-known pietist, cabbalist and
frequent contributor to the Jewish press on ritual and
astronomical calculations. While a member of the Great
Synagogue, the leading establishment congregation in East
London, he was also a founder of the Federation of (Minor)
Synagogues, and this is paralleled by Karlkammer's interest
in the conventicles, while remaining a member of a larger
congregation. Simon Wolf, the labour leader, is based on
Lewis Lyons, whose anti-anarchism and understanding of
the small masters' problems led Rudolph Rocker, the
anarchist, to call him an opportunist.[21] The bohemian
Hebrew poet, Melchizedek Pinchas, is based on Naphtali
Herz Imber (1856–1909), author of the Jewish national
hymn, now the national anthem of Israel, *Hatikvah*. Imber,
after adventures with Laurence Oliphant in Palestine and
India (where Zangwill believed he was temporarily converted), was in London from 1888 to 1892 and worked with
Zangwill on the *Jewish Standard*. He married a Protestant
woman doctor who was converted to Judaism. He died in
America, an alcoholic and in poverty, though receiving a
pension from the Judge Sulzberger who commissioned
Children of the Ghetto.[22]

One could continue with these identifications but I shall
note only one incident which shows how ready Zangwill was
to draw upon contemporary events. In 1887, Julia Davis,
Mrs Frankau (1860–1916), mother of the novelist Gilbert
Frankau, published a novel entitled *Dr Phillips: a Maida
Vale Idyll*.[23] It provoked a storm of criticism in the Jewish
community because of its unflattering portrayal of Jewish
middle-class life. Julia Frankau used the pseudonym Frank

Danby and there is an obvious parallel with Esther Ansell's authorship, under a male pseudonym, of *Mordecai Josephs*. The most 'documentary' of all the characters is Esther Ansell herself, through whom Zangwill projects the conflicts in his own life, between the attracting and the repelling aspects of his Jewish upbringing. These conflicts were to continue throughout the rest of his life.

The reception of *Children of the Ghetto* by the press, when it was published in 1892, was such as to encourage Zangwill to persist in writing novels of this genre for the English reading public. For the *Daily News* this was the book by which Zangwill had 'arrived' as a successful writer: 'admirable throughout, the theme original, the treatment no less felicitous. Often a work is saved by possessing one of these two qualities – Mr Zangwill's possesses both.' Even the magisterial *Athenaeum* found the 'vividness and force' of the book 'admirable'. To the *Manchester Guardian* it was 'the best Jewish novel ever written'. Zangwill followed *Children of the Ghetto* with perhaps his greatest humorous novel, *The King of Schnorrers* (1894), an evocation of the eighteenth-century London ghetto, centred around the character of the greatest Jewish beggar of fiction, who turned begging into a fine art. Shorter pieces dealing with Jewish life in England and Russia were collected in *Ghetto Tragedies* (1893) and *Ghetto Comedies* (1907), although in Zangwillian fiction the comedies are often tragic and the tragedies sometimes have an element of comedy. *Dreamers of the Ghetto* (1898) was a different type of work: sketches based on the lives of great figures of Jewish history from Shabbetai Zevi, the seventeenth-century false Messiah of Izmir, and Spinoza, to Disraeli and Lassalle. It is significant that most of these characters abandoned Judaism. Meanwhile, Zangwill published various novels on non-Jewish subjects: *The Master* (1895) about the making of an artist; *The Mantle of Elijah* (1900), a political novel; and *Jinny the Carrier* (1919) about life in mid-nineteenth-century rural Essex, a county also the subject of the novels of Zangwill's Anglo-Jewish contemporary, S. L. Bensusan. Zangwill also wrote for the stage, not always successfully. His most famous play is *The Melting Pot* (1909) which, in a long Broadway run, popularized the theory of America as the crucible of the races of Europe.

Despite his extensive output as novelist and dramatist, Zangwill was no literary recluse. He threw himself into the fight for causes: women's suffrage, pacifism in the First World War and, above all, Jewish Territorialism. Although a very early supporter of Theodor Herzl and Zionism, Zangwill came to believe that it was more urgent to find a home for Jewish refugees, and to create a Jewish territory, anywhere in the world, than to continue the long struggle for a Jewish national home in Palestine. In 1905 he founded the Jewish Territorial Organisation, gathered for it influential support and was largely responsible for its one concrete achievement, the settlement of several thousand Jews in Galveston, Texas.

Zangwill was much in demand as a public speaker because he was not only amusing but a challenger of established ideas. He was a controversial figure in Jewish life and the recurring dichotomy of his attitude to Judaism was shown by events in the 1900s when his translation into verse of much of a new official edition of the Jewish festival prayer book was followed by his marriage to a non-Jewess.[24]

Zangwill's pre-occupation with Jewish politics was such that H. G. Wells described him as adopting 'the role of champion of the Jewish race'; and Zangwill himself said that the middle decade of his working life was monopolised by Jewish public work. It was perhaps this that prevented him from achieving the literary distinction that his imagination, his wit and his facility as a story-teller might otherwise have ensured. His last years were overshadowed by 'his disastrous experiment of producing his own plays', in which, as his faithful friend and biographer wrote, 'he lost his money, his health and perhaps his reason'. He died, 'burnt out', in 1926, aged 62.[25]

And what of Zangwill's Anglo-Jewry? With the recurrence of forced shifts of population, economic restrictions and sheer terror by pogrom, the Russo-Jewish immigration continued. The 'Aliens' Question' again became for a few years an issue in British politics, the subject of an inquiry by a Royal Commission, and of an Aliens Act in 1905 which sought to check the flood. But because the Act contained loopholes for genuine refugees from religious or racial persecution it only stemmed the flow for a little while, after which immigration resumed, until it was ended by the outbreak of war in 1914. By then the Anglo-Jewry of 60,000 souls of 1881 had been transformed into one of nearly a quarter of a million. During these years, the immigrants had sought to anglicize themselves; and their children were not only legally but mentally British, from birth in Britain or from education in British schools, a process in which Zangwill's great Jews' Free School in Spitalfields played a notable part. With anglicization came social mobility and increasing prosperity. The immigrants moved out of East London to the lower-middle-class areas of North London or to the newer middle-class colonies of North-West London, if not to the more affluent areas of the West End. The East End began to empty and, when a fresh wave of refugees came from Central Europe in the 1930s, they comprised a middle-class immigration which went direct to middle-class areas and did not replenish the reservoir of East London as their Russo-Polish precursors had done. The evacuation and bombing of Zangwill's East End in the Second World War completed the process and by the 1950s it was largely empty of Jews and left to immigrants of other races and colours.

Anglo-Jewry, and particularly London Jewry, thus became predominantly a middle-class and suburban community. In these comfortable residential areas, the congregations built themselves large synagogues and, apart from some very recent immigrants, abandoned the life of the small conventicles of East London: in terms of the *Children of the Ghetto* it was not the 'Sons of the Covenant' but the 'Kensington Synagogue' that provided the model. But the suburban communities retained much of the social cohesion of the old East End, if not all of its religious devotion or learning. Contemporary novelists (like the Victorian authors of *Dr Phillips* or *Mordecai Josephs*) have castigated what they regard as the clannishness, the materialism and the lack of true culture of these suburban communities: perhaps only Miss Gerda Charles has portrayed them with the true knowledge of Jewish life and the sympathy which Zangwill had for the Jews of East London over half a century earlier. But if the typical Anglo-Jew, living within the confines of organized Judaism in late-Victorian London, was a working-class Jew in an East London slum, his counterpart nearly a century later is a middle-class resident of a spacious suburb. The children of the ghetto have become its grandchildren.

V. D. Lipman
April 1976

NOTES

1. *Transactions of the Jewish Historical Society of England*, XI (1928), 255.

2. Ibid XVIII (1958), 83.

3. The use of the term 'Ghetto' for the quarter of a town assigned by law or regulation for residence by Jews probably originated in the *getto nuovo* or 'new foundry', which was the name of the first area in Venice assigned for Jewish residence in 1516. Jewish quarters, whether compulsory or voluntary, had existed previously in medieval times but were generally known as 'Jewries'. The term 'ghetto' was generally applied to quarters of compulsory Jewish residence until the mid-nineteenth century and from then on also to quarters in which Jews tended to settle voluntarily. In the twentieth century it is applied also to any immigrant quarter. The classic sociological study of the ghetto, from restricted area of residence to immigrant quarter, is by Louis Wirth, *The Ghetto*, first published in 1928.

4. V. D. Lipman, *Social History of the Jews in England* (1954), 88; L. P. Gartner, *The Jewish Immigrant in England* (1960), Ch. II; *Jewish Encyclopaedia* (New York 1905), s. v. 'Migration'.

5. See I. Finestein, 'Jewish Immigration in British Party Politics in the 1890s' in *Migration and Settlement*, ed. A. Newman (1971).

6. This street in Spitalfields dates from the early eighteenth century. With the similarity of name, it is tempting to identify one of these flat-faced yellow-brick houses, with their wooden classical doorcases and regularly spaced windows, and panelled interiors, with No. 1 Royal Street, 'in its time one of the great mansions of the Ghetto. . . stoutly built, and its balusters were of covered oak'; and No. 19 Princelet Street (formerly 18 Princes Street) even housed the United Friends' (later Princes, then Princelet Street) Synagogue from 1862, like the Sons of the Covenant in No. 1 Royal Street. But Israel Zangwill's

brother stated that No. 1 Royal Street was not the Zangwill home in Princelet Street but a house in another street. See *Survey of London*, Vol. xxvii, *Spitalfields and Mile End New Town* (1957), 184 ff; J. Leftwich, *Israel Zangwill* (1957), 41.

7. Norman Bentwich, 'The Wanderers', *Trans. J.H.S.E.*, xx (1964), 51 ff.

8. See the article on Zangwill in *Jewish Encyclopaedia* (1905) by Joseph Jacobs.

9. Joseph Leftwich, *Trans. J.H.S.E.*, xviii (1958), 81.

10. *Jewish Quarterly Review*, i, (1889), 401.

11. Harold Fisch, 'Israel Zangwill' in *Encyclopaedia Judaica*, xvi, col. 930; J. Leftwich, *Trans. J.H.S.E.*, xviii (1958), 83.

12. Board of Guardians report for 1874 (35) quoted in V. D. Lipman, *A Century of Social Service* (1959), 34-5, which gives the general background for the period.

13. I do not know of any study showing the percentage of London Jews about 1870-80 who were British born. A study of a sample from the 1851 Census returns suggests that 20 years before 1870 the figure was about 90 per cent (V. D. Lipman, 'The Structure of London Jewry in the Mid-Nineteenth Century', in *Essays Presented to Sir Israel Brodie* (1967), 267).

14. For a discussion of the figures see V. D. Lipman, *Social History of the Jews in England* (1954), 87-90, 94-99.

15. Ibid, 71-5, 98.

16. The *Jewish Standard: The English Organ of Orthodoxy* was established in 1888 by Harry S. Lewis. Zangwill contributed a column 'Morour and Charosseth' (Bitter-Sweet, from the Bitter Herbs and sweet 'mortar' used at the Passover Seder table) under the pseudonym *Marshallik* (Yiddish for the medieval Jewish jester who performed at wedding celebrations). It was not very successful commercially and, after the editorship had been transferred in 1890 to the scholarly Dr S. A. Hirsch of Jews' College, it came to an end in 1891 (C. Roth, *Jewish Chronicle* (1949), 161).

17. The Lovers of Zion were a movement of the 1880s and 1890s (when they were taken over by Herzl's Zionist movement)

devoted to the spreading of the national idea, Jewish colonization in Palestine, the Hebrew language and moral improvement of Jews generally. Although mainly an East European movement, they had branches in Western countries, notably in England from 1887, led by Colonel A. E. W. Goldsmid, an army officer of Jewish origins who returned to Judaism.

18. The strike was aimed at conditions in the small workshops from which many of the small masters suffered as well. Sir Samuel Montagu, M.P. for Whitechapel, supported the strikers financially and helped to settle the dispute on terms which included an 8 a.m. to 8 p.m. day (with $1\frac{1}{2}$ hours off for meals). Lord Rothschild helped by paying the strikers' debts after settlement. Although propaganda for the strike, which included mass meetings and marches to Victoria Park, was spread by the anarchist Yiddish paper *Arbeter Freint* (Workers' Friend), the leadership of the strike by Lewis Lyons was trade unionist rather than anarchist or even socialist (L. P. Gartner, *Jewish Immigrant in England* (1960), 122-4; W. J. Fishman, *East End Jewish Radicals 1875-1914* (1975).

19. The articles in the *Jewish Encyclopaedia* of 1905 which identify Reinowitz as Reb Shmuel and Karlkammer as N. L. D. Zimmer are by Lipkind.

20. He died in 1940.

21. R. Rocker, *The London Years* (1956), 130

22. See *Jewish Encyclopaedia* (1905) and *Encyclopaedia Judaica*, s. v.

23. M. Modder, *The Jew in the Literature of England* (1960 edn), 325.

24. She was not converted to Judaism nor was his eldest son initiated into the Jewish faith.

25. J. Leftwich, *Trans. J.H.S.E.*, XVIII (1958), 86-7.

BIBLIOGRAPHICAL NOTE

Children of the Ghetto was published in London by William Heinemann in a three-volume edition in September 1892. A 'second edition', also in three volumes, followed in December 1892 with a 'third edition' in one volume in May 1893.

In the United States the work was first published in Philadelphia in two volumes by the Jewish Publication Society in 1892.

The present edition reprints photographically the text of the third British edition of 1893. A map of 'The East End of London c. 1900' is added from V. D. Lipman, *Social History of the Jews in England 1850–1950* (London, Watts, 1954). This is adapted from an earlier map by C. Russell and H. S. Lewis in their *The Jew in London* (London, Fisher Unwin, 1901).

CHILDREN OF THE GHETTO

𝔄 Study of a Peculiar People

BY

I. ZANGWILL

AUTHOR OF
THE OLD MAIDS' CLUB,'
ETC. ETC.

LONDON

WILLIAM HEINEMANN

1893

THIRD EDITION.

———

FIRST EDITION, 3 *Volumes, September* 1892.
SECOND EDITION, 3 *Volumes, December* 1892.

PREFACE TO THE THIRD EDITION.

THE issue of a one-volume edition gives me the opportunity of thanking the public and the critics for their kindly reception of this chart of a *terra incognita*, and of restoring the original sub-title, which is a reply to some criticisms upon its artistic form. The book is intended as a study through typical figures of a race whose persistence is the most remarkable fact in the history of the world, the faith and morals of which it has so largely moulded. At the request of numerous readers I have reluctantly added a glossary of ' Yiddish ' words and phrases, based on one supplied to the American edition by another hand. I have omitted only those words which occur but once and are then explained in the text; and to each word I have added an indication of the language from which it was drawn. This may please those who share Mr. Andrew Lang's and Miss Rosa Dartle's desire for information. It will be seen that most of these despised words are pure Hebrew; a language which never died off the lips of men, and which is the medium in which books are written all the world over even unto this day.   I. Z.

LONDON, *March* 1893.

CONTENTS

BOOK I.—THE CHILDREN OF THE GHETTO

CHAP.   PAGE

Chap.	Title	Page
	PROEM,	1
I.	THE BREAD OF AFFLICTION,	9
II.	THE SWEATER,	14
III.	MALKA,	29
IV.	THE REDEMPTION OF THE SON AND THE DAUGHTER,	42
V.	THE PAUPER ALIEN,	54
VI.	'REB' SHEMUEL,	63
VII.	THE NEO-HEBREW POET,	69
VIII.	ESTHER AND HER CHILDREN,	79
IX.	DUTCH DEBBY,	90
X.	A SILENT FAMILY,	96
XI.	THE PURIM BALL,	100
XII.	THE SONS OF THE COVENANT,	110
XIII.	SUGARMAN'S BAR-MITZVAH PARTY,	120
XIV.	THE HOPE OF THE FAMILY,	128
XV.	THE HOLY LAND LEAGUE,	138
XVI.	THE COURTSHIP OF SHOSSHI SHMENDRIK,	148
XVII.	THE HYAMSES' HONEYMOON,	160
XVIII.	THE HEBREW'S FRIDAY NIGHT,	169
XIX.	WITH THE STRIKERS,	179
XX.	THE HOPE EXTINCT,	189
XXI.	THE JARGON PLAYERS,	197
XXII.	'FOR AULD LANG SYNE, MY DEAR,'	202
XXIII.	THE DEAD MONKEY,	208
XXIV.	THE SHADOW OF RELIGION,	215
XXV.	SEDER NIGHT,	224

BOOK II.—THE GRANDCHILDREN OF THE GHETTO

CHAP.   PAGE
    I. THE CHRISTMAS DINNER, ... 238
   II. RAPHAEL LEON, ... 252
  III. 'THE FLAG OF JUDAH,'   .   .   . 266
   IV. THE TROUBLES OF AN EDITOR,   .   . 279
    V. A WOMAN'S GROWTH, ... 289
   VI. COMEDY OR TRAGEDY?   .   .   . 297
  VII. WHAT THE YEARS BROUGHT, .   .   . 314
 VIII. THE ENDS OF A GENERATION,   .   . 321
   IX. THE 'FLAG' FLUTTERS,   .   .   . 324
    X. ESTHER DEFIES THE UNIVERSE,   .   . 331
   XI. GOING HOME, ... 340
  XII. A SHEAF OF SEQUELS, ... 348
 XIII. THE DEAD MONKEY AGAIN,   .   . 365
  XIV. SIDNEY SETTLES DOWN,   .   .   . 370
   XV. FROM SOUL TO SOUL, ... 375
  XVI. LOVE'S TEMPTATION, ... 389
 XVII. THE PRODIGAL SON,   .   .   . 398
XVIII. HOPES AND DREAMS, ... 403

PROEM

NOT here in our London Ghetto the gates and gaberdines of the olden Ghetto of the Eternal City; yet no lack of signs external by which one may know it, and those who dwell therein. Its narrow streets have no speciality of architecture; its dirt is not picturesque. It is no longer the stage for the high-buskined tragedy of massacre and martyrdom; only for the obscurer, deeper tragedy that evolves from the pressure of its own inward forces, and the long-drawn-out tragi-comedy of sordid and shifty poverty. Natheless, this London Ghetto of ours is a region where, amid uncleanness and squalor, the rose of romance blows yet a little longer in the raw air of English reality; a world which hides beneath its stony and unlovely surface an inner world of dreams, fantastic and poetic as the mirage of the Orient where they were woven, of superstitions grotesque as the cathedral gargoyles of the Dark Ages in which they had birth. And over all lie tenderly some streaks of celestial light shining from the face of the great Lawgiver.

The folk who compose our pictures are Children of the Ghetto. Their faults are bred of its hovering miasma of persecution, their virtues straitened and intensified by the narrowness of its horizon. And they who have won their way beyond its boundaries must still play their parts in tragedies and comedies—tragedies of spiritual struggle, comedies of material ambition—which are the aftermath of its centuries of dominance, the sequel of that long cruel night in Jewry which coincides with the Christian Era. If they are not the Children, they are at least the Grandchildren of the Ghetto.

The particular Ghetto that is the dark background upon which our pictures will be cast is of voluntary formation.

People who have been living in a Ghetto for a couple of centuries are not able to step outside merely because the gates are thrown down, nor to efface the brands on their souls by putting off the yellow badges. The isolation imposed from without will have come to seem the law of their being. But a minority will pass, by units, into the larger, freer, stranger life amid the execrations of an ever-dwindling majority. For better or for worse, or for both, the Ghetto will be gradually abandoned, till at last it becomes only a swarming-place for the poor and the ignorant, huddling together for social warmth. Such people are their own Ghetto gates ; when they migrate they carry them across the sea to lands where they are not. Into the heart of East London there poured from Russia, from Poland, from Germany, from Holland, streams of Jewish exiles, refugees, settlers, few as well-to-do as the Jew of the proverb, but all rich in their cheerfulness, their industry, and their cleverness. The majority bore with them nothing but their phylacteries and praying shawls, and a good-natured contempt for Christians and Christianity. For the Jew has rarely been embittered by persecution. He knows that he is in *Goluth*, in exile, and that the days of the Messiah are not yet, and he looks upon the persecutor merely as the stupid instrument of an all-wise Providence. So that these poor Jews were rich in all the virtues, devout yet tolerant, and strong in their reliance on Faith, Hope, and, more especially, Charity.

In the early days of the nineteenth century all Israel were brethren. Even the pioneer colony of wealthy Sephardim, descendants of the Spanish crypto-Jews who had reached England *via* Holland, had modified its boycott of the poor Ashkenazic immigrants, now they were become an overwhelming majority. There was a superior stratum of Anglo-German Jews who had had time to get on, but all the Ashkenazic tribes lived very much like a happy family, the poor not stand-offish towards the rich, and anxious to afford them opportunities for well-doing. The *Schnorrer* felt no false shame in his begging. He knew it was the rich man's duty to give him unleavened bread at Passover, and coals in the winter, and odd half-crowns at all seasons ; and he regarded himself as the Jacob's ladder by which the rich man mounted to Paradise. But, like all genuine philanthropists, he did not look for gratitude. He felt that virtue was its own reward, especially when he sat in Sabbath vesture at the head of his table on Friday nights, and thanked God in an operatic aria for the white cotton tablecloth and the fried sprats. He sought personal interview with the most majestic magnates, and had humorous repartees for their lumbering censure.

As for the rich, they gave charity unscrupulously—in the same Oriental, unscientific, informal spirit in which the Dayanim, those cadis of the East End, administered justice. The *Takif*, or man of substance, was as accustomed to the palm of the mendicant outside the Great Synagogue as to the rattling pyx within. They lived in Bury Street, and Prescott Street, and Finsbury—these aristocrats of the Ghetto—in mansions that are now but congeries of 'apartments.' Few relations had they with Belgravia, but many with Petticoat Lane and the Great Shool, the stately old synagogue which has always been illuminated by candles and still refuses all modern light. The Spanish Jews had a more ancient *snoga*, but it was within a stone's-throw of the 'Duke's Place' edifice.

Decorum was not a feature of synagogue worship in those days, nor was the Almighty yet conceived as the holder of formal receptions once a week. Worshippers did not pray with bated breath, as if afraid that the Deity would overhear them They were at ease in Zion. They passed snuff-boxes and remarks about the weather. The opportunities of skipping afforded by a too exuberant liturgy promoted conversation, and even stocks were discussed in the terrible *longueurs* induced by the meaningless ministerial repetition of prayers already said by the congregation, or by the official recitations of catalogues of purchased benedictions. Sometimes, of course, this announcement of the offertory was interesting, especially when there was sensational competition. The great people bade in guineas for the privilege of rolling up the Scroll of the Law, or drawing the Curtain of the Ark, or saying a particular *Kaddish* if they were mourners, and then thrills of reverence went round the congregation. The social hierarchy was to some extent graduated by synagogal contributions, and whoever could afford only a little offering had it announced as a ' gift '—a vague term which might equally be the covering of a reticent munificence.

Very few persons ' called up ' to the reading of the Law escaped at the cost they had intended, for one is easily led on by an insinuative official incapable of taking low views of the donor's generosity and a little deaf. The moment prior to the declaration of the amount was quite exciting for the audience. On Sabbaths and Festivals the authorities could not write down these sums, for writing is work, and work is forbidden ; even to write them in the book and volume of their brain would have been to charge their memories with an illegitimate if not an impossible burden. Parchment books on a peculiar system, with holes in the pages, and laces to go through the holes, solved the problem of book-keeping without pen and ink. It is possible that many of the worshippers were tempted to give beyond their means for fear of losing the esteem of the *Shammos*, or beadle, a potent personage only next in influence to the President, whose overcoat he obsequiously removed on the greater man's annual visit to the synagogue. The beadle's eye was all over the *Shool* at once, and he could settle an altercation about seats without missing a single response. His automatic amens resounded magnificently through the synagogue, at once a stimulus and a rebuke. It was probably as a concession to him that poor men, who were neither seat-holders nor wearers of chimney-pot hats, were penned within an iron enclosure near the door of the building, and ranged on backless benches, and it says much for the authority of the *Shammos* that not even the *Schnorrer* contested it. Prayers were shouted rapidly by the congregation, and elaborately sung by the *Chazan*. The minister was *vox et præterea nihil*. He was the only musical instrument permitted, and on him devolved the whole onus of making the service attractive. He succeeded. He was helped by the sociability of the gathering, for the synagogue was virtually a Jewish club, the focus of the sectarian life.

Hard times and bitter had some of the fathers of the Ghetto, but they ate their dry bread with the salt of humour, loved their wives, and praised God for His mercies. Unwitting of the genealogies that would be found for them by their prosperous grandchildren, 'old clo'' men plied their trade in ambitious content. They were meek and timorous outside the Ghetto, walking warily for fear of the Christian. Sufferance was still the badge of all their tribe. Yet that there were Jews who held their heads high, let the following legend tell. Few men could shuffle along more inoffensively or cry 'old clo'' with a meeker twitter than Sleepy Sol. The old man crawled one day, bowed with humility and clo'-bag, into a military mews and uttered his tremulous chirp. To him came one of the hostlers with insolent beetling brow.

'Any gold lace?' faltered Sleepy Sol.

'Get out!' roared the hostler.

'I'll give you de best prices,' pleaded Sleepy Sol.

'Get out!' repeated the hostler, and hustled the old man into the street. 'If I catch you 'ere again, I'll break your neck.'

Sleepy Sol loved his neck, but the profit on gold lace torn from old uniforms was high. Next week he crept into the mews again, trusting to meet another hostler.

'Clo'! clo'!' he chirped faintly.

Alas! the brawny bully was to the fore again, and recognised him.

'You dirty old Jew!' he cried. 'Take that, and that! The next time I sees you, you'll go 'ome on a shutter.'

The old man took 'that,' and 'that,' and went on his way. The next day he came again.

'Clo'! clo'!' he whimpered.

'What!' said the ruffian, his coarse cheeks flooded with angry blood. 'Ev yer forgotten what I promised yer?'

He seized Sleepy Sol by the scruff of the neck.

'I say, why can't you leave the old man alone?'

The hostler stared at the protester, whose presence he had not noticed in the pleasurable excitement of the moment. It was a Jewish young man, indifferently attired in a pepper-and-salt suit. The muscular hostler measured him scornfully with his eye.

'What's to do with you?' he said, with studied contempt.

'Nothing,' admitted the intruder. 'And what harm is he doing you?'

'That's my bizness,' answered the hostler, and tightened his clutch of Sleepy Sol's nape.

'Well, you'd better not mind it,' answered the young man calmly. 'Let go.'

The hostler's thick lips emitted a disdainful laugh.

'Let go, d'you hear?' repeated the young man.

'I'll let go at your nose,' said the hostler, clenching his knobby fist.

'Very well,' said the young man. 'Then I'll pull yours.'

'Oho !' said the hostler, his scowl growing fiercer. 'Yer means bizness, does yer ?'

With that he sent Sleepy Sol staggering along the road, and rolled up his shirt-sleeves. His coat was already off.

The young man did not remove his ; he quietly assumed the defensive. The hostler sparred up to him with grim earnestness, and launched a terrible blow at his most characteristic feature. The young man blandly put it on one side, and planted a return blow on the hostler's ear. Enraged, his opponent sprang upon him. The young Jew paralysed him by putting his left hand negligently into his pocket. With his remaining hand he closed the hostler's right eye, and sent the flesh about it into mourning. Then he carelessly tapped a little blood from the hostler's nose, gave him a few thumps on the chest as if to test the strength of his lungs, and laid him sprawling in the courtyard. A brother hostler ran out from the stables, and gave a cry of astonishment.

'You 'd better wipe his face,' said the young man curtly.

The new-comer hurried back towards the stables.

'Vait a moment,' said Sleepy Sol. 'I can sell you a sponge sheap ; I 've got a beauty in my bag.'

There were plenty of sponges about, but the new-comer bought the second-hand sponge.

'Do you want any more ?' the young man affably inquired of his prostrate adversary.

The hostler gave a groan. He was shamed before a friend whom he had early convinced of his fistic superiority.

'No, I reckon he don't,' said the friend, with a knowing grin at the conqueror.

'Then I will wish you a good-day,' said the young man. 'Come along, father.'

'Yes, ma son-in-law,' said Sleepy Sol.

'Do you know who that was, Joe ?' said his friend, as he sponged away the blood.

Joe shook his head.

'That was Dutch Sam,' said his friend in an awe-struck whisper.

All Joe's body vibrated with surprise and respect. Dutch Sam was the champion bruiser of his time—in private life an eminent dandy and a prime favourite of His Majesty George IV. And Sleepy Sol had a beautiful daughter, and was perhaps prepossessing himself when washed for the Sabbath.

'Dutch Sam !' Joe repeated.

'Dutch Sam ! Why, we 've got his picter hanging up inside, only he 's naked to the waist.'

'Well, strike me lucky ! What a fool I was not to rekkernize 'im !' His battered face brightened up. No wonder he licked me !'

Except for the comparative infrequency of the more bestial types of men and women, Judæa has always been a cosmos in little, and its prize-fighters and scientists, its philosophers and 'fences,' its gymnasts and money-lenders, its scholars and stockbrokers, its

musicians, its chess-players, poets, comic singers, lunatics, saints,
publicans, politicians, warriors, poltroons, mathematicians, actors,
foreign correspondents, have always been in the first rank.   *Nihil
alienum a se Judæus putat.*

Joe and his friend fell to recalling Dutch Sam's great feats.
Each out-vied the other in admiration for the supreme pugilist.

Next day Sleepy Sol came rampaging down the courtyard.   He
walked at the rate of five miles to the hour, and despite the weight
of his bag his head pointed to the zenith.

' Clo' !' he shrieked.   ' Clo' !'

Joe, the hostler, came out ; his head was bandaged, and in his
hand was gold lace.   It was something even to do business with
a hero's father-in-law.

But it is given to few men to marry their daughters to champion
boxers ; and as Dutch Sam was not a Don Quixote, the average
pedlar or huckster never enjoyed the luxury of prancing gait and
cock-a-hoop business cry.   The primitive fathers of the Ghetto
might have borne themselves more jauntily had they foreseen that
they were to be the ancestors of mayors and aldermen descended
from Castilian hidalgos and Polish kings, and that an unborn
historian would conclude that the Ghetto of their day was peopled
by princes in disguise.   They would have been as surprised to
learn who they were as to be informed that they were orthodox.
The great Reform split did not occur till well on towards the
middle of the century, and the Jews of those days were unable to
conceive that a man could be a Jew without eating *kosher* meat,
and they would have looked upon the modern distinctions between
racial and religious Jews as the sophistries of the convert or the
missionary.   If their religious life converged to the Great Shool,
their social life focussed on Petticoat Lane, a long, narrow
thoroughfare which as late as Strype's day was lined with beautiful
trees ; vastly more pleasant they must have been than the faded
barrows and beggars of after days.   The Lane —such was its
affectionate sobriquet—was the stronghold of hard-shell Judaism,
the Alsatia of ' infidelity,' into which no missionary dared set foot,
especially no apostate apostle.   Even in modern days the new-
fangled Jewish minister of the fashionable suburb, rigged out like
the Christian clergyman, has been mistaken for such a *Meshumad*,
and pelted with gratuitous vegetables and eleemosynary eggs.
The Lane was always the great market-place, and every in-
salubrious street and alley abutting on it was covered with the
overflowings of its commerce and its mud.   Wentworth Street and
Goulston Street were the chief branches, and in festival times the
latter was a pandemonium of caged poultry, clucking and quack-
ing, and cackling and screaming.   Fowls and geese and ducks
were bought alive, and taken to have their throats cut for a fee by
the official slaughterer.   At Purim a gaiety, as of the Roman
carnival, enlivened the swampy Wentworth Street, and brought a
smile into the unwashed face of the pavement.   The confectioners

shops, crammed with 'stuffed monkeys' and 'bolas,' were besieged by hilarious crowds of handsome girls and their young men, fat women and their children, all washing down the luscious spicy compounds with cups of chocolate ; temporarily erected swinging cradles bore a vociferous many-coloured burden to the skies ; cardboard noses, grotesque in their departure from truth, abounded. The Purim *Spiel*, or Purim play, never took root in England, nor was Haman ever burnt in the streets, but *Shalachmonos*, or gifts of the season, passed between friend and friend, and masquerading parties burst into neighbours' houses. But the Lane was lively enough on the ordinary Friday and Sunday. The famous Sunday Fair was an event of metropolitan importance, and thither came buyers of every sect. The Friday Fair was more local, and confined mainly to edibles. The ante-festival fairs combined something of the other two, for Jews desired to sport new hats and clothes for the holidays as well as to eat extra luxuries, and took the opportunity of a well-marked epoch to invest in new every-things, from oil-cloth to cups and saucers. Especially was this so at Passover, when for a week the poorest Jew must use a supple-mentary set of crockery and kitchen utensils. A babel of sound, audible for several streets around, denoted market day in Petticoat Lane, and the pavements were blocked by serried crowds going both ways at once.

It was only gradually that the community was Anglicised. Under the sway of centrifugal impulses, the wealthier members began to form new colonies, moulting their old feathers and replacing them by finer, and flying ever further from the centre. Men of organising ability founded unrivalled philanthropic and educational institutions on British lines ; millionaires fought for municipal and their own political emancipation ; brokers brazenly foisted themselves on 'Change ; ministers gave sermons in bad English ; an English journal was started ; very slowly the con-ventional Anglican tradition was established ; and on that human palimpsest, which has borne the inscriptions of all languages and all epochs, was writ large the sign-manual of England. Judæa prostrated itself before the Dagon of its hereditary foe, the Philistine, and respectability crept on to freeze the blood of the Orient with its frigid finger, and to blur the vivid tints of the East into the uniform grey of English middle-class life. In the period within which our story moves, only vestiges of the old gaiety and brotherhood remained ; the full *al-fresco* flavour was evaporated.

And to-day they are all dead—the *Takeefim* with big hearts and bigger purses, and the humorous *Schnorrers*, who accepted their gold, and the cheerful pious pedlars who rose from one extreme to the other, building up fabulous fortunes in marvellous ways. The young mothers, who suckled their babes in the sun, have passed out in the sunshine ; yea, and the babes, too, have gone down with gray heads to the dust. Dead are the fair fat women, with tender hearts, who waddled benignantly through life, ever ready to shed the sympathetic tear, best of wives, and cooks, and mothers; dead are the bald, ruddy old men, who ambled about in faded carpet slippers, and passed the snuff-box of peace; dead are the stout-hearted youths who sailed away to Tom Tiddler's ground, and dead are the buxom maidens they led under the wedding canopy when they returned. Even the great Dr. Sequira, pompous in white stockings, Physician Extraordinary to the Prince Regent of Portugal, lies vanquished by his life-long adversary, and the Baal Shem himself, King of Cabalists, could command no countervailing miracle.

Where are the little girls in white pinafores with pink sashes who brightened the Ghetto on high days and holidays? Where is the beauteous Betsy of the Victoria Ballet? and where the jocund synagogue dignitary who led off the cotillon with her at the annual Rejoicing of the Law? Worms have long since picked the great financier's brain, the embroidered waistcoats of the bucks have passed even beyond the stage of adorning sweeps on May Day, and Dutch Sam's fist is bonier than ever. The same mould covers them all—those who donated guineas and those who donated 'gifts,' the rogues and the hypocrites and the wedding-drolls, the observant and the lax, the purse-proud and the lowly, the coarse and the genteel, the wonderful chapmen and the luckless *Schlemihls*, Rabbi and Dayan and Shochet, the scribes who wrote the sacred scroll and the cantors who trolled it off mellifluous tongues, and the betting-men who never listened to it; the grimy Russians, of the capotes and the earlocks, and the blue-blooded Dons, 'the gentlemen of the Mahamad,' who ruffled it with swords and knee-breeches in the best Christian Society. Those who kneaded the toothsome 'bolas' lie with those who ate them; and the marriage-brokers repose with those they mated. The olives and the cucumbers grow green and fat as of yore, but their lovers are mixed with a soil that is barren of them. The restless, bustling crowds that jostled laughingly in Rag Fair are at rest in the 'House of Life'; the pageant of their strenuous generation is vanished as a dream. They died with the declaration of God's unity on their stiffening lips, and the certainty of resurrection in their pulseless hearts, and a faded Hebrew inscription on a tomb or an unread entry on a synagogue brass is their only record. And yet, perhaps, their generation is not all dust. Perchance, here and there, some decrepit centenarian rubs his purblind eyes with the ointment of memory, and sees these pictures of the past, hallowed by the consecration of time, and finds his shrivelled cheek wet with the pathos sanctifying the joys that have been.

BOOK I

THE CHILDREN OF THE GHETTO

CHAPTER I

THE BREAD OF AFFLICTION

A DEAD and gone wag called the street 'Fashion Street,' and most of the people who live in it do not even see the joke. If it could exchange names with 'Rotten Row,' both places would be more appropriately designated. It is a dull, squalid, narrow thoroughfare in the East End of London, connecting Spitalfields with Whitechapel, and branching off in blind alleys. In the days when little Esther Ansell trudged its unclean pavements, its extremities were within earshot of the blasphemies from some of the vilest quarters and filthiest rookeries in the capital of the civilised world. Some of these clotted spiders'-webs have since been swept away by the besom of the social reformer, and the spiders have scurried off into darker crannies.

There were the conventional touches about the London street-picture, as Esther Ansell sped through the freezing mist of the December evening, with the pitcher in her hand, looking in her Oriental colouring like a miniature of Rebecca going to the well. A female street-singer, with a trail of infants of dubious maternity, troubled the air with a piercing melody ; a pair of slatterns with arms akimbo reviled each other's relatives ; a drunkard lurched along, babbling amiably ; an organ-grinder, blue-nosed as his monkey, set some ragged children jigging under the watery rays of a street-lamp. Esther drew her little plaid shawl tightly around her, and ran on without heeding these familiar details, her chilled feet absorbing the damp of the murky pavement through the worn soles of her cumbrous boots. They were masculine boots, kicked off by some intoxicated tramp, and picked up by Esther's father. Moses Ansell had a habit of lighting on windfalls, due, perhaps, to his meek manner of walking with bent head, as though literally bowed beneath the yoke of the Captivity. Providence rewarded him for his humility by occasional treasure-trove. Esther had received a pair of new boots from her school a week before, and the substitution of the tramp's foot-gear for her own resulted in a net profit of half a crown, and kept Esther's little brothers and sisters in bread for a week. At school, under her teacher's eye, Esther was very unobtrusive about the feet for the next fortnight, but as the fear of being found out died away, even her rather morbid conscience condoned the deception in view of the stomachic gain.

They gave away bread and milk at the school, too, but Esther and her brothers and sisters never took either, for fear of being thought in want of them. The superiority of a class-mate is hard to bear, and a high-spirited child will not easily acknowledge starvation in presence of a roomful of purse-proud urchins, some of them able to spend a farthing a day on pure luxuries. Moses Ansell would have been grieved had he known his children were refusing the bread he could not give them. Trade was slack in the sweating dens, and Moses, who had always lived from hand to mouth, had latterly held less than ever between the one and the other. He had applied for help to the Jewish Board of Guardians, but red-tape rarely unwinds as quickly as hunger coils itself; moreover, Moses was an old offender in poverty at the Court of Charity. But there was one species of alms which Moses could not be denied, and the existence of which Esther could not conceal from him as she concealed that of the eleemosynary breakfasts at the school. For it was known to all men that soup and bread were to be had for the asking thrice a week at the institution in Fashion Street, and in the Ansell household the opening of the soup-kitchen was looked forward to as the dawn of a golden age, when it would be impossible to pass more than one day without bread. The vaguely-remembered smell of the soup threw a poetic fragrance over the coming winter. Every year since Esther's mother had died, the child had been sent to fetch home the provender, for Moses, who was the only other available member of the family, was always busy praying when he had nothing better to do. And so to-night Esther fared to the kitchen with her red pitcher, passing in her childish eagerness numerous women shuffling along on the same errand, and bearing uncouth tin cans supplied by the institution. An individualistic instinct of cleanliness made Esther prefer the family pitcher. To-day this liberty of choice has been taken away, and the regulation can, numbered and stamped, serves as a soup-ticket.

There was quite a crowd of applicants outside the stable-like doors of the kitchen when Esther arrived, a few with well-lined stomachs, perhaps, but the majority famished and shivering. The feminine element swamped the rest, but there were about a dozen men and a few children among the group, most of the men scarce taller than the children—strange, stunted, swarthy, hairy creatures, with muddy complexions illumined by black, twinkling eyes. A few were of imposing stature, wearing coarse, dusty felt hats or peaked caps, with shaggy beards or faded scarfs around their throats. Here and there, too, was a woman of comely face and figure, but for the most part it was a collection of crones, prematurely aged, with weird, wan, old-world features, slipshod and draggle-tailed, their heads bare, or covered with dingy shawls in lieu of bonnets—red shawls, gray shawls, brick-dust shawls, mud-coloured shawls. Yet there was an indefinable touch of romance and pathos about the tawdriness and witch-like ugliness, and an underlying identity about the crowd of Polish, Russian, German, Dutch Jewesses, mutually apathetic, and pressing forwards. Some of them had infants at their bare breasts, who drowsed quietly with intervals of ululation. The women devoid of shawls had nothing around their necks to protect them from the cold ; the dusky throats were exposed, and sometimes even the first hooks and eyes of the bodice were unnecessarily undone. The majority wore cheap earrings and black wigs with preternaturally polished hair ; where there was no wig the hair was touzled.

At half-past five the stable-doors were thrown open, and the crowd pressed through a long, narrow, whitewashed stone corridor into a barn-like compartment, with a whitewashed ceiling traversed by wooden beams. Within this compartment, and leaving but a narrow, circumscribing border, was a sort of cattle-pen, into which the paupers crushed, awaiting amid discomfort and universal jabber the divine moment. The single jet of gas-light depending from the ceiling flared upon the strange simian faces, and touched them into a grotesque picturesqueness that would have delighted Doré.

They felt hungry, these picturesque people ; their near and dear ones were hungering at home. Voluptuously savouring in imagination the operation of the soup, they forgot its operation as a dole in aid of wages ; were unconscious of the grave economical possibilities of pauperisation and the rest, and quite willing to swallow their independence with the soup. Even Esther, who had read much and was sensitive, accepted unquestioningly the theory of the universe that was held by most people about her, that human beings were distinguished from animals in having to toil terribly for a meagre crust, but that their lot was lightened by the existence of a small and semi-divine class called *Takeefim*, or rich people, who gave away what they didn't want. How these rich people came to be Esther did not inquire ; they were as much a part of the constitution of things as clouds and horses. The semi-celestial variety was rarely to be met with. It lived far away from the Ghetto, and a small family of it was said to occupy a whole house. Representatives of it, clad in rustling silks or impressive broadcloth, and radiating an indefinable aroma of superhumanity, sometimes came to the school, preceded by the beaming head-mistress ; and then all the little girls rose and curtseyed, and the best of them, passing as average members of the class, astonished the semi-divine persons by their intimate acquaintance with the topography of the Pyrenees and the disagreements of Saul and David, the intercourse of the two species ending in effusive smiles and general satisfaction. But the dullest of the girls was alive to the comedy, and had a good-humoured contempt for the unworldliness of the semi-divine persons, who spoke to them as if they were not going to recommence squabbling, and pulling one another's hair, and copying one another's sums, and stealing one another's needles the moment the semi-celestial backs were turned.

To-night, semi-divine persons were to be seen in a galaxy of splendour, for in the reserved standing-places, behind the white deal counter, was gathered a group of philanthropists. The room was an odd-shaped polygon, partially lined with eight boilers, whose great wooden lids were raised by pulleys and balanced by red-painted iron balls. In the corner stood the cooking-engine. Cooks in white caps and blouses stirred the steaming soup with long wooden paddles. A tradesman besought the attention of the Jewish reporters to the improved boiler he had manufactured, and the superintendent adjured the newspaper men not to omit his name; while amid the soberly-clad clergymen flitted, like gorgeous humming-birds through a flock of crows, the marriageable daughters of an East End minister.

When a sufficient number of semi-divinities was gathered together, the President addressed the meeting at considerable length, striving to impress upon the clergymen and other philanthropists present that charity was a virtue, and appealing to the Bible, the Koran, and even the Vedas, for confirmation of his proposition. Early in his speech the sliding-door that separated the cattle-pen from the kitchen proper had to be closed, because the jostling crowd jabbered so much and inconsiderate infants squalled, and there did not seem to be any general desire to hear the President's ethical views. They were a low material lot, who thought only of their bellies, and did but chatter the louder when the speech was shut out. They had overflowed their barriers by this time, and were surging cruelly to and fro, and Esther had to keep her elbows close to her sides lest her arms should be dislocated. Outside the stable doors a shifting array of boys and girls hovered hungrily and curiously. When the President had finished, the Rabbinate was invited to address the philanthropists, which it did at not less length, eloquently seconding the proposition that charity was a virtue. Then the door was slid back, and the first two paupers were admitted, the rest of the crowd being courageously kept at bay by the superintendent. The head cook filled a couple of plates with soup, dipping a great pewter pot into the caldron. The Rabbinate then uplifted its eyes heavenwards, and said the grace:

'Blessed art Thou, O Lord, King of the universe, according to whose word all things exist.'

It then tasted a spoonful of the soup, as did also the President and several of the vistors, the passage of the fluid along the palate invariably evoking approving ecstatic smiles; and, indeed, there was more body in it this opening night than there would be later, when, in due course, the bulk of the meat would take its legitimate place among the pickings of office. The sight of the delighted deglutition of the semi-divine persons made Esther's mouth water

as she struggled for breathing space on the outskirts of Paradise.
The impatience, which fretted her was almost allayed by visions
of stout-hearted Solomon and gentle Rachel and whimpering little
Sarah and Ikey all gulping down the delicious draught. Even
the more stoical father and grandmother were a little in her
thoughts. The Ansells had eaten nothing but a slice of dry bread
each in the morning. Here before her, in the land of Goshen,
flowing with soup, was piled up a heap of halves of loaves, while
endless other loaves were ranged along the shelves as for a giant's
table. Esther looked ravenously at the four-square tower built of
edible bricks, shivering as the biting air sought out her back
through a sudden interstice in the heaving mass. The draught
reminded her more keenly of her little ones huddled together in
the fireless garret at home. Ah, what a happy night was in store !
She must not let them devour the two loaves to-night ; that would
be criminal extravagance. No, one would suffice for the banquet ;
the other must be carefully put by. 'To-morrow is also a day,'
as the old grandmother used to say in her quaint jargon. But the
banquet was not to be spread so fast as Esther's fancy could fly ;
the doors must be shut again, and other semi-divine and wholly
divine persons (in white ties) must move and second (with eloquence and length) votes of thanks to the President, the Rabbinate,
and all other available recipients ; a French visitor must express
his admiration of English charity. But at last the turn of the
gnawing stomachs came. The motley crowd, still babbling, made
a slow forward movement, squeezing painfully through the narrow
aperture, and shivering at a plate-glass window-pane at the side of
the cattle-pen, in the crush ; the semi-divine persons rubbed their
hands and smiled genially ; ingenious paupers tried to dodge
round to the caldrons by the semi-divine entrance ; the tropical
humming-birds fluttered among the crows ; there was a splashing
of ladles and a gurgling of cascades of soup into the cans, and
a hubbub of voices ; a toothless, white-haired, blear-eyed hag
lamented in excellent English that soup was refused her, owing
to her case not having yet been investigated, and her tears
moistened the one loaf she received. In like hard case a Russian
threw himself on the stones and howled. But at last Esther was
running through the mist, warmed by the pitcher which she
hugged to her bosom, and suppressing the blind impulse to pinch
the pair of loaves tied up in her pinafore. She almost flew up the
dark flight of stairs to the attic in Royal Street. Little Sarah was
sobbing querulously. Esther, conscious of being an angel of
deliverance, tried to take the last two steps at once, tripped and
tumbled ignominiously against the garret-door, which flew back
and let her fall into the room with a crash. The pitcher shivered
into fragments under her aching little bosom, the odorous soup
spread itself in an irregular pool over the boards, and flowed
under the two beds and dripped down the crevices into the room
beneath. Esther burst into tears ; her frock was wet and greased

her hands were cut and bleeding. Little Saɪah checked her sobs at the disaster. Moses Ansell was not yet returned from evening service, but the withered old grandmother, whose wizened face loomed through the gloom of the cold, unlit garret, sat up on the bed and cursed her angrily for a *Schlemihl*. A sense of injustice made Esther cry more bitterly. She had never broken anything for years past. Ikey, an eerie-looking dot of four and a half years, tottered towards her (all the Ansells had learnt to see in the dark), and, nestling his curly head against her wet bodice, murmured :

'Neva mind, Esty; I lat oo teep in my new bed.'

The consolation of sleeping in that imaginary new bed to the possession of which Ikey was always looking forward was apparently adequate ; for Esther got up from the floor and untied the loaves from her pinafore. A reckless spirit of defiance possessed her, as of a gambler who throws good money after bad. They should have a mad revelry to-night—the two loaves should be eaten at once. One (minus a hunk for father's supper) would hardly satisfy six voracious appetites. Solomon and Rachel, irrepressibly excited by the sight of the bread, rushed at it greedily, snatched a loaf from Esther's hand, and tore off a crust each with their fingers.

'Heathen,' cried the old grandmother. Washing and benediction !'

Solomon was used to being called a heathen by the *Bube.* He put on his cap and went grudgingly to the bucket of water that stood in a corner of the room, and tipped a drop over his fingers. It is to be feared that neither the quantity of water nor the area of hand covered reached even the minimum enjoined by Rabbincal law. He murmured something intended for Hebrew during the operation, and was beginning to mutter the devout little sentence which precedes the eating of bread, when Rachel, who as a female was less driven to the lavatory ceremony, and had thus got ahead of him, paused in her ravenous mastication and made a wry face. Solomon took a huge bite at his crust, then he uttered an inarticulate 'Pooh !' and spat out his mouthful.

There was no salt in the bread.

CHAPTER II

THE SWEATER

THE catastrophe was not complete. There were some long thin fibres of pale boiled meat, whose juices had gone to enrich the soup, lying about the floor or adhering to the fragments of the pitcher. Solomon, who was a curly-headed chap of infinite resource, discovered them, and it had just been decided to neutralise the insipidity of the bread by the far-away flavour of the meat, when a

peremptory knocking was heard at the door, and a dazzling vision
of beauty bounded into the room.

''Ere ! What are you doin', leavin' things leak through our
ceiling ? '

Becky Belcovitch was a buxom, bouncing girl, with cherry cheeks
that looked exotic in a land of pale faces. She wore a mass of
black crisp ringlets aggressively suggestive of singeing and curl-
papers. She was the belle of Royal Street in her spare time, and
womanly triumphs dogged even her working hours. She was sixteen
years old, and devoted her youth and beauty to buttonholes. In the
East End, where a spade is a spade, a buttonhole is a buttonhole,
and not a primrose or a pansy. There are two kinds of buttonhole
—the coarse for slop goods, and the fine for gentlemanly wear.
Becky concentrated herself on superior buttonholes, which are
worked with fine twist. She stitched them in her father's workshop, which was more comfortable than a stranger's, and better
fitted for evading the Factory Acts. To-night she was radiant
in silk and jewellery, and her pert snub nose had the insolence of
felicity which Agamemnon deprecated. Seeing her, you would
have as soon connected her with Esoteric Buddhism as with
buttonholes.

The *Bube* explained the situation in voluble Yiddish, and made
Esther wince again under the impassioned invective on her clumsi-
ness. The old beldame expended enough Oriental metaphor on
the accident to fit up a minor poet. If the family died of starvation,
their blood would be upon their grand-daughter's head.

' Well, why don't you wipe it up, stupid ? ' said Becky. ' 'Ow
would you like to pay for Pesach's new coat ? It just dripped past
his shoulder.'

' I 'm so sorry, Becky,' said Esther, striving hard to master the
tremor in her voice. And drawing a house-cloth from a mysterious recess, she went down on her knees in a practical prayer for
pardon.

Becky snorted and went back to her sister's engagement party.
For this was the secret of her gorgeous vesture, of her glittering
earrings, and her massive brooch, as it was the secret of the transformation of the Belcovitch workshop (and living room) into a hall
of dazzling light. Four separate gaunt bare arms of iron gas-pipe
lifted hymeneal torches. The labels from reels of cotton, pasted
above the mantelpiece as indexes of work done, alone betrayed the
past and future of the room. At a long narrow table, covered with
a white tablecloth spread with rum, gin, biscuits and fruit, and
decorated with two wax candles in tall brass candlesticks, stood or
sat a group of swarthy, neatly-dressed Poles, most of them in high
hats. A few women wearing wigs, silk dresses, and gold chains
wound round half-washed necks, stood about outside the inner
circle. A stooping black-bearded, blear-eyed man in a long
threadbare coat and a black skull-cap, on either side of which hung
a corkscrew curl, sat abstractedly eating the almonds and raisins,

in the central place of honour which befits a Maggid.   Before him were pens and ink and a roll of parchment.   This was the engagement contract.

The damages of breach of promise were assessed in advance and without respect to sex.   Whichever side repented of the bargain undertook to pay ten pounds by way of compensation for the broken pledge.   As a nation, Israel is practical and free from cant.   Romance and moonshine are beautiful things, but behind the glittering veil are always the stern realities of things and the weaknesses of human nature.

The high contracting parties were signing the document as Becky returned.   The bridegroom, who halted a little on one leg, was a tall, sallow man named Pesach Weingott.   He was a bootmaker, who could expound the Talmud and play the fiddle, but was unable to earn a living.   He was marrying Fanny Belcovitch because his parents-in-law would give him free board and lodging for a year, and because he liked her.   Fanny was a plump, pulpy girl, not in the prime of youth.   Her complexion was fair, and her manner lymphatic ; and if she was not so well favoured as her sister, she was more amiable and pleasant.   She could sing sweetly in Yiddish and in English, and had once been a pantomine fairy at ten shillings a week, and had even flourished a cutlass as a midshipman.   But she had long since given up the stage, to become her father's right-hand woman in the workshop.   She made coats from morning till midnight at a big machine with a massive treadle, and had pains in her chest even before she fell in love with Pesach Weingott.

There was a hubbub of congratulation ('*Mazzoltov, Mazzoltov,*' 'Good Luck'), and a palsy of handshaking, when the contract was signed.   Remarks, grave and facetious, flew about in Yiddish, with phrases of Polish and Russian thrown in for auld lang syne, and cups and jugs were broken in reminder of the transiency of things mortal.   The Belcovitches had been saving up their already broken crockery for the occasion.   The hope was expressed that Mr. and Mrs. Belcovitch would live to see 'rejoicings' on their other daughter, and to see their daughters' daughters under the *Chuppah*, or wedding canopy.

Becky's hardened cheek blushed under the oppressive jocularity.   Everybody spoke Yiddish habitually at No. 1 Royal Street, except the younger generation, and that spoke it to the elder.

'I always said no girl of mine should marry a Dutchman.'

It was a dominant thought of Mr. Belcovitch's, and it rose spontaneously to his lips at this joyful moment.   Next to a Christian, a Dutch Jew stood lowest in the gradation of potential sons-in-law.   Spanish Jews, earliest arrivals by way of Holland, after the Restoration, are a class apart, and look down on the later imported Ashkenazim, embracing both Poles and Dutchmen in their impartial contempt.   But this does not prevent the Pole and the Dutchman from despising each other.   To a Dutch or Russian

Jew, the 'Pullack,' or Polish Jew, is a poor creature ; and scarce anything can exceed the complacency with which the 'Pullack' looks down upon the 'Litvok,' or Lithuanian, the degraded being whose Shibboleth is literally Sibboleth, and who says 'ee' where rightly-constituted persons say 'oo.' To mimic the mincing pronunciation of the 'Litvok' affords the 'Pullack' a sense of superiority almost equalling that possessed by the English Jew, whose mispronunciation of the Holy Tongue is his title to rank far above all foreign varieties. Yet a vein of brotherhood runs beneath all these feelings of mutual superiority ; like the cliqueism which draws together 'old clo'' dealers, though each gives fifty per cent. more than any other dealer in the trade. The Dutch foregather in a district called 'The Dutch Tenters'; they eat voraciously, and almost monopolise the ice cream, hot pea, diamond-cutting, cucumber, herring, and cigar trades. They are not so cute as the Russians. Their women are distinguished from other women by the flaccidity of their bodices ; some wear small woollen caps and sabots.

When Esther read in her school-books that the note of the Dutch character was cleanliness, she wondered. She looked in vain for the scrupulously scoured floors and the shining caps and faces. Only in the matter of tobacco-smoke did the Dutch people she knew live up to the geographical 'Readers.'

German Jews gravitate to Polish and Russian ; and French Jews mostly stay in France. *Ici on ne parle pas Français* is the only lingual certainty in the London Ghetto, which is a cosmopolitan quarter.

'I always said no girl of mine should marry a Dutchman.'

Mr. Belcovitch spoke as if at the close of a long career devoted to avoiding Dutch alliances, forgetting that not even one of his daughters was yet secure.

'Nor any girl of mine,' said Mrs. Belcovitch, as if starting a separate proposition. 'I would not trust a Dutchman with my medicine-bottle, much less with my Alte or my Becky. Dutchmen were not behind the door when the Almighty gave out noses, and their deceitfulness is in proportion to their noses.'

The company murmured assent, and one gentleman, with a rather large organ, concealed it in a red cotton handkerchief, trumpeting uneasily.

'The Holy One, blessed be He, has given them larger noses than us,' said the Maggid, 'because they have to talk through them so much.'

A guffaw greeted this sally. The Maggid's wit was relished even when not coming from the pulpit. To the outsider this disparagement of the Dutch nose might have seemed a case of pot calling kettle black. The Maggid poured himself out a glass of rum, under cover of the laughter, and murmuring 'Life to you,' in Hebrew, gulped it down, and added, 'They oughtn't to call it the Dutch tongue, but the Dutch nose.'

'Yes, I always wonder how they can understand one another,' said Mrs. Belcovitch, 'with their *chatuchayacatigewesepoopa.*'

She laughed heartily over her onomatopœtic addition to the Yiddish vocabulary, screwing up her nose to give it due effect. She was a small, sickly-looking woman, with black eyes and shrivelled skin, and the wig without which no virtuous wife is complete. For a married woman must sacrifice her tresses on the altar of home, lest she snare other men with such sensuous baits. As a rule, she enters into the spirit of the self-denying ordinance so enthusiastically as to become hideous hastily in every other respect. It is forgotten that a husband is also a man. Mrs. Belcovitch's head was not completely shaven and shorn, for a lower stratum of an unmatched shade of brown peeped out in front of the *Shaitel*, not even coinciding as to the route of the central parting.

Meantime Pesach Weingott and Alte (Fanny) Belcovitch held each other's hand, guiltily conscious of Batavian corpuscles in the young man's blood. Pesach had a Dutch uncle, but as he had never talked like him Alte alone knew. Alte wasn't her real name, by the way, and Alte was the last person in the world to know what it was. She was the Belcovitches' first successful child ; the others all died before she was born. Driven frantic by a fate crueller than barrenness the Belcovitches consulted an old Polish Rabbi, who told them they displayed too much fond solicitude for their children, provoking Heaven thereby ; in future, they were to let no one but themselves know their next child's name, and never to whisper it till the child was safely married. In such wise, Heaven would not be incessantly reminded of the existence of their dear one, and would not go out of its way to castigate them.

The ruse succeeded, and Alte was anxiously waiting to change both her names under the *Chuppah*, and to gratify her life-long curiosity on the subject. Meantime, her mother had been calling her 'Alte,' or 'old un,' which sounded endearing to the child, but grated on the woman arriving ever nearer to the years of discretion. Occasionally, Mrs. Belcovitch succumbed to the prevailing tendency, and called her 'Fanny,' just as she sometimes thought of herself as Mrs. Belcovitch, though her name was Kosminski.

When Alte first went to school in London, the head-mistress said, 'What's your name?' The little 'old un' had not sufficient English to understand the question, but she remembered that the head-mistress had made the same sounds to the preceding applicant, and, where some little girls would have put their pinafores to their eyes and cried, Fanny showed herself full of resource. As the last little girl, though patently awe-struck, had come off with flying colours, merely by whimpering, 'Fanny Belcovitch,' Alte imitated these sounds as well as she was able.

'Fanny Belcovitch, did you say?' said the head-mistress, pausing with arrested pen.

Alte nodded her flaxen poll vigorously.

'Fanny Belcovitch,' she repeated, getting the syllables better on a second hearing.

The head-mistress turned to an assistant.

'Isn't it astonishing how names repeat themselves? Two girls, one after the other, both with exactly the same name!'

They were used to coincidences in the school, where, by reason of the tribal relationship of the pupils, there was a great run on some half a dozen names.

Mr. Kosminski took several years to understand that Alte had disowned him. When it dawned upon him he was not angry, and acquiesced in his fate. It was the only domestic detail in which he had allowed himself to be led by his children. Like his wife, Chayah, he was gradually persuaded into the belief that he was a born Belcovitch, or, at least, that Belcovitch was Kosminski translated into English.

Blissfully unconscious of the Dutch taint in Pesach Weingott, Bear Belcovitch bustled about in reckless hospitality. He felt that engagements were not everyday events, and that, even if his whole half-sovereign's worth of festive provision was swallowed up, he would not mind much. He wore a high hat, a well-preserved black coat, with a cutaway waistcoat, showing a quantity of glazed shirt-front and a massive watch-chain. They were his Sabbath clothes, and, like the Sabbath they honoured, were of immemorial antiquity. The shirt served him for seven Sabbaths, or a week of Sabbaths, being carefully folded after each. His boots had the Sabbath polish. The hat was the one he bought when he first set up as a *Baal Habaas*, or respectable pillar of the synagogue; for even in the smallest *Chevrah* the high hat comes next in sanctity to the Scroll of the Law, and he who does not wear it may never hope to attain to congregational dignities. The gloss on that hat was wonderful, considering it had been out unprotected in all winds and weathers. Not that Mr. Belcovitch did not possess an umbrella. He had two—one of fine new silk, the other a medley of broken ribs and cotton rags. Becky had given him the first to prevent the family disgrace of the spectacle of his promenades with the second. But he would not carry the new one on week-days because it was too good. And on Sabbaths it is a sin to carry any umbrella. So Becky's self-sacrifice was vain, and her umbrella stood in the corner, a standing gratification to the proud possessor.

Kosminski had had a hard fight for his substance, and was not given to waste. He was a tall, harsh-looking man of fifty, with grizzled hair, to whom life meant work, and work meant money, and money meant savings. In Parliamentary blue-books, English newspapers, and the Berner Street Socialistic Club, he was called a 'sweater,' and the comic papers pictured him with a protuberant paunch and a greasy smile; but he had not the remotest idea that he was other than a God-fearing, industrious, and even philanthropic citizen. The measure that had been dealt to him he did but deal to others. He saw no reason why immigrant paupers should not live on a crown a week while he taught them how to handle a press-iron or work a sewing-machine. They were much better off than in Poland. He would have been glad of such an income himself in those terrible first days of English life, when he saw his wife and his two babes starving before his eyes, and was only precluded from investing a casual twopence in poison by ignorance of the English name for anything deadly. And what did he live on now? The fowl, the pint of haricot beans, and the haddocks which Chayah purchased for the Sabbath overlapped into the middle of next week; a quarter of a pound of coffee lasted the whole week, the grounds being decocted till every grain of virtue was extracted. Black bread and potatoes and pickled herrings made up the bulk of the every-day diet. No, no one could accuse Bear Belcovitch of fattening on the entrails of his employés.

The furniture was of the simplest and shabbiest—no æsthetic instinct urged the Kosminskis to overpass the bare necessities of existence, except in dress. The only concessions to art were a crudely-coloured *Mizrach* on the east wall, to indicate the direction towards which the Jew should pray, and the mantelpiece mirror, which was bordered with yellow scalloped paper (to save the gilt), and ornamented at each corner with paper roses that bloomed afresh every Passover. And yet Bear Belcovitch had lived in much better style in Poland, possessing a brass wash-hand basin, a copper saucepan, silver spoons, a silver consecration beaker, and a cupboard with glass doors, and he frequently adverted to their fond memories. But he brought nothing away except his bedding, and that was pawned in Germany on the route. When he arrived in London he had with him three groschen and a family.

'What do you think, Pesach!' said Becky, as soon as she could get at her prospective brother-in-law through the barriers of congratulatory countrymen. 'The stuff that came through there'— she pointed to the discoloured fragment of ceiling—'was soup. That silly little Esther spilt all she got from the Kitchen.

'*Achi nebbich*, poor little thing!' cried Mrs. Kosminski, who was in a tender mood; 'very likely it hungers them sore upstairs. The father is out of work.'

'Knowest thou what, mother,' put in Fanny. 'Suppose we give them our soup. Aunt Leah has just fetched it for us. Have we not a special supper to-night?'

'But father?' murmured the little woman dubiously.

'Oh, he won't notice it. I don't think he knows the Soup Kitchen opens to-night. Let me, mother.'

And Fanny, letting Pesach's hand go, slipped out to the bedroom that served as a kitchen, and bore the still steaming pot upstairs. Pesach, who had pursued her, followed with some hunks of bread and a piece of lighted candle, which, while intended only to illumine the journey, came in handy at the terminus. And the festive company grinned and winked when the pair disappeared, and made jocular quotations from the Old Testament and the

Rabbis. But the lovers did not kiss when they came out of the garret of the Ansells ; their eyes were wet, and they went softly downstairs hand-in-hand, feeling linked by a deeper love than before.

Thus did Providence hand over the soup the Belcovitches took, from old habit, to a more necessitous quarter, and demonstrate in double sense that charity never faileth. Nor was this the only mulct which Providence exacted from the happy father, for later on a townsman of his appeared on the scene in a long capote, and with a grimy, woebegone expression. He was a 'greener' of the greenest order, having landed at the docks only a few hours ago, bringing over with him a great deal of luggage in the shape of faith in God and in the auriferous character of London pavements. On arriving in England he gave a casual glance at the Metropolis, and demanded to be directed to a synagogue, wherein to shake himself after the journey. His devotions over, he tracked out Mr. Kosminski, whose address, on a much-creased bit of paper, had been his talisman of hope during the voyage. In his native town, where the Jews groaned beneath divers and sore oppressions, the fame of Kosminski, the pioneer, the Crœsus, was a legend. Mr. Kosminski was prepared for these contingencies. He went to his bedroom, dragged out a heavy wooden chest from under the bed, unlocked it, and plunged his hand into a large dirty linen bag full of coins. The instinct of generosity which was upon him made him count out forty-eight of them. He bore them to the 'greener' in over-brimming palms, and the foreigner, unconscious how much he owed to the felicitous coincidence of his visit with Fanny's betrothal, saw fortune visibly within his grasp. He went out, his heart bursting with gratitude, his pocket with four dozen farthings. They took him in and gave him hot soup at a Poor Jews' Shelter, whither his townsman had directed him. Kosminski returned to the banqueting room, thrilling from head to foot with the approval of his conscience. He patted Becky's curly head, and said :

' Well, Becky, when shall we be dancing at your wedding ? '

Becky shook her curls. Her young men could not have a poorer opinion of one another than Becky had of them all. Their homage pleased her, though it did not raise them in her esteem. Lovers grew like blackberries—only more so ; for they were an evergreen stock. Or, as her mother put it in her coarse, pleasant manner, *Chasanim* were as plentiful as the street-dogs, Becky's beaux sat on the stairs before she was up, and became early risers in their love for her, each anxious to be the first to bid their Penelope of the buttonholes good-morrow. It was said that Kosminski's success as a 'sweater' was due to his beauteous Becky, the flower of sartorial youth gravitating to the workroom of this East London Laban. What they admired in Becky was that there was so much of her. Still, it was not enough to go round, and, though Becky might keep nine lovers in hand without fear of being set down as a flirt, a larger number of tailors would have been less consistent with prospective monogamy.

'I'm not going to throw myself away like Fanny,' said she confidentially to Pesach Weingott in the course of the evening.

He smiled apologetically.

'Fanny always had low views,' continued Becky. 'But I always said I would marry a gentleman.'

'And I dare say,' answered Pesach, stung into the retort, 'Fanny could marry a gentleman, too, if she wanted.'

Becky's idea of a gentleman was a clerk or a schoolmaster, who had no manual labour except scribbling or flogging. In her matrimonial views Becky was typical. She despised the status of her parents, and looked to marry out of it. They, for their part, could not understand the desire to be other than themselves.

'I don't say Fanny couldn't,' she admitted. 'All I say is, nobody could call this a luck-match.'

'Ah, thou hast me too many flies in thy nose,' reprovingly interposed Mrs. Belcovitch, who had just crawled up. 'Thou art too high-class.'

Becky tossed her head. 'I've got a new dolman,' she said, turning to one of her young men, who was present by special grace. 'You should see me in it. I look noble.'

'Yes,' said Mrs. Belcovitch proudly. 'It shines in the sun.'

'Is it like the one Bessie Sugarman's got?' inquired the young man.

'Bessie Sugarman!' echoed Becky scornfully. 'She gets all her things from the tallyman. She pretends to be so grand, but all her jewellery is paid for at so much a week.'

'So long as it is paid for,' said Fanny, catching the words, and turning a happy face on her sister.

'Not so jealous, Alte,' said her mother. 'When I shall win on the lotter*ee*, I will buy thee also a dolman.'

Almost all the company speculated on the Hamburg lottery, which, whether they were speaking Yiddish or English, they invariably accentuated on the last syllable. When an inhabitant of the Ghetto won even his money back, the news circulated like wild-fire, and there was a rush to the agents for tickets. The chances of sudden wealth floated like dazzling will-o'-the-wisps on the horizon, illumining the grey perspectives of the future. The lotter*ee* took the poor ticket-holders out of themselves, and gave them an interest in life apart from machine-cotton, lasts, or tobacco-leaf. The English labourer, who has been forbidden State lotteries, relieves the monotony of existence by an extremely indirect interest in the achievements of a special breed of horses.

'*Nu*, Pesach, another glass of rum,' said Mr. Belcovitch genially to his future son-in-law and boarder.

'Yes, I will,' said Pesach. 'After all, this is the first time I've got engaged.'

The rum was Mr. Belcovitch's own manufacture; its ingredients were unknown, but the fame of it travelled on currents of air to the remotest parts of the house. Even the inhabitants of the garrets sniffed and thought of turpentine.   Pesach swallowed the decoction, murmuring 'To life' afresh.   His throat felt like the funnel of a steamer, and there were tears in his eyes when he put down the glass.

'Ah, that was good !' he murmured.

'Not like thy English drinks, eh ?' said Mr. Belcovitch.

'England !' snorted Pesach, in royal disdain.   'What a country ! Daddle-doo is a language, and gingerbeer a liquor.'

'Daddle-doo' was Pesach's way of saying 'That 'll do.'   It was one of the first English idioms he picked up, and its puerility made him facetious.   It seemed to smack of the nursery.   When a nation expressed its soul thus, the existence of a beverage like gingerbeer could occasion no further surprise.

'You shan't have anything stronger than gingerbeer when we 're married,' said Fanny laughingly.   'I am not going to have any drinking.'

'But I 'll get drunk on gingerbeer,' Pesach laughed back.

'You can't,' Fanny said, shaking her large fond smile to and fro. 'By me health, not.'

'Ha ! ha ! ha !   Can't even get *shikkur* on it.   What a liquor !'

In the first Anglo-Jewish circles with which Pesach had scraped acquaintance, gingerbeer was the prevalent drink ; and, generalising almost as hastily as if he were going to write a book on the country, he concluded that it was the national beverage.   He had long since discovered his mistake, but the drift of the discussion reminded Becky of a chance for an arrow.

'On the day when you sit for joy, Pesach,' she said slyly, 'I shall send you a valentine.'

Pesach coloured up, and those in the secret laughed.   The reference was to another of Pesach's early ideas.   Some mischievous gossip had heard him arguing with another 'greener' outside a stationer's shop blazing with comic valentines.   The two foreigners were extremely puzzled to understand what these monstrosities portended.   Pesach, however, laid it down that the microcephalous gentlemen with tremendous legs, and the ladies five-sixths head and one-sixth skirt, were representations of the English peasants who lived in the little villages up country.

'When I sit for joy,' retorted Pesach, 'it will not be the season for valentines.'

'Won't it, though !' cried Becky, shaking her frizzy black curls. 'You 'll be a pair of comic uns.'

'All right, Becky,' said Alte good-humouredly.   'Your turn 'll come, and then we shall have the laugh of you.'

'Never,' said Becky.   'What do I want with a man ?'

The arm of the specially-invited young man was round her as she spoke.

'Don't make *Schnecks*,' said Fanny.

'It's not affectation.   I mean it.   What's the good of the men who visit father ?   There isn't a gentleman among them.'

'Ah, wait till I win on the lotter*ee*,' said the special young man.

'Then, vy not take another eighth of a ticket?' inquired Sugarman the Shadchan, who seemed to spring from the other end of the room. He was one of the greatest Talmudists in London—a lean, hungry-looking man, sharp of feature and acute of intellect. 'Look at Mrs. Robinson—I 've just won her over twenty pounds, and she only gave me two pounds for myself. I call it a *Cherpah*—a shame.'

'Yes, but you stole another two pounds,' said Becky.

'How do you know?' said Sugarman, startled.

Becky winked, and shook her head sapiently. 'Never *you* mind.'

The published list of the winning numbers was so complex in construction that Sugarman had ample opportunities of bewildering his clients.

'I von't sell you no more tickets,' said Sugarman, with righteous indignation.

'A fat lot I care,' said Becky, tossing her curls.

'Thou carest for nothing, said Mrs. Belcovitch, seizing the opportunity for maternal admonition. 'Thou hast not even brought me my medicine to-night. Thou wilt find it on the chest of drawers in the bedroom.'

Becky shook herself impatiently.

'I will go,' said the special young man.

'No ; it is not beautiful that a young man shall go into my bedroom in my absence,' said Mrs. Belcovitch, blushing.

Becky left the room.

'Thou knowest,' said Mrs. Belcovitch, addressing herself to the special young man, 'I suffer greatly from my legs. One is a thick one, and one a thin one.'

The young man sighed sympathetically.

'Whence comes it?' he asked.

'Do I know? I was born so. My poor lambkin' (this was the way Mrs. Belcovitch always referred to her dead mother) 'had well-matched legs. If I had Aristotle's head I might be able to find out why my legs are inferior. And so one goes about !'

The reverence for Aristotle enshrined in Yiddish idiom is probably due to his being taken by the vulgar for a Jew. At any rate, the theory that Aristotle's philosophy was Jewish was advanced by the mediæval poet, Jehuda Halevi, and sustained by Maimonides. The legend runs that when Alexander went to Palestine, Aristotle was in his train. At Jerusalem the philosopher had sight of King Solomon's manuscripts, and he forthwith edited them and put his name to them. But it is noteworthy that the story was only accepted by those Jewish scholars who adopted the Aristotelian philosophy, those who rejected it declaring that Aristotle in his last testament had admitted the inferiority of his writings to the Mosaic, and had asked that his works should be destroyed.

When Becky returned with the medicine, Mrs. Belcovitch mentioned that it was extremely nasty, and offered the young man a taste, whereat he rejoiced inwardly, knowing he had found favour

in the sight of the parent. Mrs. Belcovitch paid a penny a week
to her doctor in sickness or health, so that there was a loss on
being well. Becky used to fill up the bottles with water. to save
herself the trouble of going to fetch the medicine, but, as Mrs.
Belcovitch did not know this, it made no difference.

'Thou livest too much indoors, Mrs Kosminski,' said Mr. Sugarman, in Yiddish.

'Shall I march about in this weather—black and slippery, and
the Angel going a-hunting?'

'Ah!' said Mr. Sugarman, relapsing proudly into the vernacular;
've English valk about in all vedders.'

Meanwhile, Moses Ansell had returned from evening service,
and sat down, unquestioningly, by the light of an unexpected
candle to his expected supper of bread and soup, blessing God
for both gifts. The rest of the family had supped. Esther had
put the two youngest children to bed (Rachel had arrived at years
of independent undressing), and she and Solomon were doing
home-lessons in copy-books, the candle saving them from a caning
on the morrow. She held her pen clumsily, for several of her
fingers were swathed in bloody rags lined with cobweb. The
grandmother dozed in her chair. Everything was quiet and peaceful, though the atmosphere was chilly.

Moses ate his supper with a great smacking of the lips and an
equivalent enjoyment. When it was over he sighed deeply, and
thanked God in a prayer lasting ten minutes, and delivered in a
rapid, sing-song manner. He then inquired of Solomon whether
he had said his evening prayer. Solomon looked out of the
corners of his eyes at his *Bube*, and, seeing that she was asleep on
the bed he had, and kicked Esther significantly, but hurtfully,
under the table.

'Then you had better say your night-prayer.'

There was no getting out of that, so Solomon finished his sum,
writing the figures of the answer rather faint, in case he should
discover from another boy next morning that they were wrong ;
then, producing a Hebrew prayer-book from his inky cotton satchel,
he made a mumbling sound, with occasional enthusiastic bursts of
audible coherence, for a length of time proportioned to the number
of pages. Then he went to bed. After that Esther put her
grandmother to bed, and curled herself up at her side. She lay
awake a long time, listening to the quaint sounds emitted by
her father in his study of Rashi's *Commentary on the Book of Job*,
the measured drone blending not disagreeably with the far-away
sounds of Pesach Weingott's fiddle.

Pesach's fiddle played the accompaniment to many other people's
thoughts.   The respectable master-tailor sat behind his glazed
shirt-front, beating time with his foot. His little sickly-looking wife
stood by his side, nodding her bewigged head joyously. To both
the music brought the same recollection—a Polish market-place.

Belcovitch, or rather Kosminski, was the only surviving son of a widow. It was curious, and suggestive of some grim law of heredity, that his parents' elder children had died off as rapidly as his own, and that his life had been preserved by some such expedient as Alte's.   Only, in his case, the Rabbi consulted had advised his father to go into the woods and call his new-born son by the name of the first animal that he saw. This was why the future sweater was named Bear.   To the death of his brothers and sisters Bear owed his exemption from military service. He grew up to be a stalwart, well-set-up young baker, a loss to the Russian army.

Bear went out into the market-place one fine day and saw Chayah in maiden ringlets. She was a slim, graceful little thing, with nothing obviously odd about the legs, and was buying onions. Her back was towards him, but in another moment she turned her head and Bear's. As he caught the sparkle of her eye, he felt that without her life were worse than the conscription. Without delay, he made inquiries about the fair young vision, and, finding its respectability unimpeachable, he sent a *Shadchan* to propose to her, and they were affianced. Chayah's father undertaking to give a dowry of two hundred gulden. Unfortunately he died suddenly in the attempt to amass them, and Chayah was left an orphan.   The two hundred gulden were nowhere to be found. Tears rained down both Chayah's cheeks, on the one side for the loss of her father, on the other for the prospective loss of a husband. The Rabbi was full of tender sympathy. He bade Bear come to the dead man's chamber. The venerable white-bearded corpse lay on the bed, swathed in shroud, and *Talith*, or praying-shawl.

'Bear,' he said, 'thou knowest that I saved thy life.'

'Nay,' said Bear ; 'indeed I know not that.'

'Yea, of a surety,' said the Rabbi. 'Thy mother hath not told thee, but all thy brothers and sisters perished, and, lo ! thou alone art preserved ! It was I that called thee a beast.'

Bear bowed his head in grateful silence.

'Bear,' said the Rabbi, 'thou didst contract to wed this dead man's daughter, and he did contract to pay over to thee two hundred gulden.

'Truth,' replied Bear.

'Bear,' said the Rabbi, 'there are no two hundred gulden.'

A shadow flitted across Bear's face, but he said nothing.

'Bear,' said the Rabbi again, 'there are not two gulden.'

Bear did not move.

'Bear,' said the Rabbi, 'leave thou my side, and go over to the other side of the bed, facing me.'

So Bear left his side and went over to the other side of the bed facing him.

'Bear,' said the Rabbi, 'give me thy right hand.'

The Rabbi stretched his own right hand across the bed, but Bear kept his obstinately behind his back.

'Bear,' repeated the Rabbi, in tones of more penetrating solemnity, 'give me thy right hand.'

' Nay,' replied Bear sullenly. ' Wherefore should I give thee my right hand ? '

' Because,' said the Rabbi, and his tones trembled, and it seemed to him that the dead man's face grew sterner, ' because I wish thee to swear across the body of Chayah's father that thou wilt marry her.'

' Nay, that I will not ! ' said Bear.

' Will not ? ' repeated the Rabbi, his lips growing white with pity.

' Nay, I will not take any oaths,' said Bear hotly. ' I love the maiden, and I will keep what I have promised. But, by my father's soul, I will take no oaths ! '

' Bear,' said the Rabbi in a choking voice, ' give me thy hand. Nay, not to swear by, but to grip. Long shalt thou live, and the Most High shall prepare thy seat in Gan Iden.'

So the old man and the young clasped hands across the corpse, and the simple old Rabbi perceived a smile flickering over the face of Chayah's father. Perhaps it was only a sudden glint of sunshine.

The wedding-day drew nigh, but lo ! Chayah was again dissolved in tears.

' What ails thee ? ' said her brother Naphtali.

' I cannot follow the custom of the maidens,' wept Chayah. ' Thou knowest we are blood-poor, and I have not the wherewithal to buy my Bear a *Talith* for his wedding-day ; nay, not even to make him a *Talith*-bag. And when our father (the memory of the righteous for a blessing) was alive, I had dreamed of making my *Chosan* a beautiful velvet satchel lined with silk, and I would have embroidered his initials thereon in gold, and sewn him beautiful white corpse-clothes. Perchance he will rely upon me for his wedding *Talith*, and we shall be shamed in the sight of the congregation.'

' Nay, dry thine eyes, my sister,' said Naphtali. ' Thou knowest that my Leah presented me with a costly *Talith* when I led her under the canopy. Wherefore, do thou take my praying-shawl and lend it to Bear for the wedding-day, so that decency may be preserved in the sight of the congregation. The young man has a great heart, and he will understand.'

So Chayah, blushing prettily, lent Bear Naphtali's delicate *Talith*, and Beauty and the Beast made a rare couple under the wedding canopy. Chayah wore the gold medallion and the three rows of pearls which her lover had sent her the day before. And when the Rabbi had finished blessing husband and wife, Naphtali spake the bridegroom privily, and said :

' Pass me my *Talith* back.'

But Bear answered :

' Nay, nay ; the *Talith* is in my keeping, and there it shall remain.'

' But it is my *Talith*,' protested Naphtali in an angry whisper. ' I only lent it to Chayah to lend it thee.'

' It concerns me not,' Bear returned in a decisive whisper. ' The *Talith* is my due, and I shall keep it. What ! have I not

lost enough by marrying thy sister? Did not thy father—peace
be upon him!—promise me two hundred gulden with her?'

Naphtali retired discomfited; but he made up his mind not to
go without some compensation. He resolved that during the progress of the wedding procession, conducting the bridegroom to
the chamber of the bride, he would be the man to snatch off Bear's
new hat. Let the rest of the riotous escort essay to snatch whatever other article of the bridegroom's attire they would, the hat
was the easiest to dislodge, and he, Naphtali, would straightway
reimburse himself partially with that. But the instant the procession formed itself, behold the shifty bridegroom forthwith removed
his hat, and held it tightly under his arm.

A storm of protestations burst forth at this daring departure
from hymeneal tradition.

'Nay, nay, put it on!' arose from every mouth.

But Bear closed his, and marched mutely on.

'Heathen!' cried the Rabbi. 'Put on your hat!'

The attempt to enforce the religious sanction failed too. Bear
had spent several gulden upon his headgear, and could not see
the joke. He plodded towards his blushing Chayah through a
tempest of disapprobation.

Throughout life Bear Belcovitch retained the contrariety of
character that marked his matrimonial beginnings. He hated to
part with money; he put off paying bills to the last moment, and
he would even beseech his 'hands' to wait a day or two longer for
their wages. He liked to feel that he had all that money in his
possession. Yet 'at home' in Poland, he had always lent money
to the officers and gentry, when they ran temporarily short at cards.
They would knock him up in the middle of the night to obtain the
means of going on with the game. And in England he never refused to become surety for a loan when any of his poor friends
begged the favour of him. These loans ran from three to five
pounds, but whatever the amount, they were very rarely paid.
The loan-offices came down upon him for the money. He paid it
without a murmur, shaking his head compassionately over the poor
ne'er-do-wells, and perhaps not without a compensating consciousness of superior practicality.

Only, if the borrower had neglected to treat him to a glass of
rum to clench his signing as surety, the shake of Bear's head would
become more reproachful than sympathetic, and he would mutter
bitterly :

'Five pounds, and not even a drink for the money.'

The jewellery he generously lavished on his womankind was in
essence a mere channel of investment for his savings, avoiding the
risks of a banking-account, and aggregating his wealth in a port-
able shape, in obedience to an instinct generated by centuries of
insecurity. The interest on the sums thus invested was the gratification of the other Oriental instinct for gaudiness.

CHAPTER III

MALKA

THE Sunday Fair so long associated with Petticoat Lane is dying hard, and is still vigorous ; its glories were in full swing on the dull gray morning when Moses Ansell took his way through the Ghetto. It was near eleven o'clock, and the throng was thickening momently.   The vendors cried their wares in stentorian tones, and the babble of the buyers was like the confused roar of a stormy sea.   The dead walls and hoardings were placarded with bills from which the life of the inhabitants could be constructed.   Many were in Yiddish, the most hopelessly corrupt and hybrid jargon ever evolved.   Even when the language was English the letters were Hebrew.   Whitechapel, Public Meeting, Board School, Sermon, Police, and other modern banalities, glared at the passer-by in the sacred guise of the Tongue associated with miracles and prophecies, palm-trees and cedars and seraphs, lions and shepherds and harpists.

Moses stopped to read these hybrid posters—he had nothing better to do—as he slouched along.   He did not care to remember that dinner was due in two hours.   He turned aimlessly into Wentworth Street, and studied a placard that hung in a bootmaker's window.   This was the announcement it made in jargon :

> ' Riveters, Clickers, Lasters, Finishers,
> Wanted.
> BARUCH EMANUEL,
> Cobbler,
> Makes and Repairs Boots
> Every Bit as Cheaply
> as
> MORDECAI SCHWARTZ,
> of 12 Goulston Street.'

Mordecai Schwartz was written in the biggest and blackest of Hebrew letters, and quite dominated the little shop-window.   Baruch Emanuel was visibly conscious of his inferiority to his powerful rival, though Moses had never heard of Mordecai Schwartz before.   He entered the shop, and said in Hebrew, ' Peace be to you.'   Baruch Emanuel, hammering a sole, answered in Hebrew : ' Peace be to you.'

Moses dropped into Yiddish.

' I am looking for work.   Peradventure have you something for me.'

' What can you do ? '

' I have been a riveter.'

' I cannot engage any more riveters.'

Moses looked disappointed.

'I have also been a clicker,' he said.

'I have all the clickers I can afford,' Baruch answered.

Moses's gloom deepened.

'Two years ago I worked as a finisher.'

Baruch shook his head silently.   He was annoyed at the man's persistence.   There was only the laster resource left.

'And before that I was a laster for a week,' Moses answered.

'I don't want any !' cried Baruch, losing his temper.

'But in your window it stands that you do,' protested Moses feebly.

'I don't care what stands in my window,' said Baruch hotly. 'Have you not head enough to see that that is all bunkum? Unfortunately I work single-handed, but it looks good and it isn't lies.   Naturally I want Riveters and Clickers and Lasters and Finishers.   Then I could set up a big establishment and gouge out Mordecai Schwartz's eyes.   But the Most High denies me assistants, and I am content to want.'

Moses understood that attitude towards the nature of things. He went out and wandered down another narrow dirty street in search of Mordecai Schwartz, whose address Baruch Emanuel had so obligingly given him.   He thought of the Maggid's sermon on the day before.   The Maggid had explained a verse of Habakkuk in quite an original way which gave an entirely new colour to a passage in Deuteronomy.   Moses experienced acute pleasure in musing upon it, and went past Mordecai's shop without going in, and was only awakened from his day-dream by the brazen clanging of a bell.   It was the bell of the great Ghetto school, summoning its pupils from the reeking courts and alleys, from the garrets and the cellars, calling them to come and be Anglicised. And they came—in a great straggling procession recruited from every lane and by-way ; big children and little children ; boys in blackening corduroy and girls in washed-out cotton ; tidy children and ragged children ; children in great shapeless boots gaping at the toes ; sickly children and sturdy children and diseased children ; bright-eyed children and hollow-eyed children ; quaint, sallow, foreign-looking children and fresh-coloured, English-looking children ; with great pumpkin heads, with oval heads, with pear-shaped heads ; with old men's faces, with cherubs' faces, with monkeys' faces ; cold and famished children and warm and well-fed children ; children conning their lessons and children romping carelessly ; the demure and the anæmic ; the boisterous and the blackguardly, the insolent, the idiotic, the vicious, the intelligent, the exemplary, the dull—spawn of all countries—all hastening at the inexorable clang of the big school-bell to be ground in the same great, blind, inexorable Governmental machine.   Here, too, was a miniature fair, the path being lined by itinerant temptations. There was brisk traffic in toffy and gray peas and monkey-nuts, and the crowd was swollen by anxious parents seeing tiny or truant offspring safe within the school-gates.   The women were

bare-headed or beshawled, with infants at their breasts and little
ones toddling at their sides ; the men were greasy and musty and
squalid.   Here a bright, earnest little girl held her vagrant big
brother by the hand, not to let go till she had seen him in the
bosom of his class-mates.   There a sullen wild-eyed mite in petticoats was being dragged along, screaming, towards distasteful
durance.   It was a drab picture—tne bleak, leaden sky above, the
sloppy, miry stones below, the frowsy mothers and fathers, the
motley children.

'Monkey-nuts ! Monkey-nuts !' croaked a wizened old woman.
'Oppea ! Oppea !' droned a doddering old Dutchman.

He bore a great can of hot peas in one hand and a lighthouse-
looking pepper-pot in the other.   Some of the children swallowed
the dainties hastily out of miniature basins, others carried them
within in paper packets for surreptitious munching.

'Call that a ay-puth ?' a small boy would say.

'Not enough !' the old man would exclaim in surprise.   'Here
you are then !'

And he would give the peas another sprinkling from the
pepper-pot.

Moses Ansell's progeny were not in the picture.   The younger
children were at home ; the elder had gone to school an hour
before to run about and get warm in the spacious playgrounds.
A slice of bread each and the wish-wash of a thrice-brewed
pennyworth of tea had been their morning meal, and there
was no prospect of dinner.   The thought of them made Moses's
heart heavy again ; he forgot the Maggid's explanation of the
verse in Habakkuk, and he retraced his steps towards Mordecai
Schwartz's shop.   But, like his humbler rival, Mordecai had no use
for the many-sided Moses ; he was 'full up' with swarthy 'hands,'
though, as there were rumours of strikes in the air, he prudently
took note of Moses's address.   After this rebuff, Moses shuffled
hopelessly about for more than an hour ; the dinner-hour was
getting desperately near ; already children passed him, carrying
the Sunday dinners from the bakeries, and there were wafts of
vague poetry in the atmosphere.   Moses felt he could not face
his own children.

At last he nerved himself to an audacious resolution, and
elbowed his way blusterously towards the Ruins, lest he might
break down if his courage had time to cool.

'The Ruins' was a great stony square, partly bordered by
houses, and only picturesque on Sundays, when it became a
branch of the all-ramifying Fair.   Moses could have bought anything there, from elastic braces to green parrots in gilt cages—
that is to say, if he had had money.   At present he had nothing in
his pocket except holes.

What he might be able to do on his way back was another
matter ; for it was Malka that Moses Ansell was going to see.
She was the cousin of his deceased wife, and lived in Zachariah

Square. Moses had not been there for a month, for Malka was a wealthy twig of the family tree, to be approached with awe and trembling. She kept a second-hand clothes store in Houndsditch, a supplementary stall in the Halfpenny Exchange, and a barrow on the 'Ruins' of a Sunday ; and she had set up Ephraim, her newly-acquired son-in-law, in the same line of business in the same district. Like most things she dealt in, her son-in-law was second-hand, having lost his first wife four years ago in Poland. But he was only twenty-two, and a second-hand son-in-law of twenty-two is superior to many brand-new ones.

The two domestic establishments were a few minutes away from the shops, facing each other diagonally across the square. They were small three-roomed houses, without basements, the ground-floor window in each being filled up with a black gauze blind (an invariable index of gentility) which allowed the occupants to see all that was passing outside, but confronted gazers with their own reflections. Passers-by postured at these mirrors, twisting moustaches perkily, or giving coquettish pats to bonnets, unwitting of the grinning inhabitants. Most of the doors were ajar, wintry as the air was, for the Zachariah Squareites lived a good deal on the door-step. In the summer the housewives sat outside on chairs, and gossiped and knitted, as if the sea foamed at their feet, and wrinkled, good-humoured old men played nap on tea-trays. Some of the doors were blocked below with sliding barriers of wood, a sure token of infants inside given to straying. More obvious tokens of child-life were the swings nailed to the lintels of a few doors, in which, despite the cold, toothless babes swayed like monkeys on a branch. But the Square, with its broad area of quadrangular pavement, was an ideal playing-ground for children, since other animals came not within its precincts, except an inquisitive dog or a local cat. Solomon Ansell knew no greater privilege than to accompany his father to these fashionable quarters and whip his humming-top across the ample spaces, the while Moses transacted his business with Malka. Last time the business was psalm-saying. Milly had been brought to bed of a son, but it was doubtful if she would survive, despite the charms hung upon the bed-post to counteract the nefarious designs of Lilith, the wicked first wife of Adam, and of the Not-Good Ones who hover about women in childbirth. So Moses was sent for, post-haste, to intercede with the Almighty. His piety, it was felt, would command attention. For an average of three hundred and sixty-two days a year Moses was a miserable worm, a nonentity ; but on the other three, when death threatened to visit Malka or her little clan, Moses became a personage of prime importance, and was summoned at all hours of the day and night to wrestle with the angel Azrael. When the angel had retired worsted, after a match sometimes protracted into days, Moses relapsed into his primitive insignificance, and was dismissed with a mouthful of rum and a shilling. It never seemed to him an unfair equivalent, for nobody could make less demands on the universe than Moses. Give him two solid meals and three solid services a day, and he was satisfied, and he craved more for spiritual snacks between meals than for physical.

The last crisis had been brief, and there was so little danger that, when Milly's child was circumcised, Moses had not even been bidden to the feast, though his piety would have made him the ideal *Sandek*, or godfather. He did not resent this, knowing himself dust—and that anything but gold-dust.

Moses had hardly emerged from the little arched passage which led to the Square, when sounds of strife fell upon his ears. Two stout women, chatting amicably at their doors, had suddenly developed a dispute. In Zachariah Square, when you wanted to get to the bottom of a quarrel, the cue was not 'find the woman,' but find the child. The high-spirited bantlings had a way of pummelling one another in fistic duels, and of calling in their respective mothers when they got the worst of it—which is cowardly, but human. The mother of the beaten belligerent would then threaten to wring the 'year,' or to twist the nose, of the victorious party—sometimes she did it. In either case, the other mother would intervene, and then the two bantlings would retire into the background, and leave their mothers to take up the duel, while they resumed their interrupted game.

Of such sort was the squabble betwixt Mrs. Isaacs and Mrs. Jacobs. Mrs. Isaacs pointed out with superfluous vehemence that her poor lamb had been mangled beyond recognition. Mrs. Jacobs, *per contra*, asseverated with superfluous gesture that it was her poor lamb who had received irreparable injury. These statements were not in mutual contradiction, but Mrs. Isaacs and Mrs. Jacobs were, and so the point at issue was gradually absorbed in more personal recriminations.

'By my life, and by my Fanny's life, I'll leave my seal on the first child of yours that comes across my way! There!' Thus Mrs. Isaacs.

'Lay a finger on a hair of a child of mine, and, by my husband's life, I'll summons you, I'll have the law on you!' Thus Mrs. Jacobs, to the gratification of the resident populace.

Mrs. Isaacs and Mrs. Jacobs rarely quarrelled with each other, uniting rather in opposition to the rest of the Square. They were English, quite English, their grandfather having been born in Dresden; and they gave themselves airs in consequence, and called their *Kinder* 'children,' which annoyed those neighbours who found a larger admixture of Yiddish necessary for conversation. These very *Kinder*, again, attained considerable importance among their school-fellows by refusing to pronounce the guttural 'ch' of the Hebrew otherwise than as an English 'k.'

'Summons me, indeed!' laughed back Mrs. Isaacs. 'A fat lot I'd care for that. You'd jolly soon expose your character to the magistrate. Everybody knows what *you* are!'

'Your mother!' retorted Mrs. Jacobs mechanically, the elliptical method of expression being greatly in vogue for conversation of a loud character.   Quick as lightning came the parrying stroke.

'Yah! And what was your father, I should like to know?'

Mrs. Isaacs had no sooner made this inquiry than she became conscious of an environment of suppressed laughter ; Mrs. Jacobs awoke to the situation a second later, and the two women stood suddenly dumfounded, petrified, with arms akimbo, staring at each other.

The wise if apocryphal Ecclesiasticus sagely and pithily remarked, many centuries before modern civilisation was invented, 'Jest not with a rude man, lest thy ancestors be disgraced.'   To this day the Oriental methods of insult have survived in the Ghetto. The dead past is never allowed to bury its dead ; the genealogical dust-heap is always liable to be raked up, and even innocuous ancestors may be traduced to the third and fourth generation.

Now, it so happened that Mrs. Isaacs and Mrs. Jacobs were sisters.   And when it dawned upon them into what dilemma their automatic methods of carte and tierce had inveigled them, they were frozen with confusion.   They retired crestfallen to their respective parlours, and sported their oaks.   The resources of repartee were dried up for the moment.   Relatives are unduly handicapped in these verbal duels, especially relatives with the same mother and father.

Presently Mrs. Isaacs reappeared.   She had thought of something she ought to have said.   She went up to her sister's closed door and shouted into the keyhole, 'None of my children ever had bandy-legs!'

Almost immediately the window of the front bedroom was flung up, and Mrs. Jacobs leant out of it waving what looked like an immense streamer.

'Aha!' she observed, dangling it tantalisingly up and down. 'Morry antique!'

The dress fluttered in the breeze.   Mrs. Jacobs caressed the stuff between her thumb and forefinger.

'Aw-aw-aw-aw-aw-awl silk,' she announced with a long ecstatic quaver.

Mrs. Isaacs stood paralysed by the brilliancy of the repartee.

Mrs. Jacobs withdrew the moiré antique and exhibited a mauve gown.

'Aw-aw-aw-aw-aw-awl silk.'

The mauve fluttered for a triumphant instant, the next a puce and amber dress floated on the breeze.

'Aw-aw-aw-aw-aw-awl silk.'   Mrs. Jacob's fingers smoothed it lovingly, then it was drawn within, to be instantly replaced by a green dress.   Mrs. Jacobs passed the skirt slowly through her fingers.   'Aw-aw-aw-aw-aw-awl silk!' she quavered mockingly.

By this time Mrs. Isaacs's face was the colour of the latest flag of victory.

'The tallyman!' she tried to retort, but the words stuck in her throat. Fortunately just then she caught sight of her poor lamb playing with the other poor lamb. She dashed at her offspring, boxed its ears, and crying, 'You little blackguard, if I ever catch you playing with blackguards again I'll wring your neck for you,' she hustled the infant into the house, and slammed the door viciously behind her.

Moses had welcomed this every-day scene, for it put off for a few moments his encounter with the formidable Malka. As she had not appeared at door or window, he concluded she was in a bad temper or out of London; neither alternative was pleasant.

He knocked at the door of Milly's house, where her mother was generally to be found, and an elderly charwoman opened it. There were some bottles of spirit standing on a wooden side-table covered with a coloured cloth, and some unopened biscuit-bags. At these familiar premonitory signs of a festival, Moses felt tempted to beat a retreat. He could not think for the moment what was up, but whatever it was he had no doubt the well-to-do persons would supply him with ice. The charwoman, with brow darkened by soot and gloom, told him that Milly was upstairs, but that her mother had gone across to her own house with the clothes-brush.

Moses's face fell. When his wife was alive, she had been a link of connection between 'The Family' and himself, her cousin having generously employed her as charwoman. So Moses knew the import of the clothes-brush. Malka was very particular about her appearance, and loved to be externally speckless, but somehow or other she had no clothes-brush at home. This deficiency did not matter ordinarily, for she practically lived at Milly's. But when she had words with Milly or her husband, she retired to her own house to sulk or *schmull*, as they called it. The carrying away of the clothes-brush was, thus, a sign that she considered the breach serious, and hostilities likely to be protracted. Sometimes a whole week would go by without the two houses ceasing to stare sullenly across at each other, the situation in Milly's camp being aggravated by the lack of a clothes-brush. In such moments of irritation, Milly's husband was apt to declare that his mother-in-law had abundance of clothes-brushes, for, he pertinently asked, how did she manage during her frequent business tours in the country? He gave it as his conviction that Malka merely took the clothes-brush away to afford herself a handle for returning. But, then, Ephraim Phillips was a graceless young fellow, the death of whose first wife was probably a judgment on his levity, and everybody, except his second mother-in-law, knew that he had a book of tickets for the Oxbridge Music-Hall, and went there on Friday nights. Still, in spite of these facts, experience did show that whenever Milly's camp had out-sulked Malka's, the old woman's surrender was always veiled under the formula of: 'Oh, Milly, I've brought you over your clothes-brush! I just noticed it, and thought you might be wanting it.' After this, conversation was comparatively easy.

Moses hardly cared to face Malka in such a crisis of the clothes-brush. He turned away despairingly, and was going back through the small archway which led to the Ruins and the outside world, when a grating voice startled his ear.

'Well, Méshe, whither fliest thou? Has my Milly forbidden thee to see me?'

He looked back. Malka was standing at her house-door. He retraced his steps.

'N-n-o,' he murmured. I thought you still out with your stall.'

That was where she should have been, at any rate till half an hour ago. She did not care to tell herself, much less Moses, that she had been waiting at home for the envoy of peace from the filial camp summoning her to the ceremony of the Redemption of her grandson.

'Well, now thou seest me,' she said, speaking Yiddish for his behoof, 'thou lookest not outwardly anxious to know how it goes with me.'

'How goes it with you?'

'As well as an old woman has a right to expect. The Most High is good!' Malka was in her most amiable mood, to emphasise to outsiders the injustice of her kin in quarrelling with her. She was a tall woman of fifty, with a tanned equine gipsy face, surmounted by a black wig, and decorated laterally by great gold earrings. Great black eyes blazed beneath great black eyebrows, and the skin between them was capable of wrinkling itself black with wrath. A gold chain was wound thrice round her neck, and looped up within her black silk bodice. There were numerous rings on her fingers, and she perpetually smelt of peppermint. '*Nu*, stand not chattering there,' she went on. 'Come in. Dost thou wish me to catch my death of cold?'

Moses slouched timidly within, his head bowed as if in dread of knocking against the top of the door. The room was a perfect facsimile of Milly's parlour at the other end of the diagonal, save that, instead of the festive bottles and paper bags on the small side-table, there was a cheerless clothes-brush. Like Milly's the room contained a round table, a chest of drawers, with decanters on the top, and a high mantelpiece decorated with pendant green fringes, fastened by big-headed brass nails. Here cheap china dogs, that had had more than their day, squatted amid lustres with crystal drops. Before the fire was a lofty steel guard, which, useful enough in Milly's household, had survived its function in Malka's, where no one was ever likely to tumble into the grate. In a corner of the room a little staircase began to go upstairs. There was oil-cloth on the floor. In Zachariah Square anybody could go into anybody else's house and feel at home. There was no visible difference between one and another. Moses sat down awkwardly on a chair, and refused a peppermint. In the end he accepted an apple, blessed God for creating the fruit of the tree, and made a ravenous bite at it.

'I must take peppermints,' Malka explained. 'It's for the spasms!'

'But you said you were well,' murmured Moses.

'And suppose? If I did not take peppermint I should have the spasms. My poor sister Rosina—peace be upon him!—who died of typhoid, suffered greatly from the spasms. It's in the family. She would have died of asthma if she had lived long enough. *Nu*, how goes it with thee?' she went on, suddenly remembering that Moses, too, had a right to be ill. At bottom, Malka felt a real respect for Moses, though he did not know it. It dated from the day he cut a chip of mahogany out of her best round table. He had finished cutting his nails, and wanted a morsel of wood to burn with them, in witness of his fulfilment of the pious custom. Malka raged, but in her inmost heart there was admiration for such unscrupulous sanctity.

'I have been out of work for three weeks,' Moses answered, omitting to expound the state of his health in view of more urgent matters.

'Unlucky fool! What my silly cousin Gittel—peace be upon him!—could see to marry in thee, I know not.'

Moses could not enlighten her. He might have informed her that *Olov Hasholom*! 'peace be upon him!' was an absurdity when applied to a woman; but then he used the pious phrase himself, although aware of its grammatical shortcomings.

'I told her thou wouldst never be able to keep her, poor lamb!' Malka went on. 'But she was always an obstinate pig. And she kept her head high up, too, as if she had five pounds a week! Never would let her children earn money like other people's children. But thou oughtest not to be so obstinate. Thou shouldst have more sense, Méshe; *thou* belongest not to my family. Why can't Solomon go out with matches?'

'Gittel's soul would not like it.'

'But the living have bodies! Thou rather seest thy children starve than work. There's Esther—an idle, lazy brat, always reading story-books; why doesn't she sell flowers or pull out bastings in the evening?'

'Esther and Solomon have their lessons to do.'

'Lessons!' snorted Malka. 'What's the good of lessons? It's English, not Judaism, they teach them in that godless school. I could never read or write anything but Hebrew in all my life; but, God be thanked, I have thriven without it. All they teach them in the school is English nonsense. The teachers are a pack of heathens, who eat forbidden things; but the good Yiddishkeit goes to the wall. I'm ashamed of thee, Méshe; thou dost not even send thy boys to a Hebrew class in the evening.'

'I have no money, and they must do their English lessons; else, perhaps, their clothes will be stopped. Besides, I teach them myself every Shabbos afternoon and Sunday. Solomon translates into Yiddish the whole Pentateuch with Rashi.'

'Yes, he may know *Térah*,' said Malka, not to be baffled ; 'but he'll never know *Gemorah* or *Mishnayis*.'

Malka herself knew very little of these abstruse subjects beyond their names, and the fact that they were studied out of minutely-printed folios by men of extreme sanctity.

'He knows a little *Gemorah*, too,' said Moses. 'I can't teach him at home, because I haven't got a *Gemorah*—it's so expensive, as you know. But he went with me to the Beth-Medrash, when the Maggid was studying it with a class free of charge, and we learnt the whole of the Tractate *Niddah*. Solomon understands very well all about the Divorce Laws, and he could adjudicate on the duties of women to their husbands.'

'Ah, but he'll never know *Cabbulah*,' said Malka, driven to her last citadel. 'But, then, no one in England can study *Cabbulah* since the days of Rabbi Falk (the memory of the righteous for a blessing), any more than a born Englishman can learn Talmud. There's something in the air that prevents it. In my town there was a Rabbi who could do *Cabbulah* ; he could call Abraham our father from the grave. But in this pig-eating country no one can be holy enough for the Name—blessed be It !—to grant him the privilege. I don't believe the *Shochetim* kill the animals properly ; the statutes are violated ; even pious people eat *tripha* cheese and butter. I don't say thou dost, Méshe, but thou lettest thy children.'

'Well, your own butter is not *kosher*,' said Moses nettled.

'My butter ? What does it matter about my butter ? I never set up for a purist. I don't come of a family of Rabbonim. I'm only a business woman. It's the *froom* people that I complain of —the people who ought to set an example, and are lowering the standard of *Froomkeit*. I caught a beadle's wife the other day washing her meat and butter plates in the same bowl of water. In time they will be frying steaks in butter, and they will end by eating *tripha* meat out of butter plates, and the judgment of God will come. But what is become of thine apple? Thou hast not gorged it already ?'

Moses nervously pointed to his trousers-pocket, bulged out by the mutilated globe. After his first ravenous bite, Moses had bethought himself of his responsibilities.

'It's for the *Kinder*,' he explained.

'*Nu*, the *Kinder* !' snorted Malka disdainfully. And what will they give thee for it ? Verily, not a thank you. In my young days we trembled before the father and the mother, and my mother—peace be upon him !—*potched* my face after I was a married woman. I shall never forget that slap—it nearly made me adhere to the wall. But nowadays our children sit on our heads. I gave my Milly all she has in the world—a house, a shop, a husband, and my best bed-linen. And now, when I want her to call the child Yosef, after my first husband—peace be on him !—her own father, she would, out of sheer vexatiousness, call it Yechezkel.'

Malka's voice became more strident than ever. She had been anxious to make a species of vicarious reparation to her first husband, and the failure of Milly to acquiesce in the arrangement was a source of real vexation.

Moses could think of nothing better to say than to inquire how her present husband was.

'He overworks himself,' Malka replied, shaking her head. 'The misfortune is that he thinks himself a good man of business, and he is always starting new enterprises without consulting me. If he would only take my advice more!'

Moses shook his head in sympathetic deprecation of Michael Birnbaum's wilfulness.

'Is he at home?' he asked.

'No; but I expect him back from the country every minute. I believe they have invited him for the *Pidyun Haben* to-day.'

'Oh, is that to-day?'

'Of course. Didst thou not know?'

'No; no one told me.'

'Thine own sense should have told thee. Is it not the thirty-first day since the birth? But, of course, he won't accept when he knows that my own daughter has driven me out of her house.'

'You say not!' exclaimed Moses in horror.

'I do say,' said Malka, unconsciously taking up the clothes-brush and thumping with it on the table to emphasise the outrage. 'I told her that when Yechezkel cried so much it would be better to look for the pin than to dose the child for gripes. "I dressed it myself, mother," says she. "Thou art an obstinate cat's head, Milly," says I. "I say there *is* a pin." "And I know better," says she. "How canst thou know better than I?" says I. "Why, I was a mother before thou wast born." So I unrolled the child's flannel, and sure enough underneath it, just over the stomach, I found——'

'The pin,' concluded Moses, shaking his head gravely.

'No, not exactly. But a red mark where the pin had been pricking the poor little thing.'

'And what did Milly say then?' said Moses, in sympathetic triumph.

'Milly insisted it was a flea-bite; and I said, "Gott in Himmel, Milly, dost thou want to swear my eyes away? My enemies shall have such a flea-bite." And because Red Rivkah was in the room, Milly said I was shedding her blood in public, and she began to cry as if I had committed a crime against her in looking after her child. And I rushed out, leaving the two babies howling together. That was a week ago.'

'And how is the child?'

'How should I know? I am only the grandmother. I only supplied the bed-linen it was born on.'

'But is it recovered from the circumcision?'

'Oh yes; all our family have good healing flesh. It's a fine child,

imbeshreer. It's got my eyes and nose. It's a rare handsome
baby, *imbeshreer.* Only it wont be its mother's fault if the Almighty takes it not back again. Milly has picked up so many
ignorant Lane women, who come in and blight the child by admiring it aloud, not even saying *imbeshreer.* And then there's an old
witch, a beggar-woman that Ephraim, my son-in-law, used to give
a shilling a week to. Now he only gives her ninepence. She
asked him "Why?" and he said, "I'm married now. I can't afford
more." "What!" she shrieked; "you got married on my money!"
And one Friday, when the nurse had baby down-stairs, the old
beggar-woman knocked for her weekly allowance, and opened the
door, and she saw the child, and she looked at it with her Evil
Eye! I hope to heaven nothing will come of it!'

'I will pray for Yechezkel,' said Moses.

'Pray for Milly also while thou art about it, that she may remember what is owing to a mother before the earth covers me. I don't
know what's coming over children. Look at my Leah. She *will*
marry that Sam Levine, though he belongs to a lax English family,
and I suspect his mother never was a proselyte. She can't fry fish, any
way. I don't say anything against Sam, but still I do think my
Leah might have told me before falling in love with him. And yet,
see how I treat them! My Michael made a *Missheberach* for them
in synagogue the Sabbath after the engagement; not a common
eighteenpenny benediction, but a guinea one, with half-crown
blessings thrown in for his parents and the congregation, and a
gift of five shillings to the minister. That was, of course, in our
own *Chevrah*, not reckoning the guinea my Michael *shnodared* at
Duke's Plaizer *Shool.* You know, we always keep two seats at
Duke's Plaizer as well.'

Duke's Plaizer was the current distortion of Duke's Place.

'What magnanimity!' said Moses, overawed.

'I like to do everything with decorum,' said Malka. 'No one
can say I have ever acted otherwise than as a fine person. I dare
say thou couldst do with a few shillings thyself now.'

Moses hung his head still lower.

'You see my mother is so poorly,' he stammered. 'She is a
very old woman, and without anything to eat she may not live long.'

'They ought to take her into the Aged Widows' Home. I'm
sure I gave her *my* votes.'

'God shall bless you for it. But people say I was lucky enough
to get my Benjamin into the Orphan Asylum, and that I ought
not to have brought her from Poland. They say we grow enough
poor old widows here.'

'People say quite right—at least, she would have starved in a
Yiddishë country, not in a land of heathens.'

'But she was lonely and miserable out there, exposed to all the
malice of the Christians. And I was earning a pound a week.
Tailoring was a good trade then. The few roubles I used to send
her did not always reach her.'

'Thou hadst no right to send her anything, nor to send for her. Mothers are not everything. Thou didst marry my cousin Gittel —peace be upon him!—and it was thy duty to support *her* and her children. Thy mother took the bread out of the mouth of Gittel, and but for her my poor cousin might have been alive to-day. Believe me it was no *Mitzvah.*'

Mitzvah is a 'portmanteau-word.' It means a commandment and a good deed, the two conceptions being regarded as interchangeable.

'Nay, thou errest there,' answered Moses. 'Gittel was not a phœnix, which alone ate not of the Tree of Knowledge and so lives for ever. Women have no need to live as long as men, for they have not so many *Mitzvahs* to perform as men ; and inasmuch as '—here his tones involuntarily assumed the argumentative sing-song—'their souls profit by all the *Mitzvahs* performed by their husbands and children, Gittel will profit by the *Mitzvah* I did in bringing over my mother, so that even if she did die through it, she will not be the loser thereby. It stands in the Verse that *man* shall do the *Mitzvahs* and live by them. To live is a *Mitzvah*, but it is plainly one of those *Mitzvahs* that have to be done at a definite time, from which species women, by reason of their household duties, are exempt ; wherefore I would deduce by another circuit that it is not so incumbent upon women to live as upon men. Nevertheless, if God had willed it, she would have been still alive. The Holy One—blessed be He !—will provide for the little ones He has sent into the world. He fed Elijah the prophet by ravens, and He will never send me a black Sabbath.'

'Oh, you are a saint, Méshe !' said Malka, so impressed that she admitted him to the equality of the second person plural. 'If everybody knew as much *Térah* as you the Messiah would soon be here. Here are five shillings. For five shillings you can get a basket of lemons in the Orange Market in Duke's Place, and if you sell them in the Lane at a halfpenny each, you will make a good profit. Put aside five shillings of your takings and get another basket, and so you will be able to live till the tailoring picks up a bit.'

Moses listened as if he had never heard of the elementary principles of barter.

'May the Name—blessed be It !—bless you, and may you see rejoicings on your children's children !'

So Moses went away and bought dinner, treating his children to some *Beuglich*, or circular twisted rolls, in his joy. But on the morrow he repaired to the Market, thinking on the way of the ethical distinction between 'duties of the heart' and 'duties of the limbs,' as expounded in choice Hebrew by Rabbenu Bachja, and he laid out the remnant in lemons. Then he stationed himself in Petticoat Lane, crying, in his imperfect English, 'Lemans, verra good lemans, two a penny each, two a penny each !'

CHAPTER IV

THE REDEMPTION OF THE SON AND THE DAUGHTER

MALKA did not have long to wait for her liege lord.   He was a fresh-coloured young man of thirty, rather good-looking, with side-whiskers, keen, eager glance, and an air of perpetually doing business.   Though a native of Germany, he spoke English as well as many Lane Jews whose comparative impiety was a certificate of British birth.   Michael Birnbaum was a great man in the local little synagogue, if only one of the crowd at ' Duke's Plaizer.'   He had been successively *Gabbai* and *Parnass*, or treasurer and presi-dent, and had presented the plush curtain, with its mystical decoration of intersecting triangles, woven in silk, that hung before the Ark in which the scrolls of the Law were kept.   He was the very antithesis of Moses Ansell.   His energy was restless.   From hawking he had risen to a profitable traffic in gold lace and Brummagem jewellery, with a large *clientèle* all over the country, before he was twenty.   He touched nothing which he did not profit by ; and when he married, at twenty-three, a woman nearly twice his age, the transaction was not without the usual per-centage.   Very soon his line was diamonds—real diamonds.   He carried a pocket-knife which was a combination of a corkscrew, a pair of scissors, a file, a pair of tweezers, a tooth-pick, and half a dozen other things, and which seemed an epitome of his character. His temperament was lively, and, like Ephraim Phillips, he liked music-halls.   Fortunately, Malka was too conscious of her charms to dream of jealousy.

Michael smacked her soundly on the mouth with his lips, and said : ' Well, mother !'

He called her mother, not because he had any children, but because she had, and it seemed a pity to multiply domestic nomenclature.

'Well, my little one,' said Malka, hugging him fondly.   ' Have you made a good journey this time ? '

' No, trade is so dull.   People won't put their hands in their pockets.   And here ? '

' People won't take their hands out of their pockets, lazy dogs ! Everybody is striking—Jews with them.   Unheard-of things ! The bootmakers, the cap-makers, the furriers !   And now they say the tailors are going to strike ; more fools, too, when the trade is so slack !   What with one thing and another (let me put your cravat-pin straight, my little love !), it 's just the people who can't afford to buy new clothes that are hard up, so that they can't afford to buy second-hand clothes either.   If the Almighty is not good to us, we shall come to the Board of Guardians ourselves.'

' Not quite so bad as that, mother,' laughed Michael, twirling the

massive diamond ring on his finger. ' How 's baby ? Is it ready
to be redeemed ?'

'Which baby?' said Malka, with well-affected agnosticism.

' Phew !' whistled Michael. What 's up now, mother?'

'Nothing, my pet, nothing.'

'Well, I 'm going across. Come along, mother. Oh, wait a minute.
I want to brush this mud off my trousers. Is the clothes-brush here?'

' Yes, dearest one,' said the unsuspecting Malka.

Michael winked imperceptibly, flicked his trousers, and without
further parley ran across the diagonal to Milly's house. Five
minutes afterwards a deputation, consisting of the charwoman,
waited upon Malka, and said :

' Missus says will you please come over, as baby is a-cryin' for
its grandma.'

'Ah, that must be another pin,' said Malka, with a gleam of
triumph at her victory. But she did not budge. At the end of
five minutes she rose solemnly, adjusted her wig and her dress in
the mirror, put on her bonnet, brushed away a non-existent speck
of dust from her left sleeve, put a peppermint in her mouth, and
crossed the Square, carrying the clothes-brush in her hand.
Milly's door was half open, but she knocked at it, and said to the
charwoman :

' Is Mrs. Phillips in ?'

' Yes, mum, the company 's all upstairs.'

' Oh, then I will go up and return her this myself.'

Malka went straight through the little crowd of guests to Milly,
who was sitting on a sofa with Ezekiel, quiet as a lamb and as
good as gold, in her arms.

' Milly, my dear,' she said ; ' I have come to bring you back your
clothes-brush. Thank you so much for the loan of it.'

' You know you 're welcome, mother,' said Milly with unintentionally dual significance. The two ladies embraced. Ephraim
Phillips, a sallow-looking, close-cropped Pole, also kissed his
mother-in-law, and the gold chain that rested on Malka's bosom
heaved with the expansion of domestic pride. Malka thanked
God she was not a mother of barren or celibate children, which is
only one degree better than personal unfruitfulness, and testifies
scarce less to the celestial curse.

' Is that pin-mark gone away yet, Milly, from the precious little
thing ?' said Malka, taking Ezekiel in her arms, and disregarding
the transformation of face which in babies precedes a storm.

'Yes, it was a mere flea-bite,' said Milly incautiously, adding
hurriedly, ' I always go through his flannels and things most
carefully to see there are no more pins lurking about.'

'That is right ! Pins are like fleas—you never know where
they get to,' said Malka in an insidious spirit of compromise.
' Where is Leah ?'

'She is in the back-yard frying the last of the fish. Don't you
smell it ?'

'It will hardly have time to get cold.'

'Well, but I did a dishful myself last night. She is only preparing a reserve in case the attack be too deadly.'

'And where is the *Cohen*?'

'Oh, we have asked old Hyams across the Ruins. We expect him round every minute.'

At this point the indications of Ezekiel's facial barometer were fulfilled, and a tempest of weeping shook him.

'*Na*! Go then! Go to the mother!' said Malka angrily. 'All my children are alike. It's getting late. Hadn't you better send across again for old Hyams?'

'There's no hurry, mother,' said Michael Birnbaum soothingly. 'We must wait for Sam.'

'And who's Sam?' cried Malka unappeased.

'Sam is Leah's *Chosan*,' replied Michael ingenuously.

'Clever!' sneered Malka. 'But my grandson is not going to wait for the son of a proselyte. Why doesn't he come?'

'He'll be here in one minute.'

'How do you know?'

'We came up in the same train. He got in at Middlesborough. He's just gone home to see his folks, and get a wash and a brush-up. Considering he's coming up to town merely for the sake of the family ceremony, I think it would be very rude to commence without him. It's no joke, a long railway journey this weather. My feet were nearly frozen, despite the foot-warmer.'

'My poor lambkin!' said Malka, melting. And she patted his side-whiskers.

Sam Levine arrived almost immediately, and Leah, fishfork in hand, flew out of the back-yard kitchen to greet him. Though a member of the tribe of Levi, he was anything but ecclesiastical in appearance, rather a representative of muscular Judaism. He had a pink-and-white complexion and a tawny moustache, and bubbled over with energy and animal spirits. He could give most men thirty in a hundred in billiards, and fifty in anecdote. He was an advanced Radical in politics, and had a high opinion of the intelligence of his party. He paid Leah lip-fealty on his entry.

'What a pity it's Sunday!' was Leah's first remark when the kissing was done.

'No going to the play,' said Sam ruefully, catching her meaning.

They always celebrated his return from a commercial round by going to the theatre—'the-etter' they pronounced it. They went to the pit of the West End houses rather than patronise the local dress-circles for the same money. There were two strata of Ghetto girls: those who strolled in the Strand on Sabbath, and those who strolled in the Whitechapel Road. Leah was of the upper stratum. She was a tall lovely brunette, exuberant of voice and figure, with coarse red hands. She doted on ice-cream in the summer, and hot chocolate in the winter, but her love of the theatre was a perennial passion. Both Sam and she had good ears, and were always first in the field with the latest comic opera tunes. Leah's healthy vitality was prodigious. There was a legend in the Lane of such a maiden having been chosen by a coronet ; Leah was satisfied with Sam, who was just her match. On the heels of Sam came several other guests, notably Mrs. Jacobs (wife of 'Reb' Shemuel), with her pretty daughter, Hannah. Mr. Hyams, the *Cohen*, came last—the Priest whose functions had so curiously dwindled since the times of the Temples. To be called first to the reading of the Law, to bless his brethren with symbolic spreadings of palms and fingers in a mystic incantation delivered standing shoeless before the Ark of the Covenant at festival seasons, to redeem the mother's first-born son when neither parent was of priestly lineage—these privileges, combined with a disability to be with or near the dead, differentiated his religious position from that of the Levite or the Israelite. Mendel Hyams was not puffed up about his tribal superiority, though, if tradition were to be trusted, his direct descent from Aaron, the High Priest, gave him a longer genealogy than Queen Victoria's. He was a meek sexagenarian, with a threadbare black coat and a child-like smile. All the pride of the family seemed to be monopolised by his daughter, Miriam, a girl whose very nose Heaven had fashioned scornful. Miriam had accompanied him out of contemptuous curiosity. She wore a stylish feather in her hat, and a boa round her throat, and earned thirty shillings a week, all told, as a school teacher. (Esther Ansell was in her class just now.) Probably her toilette had made old Hyams unpunctual. His arrival was the signal for the commencement of the proceedings, and the men hastened to assume their head-gear.

Ephraim Phillips cautiously took the swaddled-up infant from the bosom of Milly, where it was suckling, and presented it to old Hyams. Fortunately Ezekiel had already had a repletion of milk, and was drowsy and manifested very little interest in the whole transaction.

'This, my first-born son,' said Ephraim in Hebrew as he handed Ezekiel over, 'is the first-born of his mother, and the Holy One —blessed be He !—hath given command to redeem him, as it is said, and those that are to be redeemed of them from a month old shalt thou redeem according to thine estimation for the money of five shekels after the shekel of the sanctuary, the shekel being twenty gerahs : and it is said, " Sanctify unto Me all the first-born, whatsoever openeth the womb among the children of Israel, both of man and of beast ; it is Mine."'

Ephraim Phillips then placed fifteen shillings in silver before old Hyams, who thereupon inquired in Chaldaic :

'Which wouldst thou rather—give me thy first-born son, the first-born of his mother, or redeem him for five selaim, which thou art bound to give according to the Law?'

Ephraim replied in Chaldaic :

'I am desirous rather to redeem my son, and here thou hast

the value of his redemption, which I am bound to give according
to the Law.'

Thereupon Hyams took the money tendered, and gave back
the child to his father, who blessed God for His sanctifying commandments, and thanked Him for His mercies ; after which the
old *Cohen* held the fifteen shillings over the head of the infant,
saying : 'This instead of that, this in exchange for that, this in
remission of that.   May this child enter into life, into the law,
and into the fear of Heaven !   May it be God's will that even as he
has been admitted to redemption, so may he enter into the Law,
the nuptial canopy, and into good deeds ! Amen.'   Then, placing
his hand in benediction upon the child's head, the priestly layman
added : 'God make thee as Ephraim and Manasseh.   The Lord
bless thee and keep thee.   The Lord make His face to shine upon
thee, and be gracious unto thee.   The Lord turn His face to thee
and grant thee peace.   The Lord is thy guardian ; the Lord is
thy shade upon thy right hand.   For length of days and years of
life and peace shall they add to thee.   The Lord shall guard thee
from all evil.   He shall guard thy soul.'

'Amen,' answered the company, and then there was a buzz of
secular talk, general rapture being expressed at the stolidness of
Ezekiel's demeanour.   Cups of tea were passed round by the lovely
Leah, and the secrets of the paper bags were brought to light.
Ephraim Phillips talked horses with Sam Levine, and old Hyams
quarrelled with Malka over the disposal of the fifteen shillings.
Knowing that Hyams was poor, Malka refused to take back the
money, retendered by him under pretence of a gift to the child.
The *Cohen*, however, was a proud man, and, under the eye of
Miriam, a firm one.   Ultimately it was agreed the money should
be expended on a *Missheberach*, for the infant's welfare and the
synagogue's.   Birds of a feather flock together, and Miriam for-
gathered with Hannah Jacobs, who also had a stylish feather in
her hat, and was the most congenial of the company.   Mrs. Jacobs
was left to discourse of the ailments of childhood and the iniquities
of servants with Mrs. Phillips.   Reb Shemuel's wife, commonly
known as the Rebbitzin, was a tall woman with a bony nose and
shrivelled cheeks, whereon the paths of the blood-vessels were
scrawled in red.   The same bones were visible beneath the
plumper padding of Hannah's face.   Mrs. Jacobs had escaped the
temptation to fatness, which is the besetting peril of the Jewish
matron.   If Hannah could escape her mother's inclination to
angularity she would be a pretty woman.   She dressed with taste,
which is half the battle, and for the present she was only nineteen.

'Do you think it's a good match?' said Miriam Hyams, indicating Sam Levine with a movement of the eyebrow.

A swift, scornful look flitted across Hannah's face.   'Among
the Jews,' she said, 'every match is a grand *Shidduch* before the
marriage ; after, we hear another tale.'

'There is a good deal in that,' admitted Miriam thoughtfully.

' The girl's family cries up the capture shamelessly. I remember, when Clara Emanuel was engaged, her brother Jack told me it was a splendid *Shidduch.* Afterwards I found he was a widower of fifty-five with three children.'

' But that engagement went off,' said Hannah.

' I know,' said Miriam. ' I'm only saying I can't fancy myself doing anything of the kind.'

' What! breaking off an engagement?' said Hannah, with a cynical little twinkle about her eye.

' No; taking a man like that,' replied Miriam. ' I wouldn't look at a man over thirty-five, or with less than two hundred and fifty a year.'

' You'll never marry a teacher, then,' Hannah remarked.

' Teacher!' Miriam Hyams repeated, with a look of disgust. ' How can one be respectable on three pounds a week? I must have a man in a good position.' She tossed her piquant nose and looked almost handsome. She was five years older than Hannah, and it seemed an enigma why men did not rush to lay five pounds a week at her daintily shod feet.

' I'd rather marry a man with two pounds a week, if I loved him,' said Hannah, in a low tone.

' Not in this century,' said Miriam, shaking her head incredulously. ' We don't believe in that nonsense nowadays. There was Alice Green—she used to talk like that: now look at her, riding about in a gig side by side with a bald monkey.'

' Alice Green's mother,' interrupted Malka, pricking up her ears, ' married a son of Mendel Weinstein by his third wife, Dinah, who had ten pounds left her by her uncle Shloumi.'

' No, Dinah was Mendel's second wife,' corrected Mrs. Jacobs, cutting short a remark of Mrs. Phillips's in favour of the new interest.

' Dinah was Mendel's third wife,' repeated Malka, her tanned cheeks reddening. ' I know it because my Simon—God bless him! —was breeched the same month.'

Simon was Malka's eldest, now a magistrate in Melbourne.

' His third wife was Kitty Green, daughter of the yellow Melammed,' persisted the Rebbitzin. ' I know it for a fact, because Kitty's sister Annie was engaged for a week to my brother-in-law Nathaniel.'

' His first wife,' put in Malka's husband, with the air of arbitrating between the two, ' was Shmool, the publican's eldest daughter.'

' Shmool, the publican's daughter,' said Malka, stirred to fresh indignation, ' married Hyam Robins, the grandson of old Benjamin, who kept the cutlery shop at the corner of Little Eden Alley, there where the pickled cucumber store stands now.'

' It was Shmool's sister that married Hyam Robins, wasn't it, mother?' asked Milly incautiously.

' Certainly not,' thundered Malka. ' I knew old Benjamin well, and he sent me a pair of chintz curtains when I married your father.'

' Poor old Benjamin! How long has he been dead?' mused Reb Shemuel's wife.

'He died the year I was confined with my Leah——'

'Stop! stop,' interrupted Sam Levine boisterously. 'There's Leah getting as red as fire for fear you'll blab out her age.'

'Don't be a fool, Sam!' said Leah, blushing violently, and looking the lovelier for it.

The attention of the entire company was now concentrated upon the question at issue, whatever it might be. Malka fixed her audience with her piercing eye, and said in a tone that scarce brooked contradiction:

'Hyam Robins couldn't have married Shmool's sister, because Shmool's sister was already the wife of Abraham the fishmonger.'

'Yes, but Shmool had two sisters,' said Mrs. Jacobs, audaciously asserting her position as the rival genealogist.

'Nothing of the kind,' replied Malka warmly.

'I'm quite sure,' persisted Mrs. Jacobs. 'There was Phœby, and there was Harriet.'

'Nothing of the kind,' repeated Malka. 'Shmool had three sisters. Only two were in the deaf and dumb home.'

'Why, that wasn't Shmool at all,' Milly forgot herself so far as to say; 'that was Block, the baker.'

'Of course,' said Malka in her most acid tone. 'My *Kinder* always know better than me.'

There was a moment of painful silence. Malka's eye mechanically sought the clothes-brush. Then Ezekiel sneezed. It was a convulsive 'atichoo,' and agitated the infant to its most intimate flannel roll.

'For Thy salvation do I hope, O Lord,' murmured Malka piously, adding triumphantly aloud: 'There! the *Kind* has sneezed to the truth of it. I knew I was right!'

The sneeze of an innocent child silences everybody who is not a blasphemer. In the general satisfaction at the unexpected solution of the situation, no one even pointed out that the actual statement to which Ezekiel had borne testimony was an assertion of the superior knowledge of Malka's children. Shortly afterwards the company trooped downstairs to partake of high tea, which in the Ghetto need not include anything more fleshly than fish. Fish was, indeed, the staple of the meal. Fried fish, and such fried fish! Only a great poet could sing the praises of the national dish, and the golden age of Hebrew poetry is over. Strange that Gebirol should have lived and died without the opportunity of the theme, and that the great Jehuda Halevi himself should have had to devote his genius merely to singing the glories of Jerusalem. 'Israel is among the other nations,' he sang, 'as the heart among the limbs.' Even so is the fried fish of Judea to the fried fish of Christendom and Heathendom. With the audacity of true culinary genius, Jewish fried fish is always served cold. The skin is a beautiful brown, the substance firm and succulent. The very bones thereof are full of marrow; yea, and charged with memories of the happy past. Fried fish binds Anglo-Judea more than all the lip-professions of unity. Its savour is early known of youth, and the divine flavour, endeared by a thousand childish recollections, entwined with the most sacred associations, draws back the hoary sinner into the paths of piety. It is on fried fish, mayhap, that the Jewish matron grows fat. In the days of the Messiah, when the saints shall feed off the Leviathan, and the Sea Serpent shall be dished up for the last time, and the world and the silly season shall come to an end, in those days it is probable that the saints will prefer their Leviathan fried. Not that any physical frying will be necessary, for in those happy times (for whose coming every faithful Israelite prays three times a day) the Leviathan will have what taste the eater will. Possibly a few highly respectable saints, who were fashionable in their day, and contrived to live in Kensington without infection of paganism, will take their Leviathan in conventional courses, and beginning with *hors d'œuvres* may *will* him everything by turns and nothing long ; making him soup and sweets, joint and *entrée*, and even ices and coffee, for in the millennium the harassing prohibition which bars cream after meat will fall through. But, however this be, it is beyond question that the bulk of the faithful will mentally fry him ; and though the Christian saints, who shall be privileged to wait at table, hand them plate after plate, fried fish shall be all the fare. One suspects that the Hebrew gained the taste in the Desert of Sinai, for the manna that fell there was not monotonous to the palate as the sciolist supposes, but likewise mutable under volition. It were incredible that Moses, who gave so many imperishable things to his people, did not also give them the knowledge of fried fish, so that they might obey his behest, and rejoice before the Lord. Nay, was it not because, while the manna fell, there could be no lack of fish to fry, that they lingered forty years in a dreary wilderness?

Other delicious things there are in Jewish cookery—*Lockschen*, which are the apotheosis of vermicelli ; *Ferfel*, which are *Lockschen* in an atomic state ; and *Creplich*, which are triangular meat pasties ; and *Kuggol*, to which pudding has a far-away resemblance ; and there is even *gefüllte Fisch*, which is stuffed fish without bones —but fried fish reigns above all in cold, unquestioned sovereignty. No other people possesses the recipe. As a poet of the commencement of the century sings :

> ' The Christians are ninnies, they can't fry Dutch plaice,
> Believe me, they can't tell a carp from a dace.'

It was while discussing a deliciously brown oblong of the Dutch plaice of the ballad that Samuel Levine appeared to be struck by an idea. He threw down his knife and fork, and exclaimed in Hebrew :

' *Shemah beni* !'

Everyone looked at him.

' Hear, my son !' he repeated in comic horror. Then relapsing into English, he explained. ' I 've forgotten to give Leah a present from her *Chosan*.'

' A-h-h ! '

Everybody gave a sigh of deep interest.   Leah, whom the exigencies of service had removed from his side to the head of the table, half rose from her seat in excitement.

Now, whether Samuel Levine had really forgotten, or whether he had chosen the most effective moment, will never be known ; certain it is that the Semitic instinct for drama was gratified within him as he drew a little folded white paper out of his waistcoat pocket, amid the keen expectation of the company.

' This,' said he, tapping the paper as if he were a conjurer, ' was purchased by me yesterday morning for my little girl.   I said to myself, says I, " Look here, old man, you 've got to go up to town for a day in honour of Ezekiel Phillips, and your poor girl, who had looked forward to your staying away till Passover, will want some compensation for her disappointment at seeing you earlier." So I thinks to myself, thinks I, " Now what is there that Leah would like ?   It must be something appropriate, of course, and it mustn't be of any value, because I can't afford it."   It 's a ruinous business getting engaged, the worst bit of business I ever did in all my born days.'   Here Sam winked facetiously at the company. ' And I thought and thought of what was the cheapest thing I could get out of it with, and, lo and behold ! I suddenly thought of a ring.'

So saying, Sam, still with the same dramatic air, unwrapped the thick gold ring and held it up so that the huge diamond in it sparkled in the sight of all.   A long ' O—h—h ! ' went round the company, the majority instantaneously pricing it mentally, and wondering at what reduction Sam had acquired it from a brother commercial.   For that no Jew ever pays full retail price for jewellery is regarded as axiomatic.   Even the engagement-ring is not required to be first-hand—or should it be first-finger ?—so long as it is solid, which perhaps accounts for the superiority of the Jewish marriage-rate.   Leah rose entirely to her feet, the light of the diamond reflected in her eager eyes.   She lent across the table, stretching out a finger to receive her lover's gift.   Sam put the ring near her finger, then drew it away teasingly.

' Them as asks shan't have,' he said in high good humour. ' You 're too greedy !   Look at the number of rings you 've got already.'   The fun of the situation diffused itself along the table.

' Give it me,' laughed Miriam Hyams, stretching out her finger. ' I 'll say " ta " so nicely.'

' No,' he said, ' you 've been naughty ; I 'm going to give it to the little girl who has sat quiet all the time.   Miss Hannah Jacobs, rise to receive your prize.'

Hannah, who was sitting two places to the left of him, smiled quietly, but went on carving her fish.   Sam, growing quite boisterous under the appreciation of a visibly amused audience, leaned towards her, captured her right hand, and forcibly adjusted the ring on the forefinger, exclaiming in Hebrew, with mock solemnity, ' Behold, thou art consecrated unto me by this ring according to the Law of Moses and Israel.'

It was the formal marriage speech he had learnt up for his approaching marriage. The company roared with laughter, and pleasure and enjoyment of the fun made Leah's lovely, smiling cheeks flush to a livelier crimson. Badinage flew about from one end of the table to the other ; burlesque congratulations were showered on the couple, flowing over even unto Mrs. Jacobs, who appeared to enjoy the episode as much as if her daughter were really off her hands. The little incident added the last touch of high spirits to the company and extorted all their latent humour. Samuel excelled himself in vivacious repartee, and responded comically to the toast of his health as drunk in coffee. Suddenly, amid the hubbub of chaff and laughter and the clatter of cutlery, a still, small voice made itself heard. It came from old Hyams, who had been sitting quietly with brow corrugated under his black velvet *Koppel.*

' Mr. Levine,' he said, in low, grave tones, ' I have been thinking, and I am afraid that what you have done is serious.'

The earnestness of his tones arrested the attention of the company. The laughter ceased.

' What do you mean ? ' said Samuel. He understood the Yiddish, which old Hyams almost invariably used, though he did not speak it himself. Contrariwise, old Hyams understood much more English than he spoke.

' You have married Hannah Jacobs.'

There was a painful silence, dim recollections surging in everybody's brain.

' Married Hannah Jacobs ! ' repeated Samuel incredulously.

' Yes,' affirmed old Hyams. ' What you have done constitutes a marriage according to Jewish law. You have pledged yourself to her in the presence of two witnesses.'

There was another tense silence. Samuel broke it with a boisterous laugh.

' No, no, old fellow,' he said ; ' you don't have me like that ! '

The tension was relaxed. Everybody joined in the laugh with a feeling of indescribable relief. Facetious old Hyams had gone near scoring one. Hannah smilingly plucked off the glittering bauble from her finger and slid it on to Leah's. Hyams alone remained grave.

' Laugh away ! ' he said. ' You will soon find I am right. Such is our law.'

' Maybe,' said Samuel, constrained to seriousness despite himself. ' But you forget that I am already engaged to Leah.'

' I do not forget it,' replied Hyams ; ' but it has nothing to do with the case. You are both single, or, rather, you *were* both single, for now you are man and wife.'

Leah, who had been sitting pale and agitated, burst into tears. Hannah's face was drawn and white. Her mother looked the least alarmed of the company.

'Droll person!' cried Malka, addressing Sam angrily in jargon. 'What hast thou done?'

'Don't let us all go mad!' said Samuel, bewildered. 'How can a piece of fun, a joke, be a valid marriage?'

'The law takes no account of jokes,' said old Hyams solemnly.

'Then why didn't you stop me?' asked Sam, exasperated. 'It was all done in a moment. I laughed myself; I had no time to think.'

Sam brought his fist down on the table with a bang.

'Well, I'll never believe this! If this is Judaism——'

'Hush!' said Malka angrily. 'These are your English Jews, who make mock of holy things. I always said the son of a proselyte was——'

'Look here, mother,' put in Michael soothingly. 'Don't let us make a fuss before we know the truth. Send for someone who is likely to know.' He played agitatedly with his complex pocket-knife.

'Yes; Hannah's father, Reb Shemuel, is just the man!' cried Milly Phillips.

'I told you my husband was gone to Manchester for a day or two,' Mrs. Jacobs reminded her.

'There's the Maggid of the Sons of the Covenant,' said one of the company. 'I'll go and fetch him.'

The stooping black-bearded Maggid was brought. When he arrived, it was evident from his look that he knew all and brought confirmation of their worst fears. He explained the law at great length, and cited precedent upon precedent. When he ceased, Leah's sobs alone broke the silence. Samuel's face was white. The merry gathering had been turned to a wedding-party.

'You rogue!' burst forth Malka at last. 'You planned all this —you thought my Leah didn't have enough money, and that Reb Shemuel will heap you up gold in the hands. But you don't take me in like this.'

'May this piece of bread choke me if I had the slightest iota of intention!' cried Samuel passionately, for the thought of what Leah might think was like fire in his veins. He turned appealingly to the Maggid: 'But there must be some way out of this— surely there must be some way out. I know you Maggidim can split hairs. Can't you make one of your clever distinctions even when there's more than a trifle concerned?'

There was a savage impatience about the bridegroom which boded ill for the law.

'Of course there's a way out,' said the Maggid calmly. 'Only one way, but a very broad and simple one.'

'What's that?' everybody asked breathlessly.

'He must give her *Gett*!'

'Of course!' shouted Sam, in a voice of thunder. 'I divorce her at once!' He guffawed hysterically. 'What a pack of fools we are! Good old Jewish law!'

Leah's sobs ceased. Everybody except Mrs. Jacobs was smiling once more. Half a dozen hands grasped the Maggid's; half a dozen others thumped him on the back. He was pushed into a chair. They gave him a glass of brandy; they heaped a plate with fried fish. Verily the Maggid, who was in truth sore a-hungered, was in luck's way. He blessed Providence and the Jewish marriage law.

'But you had better not reckon that a divorce,' he warned them between two mouthfuls. 'You had better go to Reb Shemuel, the maiden's father, and let him arrange the *Gett* beyond reach of cavil.'

'But Reb Shemuel is away,' said Mrs. Jacobs.

'And I must go away, too, by the first train to-morrow,' said Sam. 'However, there's no hurry. I'll arrange to run up to town again in a fortnight or so, and then Reb Shemuel shall see that we are properly untied. You don't mind being my wife for a fortnight, I hope, Miss Jacobs?' asked Sam, winking gleefully at Leah.

She smiled back at him, and they laughed together over the danger they had just escaped. Hannah laughed, too, in contemptuous amusement at the rigidity of Jewish law.

'I'll tell you what, Sam: can't you come back for next Saturday week?' said Leah.

'Why?' asked Sam. 'What's on?'

'The Purim ball at the Club. As you've got to come back to give Hannah *Gett*, you might as well come in time to take me to the ball.'

'Right you are!' said Sam cheerfully.

Leah clapped her hands.

'Oh, that will be jolly!' she said. 'And we'll take Hannah with us,' she added as an after-thought.

'Is that by way of compensation for losing my husband?' Hannah asked with a smile.

'Leah gave a happy laugh, and turned the new ring on her finger in delighted contemplation.

'All's well that ends well,' said Sam. 'Through this joke Leah will be the belle of the Purim ball. I think I deserve another piece of plaice, Leah, for that compliment. As for you, Mr. Maggid, you're a saint and a Talmud sage!'

The Maggid's face was brightened by a smile. He intoned the grace with unction when the meal ended, and everybody joined in heartily at the specifically vocal portions. Then the Maggid left, and the cards were brought out.

It is inadvisable to play cards *before* fried fish, because it is well known that you may lose, and losing may ruffle your temper, and you may call your partner an ass or your partner may call you an ass. To-night the greatest good humour prevailed, though several pounds changed hands. They played loo, 'klobbiyos,' napoleon, vingt-et-un, and especially brag. Solo-whist had not yet come in to drive everything else out. Old Hyams did not *spiel*, because he could not afford to, and Hannah Jacobs because she did not care to. These and a few other guests left early, but the family party stayed late. On a warm green table, under a cheerful gaslight, with brandy and whisky and sweets and fruit to hand, with no trains or 'buses to catch, what wonder if the light-hearted assembly played far into the new day?

Meanwhile, the redeemed son slept peacefully in his crib with his legs curled up, and his little fists clenched beneath the coverlet.

CHAPTER V

THE PAUPER ALIEN

MOSES ANSELL married mainly because all men are mortal. He knew he would die, and he wanted an heir. Not to inherit anything, but to say *Kaddish* for him. *Kaddish* is the most beautiful and wonderful mourning prayer ever written. Rigidly excluding all references to death and grief, it exhausts itself in supreme glorification of the Eternal, and in supplication for peace upon the House of Israel. But its significance has been gradually transformed ; human nature, driven away with a pitchfork, has avenged itself by regarding the prayer as a mass, not without purgatorial efficacy, and so the Jew is reluctant to die without leaving someone qualified to say *Kaddish* after him every day for a year, and then one day a year. That is one reason why sons are of such domestic importance.

Moses had only a mother in the world when he married Gittel Silverstein, and he hoped to restore the balance of male relatives by this reckless measure. The result was six children, three girls and three *Kaddishim*. In Gittel Moses found a tireless helpmate. During her lifetime the family always lived in two rooms, for she had various ways of supplementing the household income. When in London, she charred for her cousin, Malka, at a shilling a day. Likewise she sewed underlinen and stitched slips of fur into caps in the privacy of home and midnight. For all Mrs. Ansell's industry, the family had been a typical group of wandering Jews, straying from town to town in search of better things. The congregation they left (every town which could muster the minimum of ten men for worship boasted its *Kehillah*) invariably paid their fare to the next congregation, glad to get rid of them so cheaply ; and the new *Kehillah* jumped at the opportunity of gratifying their restless migratory instinct and sent them to a newer. Thus were they tossed about on the battledores of philanthropy, often reverting to their starting-point, to the disgust of the charitable committees. Yet Moses always made loyal efforts to find work. His versatility was marvellous. There was nothing he could not do badly. He had been glazier, synagogue beadle, picture-frame manufacturer, cantor, pedlar, shoemaker in all branches, coat-seller, official executioner of fowls and cattle, Hebrew teacher, fruiterer, circumciser, professional corpse-watcher, and now he was a tailor out of work.

Unquestionably Malka was right in considering Moses a *Schlemihl* in comparison with many a fellow-immigrant, who brought indefatigable hand and subtle brain to the struggle for existence, and discarded the prop of charity as soon as he could, and sometimes earlier.

It was as a hawker that Moses believed himself most gifted, and he never lost the conviction that, if he could only get a fair start, he had in him the makings of a millionaire. Yet there was scarcely anything cheap with which he had not tramped the country ; so that when poor Benjamin, who profited by his mother's death to get into the Orphan Asylum, was asked to write a piece of composition on 'The Methods of Travelling,' he excited the hilarity of the class-room by writing that there were numerous ways of travelling, for you could travel with sponge, lemons, rhubarb, old clothes, jewellery, and so on for a page of a copy-book. Benjamin was a brilliant boy, yet he never shook off some of the misleading associations engendered by the parental jargon. For Mrs. Ansell had diversified her corrupt German by streaks of incorrect English, being of a much more energetic and ambitious temperament than the conservative Moses, who dropped nearly all his burden of English into her grave. For Benjamin 'to travel' meant to wander about selling goods, and when in his books he read of African travellers, he took it for granted that they were but exploiting the Dark Continent for small profits and quick returns.

And who knows? Perhaps of the two species, it was the old Jewish pedlars who suffered the more and made the less profit on the average. For the despised three-hatted scarecrow of Christian caricature, who shambled along snuffling 'Old clo',' had a strenuous inner life, which might possibly have vied in intensity, elevation, and even sense of humour, with that of the best of the jeerers on the highway. To Moses 'travelling' meant straying forlornly in strange towns and villages, given over to the worship of an alien deity, and ever ready to avenge his crucifixion ; in a land of whose tongue he knew scarce more than the Saracen damsel married by legend to A'Becket's father. It meant praying brazenly in crowded railway trains, winding the phylacteries sevenfold round his left arm, and crowning his forehead with a huge leather bump of righteousness, to the bewilderment or irritation of unsympathetic fellow-passengers. It meant living chiefly on dry bread and drinking black tea out of his own cup, with meat and fish and the good things of life utterly banned by the traditional law, even if he

were flush.   It meant carrying the red rag of an obnoxious
personality through a land of bulls.   It meant passing months
away from wife and children, in a solitude only occasionally
alleviated by a Sabbath spent in a synagogue-town.   It meant
putting up at low public-houses and common lodging-houses,
where rowdy disciples of the Prince of Peace often sent him
bleeding to bed, or shamelessly despoiled him of his merchandise,
or bullied and blustered him out of his fair price, knowing he
dared not resent.   It meant being chaffed and gibed at in language
of which he only understood that it was cruel, though certain trite
facetiæ grew intelligible to him by repetition.

Thus, once when he had been interrogated as to the locality of
Moses when the light went out, he replied in Yiddish that the
light could not go out, for 'it stands in the verse that round the
head of Moses, our Teacher, the great Lawgiver, was a perpetual
halo.'

An old German happened to be smoking at the bar of the
public-house when the pedlar gave this acute answer.   He laughed
heartily, slapped the Jew on the back, and translated the repartee
to the convivial crew.   For once intellect told, and the rough
drinkers, with a pang of shame, vied with one another in pressing
bitter beer upon the temperate Semite.   But, as a rule, Moses
Ansell drank the cup of affliction instead of hospitality, and bore
his share to the full, without the remotest intention of being heroic,
in the long agony of his race, doomed to be a byword and a
mockery amongst the heathen.   Assuredly to die for a religion is
easier than to live for it.   Yet Moses never complained nor lost
faith.   To be spat upon was the very condition of existence of the
modern Jew, deprived of Palestine and his Temple—a footsore
mendicant, buffeted and reviled, yet the dearer to the Lord God
who had chosen him from the nations.   Bullies might break
Moses's head in this world, but in the next he would sit on a gold
chair in Paradise among the saints, and sing exegetical acrostics
to all eternity.

It was some dim perception of these things that made Esther
forgive her father when the Ansells waited weeks and weeks for a
postal order, and landlords were threatening to bundle them out
neck and crop, and her mother's hands were worn to the bone
slaving for her little ones.

Things improved a little just before the mother died, for they
had settled down in London, and Moses earned eighteen shillings
a week as a machinist and presser, and no longer roamed the
country.   But the interval of happiness was brief.   The grandmother, imported from Poland, did not take kindly to her son's
wife, whom she found wanting in the minutiæ of ceremonial piety,
and godless enough to wear her own hair.   There had been,
indeed, a note of scepticism, of defiance, in Esther's mother—a
hankering after the customs of the heathen, which her grandmother
divined instinctively, and resented for the sake of her son and

the post-mundane existence of her grandchildren.   Mrs. Ansell's
scepticism based itself upon the uncleanliness which was so
generally next to godliness in the pious circles round them, and
she had been heard to express contempt for the learned and
venerable Israelite who, being accosted by an acquaintance when
the shadows of eve were beginning to usher in the Day of Atonement, exclaimed :

'For Heaven's sake don't stop me—I missed my bath last year!'

Mrs. Ansell bathed her children from head to foot once a month,
and even profanely washed them on the Sabbath, and had other
strange, uncanny notions.   She professed not to see the value to
God, man, or beast of the learned Rabbonim, who sat shaking
themselves all day in the Beth Hamidrash, and said they would be
better occupied in supporting their families—a view which, though
mere surface-blasphemy on the part of the good woman, and
primarily intended as a hint to Moses to study less and work
longer, did not fail to excite lively passages of arms between the
two women.   But death ended these bickerings, and the *Bube*, who
had frequently reproached her son for bringing her into such an
atheistic country, was left a drag the more upon a family deprived
at once of a mother and a bread-winner.   Old Mrs. Ansell was
unfit for anything save grumbling, and so the headship naturally
devolved upon Esther, whom her mother's death left a woman
getting on for eight.   The commencement of her reign coincided
with a sad bisection of territory.   Shocking as it may be to better-
regulated minds, these seven people lived in one room.   Moses
and the two boys slept in one bed, and the grandmother and the
three girls in another.   Esther had to sleep with her head on a
supplementary pillow at the foot of the bed.   But there can be
much love in a little room.

The room was not, however, so very little, for it was of ungainly,
sprawling structure, pushing out an odd limb that might have been
cut off with a curtain.   The walls nodded fixedly to one another,
so that the ceiling was only half the size of the floor.   The furniture
comprised but the commonest necessities.   This attic of the
Ansells was nearer heaven than most earthly dwelling-places, for
there were four tall flights of stairs to mount before you got to it.

No. 1 Royal Street had been in its time one of the great mansions of the Ghetto ; pillars of the synagogue had quaffed *kosher*
wine in its spacious reception rooms, and its corridors had echoed
with the gossip of portly dames in stiff brocades.   It was stoutly
built, and its balusters were of carved oak.   But now the threshold of the great street door, which was never closed, was
encrusted with black mud, and a musty odour permanently clung
to the wide staircases, and blent subtly with far-away reminiscences
of Mr. Belcovitch's festive turpentine.

The Ansells had numerous housemates, for No. 1 Royal Street
was a Jewish colony in itself, and the resident population was
periodically swollen by the 'hands' of the Belcovitches, and by

the Sons of the Covenant, who came to worship at their synagogue on the groundfloor.

What with Sugarman the Shadchan on the first-floor, Mrs. Simons and Dutch Debby on the second, the Belcovitches on the third, and the Ansells and Gabriel Hamburg, the great scholar, on the fourth, the doorposts twinkled with *Mezuzahs*—cases or cylinders containing sacred script, with the word *Shaddai* (Almighty) peering out of a little glass eye at the centre. Even Dutch Debby, abandoned wretch as she was, had this protection against evil spirits (so it has come to be regarded) on her lintel, though she probably never touched the eye with her finger to kiss the place of contact after the manner of the faithful.

Thus was No. 1 Royal Street close-packed with the stuff of human life, homespun and drab enough, but not altogether profitless, maybe, to turn over and examine ; so close-packed was it that there was scarce breathing space. It was only at immemorial intervals that our pauper alien made a pun, but one day he flashed upon the world the pregnant remark that England was well named, for to the Jew it was verily the Enge-land, which in German signifies the country without elbow-room. Moses Ansell chuckled softly and beatifically when he emitted the remark that surprised all who knew him. But then it was the Rejoicing of the Law, and the Sons of the Covenant had treated him to rum and currant cake. He often thought of his witticism afterwards, and it always lightened his unwashed face with a happy smile. The recollection usually caught him when he was praying.

For fours years after Mrs. Ansell's charity funeral, the Ansells, though far from happy, had no history to speak of.

Benjamin accompanied Solomon to *Shool* morning and evening, to say *Kaddish* for their mother, till he passed into the Orphan Asylum and out of the lives of his relatives. Solomon and Rachel and Esther went to the great school and Isaac to the infant school ; while the tiny Sarah, whose birth had cost Mrs. Ansell's life, crawled and climbed about in the garret, the grandmother coming in negatively useful as a safeguard against fire on the days when the grate was not empty. The *Bube's* own conception of her function as a safeguard against fire was quite other.

Moses was out all day working, or looking for work, or praying, or listening to '*Droshes*' by the Maggid or other great preachers. Such charities as brightened and warmed the Ghetto Moses usually came in for. Bread, meat, and coal-tickets, godsends from the Society for Restoring the Soul, made odd days memorable ; blankets were not so easy to get as in the days of poor Gittel's confinements.

What little cooking there was to do was done by Esther before or after school ; she and her children usually took their mid-day meal with them in the shape of bread, occasionally made ambrosial by treacle. The Ansells had more fast-days than the Jewish calendar, which is saying a good deal. Providence, however, generally stepped in before the larder had been bare twenty-four hours.

As the fast-days of the Jewish calendar did not necessarily fall upon the Ansell fast-days, they were an additional tax on Moses and his mother. Yet neither ever wavered in the scrupulous observance of them, not a crumb of bread nor a drop of water passing their lips. In the keen search for facts detrimental to the Ghetto, it is surprising that no political economist has hitherto exposed the abundant fasts with which Israel has been endowed, and which obviously operate as a dole in aid of wages. So does the Lenten period of the 'three weeks,' when meat is prohibited in memory of the shattered Temples. The Ansells kept the 'three weeks' pretty well all the year round. On rare occasions they purchased pickled Dutch herrings, or brought home pennyworths of pea-soup, or of baked potatoes and rice, from a neighbouring cookshop. For Festival days, if Malka had subsidised them with a half-sovereign, Esther sometimes compounded *Tzimmus*, a dainty blend of carrots, pudding, and potatoes. She was prepared to write an essay on *Tzimmus*, as a gastronomic ideal. There were other pleasing Polish combinations which were baked for twopence by the local bakers. *Tabechas*, or stuffed entrails, and liver, lights or milt, were good substitutes for meat. A favourite soup was *Borsch*, which was made with beetroot, fat taking the place of the more fashionable cream.

The national dish was seldom their lot. When fried fish came it was usually from the larder of Mrs. Simons, a motherly old widow who lived in the second floor front, and presided over the confinements of all the women, and the sicknesses of all the children, in the neighbourhood. Her married daughter, Dinah, was providentially suckling a black-eyed boy when Mrs. Ansell died, so Mrs. Simons converted her into a foster-mother of little Sarah, regarding herself ever afterwards as under special responsibilities towards the infant, whom she occasionally took to live with her for a week, and for whom she saw heaven encouraging a future alliance with the black-eyed foster-brother. Life would have been gloomier still in the Ansell garret if Mrs. Simons had not been created to bless and sustain. Even old garments somehow arrived from Mrs. Simons to eke out the corduroys and the print gowns which were the gift of the school. There were few pleasanter events in the Ansell household than the falling ill of one of the children, for not only did this mean a supply of broth, port wine, and other incredible luxuries from the charity doctor (of which all could taste), but it brought in its train the assiduous attendance of Mrs. Simons. To see the kindly brown face bending over it with smiling eyes of jet, to feel the soft cool hand pressed to its forehead, was worth a fever to a motherless infant. Mrs. Simons was a busy woman, and a poor withal, and the Ansells were a reticent pack, not given to expressing either their love or their hunger to outsiders ; so altogether the children did not see so much of Mrs. Simons or her bounties as they would have liked. Nevertheless, in a grave crisis she was always to be counted upon.

'I tell thee what, Méshe,' said old Mrs. Ansell often, 'that woman wants to marry thee. A blind man could see it.'

'She cannot want it, mother,' Moses would reply with infinite respect.

'What art thou saying? A wholly fine young man like thee,' said his mother, fondling his side ringlets, 'and one so *froom*, too, and with such worldly wisdom. But thou must not have her, Méshe.'

'What kind of idea thou stuffest into my head! I tell thee she would not have me if I sent to ask.'

'Talk not thyself thereinto. Who wouldn't like to catch hold of thy cloak to go to heaven by? But Mrs. Simons is too much of an English-woman for me. Your last wife had English ideas, and made mock of pious men, and God's judgment took her. What says the Prayer-Book? For three things a woman dies in child-birth, for not separating the dough, for not lighting the Sabbath lamps, for not——'

'How often have I told thee she did do all these things!' interrupted Moses.

'Dost thou contradict the Prayer-Book?' said the *Bube* angrily. 'It would have been different if thou hadst let me pick a woman for thee. But this time thou wilt honour thy mother more. It must be a respectable, virtuous maiden, with the fear of Heaven; not an old woman like Mrs. Simons, but one who can bear me robust grandchildren. The grandchildren thou hast given me are sickly, and they fear not the Most High. Ah! why didst thou drag me to this impious country? Couldst thou not let me die in peace? Thy girls think more of English story-books and lessons than of Yiddishkeit, and the boys run out under the naked sky with bare heads, and are loath to wash their hands before meals, and they do not come home in the dinner-hour for fear they should have to say the afternoon prayer. Laugh at me, Moses, as thou wilt; but, old as I am, I have eyes, and not two blotches of clay in in my sockets. Thou seest not how thy family is going to destruction. Oh, the abominations!'

Thus warned and put on his mettle, Moses would keep a keen look-out on his hopeful family for the next day, and the seed which the grandmother had sown came up in black and blue bruises on the family anatomy, especially on that portion of it which belonged to Solomon. For Moses's crumbling trousers were buckled with a stout strap, and Solomon was a young rogue who did his best to dodge the Almighty, and had never heard of Lowell's warning:

> 'You've gut to git up airly,
> Ef you want to take in God.'

Even if he had heard of it, he would probably have retorted that he usually got up early enough to take in his father, who was the more immediately terrible of the two. Nevertheless, Solomon learnt many lessons at his father's knee or rather across it. In earlier days Solomon had had a number of confidential transactions with his father's God, making bargains with Him according to his childish sense of equity. If, for instance, God would ensure his doing his sums correctly, so that he should neither be caned nor 'kept in,' he would say his morning prayers, without skipping the aggravating *Longe Verachum* which bulked so largely on Mondays and Thursdays ; otherwise he could not be bothered.

By the terms of the contract, Solomon threw all the initiative on the Deity, and whenever the Deity undertook His share of the contract, Solomon honourably fulfilled his. Thus was his faith in Providence never shaken like that of some boys, who expect the Deity to follow their lead. Still, by declining to praise his Maker at extraordinary length except in acknowledgment of services rendered, Solomon gave early evidence of his failure to inherit his father's business incapacity.

On days when things at the school went well, no one gabbled through the weary Prayer-Book more conscientiously than he ; he said all the things in large type, and all the funny little bits in small type, and even some passages without vowels. Nay, he included the very prefaces, and was lured on and coaxed on, and enticed by his father to recite the appendices which shot up one after the other on the devotional horizon like the endless-seeming terraces of a deceptive ascent ; just another little bit, and now that little bit, and just that last bit, and one more very last little bit. It was like the infinite inclusiveness of a Chinese sphere, or the farewell performances of a distinguished singer.

For the rest Solomon was a *Chine-ponim*, or droll, having that inextinguishable sense of humour which has made the saints of the Jewish Church human, and has lit up dry technical Talmudic discussions with flashes of freakish fun—with pun and jest and merry quibble—and has helped the race to survive (*pace* Dr. Wallace) by dint of a humorous acquiescence in the inevitable.

His *Chine* helped Solomon to survive synagogue, where the only drop of sweetness was in the beaker of wine for the santification service. Solomon was always in the van of the brave boys who volunteered to take part in the ceremonial quaffing of it. Decidedly Solomon was not spiritual ; he would not even kiss a Hebrew Pentateuch that he had dropped, unless his father was looking, and but for the personal supervision of the *Bube*, the dirty white fringes of his 'four-corners' might have got tangled and irredeemably invalidated, for all he cared.

In the direst need of the Ansells, Solomon held his curly head high among his schoolfellows, and never lacked personal possessions, though they were not negotiable at the pawnbroker's. He had a peep-show, made out of an old cocoa-box, and representing the sortie from Plevna, a permit to view being obtainable for a fragment of slate pencil. For two pins he would let you look a whole minute. He also had bags of brass buttons, marbles, both commoners and alleys, nibs, beer-bottle labels, and cherry 'hogs,' besides bottles of liquorice-water, vendible either by the sip or the teaspoonful ; and he dealt in 'assy tassy' which consisted of little packets of acetic acid blent with brown sugar. The character of his stock varied according to the time of year, for Nature and Belgravia are less stable in their seasons than the Jewish school-boy, to whom buttons in March are as inconceivable as snowballing in July.

On Purim Solomon always had nuts to gamble with, just as if he had been a banker's son, and on the Day of Atonement he was never without a little tin fusee-box filled with savings of snuff. This, when the fast racked them most sorely, he would pass round among the old men with a grand manner. They would take a pinch and say, ' May thy strength increase,' and blow their delighted noses with great coloured handkerchiefs, and Solomon would feel about fifty, and sniff a few grains himself with the air of an aged connoisseur.

He took little interest in the subtle disquisitions of the Rabbis, which added their burden to his cross of secular learning. He wrestled but perfunctorily with the theses of the Bible commen-tators, for Moses Ansell was so absorbed in translating and enjoy-ing the intellectual tangles, that Solomon had scarce more to do than to play the part of chorus. He was fortunate in that his father could not afford to send him to a *Chedar*, an insanitary insti-tution that made Jacob a dull boy by cutting off his playtime and his oxygen, and delivering him over to the leathery mercies of an unintelligently learned zealot, scrupulously unclean.

The literature and history Solomon really cared for was not of the Jews. It was the history of Daredevil Dick and his congeners, whose surprising adventures, second-hand, in ink-stained sheets, were bartered to him for buttons, which shows the advantages of not having a soul above such. These deeds of derring-do (usually start-ing in the *Sturm und Drang* school-room period, in which teachers were thankfully accepted as created by Providence for the sport of schoolboys) Solomon conned at all hours, concealing them under his locker when he was supposed to be studying the Irish Question from an atlas, and even hiding them between the leaves of his dog-eared Prayer-Book for use during the morning service. The only harm they did him was that inflicted through the medium of the educational rod, when his surreptitious readings were discovered and his treasures thrown to the flames amid tears copious enough to extinguish them.

CHAPTER VI

'REB' SHEMUEL

'The Torah is greater than the priesthood and than royalty, seeing that royalty demands thirty qualifications, the priesthood twenty-four, while the Torah is acquired by forty-eight.   And these are they: by audible study; by distinct pronunciation; by understanding and discernment of the heart; by awe, reverence, meekness, cheerfulness; by ministering to the sages; by attaching one's self to colleagues, by discussion with disciples, by sedateness; by knowledge of the Scripture and of the Mishnah; by moderation in business, in intercourse with the world, in pleasure, in sleep, in conversation, in laughter; by long suffering, by a good heart, by faith in the wise; by resignation under chastisement; by recognising one's place, rejoicing in one's portion, putting a fence to one's words, claiming no merit for one's self; by being beloved, loving the All-present, loving mankind, loving just courses, rectitude and reproof; by keeping one's self far from honours, not boasting of one's learning, nor delighting in giving decisions; by bearing the yoke with one's fellow, judging him favourably, and leading him to truth and peace; by being composed in one's study; by asking and answering, hearing and adding thereto (by one's own reflection); by learning with the object of teaching and learning with the object of practising; by making one's master wiser, fixing attention upon his discourse, and reporting a thing in the name of him who said it.   So thou hast learnt. Whosoever reports a thing in the name of him that said it brings deliverance into the world, as it is said: And Esther told the King in the name of Mordecai.'   (*Ethics of the Fathers*, Singer's translation.)

MOSES ANSELL only occasionally worshipped at the synagogue of the Sons of the Covenant, for it was too near to make attendance a *Mitzvah*, pleasing in the sight of Heaven.   It was like having the prayer-quorum brought to you, instead of your going to it. The pious Jew must speed to *Shool* to show his eagerness, and return slowly, as with reluctant feet, lest Satan draw the attention of the Holy One to the laches of His chosen people.   It was not easy to express these varying emotions on a few flights of stairs, and so Moses went farther afield.   In subtle minutiæ like this Moses was *facile princeps*, being as Wellhausen puts it, of the *virtuosi* of religion.   If he put on his right stocking (or rather foot-lappet, for he did not wear stockings), first, he made amends by putting on the left boot first, and if he had lace-up boots, then the boot put on second would have a compensatory precedence in the lacing.   Thus was the divine principle of justice symbolised even in these small matters.

Moses was a great man in several of the more distant *Chevrahs* among which he distributed the privilege of his presence.   It was only when by accident the times of service did not coincide that Moses favoured the Sons of the Covenant, making an appearance either at the commencement or the fag-end, for he was not above praying odd bits of the service twice over, and even sometimes prefaced or supplemented his synagogal performances by solo renditions of the entire ritual of a hundred pages at home.   The

morning services began at six in summer and seven in winter, so
that the working man might start his long day's work fortified.

At the close of the service at the Beth Hamidrash, a few morn-
ings after the Redemption of Ezekiel, Solomon went up to Reb
Shemuel, who in return for the privilege of blessing the boy, gave
him a halfpenny. Solomon passed it on to his father, whom he
accompanied.

'Well, how goes it, Reb Moshé?' said Reb Shemuel with his
cheery smile, noticing Moses loitering. He called him 'Reb' out
of courtesy and in acknowledgment of his piety. The real 'Reb'
was a fine figure of a man, with matter, if not piety, enough for two
Moses Ansells. 'Reb' was a popular corruption of 'Rav' or
'Rabbi.'

'Bad,' replied Moses. 'I haven't had any machining to do for
a month. Work is very slack at this time of year. But God is
good!'

'Can't you sell something?' said Reb Shemuel, thoughtfully
caressing his long gray-streaked black beard.

'I have sold lemons; but the four or five shillings I made went
in bread for the children and in rent. Money runs through the
fingers, somehow, with a family of five and a frosty winter! When
the lemons were gone, I stood where I started.'

The Rabbi sighed sympathetically, and slipped half a crown
into Moses's palm. Then he hurried out. His boy, Levi, stayed
behind a moment to finish a transaction involving the barter of a
pea-shooter for some of Solomon's buttons. Levi was two years
older than Solomon, and was further removed from him by going
to a 'middle-class' school. His manner towards Solomon was of
a corresponding condescension. But it took a great deal to overawe Solomon, who, with the national humour, possessed the national *Chutzbah*, which is variously translated enterprise, audacity,
brazen impudence, and cheek.

'I say, Levi,' he said, 'we've got no school to-day! Won't you
come round this morning and play I-spy-I in our street? There
are some splendid corners for hiding, and they are putting up new
buildings all round with lovely hoardings, and they're knocking
down a pickle warehouse; and while you are hiding in the rub-
bish you sometimes pick up scrumptious bits of pickled walnut.
Oh, golly, ain't they prime!'

Levi turned up his nose.

'We've got plenty of whole walnuts at home,' he said.

Solomon felt snubbed. He became aware that this tall boy
had smart black clothes, which would not be improved by rubbing
against his own greasy corduroys.

'Oh, well,' he said, 'I can get lots of boys, and girls too!'

'Say,' said Levi, turning back a little. 'That little girl your
father brought upstairs here on the Rejoicing of the Law—that
was your sister, wasn't it?'

'Esther, d'ye mean?'

'How should I know? A little dark girl, with a print dress; rather pretty—not a bit like you.'

'Yes, that's our Esther; she's in the sixth standard, and only eleven!'

'We don't have standards in our school!' said Levi contemptuously. 'Will your sister join in the I-spy-I?'

'No, she can't run,' replied Solomon, half apologetically. 'She only likes to read. She reads all my *Boys of Englands* and things; and now she's got hold of a little brown book she keeps all to herself. I like reading, too; but I do it in school or in *Shool*, when there's nothing better to do.'

'Has she got a holiday to-day, too?'

'Yes,' said Solomon.

'But my school's open,' said Levi enviously; and Solomon lost the feeling of inferiority, and felt avenged.

'Come, then, Solomon,' said his father, who had reached the door. The two converted part of the half-crown into French loaves, and carried them home to form an unexpected breakfast.

Meantime Reb Shemuel, whose full name was the Reverend Samuel Jacobs, also proceeded to breakfast. His house lay near the *Shool*, and was approached by an avenue of mendicants. He arrived in his shirt-sleeves.

'Quick, Simcha, give me my new coat! It is very cold this morning.'

'You've given away your coat again!' shrieked his wife, who, though her name meant 'Rejoicing,' was more often upbraiding.

'Yes, it was only an old one, Simcha,' said the Rabbi deprecatingly. He took off his high hat, and replaced it by a little black cap.

'You'll ruin me, Shemuel!' moaned Simcha, wringing her hands. 'You'd give away the shirt off your skin to a pack of good-for-nothing *Schnorrers*!'

'Yes, if they had only their skin in the world. Why not?' said the old Rabbi, a pacific gleam in his large gazelle-like eyes. 'Perhaps my coat may have the honour to cover Elijah the prophet.'

'Elijah the prophet!' snorted Simcha. 'Elijah has sense enough to stay in heaven, and not go wandering about shivering in the fog and frost of this God-accursed country!'

The old Rabbi answered, 'Atschew!'

'For Thy salvation do I hope, O Lord!' murmured Simcha piously in Hebrew, adding excitedly in English: 'Ah, you'll kill yourself, Shemuel!' She rushed upstairs and returned with another coat and a new terror.

'Here, you fool, you've been and done a fine thing this time! All your silver was in the coat you've given away!'

'Was it?' said Reb Shemuel, startled. Then the tranquil look returned to his brown eyes: 'No, I took it all out before I gave away the coat.'

'God be thanked!' said Simcha fervently in Yiddish. 'Where is it? I want a few shillings for grocery.'

'I gave it away before, I tell you!'

Simcha groaned, and fell into her chair with a crash that rattled the tray and shook the cups.

'Here's the end of the week coming,' she sobbed, 'and I shall have no fish for Shabbos.'

'Do not blaspheme!' said Reb Shemuel, tugging a little angrily at his venerable beard. 'The Holy One—blessed be He!—will provide for our Shabbos.'

Simcha made a sceptical mouth, knowing that it was she, and nobody else, whose economies would provide for the due celebration of the Sabbath. Only by a constant course of vigilance, mendacity, and petty peculation at her husband's expense could she manage to support the family of four comfortably on his pretty considerable salary. Reb Shemuel went and kissed her on the sceptical mouth, because in another instant she would have him at her mercy. He washed his hands, and durst not speak between that and the first bite.

He was an official of heterogeneous duties—he preached and taught and lectured. He married people and divorced them. He released bachelors from the duty of marrying their deceased brothers' wives. He superintended a slaughtering department, licensed men as competent killers, examined the sharpness of their knives that the victims might be put to as little pain as possible, and inspected dead cattle in the shambles to see if they were perfectly sound and free from pulmonary disease. But his greatest function was *paskening*, or answering inquiries, ranging from the simplest to the most complicated problems of ceremonial ethics and civil law. He had added a volume of *Shaaloth u-Teshuvoth*, or 'Questions and Answers,' to the colossal casuistic literature of his race. His aid was also invoked as a Shadchan, though he forgot to take his commissions and lacked the restless zeal for the mating of mankind which animated Sugarman, the professional match-maker. In fine, he was a witty old fellow, and everybody loved him. He and his wife spoke English with a strong foreign accent; in their more intimate causeries they dropped into Yiddish.

The Rebbitzin poured out the Rabbi's coffee, and whitened it with milk drawn direct from the cow into her own jug. The butter and cheese were equally *kosher*, coming straight from Hebrew Hollanders, and having passed through none but Jewish vessels. As the Reb sat himself down at the head of the table, Hannah entered the room.

'Good-morning, father,' she said, kissing him. 'What have you got your new coat on for? Any weddings to-day?'

'No, my dear,' said Reb Shemuel; 'marriages are falling off. There hasn't even been an engagement since Belcovitch's eldest daughter betrothed herself to Pesach Weingott.'

'Oh, these Jewish young men!' said the Rebbitzin. 'Look at my Hannah,—as pretty a girl as you could meet in the whole Lane,—and yet here she is wasting her youth.'

Hannah bit her lip instead of her bread-and-butter, for she felt she had brought the talk on herself. She had heard the same grumblings from her mother for two years. Mrs. Jacobs's maternal anxiety had begun when her daughter was seventeen.

'When *I* was seventeen,' she went on, 'I was a married woman. Nowadays the girls don't begin to get a *Chosan* till they 're twenty.'

'We are not living in Poland,' the Reb reminded her.

'What 's that to do with it? It 's the Jewish young men who want to marry gold.'

'Why blame them? A Jewish young man can marry several pieces of gold, but since Rabbenu Gershom he can marry only one woman,' said the Reb, laughing feebly, and forcing his humour for his daughter's sake.

'One woman is more than thou canst support,' said the Rebbitzin, irritated into Yiddish; 'giving away the flesh from off thy children's bones! If thou hadst been a proper father, thou wouldst have saved thy money for Hannah's dowry instead of wasting it on a parcel of vagabond *Schnorrers*. Even so I can give her a good stock of bedding and under-linen. It 's a reproach and a shame that thou hast not yet found her a husband. Thou canst find husbands quick enough for other men's daughters!'

'I found a husband for thy father's daughter,' said the Reb, with a roguish gleam in his brown eyes.

'Don't throw that up to me! I could have got plenty better. And my daughter wouldn't have known the shame of finding nobody to marry her. In Poland at least the youths would have flocked to marry her because she was a Rabbi's daughter, and they 'd think it an honour to be a son-in-law of a Son of the Law. But in this godless country! Why, in my village the Chief Rabbi's daughter, who was so ugly as to make one spit out, carried off the finest man in the district.'

'But thou, my Simcha, hadst no need to be connected with Rabbonim.'

'Oh yes, make mockery of me!'

'I mean it. Thou art as a lily of Sharon.'

'Wilt thou have another cup of coffee, Shemuel?'

'Yes, my life. Wait but a little and thou shalt see our Hannah under the *Chuppah*.'

'Hast thou anyone in thine eye?'

The Reb nodded his head mysteriously, and winked the eye as if nudging the person in it.

'Who is it, father?' said Levi. 'I do hope it 's a real swell who talks English properly.'

'And mind you make yourself agreeable to him, Hannah,' said the Rebbitzin. 'You spoil all the matches I 've tried to make for you by your stupid stiff manner.'

'Look here, mother!' cried Hannah, pushing aside her cup violently. 'Am I going to have my breakfast in peace? I don't want to be married at all. I don't want any of your Jewish men coming round to examine me as if I were a horse, and wanting to know how much money you'll give them as a set-off. Let me be! Let me be single! It's my business, not yours.'

The Rebbitzin bent eyes of angry reproach on the Reb.

'What did I tell thee, Shemuel? She's *meshuggah*—quite mad! Healthy and fresh and mad!'

'Yes, you'll drive me mad,' said Hannah savagely. 'Let me be! I'm too old now to get a *Chosan*, so let me be as I am. I can always earn my own living.'

'Thou seest, Shemuel?' said Simcha. 'Thou seest my sorrows? Thou seest how impious our children wax in this godless country!'

'Let her be, Simcha; let her be,' said the Reb. 'She is young yet. If she hasn't any inclination thereto——'

'And what is *her* inclination? A pretty thing, forsooth! Is she going to make her mother a laughing-stock! Are Mrs. Jewell and Mrs. Abrahams to dandle grandchildren in my face, to gouge out my eyes with them? It isn't that she can't get young men. Only she is so high-blown. One would think she had a father who earned five hundred a year, instead of a man who scrambles half his salary among dirty *Schnorrers*.'

'Talk not like an Epicurean,' said the Reb. 'What are we all but *Schnorrers*, dependent on the charity of the Holy One— blessed be He! What! have we made ourselves? Rather fall prostrate and thank Him that His bounties to us are so great that they include the privilege of giving charity to others.'

'But we work for our living,' said the Rebbitzin. 'I wear my knees away scrubbing.'

External evidence pointed rather to the defrication of the nose.

'But, mother,' said Hannah, 'you know we have a servant to do the rough work.'

'Yes, servants!' said the Rebbitzin contemptuously. 'If you don't stand over them as the Egyptian taskmasters over our fore-fathers, they don't do a stroke of work except breaking the crock-ery. I'd much rather sweep a room myself than see a *Shiksah* pottering about for an hour, and end by leaving all the dust on the window ledges and the corners of the mantelpiece. As for beds, I don't believe *Shiksahs* ever shake them. If I had my way, I'd wring all their necks.'

'What's the use of always complaining!' said Hannah im-patiently. 'You know we must keep a *Shiksah* to attend to the Shabbos fire. The women or the little boys you pick up in the street are so unsatisfactory. When you call in a little barefoot street Arab and ask him to poke the fire, he looks at you as if you must be an imbecile not to be able to do it yourself. And then you can't always get hold of one.'

The Sabbath fire was one of the great difficulties of the Ghetto.

The Rabbis had modified the Biblical prohibition against having any fire whatever, and allowed it to be kindled by non-Jews. Poor women, frequently Irish, known as *Shabbos-goyahs* or *fire-goyahs*, acted as stokers to the Ghetto at twopence a hearth. No Jew ever touched a match or a candle, or burnt a piece of paper, or even opened a letter. The *Goyah*, which is literally heathen female, did everything required on the Sabbath. His grandmother once called Solomon Ansell a Sabbath female merely for fingering the shovel when there was nothing in the grate.

The Reb liked his fire. When it sank on the Sabbath he could not give orders to the *Shiksah* to replenish it, but he would rub his hands and remark casually (in her hearing) : 'Ah, how cold it is !'

'Yes,' he said now. 'I always freeze on Shabbos when thou hast dismissed thy *Shiksah*. Thou makest me catch one cold a month.'

' *I* make thee catch cold !' retorted the Rebbitzin. ' When thou comest through the air of winter in thy shirt-sleeves ! Thou 'lt fall back upon me for poultices and mustard plasters, and then thou expectest me to have enough money to pay a *Shiksah* into the bargain ! If I have any more of thy *Schnorrers* coming here, I shall bundle them out neck and crop.'

This was the moment selected by Fate and Melchitzedek Pinchas for the latter's entry.

CHAPTER VII

THE NEO-HEBREW POET

HE came through the open street-door, knocked perfunctorily at the door of the room, opened it, and then kissed the *Mezuzah* outside the door. Then he advanced, snatched the Rebbitzin's hand away from the handle of the coffee-pot, and kissed it with equal devotion. He then seized upon Hannah's hand and pressed his grimy lips to that, murmuring in German :

'Thou lookest so charming this morning, like the roses of Carmel.' Next he bent down and pressed his lips to the Reb's coat-tail. Finally he said ' Good-morning, sir,' to Levi, who replied very affably : ' Good-morning, Mr. Pinchas.'

'Peace be unto you, Pinchas !' said the Reb. ' I did not see you in *Shool* this morning, though it was the New Moon.'

'No, I went to the Great *Shool*,' said Pinchas in German. ' If you do not see me at your place, you may be sure I 'm somewhere else. Anyone who has lived so long as I in the Land of Israel cannot bear to pray without a quorum. In the Holy Land I used to learn for an hour in the *Shool* every morning before the service began. But I am not here to talk about myself. I came to ask you to do me the honour to accept a copy of my new volume of poems, entitled *Metatoron's Flames.* Is it not a beautiful title? When Enoch was taken up to heaven while yet alive, he was converted to flames of fire and became Metatoron, the great Spirit of the Cabbalah. So am I rapt up into the heaven of lyrical poetry, and become all fire and flame and light.'

The poet was a slim, dark little man, with long matted black hair. His face was hatchet-shaped, and not unlike an Aztec's; the eyes were informed by an eager brilliance. He had a heap of little paper-covered books in one hand and an extinct cigar in the other. He placed the books upon the breakfast-table.

'At last,' he said. 'See, I have got it printed—the great work which this ignorant English Judaism has left to moulder, while it pays its stupid reverends thousands a year for wearing white ties.'

'And who paid for it now, Mr. Pinchas?' said the Rebbitzin.

'Who? Who-o-o?' stammered Melchitzedek. 'Who but myself?'

'But you say you are blood-poor.'

'True as the Law of Moses! But I have written articles for the jargon-papers. They jump at me—there is not a man on the staff of them all who has the pen of a ready writer. I can't get any money out of them, my dear Rebbitzin, else I shouldn't be without breakfast this morning; but the proprietor of the largest of them is also a printer, and he has printed my little book in return. But I don't think I shall fill my stomach with the sales—oh, the Holy One—blessed be He!—bless you, Rebbitzin, of course I'll take a cup of coffee. I don't know anyone else who makes coffee with such a sweet savour; it would do for a spice-offering when the Almighty restores us our Temple. You are a happy mortal, Rebbi. You will permit that I seat myself at the table?'

Without awaiting permission he pushed a chair between Levi and Hannah and sat down; then he got up again and washed his hands, and helped himself to a spare egg.

'Here is your copy, Reb Shemuel,' he went on, after an interval. 'You see, it is dedicated generally, "To the Pillars of English Judaism." They are a set of donkey-heads, but one must give them a chance of rising to higher things. It is true that not one of them understands Hebrew, not even the Chief Rabbi, to whom courtesy made me send a copy. Perhaps he will be able to read my poems with a dictionary; he certainly can't write Hebrew without two grammatical blunders to every word. No, no, don't defend him, Reb Shemuel, because you're under him. He ought to be under you—only he expresses his ignorance in English, and the fools think to talk nonsense in good English is to be qualified for the Rabbinate.'

The remark touched the Rabbi in a tender place. It was the one worry of his life, the consciousness that persons in high quarters disapproved of him as a force impeding the Anglicisation of the Ghetto. He knew his shortcomings, but could never quite comprehend the importance of becoming English. He had a latent feeling that Judaism had flourished before England was invented, and so the poet's remark was secretly pleasing to him.

'You know very well,' went on Pinchas, 'that I and you are the only two persons in London who can write correct Holy Language.'

'No, no !' said the Rabbi deprecatingly.

'Yes, yes,' said Pinchas emphatically. 'You can write quite as well as I. But just cast your eye now on the special dedication which I have written to you in my own autograph.

'"To the light of his generation, the great Gaon, whose excellency reaches to the ends of the earth, from whose lips all the people of the Lord seek knowledge, the never-failing well, the mighty eagle who soars to heaven on the wings of understanding, to Rav Shemuel, may whose light never be dimmed, and in whose day may the Redeemer come unto Sion."

'There, take it ; honour me by taking it. It is the homage of the man of genius to the man of learning—the humble offering of the one Hebrew scholar in England to the other.'

'Thank you,' said the old Rabbi, much moved. 'It is too handsome of you, and I shall read it at once and treasure it amongst my dearest books, for you know well that I consider that you have the truest poetic gift of any son of Israel since Jehuda Halevi.'

'I have ! I know it ! I feel it ! It burns me. The sorrow of our race keeps me awake at night ; the national hopes tingle like electricity through me ; I bedew my couch with tears in the darkness ;' Pinchas paused to take another slice of bread-and-butter. 'It is then that my poems are born ; the words burst into music in my head, and I sing, like Isaiah, the restoration of our land, and become the poet-patriot of my people. But these English ! they care only to make money, and to stuff it down the throats of gorging reverends. My scholarship, my poetry, my divine dreams, what are these to a besotted, brutal congregation of Men-of-the-Earth ? I sent Buckledorf, the rich banker, a copy of my little book, with a special dedication, written in my own autograph, in German, so that he might understand it. And what did he send me ? A beggarly five shillings ! Five shillings to the one poet in whom the heavenly fire lives ! How can the heavenly fire live on five shillings ? I had almost a mind to send it back. And then there was Gideon, the Member of Parliament. I made one of the poems an acrostic on his name, so that he might be handed down to posterity. There, that's the one. No ; the one on the page you were just looking at. Yes, that's it, beginning :

> '"G reat leader of our Israel's host,
>   I sing thy high heroic deeds,
>   D ivinely-gifted learned man."

'I wrote his dedication in English, for he understands neither Hebrew nor German, the miserable, purse-proud, vanity-eaten Man-of-the-Earth.'

'Why, didn't he give you anything at all?' said the Reb.

'Worse! he sent me back the book. But I'll be revenged on him. I'll take the acrostic out of the next edition and let him rot in oblivion. I have been all over the world to every great city where Jews congregate. In Russia, in Turkey, in Germany, in Roumania, in Greece, in Morocco, in Palestine. Everywhere the greatest Rabbis have leapt like harts on the mountains with joy at my coming. They have fed and clothed me like a prince. I have preached at the synagogues, and everywhere people have said it was like the Wilna Gaon come again. From the neighbouring villages for miles and miles the pious have come to be blessed by me. Look at my testimonials from all the greatest saints and savants. But in England—in England alone—what is my welcome? Do they say "Welcome, Melchitzedek Pinchas? Welcome as the bridegroom to the bride, when the long day is done and the feast is o'er! Welcome to you with the torch of your genius, with the burden of your learning, that is rich with the whole wealth of Hebrew literature in all ages and countries. Here we have no great and wise men. Our Chief Rabbi is an idiot. Come thou, and be our Chief Rabbi." Do they say this? No! They greet me with scorn, coldness, slander. As for the Rev. Elkan Benjamin, who makes such a fuss of himself because he sends a wealthy congregation to sleep with his sermons, I'll expose him, as sure as there's a guardian of Israel. I'll let the world know about his four mistresses.'

'Nonsense! Guard yourself against the evil tongue,' said the Reb. 'How do you know he has?'

'It's the Law of Moses,' said the little poet. 'True as I stand here! You ask Jacob Hermann; it was he who told me about it. Jacob Hermann said to me one day, that Benjamin has a mistress for every fringe of his "four-corners." And how many is that, eh? I do not know why he should be allowed to slander me, and I not be allowed to tell the truth about him. One day I will shoot him. You know he said that when I first came to London I joined the *Meshumadim* in Palestine Place!'

'Well, he had at least some foundation for that,' said Reb Shemuel.

'Foundation! Do you call that foundation? because I lived there for a week, hunting out their customs and their ways of ensnaring the souls of our brethren, so that I might write about them one day. Have I not already told you not a morsel of their food passed my lips, and that the money which I had to take so as not to excite suspicion I distributed in charity among the poor Jews? Why not? From pigs we take bristles.'

'Still, you must remember that if you had not been such a saint and such a great poet, I might myself have believed that you sold your soul for money to escape starvation. I know how these devils set their baits for the helpless immigrant, offering bread in return for a lip-conversion. They are grown so cunning now they print their hellish appeals in Hebrew, knowing we reverence the holy tongue.'

'Yes ; the ordinary Man-of-the-Earth believes everything that 's in Hebrew. That was the mistake of the Apostles—to write in Greek. But, then, they too were such Men-of-the-Earth.'

'I wonder who writes such good Hebrew for the missionaries,' said Reb Shemuel.

'I wonder !' gurgled Pinchas, deep in his coffee.

'But, father,' asked Hannah, 'don't you believe any Jew ever really believes in Christianity ? '

'How is it possible ?' answered Reb Shemuel. 'A Jew who has the Law from Sinai, the Law that will never be changed, to whom God has given a sensible religion and common sense—how can such a person believe in the farrago of nonsense that makes up the worship of the Christians ? No Jew has ever apostatised except to fill his purse or his stomach, or to avoid persecution. Getting grace, they call it in English ; but with poor Jews it is always grace after meals. Look at the crypto-Jews, the Marranos, who for centuries lived a double life, outwardly Christians, but handing down secretly from generation to generation the faith, the traditions, the observances of Judaism.'

'Yes, no Jew was ever fool enough to turn Christian unless he was a clever man,' said the poet paradoxically. ' Have you not, my sweet, innocent young lady, heard the story of the two Jews in Burgos Cathedral ? '

'No ; what is it ?' said Levi eagerly.

'Well, pass my cup up to your highly superior mother, who is waiting to fill it with coffee. Your eminent father knows the story —I can see by the twinkle in his learned eye.'

'Yes, that story has a beard,' said the Reb.

'Two Spanish Jews,' said the poet, addressing himself deferentially to Levi, 'who had got grace, were waiting to be baptized at Burgos Cathedral. There was a great throng of Catholics, and a special Cardinal was coming to conduct the ceremony, for their conversion was a great triumph. But the Cardinal was late, and the Jews fumed and fretted at the delay. The shadows of evening were falling on vault and transept. At last one turned to the other, and said, "Knowest thou what, Moses ? If the holy father does not arrive soon, we shall be too late to say *Minchah*." '

Levi laughed heartily ; the reference to the Jewish afternoon prayer went home to him.

'That story sums up in a nutshell the whole history of the great movement for the conversion of the Jews. We dip ourselves in baptismal water and wipe ourselves with a *Talith*. We are not a race to be lured out of the fixed feelings of countless centuries by the empty spirituality of a religion in which—as I soon found out when I lived among the soul-dealers —its very professors no longer believe. We are too fond of solid things,' said the poet, upon whom a good breakfast was beginning to produce a soothing, materialistic effect. 'Do you know that anecdote about the two Jews in the Transvaal?' Pinchas went on. 'That's a real *Chine*.'

'I don't think I know that *Maaseh*,' said Reb Shemuel.

'Oh, the two Jews had made a *trek*, and were travelling onwards exploring unknown country. One night they were sitting by their camp-fire playing cards, when suddenly one threw up his cards, tore his hair, and beat his breast in terrible agony. "What's the matter?" cried the other. "Woe, woe!" said the first. "To-day was the Day of Atonement, and we have eaten and gone on as usual!" "Oh, don't take on so," said his friend. "After all, Heaven will take into consideration that we lost count of the Jewish calendar and didn't mean to be so wicked. And we can make up for it by fasting to-morrow." "Oh no, not for me!" said the first. "To-day was the Day of Atonement."'

All laughed, the Reb appreciating most keenly the sly dig at his race. He had a kindly sense of human frailty. Jews are very fond of telling stories against themselves—for their sense of humour is too strong not to be aware of their own foibles—but they tell them with closed doors, and resent them from the outside. They chastise themselves because they love themselves, as members of the same family insult one another. The secret is, that insiders understand the limitations of the criticism, which outsiders are apt to take in bulk. No race in the world possesses a richer anecdotal lore than the Jews—such pawky, even blasphemous humour, not understandable of the heathen; and to a suspicious mind, Pinchas's overflowing cornucopia of such would have suggested a prior period of Continental wandering from town to town, like the *Minnesingers* of the Middle Ages, repaying the hospitality of his Jewish entertainers with a budget of good stories and gossip from the scenes of his pilgrimages.

'Do you know the story,' he went on, encouraged by Simcha's smiling face, 'of the old Rav and the *Havdalah*? His wife left town for a few days, and when she returned the Rav took out a bottle of wine, poured some into the consecration cup, and began to recite the blessing. "What art thou doing?" demanded his wife, in amaze. "I am making *Havdalah*," replied the Rav. "But it is not the conclusion of a Festival to-night," she said. "Oh yes, it is," he answered. "My festival's over. You've come back."'

The Reb laughed so much over this story that Simcha's brow grew as the solid Egyptian darkness, and Pinchas perceived he had made a mistake.

'But listen to the end,' he said, with a creditable impromptu. 'The wife said, "No, you're mistaken. Your Festival's only beginning. You get no supper. It's the commencement of the Day of Atonement."'

Simcha's brow cleared, and the Reb laughed heartily.

'But I don't see the point, father,' said Levi.

'Point! Listen, my son. First of all, he was to have a Day of

Atonement, beginning with no supper, for his sin of rudeness to his faithful wife. Secondly, dost thou not know that with us the Day of Atonement is called a Festival, because we rejoice at the Creator's goodness in giving us the privilege of fasting? That's it, Pinchas, isn't it?'

'Yes, that's the point of the story, and I think the Rebbitzin had the best of it, eh?'

'Rebbitzins always have the last word,' said the Reb. 'But did I tell you the story of the woman who asked me a question the other day? She brought me a fowl in the morning, and said that in cutting open the gizzard she had found a rusty pin, which the fowl must have swallowed. She wanted to know whether the fowl might be eaten. It was a very difficult point, for how could you tell whether the pin had in any way contributed to the fowl's death? I searched the *Shass* and a heap of *Shaaloth u-Teshu-voth*. I went and consulted the Maggid, and Sugarman the Shadchan, and Mr. Karlkammer, and at last we decided that the fowl was *tripha* and could not be eaten. So the same evening I sent for the woman, and, when I told her of our decision, she burst into tears and wrung her hands. "Do not grieve so," I said taking compassion upon her; "I will buy thee another fowl." But she wept on uncomforted. "Oh, woe! woe!" she cried. "We ate it all up yesterday!"'

Pinchas was convulsed with laughter. Recovering himself, he lit his half-smoked cigar without asking leave.

'I thought it would turn out differently,' he said—'like that story of the peacock. A man had one presented to him, and as this is such rare diet, he went to the Rav to ask if it was *kosher*. The Rabbi said "No," and confiscated the peacock. Later on the man heard that the Rabbi had given a banquet, at which his peacock was the crowning dish. He went to the Rabbi, and reproached him. "*I* may eat it," replied the Rabbi, "because my father considers it permitted, and we may always go by what some eminent Son of the Law decides. But you, unfortunately, came to *me* for an opinion, and the permissibility of peacock is a point on which I have always disagreed with my father."'

Hannah seemed to find peculiar enjoyment in the story.

'Anyhow,' concluded Pinchas, 'you have a more pious flock than the Rabbi of my native place, who one day announced to his congregation that he was going to resign. Startled, they sent to him a delegate, who asked, in the name of the congregation, why he was leaving them. "Because," answered the Rabbi, "this is the first question anyone has ever asked me!"'

'Tell Mr. Pinchas your repartee about the donkey,' said Hannah, smiling.

'Oh no, it's not worth while,' said the Reb.

'Thou art always so backward with thine own,' cried the Rebbitzin warmly. 'Last Purim an impudent of face sent my husband a donkey made of sugar. My husband had a Rabbi baked in gingerbread, and sent it in exchange to the donor, with the inscription, "A Rabbi sends a Rabbi"!'

Reb Shemuel laughed heartily, hearing this afresh at the lips of his wife. But Pinchas was bent double, like a convulsive note of interrogation.

The clock on the mantelshelf began to strike nine. Levi jumped to his feet.

'I shall be late for school!' he cried, making for the door.

'Stop! stop!' shouted his father. 'Thou hast not yet said grace.'

'Oh yes, I have, father. While you were all telling stories I was *benshing* quietly to myself.'

'Is Saul also among the prophets? is Levi also among the story-tellers?' murmured Pinchas to himself. Aloud he said: 'The child speaks truth. I saw his lips moving.'

Levi gave the poet a grateful look, snatched up his satchel, and ran off to No. 1 Royal Street. Pinchas followed him soon, inwardly upbraiding Reb Shemuel for meanness. He had only as yet had his breakfast for his book. Perhaps it was Simcha's presence that was to blame. She was the Reb's right hand, and he did not care to let her know what his left was doing.

He retired to his study when Pinchas departed, and the Rebbitzin clattered about with a besom.

The study was a large square room lined with book-shelves, and hung with portraits of the great Continental Rabbis. The books were bibliographical monsters to which the Family Bibles of the Christian are mere pocket-books. They were all printed purely with the consonants, the vowels being divined grammatically or known by heart. In each there was an island of text in a sea of commentary, itself lost in an ocean of super-commentary that was bordered by a continent of super-super-commentary. Reb Shemuel knew many of these immense folios—with all their tortuous windings of argument and anecdote—much as the child knows the village it was born in, the crooked byways and the field-paths. Such-and-such a Rabbi gave such-and-such an opinion on such-and-such a line from the bottom of such-and-such a page—his memory of it was a visual picture. And just as the child does not connect its native village with the broader world without, does not trace its streets and turnings till they lead to the great towns, does not inquire as to its origins and its history, does not view it in relation to other villages, to the country, to the continent, to the world, but loves it for itself and in itself, so Reb Shemuel regarded and reverenced and loved these gigantic pages, with their serried battalions of varied type. They were facts—absolute as the globe itself—regions of wisdom, perfect and self-sufficing. A little obscure here and there, perhaps, and in need of amplification or explication for inferior intellects—a half-finished manuscript commentary on one of the super-commentaries, to be called 'The Garden of Lilies' was lying open on Reb Shemuel's own desk—but yet the only true encyclopædia of things terrestrial and divine. And, indeed, they were wonderful books. It was as difficult to say what was not in them as what was. Through them the old Rabbi held communion with his God, whom he loved with all his heart and soul, and thought of as a genial Father, watching tenderly over His froward children, and chastising them because He loved them. Generations of saints and scholars linked Reb Shemuel with the marvels of Sinai. The infinite network of ceremonial never hampered his soul; it was his joyous privilege to obey his Father in all things, and, like the king who offered to reward the man who invented a new pleasure, he was ready to embrace the sage who could deduce a new commandment. He rose at four every morning to study, and snatched every odd moment he could during the day. Rabbi Meir, that ancient ethical teacher, wrote : 'Whosoever labours in the Torah for its own sake, the whole world is indebted to him ; he is called friend, beloved, a lover of the All-present, a lover of mankind : it clothes him in meekness and reverence ; it fits him to become just, pious, upright, and faithful ; he becomes modest, long-suffering, and forgiving of insult.'

Reb Shemuel would have been scandalised if anyone had applied these words to him.

At about eleven o'clock Hannah came into the room, an open letter in her hand.

'Father,' she said, 'I have just had a letter from Mr. Samuel Levine.'

'Your husband?' he said, looking up with a smile.

'My husband,' she replied, with a fainter smile.

'And what does he say?'

'It isn't a very serious letter. He only wants to reassure me that he is coming back by Sunday week to be divorced.'

'All right. Tell him it shall be done at cost price,' he said, with the foreign accent that made him somehow seem more lovable to his daughter when he spoke English. ' He shall only be charged for the scribe.'

'He'll take that for granted,' Hannah replied. 'Fathers are expected to do these little things for their own children. But how much nicer it would be if you could give me the *Gett* yourself.'

'I would marry you with pleasure,' said Reb Shemuel ; 'but divorce is another matter. The *Din* has too much regard for a father's feelings to allow that.'

'And you really think I am Sam Levine's wife?'

'How many times shall I tell you? Some authorities do take the *intention* into account, but the letter of the law is clearly against you. It is far safer to be formally divorced.'

'Then, if he were to die——'

'Save us and grant us peace !' interrupted the Reb in horror.

'I should be his widow.'

'Yes, I suppose you would. But what *Narrischkeit* ! Why

should he die? It isn't as if you were really married to him,' said the Reb, his eye twinkling.

'But isn't it all absurd, father?'

'Do not talk so,' said Reb Shemuel, resuming his gravity. 'Is it absurd that you should be scorched if you play with fire?'

Hannah did not reply to the question.

'You never told me how you got on at Manchester,' she said. 'Did you settle the dispute satisfactorily?'

'Oh yes,' said the Reb; 'but it was very difficult. Both parties were so envenomed, and it seems that the feud has been going on in the congregation ever since the Day of Atonement, when the minister refused to blow the *Shofar* three minutes too early, as the president requested. The treasurer sided with the minister, and there has almost been a split.'

'The sounding of the New Year trumpet seems often to be the signal for war,' said Hannah sarcastically.

'It is so,' said the Reb sadly.

'And how did you repair the breach?'

'Just by laughing at both sides. They would have turned a deaf ear to reasoning. I told them that *Midrash* about Jacob's journey to Laban.'

'What is that?'

'Oh, it's an amplification of the Biblical narrative. The verse in Genesis says that he lighted on the place, and he put up there for the night because the sun had set, and he took of the stones of the place, and he made them into pillows. But later on it says that he rose up in the morning, and he took *the* stone which he had put as his pillows. Now, what is the explanation?' Reb Shemuel's tone became momently more sing-song. 'In the night the stones quarrelled for the honour of supporting the patriarch's head, and so by a miracle they were turned into one stone to satisfy them all. Now, you remember that when Jacob arose in the morning, he said: How fearful is this place! this is none other than the house of God. So I said to the wranglers: Why did Jacob say that? He said it because his rest had been so disturbed by the quarrelling stones that it reminded him of the house of God, the synagogue. I pointed out how much better it would be if they ceased their quarrellings and became one stone. And so I made peace again in the *Kehillah*.'

'Till next year,' said Hannah, laughing. 'But, father, I have often wondered why they allow the ram's horn in the service. I thought all musical instruments were forbidden.'

'It is not a musical instrument in practice,' said the Reb with evasive facetiousness. And, indeed, the performers were nearly always incompetent, marring the solemnity of great moments by asthmatic wheezings and thin far-away tootlings.

'But it would be if we had trained trumpeters,' persisted Hannah, smiling.

'If you really want the explanation, it is that, since the fall of the second Temple, we have dropped out of our worship all musical instruments connected with the old Temple worship, especially such as have become associated with Christianity. But the ram's horn on the New Year is an institution older than the Temple, and specially enjoined in the Bible.

'But surely there is something spiritualising about an organ?'

For reply the Reb pinched her ear.

'Ah, you are a sad *Epikouros*,' he said half seriously. 'If you loved God, you would not want an organ to take your thoughts to heaven.'

He released her ear and took up his pen, humming with unction a synagogue air full of joyous flourishes.

Hannah turned to go, then turned back.

'Father,' she said nervously, blushing a little, 'who was that you said you had in your eye?'

'Oh, nobody in particular,' said the Reb, equally embarrassed, and avoiding meeting her eye, as if to conceal the person in his.

'But you must have meant something by it,' she said gravely. 'You know I'm not going to be married off to please—other people.'

The Reb wriggled uncomfortably in his chair.

'It was only a thought, an idea. If it does not come to you, too, it shall be nothing. I didn't mean anything serious; really, my dear, I didn't. To tell the truth'—he finished suddenly, with a frank, heavenly smile—'the person I had mainly in my eye when I spoke was your mother.'

This time his eye met hers, and they smiled at each other with the consciousness of the humours of the situation. The Rebbitzin's broom was heard banging viciously in the passage. Hannah bent down and kissed the ample forehead beneath the black skull-cup.

'Mr. Levine also writes insisting that I must go to the Purim ball with him and Leah,' she said, glancing at the letter.

'A husband's wishes must be obeyed,' answered the Reb.

'No, I will treat him as if he were really my husband,' retorted Hannah. 'I will have my own way. I shan't go.'

The door was thrown open suddenly.

'Oh yes, thou wilt,' said the Rebbitzin. 'Thou art not going to bury thyself alive.'

CHAPTER VIII

ESTHER AND HER CHILDREN

ESTHER ANSELL did not welcome Levi Jacobs warmly. She had just cleared away the breakfast things, and was looking forward to a glorious day's reading, and the advent of a visitor did not gratify her. And yet Levi Jacobs was a good-looking boy, with

brown hair and eyes, a dark glowing complexion and ruddy lips—
a sort of reduced masculine edition of Hannah.

'I've come to play I-spy-I, Solomon,' he said when he entered.
'My, don't you live high up !'

'I thought you had to go to school,' Solomon observed with a stare.

'Ours isn't a board school,' Levi explained. 'You might introduce a fellow to your sister.'

'Garn ! You know Esther right enough,' said Solomon, and
began to whistle carelessly.

'How are you, Esther ?' said Levi awkwardly.

'I'm very well, thank you,' said Esther, looking up from a little
brown-covered book, and looking down at it again.

She was crouching on the fender, trying to get some warmth at
the little fire extracted from Reb Shemuel's half-crown. December continued gray; the room was dim, and a spurt of flame
played on her pale, earnest face. It was a face that never lost
a certain ardency of colour even at its palest ; the hair was dark
and abundant, the eyes were large and thoughtful, the nose
slightly aquiline, and the whole cast of the features betrayed the
Polish origin. The forehead was rather low. Esther had nice
teeth, which accident had preserved white. It was an arrestive
rather than a beautiful face, though charming enough when she
smiled. If the grace and candour of childhood could have been disengaged from the face, it would have been easier to say whether
it was absolutely pretty. It came nearer being so on Sabbaths
and holidays, when scholastic supervision was removed, and the
hair was free to fall loosely about the shoulders instead of being
screwed up into the pendulous plait so dear to the educational eye.
Esther could have earned a penny quite easily by sacrificing her
tresses, and going about with close-cropped head like a boy, for
her teacher never failed thus to reward the shorn, but in the
darkest hours of hunger she held on to her hair as her mother
had done before her. The prospects of Esther's post-nuptial wig
were not brilliant. She was not tall for a girl who is getting on
for twelve ; but some little girls shoot up suddenly, and there
was considerable room for hope.

Sarah and Isaac were romping noisily about and under the
beds ; Rachel was at the table, knitting a scarf for Solomon ; the
grandmother poured over a bulky enchiridion for pious women,
written in jargon. Moses was out in search of work. No one
took any notice of the visitor.

'What's that you're reading ?' he asked Esther politely.

'Oh, nothing,' said Esther with a start, closing the book, as if
fearful he might want to look over her shoulder.

'I don't see the fun of reading books out of school,' said Levi.

'Oh, but we don't read school books,' said Solomon defensively.

'I don't care. It's stupid.'

'At that rate you could never read books when you're grown
up,' said Esther contemptuously.

'No, of course not,' admitted Levi; otherwise where would be the fun of being grown up? After I leave school I don't intend to open a book.'

'No? Perhaps you'll open a shop,' said Solomon.

'What will you do when it rains?' asked Esther crushingly.

'I shall smoke,' replied Levi loftily.

'Yes, but suppose it's Shabbos?' swiftly rejoined Esther.

Levi was nonplussed. 'Well, it can't rain all day, and there are only fifty-two Sabbaths in the year,' he said lamely. 'A man can always do something.'

'I think there's more pleasure in reading than in doing something,' remarked Esther.

'Yes, you're a girl,' Levi reminded her, 'and girls are expected to stay indoors. Look at my sister Hannah; she reads too. But a man can be out doing what he pleases, eh, Solomon?'

'Yes, of course we've got the best of it,' said Solomon; 'the Prayer-Book shows that. Don't I say every morning, "Blessed art Thou, O Lord our God, who hast not made me a woman"?'

'I don't know whether you do say it. You certainly have got to,' said Esther witheringly.

'Sh!' said Solomon, winking in the direction of the grandmother.

'It doesn't matter,' said Esther calmly. 'She can't understand what I am saying.'

'I don't know,' said Solomon dubiously. 'She sometimes catches more than you bargain for.'

'And then *you* catch more than you bargain for,' said Rachel, looking up roguishly from her knitting.

Solomon stuck his tongue in his cheek and grimaced.

Isaac came behind Levi and gave his coat a pull, and toddled off with a yell of delight.

'Be quiet, Ikey!' cried Esther. 'If you don't behave better I shan't sleep in your new bed.'

'Oh yeth you mutht, Ethty,' lisped Ikey, his elfish face growing grave. He went about depressed for some seconds.

'Kids are a beastly nuisance,' said Levi; 'don't you think so, Esther?'

'Oh no, not always,' said the little girl. 'Besides, we were all kids once.'

'That's what I complain of,' said Levi. 'We ought all to be born grown-up.'

'But that's impossible!' put in Rachel.

'It isn't impossible at all,' said Esther. 'Look at Adam and Eve!'

Levi looked at Esther gratefully instead. He felt nearer to her, and thought of persuading her into playing kiss-in-the-ring. But he found it difficult to back out of his undertaking to play I-spy-I with Solomon; and in the end he had to leave Esther to her book.

She had little in common with her brother Solomon, least of all

humour and animal spirits. Even before the responsibilities of
headship had come upon her, she was a preternaturally thoughtful
little girl who had strange intuitions about things, and was doomed
to work out her own salvation as a metaphysician. When she
asked her mother who made God, a slap in the face demonstrated
to ᴐ. ʳ the limits of human inquiry. The natural instinct of the
child overrode the long travail of the race to conceive an abstract
Deity, and Esther pictured God as a Mammoth cloud. In early
years Esther imagined that the 'body' that was buried when a
person died was the corpse decapitated, and she often puzzled herself to think what was done with the isolated head. When her
mother was being tied up in grave-clothes, Esther hovered about
with a real thirst for knowledge, while the thoughts of all the
other children were sensuously concentrated on the funeral and
the glory of seeing a vehicle drive away from their own door.
Esther was also disappointed at not seeing her mother's soul fly
up to heaven, though she watched vigilantly at the death-bed for
the ascent of the long, yellow, hook-shaped thing. The genesis of
this conception of the soul was probably to be sought in the pictorial representations of ghosts in the story papers brought home
by her eldest brother, Benjamin. Strange shadowy conceptions
of things more corporeal floated up from her solitary reading.
Theatres she came across often, and a theatre was a kind of Babel
plain or Vanity Fair, in which performers and spectators were
promiscuously mingled, and wherein the richer folk, clad in evening dress, sat in thin deal boxes—the cases in Spitalfields Market
being Esther's main association with boxes. One of her day-
dreams of the future was going to the theatre in a night-gown, and
being accommodated with an orange-box.

Little rectification of such distorted views of life was to be
expected from Moses Ansell, who went down to his grave without
seeing even a circus, and had no interest in art apart from the
Police News and his Mizrach and the synagogue decorations.
Even when Esther's sceptical instinct drove her to inquire of her
father how people knew that Moses got the Law on Mount Sinai,
he could only repeat in horror that the books of Moses said so,
and could never be brought to see that his arguments travelled on
roundabouts. She sometimes regretted that her brilliant brother
Benjamin had been swallowed up by the Orphan Asylum, for she
imagined she could have discussed many a knotty point with him.
Solomon was both flippant and incompetent. But in spite of her
theoretical latitudinarianism, in practice she was pious to the
point of fanaticism, and could scarce conceive the depths of degradation of which she heard vague horror-struck talk. There were
Jews about—grown-up men and women, not insane—who struck
lucifer matches on the Sabbath, and housewives who carelessly
mixed their butter-plates with their meat-plates, even when they
did not actually eat butter with meat. Esther promised herself
that, please God, she would never do anything so wicked when

she grew up. She, at least, would never fail to light the Sabbath candles nor to *kosher* the meat. Never was child more alive to the beauty of duty, more open to the appeal of virtue, self-control, abnegation. She fasted till two o'clock on the Great White Fast when she was seven years old, and accomplished the perfect feat at nine. When she read a simple little story in a prize-book, inculcating the homely moralities at which the cynic sneers, her eyes filled with tears and her breast with unselfish and dutiful determinations. She had something of the temperament of the stoic, fortified by that spiritual pride which does not look for equal goodness in others; and though she disapproved of Solomon's dodgings of duty, she did not sneak or preach—even gave him surreptitious crusts or coffee before he had said his prayers, especially on Saturdays and Festivals, when the praying took place in *Shool* and was liable to be prolonged till mid-day.

Esther often went to synagogue, and sat in the ladies' compartment. The drone of the Sons of the Covenant downstairs was part of her consciousness of home, like the musty smell of the stairs, or Becky's young men, through whom she had to plough her way when she went for the morning milk, or the odours of Mr. Belcovitch's rum or the whirr of his machines, or the bent, snuffy personality of the Hebrew scholar in the adjoining garret, or the dread of Dutch Debby's dog that was ultimately transformed to friendly expectation. Esther led a double life, just as she spoke two tongues. The knowledge that she was a Jewish child, whose people had had a special history, was always at the back of her consciousness; sometimes it was brought to the front by the scoffing rhymes of Christian children, who informed her that they had stuck a piece of pork upon a fork and given it to a member of her race.

But far more vividly did she realise that she was an English girl; far keener than her pride in Judas Maccabæus was her pride in Nelson and Wellington; she rejoiced to find that her ancestors had always beaten the French, from the days of Cressy and Poictiers to the day of Waterloo; that Alfred the Great was the wisest of kings, and that Englishmen dominated the world and had planted colonies in every corner of it; that the English language was the noblest in the world, and men speaking it had invented railway trains, steamships, telegraphs, and everything worth inventing. Esther absorbed these ideas from the school reading-books. The experience of a month will overlay the hereditary bequest of a century. And yet, beneath all, the prepared plate remains most sensitive to the old impressions.

Sarah and Isaac had developed as distinct individualities as was possible in the time at their disposal. Isaac was just five, and Sarah, who had never known her mother, just four. The thoughts of both ran strongly in the direction of sensuous enjoyment, and they preferred baked potatoes, especially potatoes touched with gravy, to all the joys of the Kindergarten. Isaac's ambitions ran

in the direction of eider-down beds, such as he had once felt at
Malka's, and Moses soothed him by the horizon-like prospect of
such a new bed. Places of honour had already been conceded
by the generous little chap to his father and brothers. Heaven
alone knows how he had come to conceive their common bed as
his own peculiar property, in which the other three resided at
night on sufferance. He could not even plead it was his by right
of birth in it. But Isaac was not, after all, wholly given over to
worldly thoughts, for an intellectual problem often occupied his
thoughts and led him to slap little Sarah's arms. He had been
born on the fourth of December, while Sarah had been born, a
year later, on the third.

'It ain't, it can't be,' he would say. 'Your birfday can't be afore
mine.'

''Tis, Esty thays so,' Sarah would reply.

'Esty's a liar,' Isaac responded imperturbably.

'Arx *Tatah*.'

'*Tatah* dunno. Ain't I five?'

'Yeth.'

'And ain't you four?'

'Yeth.'

'And ain't I older than you?'

'Courth.'

'And wasn't I born afore you?'

'Yeth, Ikey.'

'Then 'ow can your birfday come afore mine?'

'Cos it doth.'

'Stoopid!'

'It doth, arx Esty,' Sarah would insist.

'Than't teep in my new bed,' Ikey would threaten.

'Thall if I like.'

'Than't!'

Here Sarah would generally break down in tears, and Isaac
with premature economic instinct, feeling it wicked to waste a cry,
would proceed to justify it by hitting her. Thereupon little Sarah
would hit him back and develop a terrible howl.

'Hi, woe is unto me,' she would wail in jargon, throwing herself on the ground in a corner and rocking herself to and fro, like
her far-away ancestresses remembering Zion by the waters of
Babylon.

Little Sarah's lamentations never ceased till she had been
avenged by a higher hand.   There were several great powers, but
Esther was the most trusty instrument of reprisal.   If Esther was
out, little Sarah's sobs ceased speedily, for she, too, felt the folly
of fruitless tears. Though she nursed in her breast the sense of
injury, she would even resume her amicable romps with Isaac.
But the moment the step of the avenger was heard on the stairs,
little Sarah would betake herself to the corner and howl with the
pain of Isaac's pummellings. She had a strong love of abstract

justice, and felt that, if the wrong-doer were to go unpunished, there was no security for the constitution of things.

To-day's holiday did not pass without an outbreak of this sort. It occurred about tea-time. Perhaps the infants were fractious because there was no tea. Esther had to economise her resources, and a repast at seven would serve for both tea and supper. Among the poor combination meals are as common as combination beds and chests. Esther had quieted Sarah by slapping Isaac, but, as this made Isaac howl, the gain was dubious. She had to put a fresh piece of coal on the fire, and sing to them while their shadows contorted themselves grotesquely on the beds and then upwards along the sloping walls, terminating with twisted necks on the ceiling.

Esther usually sang melancholy things in minor keys. They seemed most attuned to the dim, straggling room. There was a song her mother used to sing. It was taken from a Purim Spiel, itself based upon a Midrash, one of the endless legends with which the People of One Book have broidered it, amplifying every minute detail with all the exuberance of Oriental imagination, and justifying their fancies with all the ingenuity of a race of lawyers. After his brethren sold Joseph to the Midianite merchants, the lad escaped from the caravan and wandered footsore and hungry to Bethlehem, to the grave of his mother, Rachel. And he threw himself upon the ground and wept aloud, and sang to a heart-breaking melody in Yiddish :

> ' *Und hei weh ist mir,*
> *Wie schlecht ist doch mir,*
> *Ich bin vertrieben geworen*
> *Junger heid voon dir.'*

Whereof the English runs :

> ' *Alas! woe is me!*
> *How wretched to be*
> *Driven away and banished,*
> *Yet so young, from thee!* '

Thereupon the voice of his beloved mother, Rachel, was heard from the grave, comforting him and bidding him be of good cheer, for that his future should be great and glorious.

Esther could not sing this without the tears trickling down her cheeks. Was it that she thought of her own dead mother, and applied the lines to herself? Isaac's ill-humour scarcely ever survived the anodyne of these mournful cadences. There was another melodious wail which Alte Belcovitch had brought from Poland. The chorus ran :

> ' *Man nemt awek die chasanim voon die callohs,*
> *Hi, hi, did-a-rid-a-ree!*'

> ' *They tear away their lovers from the maidens,*
> *Hi, hi, did-a-rid-a-ree!* '

The air mingled the melancholy of Polish music with the sadness of Jewish, and the words hinted of God knew what

> ' Old unhappy far-off things
> And battles long ago.'

And so over all the songs and stories was the trail of tragedy ; under all, the heartache of a hunted race.   There are few more plaintive chants in the world than the recitation of the Psalms by the Sons of the Covenant on Sabbath afternoons amid the gathering shadows of twilight.   Esther often stood in the passage to hear it, morbidly fascinated, tears of pensive pleasure in her eyes. Even the little jargon story-book, which Moses Ansell read out that night to his *Kinder* after tea-supper, by the light of the one candle, was prefaced with a note of pathos.   ' These stories have we gathered together from the Gemorah and the Midrash, wonderful stories, and we have translated the beautiful stories, using the Hebrew alphabet, so that everyone, little or big, shall be able to read them, and shall know that there is a God in the world who forsaketh not His people Israel, and who even for us will likewise work miracles and wonders, and will send us the righteous Redeemer speedily in our days.   Amen.'

Of this same Messiah the children heard endless tales.   Oriental fancy had been exhausted in picturing him for the consolation of exiled and suffering Israel.   Before his days there would be a wicked Messiah of the house of Joseph ; later, a king with one ear, deaf to hear good, but acute to hear evil ; there would be a scar on his forehead ; one of his hands would be an inch long and the other three miles ; apparently a subtle symbol of the persecutor. The jargon story-book, among its ' stories, wonderful stories,' had also extracts from the famous romance, or diary, of Eldad the Danite, who professed to have discovered the lost ten tribes. Eldad's book appeared towards the end of the ninth century, and became the ' Arabian Nights' of the Jews, and it had filtered down through the ages into the Ansell garret, in common with many other tales from the rich storehouse of mediæval folklore, in the diffusion of which the Wandering Jew has played so great a part.

Sometimes Moses read to his charmed hearers the descriptions of heaven and hell by Immanuel, the friend and contemporary of Dante, sometimes a jargon version of *Robinson Crusoe*.   Tonight he chose Eldad's account of the tribe of Moses, dwelling beyond the wonderful river Sambatyon, which never flows on the Sabbath.

' There is also the tribe of Moses, our just master, which is called the tribe that flees, because it fled from idol worship and clung to the fear of God.   A river flows round their land for a distance of four days' journey on every side.   They dwell in beautiful houses provided with handsome towers, which they have built themselves.   There is nothing unclean among them, neither in the case of birds, venison, nor domesticated animals ; there are no wild animals, no flies, no foxes, no vermin, no serpents, no dogs, and in general nothing which does harm ; they have only sheep and cattle, which bear twice a year. They sow and reap ; there are all sorts of gardens with all kinds of fruit and cereals, viz. beans, melons, gourds, onions, garlic, wheat, and barley, and the seed grows a hundredfold. They have faith ; they know the law, the Mishnah, the Talmud, and the Agadah ; but their Talmud is in Hebrew. They introduce their sayings in the name of the Fathers, the wise men, who heard them from the mouth of Joshua, who himself heard them from the mouth of God. They have no knowledge of the Tanaim (doctors of the Mishnah) and Amoraim (doctors of the Talmud), who flourished during the time of the second Temple, which was, of course, not known to these tribes. They speak only Hebrew, and are very strict as regards the use of wine made by others than themselves, as well as the rules of slaughtering animals ; in this respect the law of Moses is much more rigorous than that of the tribes. They do not swear by the name of God, for fear that their breath may leave them, and they become angry with those who swear ; they reprimand them, saying, " Woe, ye poor, why do you swear with the mention of the name of God upon your lips? Use your mouth for eating bread and drinking water. Do you not know that for the sin of swearing your children die young?" And in this way they exhort everyone to serve God with fear and integrity of heart. Therefore the children of Moses, the servant of God, live long, to the age of one hundred or one hundred and twenty years. No child, be it son or daughter, dies during the lifetime of its parent, but they reach a third and a fourth generation, and see grandchildren and great-grandchildren with their offspring. They do all field-work themselves, having no male or female servants ; there are also merchants among them. They do not close their houses at night, for there is no thief nor any wicked man among them. Thus a little lad might go for days with his flock without fear of robbers, demons, or danger of any other kind ; they are indeed all holy and clean. These Levites busy themselves with the Law and with the commandments, and they still live in the holiness of our master, Moses ; therefore God has given them all this good. Moreover, they see nobody and nobody sees them, except the four tribes who dwell on the other side of the rivers of Cush ; they see them and speak to them, but the river Sambatyon is between them, as it is said : " That thou mayest say to prisoners, Go forth" (Isaiah xlix. 9). They have plenty of gold and silver ; they sow flax, and cultivate the crimson worm, and make beautiful garments. Their number is double or four times the number that went out from Egypt.

' The river Sambatyon is two hundred yards broad—"about as far as a bowshot" (Gen. xxi. 16)—full of sand and stones, but without water; the stones make a great noise like the waves of the sea and a stormy wind, so that in the night the noise is heard at a distance of half a day's journey. There are sources of water which collect themselves in one pool, out of which they water the fields. There are fish in it, and all kinds of clean birds fly round it. And this river of stone and sand rolls during the six working days, and rests on the Sabbath day. As soon as the Sabbath begins, fire surrounds the river, and the flames remain till the next evening, when the Sabbath ends. Thus no human being can reach the river for a distance of half a mile on either side ; the fire consumes all that grows there. The four tribes, Dan, Naphtali, Gad, and Asher, stand on the borders of the river. When shearing their flocks here—for the land is flat and clean, without any thorns—if the children of Moses see them gathered together on the border, they shout, saying, "Brethren, tribes of Jeshurum, show us your camels, dogs, and asses," and they make their remarks about the length of the camel's neck and the shortness of the tail. Then they greet one another and go their way.'

When this was done, Solomon called for hell. He liked to hear about the punishment of the sinners ; it gave a zest to life. Moses hardly needed a book to tell them about hell. It had no secrets for him. The Old Testament has no reference to a future existence, but the poor Jew has no more been able to live without the hope of hell than the poor Christian. When the wicked man has waxed fat and kicked the righteous skinny man, shall the two lie down in the same dust and the game be over ? Perish the thought ! One of the hells was that in which the sinner was condemned to do over and over again the sins he had done in life.

'Why, that must be jolly !' said Solomon.

'No, that is frightful,' maintained Moses Ansell.

He spoke Yiddish, the children English.

'Of course it is,' said Esther. 'Just fancy, Solomon, having to eat toffy all day !'

'It 's better than eating nothing all day,' replied Solomon.

'But to eat it every day for ever and ever!' said Moses. 'There's no rest for the wicked.'

'What ! not even on the Sabbath ?' said Esther.

'Oh yes, of course then. Like the river Sambatyon, even the flames of hell rest on Shabbos.'

'Haven't they got no *fire-goyahs* ?' inquired Ikey, and everybody laughed.

'Shabbos is a holiday in hell,' Moses explained to the little one. 'So thou seest the result of thy making out Sabbath too early on Saturday night ; thou sendest the poor souls back to their tortures before the proper time.'

Moses never lost an opportunity of enforcing the claims of the ceremonial law. Esther had a vivid picture flashed upon her of poor yellow hook-shaped souls floating sullenly back towards the flames.

Solomon's chief respect for his father sprang from the halo of military service encircling Moses ever since it leaked out through the lips of the *Bube* that he had been a conscript in Russia and been brutally treated by the sergeant. But Moses could not be got to speak of his exploits. Solomon pressed him to do so, especially when his father gave symptoms of inviting him to the study of Rashi's Commentary. To-night Moses brought out a Hebrew tome, and said :

'Come, Solomon, enough of stories. We must learn a little.'

'To-day is a holiday,' grumbled Solomon.

'It is never a holiday for the study of the Law.'

'Only this once, father ; let 's play draughts.'

Moses weakly yielded. Draughts was his sole relaxation, and when Solomon acquired a draughtboard by barter, his father taught him the game. Moses played the Polish variety, in which the men are like English kings, that leap backwards and forwards, and the kings shoot diagonally across, like bishops at chess. Solomon could not withstand these gigantic grasshoppers, whose stopping-places he could never anticipate. Moses won every game to-night, and was full of glee, and told the *Kinder* another story. It was about the Emperor Nicholas, and is not to be found in the official histories of Russia.

'Nicholas was a wicked king, who oppressed the Jews, and made their lives sore and bitter. And one day he made it known to the Jews that, if a million roubles were not raised for him in a month's time, they should be driven from their homes. Then the Jews prayed unto God, and besought Him to help them for the merits of the forefathers, but no help came. Then they tried to bribe the officials ; but the officials pocketed their gold, and the Emperor still demanded his tax. Then they went to the great Masters of Cabbalah, who by pondering day and night on the Name and its transmutations had won the control of all things, and they said, " Can ye do naught for us ? " Then the Masters of Cabbalah took counsel together, and at midnight they called up the spirits of Abraham our father, and Isaac and Jacob, and Elijah the Prophet, who wept to hear of their children's sorrows. And Abraham our father, and Isaac and Jacob, and Elijah the Prophet, took the bed whereon Nicholas the Emperor slept, and transported it to a wild place. And they took Nicholas the Emperor out of his warm bed, and whipped him soundly, so that he yelled for mercy. Then they asked : " Wilt thou rescind the edict against the Jews ? " And he said, " I will." But in the morning Nicholas the Emperor woke up and called for the chief of the bed-chamber, and said : " How darest thou allow my bed to be carried out in the middle of the night into the forest ? " And the chief of the bed-chamber grew pale, and said that the Emperor's guards had watched all night outside the door ; neither was there space for the bed to pass out. And Nicholas the Emperor, thinking he had dreamed, let the man go unhung. But the next night, lo ! the bed was transported again to the wild place, and Abraham our father, and Isaac and Jacob, and Elijah the Prophet, drubbed him doubly, and again he promised to remit the tax. So in the morning the chief of the bed-chamber was hanged, and at night the guards were doubled. But the bed sailed away to the wild place, and Nicholas the Emperor was trebly whipped. Then Nicholas the Emperor annulled the edict, and the Jews rejoiced, and fell at the knees of the Masters of Cabbalah.'

'But why can't they save the Jews altogether?' queried Esther.

'Ah!' said Moses mysteriously, 'Cabbalah is a great force, and must not be abused. The Holy Name must not be made common. Moreover one might lose one's life.'

'Could the Masters make men?' inquired Esther, in awe-struck tones. She had recently come across Frankenstein.

'Certainly,' said Moses. 'And, what is more, it stands written that Rav Chanina and Rav Osheya fashioned a fine fat calf on Friday, and enjoyed it on the Sabbath.'

'Oh, father!' said Solomon piteously. 'Don't you know Cabbalah?'

CHAPTER IX

DUTCH DEBBY

A YEAR before we got to know Esther Ansell she got to know Dutch Debby, and it changed her life. Dutch Debby was a tall, sallow, ungainly girl, who lived in the wee back-room on the second floor behind Mrs. Simons, and supported herself and her dog by needlework. Nobody ever came to see her, for it was whispered that her parents had cast her out when she presented them with an illegitimate grandchild. The baby was fortunate enough to die, but she still continued to incur suspicion by keeping a dog, which is an un-Jewish trait. Bobby often squatted on the stairs guarding her door, and, as it was very dark on the staircase, Esther suffered great agonies lest she should tread on his tail and provoke reprisals. Her anxiety led her to do so one afternoon, and Bobby's teeth just penetrated through her stocking. The clamour brought out Dutch Debby, who took the girl into her room and soothed her. Esther had often wondered what uncanny mysteries lay behind that dark, dog-guarded door, and she was rather more afraid of Debby than of Bobby.

But that afternoon saw the beginning of a friendship which added one to the many factors which were moulding the future woman. For Debby turned out a very mild bogie indeed, with a good English vocabulary and a stock of old *London Journals* more precious to Esther than mines of Ind. Debby kept them under the bed, which, as the size of the bed all but coincided with the area of the room, was a wise arrangement. And on the long summer evenings and the Sunday afternoons when her little ones needed no looking after and were traipsing about playing 'Whoop!' and pussy-cat in the street downstairs, Esther slipped into the wee back-room, where the treasures lay, and there, by the open window overlooking the dingy back-yard and the slanting perspectives of sun-flecked red tiles where cats prowled and dingy sparrows hopped, in an atmosphere laden with whiffs from a neighbouring dairyman's stables, Esther lost herself in wild tales of passion and romance. She frequently read them aloud for the benefit of the sallow-faced needlewoman, who had found romance square so sadly with the realities of her own existence. And so all a summer afternoon, Dutch Debby and Esther would be rapt away to a world of brave men and fair women, a world of fine linen and purple, of champagne and wickedness and cigarettes, a world where nobody worked or washed shirts, or was hungry or had holes in boots, a world utterly ignorant of Judaism and the heinousness of eating meat with butter. Not that Esther for her part correlated her conception of this world with facts. She never realised that it was an actually possible world—never, indeed, asked herself whether it existed outside print or not. She never thought of it in that way at all, any more than it ever occurred to her that people once spoke the Hebrew she learnt to read and translate. Bobby was often present at these readings, but he kept his thoughts to himself, sitting on his hind-legs with his delight-fully ugly nose tilted up inquiringly at Esther. For the best of all this new friendship was that Bobby was not jealous. He was only a sorry dun-coloured mongrel to outsiders, but Esther learnt to see him almost through Dutch Debby's eyes. And she could run up the stairs freely, knowing that if she trod on his tail now, he would take it as a mark of *camaraderie*.

'I used to pay a penny a week for the *London Journal*,' said Debby early in their acquaintanceship, 'till one day I discovered I had a dreadful bad memory.'

'And what was the good of that?' asked Esther.

'Why, it was worth shillings and shillings to me. You see, I used to save up all the back numbers of the *London Journal*, because of the answers to correspondents, telling you how to do your hair and trim your nails and give yourself a nice complexion. I used to bother my head about that sort of thing in those days, dear; and one day I happened to get reading a story in a back number, only about a year old, and I found I was just as interested as if I had never read it before, and I hadn't the slightest remem-brance of it. After that I left off buying the *Journal*, and took to reading my big heap of back numbers. I get through them once every two years.' Debby interrupted herself with a fit of cough-ing, for lengthy monologue is inadvisable for persons who bend over needlework in dark back rooms. Recovering herself, she added, 'And then I start afresh. You couldn't do that, could you?'

'No,' admitted Esther, with a painful feeling of inferiority. 'I remember all I've ever read.'

'Ah, you will grow up a clever woman,' said Debby, patting her hair.

'Oh, do you think so?' said Esther, her dark eyes lighting up with pleasure.

'Oh yes; you're always first in your class, ain't you?'

'Is that what you judge by, Debby?' said Esther, disappointed. 'The other girls are so stupid, and take no thought for anything but their hats and their frocks. They would rather play gobs or shuttlecock or hopscotch than read about the "Forty Thieves." They don't mind being kept a whole year in one class, but I—oh, I feel so mad at getting on so slow! I could easily learn the standard work in three months. I want to know everything, so that I can grow up to be a teacher at our school.'

'And does your teacher know everything?'

'Oh yes! She knows the meaning of every word and all about foreign countries.'

'And would you like to be a teacher?'

'If I could only be clever enough?' sighed Esther. 'But then, you see, the teachers at our school are real ladies, and they dress, oh, so beautifully! with fur tippets and six-buttoned gloves. I could never afford it, for even when I was earning five shillings a week I should have to give most of it to father and the children.'

'But if you're very good I dare say some of the great ladies like the Rothschilds will buy you nice clothes; I have heard they are very good to clever children.'

'No; then the other teachers would know I was getting charity! And they would mock at me. I heard Miss Hyams make fun of a teacher because she wore the same dress as last winter. I don't think I should like to be a teacher, after all, though it is nice to be able to stand with your back to the fire in the winter. The girls would know——' Esther stopped and blushed.

'Would know what, dear?'

'Well, they would know father,' said Esther, in low tones. 'They would see him selling things in the Lane, and they wouldn't do what I told them.'

'Nonsense, Esther! I believe most of the teachers' fathers are just as bad—I mean as poor. Look at Miss Hyam's own father.'

'Oh, Debby! I do hope that's true. Besides, when I was earning five shillings a week I could buy father a new coat, couldn't I? And then there would be no need for him to stand in the Lane with lemons or "four-corner" fringes, would there?'

'No, dear. You shall be a teacher, I prophesy; and—who knows?—some day you may be head-mistress!'

Esther laughed a startled little laugh of delight, with a suspicion of a sob in it.

'What, me! Me go round and make all the teachers do their work! Oh, wouldn't I catch them gossiping! I know their tricks!'

'You seem to look after your teacher well. Do you ever call her over the coals for gossiping?' inquired Dutch Debby amused.

'No, no,' protested Esther, quite seriously. 'I like to hear them gossiping. When my teacher and Miss Davis, who's in the next room, and a few other teachers get together, I learn, oh, such a lot from their conversation!'

'Then they do teach you, after all,' laughed Debby.

'Yes, but it's not on the time-table,' said Esther, shaking her little head sapiently. 'It's mostly about young men. Did you ever have a young man, Debby?'

'Don't—don't ask such questions, child!'

Debby bent over her needlework.

'Why not?' persisted Esther. 'If I only had a young man when I grew up, I should be proud of him Yes, you're trying to turn your head away. I'm sure you had. Was he nice, like Lord Eversmonde, or Captain Andrew Sinclair? Why, you're crying, Debby!'

'Don't be a little fool, Esther! A tiny fly has just flown into my eye, poor little thing! He hurts me, and does himself no good.'

'Let me see, Debby!' said Esther. 'Perhaps I shall be in time to save him.'

'No, don't trouble.'

'Don't be so cruel, Debby. You're as bad as Solomon, who pulls off flies' wings to see if they can fly without them.'

'He's dead now. Go on with "Lady Ann's Rival." We've been wasting the whole afternoon talking. Take my advice, Esther, and don't stuff your head with ideas about young men. You're too young. Now, dear, I'm ready. Go on.'

'Where was I? Oh yes. "Lord Eversmonde folded the fair young form to his manly bosom, and pressed kiss after kiss upon her ripe young lips, which responded passionately to his own. At last she recovered herself, and cried reproachfully: 'Oh, Sigismund, why do you persist in coming here when the duke forbids it?'" Oh, do you know, Debby, father said the other day I oughtn't to come here.'

'Oh no, you must!' cried Debby impulsively. 'I couldn't part with you now!'

'Father says people say you are not good,' said Esther candidly.

Debby breathed painfully.

'Well!' she whispered.

'But I said people were liars. You *are* good!'

'Oh, Esther, Esther!' sobbed Debby, kissing the earnest little face with a vehemence that surprised the child.

'I think father only said that,' Esther went on, 'because he fancies I neglect Sarah and Isaac when he's at *Shool*, and they quarrel so about their birthdays when they're together. But they don't slap one another hard. I'll tell you what. Suppose I bring Sarah down here!'

'Well, but won't she cry and be miserable here if you read, and with no Isaac to play with?'

'Oh no,' said Esther confidently. 'She'll keep Bobby company.'

Bobby took kindly to little Sarah also. He knew no other dogs, and in such circumstances a sensible animal falls back on human beings. He had first met Debby herself quite casually, and the two lonely beings took to each other. Before that meeting Dutch Debby was subject to wild temptations. Once she half starved herself and put aside ninepence a week for almost three months, and purchased one-eighth of a lottery ticket from Sugarman the Shadchan, who recognised her existence for the occasion. The fortune did not come off.

Debby saw less and less of Esther as the months crept on again towards winter, for the little girl feared her hostess might feel constrained to offer her food, and the children required more soothing. Esther would say very little about her home-life, though Debby got to know a great deal about her school-mates and her teacher.

One summer evening, after Esther had passed into the hands of Miss Miriam Hyams, she came to Dutch Debby with a grave face, and said:

'Oh, Debby, Miss Hyams is not a heroine.'

'No?' said Debby, amused. 'You were so charmed with her at first.'

'Yes, she is very pretty, and her hats are lovely; but she is not a heroine.'

'Why, what's happened?'

'You know what lovely weather it's been all day?'

'Yes.'

'Well, this morning, all in the middle of the Scripture lesson, she said to us: "What a pity, girls, we've got to stay cooped up here this bright weather!"—you know how she chats to us so nicely. "In some schools they have half-holidays on Wednesday afternoons in the summer. Wouldn't it be nice if we could have them, and be out in the sunshine in Victoria Park?" "Hoo, yes, teacher, wouldn't that be jolly!" we all cried. Then teacher said: "Well, why not ask the head-mistress for a holiday this afternoon? You're the highest standard in the school. I dare say if you ask for it the whole school will get a holiday. Who will be spokeswoman?" Then all the girls said I must be, because I was the first girl in the class and sounded all my *h's*; and when the head-mistress came into the room I up and curtseyed, and asked her if we could have a holiday this afternoon on account of the beautiful sunshine. Then the head-mistress put on her eye-glasses, and her face grew black, and the sunshine seemed to go out of the room. And she said: "What! After all the holidays we have here, a month at New Year, and a fortnight at Passover, and all the Fast-days! I am surprised that you girls should be so lazy and idle, and ask for more. Why don't you take example by your teacher? Look at Miss Hyams!" We all looked at Miss Hyams, but she was looking for some papers in her desk. "Look how Miss Hyams works!" said the head-mistress.   "*She* never grumbles, *she* never asks for a holiday ! "   We all looked again at Miss Hyams, but she hadn't yet found the papers.   There was an awful silence ; you could have heard a pin drop.   There wasn't a single cough or rustle of a dress.   Then the head-mistress turned to me, and she said : "And you, Esther Ansell, whom I always thought so highly of ; I 'm surprised at your being the ringleader in such a disgraceful request !   You ought to know better.   I shall bear it in mind, Esther Ansell."   With that she sailed out, stiff and straight as a poker, and the door closed behind her with a bang.'

'Well, and what did Miss Hyams say then ? ' asked Debby, deeply interested.

'She said : " Selina Green, and what did Moses do when the Children of Israel grumbled for water ? "   She just went on with the Scripture lesson as if nothing had happened.'

'I should tell the head mistress who set me on,' cried Debby indignantly.

'Oh no,' said Esther, shaking her head.   'That would be mean. It 's a matter for her own conscience.   Oh, but I do wish,' she concluded, 'we had had a holiday !   It would have been so lovely out in the park.'

Victoria Park was 'the Park' to the Ghetto.   A couple of miles off, far enough to make a visit to it an excursion, it was a perpetual blessing to the Ghetto.   On rare Sunday afternoons, the Ansell family minus the *Bube* toiled there and back *en masse*, Moses carrying Isaac and Sarah by turns upon his shoulder.   Esther loved the Park in all weathers, but best of all in the summer, when the great lake was bright and busy with boats, and the birds twittered in the leafy trees, and lobelias and calceolarias were woven into wonderful patterns by the gardeners.

Then she would throw herself down on the thick grass and look up in mystic rapture at the brooding blue sky, and forget to read the book she had brought with her, while the other children chased one another about in savage delight.   Only once on a Saturday afternoon, when her father was not with them, did she get Dutch Debby to break through her retired habits and accompany them, and then it was not summer, but late autumn.   There was an indefinable melancholy about the sere landscape.   Russet refuse strewed the paths, and the gaunt trees waved fleshless arms in the breeze ; the November haze rose from the moist ground and dulled the blue of heaven with smoky clouds amid which the sun, a red sailless boat, floated at anchor among golden and crimson furrows and glimmering far-dotted fleeces.   The small lake was slimy, reflecting the trees on its borders as a network of dirty branches. A solitary swan ruffled its plumes and elongated its throat, doubled in quivering outlines beneath the muddy surface.   All at once the splash of oars was heard and the sluggish waters were stirred by the passage of a boat, in which a heroic young man was rowing a no less heroic young woman.

Dutch Debby burst into tears and went home. After that she fell back entirely on Bobby and Esther and the *London Journal*, and never even saved up nine shillings again.

CHAPTER X

A SILENT FAMILY

SUGARMAN the Shadchan arrived one evening a few days before Purim at the tiny two-storied house in which Esther's teacher lived, with little Nehemiah tucked under his arm. Nehemiah wore shoes and short red socks. The rest of his legs were bare ; Sugarman always carried him so as to demonstrate this fact. Sugarman himself was rigged out in a handsome manner, and the day not being holy, his blue bandanna peeped out from his left coat-tail, instead of being tied round his trouser-band.

'Good-morning, marm,' he said cheerfully.

'Good-morning, Sugarman,' said Mrs Hyams.

She was a little careworn old woman of sixty, with white hair. Had she been more pious, her hair would never have turned gray. But Miriam had long since put her veto on her mother's black wig. Mrs. Hyams was a meek, weak person, and submitted in silence to the outrage on her deepest instincts. Old Hyams was stronger, but not strong enough. He, too, was a silent person.

'P'raps you're surprised,' said Sugarman, 'to get a call from me in my sealskin vestcoat. But de fact is, marm, I put it on to call on a lady. I only dropped in here on my vay.'

'Won't you take a chair ?' said Mrs Hyams. She spoke English painfully and slowly, having been schooled by Miriam.

'No, I'm not tired. But I vill put Nechemyah down on one, if you permit. Dere ! sit still or I *potch* you ! P'raps you could lend me your corkscrew.'

'With pleasure,' said Mrs Hyams.

'I dank you. You see, my boy, Ebenezer, is *Bar-mitzvah* next Shabbos a veek, and I may not be passing again. You vill come ?'

'I don't know,' said Mrs Hyams hesitatingly. She was not certain whether Miriam considered Sugarman on their visiting-list.

'Don't say dat. I expect to open dirteen bottles of lemonade ! You must come, you and Mr. Hyams and the whole family.'

'Thank you ; I will tell Miriam and Daniel, and my husband.'

'Dat's right.—Nechemyah, don't dance on de good lady's chair. —Did you hear, Mrs. Hyams, of Mrs. Jonas's luck ?'

'No.'

'I won her eleven pounds on the lotter*ee*.'

'How nice !' said Mrs. Hyams, a little fluttered.

'I would let you have half a ticket for two pounds.'

' I haven't the money.'

'Vell, dirty-six shillings ! Dere ! I have to pay dat myself.'

' I would if I could, but I can't.'

' But you can have an eighth for nine shillings.'

Mrs. Hyams shook her head hopelessly.

' How is your son Daniel?' Sugarman asked.

' Pretty well, thank you. How is your wife?'

'Tank Gawd !'

' And your Bessie?'

'Tank Gawd ! Is your Daniel in?'

' Yes.'

'Tank Gawd ! I mean, can I see him?'

' It won't do any good.'

'No, not dat,' said Sugarman. 'I should like to ask him to de Confirmation myself.'

'Daniel !' called Mrs. Hyams.

He came from the back-yard in rolled-up shirt-sleeves, soap-suds drying on his arms. He was a pleasant-faced, flaxen-haired young fellow, the junior of Miriam by eighteen months. There was will in the lower part of the face, and tenderness in the eyes.

' Good-morning, sir,' said Sugarman. ' My Ebenezer is *Bar-mitzvah* next Shabbos week ; vill you do me the honour to drop in vid your moder and fader after *Shool*?'

Daniel crimsoned suddenly. He had 'No' on his lips, but suppressed it, and ultimately articulated it in some polite periphrasis. His mother noticed the crimson. On a blonde face it tells.

'Don't say dat,' said Sugarman. ' I expect to open dirteen bottles of lemonade. I have lent your good moder's cork-screw.'

' I shall be pleased to send Ebenezer a little present ; but I can't come—I really can't. You must excuse me.' Daniel turned away.

'Vell,' said Sugarman, anxious to assure him he bore no malice, ' if you send a present, I reckon it de same as if you come.'

'That's all right,' said Daniel, with strained heartiness.

Sugarman tucked Nehemiah under his arm, but lingered on the threshold. He did not know how to broach the subject. But the inspiration came.

'Do you know I have summonsed Morris Kerlinski?'

' No,' said Daniel. ' What for?'

' He owes me dirty shillings. I found him a very fine maiden, but now he is married he says it was only worth a suvran. He offered it me, but I vouldn't take it. A poor man he vas, too, and got ten pun from a Marriage Portion Society.'

' Is it worth while bringing a scandal on the community for the sake of ten shillings? It will be in all the papers, and shadchan will be spelt "shatcan," "shodkin," "shatkin," "chodcan," "shot-gun," and goodness knows what else.'

'Yes, but it isn't ten shillings,' said Sugarman ; its dirty shillings '

' But you say he offered you a sovereign?'

'So he did.   He arranged for two-pun-ten.   I took the suvran, but not in full payment.'

'You ought to settle it before the Beth-din,' said Daniel vehemently, ' or get some Jew to arbitrate.   You make the Jews a laughing stock.   It is true all marriages depend on money,' he added bitterly ;   ' only it is the fashion of police-court reporters to pretend the custom is limited to the Jews.'

'Vell, I did go to Reb Shemuel,' said Sugarman.   I dought he 'd be the very man to arbitrate.'

' Why ? ' asked Daniel.

'Vy? Hasn't he been a *Shadchan* himself?   From who else shall ve look for sympaty ? '

' I see,' said Daniel, smiling a little ; 'and apparently you got none.'

' No,' said Sugarman, growing wroth at the recollection.   ' He said ve are not in Poland.'

' Quite true.'

'Yes ; but I gave him an answer he didn't like,' said Sugarman. ' I said, "And ven ve are not in Poland, musn't ve keep *none* of our religion ? "'   His tone changed from indignation to insinuation. 'Vy vill you not let me get *you* a vife, Mr. Hyams?   I have several extra fine maidens in my eye.   Come now, don't look so angry.   How much commission vill you give me if I find you a maiden vid a hundred pound ?'

' The maiden !' thundered Daniel.   Then it dawned upon him that he had said a humorous thing, and he laughed.   There was merriment as well as mysticism in Daniel's blue eye.

But Sugarman went away downhearted.   Love is blind, and even marriage-brokers may be myopic.   Most people not concerned knew that Daniel Hyams was ' sweet ' on Sugarman's Bessie.   And it was so.   Daniel loved Bessie, and Bessie loved Daniel.   Only Bessie did not speak because she was a woman, and Daniel did not speak because he was a man.   They were a quiet family, the Hyamses.   They all bore their crosses in a silence unbroken even at home.   Miriam herself, the least reticent, did not give the impression that she could not have husbands for the winking.   Her demands were so high—that was all.   Daniel was proud of her and her position and her cleverness, and was confident she would marry as well as she dressed.   He did not expect her to contribute towards the expenses of the household, though she did, for he felt he had broad shoulders.   He bore his mother and father on those shoulders—semi-invalids both.   In the bold, bad years of shameless poverty, Hyams had been a wandering metropolitan glazier ; but this open degradation became intolerable as Miriam's prospects improved.   It was partly for her sake that Daniel ultimately supported his parents in idleness, and refrained from speaking to Bessie.   For he was only an employé in a fancy-goods warehouse, and on forty-five shillings a week you cannot keep up two respectable establishments.

Bessie was a bonnie girl, and could not in the nature of things be long uncaught. There was a certain night on which Daniel did not sleep—hardly a white night, as our French neighbours say ; a tear-stained night, rather. In the morning he was resolved to deny himself Bessie. Peace would be his instead. If it did not come immediately, he knew it was on the way ; for once before he had struggled and been so rewarded. That was in his eighteenth year, when he awoke to the glories of freethought, and knew himself a victim to the Moloch of the Sabbath, to which fathers sacrifice their children. The proprietor of the fancy goods was a Jew, and, moreover, closed on Saturdays. But for this anachronism of keeping Saturday holy when you had Sunday also to laze on, Daniel felt a hundred higher careers would have been open to him. Later, when freethought waned (it was after Daniel had met Bessie), although he never returned to his father's narrowness, he found the abhorred Sabbath sanctifying his life. It made life a conscious voluntary sacrifice to an ideal, and the reward was a touch of consecration once a week. Daniel could not have described these things, nor did he speak of them, which was a pity. Once, and once only, in the ferment of freethought he had uncorked his soul, and it had run over with much froth, and thenceforward old Mendel Hyams and Beenah, his wife, opposed more furrowed foreheads to a world too strong for them. If Daniel had taken back his words, and told them he was happier for the ruin they had made of his prospects, their gait might not have been so listless. But he was a silent man.

'You will go to Sugarman's, mother,' he said now. 'You and father. Don't mind that I 'm not going. I have another appointment for the afternoon.'

It was a superfluous lie for so silent a man.

'He doesn't like to be seen with us,' Beenah Hyams thought. But she was silent.

'He has never forgiven my putting him to the fancy goods,' thought Mendel Hyams when told. But he was silent.

It was of no good discussing it with his wife. These two had rather halved their joys than their sorrows. They had been married forty years, and had never had an intimate moment. Their marriage had been a matter of contract. Forty years ago, in Poland, Mendel Hyams had awoke one morning to find a face he had never seen before on the pillow beside his. Not even on the wedding-day had he been allowed a glimpse of his bride's countenance. That was the custom of the country and the time. Beenah bore her husband four children, of whom the elder two died ; but the marriage did not beget affection, often the inverse offspring of such unions. Beenah was a dutiful housewife, and Mendel Hyams supported her faithfully as long as his children would let him. Love never flew out of the window, for he was never in the house.

They did not talk to each other much. Beenah did the house-work unaided by the sprig of a servant who was engaged to satisfy the neighbours. In his enforced idleness Mendel fell back on his religion, almost a profession in itself. They were a silent couple.

At sixty there is not much chance of a forty-year-old silence being broken on this side of the grave. So far as his personal happiness was concerned, Mendel had only one hope left in the world—to die in Jerusalem. His feeling for Jerusalem was unique. All the hunted Jew in him combined with all the battered man to transfigure Zion with the splendour of sacred dreams, and girdle it with the rainbows that are builded of bitter tears. And with it all a dread that, if he were buried elsewhere, when the last trump sounded he would have to roll under the earth and under the sea to Jerusalem, the rendezvous of Resurrection.

Every year at the Passover table he gave his hope voice : ' Next year—in Jerusalem !' In her deepest soul Miriam echoed this wish of his. She felt she could like him better at a distance. Beenah Hyams had only one hope left in the world—to die.

CHAPTER XI

THE PURIM BALL

SAM LEVINE duly returned for the Purim ball. Malka was away, and so it was safe to arrive on the Sabbath. Sam and Leah called for Hannah in a cab, for the pavements were unfavourable to dancing-shoes, and the three drove to the Club, which was not a sixth of a mile off.

The Club was the People's Palace of the Ghetto ; but that it did not reach the bed-rock of the inhabitants was sufficiently evident from the fact that its language was English. The very lowest stratum of secondary formation—the children of immigrants—while the highest touched the lower middle class on the mere fringes of the Ghetto. It was a happy place, where young men and maidens met on equal terms and similar subscriptions ; where billiards and flirtations and concerts and laughter and gay gossip were always on, and lemonade and cakes never off ; a heaven where marriages were made, books borrowed, and newspapers read. Muscular Judaism was well to the fore at the Club, and entertainments were frequent. The middle classes of the community, overflowing with artistic instinct, supplied a phenomenal number of reciters, vocalists, and instrumentalists ready to oblige, and the greatest favourites of the London foot-lights were pleased to come down, partly because they found such keenly appreciative audiences, and partly because they were so much mixed up with the race, both professionally and socially. There were serious lectures now and again, but few of the members took them seriously; they came to the Club not to improve their minds, but to relax them.

The Club was a blessing without disguise to the daughters of Judah, and certainly kept their brothers from harm. The ballroom, with its decorations of evergreens and winter blossoms, was a gay sight. Most of the dancers were in evening dress, and it would have been impossible to tell the ball from a Belgravian gathering, except by the preponderance of youth and beauty. Where could you match such a bevy of brunettes, where find such blondes? They were anything but lymphatic, these Oriental blondes, if their eyes did not sparkle so intoxicatingly as those of the darker majority. The young men had carefully-curled moustaches and ringlets oiled like the Assyrian bull, and figure-six noses, and studs glittering on their creamy shirt-fronts. How they did it on their wages was one of the many miracles of Jewish history. For socially, and even in most cases financially, they were only on the level of the Christian artisan. These young men in dress-coats were epitomes of one aspect of Jewish history. Not in every respect improvements on the Sons of the Covenant, though; replacing the primitive manners and the piety of the foreign Jew by a veneer of cheap culture and a laxity of ceremonial observance.

It was a merry party, almost like a family gathering, not merely because most of the dancers knew one another, but because 'all Israel are brothers'—and sisters. They danced very buoyantly, not boisterously, the square dances symmetrically executed, every performer knowing his part, the waltzing full of rhythmic grace. When the music was popular, they accompanied it on their voices. After supper their heels grew lighter, and the laughter and gossip louder, but never beyond the bounds of decorum. A few Dutch dancers tried to introduce the more gymnastic methods in vogue in their own clubs, where the kangaroo is dancing-master, but the sentiment of the floor was against them. Hannah danced little, a voluntary wall-flower; for she looked radiant in tussore silk, and there was an air of refinement about the slight, pretty girl that attracted the beaux of the Club. But she only gave a duty dance to Sam and a waltz to Daniel Hyams, who had been brought by his sister, though he did not boast a swallow-tail to match her flowing draperies. Hannah caught a rather unamiable glance from pretty Bessie Sugarman, whom poor Daniel was trying hard not to see in the crush.

'Is your sister engaged yet?' Hannah asked, for want of something to say.

'You would know it if she was,' said Daniel, looking so troubled that Hannah reproached herself for the meaningless remark.

'How well she dances!' she made haste to say.

'Not better than you,' said Daniel gallantly.

'I see compliments are among the fancy goods you deal in. Do you reverse?' she added, as they came to an awkward corner.

'Yes—but not my compliments,' he said, smiling.   'Miriam taught me.'

'She makes me think of Miriam dancing by the Red Sea,' she said, laughing at the incongruous idea.

'She played a timbrel, though, didn't she?' he asked.   'I confess I don't quite know what a timbrel is.'

'A sort of tambourine, I suppose,' said Hannah merrily ; 'and she sang because the children of Israel were saved.'

They both laughed heartily, but when the waltz was over they returned to their individual gloom.   Towards supper-time, in the middle of a square dance, Sam, suddenly noticing Hannah's solitude, brought her a tall, bronzed, gentlemanly young man in a frock-coat, mumbled an introduction, and rushed back to the arms of the exacting Leah.

'Excuse me, I am not dancing to-night,' Hannah said coldly, in reply to the stranger's demand for her programme.

'Well, I 'm not half sorry,' he said, with a frank smile.   'I had to ask you, you know.   But I should feel quite out of place bumping such a lot of swells.'

There was something unusual about the words and the manner which impressed Hannah agreeably, in spite of herself.   Her face relaxed a little as she said : 'Why, haven't you been to one of these affairs before?'

'Oh yes, six or seven years ago ; but the place seems quite altered.   They 've rebuilt it, haven't they?   Very few of us sported dress-coats here in the days before I went to the Cape. I only came back the other day, and somebody gave me a ticket, and so I 've looked in for auld lang syne.'

An unsympathetic hearer would have detected a note of condescension in the last sentence.   Hannah detected it, for the announcement that the young man had returned from the Cape froze all her nascent sympathy.   She was turned to ice again. Hannah knew him well—the young man from the Cape.   He was a higher and more disagreeable development of the young man in the dress-coat.   He had put South African money in his purse—whether honestly or not, no one inquired : the fact remained, he had put it in his purse.   Sometimes the law confiscated it, pretending he had purchased diamonds illegally or whatnot, but then the young man did *not* return from the Cape.   But, to do him justice, the secret of his success was less dishonesty than the opportunities for initiative energy in unexploited districts.   Besides, not having to keep up appearances, he descended to menial occupations, and toiled so long and terribly that he would probably have made just as much money at home, if he had had the courage. Be this as it may, there the money was ; and, armed with it, the young man set sail literally for England, home, and beauty, resuming his cast-off gentility with several extra layers of superciliousness.

Pretty Jewesses, pranked in their prettiest clothes, hastened, metaphorically speaking, to the port to welcome the wanderer, for they knew it was from among them he would make his pick. There were several varieties of him—marked by financial ciphers—but whether he married in his old station or higher up the scale, he was always faithful to the sectarian tradition of the race, and this less from religious motives than from hereditary instinct. Like the young man in the dress-coat, he held the Christian girl to be cold of heart and unsprightly of temperament. He laid it down that all Yiddishë girls possessed that warmth and *chic* which, among Christians, were the birthright of a few actresses and music-hall artistes—themselves, probably, Jewesses! And on things theatrical this young man spoke as one having authority. Perhaps, though he was scarce conscious of it, at the bottom of his repulsion was the certainty that the Christian girl could not fry fish. She might be delightful for flirtation of all degrees, but had not been formed to make him permanently happy.

Such was the conception which Hannah had formed for herself of the young man from the Cape. This latest specimen of the genus was prepossessing, into the bargain. There was no denying he was well built, with a shapely head and a lovely moustache. Good looks alone were vouchers for insolence and conceit, but, backed by the aforesaid purse—— She turned her head away, and stared at the evolutions of the Lancers with much interest.

'They've got some pretty girls in that set,' he observed admiringly.

Evidently the young man did not intend to go away.

Hannah felt very annoyed. 'Yes,' she said sharply; 'which would you like?'

'I shouldn't care to make invidious distinctions,' he replied with a little laugh.

'Odious prig!' thought Hannah. 'He actually doesn't see I'm sitting on him!' Aloud she said: 'No? But you can't marry them all.'

'Why should I marry any?' he asked in the same light tone, though there was a shade of surprise in it.

'Haven't you come back to England to get a wife? Most young men do, when they don't have one exported to them in Africa.

He laughed with genuine enjoyment, and strove to catch the answering gleam in her eyes, but she kept them averted. They were standing with their backs to the wall, and he could only see the profile and note the graceful poise of the head upon the warm-coloured neck that stood out against the white bodice. The frank ring of his laughter mixed with the merry jingle of the fifth figure.

'Well, I'm afraid I'm going to be an exception,' he said.

'You think nobody good enough, perhaps,' she could not help saying.

'Oh! Why should you think that?'

'Perhaps you're married already.'

'Oh no, I'm not,' he said earnestly. 'You're not, either, are you?'

'Me?' she asked. Then, with a barely perceptible pause, she said: 'Of course I am.'

The thought of posing as the married woman she theoretically was flashed upon her suddenly, and appealed irresistibly to her sense of fun. The recollection that the nature of the ring on her finger was concealed by her glove afforded her supplementary amusement.

'Oh!' was all he said. 'I didn't catch your name exactly.'

'I didn't catch yours,' she replied evasively.

'David Brandon,' he said readily.

'It's a pretty name,' she said, turning smilingly to him; the infinite possibilities of making fun of him latent in the joke quite warmed her towards him. 'How unfortunate for me I have destroyed my chance of getting it!'

It was the first time she had smiled, and he liked the play of light round the curves of her mouth, amid the shadows of the soft dark skin, in the black depths of the eyes.

'How unfortunate for me!' he said, smiling in return.

'Oh yes, of course,' she said, with a little toss of her head. 'There is no danger in saying that now.'

'I wouldn't care if there was.'

'It is easy to smooth down the serpent when the fangs are drawn,' she laughed back.

'What an extraordinary comparison!' he exclaimed. 'But where are all the people going? It isn't all over, I hope.'

'Why, what do you want to stay for? You're not dancing.'

'That is the reason—unless I dance with you.'

'And then you would want to go?' she flashed with mock resentment.

'I see you're too sharp for me,' he said lugubriously. 'Roughing it among the Boers makes a fellow a bit dull in compliments.'

'Dull indeed!' said Hannah, drawing herself up with great seriousness. 'I think you're far more complimentary than you have a right to be to a married woman.'

His face fell. 'Oh, I didn't mean anything,' he said apologetically.

'So I thought,' retorted Hannah.

The poor fellow grew more red and confused than ever. Hannah felt quite sympathetic with him now, so pleased was she at the humiliated condition to which she had brought the young man from the Cape.

'Well, I'll say good-bye,' he said awkwardly. 'I suppose I mustn't ask to take you down to supper. I dare say your husband will want that privilege.'

'I dare say,' replied Hannah, smiling, 'although husbands do not always appreciate their privileges.'

'I shall be glad if yours doesn't !' he burst forth.

'Thank you for your good wishes for my domestic happiness,' she said severely.

'Oh, why will you misconstrue everything I say?' he pleaded. 'You must think me an awful *Schlemihl*, putting my foot into it so often. Anyhow, I hope I shall meet you again somewhere.'

'The world is very small,' she reminded him.

'I wish I knew your husband,' he said ruefully.

'Why?' said Hannah innocently.

'Because I could call on him,' he replied, smiling.

'Well, you do know him,' she could not help saying.

'Do I? Who is it? I don't think I do !' he exclaimed.

'Well, considering he introduced you to me !'

'Sam !' cried David, startled.

'Yes.'

'But——' said David, half incredulously, half in surprise. He certainly had never credited Sam with the wisdom to select, or the merit to deserve a wife like this.

'But what?' asked Hannah, with charming *naïveté*.

'He said—I—I—at least I think he said—I—I understood that he introduced me to Miss Solomon as his intended wife.'

Solomon was the name of Malka's first husband, and so of Leah.

'Quite right,' said Hannah simply.

'Then—what—how?' he stammered.

'She *was* his intended wife,' explained Hannah, as if she were telling the most natural thing in the world ; 'before he married me, you know.'

'I—I beg your pardon if I seemed to doubt you. I really thought you were joking.'

'Why, what made you think so?'

'Well,' he blurted out, 'he didn't mention he was married, and seeing him dancing with her the whole time——'

'I suppose he thinks he owes her some attention,' said Hannah indifferently ; 'by way of compensation, probably. I shouldn't be at all surprised if he takes her down to supper instead of me.'

'There he is, struggling towards the buffet. Yes, he has her on his arm.'

'You speak as if she were his phylacteries,' said Hannah, smiling. 'It would be a pity to disturb them. So, if you like, *you* can have me on your arm, as you put it.'

The young man's face lit up with pleasure, the keener that it was unexpected.

'I am very glad to have such phylacteries on my arm, as you put it,' he responded. 'I fancy I should be a good deal *froomer* if my phylacteries were like that.'

'What ! aren't you *froom* ?' she said, as they joined the hungry procession, in which she noted Bessie Sugarman on the arm of Daniel Hyams.

'No, I'm a regular wrong un,' he replied. 'As for phylacteries, I almost forget how to lay them.'

'That *is* bad,' she admitted, though he could not ascertain her own point of view from the tone.

'Well, everybody else is just as bad,' he said cheerfully. 'All the old piety seems to be breaking down. It's Purim, but how many of us have been to hear the—the what do you call it ?—the *Megillah* read ? There is actually a minister here to-night bareheaded. And how many of us are going to wash our hands before supper, or *bensh* afterwards, I should like to know ? Why, it's as much as can be expected if the food's *kosher* and there's no ham sandwiches on the dishes. Lord ! how my old dad—God rest his soul !—would have been horrified by such a party as this !'

'Yes, it's wonderful how ashamed Jews are of their religion outside a synagogue !' said Hannah musingly. '*My* father, if he were here, would put on his hat after supper, and *bensh*, though there wasn't another man in the room to follow his example.'

'And I should admire him for it,' said David earnestly, though I admit I shouldn't follow his example myself. I suppose he's one of the old school.'

'He is Reb Shemuel,' said Hannah with dignity.

'Oh, indeed !' he exclaimed, not without surprise ; 'I know him well. He used to bless me when I was a boy, and it used to cost him a halfpenny a time. Such a jolly fellow !'

'I'm so glad you think so,' said Hannah, flushing with pleasure.

'Of course I do. Does he still have all those *Greeners* coming to propound cases ?'

'Oh yes. Their piety is just the same as ever.'

'They're poor,' observed David. 'It's always those poorest in worldly goods who are richest in religion.'

'Well, isn't that a compensation ?' returned Hannah with a little sigh. 'But from my father's point of view the truth is rather that those who have most pecuniary difficulties have most religious difficulties.'

'Ah, I suppose they come to your father as much to solve the first as the second.'

'Father is very good,' she said simply.

They had by this time obtained something to eat, and for a minute or so the dialogue became merely dietary.

'Do you know ?' he said in the course of the meal, 'I feel I ought not to have told you what a wicked person I am. I put my foot into it there, too.'

'No, why ?'

'Because you are Reb Shemuel's daughter.'

'Oh, what nonsense ! I like to hear people speak their mind. Besides, you mustn't fancy I'm as *froom* as my father !'

'I don't fancy that. Not quite,' he laughed. 'I know there's some blessed old law or other by which women haven't got the same chance of distinguishing themselves that way as men. I

have a vague recollection of saying a prayer, thanking God for not
having made me a woman.'

'Ah, that must have been a long time ago,' she said slyly.

'Yes, when I was a boy,' he admitted. Then the oddity of the
premature thanksgiving struck them both, and they laughed.

'You've got a different form provided for you, haven't you?' he
said.

'Yes, I have to thank God for having made me according to
His will.'

'You don't seem satisfied for all that,' he said, struck by something in the way she said it.

'How can a woman be satisfied?' she asked, looking up frankly.
'She has no voice in her destinies. She must shut her eyes and
open her mouth, and swallow what it pleases God to send her.'

'All right, shut your eyes,' he said, and, putting his hand over
them, he gave her a tit-bit and restored the conversation to a more
flippant level.

'You mustn't do that,' she said. 'Suppose my husband were to
see you?'

'Oh, bother!' he exclaimed. 'I don't know why it is, but I
don't seem to realise you're a married woman.'

'Am I playing the part so badly as all that?'

'Is it a part?' he cried eagerly.

She shook her head. His face fell again. She could hardly
fail to note the change.

'No, it's a stern reality,' she said. 'I wish it wasn't.'

It seemed a bold confession, but it was easy to understand.
Sam had been an old schoolfellow of his, and David had not
thought highly of him. He was silent a moment.

'Are you not happy?' he said gently.

'Not in my marriage.'

'Sam must be a regular brute!' he cried indignantly. 'He
doesn't know how to treat you. He ought to have his head
punched, the way he's going on with that fat thing in red.'

'Oh, don't run her down,' said Hannah, struggling to repress
her emotions, which were not purely of laughter. 'She's my dearest friend.'

'They always are,' said David oracularly. 'But how came you
to marry him?'

'Accident,' she said indifferently.

'Accident!' he repeated, open-eyed.

'Ah, well, it doesn't matter,' said Hannah, meditatively conveying a spoonful of trifle to her mouth. 'I shall be divorced from
him to-morrow. Be careful! You nearly broke that plate.'

David stared at her open-mouthed.

'Going to be divorced from him to-morrow!'

'Yes. Is there anything odd about it?'

'Oh,' he said, after staring at her impassive face for a full
minute. 'Now I'm sure you've been making fun of me all along.'

'My dear Mr. Brandon, why will you persist in making me out a liar?'

He was forced to apologise again, and became such a model of perplexity and embarrassment that Hannah's gravity broke down at last, and her merry peal of laughter mingled with the clatter of plates and the hubbub of voices.

'I must take pity on you and enlighten you,' she said ; 'but promise me it shall go no further. It's only our own little circle that knows about it, and I don't want to be the laughing-stock of the Lane.'

'Of course I will promise,' he said eagerly.

She kept his curiosity on the *qui vive* to amuse herself a little longer, but ended by telling him all amid frequent exclamations of surprise.

'Well, I never!' he said, when it was over. 'Fancy a religion in which only two per cent. of the people who profess it have ever heard of its laws. I suppose we're so mixed up with the English that it never occurs to us we've got marriage laws of our own— like the Scotch. Anyhow, I'm real glad, and I congratulate you.'

'On what?'

'On not being really married to Sam.'

'Well, you're a nice friend of his, I must say. I don't congratulate myself, I can tell you.'

'You don't?' he said in a disappointed tone.

She shook her head silently.

'Why not?' he inquired anxiously.

'Well, to tell the truth, this forced marriage was my only chance of getting a husband who wasn't pious. Don't look so puzzled. I wasn't shocked at your wickedness—you mustn't be at mine. You know there's such a lot of religion in our house that I thought if I ever did get married, I'd like a change.'

'Ha! ha! ha! So you're as the rest of us. Well, it's plucky of you to admit it.'

'Don't see it. My living doesn't depend on religion, thank Heaven! Father's a saint, I know, but he swallows everything he sees in his books, just as he swallows everything mother and I put before him in his plate, and in spite of it all——'

She was about to mention Levi's shortcomings, but checked herself in time. She had no right to unveil anybody's soul but her own, and she didn't know why she was doing that.

'But you don't mean to say your father would forbid you to marry a man you cared for, just because he wasn't *froom.*'

'I'm sure he would.'

'But that would be cruel.'

'He wouldn't think so. He'd think he was saving my soul, and you must remember he can't imagine anyone who has been taught to see its beauty not loving the yoke of the Law. He's the best father in the world, but, when religion's concerned, the best-hearted of mankind are liable to become hard as stone. You don't know my father as I do.   But, apart from that, I wouldn't marry a man myself who might hurt my father's position.   I should have to keep a *kosher* house, or look how people would talk!'

'And wouldn't you if you had your own way?'

'I don't know what I would do.   It's so impossible, the idea of my having my own way.   I think I should probably go in for a change.   I'm so tired, so tired of this eternal ceremony, always washing up plates and dishes.   I dare say it's all for our good, but I *am* so tired.'

'Oh, I don't see much difficulty about *Koshers*.   I always eat *kosher* meat myself when I can get it, providing it's not so beastly tough, as it has a knack of being.   Of course, it's absurd to expect a man to go without meat when he's travelling up-country just because it hasn't been killed with a knife instead of a pole-axe.   Besides, don't we know well enough that the folks who are most particular about those sort of things don't mind swindling and setting their houses on fire, and all manner of abominations?   I wouldn't be a Christian for the world, but I should like to see a little more common-sense introduced into our religion; it ought to be more up to date.   If ever I marry, I should like my wife to be a girl who wouldn't want to keep anything but the higher parts of Judaism.   Not out of laziness, mind you, but out of conviction.'

David stopped suddenly, surprised at his own sentiments, which he learnt for the first time.   However vaguely they might have been simmering in his brain, he could not honestly accuse himself of having ever bestowed any reflection on 'the higher parts of Judaism,' or even on the religious convictions, apart from the racial aspects, of his future wife.   Could it be that Hannah's earnestness was infecting him?

'Oh, then you *would* marry a Jewess?' said Hannah.

'Oh, of course!' he said in astonishment.   Then, as he looked at her pretty, earnest face, the amusing recollection that she *was* married already came over him with a sort of shock, not wholly comical.   There was a minute of silence, each pursuing a separate train of thought.   Then David wound up, as if there had been no break, with an elliptical, 'Wouldn't you?'

Hannah shrugged her shoulders and elevated her eyebrows in a gesture that lacked her usual grace.

'Not if I had only to please myself,' she added.

'Oh, come, don't say that!' he said anxiously.   'I don't believe mixed marriages are a success.   Really I don't.   Besides, look at the scandal!'

Again she shrugged her shoulders, defiantly this time.

'I don't suppose I shall ever get married,' she said.   'I never could marry a man father would approve of, so that a Christian would be no worse than an educated Jew.'

David did not quite grasp the sentence; he was trying to, when Sam and Leah passed them.   Sam winked in a friendly, if not very refined, manner.

'I see you two are getting on all right,' he said.

'Good gracious!' cried Hannah, starting up, with a blush. 'Everybody's going back. They *will* think us greedy! What a pair of fools we are to have got into such serious conversation at a ball!'

'Was it serious?' said David with a retrospective air. 'Well, I never enjoyed a conversation so much in my life.'

'You mean the supper,' Hannah said lightly.

'Well, both. It's your fault that we don't behave more appropriately.'

'How do you mean?'

'You won't dance.'

'Do you want to?'

'Rather!'

'I thought you were afraid of all the swells.'

'Supper has given me courage.'

'Oh, very well, if you want to—that's to say, if you really can waltz.'

'Try me; only you must allow for my being out of practice. I didn't get many dances at the Cape, I can tell you.'

'The Cape!' Hannah heard the words without making her usual grimace. She put her hand lightly on his shoulder, he encircled her waist with his arm, and they surrendered themselves to the intoxication of the slow, voluptuous music.

CHAPTER XII

THE SONS OF THE COVENANT

THE Sons of the Covenant sent no representatives to the Club ball, wotting neither of waltzes nor of dress-coats, and preferring death to the embrace of a strange dancing woman. They were the congregation of which Mr. Belcovitch was president, and their synagogue was the ground-floor of No. 1 Royal Street—two large rooms knocked into one, and the rear partitioned off for the use of the bewigged, heavy-jawed women who might not sit with the men lest they should fascinate their thoughts away from things spiritual. Its furniture was bare benches, a raised platform with a reading desk in the centre, and a wooden curtained ark at the end, containing two parchment scrolls of the Law, each with a silver pointer and silver bells and pomegranates. The scrolls were in manuscript, for the printing-press has never yet sullied the sanctity of the synagogue editions of the Pentateuch. The room was badly ventilated, and what little air there was was generally sucked up by a greedy company of wax-candles, big and little, stuck in brass holders. The back-window gave on the yard

and the contiguous cow-sheds, and 'moos' mingled with the
impassioned supplications of the worshippers, who came hither
two, and often three, times a day to batter the gates of heaven and
to listen to sermons more exegetical than ethical.   They dropped
in, mostly in their workaday garments and grime, and rumbled
and roared and chorused prayers with a zeal that shook the
window-panes, and there was never lack of *Minyan*—the congregational quorum of ten.   In the West End synagogues are built
to eke out the incomes of poor *Minyan*-men or professional congregants ; in the East End rooms are tricked up for prayer.   This
synagogue was all of luxury many of its Sons could boast.   It was
their salon and their lecture-hall.   It supplied them not only with
their religion, but their art and letters, their politics and their
public amusements.   It was their home as well as the Almighty's,
and on occasions they were familiar, and even a little vulgar, with
Him.   It was a place in which they could sit in their slippers—
metaphorically, that is ; for though they frequently did so literally,
it was by way of reverence, not ease.   They enjoyed themselves
in this *Shool* of theirs ; they shouted and skipped and shook and
sang, they wailed and moaned, they clenched their fists and
thumped their breasts, and they were not least happy when they
were crying.   There is an apocryphal anecdote of one of them
being in the act of taking a pinch of snuff, when the Confession
caught him unexpectedly.

'We have trespassed,' he wailed mechanically, as he spas-
modically put the snuff in his bosom and beat his nose with his
clenched fist.

They prayed metaphysics, acrostics, angelology, Cabbalah, history,
exegetics, Talmudical controversies, menus, recipes, priestly pre-
scriptions, the canonical books, psalms, love-poems, an undigested
hotch-potch of exalted and questionable sentiments, of communal
and egoistic aspirations of the highest order.   It was a wonderful
liturgy, as grotesque as it was beautiful ; like an old cathedral, in
all styles of architecture, stored with shabby antiquities and side-
shows, and overgrown with moss and lichen—a heterogeneous
blend of historical strata of all periods, in which gems of poetry
and pathos and spiritual fervour glittered, and pitiful records of
ancient persecution lay petrified.   And the method of praying
these things was equally complex and uncouth, equally the bond-
slave of tradition ; here a rising and there a bow, now three steps
backwards and now a beating of the breast, this bit for the congregation and that for the minister ; variants of a page, a word, a
syllable, even a vowel, ready for every possible contingency.   Their
religious consciousness was largely a musical box : the thrill of
the ram's horn, the cadenza of a psalmic phrase, the jubilance of
a festival 'Amen' and the sobriety of a workaday 'Amen,' the
Passover melodies and the Pentecost, the minor keys of Atonement and the hilarious rhapsodies of Rejoicing, the plain chant of
the Law and the more ornate intonation of the Prophets—all this

was known and loved, and was far more important than the
meaning of it all, or its relation to their real lives ; for page upon
page was gabbled off at rates that could not be excelled by
automata.   But if they did not always know what they were
saying, they always meant it.   If the service had been more intelligible it would have been less emotional and edifying.   There
was not a sentiment, however incomprehensible, for which they
were not ready to die or to damn.

'All Israel are brethren ;' and indeed there was a strange,
antique clannishness about these Sons of the Covenant, which, in
the modern world, where the ends of the ages meet, is Socialism.
They prayed for one another while alive, visited one another's
bedsides when sick, buried one another when dead.   No mercenary
hands poured the yolks of eggs over their dead faces, and arrayed
their corpses in their praying-shawls.   No hired masses were said
for the sick or the troubled, for the psalm-singing services of the
Sons of the Covenant were always available for petitioning the
heavens, even though their brother had been arrested for buying
stolen goods, and the appeal might be an invitation to Providence
to compound a felony.   Little charities of their own they had, too
—a Sabbath Meal Society, and a Marriage Portion Society, to
buy the sticks for poor couples ; and when a pauper countryman
arrived from Poland, one of them boarded him, and another lodged
him, and a third taught him a trade.   Strange exotics in a land of
prose, carrying with them through the paven highways of London
the odour of Continental Ghettos, and bearing in their eyes, through
all the shrewdness of their glances, the eternal mysticism of the
Orient, where God was born.   Hawkers and pedlars, tailors and
cigar-makers, cobblers and furriers, glaziers and cap-makers—this
was in sum their life : to pray much and to work long ; to beg a
little and to cheat a little ; to eat not over-much and to ' drink '
scarce at all ; to beget annual children by chaste wives (disallowed
them half the year), and to rear them not over-well ; to study the
Law and the Prophets, and to reverence the Rabbinical tradition
and the chaos of commentaries expounding it ; to abase themselves
before the *Life of Man* and Joseph Caro's *Prepared Table* as
though the authors had presided at the foundation of the earth ;
to wear phylacteries and fringes, to keep the beard unshaven and
the corners of the hair uncut ; to know no work on Sabbath and
no rest on week-day.   It was a series of recurrent landmarks,
ritual and historical, of intimacy with God so continuous that they
were in danger of forgetting His existence, as of the air they
breathed.   They ate unleavened bread in Passover, and blessed
the moon, and counted the days of the Omer till Pentecost saw
the synagogue dressed with flowers in celebration of an Asiatic
fruit harvest by a European people divorced from agriculture ;
they passed to the terrors and triumphs of the New Year (with its
domestic symbolism of apple and honey and its procession to the
river), and the revelry of repentance on the Great White Fast,

when they burned long candles and whirled fowls round their heads and attired themselves in grave-clothes, and saw from their seats in synagogue the long Fast-day darken slowly into dusk, while God was sealing the decrees of Life and Death; they passed to Tabernacles, when they ran up rough booths in back-yards, draped with their bed-sheets and covered with greenery, and bore through the streets citrons in boxes and a waving combination of myrtle and palm and willow branches, wherewith they made a pleasant rustling in the synagogue ; and thence to the Rejoicing of the Law, when they danced and drank rum in the House of the Lord, and scrambled sweets for the little ones, and made a seven-fold circuit with the two scrolls, supplemented by toy flags and children's candles stuck in hollow carrots ; and then on again to Dedication, with its celebration of the Maccabæan deliverance and the miracle of the unwaning oil in the Temple, and to Purim, with its masquerading and its execration of Haman's name by the banging of little hammers ; and so back to Passover.   And with these larger cycles, epicycles of minor fasts and feasts, multiplex, not to be overlooked, from the fast of the ninth of Ab—fatal day for the race—when they sat on the ground in shrouds, and wailed for the destruction of Jerusalem, to the feast of the Great Hosannah, when they whipped away willow-leaves on the *Shool* benches in symbolism of forgiven sins, sitting up the whole of the night before in a long paroxysm of prayer, mitigated by coffee and cakes ; from the period in which nuts were prohibited to the period in which marriages were commended.

And each day, too, had its cycles of religious duty, its comprehensive and cumbrous ritual, with accretions of commentary and tradition.

And every contingency of the individual life was equally provided for, and the writings that regulated all this complex ritual are a marvellous monument of the patience, piety, and juristic genius of the race—and of the persecution which threw it back upon its sole treasure, the Law.

Thus they lived and died, these Sons of the Covenant, half-automata, sternly disciplined by voluntary and involuntary privation, hemmed and mewed in by iron walls of form and poverty, joyfully ground under the perpetual rotary wheel of ritualism, good-humoured withal, and casuistic, like all people whose religion stands much upon ceremony ; inasmuch as a ritual law comes to count one equally with a moral, and a man is not half bad who does three-fourths of his duty.

And so the stuffy room, with its guttering candles and its chameleon-coloured ark-curtain, was the pivot of their narrow lives.   Joy came to bear to it the offering of its thanksgiving and to vow sixpenny-bits to the Lord, prosperity came in a high hat to chaffer for the holy privileges, and grief came with rent garments to lament the beloved dead and glorify the name of the Eternal.

The poorest life is to itself the universe and all that therein is and these humble products of a great and terrible past, strange fruits of a motley-flowering secular tree, whose roots are in Canaan, and whose boughs overshadow the earth, were all the happier for not knowing that the fulness of life was not theirs.

And the years went rolling on, and the children grew up, and here and there a parent.

    *   *   *   *   *

The Elders of the synagogue were met in council.

'He is greater than a prince,' said the Shalotten Shammos.

'If all the princes of the earth were put in one scale,' said Mr. Belcovitch, 'and our Maggid, Moses, in the other, he would outweigh them all. He is worth a hundred of the Chief Rabbi of England who has been seen bareheaded.'

'From Moses to Moses there has been none like Moses,' said old Mendel Hyams, interrupting the Yiddish with a Hebrew quotation.

'Oh no,' said the Shalotten Shammos, who was a great stickler for precision, being, as his nickname implied, a master of ceremonies. 'I can't admit that. Look at my brother Nachmann.'

There was a general laugh at the Shalotten Shammos's bull, the proverb dealing only with Moseses.

'He has the true gift,' observed Froom Karlkammer, shaking the flames of his hair pensively. 'For the letters of his name have the same numerical value as those of the great Moses da Leon.'

Froom Karlkammer was listened to with respect, for he was an honorary member of the committee, who paid for two seats in a larger congregation, and only worshipped with the Sons of the Covenant on special occasions. The Shalotten Shammos, however, was of contradictory temperament, a born dissentient, upheld by a steady consciousness of highly superior English, the drop of bitter in Belcovitch's presidential cup. He was a long, thin man, who towered above the congregation, and was as tall as the bulk of them even when he was bowing his acknowledgments to his Maker.

'How do you make that out?' he asked Karlkammer. 'Moses, of course, adds up the same as Moses; but while the other part of the Maggid's name makes seventy-three, Da Leon's makes ninety-one.'

'Ah, that's because you're ignorant of Gematriyah,' said little Karlkammer, looking up contemptuously at the cantankerous giant. 'You reckon all the letters on the same system, and you omit to give yourself the licence of deleting the ciphers.'

In philology it is well known that all consonants are interchangeable, and vowels don't count; in Gematriyah any letter may count for anything, and the total may be summed up anyhow.

Karlkammer was one of the curiosities of the Ghetto. In a land of *froom* men, he was the *froomest*. He had the very genius of fanaticism. On the Sabbath he spoke nothing but Hebrew, whatever the inconvenience and however numerous the misunder-

standings, and if he perchance paid a visit he would not perform
the 'work' of lifting the knocker.   Of course he had his handkerchief girt round his waist to save him from carrying it ; but this
compromise, being general, was not characteristic of Karlkammer,
any more than his habit of wearing two gigantic sets of phylacteries where average piety was content with one of moderate size.
One of the walls of his room had an unpapered and unpainted scrap
in mourning for the fall of Jerusalem.   He walked through the
streets to synagogue attired in his praying-shawl and phylacteries,
and knocked three times at the door of God's house when he
arrived.   On the Day of Atonement he walked in his socks, though
the heavens fell, wearing his grave-clothes.   On this day he
remained standing in synagogue from six A.M. to seven P.M., with
his body bent at an angle of ninety degrees.   It was to give him
bending space that he hired two seats.   On Tabernacles, not having
any ground whereon to erect a booth, by reason of living in an attic,
he knocked a square hole in the ceiling, covered it with branches,
through which the free air of heaven played, and hung a quad-
rangle of sheets from roof to floor.   He bore to synagogue the
tallest *Lulav* of palm-branches that could be procured, and
quarrelled with a rival pietist for the last place in the floral procession, as being the lowliest and meekest man in Israel, an ethical
pedestal equally claimed by his rival.   He insisted on bearing a
corner of the biers of all the righteous dead.   Almost every other
day was a fast-day for Karlkammer, and he had a host of supplementary ceremonial observances which are not for the vulgar.
Compared to him, Moses Ansell and the ordinary Sons of the
Covenant were mere heathens.   He was a man of prodigious distorted mental activity.   He had read omnivorously amid the vast
stores of Hebrew literature, was a great authority on Cabbalah,
understood astromony, and still more astrology, was strong on
finance, and could argue coherently on any subject outside religion.
His letters to the press on specifically Jewish subjects were the
most hopeless, involved, incomprehensible, and protracted puzzles
ever penned, bristling with Hebrew quotations from the most
varying, the most irrelevant, and the most mutually incongruous
sources, and peppered with the dates of birth and death of every
Rabbi mentioned.

No one had ever been known to follow one of these argumenta-
tions to the bitter end.   They were written in good English,
modified by a few peculiar terms used in senses unsuspected by
dictionary-makers ; in a beautiful hand, with the *t*'s uncrossed,
but crowned with the side stroke, so as to avoid the appearance
of the symbol of Christianity, and with the dates expressed according to the Hebrew calendar, for Karlkammer refused to recognise
the chronology of the Christian.   He made three copies of every
letter, and each was exactly like the others in every word and
every line.   His bill for midnight oil must have been extraordinary,
for he was a business man, and had to earn his living by day.

Kept within the limits of sanity by a religion without apocalyptic visions, he was saved from predicting the end of the world by mystic calculations ; but he used them to prove everything else, and fervently believed that endless meanings were deducible from the numerical value of Biblical words ; that not a curl at the tail of a letter of any word in any sentence but had its super-subtle significance.   The elaborate cipher, with which Bacon is alleged to have written Shakespeare's plays, were mere child's play compared with the infinite revelations which, in Karlkammer's belief, the deity left latent in writing the Old Testament from Genesis to Malachi, and in inspiring the Talmud and the holier treasures of Hebrew literature.   Nor were these ideas of his own origination. His was an eclectic philosophy and religionism, of which all the elements were discoverable in old Hebrew books, scraps of Alexandrian philosophy inextricably blent with Aristotelian, Platonic, Mystic.

He kept up a copious correspondence with scholars in other countries, and was universally esteemed and pitied.

' We haven't come to discuss the figures of the Maggid's name, but of his salary,' said Mr. Belcovitch, who prided himself on his capacity for conducting public business.

' I have examined the finances,' said Karlkammer, 'and I don't see how we can possibly put aside more for our preacher than the pound a week.'

' But he is not satisfied,' said Mr. Belcovitch.

' I don't see why he shouldn't be,' said the Shalotten Shammos. ' A pound a week is luxury for a single man.'

The Sons of the Covenant did not know that the poor, consumptive Maggid sent half his salary to his sisters in Poland, to enable them to buy back their husbands from military service ; also, they had vague, unexpressed ideas that he was not mortal, that Heaven would look after his larder, that, if the worst came to the worst, he could fall back on Cabbalah and engage himself with the mysteries of food-creation.

' I have a wife and family to keep on a pound a week,' grumbled Greenberg the *Chazan*.

Besides being reader, Greenberg blew the horn and killed cattle, and circumcised male infants, and educated children, and discharged the functions of beadle and collector.   He spent a great deal of his time in avoiding being drawn into the contending factions of the congregation, and in steering equally between Belcovitch and the Shalotten Shammos.   The Sons only gave him fifty a year for all his trouble, but they eked it out by allowing him to be on the committee, where, on the question of a rise in the reader's salary, he was always an ineffective minority of one.   His other grievance was that for the high festivals the Sons temporarily engaged a finer-voiced reader, and advertised him at raised prices to repay themselves out of the surplus congregation.   Not only had Greenberg to play second fiddle on these grand occasions,

but he had to iterate ' Pom !' as a sort of musical accompaniment
in the pauses of his rival's vocalisation.

'You can't compare yourself with the Maggid,' the Shalotten
Shammos reminded him consolingly. 'There are hundreds of
you in the market. There are several *morceaux* of the service
which you do not sing half so well as your predecessor, your
horn-blowing cannot compete with Freedman's of the Fashion
Street *Chevrah*, nor can you read the Law as quickly and accu-
rately as Prochintski. I have told you over and over again you
confound the air of the Passover *Yigdal* with the New Year
ditto. And, then, your preliminary flourish to the Confession of
Sin—it goes, " Ei, Ei, Ei, Ei, Ei, Ei, Ei "' (he mimicked Greenberg's melody), ' whereas it should be, " Oi, Oi, Oi, Oi, Oi, Oi——"'

'Oh no !' interrupted Belcovitch. 'All the *Chazanim* I've ever
heard do it : " Ei, Ei, Ei——"'

'You are not entitled to speak on this subject, Belcovitch,' said
the Shalotten Shammos warmly. 'You are a Man-of-the-Earth.
I have heard every great *Chazan* in Europe.'

'What was good enough for my father is good enough for me,'
retorted Belcovitch. 'The *Shool* he took me to at home had
a beautiful *Chazan*, and he always sang it, " Ei, Ei, Ei——"'

'I don't care what you heard at home. In England every
Chazan sings, " Oi, Oi, Oi——"'

'We can't take our tune from England,' said Karlkammer reprovingly. 'England is a polluted country by reason of the
Reformers, whom we were compelled to excommunicate.'

'Do you mean to say that my father was an Epicurean ?' asked
Belcovitch indignantly. 'The tune was as Greenberg sings it.
That there are impious Jews who pray bareheaded and sit in the
synagogue side by side with the women has nothing to do with
it.'

The Reformers did neither of these things, but the Ghetto to a
man believed they did, and it would have been countenancing
their blasphemies to pay a visit to their synagogue and see. It
was an extraordinary example of a myth flourishing in the teeth of
the facts, and as such should be useful to historians sifting ' the
evidence of contemporary writers.'

The dispute thickened ; the synagogue hummed with ' Ei's ' and
' Oi's ' not in concord.

'Shah !' said the President at last. 'Make an end, make an
end !'

'You see, he knows I 'm right,' murmured the Shalotten Shammos to his circle.

'And if you are !' burst forth the impeached Greenberg, who
had by this time thought of a retort. 'And if I do sing the Passover *Yigdal* instead of the New Year, have I not reason, seeing I
have *no bread in the house* ? With my salary I have Passover all
the year round.'

'The *Chazan's* sally made a marked impression on his audience,

if not on his salary.   It was felt that he had a just grievance, and
the conversation was hastily shifted to the original topic.

'We mustn't forget the Maggid draws crowds here every Saturday and Sunday afternoon,' said Mendel Hyams.   'Suppose he
goes over to a *Chevrah* that will pay him more?'

'No, he won't do that,' said another of the Committee.   'He
will remember that we brought him out of Poland.'

'Yes; but we shan't have room for the audiences soon,'
said Belcovitch.   'There are so many outsiders turned away
every time that I think we ought to let half the applicants enjoy
the first two hours of the sermon, and the other half the second
two hours.'

'No, no; that would be cruel,' said Karlkammer.   'He will
have to give the Sunday sermons at least in a larger synagogue.
My own *Shool*, the German, will be glad to give him facilities.'

'But what if they want to take him altogether at a higher
salary?' said Mendel.

'No, I'm on the Committee—I'll see to that,' said Karlkammer
reassuringly.

'Then do you think we shall tell him we can't afford to give him
more?' asked Belcovitch.

There was a murmur of assent, with a fainter mingling of dissent.   The motion that the Maggid's application be refused was
put to the vote, and carried by a large majority.

It was the fate of the Maggid to be the one subject on which
Belcovitch and the Shalotten Shammos agreed.   They agreed as
to his transcendent merits, and they agreed as to the adequacy of
his salary.

'But he's so weakly,' protested Mendel Hyams, who was in the
minority.   'He coughs blood.'

'He ought to go to a sunny place for a week,' said Belcovitch
compassionately.

'Yes, he must certainly have that,' said Karlkammer.   'Let us
add as a rider that, although we cannot pay him more per week,
he must have a week's holiday in the country.   The Shalotten
Shammos shall write the letter to Rothschild.'

Rothschild was a magic name in the Ghetto; it stood next to
the Almighty's as a redresser of grievances and a friend of the
poor, and the Shalotten Shammos made a large part of his income by writing lettters to it.   He charged twopence-halfpenny
per letter for his English vocabulary was larger than any other
scribe's in the Ghetto, and his words were as much longer than
theirs as his body.   He also filled up printed application forms for
soup or Passover cakes, and had a most artistic sense of the proportion of orphans permissible to widows, and a correct instinct
for the plausible duration of sicknesses.

The Committee agreed *nem. con.* to the grant of a seaside
holiday, and the Shalotten Shammos with a gratified feeling of
importance, waived his twopence-halfpenny.   He drew up a letter

forthwith, not of course in the name of the Sons of the Covenant, but in the Maggid's own.

He took the magniloquent sentences to the Maggid for signature. He found the Maggid walking up and down Royal Street waiting for the verdict. The Maggid walked with a stoop that was almost a permanent bow, so that his long black beard reached well towards his baggy knees. His curved eagle-nose was grown thinner, his long coat shinier, his look more haggard, his corkscrew earlocks were more matted, and when he spoke his voice was a tone more raucous. He wore his high hat—a tall cylinder that reminded one of a weather-beaten turret.

The Shalotten Shammos explained briefly what he had done.

' May thy strength increase ! ' said the Maggid in the Hebrew formula of gratitude.

' Nay, thine is more important,' replied the Shalotten Shammos with hilarious heartiness, and he proceeded to read the letter as they walked along together, giant and doubled-up wizard.

' But I haven't got a wife and six children,' said the Maggid, for whom one or two phrases stood out intelligible. ' My wife is dead, and I never was blessed with a *Kaddish*.'

' It sounds better so,' said the Shalotten Shammos authoritatively. ' Preachers are expected to have heavy families dependent upon them. It would sound lies if I told the truth.'

This was an argument after the Maggid's own heart, but it did not quite convince him.

' But they will send and make inquiries,' he murmured.

' Then your family are in Poland ; you send your money over there.'

' That is true,' said the Maggid feebly. ' But still it likes me not.'

' You leave it to me,' said the Shalotten Shammos impressively. ' A shamefaced man cannot learn, and a passionate man cannot teach. So said Hillel. When you are in the pulpit I listen to you ; when I have my pen in hand, do you listen to me. As the proverb says, if I were a Rabbi, the town would burn ; but if you were a scribe the letter would burn. I don't pretend to be a Maggid ; don't you set up to be a letter-writer.'

' Well, but do you think it 's honourable——'

' Hear, O Israel ! ' cried the Shalotten Shammos, spreading out his palms impatiently. ' Haven't I written letters for twenty years ?'

The Maggid was silenced. He walked on brooding.

' And what is this place—Burnmud—I ask to go to ? ' he inquired.

' Bournemouth,' corrected the other. ' It is a place on the South Coast where all the most aristocratic consumptives go.'

' But it must be very dear,' said the poor Maggid, affrighted.

' Dear ? Of course it's dear,' said the Shalotten Shammos pompously. ' But shall we consider expense where your health is concerned?'

The Maggid felt so grateful he was almost ashamed to ask whether he could eat *Kosher* there, but the Shalotten Shammos, who had the air of a tall encyclopædia, set his soul at rest on all points.

CHAPTER XIII

SUGARMAN'S BAR-MITZVAH PARTY

THE day of Ebenezer Sugarman's *Bar-mitzvah* duly arrived. All his sins would henceforth be on his own head, and everybody rejoiced. By the Friday evening so many presents had arrived —four breast-pins, two rings, six pocket-knives, three sets of Machzorim, or Festival Prayer-Books, and the like—that his father barred up the door very carefully, and in the middle of the night, hearing a mouse scampering across the floor, woke up in a cold sweat and threw open the bedroom window and cried, ' Ho ! buglers ! '   But the ' buglers ' made no sign of being scared, everything was still and nothing purloined, so Jonathan took a reprimand from his disturbed wife and curled himself up again in bed.

Sugarman did things in style, and through the influence of a client the confirmation ceremony was celebrated in ' Duke's Plaizer Shool.'   Ebenezer, who was tall and weak-eyed, with lank black hair, had a fine new black cloth suit, and a beautiful silk praying-shawl with blue stripes, and a glittering watch-chain, and a gold ring, and a nice new Prayer-Book with gilt edges, and all the boys under thirteen made up their minds to grow up and be responsible for their sins as quick as possible.   Ebenezer walked up to the reading desk with a dauntless stride and intoned his portion of the Law with no more tremor than was necessitated by the musical roulades, and then marched upstairs as bold as brass to his mother, who was sitting up in the gallery, and who gave him a loud smacking kiss that could be heard in the four corners of the synagogue, just as if she were a real lady.

Then there was the *Bar-mitzvah* breakfast, at which Ebenezer delivered an English sermon and a speech, both openly written by the Shalotten Shammos, and everybody commended the boy's beautiful sentiments, and the beautiful language in which they were couched.   Mrs. Sugarman forgot all the trouble Ebenezer had given her in the face of his assurances of respect and affection, and she wept copiously.   Having only one eye, she could not see what her Jonathan saw, and what was spoiling his enjoyment of Ebenezer's effusive gratitude to his dear parents for having trained him up in lofty principles.

It was chiefly male cronies who had been invited to breakfast, and the table had been decorated with biscuits and fruit and sweets not appertaining to the meal, but provided for the refreshment of the less-favoured visitors—such as Mr. and Mrs. Hyams —who would be dropping in during the day.   Now, nearly every one of the guests had brought a little boy with him, each of whom stood like a page behind his father's chair.

Before starting on their prandial fried fish, these trenchermen took from the dainties wherewith the ornamental plates were laden, and gave thereof to their offspring. Now, this was only right and proper, because it is the prerogative of children to '*nash*' on these occasions. But, as the meal progressed, each father from time to time, while talking briskly to his neighbour, allowed his hand to stray mechanically into the plates, and thence negligently backwards into the hand of his infant, who stuffed the treasure into his pockets. Sugarman fidgeted about uneasily; not one surreptitious seizure escaped him, and every one pricked him like a needle. Soon his soul grew punctured like a pincushion. The Shalotten Shammos was among the worst offenders, and he covered his back-handed proceedings with a ceaseless flow of complimentary conversation.

'Excellent fish, Mrs. Sugarman,' he said, dexterously slipping some almonds behind his chair.

'What?' said Mrs. Sugarman, who was hard of hearing.

'First-class plaice!' shouted the Shalotten Shammos, negligently conveying a bunch of raisins.

'So they ought to be,' said Mrs. Sugarman in her thin, tinkling accents; 'they were all alive in the pan.'

'Ah, did they twitter?' said Mr. Belcovitch, pricking up his ears.

'No,' Bessie interposed. 'What do you mean?'

'At home in my town,' said Mr. Belcovitch impressively, 'a fish made a noise in the pan one Friday.'

'Well, and suppose?' said the Shalotten Shammos, passing a fig to the rear. 'The oil frizzles.'

'Nothing of the kind,' said Belcovitch angrily; 'a real living noise. The woman snatched it out of the pan and ran with it to the Rabbi. But he did not know what to do. Fortunately, there was staying with him for the Sabbath a travelling Saint from the far city of Ridnik, a *Chassid*, very skilful in plagues and purifications, and able to make clean a creeping thing by a hundred and fifty reasons. He directed the woman to wrap the fish in a shroud, and give it honourable burial as quickly as possible. The funeral took place the same afternoon, and a lot of people went in solemn procession to the woman's back-garden, and buried it with all seemly rites, and the knife with which it had been cut was buried in the same grave, having been defiled by contact with the demon. One man said it should be burnt, but that was absurd, because the demon would be only too glad to find itself in its native element; but to prevent Satan from rebuking the woman any more, its mouth was stopped with furnace ashes. There was no time to obtain Palestine earth, which would have completely crushed the demon.'

'The woman must have committed some *Avirah*,' said Karlkammer.

'A true story!' said the Shalotten Shammos ironically. 'That tale has been over Warsaw this twelvemonth.'

'It occurred when I was a boy,' affirmed Belcovitch indignantly. 'I remember it quite well. Some people explained it favourably. Others were of opinion that the soul of the fishmonger had transmigrated into the fish, an opinion borne out by the death of the fishmonger a few days before. And the Rabbi is still alive to prove it—may his light continue to shine !—though they write that he has lost his memory.'

The Shalotten Shammos sceptically passed a pear to his son. Old Gabriel Hamburg, the scholar, came compassionately to the raconteur's assistance.

'Rabbi Solomon Maimon,' he said, 'has left it on record that he witnessed a similar funeral in Posen.'

'It was well she buried it,' said Karlkammer. 'It was an atonement for a child, and saved its life.'

The Shalotten Shammos laughed outright.

'Ah, laugh not,' said Mrs. Belcovitch, 'or you may laugh with blood. It isn't for my own sins that I was born with ill-matched legs.'

'I must laugh when I hear of God's fools burying fish anywhere but in their stomach,' said the Shalotten Shammos, transporting a Brazil nut to the rear, where it was quietly annexed by Solomon Ansell, who had sneaked in uninvited and ousted the other boy from his coign of vantage.

The conversation was becoming heated ; Breckeloff turned the topic.

'My sister has married a man who can't play cards,' he said lugubriously.

'How lucky for her !' answered several voices.

'No, it's just her black luck !' he rejoined ; 'for he *will* play.'

There was a burst of laughter, and then the company remembered that Breckeloff was a *Badchan*, or jester.

'Why, your sister's husband is a splendid player,' said Sugarman with a flash of memory, and the company laughed afresh.

'Yes, said Breckeloff. 'But he doesn't give me the chance of losing to him now, he's got such a stuck-up *Kotzon*. He belongs to Duke's Plaizer *Shool*, and comes there very late, and when you ask him his birthplace he forgets he was a *Pullack*, and says he comes from "behind Berlin."'

These strokes of true satire occasioned more merriment, and were worth a biscuit to Solomon Ansell, *vice* the son of the Shalotten Shammos.

Among the inoffensive guests were old Gabriel Hamburg, the scholar, and young Joseph Strelitski, the student, who sat together. On the left of the somewhat seedy Strelitski, pretty Bessie, in blue silk, presided over the coffee-pot. Nobody knew whence Bessie had stolen her good looks ; probably from some remote ancestress. Bessie was in every way the most agreeable member of the family, inheriting some of her father's brains, but wisely going for the rest of herself to that remote ancestress.

Gabriel Hamburg and Joseph Strelitski had both had relations with No. 1 Royal Street for some time, yet they had hardly exchanged a word, and their meeting at this breakfast-table found them as great strangers as though they had never seen each other. Strelitski came because he boarded with the Sugarmans, and Hamburg came because he sometimes consulted Jonathan Sugarman about a Talmudical passage. Sugarman was charged with the oral traditions of a chain of Rabbis, like an actor who knows all the 'business' elaborated by his predecessors, and even a scientific scholar like Hamburg found him occasionally and fortuitously illuminating. Even so Karlkammer's red hair was a pillar of fire in the trackless wilderness of Hebrew literature. Gabriel Hamburg was a mighty savant, who endured all things for the love of knowledge and the sake of six men in Europe who followed his work and profited by its results. Verily, fit audience, though few. But such is the fate of great scholars, whose readers are sown throughout the lands more sparsely than monarchs. One by one Hamburg grappled with the countless problems of Jewish literary history, settling dates and authors, disintegrating the books of the Bible into their constituent parts, now inserting a gap of centuries between two halves of the same chapter, now flashing the light of new theories upon the development of Jewish theology. He lived at Royal Street and the British Museum, for he spent most of his time groping among the folios and manuscripts, and had no need for more than the little back bedroom behind the Ansells', stuffed with mouldy books. Nobody (who was any-body) had heard of him in England, and he worked on, unencumbered by patronage or a full stomach. The Ghetto itself knew little of him, for there were but few with whom he found inter-course satisfying. He was not 'orthodox' in belief, though eminently so in practice—which is all the Ghetto demands—not from hypocrisy, but from ancient prejudice. Scholarship had not shrivelled up his humanity, for he had a genial fund of humour and a gentle play of satire, and loved his neighbours for their folly and narrowmindedness. Unlike Spinoza, too, he did not go out of his way to inform them of his heterodox views, content to comprehend the crowd rather than be misunderstood by it. He knew that the bigger soul includes the smaller, and that the smaller can never circumscribe the bigger. Such money as was indispensable for the endowment of research he earned by copying texts and hunting out references for the numerous scholars and clergymen who infest the Museum and prevent the general reader from having elbow-room. In person he was small and bent and snuffy.

Superficially more intelligible, Joseph Strelitski was really a deeper mystery than Gabriel Hamburg. He was known to be a recent arrival on English soil, yet he spoke English fluently. He studied at Jews' College by day, and was preparing for the exami-nations at the London University. None of the other students knew where he lived, nor a bit of his past history. There was a vague idea afloat that he was an only child whose parents had been hounded to penury and death by Russian persecution, but who launched it nobody knew. His eyes were sad and earnest ; a curl of raven hair fell forwards on his high brow ; his clothing was shabby, and darned in places by his own hand. Beyond accepting the gift of education at the hands of dead men, he would take no help. On several distinct occasions the magic name Rothschild was appealed to on his behalf by well-wishers, and through its avenue of almoners it responded with its eternal quenchless, unquestioning generosity to students. But Joseph Strelitski always quietly sent back these bounties. He made enough to exist upon by touting for a cigar firm in the evenings. In the streets he walked with tight-pursed lips, dreaming no one knew what.

And yet there were times when his tight-pursed lips unclenched themselves, and he drew in great breaths even of Ghetto air with the huge contentment of one who has known suffocation. ' One can breathe here,' he seemed to be saying. The atmosphere, untainted by spies, venal officials, and jeering soldiery, seemed fresh and sweet. Here the ground was stable, not mined in all directions ; no arbitrary ukase—veritable sword of Damocles—hung over the head and darkened the sunshine. In such a country, where faith was free and action untrammelled, mere living was an ecstasy when remembrance came over one ; and so Joseph Strelitski sometimes threw back his head and breathed in liberty. The voluptousness of the sensation cannot be known by born freemen.

When Joseph Strelitski's father was sent to Siberia, he took his nine-year-old boy with him, in infringement of the law that prohibits exiles from taking children above five years of age. The police authorities, however, raised no objection, and they permitted Joseph to attend the public school at Kansk, Yeniseisk province, where the Strelitski family resided. A year or so afterwards the Yeniseisk authorities accorded the family permission to reside in Yeniseisk, and Joseph, having given proof of brilliant abilities, was placed in the Yeniseisk Gymnasium. For nigh three years the boy studied here, astonishing the Gymnasium with his extraordinary ability, when suddenly the Government authorities ordered the boy to return at once ' to the place where he was born.' In vain the school directors, won over by the poor boy's talent and enthusiasm for study, petitioned the Government. The Yeniseisk authorities were again ordered to expel him. No respite was granted, and the thirteen-year-old lad was sent to Sokolk, in the government of Grodno, at the other extreme of European Russia, where he was quite alone in the world. Before he was sixteen he escaped to England, his soul branded by terrible memories and steeled by solitude to a stern strength.

At Sugarman's he spoke little, and then mainly with the father on scholastic points. After meals he retired quickly to his business

or his sleeping-den, which was across the road. Bessie loved
Daniel Hyams, but she was a woman, and Strelitski's neutrality
piqued her.   Even to-day it is possible he might not have spoken
to Gabriel Hamburg if his other neighbour had not been Bessie.
Gabriel Hamburg was glad to talk to the youth, the outlines of
whose English history were known to him.   Strelitski seemed to
expand under the sunshine of a congenial spirit ; he answered
Hamburg's sympathetic inquiries about his work without reluctance, and even made some remarks on his own initiative.

And as they spoke, an under-current of pensive thought was flowing in the old scholar's soul, and his tones grew tenderer and tenderer.   The echoes of Ebenezer's effusive speech were in his ears,
and the artificial notes rang strangely genuine.   All round him
sat happy fathers of happy children, men who warmed their hands
at the home-fire of life, men who lived while he was thinking.
Yet he, too, had had his chance far back in the dim and dusty
years, his chance of love, and money with it.   He had let it slip
away for poverty and learning, and only six men in Europe cared
whether he lived or died.   The sense of his own loneliness smote
him with a sudden aching desolation.   His gaze grew humid ; the
face of the young student was covered with a veil of mist, and
seemed to shine with the radiance of an unstained soul.   If he had
been as other men, he might have had such a son.   At this moment Gabriel Hamburg was speaking of paragoge in Hebrew grammar, but his voice faltered, and in imagination he was laying hands
of paternal benediction on Joseph Strelitski's head.   Swayed by
an overmastering impulse, he burst out at last :

'An idea strikes me.'

Strelitski looked up in silent interrogation at the old man's
agitated face.

'You live by yourself.   I live by myself.   We are both students.
Why should we not live together as students, too ?'

A swift wave of surprise crossed Strelitski's face, and his eyes
grew soft.   For an instant the one solitary soul visibly yearned
towards the other.   He hesitated.

'Do not think I am too old,' said the great scholar, trembling
all over.   'I know it is the young who chum together, but still I
am a student.   And you shall see how lively and cheerful I will be.'
He forced a smile that hovered on tears.   'We shall be two
rackety young students, every night raising a thousand devils.
Gaudeamus igitur.'

He began to hum in his cracked hoarse voice the *Burschen-lied*
of his early days at the Berlin Gymnasium.

But Strelitski's face had grown dusky with a gradual flush and
a deepening gloom.   His black eyebrows were knit, and his lips
set together, and his eyes full of sullen ire.   He suspected a snare
to assist him.

He shook his head.

'Thank you,' he said slowly.   But I prefer to live alone.'

And he turned and spoke to the astonished Bessie, and so the two strange lonely vessels that had hailed each other across the darkness drifted away and apart for ever in the waste of waters.

But Jonathan Sugarman's eye was on more tragic episodes. Gradually the plates emptied, for the guests openly followed up the more substantial elements of the repast by dessert, more devastating even than the rear manœuvres. At last there was nothing but an aching china blank. The men looked round the table for something else to '*nash*,' but everywhere was the same depressing desolation. Only in the centre of the table towered in awful intact majesty the great *Bar-mitzvah* cake, like some mighty sphinx of stone surveying the ruins of empires, and the least reverent shrank before its austere gaze. But at last the Shalotten Shammos shook off his awe and stretched out his hand leisurely towards the cake, as became a master of ceremonies. But when Sugarman the Shadchan beheld his hand moving like a creeping flame forward, he sprang towards him as the tigress springs when the hunter threatens her cub. And, speaking no word, he snatched the great cake from under the hand of the spoiler, and tucked it under his arm, in the place where he carried Nehemiah, and sped therewith from the room. Then consternation fell upon the scene till Solomon Ansell, crawling on hands and knees in search of wind-falls, discovered a basket of apples stored under the centre of the table, and the Shalotten Shammos's son told his father thereof ere Solomon could do more than secure a few for his brother and sisters. Then the Shalotten Shammos laughed joyously, 'Apples!' and dived under the table, and his long form reached to the other side and beyond, and gray-bearded men echoed the joyous cry and scrambled on the ground like school-boys

'*Leolom tikkach*—always take,' quoted the *Badchan* gleefully.

When Sugarman returned, radiant, he found his absence had been fatal.

'Piece of fool! Two-eyed lump of flesh!' said Mrs. Sugarman in a loud whisper. 'Flying out of the room as if thou hadst the ague!'

'Shall I sit still like thee while our home is eaten up around us?' Sugarman whispered back. 'Couldst thou not look to the apples? Plaster image! Leaden fowl! See, they have emptied the basket, too.'

'Well, dost thou expect luck and blessing to crawl into it? Even five shillings worth of *Nash* cannot last for ever. May ten ammunition-waggons of black curses be discharged on thee!' replied Mrs. Sugarman, her one eye shooting fire.

This was the last straw of insult added to injury. Sugarman was exasperated beyond endurance. He forgot that he had a wider audience than his wife. He lost all control of himself, and cried aloud in a frenzy of rage :

'What a pity thou hadst not a fourth uncle!'

Mrs. Sugarman collapsed, speechless.

'A greedy lot, marm!' Sugarman reported to Mrs. Hyams on the Monday. 'I was very glad you and your people didn't come. Dere was noding left, except de prospectuses of de Hamburg lotteree vich I left laying all about for de guests to take. Being Shabbos, I could not give dem out.'

'We were sorry not to come, but neither Mr. Hyams nor myself felt well,' said the white-haired, broken-down old woman, with her painfully slow enunciation. Her English words rarely went beyond two syllables

'Ah!' said Sugarman. 'But I've come to give you back your corkscrew.'

'Why it's broken!' said Mrs. Hyams as she took it.

'So it is, marm,' he admitted readily. 'But if you taink dat I ought to pay for de damage, you're mistaken. If you lend me your cat'—here he began to make the argumentative movement with his thumb, as though scooping out imaginary *kosher* cheese with it—'if you lend me your cat to kill my rat'—his tones took on the strange Talmudic sing-song—'and my rat, instead, kills your cat, then it is the fault of your cat, and not the fault of my rat.'

Poor Mrs. Hyams could not meet this argument. If Mendel had been at home, he might have found a counter-analogy. As it was, Sugarman retucked Nehemiah under his arm and departed triumphant, almost consoled for the raid on his provisions by the thought of money saved. In the street he met the Shalotten Shammos.

'Blessed art thou who comest!' said the giant in Hebrew; then, relapsing into Yiddish, he cried : 'I've been wanting to see you! What did you mean by telling your wife you were sorry she had not a fourth uncle?'

'Soorka knew what I meant,' said Sugarman, with a little croak of victory. 'I have told her the story before. When the Almighty Shadchan was making marriages in heaven, before we were yet born, the name of my wife was coupled with my own. The spirit of her eldest uncle, hearing this, flew up to the angel who made the proclamation, and said, "Angel, thou art making a mistake! The man of whom thou makest mention will be of a lower status than this future niece of mine." Said the angel, "Sh! It is all right. She will halt on one leg." Came then the spirit of her second uncle, and said, "Angel, what blazonest thou? A niece of mine marry a man of such family!" Says the angel "Sh! It is all right. She will be blind in one eye." Came the spirit of her third uncle, and said, "Angel, hast thou not erred? Surely thou canst not mean to marry my future niece into such a humble family!" Says the angel, "Sh! It is all right. She will be deaf in one ear." Now do you see? If she had only had a fourth uncle, she would have been dumb into the bargain ; there is only one mouth, and my life would have been a happy one. Before I told Soorka that history she used to throw up her better breeding and finer family to me. Even in public she would shed my blood. Now she does not do it even in private.'

Sugarman the Shadchan winked, readjusted Nehemiah, and went his way.

CHAPTER XIV

THE HOPE OF THE FAMILY

IT was a cold, bleak Sunday afternoon, and the Ansells were spending it as usual. Little Sarah was with Mrs. Simons, Rachel had gone to Victoria Park with a party of school-mates ; the grandmother was asleep on the bed, covered with one of her son's old coats (for there was no fire in the grate), with her pious vade-mecum in her hand ; Esther had prepared her lessons, and was reading a little brown book at Dutch Debby's, not being able to forget the *London Journal* sufficiently ; Solomon had not prepared his, and was playing 'rounder' in the street, Isaac being permitted to 'feed' the strikers in return for a prospective occupation of his new bed ; Moses Ansell was at *Shool*, listening to a *Hesped* or funeral oration at the German synagogue, preached by Reb Shemuel over one of the lights of the Ghetto, prematurely gone out—no other than the consumptive Maggid, who had departed suddenly for a less fashionable place than Bournemouth. 'He has fallen,' said the Reb, 'not laden with age, nor sighing for release because the grasshopper was a burden. But he who holds the keys said : 'Thou hast done thy share of the work ; it is not thine to complete it. It was in thy heart to serve Me ; from Me thou shalt receive thy reward.''

And all the perspiring crowd in the black-draped hall shook with grief, and thousands of working men followed the body weeping to the grave, walking all the way to the great cemetery in Bow.

A slim, black-haired handsome lad of about twelve, dressed in a neat black suit with a shining white Eton collar, stumbled up the dark stairs of No. 1 Royal Street, with an air of unfamiliarity and disgust. At Dutch Debby's door he was delayed by a brief altercation with Bobby. He burst open the door of the Ansell apartment without knocking, though he took off his hat involuntarily as he entered. Then he stood still with an air of disappointment. The room seemed empty.

'What dost thou want, Esther?' murmured the grandmother, rousing herself sleepily.

The boy looked towards the bed with a start. He could not make out what the grandmother was saying. It was four years since he had heard Yiddish spoken, and he had almost forgotten the existence of the dialect. The room, too, seemed chill and alien—so unspeakably poverty-stricken.

'Oh, how are you, grandmother?' he said, going up to her and kissing her perfunctorily. 'Where's everybody?'

'Art thou Benjamin?' said the grandmother, her stern wrinkled face shadowed with surprise and doubt.

Benjamin guessed what she was asking, and nodded.

'But how richly they have dressed thee! Alas, I suppose they have taken away thy Judaism instead. For four whole years—is it not?—thou hast been with English folk. Woe! woe! If thy father had married a pious woman she would have been living still, and thou wouldst have been able to live happily in our midst, instead of being exiled among strangers, who feed thy body and starve thy soul. If thy father had left me in Poland I should have died happy, and my old eyes would never have seen the sorrow. Unbutton thy waistcoat; let me see if thou wearest the "four-corners" at least.'

Of this harangue, poured forth at the rate natural to thoughts running ever in the same grooves, Benjamin understood but a word here and there. For four years he had read and read and read English books, absorbed himself in English composition, heard nothing but English spoken about him—nay, he had even deliberately put the jargon out of his mind at the commencement, as something degrading and humiliating. Now it struck vague notes of old out-grown associations, but called up no definite images.

'Where's Esther?' he said.

'Esther?' grumbled the grandmother, catching the name. 'Esther is with Dutch Debby. She's always with her. Dutch Debby pretends to love her like a mother. And why?—because she wants to *be* her mother. She aims at marrying my Moses. But not for us. This time we shall marry the woman I select. No person like that, who knows as much about Judaism as the cow of Sunday—nor like Mrs. Simons, who coddles our little Sarah because she thinks my Moses will have her. It's plain as the eye in her head what she wants. But the Widow Finkelstein is the woman we're going to marry. She is a true Jewess—shuts up her shop the moment Shabbos comes in, not works right into the Sabbath like so many, and goes to *Shool* even on Friday nights. Look how she brought up her Avromkely, who intoned the whole portion of the Law and the Prophets in *Shool* before he was six years old. Besides, she has money and has cast eyes upon him.'

The boy, seeing conversation was hopeless, murmured something inarticulate and ran down the stairs to find some traces of the intelligible members of his family. Happily Bobby, remembering their former altercation and determining to have the last word, barred Benjamin's path with such pertinacity that Esther came out to quiet him, and leapt into her brother's arms with a great cry of joy, dropping the book she held full on Bobby's nose.

'Oh, Benjy! Is it really you? Oh, I am so glad! I am so

glad ! I knew you would come some day. Oh, Benjy !—Bobby, you bad dog, this is Benjy, my brother. Debby, I'm going upstairs; Benjamin's come back ! Benjamin's come back !'

'All right, dear,' Debby called out. 'Let me have a look at him soon. Send me in Bobby, if you're going away.' The words ended in a cough.

Esther hurriedly drove in Bobby, and then half led, half dragged, Benjamin upstairs. The grandmother had fallen asleep again, and was snoring peacefully.

'Speak low, Benjy,' said Esther ; 'grandmother's asleep.'

'All right, Esther. I don't want to wake her, I'm sure. I was up here just now, and I couldn't make out a word she was jabbering.'

'I know. She's losing all her teeth, poor thing !'

'No, it isn't that. She speaks that beastly Yiddish. I made sure she'd have learnt English by this time. I hope *you* don't speak it, Esther.'

'I must, Benjy. You see, father and grandmother never speak anything else at home, and only know a few words of English. But I don't let the children speak it, except to them. You should hear little Sarah speak English. It's beautiful. Only when she cries she says "Woe is me !" in Yiddish. I have had to slap her for it, but that makes her cry "Woe is me !" all the more. Oh, how nice you look, Benjy, with your white collar—just like the pictures of little Lord Launceston in the Fourth Standard Reader ! I wish I could show you to the girls ! Oh my ! what'll Solomon say when he sees you? He's always wearing his corduroys away at the knees.'

'But where is everybody? And why is there no fire?' said Benjamin impatiently. 'It's beastly cold.'

'Father hopes to get a bread, coal, and meat ticket to-morrow, dear.'

'Well, this is a pretty welcome for a fellow !' grumbled Benjamin.

'I'm so sorry, Benjy ! If I'd only known you were coming I might have borrowed some coals from Mrs. Belcovitch. But just stamp your feet a little if they freeze. No, do it outside the door—grandmother's asleep. Why didn't you write to me you were coming ?'

'I didn't know. Old Four-Eyes—that's one of our teachers—was going up to London this afternoon, and he wanted a boy to carry some parcels, and as I'm the best boy in my class he let me come. He let me run up and see you all, and I'm to meet him at London Bridge Station at seven o'clock. You're not much altered, Esther.'

'Ain't I ?' she said, with a little pathetic smile. 'Ain't I bigger ?'

'Not four years bigger. For a moment I could fancy I'd never been away. How the years slip by ! I shall be *Bar-mitzvah* soon.'

'Yes ; and now I've got you again I've so much to say I don't know where to begin. That time father went to see you I couldn't get much out of him about you, and your own letters have been so few.'

'A letter costs a penny, Esther. Where am I to get pennies from?'

'I know, dear. I know you would have liked to write. But now you shall tell me everything. Have you missed us very much?'

'No, I don't think so,' said Benjamin.

'Oh, not at all?' asked Esther, in disappointed tones.

'Yes; I missed *you*, Esther, at first,' he said soothingly. 'But there's such a lot to do and to think about. It's a new life.'

'And have you been happy, Benjy?'

'Oh yes; quite. Just think! Regular meals, with oranges and sweets and entertainments every now and then, a bed all to yourself, good fires, a mansion with a noble staircase and hall, a field to play in, with balls and toys——'

'A field!' echoed Esther. 'Why, it must be like going to Greenwich every day.'

'Oh, better than Greenwich, where they take you girls for a measly day's holiday once a year.'

'Better than the Crystal Palace, where they take the boys?'

'Why, the Crystal Palace is quite near. We can see the fireworks every Thursday night in the season.'

Esther's eyes opened wider.

'And have you been inside?'

'Lots of times.'

'Do you remember the time you didn't go?' Esther said softly.

'A fellow doesn't forget that sort of thing,' he grumbled. 'I so wanted to go—I had heard such a lot about it from the boys who had been. When the day of the excursion came my Shabbos coat was in pawn, wasn't it?'

'Yes,' said Esther, her eyes growing humid. 'I was so sorry for you, dear. You didn't want to go in your corduroy coat and let the boys know you didn't have a best coat. It was quite right, Benjy.'

'I remember mother gave me a treat instead,' said Benjamin, with a comic grimace. 'She took me round to Zachariah Square and let me play there while she was scrubbing Malka's floor. I think Milly gave me a penny, and I remember Leah let me take a couple of licks from a glass of ice-cream she was eating on the Ruins. It was a hot day—I shall never forget that ice-cream. But fancy parents pawning a chap's only decent coat!' He smoothed his well-brushed jacket complacently.

'Yes; but don't you remember mother took it out the very next morning before school with the money she earnt at Malka's?'

'But what was the use of that? I put it on, of course, when I went to school, and told the teacher I was ill the day before, just to show the boys I was telling the truth. But it was too late to take me to the Palace.'

'Ah, but it came in handy. Don't you remember, Benjy, how one of the great ladies died suddenly the next week?'

'Oh yes! Yoicks! tally-ho!' cried Benjamin with sudden excitement. 'We went down on hired omnibuses to the cemetery, ever so far into the country, six of the best boys in each class; and I was on the box-seat next to the driver, and I thought of the old mail-coach days and looked out for highwaymen. We stood along the path in the cemetery, and the sun was shining, and the grass was so green, and there were such lovely flowers on the coffin when it came past, with the gentlemen crying behind it. And then we had lemonade and cakes on the way back. Oh, it was just beautiful! I went to two other funerals after that, but that was the one I enjoyed most. Yes, that coat did come in useful, after all, for a day in the country.'

Benjamin evidently did not think of his own mother's interment as a funeral. Esther did, and she changed the subject quickly.

'Well, tell me more about your place.'

'Well, it's like going to funerals every day. It's all country all round about, with trees and flowers and birds. Why, I've helped to make hay in the autumn!'

Esther drew a sigh of ecstasy.

'It's like a book!' she said.

'Books!' he said. 'We've got hundreds and hundreds—a whole library. Dickens, Mayne Reid, George Eliot, Captain Marryat, Thackeray—I've read them all.'

'Oh, Benjy!' said Esther, clapping her hands in admiration both of the library and her brother. 'I wish I were you.'

'Well, you could be me easily enough.'

'How?' said Esther eagerly.

'Why, we have a girls' department too. You're an orphan as much as me. You get father to enter you as a candidate.'

'Oh, how could I, Benjy?' said Esther, her face falling. 'What would become of Solomon and Ikey and little Sarah?'

'They've got a father, haven't they, and a grandmother?'

'Father can't do washing and cooking, you silly boy! and grandmother's too old.'

'Well, I call it a beastly shame. Why can't father earn a living and give out the washing? He never has a penny to bless himself with.'

'It isn't his fault, Benjy. He tries hard. I'm sure he often grieves that he's so poor that he can't afford the railway-fare to visit you on visiting-days. That time he did go, he only got the money by selling a work-box I had for a prize. But he often speaks about you.'

'Well, I don't grumble at his not coming,' said Benjamin. 'I forgive him that, because, you know, he's not very presentable, is he, Esther?'

Esther was silent.

'Oh, well, everybody knows he's poor. They don't expect father to be a gentleman.'

'Yes, but he might look decent. Does he still wear those two

beastly little curls at the side of his head? Oh, I did hate it when
I was at school here and he used to come to see the master about
something. Some of the boys had such respectable fathers; it
was quite a pleasure to see them come in and overawe the teacher.
Mother used to be as bad, coming in with a shawl over her head!'

'Yes, Benjy, but she used to bring us in bread-and-butter when
there had been none in the house at breakfast-time. Don't you
remember, Benjy?'

'Oh yes, I remember. We've been through some beastly bad
times, haven't we, Esther? All I say is, you wouldn't like father
coming in before all the girls in your class, would you, now?'

Esther blushed.

'There is no occasion for him to come,' she said evasively.

'Well, I know what I shall do!' said Benjamin decisively. 'I
am going to be a very rich man.'

'Are you, Benjy?' inquired Esther.

'Yes, of course. I'm going to write books—like Dickens and
those fellows. Dickens made a pile of money just by writing
down plain everyday things going on around.'

'But you can't write!'

Benjamin laughed a superior laugh.

'Oh, can't I? What about *Our Own*, eh?'

'What's that?'

'That's our journal. I edit it. Didn't I tell you about it?
Yes, I'm running a story through it called "The Soldier's Bride"
—all about life in Afghanistan.'

'Oh, where could I get a number?'

'You can't get one. It ain't printed, stupid! It's all copied
by hand, and we've only got a few copies. If you came down,
you could see it.'

'Yes, but I can't come down,' said Esther, with tears in her eyes.

'Well, never mind. You'll see it some day. Well, what was
I telling you? Oh yes—about my prospects. You see, I'm going
in for a scholarship in a few months, and everybody says I shall
get it. Then perhaps I might go to a higher school, and then
to Oxford or Cambridge.'

'And row in the boat-race!' said Esther, flushing with excitement.

'No; bother the boat-race! I'm going in for Latin and Greek.
I've begun to learn French already. So I shall know three
languages.'

'Four!' said Esther. 'You forget Hebrew!'

'Oh, of course, Hebrew. I don't reckon Hebrew. Everybody
knows Hebrew. Hebrew's no good to any one. What I want is
something that'll get me on in the world and enable me to write
my books.'

'But Dickens—did he know Latin or Greek?' asked Esther.

'No, he didn't,' said Benjamin proudly. 'That's just where I
shall have the pull of him. Well, when I've got rich I shall buy
father a new suit of clothes and a high hat—it *is* so beastly cold

here, Esther ; just feel my hands, like ice !—and I shall make him
live with grandmother in a decent room, and give him an allowance,
so that he can study beastly big books all day long—does he still
take a week to read a page ? And Sarah and Isaac and Rachel
shall go to a proper boarding-school, and Solomon—how old will
he be then ?'

Esther looked puzzled.

' Oh, but suppose it takes you ten years getting famous ? Solomon
will be nearly twenty.'

' It can't take me ten years. But never mind ! We shall see
what is to be done with Solomon when the time comes. As for
you——'

' Well, Benjy?' she said, for his imagination was breaking down.

' I 'll give you a dowry and you 'll get married. See !' he concluded triumphantly.

' Oh, but suppose I shan't want to get married ?'

' Nonsense ! every girl wants to get married. I overheard old
Four-Eyes say all the teachers in the girls' department were
dying to marry him. I 've got several sweethearts already, and I
dare say you have.' He looked at her quizzingly.

' No, dear,' she said earnestly. ' There 's only Levi Jacobs, Reb
Shemuel's son, who 's been coming round sometimes to play with
Solomon, and brings me almond-rock. But I don't care for him—
at least, not in that way. Besides, he 's quite above us.'

' *Oh*, is he ? Wait till I write my novels !'

' I wish you 'd write them now—because then I should have
something to read. Oh !'

' What 's the matter ?'

' I 've lost my book. What have I done with my little brown
book ?'

' Didn't you drop it on that beastly dog ?'

' Oh, did I ? People 'll tread on it on the stairs. Oh dear ! I'll
run down and get it. But don't call Bobby beastly, please.'

' Why not ? Dogs are beasts, aren't they ?'

Esther puzzled over the retort as she flew downstairs, but could
find no reply. She found the book, however, and that consoled her.

' What have you got hold of?' said Benjamin when she returned.

' Oh, nothing ! It wouldn't interest you.'

' All books interest me,' announced Benjamin with dignity.

Esther reluctantly gave him the book. He turned over the
pages carelessly, then his face grew serious and astonished.

' Esther,' he said, ' how did you come by this ?'

' One of the girls gave it me in exchange for a stick of slate-
pencil. She said she got it from the missionaries—she went to
their night-school for a lark, and they gave her it, and a pair of
boots as well.'

' And you have been reading it ?'

' Yes, Benjy,' said Esther meekly.

' You naughty girl ! Don't you know the New Testament is a

wicked book? Look here! There's the word "Christ" on nearly every page, and the word "Jesus" on every other. And you haven't even scratched them out! Oh, if anyone was to catch you reading this book!'

'I don't read it in school-hours,' said the little girl deprecatingly.

'But you have no business to read it at all.'

'Why not?' she said doggedly. 'I like it. It seems just as interesting as the Old Testament, and there are more miracles to the page.'

'You wicked girl!' said her brother, overwhelmed by her audacity. 'Surely you know that all those miracles were false?'

'Why were they false?' persisted Esther.

'Because miracles left off after the Old Testament! There are no miracles nowadays, are there?'

'No,' admitted Esther.

'Well, then,' he said triumphantly, 'if miracles had gone overlapping into New Testament times, we might just as well expect to have them now.'

'But why shouldn't we have them now?'

'Esther, I'm surprised at you! I should like to set Old Four-Eyes on to you. He'd soon tell you why. Religion all happened in the past. God couldn't be always talking to His creatures.'

'I wish I'd lived in the past, when religion was happening,' said Esther ruefully. 'But why do Christians all reverence this book? I'm sure there are many more millions of them than of Jews!'

'Of course there are, Esther. Good things are scarce. We are so few because we are God's chosen people.'

'But why do I feel good when I read what Jesus said?'

'Because you are so bad,' he answered, in a shocked tone. 'Here, give me the book; I'll burn it!'

'No, no!' said Esther. 'Besides, there's no fire.'

'No, hang it!' he said, rubbing his hands. 'Well, it'll never do if you have to fall back on this sort of thing. I'll tell you what I'll do—I'll send you *Our Own*.'

'Oh, will you, Benjy? That is good of you!' she said joyfully, and was kissing him, when Solomon and Isaac came romping in and woke up the grandmother.

'How are you, Solomon?' said Benjamin. 'How are you, my little man?' he added, patting Isaac on his curly head.

Solomon was overawed for a moment. Then he said: 'Hullo, Benjy! Have you got any spare buttons?'

But Isaac was utterly ignorant who the stranger could be, and hung back with his finger in his mouth.

'That's your brother Benjamin, Ikey,' said Solomon.

'Don't want no more brovers,' said Ikey.

'Oh, but I was here before you,' said Benjamin, laughing.

'Does oor birfday come before mine, then?'

'Yes, if I remember.'

Isaac looked tauntingly at the door.

'See !' he cried to the absent Sarah.   Then, turning graciously to Benjamin, he said, 'I thant kiss oo, but I'll lat oo teep in my new bed.'

'But you *must* kiss him,' said Esther, and saw that he did it before she left the room to fetch little Sarah from Mrs. Simons.

When she came back Solomon was letting Benjamin inspect his Plevna peep-show without charge, and Moses Ansell was back, too.   His eyes were red with weeping, but that was on account of the Maggid.   His nose was blue with the chill of the cemetery.

'He was a great man,' he was saying to the grandmother.   'He could lecture for four hours together on any text, and he would always manage to get back to the text before the end.   Such exegetics ! such homiletics !   He was greater than the Emperor of Russia.   Woe ! woe !'

'Woe ! woe !' echoed the grandmother.   'If women were allowed to go to funerals, I would gladly have followed him.   Why did he come to England ?   In Poland he would still have been alive.   And why did I come to England ?   Woe ! woe !'

Her head dropped back on the pillow, and her sighs passed gently into snores.   Moses turned again to his eldest-born, feeling that he was secondary in importance only to the Maggid, and proud at heart of his genteel English appearance.

'Well, you'll soon be *Bar-mitzvah*, Benjamin,' he said with clumsy geniality, blent with respect, as he patted his boy's cheek with his discoloured fingers.

Benjamin caught the last two words, and nodded his head.

'And then you'll be coming back to us.   I suppose they will apprentice you to something ?'

'What does he say, Esther ?' asked Benjamin impatiently.

Esther interpreted.

'Apprentice me to something !' he repeated, disgusted. 'Father's ideas are so beastly humble.   He would like everybody to dance on him.   Why, he'd be content to see me a cigar-maker or a presser.   Tell him I'm not coming home—that I'm going to win a scholarship and go to the University.'

Moses's eyes dilated with pride.   'Ah, you will become a Rav !' he said, and lifted up his boy's chin and looked lovingly into the handsome face.

'What's that about a Rav, Esther ?' said Benjamin.   'Does he want me to become a Rabbi ?   Ugh !   Tell him I'm going to write books.'

'My blessed boy !   A good commentary on the Song of Songs is much needed.   Perhaps you will begin by writing that.'

'Oh, it's no use talking to him, Esther !   Let him be.   Why can't he speak English ?'

'He can, but you'd understand even less,' said Esther, with a sad smile.

'Well, all I say is it's a beastly disgrace !   Look at the years he's been in England—just as long as we have.'   Then the humour of the remark dawned upon him, and he laughed. 'I suppose he's out of work, as usual?' he added.

Moses's ears pricked up at the syllables 'out-of-work,' which to him was a single word of baleful meaning.

'Yes,' he said in Yiddish. 'But if I only had a few pounds to start with, I could work up a splendid business.'

'Wait! He shall have a business,' said Benjamin when Esther interpreted.

'Don't listen to him,' said Esther. 'The Board of Guardians has started him again and again. But he likes to think he is a man of business.'

Meantime Isaac had been busy explaining Benjamin to Sarah, and pointing out the remarkable confirmation of his own views as to birthdays. This will account for Esther's next remark being:

'Now, dears, no fighting to-day? We must celebrate Benjy's return. We ought to kill a fatted calf—like the man in the Bible.'

'What are you talking about, Esther?' said Benjamin suspiciously.

'I'm so sorry—nothing—only foolishness,' said Esther. 'We really must do something to make a holiday of the occasion. Oh, I know! we'll have tea before you go, instead of waiting till supper-time. Perhaps Rachel'll be back from the park. You haven't seen her yet.'

'No, I can't stay,' said Benjy. 'It'll take me three-quarters of an hour getting to the station. And you've got no fire to make tea with, either.'

'Nonsense, Benjy! You seem to have forgotten everything; we've got a loaf and a penn'uth of tea in the cupboard. Solomon, fetch a farthing's-worth of boiling water from the Widow Finkelstein.'

At the words 'Widow Finkelstein' the grandmother awoke and sat up.

'No, I'm too tired,' said Solomon. 'Isaac can go.'

'No,' said Isaac. 'Let Esty go.'

Esther took a jug and went to the door.

'Méshe,' said the grandmother, 'go thou to the Widow Finkelstein.'

'But Esther can go,' said Moses.

'Yes, I'm going,' said Esther.

'Méshe!' repeated the *Bube* inexorably, 'go thou to the Widow Finkelstein.'

Moses went.

'Have you said the afternoon prayer, boys?' the old woman asked.

'Yes,' said Solomon, 'while you were asleep.'

'Oh-h-h!' said Esther under her breath. And she looked reproachfully at Solomon.

'Well, didn't you say we must make a holiday to-day?' he whispered back.

CHAPTER XV

THE HOLY LAND LEAGUE

'OH, these English Jews!' said Melchitzedek Pinchas in German.

'What have they done to you now?' said Guedalyah the Greengrocer in Yiddish.

The two languages are relatives, and often speak as they pass by.

'I have presented my book to every one of them, but they have paid me scarce enough to purchase poison for them all,' said the little poet, scowling. The cheek-bones stood out sharply beneath the tense bronzed skin; the black hair was tangled and unkempt, and the beard untrimmed; the eyes darted venom. 'One of them —Gideon, M.P., the stockbroker—engaged me to teach his son for his *Bar-mitzvah*. But the boy is so stupid—so stupid! Just like his father. I have no doubt he will grow up to be a Rabbi. I teach him his portion—I sing the words to him with a most beautiful voice, but he has as much ear as soul. Then I write him a speech—a wonderful speech for him to make to his parents and the company at the breakfast—and in it, after he thanks them for their kindness, I make him say how, with the blessing of the Almighty, he will grow up to be a good Jew and munificently support Hebrew literature and learned men, like his revered teacher, Melchitzedek Pinchas. And then he shows it to his father, and his father says it is not written in good English, and that another scholar has already written him a speech. Good English! Gideon has as much knowledge of style as the Rev. Elkan Benjamin of decency. Ah, I will shoot them both! I know I do not speak English like a native, but what language under the sun is there I cannot write? French, German, Spanish, Arabic—they flow from my pen like honey from a rod. As for Hebrew, you know, Guedalyah, I and you are the only two men in England who can write Holy Language grammatically. And yet these miserable stockbrokers, Men-of-the-Earth, they dare to say I cannot write English, and they have given me the sack—I who was teaching the boy true Judaism and the value of Hebrew literature.'

'What! they didn't let you finish teaching the boy his Hebrew portion because you couldn't write English!'

'No; they had another pretext. One of the servant girls said I wanted to kiss her—lies and falsehoods! I was kissing my finger after kissing the *Mezuzah*, and the stupid abomination thought I was kissing my hand to her. It sees itself that they don't kiss the *Mezuzahs* often in that house—the impious crew! And what will be now? The stupid boy will go home to breakfast in a bazaar of costly presents, and he will make the stupid speech written by the fool of an Englishman, and the ladies will weep. But where will be the Judaism in all this? Who will vaccinate him against free-thinking as I would have done ? Who will infuse into him the true patriotic fervour, the love of his race, the love of Zion, the land of his fathers?'

'Ah, you are verily a man after my own heart !' said Guedalyah the Greengrocer, overswept by a wave of admiration. 'Why should you not come with me to my Beth-Hamidrash to-night, to the meeting for the foundation of the Holy Land League?—That cauliflower will be fourpence, mum.'

'Ah, what is that?' said Pinchas.

'I have an idea. A score of us meet to-night to discuss it.'

'Ah, yes ! You have always ideas. You are a sage and a saint, Guedalyah. The Beth-Hamidrash which you have established is the only centre of real orthodoxy and Jewish literature in London. The ideas you expound in the Jewish papers for the amelioration of the lot of our poor brethren are most statesmanlike. But these donkey-head English rich people—what help can you expect from them ? They do not even understand your plans. They have only sympathy with needs of the stomach.'

'You are right—you are right, Pinchas !' said Guedalyah the Greengrocer eagerly.

He was a tall, loosely built man, with a pasty complexion capable of shining with enthusiasm. He was dressed shabbily, and in the intervals of selling cabbages projected the regeneration of Judah.

'That is just what is beginning to dawn upon me, Pinchas,' he went on. 'Our rich people give plenty away in charity ; they have good hearts, but not Jewish hearts. As the verse says.—A bundle of rhubarb and two pounds of Brussels sprouts, and threepence-half-penny change. Thank you ; much obliged.—Now, I have bethought myself, why should we not work out our own salvation ? It is the poor, the oppressed, the persecuted, whose souls pant after the land of Israel as the hart after the water-brooks. Let us help ourselves ; let us put our hands in our own pockets. With our *Groschen* let us rebuild Jerusalem and our holy Temple. We will collect a fund, slowly but surely ; from all parts of the East End and the provinces the pious will give. With the first-fruits we will send out a little party of persecuted Jews to Palestine, and then another and another. The movement will grow like a sliding snowball that becomes an avalanche.'

'Yes ; then the rich will come to you,' said Pinchas, intensely excited. 'Ah ! it is a great idea, like all yours. Yes, I will come —I will make a mighty speech, for my lips, like Isaiah's, have been touched with the burning coal. I will inspire all hearts to start the movement at once. I will write its "Marseillaise" this very night, bedewing my couch with a poet's tears. We shall no longer be dumb ; we shall roar like the lions of Lebanon. I shall be the trumpet to call the dispersed together from the four corners of the earth—yea, I shall be the Messiah himself !' said Pinchas, rising on the wings of his own eloquence, and forgetting to puff at his cigar.

' I rejoice to see you so ardent, but mention not the word Messiah, for I fear some of our friends will take alarm and say that these are not Messiah times, that neither Elias, nor Gog, King of Magog, nor any of the portents have yet appeared.—Kidneys or regents, my child?'

' Stupid people! Hillel said more wisely : " If I help not myself, who will help me?" Do they expect the Messiah to fall from heaven? Who knows but I am the Messiah? Was I not born on the ninth of Ab?'

' Hush, hush!' said Guedalyah the Greengrocer. ' Let us be practical. We are not yet ready for Marseillaises or Messiahs. The first step is to get funds enough to send one family to Palestine.'

' Yes, yes,' said Pinchas, drawing vigorously at his cigar to rekindle it. ' But we must look ahead. Already I see it all. Palestine in the hands of the Jews, the holy Temple rebuilt, a Jewish state, a president who is equally accomplished with the sword and the pen—the whole campaign stretches before me. I see things like Napoleon, general and dictator alike.'

' Truly we wish that,' said the Greengrocer cautiously. But to-night it is only a question of a dozen men founding a collecting society.'

' Of course, of course ; that I understand. You 're right ; people about here say Guedalyah the Greengrocer is always right. I will come beforehand to supper with you to talk it over, and you shall see what I will write for the *Mizpeh* and the *Arbeiter-freund.* You know, all these papers jump at me ; their readers are the class to which you appeal ; in them will I write my burning verses and leaders advocating the Cause. I shall be your Tyrtæus, your Mazzini, your Napoleon. How blessed that I came to England just now ! I have lived in the Holy Land—the genius of the soil is blent with mine. I can describe its beauties as none other can. I am the very man at the very hour. And yet I will not go rashly —slow and sure—my plan is to collect small amounts from the poor, to start by sending one family at a time to Palestine. That is how we must do it. How does that strike you, Guedalyah? You agree?'

' Yes, yes. That is also my opinion.'

' You see, I am not a Napoleon only in great ideas. I understand detail, though as a poet I abhor it. Ah, the Jew is king of the world ! He alone conceives great ideas, and executes them by petty means. The heathen are so stupid—so stupid ! Yes, you shall see at supper how practically I will draw up the scheme. And then I will show you, too, what I have written about Gideon, M.P., the dog of a stockbroker—a satirical poem have I written about him in Hebrew—an acrostic with his name for the mockery of posterity. Stocks and shares have I translated into Hebrew, with new words which will at once be accepted by the Hebraists of the world and added to the vocabulary of modern Hebrew. Oh, I am terrible in satire ! I sting like the hornet—witty as Immanuel, but mordant as his friend Dante. It will appear in the *Mizpeh* to-morrow. I will show this Anglo-Jewish community that I am a man to be reckoned with. I will crush it—not it me !'

'But they don't see the *Mizpeh*, and couldn't read it if they did.'

'No matter. I send it abroad—I have friends, great Rabbis, great scholars, everywhere, who send me their learned manuscripts, their commentaries, their ideas, for revision and improvement. Let the Anglo-Jewish community hug itself in its stupid prosperity, but I will make it the laughing-stock of Europe and Asia. Then some day it will find out its mistake ; it will not have ministers like the Rev. Elkan Benjamin, who keeps four mistresses ; it will depose the lump of flesh who reigns over it, and it will seize the hem of my coat and beseech me to be its Rabbi.'

'We should have a more orthodox Chief Rabbi certainly,' admitted Guedalyah.

'Orthodox ? Then, and only then, shall we have true Judaism in London, and a burst of literary splendour far exceeding that of the much overpraised Spanish school, none of whom had that true lyrical gift which is like the carol of the bird in the pairing season. Oh, why have I not the bird's privileges as well as its gift of song ? Why can I not pair at will ? Oh, the stupid Rabbis who forbade polygamy ! Verily as the verse says : " The law of Moses is perfect, enlightening the eyes "— marriage, divorce, all are regulated with the height of wisdom. Why must we adopt the stupid customs of the heathens ? At present I have not even one mate. But I love—ah, Guedalyah ! I love ! The women are so beautiful ! You love the women--hey ?'

'I love my Rivkah,' said Guedalyah.—'A penny on each gingerbeer-bottle.'

'Yes ; but why haven't *I* got a wife—eh ?' demanded the little poet fiercely, his black eyes glittering. 'I am a fine, tall, well-built good-looking man. In Palestine and on the Continent all the girls would go about sighing and casting sheep's-eyes at me, for there the Jews love poetry and literature. But here ! I can go into a room with a maiden in it, and she makes herself unconscious of my presence. There is Reb Shemuel's daughter, a fine beautiful virgin. I kiss her hand and it is ice to my lips. Ah, if I only had money ! And money I should have, if these English Jews were not so stupid, and if they elected me Chief Rabbi. Then I would marry—one, two, three maidens.'

'Talk not such foolishness !' said Guedalyah, laughing, for he thought the poet jested.

Pinchas saw his enthusiasm had carried him too far ; but his tongue was the most reckless of organs, and often slipped into the truth. He was a real poet, with an extraordinary faculty for language, and a gift of unerring rhythm. He wrote after the mediæval model, with a profusion of acrostics and double-rhyming, not with the bald duplications of primitive Hebrew poetry. Intellectually he divined things like a woman, with marvellous rapidity, shrewdness, and inaccuracy. He saw into people's souls through a dark refracting suspiciousness. The same bent of mind, the same individuality of distorted insight, made him overflow with ingenious explanations of the Bible and the Talmud, with new views and new lights on history, philology, medicine—anything, everything. And he believed in his ideas, because they were his, and in himself, because of his ideas. To himself his stature sometimes seemed to expand till his head touched the sun—but that was mostly after wine—and his brain retained a permanent glow from the contact.

'Well, peace be with you !' said Pinchas. ' I will leave you to your customers, who besiege you as I have been besieged by the maidens. But what you have just told me has gladdened my heart. I always had an affection for you, but now I love you like a woman. We will found this Holy Land League, I and you. You shall be president—I waive all claims in your favour—and I will be treasurer—hey ?'

'We shall see—we shall see,' said Guedalyah the Greengrocer.

'No, we cannot leave it to the mob—we must settle it before-hand. Shall we say done ?'

He laid his finger cajolingly to the side of his nose.

'We shall see,' repeated Guedalyah the Greengrocer impatiently.

'No ; say ! I love you like a brother. Grant me this favour, and I will never ask anything of you so long as I live.'

'Well, if the others——' began Guedalyah feebly.

'Ah ! you are a prince in Israel,' Pinchas cried enthusiastically. ' If I could only show you my heart—how it loves you !'

He capered off at a sprightly trot, his head haloed by huge volumes of smoke. Guedalyah the Greengrocer bent over a bin of potatoes. Looking up suddenly, he was startled to see the head fixed in the open front of the shop-window. It was a narrow, dark-bearded face, distorted with an insinuative smile. A dirty-nailed forefinger was laid on the right of the nose.

'You won't forget ?' said the head coaxingly.

'Of course I won't forget,' cried the Greengrocer querulously.

The meeting took place at ten that night at the Beth-Hamidrash founded by Guedalyah, a large unswept room, rudely fitted up as a synagogue, and approached by reeking staircases unsavoury as the neighbourhood. On one of the back benches a shabby youth with very long hair and lank fleshless limbs shook his body violently to and fro while he vociferated the sentences of the Mishnah in the traditional argumentative sing-song. Near the central raised platform was a group of enthusiasts, among whom Froom Karl-kammer, with his thin, ascetic body and the mass of red hair that crowned his head like the light of a pharos, was a conspicuous figure.

'Peace be to you, Karlkammer!' said Pinchas to him in Hebrew.

'To you be peace, Pinchas !' replied Karlkammer.

'Ah !' went on Pinchas, ' sweeter than honey it is to me—yea,

than fine honey—to talk to a man in the Holy Tongue. Woe!
the speakers are few in these latter days. I and thou, Karlkammer, are the only two people who can speak the Holy Tongue
grammatically on this isle of the sea. Lo, it is a great thing we
are met to do this night. I see Zion laughing on her mountains,
and her fig-trees skipping for joy. I will be the treasurer of
the fund, Karlkammer—do thou vote for me, for so our society
shall flourish as the green bay-tree.'

Karlkammer grunted vaguely, not having humour enough to
recall the usual associations of the simile, and Pinchas passed on
to salute Hamburg. To Gabriel Hamburg Pinchas was occasion
for half-respectful amusement. He could not but reverence the
poet's genius, even while he laughed at his pretensions to omni-
science, and at the daring and unscientific guesses which the poet
offered as plain prose. For when in their arguments Pinchas
came upon Jewish ground, he was in presence of a man who
knew every inch of it.

'Blessed art thou who arrivest!' he said when he perceived
Pinchas. Then, dropping into German, he continued : ' I did not
know you would join in the rebuilding of Zion.'

'Why not?' inquired Pinchas.

'Because you have written so many poems thereupon.'

'Be not so foolish,' said Pinchas, annoyed. ' Did not King
David fight the Philistines as well as write the Psalms?'

'Did he write the Psalms?' said Hamburg quietly, with a smile.

'No, not so loud! Of course he didn't! The Psalms were
written by Judas Maccabæus, as I proved in the last issue of the
Stuttgard *Zeitschrift*. But that only makes my analogy more
forcible. You shall see how I will gird on sword and armour,
and I shall yet see even you in the forefront of the battle. I will
be treasurer ; you shall vote for me, Hamburg, for I and you are
the only two people who know the Holy Tongue grammatically,
and we must work shoulder to shoulder, and see that the balance-
sheets are drawn up in the language of our fathers.'

In like manner did Melchitzedek Pinchas approach Hiram
Lyons and Simon Gradkoski, the former a poverty-stricken pietist,
who added day by day to a furlong of crabbed manuscript, em-
bodying a useless commentary on the first chapter of Genesis ;
the latter the portly fancy-goods dealer in whose warehouse
Daniel Hyams was employed. Gradkoski rivalled Reb Shemuel
in his knowledge of the exact *loci* of Talmudical remarks—page
this and line that—and, secretly a tolerant latitudinarian, enjoyed
the reputation of a bulwark of orthodoxy too well to give it up.
Gradkoski passed easily from writing an invoice to writing a
learned article on Hebrew astronomy. Pinchas ignored Joseph
Strelitski, whose raven curl floated wildly over his forehead like a
pirate's flag, though Hamburg, who was rather surprised to see
the taciturn young man at a meeting, strove to draw him into
conversation. The man to whom Pinchas ultimately attached

himself was only a man in the sense of having attained his religious majority. He was a Harrow boy, named Raphael Leon, a scion of a wealthy family. The boy had manifested a strange premature interest in Jewish literature, and had often seen Gabriel Hamburg's name in learned footnotes, and discovering that he was in England, had just written to him. Hamburg had replied ; they had met that day for the first time, and at the lad's own request the old scholar brought him on to this strange meeting. The boy grew to be Hamburg's one link with wealthy England, and though he rarely saw Leon again, the lad came in a shadowy way to take the place he had momentarily designed for Joseph Strelitski. To-night it was Pinchas who assumed the paternal manner, but he mingled it with a subtle obsequiousness that made the shy, simple lad uncomfortable, though when he came to read the poet's lofty sentiments, which arrived (with an acrostic dedication) by the first post next morning, he conceived an enthusiastic admiration for the neglected genius.

The rest of the 'remnant' that was met to save Israel looked more commonplace—a furrier, a slipper-maker, a locksmith, an ex-glazier (Mendel Hyams), a confectioner, a *Melammed*, or Hebrew teacher, a carpenter, a presser, a cigar-maker, a small shopkeeper or two, and last and least, Moses Ansell. They were of many birthplaces—Austria, Holland, Poland, Russia, Germany, Italy, Spain—yet felt themselves of no country and of one. Encircled by the splendours of Modern Babylon, their hearts turned to the East like passion-flowers seeking the sun. Palestine, Jerusalem, Jordan, the Holy Land, were magic syllables to them ; the sight of a coin struck on one of Baron Edmund's colonies filled their eyes with tears ; in death they craved no higher boon than a handful of Palestine earth sprinkled over their graves.

But Guedalyah the Greengrocer was not the man to encourage idle hopes. He explained his scheme lucidly, without high falutin. They were to rebuild Judaism as the coral insect builds its reefs— not, as the prayer went, ' speedily and in our days.'

They had brought themselves up to expect more, and were disappointed. Some protested against peddling little measures ; like Pinchas, they were for high, heroic deeds. Joseph Strelitski, student and cigar commission-agent, jumped to his feet and cried passionately in German : ' Everywhere Israel groans and travails —must we indeed wait and wait till our hearts are sick, and strike never a decisive blow ? It is nigh two thousand years since across the ashes of our holy Temple we were driven into the Exile, clanking the chains of pagan conquerors. For nigh two thousand years have we dwelt on alien soils, a mockery and a byword for the nations, hounded out from every worthy employ and persecuted for turning to the unworthy, spat upon and trodden under foot, suffusing the scroll of history with our blood, and illuminating it with the lurid glare of the fires to which our martyrs have ascended gladly for the Sanctification of the Name. We, who twenty centuries ago were a mighty nation, with a law and a constitution and a religion which have been the key-notes of the civilisation of the world, we who sat in judgment by the gates of great cities, clothed in purple and fine linen, are the sport of peoples who were then roaming wild in woods and marshes, clothed in the skins of the wolf and the bear. Now in the East there gleams again a star of hope, why shall we not follow it ? Never has the chance of the Restoration flamed so high as to-day.   Our capitalists rule the markets of Europe, our generals lead armies, our great men sit in the councils of every State.   We are everywhere—a thousand thousand stray rivulets of power that could be blent into a mighty ocean.   Palestine is one if we wish—the whole house of Israel has but to speak with a mighty unanimous voice.   Poets will sing for us, journalists write for us, diplomatists haggle for us, million-aires pay the price for us.   The Sultan would restore our land to us to-morrow, did we but essay to get it.   There are no obstacles but ourselves.   It is not the heathen that keep us out of our land —it is the Jews, the rich and prosperous Jews, Jeshurun grown fat and sleepy, dreaming the false dream of Assimilation with the people of the pleasant places in which their lines have been cast. Give us back our country ; this alone will solve the Jewish question. Our paupers shall become agriculturists, and like Antæus, the genius of Israel shall gain fresh strength by contact with Mother Earth.   And for England it will help to solve the Indian question. Between European Russia and India there will be planted a people fierce, terrible, hating Russia for her wild-beast deeds.   And if we cannot buy it back with gold, we must buy it back with steel. Into the Exile we took with us, of all our glories, only a spark of the fire by which our Temple, the abode of our great One, was engirdled, and this little spark kept us alive while the towers of our enemies crumbled to dust, and this spark leapt into celestial flame, and shed light upon the faces of the heroes of our race, and inspired them to endure the horrors of the Dance of Death and the tortures of the *auto-da-fé*.   Let us fan the spark again, till it leap up and become a pillar of flame, going before us and showing us the way to Jerusalem, the city of our sires.   As the national poet of Israel, Naphtali Herz Imber, has so nobly sung.'   Here he broke into the Hebrew *Wacht am Rhein*, of which an English version would run thus :

THE WATCH ON THE JORDAN.

I.

Like the crash of the thunder
Which splitteth asunder
  The flame of the cloud,
On our ears ever falling,
A voice is heard calling
  From Zion aloud.

' Let your spirits' desires
For the land of your sires
   Eternally burn.
From the foe to deliver
Our own holy river,
   To Jordan return.'
Where the soft-flowing stream
Murmurs low as in dream,
There set we our watch !
Our watchword, ' The sword
Of our land and our Lord ' :
By Jordan then set we our watch.

II.

Rest in peace, lovèd land,
For we rest not, but stand,
   Off-shaken our sloth.
When the bolts of war rattle
To shirk not the battle,
   We make thee our oath.
As we hope for a heaven,
Thy chains shall be riven,
   Thine ensign unfurled.
And in pride of our race
We will fearlessly face
   The might of the world.
When our trumpet is blown,
And our standard is flown,
   Then set we our watch !
Our watchword, ' The sword
Of our land and our Lord ' :
By Jordan then set we our watch.

III.

Yea, as long as there be
Birds in air, fish in sea,
   And blood in our veins ;
And the lions in might,
Leaping down from the height,
   Shake, roaring, their manes ;
And the dew nightly laves
The forgotten old graves
   Where Judah's sires sleep,
We swear, who are living,
To rest not in striving,
   To pause not to weep.
Let the trumpet be blown,
Let the standard be flown,
   Now set we our watch !
Our watchword, ' The sword
Of our land and our Lord ' :
In Jordan now set we our watch.

He sank upon the rude wooden bench, exhausted, his eyes glittering, his raven hair dishevelled by the wildness of his gestures. He had said. For the rest of the evening he neither moved nor spake. The calm, good-humoured tones of Simon Gradkoski followed like a cold shower.

'We must be sensible,' he said, for he enjoyed the reputation of a shrewd conciliatory man of the world as well as of a pillar of orthodoxy. 'The great people will come to us, but not if we abuse them. We must flatter them up, and tell them they are the descendants of the Maccabees. There is much political kudos to be got out of leading such a movement; this, too, they will see. Rome was not built in a day, and the Temple will not be rebuilt in a year. Besides, we are not soldiers now. We must recapture our land by brain, not sword. Slow and sure, and the blessing of God over all.'

After such wise Simon Gradkoski. But Gronovitz, the Hebrew teacher, crypto-atheist and overt revolutionary, who read a Hebrew edition of the *Pickwick Papers* in synagogue on the Day of Atonement, was with Joseph Strelitski, and a bigot whose religion made his wife and children wretched was with the cautious Simon Gradkoski. Froom Karlkammer followed, but his drift was uncertain. He apparently looked forward to miraculous interpositions. Still, he approved of the movement from one point of view. The more Jews lived in Jerusalem, the more would be enabled to die there, which was the aim of a good Jew's life. As for the Messiah, he would come assuredly 'in God's good time.' Thus Karlkammer at enormous length, with frequent intervals of unintelligibility and huge chunks of irrelevant quotation and much play of cabalistic conceptions. Pinchas, who had been fuming throughout this speech, for to him Karlkammer stood for the archetype of all donkeys, jumped up impatiently when Karlkammer paused for breath, and then denounced as an interruption that gentleman's indignant continuance of his speech. The sense of the meeting was with the poet, and Karlkammer was silenced. Pinchas was dithyrambic, sublime, with audacities which only genius can venture on. He was pungently merry over Imber's pretensions to be the National Poet of Israel, declaring that his prosody, his vocabulary, and even his grammar, were beneath contempt. He, Pinchas, would write Judea a real patriotic poem, which should be sung from the slums of Whitechapel to the *veldts* of South Africa, and from the *Mellah* of Morocco to the Judengassen of Germany, and should gladden the hearts and break from the mouths of the poor immigrants saluting the statue of Liberty in New York harbour. When he, Pinchas, walked in Victoria Park of a Sunday afternoon and heard the band play, the sound of the cornet always seemed to him, said he, like the sound of Bar Cochba's trumpet calling the warriors to battle. And when it was all over, and the band played 'God save the Queen,' it sounded like the pæan of victory when he marched, a conqueror, to the gates of Jerusalem. Wherefore he, Pinchas, would be their leader. Had not the Providence which concealed so many revelations in the letters of the Torah given him the name Melchitzedek Pinchas, whereof one initial stood for Messiah and the other for Palestine? Yes, he would be their Messiah. But money nowadays was the sinews of war, and the first step to Messiahship was the keeping of the funds. The Redeemer must in the first instance be the treasurer. With this anti-climax Pinchas wound up, his childishness and *naïveté* conquering his cunning.

Other speakers followed, but in the end Guedalyah the Greengrocer prevailed. They appointed him President, and Simon Gradkoski Treasurer, collecting twenty-five shillings on the spot, ten from the lad Raphael Leon. In vain Pinchas reminded the President they would need Collectors to make house-to-house calls ; three other members were chosen to trisect the Ghetto. All felt the incongruity of hanging money-bags at the saddle-bow of Pegasus. Whereupon Pinchas re-lit his cigar, and, muttering that they were all fool-men, betook himself unceremoniously without.

Gabriel Hamburg looked on throughout with something like a smile on his shrivelled features. Once while Joseph Strelitski was holding forth he blew his nose violently. Perhaps he had taken too large a pinch of snuff. But not a word did the great scholar speak. He would give up his last breath to promote the Return (provided the Hebrew manuscripts were not left behind in alien museums) ; but the humours of the enthusiasts were part of the great comedy in the only theatre he cared for. Mendel Hyams was another silent member. But he wept openly under Strelitski's harangue.

When the meeting adjourned, the lank, unhealthy, swaying creature in the corner, who had been mumbling the tractate Baba Kama out of courtesy, now burst out afresh in his quaint argumentative recitative :

' What, then, does it refer to ? To his stone, or his knife, or his burden, which he has left on the highway, and it injured a passerby. How is this ? If he gave up his ownership thereof, whether according to Rav or according to Shemuel, it is a pit, and if he retained his ownership, if according to Shemuel, who holds that all are derived from "his pit," then it is "a pit." And if according to Rav, who holds that all are derived from "his ox," then it is "an ox," therefore the derivatives of "an ox" are the same as "an ox" itself.'

He had been at it all day, and he went on far into the small hours, shaking his body backwards and forwards without remission.

CHAPTER XVI

THE COURTSHIP OF SHOSSHI SHMENDRIK

MECKISH was a Chassid, which in the vernacular is a saint, but in the actual a member of the sect of the Chassidim, whose centre is Galicia. In the eighteenth century Israel Baalshem, 'the Master of the Name,' retired to the mountains to meditate on philosophical truths.   He arrived at a creed of cheerful and even stoical acceptance of the cosmos in all its aspects, and a conviction that the incense of an enjoyed pipe was grateful to the Creator.   But it is the inevitable misfortune of religious founders to work apocryphal miracles, and to raise up an army of disciples who squeeze the teaching of their master into their own mental moulds, and are ready to die for the resultant distortion.   It is only by being misunderstood that a great man can have any influence upon his kind.   Baalshem was succeeded by an army of thaumaturgists, and the wonder-working Rabbis of Sadagora, who are in touch with all the spirits of the air, enjoy the revenue of princes and the reverence of popes.   To snatch a morsel of such a Rabbi's Sabbath *Kuggol*, or pudding, is to ensure paradise, and the scramble is a scene to witness.   Chassidism is the extreme expression of Jewish optimism.   The Chassidim are the Corybantes or Salvationists of Judaism.   In England their idiosyncrasies are limited to noisy jubilant services in their *Chevrah*, the worshippers dancing, or leaning, or standing, or writhing, or beating their heads against the wall as they will, and playing like happy children in the presence of their Father.

Meckish also danced at home and sang ' Tiddy, riddy, roi, toi, toi, toi, ta,' varied by ' Rom, pom, pom ' and ' Bim-bom ' in a quaint melody, to express his personal satisfaction with existence.   He was a weazened little widower with a deep yellow complexion, prominent cheek-bones, a hook nose, and a scrubby, straggling little beard.   Years of professional practice as a mendicant had stamped his face with an anguished, suppliant, conciliatory grin, which he could not now erase even after business hours.   It might, perhaps, have yielded to soap and water, but the experiment had not been tried.   On his head he always wore a fur cap, with lappets for his ears.   Across his shoulders was strung a lemon-basket filled with grimy, gritty bits of sponge, which nobody ever bought.   Meckish's merchandise was quite other.   He dealt in sensational spectacle.   As he shambled along with extreme difficulty and by the aid of a stick, his lower limbs, which were crossed in odd contortions, appeared half paralysed, and when his strange appearance had attracted attention, his legs would give way, and he would find himself with his back on the pavement, where he waited to be picked up by sympathetic spectators shedding silver and copper.   After an indefinite number of performances, Meckish would hurry home in the darkness, to dance and sing ' Tiddy, riddy, roi, toi, Bim-bom.'

Thus Meckish lived at peace with God and man, till one day the fatal thought came into his head that he wanted a second wife.   There was no difficulty in getting one—by the aid of his friend, Sugarman the Shadchan—and soon the little man found his household goods increased by the possession of a fat Russian giantess.   Meckish did not call in the authorities to marry him ; he had a ' still wedding,' which cost nothing.   An artificial canopy, made out of a sheet and four broomsticks, was erected in the chimney-corner, and nine male friends sanctified the ceremony by their presence. Meckish and the Russian giantess fasted on their wedding-morn, and everything was in honourable order.

But Meckish's happiness and economies were short-lived. The Russian giantess turned out a Tartar. She got her claws into his savings, and decorated herself with Paisley shawls and gold necklaces. Nay, more! She insisted that Meckish must give her 'society,' and keep open house. Accordingly the bed-sitting room which they rented was turned into a salon of reception, and hither one Friday night came Peleg Shmendrik and his wife, and Mr. and Mrs. Sugarman. Over the Sabbath meal the current of talk divided itself into masculine and feminine freshets. The ladies discussed bonnets, and the gentlemen Talmud. All the three men dabbled, pettily enough, in stocks and shares, but nothing in the world would tempt them to transact any negotiation or discuss the merits of a prospectus on the Sabbath, though they were all fluttered by the allurements of the Sapphire Mines, Limited, as set forth in a whole page of advertisement in the *Jewish Chronicle*, the organ naturally perused for its religious news on Friday evenings. The share-list would close at noon on Monday.

'But when Moses, our teacher, struck the rock,' said Peleg Shmendrik, in the course of the discussion, 'he was right the first time, but wrong the second, because, as the Talmud points out, a child may be chastised when it is little, but as it grows up it should be reasoned with.'

'Yes,' said Sugarman the Shadchan quickly; 'but if his rod had not been made of sapphire he would have split that instead of the rock.'

'Was it made of sapphire?' asked Meckish, who was rather a Man-of-the-Earth.

'Of course it was, and a very fine thing, too,' answered Sugarman.

'Do you think so?' inquired Peleg Shmendrik eagerly.

'The sapphire is a magic stone,' answered Sugarman. 'It improves the vision, and makes peace between foes. Issachar, the studious son of Jacob, was represented on the breast-plate by the sapphire. Do you not know that the mist-like centre of the sapphire symbolizes the cloud that enveloped Sinai at the giving of the Law?'

'I did not know that,' answered Peleg Shmendrik; 'but I know that Moses's rod was created in the twilight of the first Sabbath, and God did everything after that with this sceptre.'

'Ah, but we are not all strong enough to wield Moses's rod; it weighs forty seahs,' said Sugarman.

'How many seahs do you think one could carry safely?' asked Meckish.

'Five or six seahs—not more,' said Sugarman. 'You see, one might drop them if he attempted more, and even sapphire may break. The first Tables of the Law were made of sapphire, and yet from a great height they fell terribly, and were shattered to pieces.'

'Gideon the M.P. may be said to desire a rod of Moses, for his secretary told me he will take forty,' said Shmendrik.

'Hush ! what are you saying?' cried Sugarman. 'Gideon is a rich man ; and, then, he is a director.'

'It seems a good lot of directors,' said Meckish.

'Good to look at. But who can tell?' said Sugarman, shaking his head. 'The Queen of Sheba probably brought sapphires to Solomon, but she was not a virtuous woman.'

'Ah, Solomon !' sighed Mrs. Shmendrik, pricking up her ears and interrupting this talk of stocks and stones. 'If he'd had a thousand daughters instead of a thousand wives, even his Treasury couldn't have held out. I had only two girls—praised be He !—and yet it nearly ruined me to buy them husbands. A dirty *Greener* comes over, without a shirt to his skin, and forsooth nothing else but he must have two hundred pounds in the hand. And then you've got to stick to his back to see that he doesn't take his breeches in his hand and off to America. In Poland he would have been glad to get a maiden, and would have said " Thank you."'

'Well, but what about your own son?' said Sugarman. 'Why haven't you asked me to find Shosshi a wife? It's a sin against the maidens of Israel. He must be long past the Talmudical age.'

'He is twenty-four,' said Peleg Shmendrik.

'Tu, tu, tu, tu, tu !' said Sugarman, clacking his tongue in horror. 'Have you, perhaps, an objection to his marrying?'

'Save us and grant us peace !' cried the father in deprecatory horror. 'Only Shosshi is so shy. You are aware, too, he is not handsome. Heaven alone knows whom he takes after !'

'Peleg, I blush for you !' said Mrs. Shmendrik. 'What is the matter with the boy? Is he deaf, dumb, blind, unprovided with legs ? If Shosshi is backward with the women, it is because he "learns" so hard when he's not at work. He earns a good living by his cabinet-making, and it is quite time he set up a Jewish household for himself. How much will you want for finding him a *Calloh*?'

'Hush !' said Sugarman sternly. 'Do you forget it is the Sabbath ? Be assured I shall not charge more than last time, unless the bride has an extra good dowry.'

On Saturday night, immediately after *Havdalah*, Sugarman went to Mr. Belcovitch, who was just about to resume work, and informed him he had seen the very *Chosan* for Becky.

'I know,' he said, 'Becky has a lot of young men after her, but what are they but a pack of bare-backs ? How much dowry will you give for a solid man ?'

After much haggling, Belcovitch consented to give twenty

pounds immediately before the marriage ceremony, and another twenty at the end of twelve months.

'But no pretending you haven't got it about you when we're at the *Shool*, no asking us to wait till we get home,' said Sugarman, 'or else I withdraw my man, even from under the *Chuppah* itself. When shall I bring him for your inspection?'

'Oh, to-morrow afternoon—Sunday—when Becky will be out in the park with her young men. It's best I shall see him first.'

Sugarman now regarded Shosshi as a married man. He rubbed his hands and went to see him. He found him in a little shed in the back-yard, where he did extra work at home. Shosshi was busy completing little wooden articles—stools and wooden spoons and money-boxes—for sale in Petticoat Lane next day. He supplemented his wages that way.

'Good-evening, Shossi,' said Sugarman.

'Good-evening,' murmured Shosshi, sawing away.

Shosshi was a gawky young man, with a blotched, sandy face, ever ready to blush deeper with the suspicion that conversations going on at a distance were all about him. His eyes were shifty and cat-like ; one shoulder over-balanced the other, and when he walked he swayed loosely to and fro. Sugarman was rarely remiss in the offices of piety, and he was nigh murmuring the prayer at the sight of monstrosities : 'Blessed art Thou who variest the creatures.' But, resisting the temptation, he said aloud :

'I have something to tell you.'

Shosshi looked up suspiciously.

Don't bother ; I am busy,' he said, and applied his plane to the leg of a stool.

'But this is more important than stools. How would you like to get married?'

Shosshi's face became like a peony.

'Don't make laughter,' he said.

'But I mean it. You are twenty-four years old, and ought to have a wife and four children by this time.'

'But I don't want a wife and four children,' said Shosshi.

'No, of course not. I don't mean a widow. It is a maiden I have in my eye.'

'Nonsense ! what maiden would have me ?' said Shosshi, a note of eagerness mingling with the diffidence of the words.

'What maiden? *Gott in Himmel!* A hundred ! A fine, strong, healthy young man like you, who can make a good living !'

Shosshi put down his plane and straightened himself. There was a moment of silence. Then his frame collapsed again into a limp mass. His head drooped over his left shoulder.

'This is all foolishness you talk. The maidens make mock.'

'Be not a piece of clay ! I know a maiden who has you quite in affection.'

The blush which had waned mantled in a full flood. Shosshi

stood breathless, gazing, half suspiciously, half credulously, at his strictly honourable Mephistopheles.

It was about seven o'clock, and the moon was a yellow crescent in the frosty heavens. The sky was punctured with clear-cut constellations. The back-yard looked poetic with its blend of shadow and moonlight.

'A beautiful fine maid,' said Sugarman ecstatically, 'with pink cheeks and black eyes and forty pounds dowry.

The moon sailed smilingly along. The water was running into the cistern with a soothing, peaceful sound. Shosshi consented to go and see Mr. Belcovitch.

Mr. Belcovitch made no parade. Everything was as usual. On the wooden table were two halves of squeezed lemons, a piece of chalk, two cracked cups, and some squashed soap. He was not overwhelmed by Shosshi, but admitted he was solid. His father was known to be pious, and both his sisters had married reputable men. Above all, he was not a Dutchman. Shosshi left No. 1 Royal Street, Belcovitch's accepted son-in-law. Esther met him on the stairs, and noticed the radiance on his pimply countenance. He walked with his head almost erect. Shosshi was indeed very much in love, and felt that all that was needed for his happiness was a sight of his future wife.

But he had no time to go and see her except on Sunday afternoons, and then she was always out. Mrs. Belcovitch, however, made amends by paying him considerable attention. The sickly-looking little woman chatted to him for hours at a time about her ailments, and invited him to taste her medicine, which was a compliment Mrs. Belcovitch passed only to her most esteemed visitors. By-and-by she even wore her night-cap in his presence, as a sign that he had become one of the family. Under this encouragement Shosshi grew confidential, and imparted to his future mother-in-law the details of his mother's disabilities. But he could mention nothing which Mrs. Belcovitch could not cap, for she was a woman extremely catholic in her maladies. She was possessed of considerable imagination, and once when Fanny selected a bonnet for her in a milliner's window, the girl had much difficulty in persuading her it was not inferior to what turned out to be the reflection of itself in a side mirror.

'I'm so weak upon my legs,' she would boast to Shosshi. 'I was born with ill-matched legs. One is a thick one and one is a thin one. And so one goes about.'

Shosshi expressed his sympathetic admiration, and the courtship proceeded apace. Sometimes Fanny and Pesach Weingott would be at home working, and they were very affable to him. He began to lose something of his shyness and his lurching gait, and he quite looked forward to his weekly visit to the Belcovitches. It was the story of Cymon and Iphigenia over again. Love improved even his powers of conversation, for when Belcovitch held forth at length, Shosshi came in several times with 'So?' and sometimes in the right place. Mr. Belcovitch loved his own voice, and listened to it, the arrested press-iron in his hand. Occasionally, in the middle of one of his harangues, it would occur to him that some one was talking and wasting time, and then he would say to the room, 'Shah! make an end, make an end!' and dry up. But to Shosshi he was especially polite, rarely interrupting himself when his son-in-law-elect was hanging on his words. There was an intimate, tender tone about these causeries.

'I should like to drop down dead suddenly,' he would say with the air of a philosopher who had thought it all out. 'I shouldn't care to lie up in bed and mess about with medicine and doctors. To make a long job of dying is so expensive.'

'So?' said Shosshi.

'Don't worry, Bear! I dare say the devil will seize you suddenly,' interposed Mrs. Belcovitch dryly.

'It will not be the devil,' said Mr. Belcovitch confidently, and in a confidential manner. 'If I had died as a young man, Shosshi, it might have been different.'

Shosshi pricked up his ears to listen to the tale of Bear's wild cubhood.

'One morning,' said Belcovitch, 'in Poland, I got up at four o'clock to go to Supplications for Forgiveness. The air was raw, and there was no sign of dawn. Suddenly I noticed a black pig trotting behind me. I quickened my pace, and the black pig did likewise. I broke into a run, and I heard the pig's paws patting furiously upon the hard frozen ground. A cold sweat broke out all over me. I looked over my shoulder, and saw the pig's eyes burning like red-hot coals in the darkness. Then I knew that the Not-Good One was after me. "Hear, O Israel!" I cried. I looked up to the heavens, but there was a cold mist covering the stars. Faster and faster I flew, and faster and faster flew the demon-pig. At last the *Shool* came in sight. I made one last wild effort, and fell exhausted upon the holy threshold, and the pig vanished.'

'So?' said Shosshi, with a long breath.

'Immediately after *Shool* I spake with the Rabbi, and he said, "Bear, are thy *Tephillin* in order?" So I said, "Yea, Rabbi; they are very large, and I bought them of the pious scribe, Naphtali, and I look to the knots weekly." But he said, "I will examine them." So I brought them to him, and he opened the head-phylactery, and, lo! in place of the holy parchment he found breadcrumbs.'

'Hoi, hoi!' said Shosshi in horror, his red hands quivering.

'Yes,' said Bear mournfully, 'I had worn them for ten years; 'and, moreover, the leaven had defiled all my Passovers.'

Belcovitch also entertained the lover with details of the internal politics of the Sons of the Covenant.

Shosshi's affection for Becky increased weekly under the stress of these intimate conversations with her family. At last his passion was rewarded, and Becky, at the violent instance of her father, consented to disappoint one of her young men, and to stay at home to meet her future husband.   She put off her consent till after dinner, though, and it began to rain immediately before she gave it.

The moment Shosshi came into the room he divined that a change had come over the spirit of the dream.   Out of the corners of his eyes he caught a glimpse of an appalling beauty standing behind a sewing-machine.   His face fired up, his legs began to quiver, he wished the ground would open and swallow him as it did Korah.

'Becky,' said Mr. Belcovitch, 'this is Mr. Shosshi Shmendrik.'

Shosshi put on a sickly grin, and nodded his head affirmatively, as if to corroborate the statement, and the round felt hat he wore slid back till the broad brim rested on his ears.   Through a sort of mist, a terribly fine maid loomed.

Becky stared at him haughtily and curled her lip.   Then she giggled.

Shosshi held out his huge red hand limply.   Becky took no notice of it.

'*Nu*, Becky!' breathed Belcovitch, in a whisper that could have been heard across the way.

'How are you?   All right?' said Becky very loud, as if she thought deafness was among Shosshi's disadvantages.

Shosshi grinned reassuringly.

There was another silence.

Shosshi wondered whether the *convenances* would permit him to take his leave now.   He did not feel comfortable at all.   Everything had been going so delightfully, it had been quite a pleasure to him to come to the house.   But now all was changed.   The course of true love never does run smooth, and the advent of this new personage into the courtship was distinctly embarrassing.

The father came to the rescue.

'A little rum?' he said.

'Yes,' said Shosshi.

'Chayah!   *Nu*.   Fetch the bottle.'

Mrs. Belcovitch went to the chest of drawers in the corner of the room and took from the top of it a large decanter.   She then produced two glasses without feet, and filled them with the home-made rum, handing one to Shosshi and the other to her husband. Shosshi muttered a blessing over it, then he leered vacuously at the company and cried, 'To life!'

'To peace!' replied the older man, gulping down the spirit.

Shosshi was doing the same when his eye caught Becky's.   He choked for five minutes, Mrs. Belcovitch thumping him maternally on the back.   When he was comparatively recovered, the sense of his disgrace rushed upon him and overwhelmed him afresh. Becky was still giggling behind the sewing-machine.   Once more Shosshi felt that the burden of the conversation was upon him.

He looked at his boots, and not seeing anything there, looked up again and grinned encouragingly at the company, as if to waive his rights. But finding the company did not respond, he blew his nose enthusiastically, as a lead-off to the conversation.

Mr. Belcovitch saw his embarrassment, and, making a sign to Chayah, slipped out of the room, followed by his wife. Shosshi was left alone with the terribly fine maid.

Becky stood still, humming a little air and looking up at the ceiling, as if she had forgotten Shosshi's existence. With her eyes in that position it was easier for Shosshi to look at her. He stole side-long glances at her, which, growing bolder and bolder, at length fused into an uninterrupted steady gaze.

How fine and beautiful she was ! His eyes began to glitter ; a smile of approbation overspread his face. Suddenly she looked down and their eyes met. Shosshi's smile hurried off and gave way to a sickly, sheepish look, and his legs felt weak. The terribly fine maid gave a kind of snort, and resumed her inspection of the ceiling. Gradually Shosshi found himself examining her again. Verily Sugarman had spoken truly of her charms. But—overwhelming thought !—had not Sugarman also said she loved him ? Shosshi knew nothing of the ways of girls, except what he had learned from the Talmud. Quite possibly Becky was now occupied in expressing ardent affection. He shuffled towards her, his heart beating violently. He was near enough to touch her. The air she was humming throbbed in his ears. He opened his mouth to speak—Becky, becoming suddenly aware of his proximity, fixed him with a basilisk glare—the words were frozen on his lips. For some seconds his mouth remained open, then the ridiculousness of shutting it again without speaking spurred him on to make some sound, however meaningless. He made a violent effort, and there burst from his lips in Hebrew :

' " Happy are those who dwell in Thy house ; ever shall they praise Thee—Selah ! " '   It was not a compliment to Becky. Shosshi's face lit up with joyous relief. By some inspiration he had started the afternoon prayer. He felt that Becky would understand the pious necessity. With fervent gratitude to the Almighty he continued the Psalm : ' Happy are the people whose lot is thus,' etc.   Then he turned his back on Becky, with his face to the east wall, made three steps forwards and commenced the silent delivery of the *Amidah*.   Usually he gabbled off the ' Eighteen Blessings ' in five minutes.   To-day they were prolonged till he heard the footsteps of the returning parents.   Then he scurried through the relics of the service at lightning speed. When Mr. and Mrs. Belcovitch re-entered the room, they saw by his happy face that all was well, and made no opposition to his instant departure.

He came again the next Sunday, and was rejoiced to find that Becky was out, though he had hoped to find her in. The courtship made great strides that afternoon, Mr. and Mrs. Belcovitch being more amiable than ever, to compensate for Becky's private refusal to entertain the addresses of such a *Shmuck*.   There had been sharp domestic discussions during the week, and Becky had only sniffed at her parents' commendations of Shosshi as a 'very worthy youth.'   She declared that it was 'remission of sins merely to look at him.'

Next Sabbath Mr. and Mrs. Belcovitch paid a formal visit to Shosshi's parents to make their acquaintance, and partook of tea and cake.   Becky was not with them ; moreover, she defiantly declared she would never be at home on a Sunday till Shosshi was married.   They circumvented her by getting him up on a weekday.   The image of Becky had been so often in his thoughts now, that by the time he saw her the second time he was quite habituated to her appearance.   He had even imagined his arm round her waist, but in practice he found he could go no further as yet than ordinary conversation.

Becky was sitting sewing buttonholes when Shosshi arrived. Everybody was there : Mr. Belcovitch pressing coats with hot irons ; Fanny shaking the room with her heavy machine ; Pesach Weingott cutting a piece of chalk-marked cloth ; Mrs. Belcovitch carefully pouring out tablespoonfuls of medicine.   There were even some outside 'hands,' work being unusually plentiful, as from the manifestoes of Simon Wolf, the labour-leader, the slop manufacturers anticipated a strike.

Sustained by their presence, Shosshi felt a bold and gallant wooer.   He determined that this time he would not go without having addressed at least one remark to the object of his affections. Grinning amiably at the company generally, by way of salutation, he made straight for Becky's corner.   The terribly fine lady snorted at the sight of him, divining that she had been out-manœuvred.   Belcovitch surveyed the situation out of the corners of his eyes, not pausing a moment in his task.

'*Nu*, how goes it, Becky?' Shosshi murmured.

Becky said :

'All right ; how are you ?'

'God be thanked, I have nothing to complain of,' said Shosshi, encouraged by the warmth of his welcome.   'My eyes are rather weak still, though much better than last year.'

Becky made no reply, so Shosshi continued :

'But my mother is always a sick person.   She has to swallow bucketfuls of cod-liver oil.   She cannot be long for this world.'

'Nonsense, nonsense !' put in Mrs. Belcovitch, appearing suddenly behind the lovers.   'My children's children shall never be any worse ; it 's all fancy with her, she coddles herself too much.'

'Oh no, she says she 's much worse than you.'   Shosshi blurted out, turning round to face his future mother-in-law.

'Oh, indeed !' said Chayah angrily.   'My enemies shall have my maladies !   If your mother had my health, she would be lying in bed with it. But I go about in a sick condition. I can hardly crawl around. Look at my legs ; has your mother got such legs ? One a thick one, and one a thin one.'

Shosshi grew scarlet ; he felt he had blundered. It was the first real shadow on his courtship, perhaps the little rift within the lute. He turned back to Becky for sympathy. There was no Becky. She had taken advantage of the conversation to slip away. He found her again in a moment, though, at the other end of the room. She was seated before a machine. He crossed the room boldly and bent over her.

'Don't you feel cold, working?'

Br-r-r-r-r-h !

It was the machine turning. Becky had set the treadle going madly, and was pushing a piece of cloth under the needle. When she paused, Shosshi said :

'Have you heard Reb Shemuel preach? He told a very amusing allegory last——'

Br-r-r-r-r-h !

Undaunted, Shosshi recounted the amusing allegory at length, and as the noise of her machine prevented Becky hearing a word, she found his conversation endurable. After several more monologues, accompanied on the machine by Becky, Shosshi took his departure in high feather, promising to bring up specimens of his handiwork for her edification.

On his next visit, he arrived with his arms laden with choice morsels of carpentry. He laid them on the table for her admiration.

They were odd knobs and rockers for Polish cradles ! The pink of Becky's cheeks spread all over her face like a blot of red ink on a piece of porous paper. Shosshi's face reflected the colour in even more ensanguined dyes. Becky rushed from the room, and Shosshi heard her giggling madly on the staircase. It dawned upon him that he had displayed bad taste in his selection.

'What have you done to my child?' Mrs. Belcovitch inquired.

'N-n-othing,' he stammered ; 'I only brought her some of my work to see.'

'And is this what one shows to a young girl?' demanded the mother indignantly.

'They are only bits of cradles,' said Shosshi deprecatingly. 'I thought she would like to see what nice workmanly things I turned out. See how smoothly these rockers are carved ! Here is a thick one and there is a thin one !'

'Ah, shameless droll ! dost thou make mock of my legs too?' said Mrs. Belcovitch. 'Out, impudent face, out with thee !'

Shosshi gathered up his specimens in his arms and fled through the door. Becky was still in hilarious eruption outside. The sight of her made confusion worse confounded. The knobs and rockers rolled thunderously down the stairs; Shosshi stumbled after them, picking them up on his course, and wishing himself dead.

All Sugarman's strenuous efforts to patch up the affair failed. Shosshi went about broken-hearted for several days. To have been so near the goal, and then not to arrive after all ! What made failure more bitter was that he had boasted of his conquest to his 'acquaintances, especially to the two who kept the stalls to the right and left of him on Sundays in Petticoat Lane. They made a butt of him as it was ; he felt he could never stand between them for a whole morning now, and have Attic salt put upon his wounds. He shifted his position, arranging to pay six-pence a time for the privilege of fixing himself outside Widow Finkelstein's shop, which stood at the corner of a street and might be presumed to intercept two streams of pedestrians. Widow Finkelstein's shop was a chandler's, and she did a large business in farthing-worths of boiling water. There was thus no possible rivalry between her ware and Shosshi's, which consisted of wooden candlesticks, little rocking-chairs, stools, ash-trays, etc., piled up artistically on a barrow.

But Shosshi's luck had gone with the change of *locus.* His clientèle went to the old spot, but did not find him. He did not even make a hansel. At two o'clock he tied his articles to the barrow with a complicated arrangement of cords. Widow Finkel-stein waddled out and demanded her sixpence. Shosshi replied that he had not taken sixpence, that the coign was not one of vantage. Widow Finkelstein stood up for her rights, and even hung on to the barrow for them. There was a short sharp argu-ment, a simultaneous jabbering as of a pair of monkeys. Shosshi Shmendrik's pimply face worked with excited expostulation ; Widow Finkelstein's cushion-like countenance was agitated by waves of righteous indignation. Suddenly Shosshi darted between the shafts and made a dash off with the barrow down the side street. But Widow Finkelstein pressed it down with all her force, arresting the motion like a drag. Incensed by the laughter of the spectators, Shosshi put forth all his strength at the shafts, jerked the widow off her feet, and see-sawed her skywards, huddled up spherically like a balloon, but clinging as grimly as ever to the defalcating barrow. Then Shosshi started off at a run, the car-pentry rattling, and the dead weight of his living burden making his muscles ache.

Right to the end of the street he dragged her, pursued by a hooting crowd. Then he stopped, worn out.

'Will you give me that sixpence, you *gonof* ?'

' No, I haven't got it. You'd better go back to your shop, else you'll suffer from worse thieves.'

It was true. Widow Finkelstein smote her wig in horror, and hurried back to purvey treacle.

But that night when she had put up the shutters she hurried off to Shosshi's address, which she had learnt in the interim. His little brother opened the door and said Shosshi was in the shed.

He was just nailing the thicker of those rockers on to the body of a cradle. His soul was full of bitter-sweet memories. Widow Finkelstein suddenly appeared in the moonlight. For a moment Shosshi's heart beat wildly. He thought the buxom figure was Becky's.

'I have come for my sixpence!'

Ah! The words awoke him from his dream. It was only the Widow Finkelstein.

And yet—— Verily the widow, too, was plump and agreeable. If only her errand had been pleasant, Shosshi felt she might have brightened his back-yard. He had been moved to his depths latterly, and a new tenderness and a new boldness towards women shone in his eyes.

He rose and put his head on one side and smiled amiably, and said:

'Be not so foolish. I did not take a copper. I am a poor young man. You have plenty of money in your stocking.'

'How know you that?' said the widow, stretching forward her right foot meditatively, and gazing at the strip of stocking revealed.

'Never mind,' said Shosshi, shaking his head sapiently.

'Well, it is true,' she admitted. 'I have two hundred and seventeen golden sovereigns besides my shop. But for all that, why should you keep my sixpence?' She asked it with the same good-humoured smile.

The logic of that smile was unanswerable. Shosshi's mouth opened, but no sound issued from it. He did not even say the evening prayer. The moon sailed slowly across the heavens. The water flowed into the cistern with a soft soothing sound.

Suddenly it occurred to Shosshi that the widow's waist was not very unlike that which he had engirdled imaginatively. He thought he would just try if the sensation was anything like what he had fancied. His arm strayed timidly round her black-beaded mantle. The sense of his audacity was delicious. He was wondering whether he ought to say *Shehechyoni*—the prayer over a new pleasure. But the Widow Finkelstein stopped his mouth with a kiss. After that Shosshi forgot his pious instincts.

Except Mrs. Ansell, Sugarman was the only person scandalised. Shosshi's irrepressible spirit of romance had robbed him of his commission. But Meckish danced with Shosshi Shmendrik at the wedding while the *Calloh* footed it with the Russian giantess. The men danced in one half of the room, the women in the other.

CHAPTER XVII

THE HYAMSES' HONEYMOON

'BEENAH, hast thou heard aught about our Daniel?'

There was a note of anxiety in old Hyams's voice.

'Naught, Mendel.'

'Thou hast not heard talk of him and Sugarman's daughter?'

'No ; is there aught between them ?'

The listless old woman spoke a little eagerly.

'Only that a man told me that his son saw our Daniel pay court to the maiden.'

'Where ?'

'At the Purim ball.'

'The man is a fool; a youth must dance with some maiden or the other.'

Miriam came in, fagged out from teaching. Old Hyams dropped from Yiddish into English.

'You are right. He must.'

Beenah replied in her slow painful English :

'Would he not have told us ?'

Mendel repeated :

'Would he not have told us ?'

Each avoided the other's eye. Beenah dragged herself about the room, laying Miriam's tea.

'Mother, I wish you wouldn't scrape your feet along the floor so. It gets on my nerves, and I *am* so worn out. Would he not have told you what ? And who's he ?'

Beenah looked at her husband.

'I heard Daniel was engaged,' said old Hyams jerkily.

Miriam started and flushed.

'To whom ?' she cried in excitement.

'Bessie Sugarman.'

'Sugarman's daughter ?' Miriam's voice was pitched high.

'Yes.'

Miriam's voice rose to a higher pitch.

'Sugarman the Shadchan's daughter ?'

'Yes.'

Miriam burst into a fit of incredulous laughter.

'As if Daniel would marry into a miserable family like that.'

'It is as good as ours,' said Mendel, with white lips.

His daughter looked at him, astonished.

'I thought your children had taught you more self-respect than that,' she said quietly. 'Mr. Sugarman is a nice person to be related to !'

'At home Mrs. Sugarman's family was highly respected,' quavered old Hyams.

'We are not at home now,' said Miriam witheringly ; 'we're in England. A bad-tempered old hag !'

'That is what she thinks me,' thought Mrs. Hyams, but she said nothing.

'Did you not see Daniel with her at the ball ?' said Mr. Hyams, still visibly disquieted.

'I'm sure I didn't notice,' Miriam replied petulantly. 'I think you must have forgot the sugar, mother, or else the tea is viler than usual. Why don't you let Jane cut the bread-and-butter instead of lazing in the kitchen ?'

'Jane has been washing all day in the scullery,' said Mrs. Hyams apologetically.

'H'm!' snapped Miriam, her pretty face looking peevish and careworn. Jane ought to have to manage sixty-three girls, whose ignorant parents let them run wild at home and haven't the least idea of discipline. As for this chit of a Sugarman, don't you know that Jews always engage every fellow and girl that look at each other across the street, and make fun of them and discuss their united prospects before they are even introduced to each other?'

She finished her tea, changed her dress, and went off to the theatre with a girl-friend. The really harassing nature of her work called for some such recreation. Daniel came in a little after she had gone out, and ate his supper, which was his dinner saved for him and warmed up in the oven.

Mendel sat studying from an unwieldy folio, which he held on his lap by the fireside, and bent over. When Daniel had done supper and was standing yawning and stretching himself, Mendel said suddenly, as if trying to bluff him:

'Why don't you ask your father to wish you *Mazzoltov*?'

'*Mazzoltov?* What for?' asked Daniel puzzled.

'On your engagement.'

'My engagement!' repeated Daniel, his heart thumping against his ribs.

'Yes; to Bessie Sugarman.'

Mendel's eye, fixed scrutinizingly on his boy's face, saw it pass from white to red and from red to white. Daniel caught hold of the mantel as if to steady himself.

'But it is a lie!' he cried hotly. Who told you that?'

'No one; a man hinted as much.'

'But I haven't even been in her company.'

'Yes; at the Purim ball.'

Daniel bit his lip.

'Damned gossips!' he cried. 'I'll never speak to the girl again.'

There was a tense silence for a few seconds, then old Hyams said:

'Why not? You love her.'

Daniel stared at him, his heart palpitating painfully; the blood in his ears throbbed mad, sweet music.

'You love her,' Mendel repeated quietly. 'Why do you not ask her to marry you? Do you fear she would refuse?'

Daniel burst into half-hysterical laughter. Then, seeing his father's half-reproachful, half-puzzled look, he said shamefacedly:

'Forgive me, father; I really couldn't help it. The idea of your talking about love! The oddity of it came over me all of a heap.'

'Why should I not talk about love?'

'Don't be so comically serious, father,' said Daniel, smiling afresh. What's come over you? What have you to do with love? One would think you were a romantic young fool on the stage. It's all nonsense about love. I don't love anybody, least of all Bessie Sugarman, so don't you go worrying your old head about *my* affairs. You get back to that musty book of yours there—I wonder if you 've suddenly come across anything about love in that —and don't forget to use the reading-glasses, and not your ordinary spectacles, else it 'll be a sheer waste of money. By the way, mother, remember to go to the Eye Hospital, on Saturday, to be tested. I feel sure it 's time you had a pair of specs, too.'

'Don't I look old enough already?' thought Mrs. Hyams. But she said, 'Very well, Daniel,' and began to clear away his supper.

'That's the best of being in the fancy,' said Daniel cheerfully. 'There's no end of articles you can get at trade prices.'

He sat for half an hour turning over the evening paper, then went to bed. Mr. and Mrs. Hyams's eyes sought each other involuntarily, but they said nothing. Mrs. Hyams fried a piece of *Wurst* for Miriam's supper and put it into the oven to keep hot ; then she sat down opposite Mendel to stitch on a strip of fur, which had got unripped, on one of Miriam's jackets. The fire burnt briskly, little flames leapt up with a crackling sound, the clock ticked quietly.

Beenah threaded her needle at the first attempt.

'I can still see without spectacles,' she thought bitterly, but she said nothing.

Mendel looked up furtively at her several times from his book. The meagreness of her parchment flesh, the thickening mesh of wrinkles, the snow-white hair, struck him with almost novel force. But he said nothing. Beenah patiently drew her needle through and through the fur, ever and anon glancing at Mendel's worn, spectacled face—the eyes deep in the sockets, the forehead that was bent over the folio furrowed painfully beneath the black *Koppel*, the complexion sickly. A lump seemed to be rising in her throat. She bent determinedly over her sewing, then suddenly looked up again. This time their eyes met. They did not droop them ; a strange subtle flash seemed to pass from soul to soul. They gazed at each other, trembling on the brink of tears.

'Beenah.'

The voice was thick with suppressed sobs.

'Yes, Mendel.'

'Thou has heard?'

'Yes, Mendel.'

'He says he loves her not.'

'So he says.'

'It is lies, Beenah.'

'But wherefore should he lie?'

'Thou askest with thy mouth, not thy heart. Thou knowest that he wishes us not to think that he remains single for our sake. All his money goes to keep up this house we live in. It is the Law of Moses. Sawest thou not his face when I spake of Sugarman's daughter?'

Beenah rocked herself to and fro, crying :

'My poor Daniel! My poor lamb! Wait a little. I shall die soon. The All-High is merciful. Wait a little.'

Mendel caught Miriam's jacket, which was slipping to the floor, and laid it aside.

'It helps not to cry,' he said gently, longing to cry with her. 'This cannot be. He must marry the maiden whom his heart desires. Is it not enough that he feels we have crippled his life for the sake of our Sabbath? He never speaks of it, but it smoulders in his veins.'

'Wait a little!' moaned Beenah, still rocking to and fro.

'Nay, calm thyself.' He rose, and passed his horny hand tenderly over her white hair. 'We must not wait. Consider how long Daniel has waited.'

'Yes, my poor lamb, my poor lamb!' sobbed the old woman.

'If Daniel marries,' said the old man, striving to speak firmly, we have not a penny to live upon. Our Miriam requires all her salary. Already she gives us more than she can spare. She is a lady, in a great position. She must dress finely. Who knows, too, but that we are in the way of a gentleman marrying her? We are not fit to mix with high people. But, above all, Daniel must marry, and I must earn your and my living as I did when the children were young.'

'But what wilt thou do?' said Beenah, ceasing to cry, and looking up with affrighted face. 'Thou canst not go glaziering. Think of Miriam. What canst thou do, what canst thou do? Thou knowest no trade!'

'No, I know no trade,' he said bitterly. 'At home, as thou art aware, I was a stone-mason; but here I could get no work without breaking the Sabbath, and my hand has forgotten its cunning. Perhaps I shall get my hand back.'

He took hers in the meantime. It was limp and chill, though so near the fire.

'Have courage,' he said. 'There is naught I can do here that will not shame Miriam. We cannot even go into an alms-house without shedding her blood; but the Holy One—blessed be He!—is good. I will go away.'

'Go away!' Beenah's clammy hand tightened her clasp of his. Thou wilt travel with ware in the country?'

'No. If it stands written that I must break with my children, let the gap be too wide for repining. Miriam will like it better. I will go to America.'

'To America!' Beenah's heart beat wildly. 'And leave me?' A strange sense of desolation swept over her.

'Yes—for a little, anyhow. Thou must not face the first hardships. I shall find something to do. Perhaps in America there are more Jewish stone-masons to get work from. God will not desert us. There I can sell ware in the streets—do as I will. At the worst, I can always fall back upon glaziering. Have faith, my dove.'

The novel word of affection thrilled Beenah through and through.

'I shall send thee a little money ; then, as soon as I can see my way clear, I shall send for thee, and thou shalt come out to me, and we will live happily together, and our children shall live happily here.'

But Beenah burst into fresh tears.

'Woe ! woe !' she sobbed. 'How wilt thou, an old man, face the sea and strange faces all alone? See how sorely thou art racked with rheumatism. How canst thou go glaziering ? Thou liest often groaning all the night. How shalt thou carry the heavy crate on thy shoulders ?'

'God will give me strength to do what is right.'

The tears were plain enough in his voice now, and would not be denied. His words forced themselves out in a husky wheeze.

Beenah threw her arms round his neck.

'No, no !' she cried hysterically. 'Thou shalt not go ! Thou shalt not leave me !'

'I must go,' his parched lips articulated.

He could not see that the snow of her hair had drifted into her eyes, and was scarce whiter than her cheeks. His spectacles were a blur of mist.

'No, no,' she moaned incoherently. 'I shall die soon. God is merciful. Wait a little, wait a little ! He will kill us both soon. My poor lamb ! My poor Daniel ! Thou shalt not leave me.'

The old man unlaced her arms from his neck.

'I must. I have heard God's word in the silence.'

'Then I will go with thee. Wherever thou goest I will go.'

'No, no ; thou shalt not face the first hardships. I will front them alone. I am strong—I am a man.'

'And thou hast the heart to leave me ?'

She looked piteously into his face, but hers was still hidden from him in the mist. But through the darkness the flash passed again. His hand groped for her waist ; he drew her again towards him, and put the arms he had unlaced round his neck and stooped his wet cheek to hers. The past was a void ; the forty years of joint housekeeping, since the morning each had seen a strange face on the pillow, faded to a point. For fifteen years they had been drifting towards each other—drifting nearer, nearer in dual lone-liness ; driven together by common suffering and growing aliena-tion from the children they had begotten in common ; drifting nearer, nearer, in silence, almost in unconsciousness. And now they had met. The supreme moment of their lives had come. The silence of forty years was broken. His withered lips sought hers, and love flooded their souls at last.

When the first delicious instants were over, Mendel drew a chair to the table and wrote a letter in Hebrew script and posted it, and Beenah picked up Miriam's jacket. The crackling flames had subsided to a steady glow, the clock ticked on quietly as before ; but something new and sweet and sacred had come into her life, and Beenah no longer wished to die.

When Miriam came home she brought a little blast of cold air into the room. Beenah rose and shut the door, and put out Miriam's supper ; she did not drag her feet now.

'Was it a nice play, Miriam ? ' said Beenah softly.

'The usual stuff and nonsense ! ' said Miriam peevishly. 'Love and all that sort of thing, as if the world never got any older.'

At breakfast next morning old Hyams received a letter by the first post. He carefully took his spectacles off and donned his reading-glasses to read it, throwing the envelope carelessly into the fire. When he had scanned a few lines, he uttered an exclamation of surprise and dropped the letter.

'What's the matter, father ? ' asked Daniel, while Miriam tilted her snub-nose curiously.

'Praised be God ! ' was all the old man could say.

'Well, what is it ? Speak ! ' said Beenah, with unusual animation, while a flush of excitement lit up Miriam's face and made it beautiful.

'My brother in America has won a thousand pounds on the lotteree, and he invites me and Beenah to come and live with him.'

'Your brother in America ! ' repeated his children, staring.

'Why, I didn't know you had a brother in America!' added Miriam.

'No ; while he was poor I didn't mention him,' replied Mendel, with unintentional sarcasm. 'But I've heard from him several times. We both came over from Poland together, but the Board of Guardians sent him and a lot of others on to New York.'

'But you won't go, father ! ' said Daniel.

'Why not ? I should like to see my brother before I die. We were very thick as boys.'

'But a thousand pounds isn't so very much,' Miriam could not refrain from saying.

Old Hyams had thought it boundless opulence, and was now sorry he had not done his brother a better turn.

'It will be enough for us all to live upon—he and Beenah and me. You see, his wife died, and he has no children.'

'You don't really mean to go ? ' gasped Daniel, unable to grasp the situation suddenly sprung upon him. 'How will you get the money to travel with ? '

'Read here,' said Mendel quietly, passing him the letter. 'He offers to send it.'

'But it's written in Hebrew ! ' cried Daniel, turning it upside down hopelessly.

'You can read Hebrew writing, surely ? ' said his father.

'I could, years and years ago. I remember you taught me the letters. But my Hebrew correspondence has been so scanty——'

He broke off with a laugh, and handed the letter to Miriam, who surveyed it with mock comprehension. There was a look of relief in her eyes as she returned it to her father.

'He might have sent something to his nephew and his niece,' she said half seriously.

'Perhaps he will when I get to America and tell him how pretty you are,' said Mendel oracularly.

He looked quite joyous, and even ventured to pinch Miriam's flushed cheek roguishly, and she submitted to the indignity without a murmur.

'Why, *you're* looking as pleased as Punch too, mother!' said Daniel, in half-rueful amazement. 'You seem delighted at the idea of leaving us.'

'I always wanted to see America,' the old woman admitted, with a smile. 'I also shall renew an old friendship in New York.'

She looked meaningly at her husband, and in his eye was an answering love-light.

'Well, that's cool!' Daniel burst forth. 'But she doesn't mean it, does she, father?'

'I mean it,' Hyams answered.

'But it can't be true,' persisted Daniel, in ever-growing bewilderment. 'I believe it's all a hoax.'

Mendel hastily drained his coffee-cup.

'A hoax!' he murmured from behind the cup.

'Yes ; I believe some one is having a lark with you.'

'Nonsense!' cried Mendel vehemently, as he put down his coffee-cup and picked up the letter from the table. 'Don't I know my own brother Yankov's writing? Besides, who else would know all the little things he writes about?'

Daniel was silenced, but lingered on after Miriam had departed to her wearisome duties.

'I shall write at once, accepting Yankov's offer,' said his father. 'Fortunately, we took the house by the week, so you can always move out if it is too large for you and Miriam. I can trust you to look after Miriam, I know, Daniel.'

Daniel expostulated yet further, but Mendel answered :

'He is so lonely. He cannot well come over here by himself, because he is half paralysed. After all, what have I to do in England? And the mother naturally does not care to leave me. Perhaps I shall get my brother to travel with me to the land of Israel, and then we shall all end our days in Jerusalem, which you know has always been my heart's desire.'

Neither mentioned Bessie Sugarman.

'Why do you make so much bother?' Miriam said to Daniel in the evening. 'It's the best thing that could have happened. Who'd have dreamt at this hour of the day of coming into possession of a relative who might actually have something to leave us? It'll be a good story to tell, too.'

After *Shool* next morning Mendel spoke to the President.

'Can you lend me six pounds?' he asked.

Belcovitch staggered.

'Six pounds!' he repeated, dazed.

'Yes. I wish to go to America with my wife. And I want you, moreover, to give your hand, as a countryman, that you will not breathe a word of this, whatever you hear. Beenah and I have sold a few little trinkets which our children gave us, and we have reckoned that with six pounds more we shall be able to take steerage passages and just exist till I get work.'

'But six pounds is a very great sum, without sureties,' said Belcovitch, rubbing his time-worn workaday high hat in his agitation.

'I know it is!' answered Mendel; 'but God is my witness that I mean to pay you. And if I die before I can do so, I vow to send word to my son, Daniel, who will pay you the balance. You know my son Daniel. His word is an oath.'

'But where shall I get six pounds from?' said Bear helplessly. 'I am only a poor tailor. And my daughter gets married soon. It is a great sum—by my honourable word it is. I have never lent so much in my life, nor even been security for such an amount.'

Mendel dropped his head. There was a moment of anxious silence. Bear thought deeply.

'I tell you what I'll do,' said Bear at last. 'I'll lend you five, if you can manage to come out with that.'

Mendel gave a great sigh of relief.

'God shall bless you!' he said. He wrung the sweater's hand passionately. 'I dare say we shall find another sovereign's-worth to sell. Mendel clinched the borrowing by standing the lender a glass of rum, and Bear felt secure against the graver shocks of doom. If the worst came to the worst now, he had still had something for his money.

And so Mendel and Beenah sailed away over the Atlantic. Daniel accompanied them to Liverpool, but Miriam said she could not get a day's holiday; perhaps she remembered the rebuke Esther Ansell had drawn down on herself, and was chary of asking.

At the dock in the chill dawn, Mendel Hyams kissed his son Daniel on the forehead, and said in a broken voice:

'Good-bye; God bless you!' He dared not add, 'and God bless your Bessie, my daughter-in-law to be;' but the benediction was in his heart. Daniel turned away heavy-hearted, but the old man touched him on the shoulder, and said in a low, tremulous voice:

'Won't you forgive me for putting you into the fancy goods?'

'Father! What do you mean?' said Daniel choking. 'Surely you are not thinking of the wild words I spoke years and years ago. I have long forgotten them.'

'Then you will remain a good Jew,' said Mendel, trembling all over, 'even when we are far away?'

'With God's help,' said Daniel.

And then Mendel turned to Beenah and kissed her, weeping, and the faces of the old couple were radiant behind their tears.

Daniel stood on the clamorous, hustling wharf watching the ship move slowly from her moorings towards the open river. And

neither he nor any one in the world but the happy pair knew that
Mendel and Beenah were on their honeymoon.

   *   *   *   *   *   *

Mrs. Hyams died two years after her honeymoon, and old Hyams
laid a lover's kiss upon her sealed eyelids.   Then, being absolutely
alone in the world, he sold off his scanty furniture, sent the balance
of the debt with a sovereign of undemanded interest to Bear
Belcovitch, and girded up his loins for the journey to Jerusalem,
which had been the dream of his life.

But the dream of his life had better have remained a dream.
Mendel saw the hills of Palestine, and the holy Jordan, and Mount
Moriah, the site of the Temple, and the tombs of Absalom and
Melchitzedek, and the gate of Zion, and the aqueduct built by
Solomon, and all that he had longed to see from boyhood.   But
somehow it was not *his* Jerusalem, scarce more than his London
Ghetto transplanted, only grown filthier, and narrower, and more
ragged, with cripples for beggars and lepers in lieu of hawkers.
The magic of his dream-city was not here.   This was something
prosaic, almost sordid ; it made his heart sink as he thought of
the sacred splendours of the Zion he had imaged in his suffering
soul.   The rainbows builded of his bitter tears did not span the
firmament of this dingy Eastern city, set amid sterile hills.   Where
were the roses and lilies, the cedars and the fountains ?   Mount
Moriah was here indeed, but it bore the Mosque of Omar, and the
Temple of Jehovah was but one ruined wall.   The Shechinah, the
Divine glory, had faded into cold sunshine.   'Who shall go up
into the mount of Jehovah ?'   Lo, the Moslem worshipper and the
Christian tourist.   Barracks and convents stood on Zion's hill.
His brethren, rulers by Divine right of the soil they trod, were
lost in the chaos of populations—Syrians, Armenians, Turks,
Copts, Abyssinians, Europeans—as their synagogues were lost
amid the domes and minarets of the Gentiles.   The city was full
of venerated relics of the Christ his people had lived—and died—
to deny, and over all flew the crescent flag of the Mussulman.

And so every Friday, heedless of scoffing onlookers, Mendel
Hyams kissed the stones of the Wailing Place, bedewing their
barrenness with tears, and every year at Passover, until he was
gathered to his fathers, he continued to pray, ' Next year—in
Jerusalem.'

CHAPTER XVIII

THE HEBREW'S FRIDAY NIGHT

' AH, the Men-of-the-Earth !' said Pinchas to Reb Shemuel.
' Ignorant fanatics ! how shall a movement prosper in their hands ?
They have not the poetic vision ; their ideas are as the mole's ;
they wish to make Messiahs out of halfpence.   What inspiration

for the soul is there in the sight of snuffy collectors that have the air of *Schnorrers*—with Karlkammer's red hair for a flag, and the sound of Gradkoski's nose-blowing for a trumpet-peal? But I have written an acrostic against Guedalyah the Greengrocer, virulent as serpents' gall. He the Redeemer, indeed, with his diseased potatoes and his flat gingerbeer! Not thus did the great prophets and teachers in Israel figure the Return. Let a great signal-fire be lit in Israel, and, lo ! the beacons will leap up on every mountain, and tongue of flame shall call to tongue. Yea, I, even I, Melchitzedek Pinchas, will light the fire forthwith.'

'Nay, not to-day,' said Reb Shemuel, with his humorous twinkle. 'It is the Sabbath.'

The Rabbi was returning from synagogue, and Pinchas was giving him his company on the short homeward journey. At their heels trudged Levi, and on the other side of Reb Shemuel walked Eliphaz Chowchoski, a miserable-looking Pole, whom Reb Shemuel was taking home to supper. In those days Reb Shemuel was not alone in taking to his hearth 'the Sabbath guest'—some forlorn starveling or other—to sit at the table in like honour with the master. It was an object-lesson in Equality and Fraternity for the children of many a well-to-do household, nor did it fail altogether in the homes of the poor. 'All Israel are brothers,' and how better honour the Sabbath than by making the lip-babble a reality?

'You will speak to your daughter?' said Pinchas, changing the subject abruptly. 'You will tell her that what I wrote to her is not a millionth part of what I feel ; that she is my sun by day, and my moon and stars by night ; that I must marry her at once or die ; that I think of nothing in the world but her ; that I can do, write, plan, nothing without her ; that once she smiles on me I will write her great love-poems, greater than Byron's, greater than Heine's—the real song of songs, which is Pinchas's ; that I will make her immortal as Dante made Beatrice, as Petrarch made Laura ; that I walk about wretched, bedewing the pavements with my tears ; that I sleep not by night nor eat by day. You will tell her this?'

He laid his finger pleadingly on his nose.

'I will tell her,' said Reb Shemuel. 'You are a son-in-law to gladden the heart of any man. But I fear the maiden looks but coldly on wooers. Besides, you are fourteen years older than she.'

'Then I love her twice as much as Jacob loved Rachel, for it is written : "Seven years were but as a day in his love for her." To me fourteen years are but as a day in my love for Hannah.'

The Rabbi laughed at the quibble, and said :

'You are like the man who, when he was accused of being twenty years older than the maiden he desired, replied : "But when I look at her I shall become ten years younger, and when she looks at me she will become ten years older, and thus we shall be even."'

Pinchas laughed enthusiastically in his turn, but replied :

'Surely you will plead my cause—you, whose motto is the Hebrew saying, "The husband help the housewife, God help the bachelor."'

'But have you the wherewithal to support her ?'

'Shall my writings not suffice ? If there are none to protect literature in England, we will go abroad—to your birthplace, Reb Shemuel, the cradle of great scholars.'

The poet spoke yet more, but in the end his excited, stridulous accents fell on Reb Shemuel's ears as a storm without on the ears of the slippered reader by the fireside. He had dropped into a delicious reverie, tasting in advance the Sabbath peace. The work of the week was over. The faithful Jew could enter on his rest—the narrow, miry streets faded before the brighter image of his brain. 'Come, my beloved, to meet the Bride ; the face of the Sabbath let us welcome.' .

To-night his sweetheart would wear her Sabbath face, putting off the mask of the shrew, which hid, not from him, the angel countenance. To-night he could in very truth call his wife (as the Rabbi in the Talmud did), 'not wife, but home.' To-night she would be in very truth *Simcha*—'rejoicing.' A cheerful warmth glowed at his heart; love for all the wonderful creation dissolved him in tenderness. As he approached the door, cheerful lights gleamed on him like a heavenly smile. He invited Pinchas to enter, but the poet, in view of his passion, thought it prudent to let others plead for him, and went off with his finger to his nose in final reminder. The Reb kissed the *Mezuzah* on the outside of the door, and his daughter, who met him, on the inside. Everything was as he had pictured it : the two tall wax candles in quaint, heavy silver candlesticks, the spotless table-cloth, the dish of fried fish made picturesque with sprigs of parsley, the Sabbath loaves shaped like boys' tip-cats—with a curious plait of crust from point to point, and thickly sprinkled with a drift of poppy-seed, and covered with a velvet cloth embroidered with Hebrew words—the flask of wine and the silver goblet. The sight was familiar, yet it always struck the simple old Reb anew, with a sense of special blessing.

'Good-Shabbos, Simcha,' said Reb Shemuel.

'Good-Shabbos, Shemuel,' said Simcha.

The light of love was in her eyes, and in her hair her newest comb. Her sharp features shone with peace and goodwill and the consciousness of having duly lit the Sabbath candles and thrown the morsel of dough into the fire. Shemuel kissed her ; then he laid his hands upon Hannah's head, and murmured : 'May God make thee as Sarah, Rebecca, Rachel, and Leah !' and upon Levi's, murmuring : 'May God make thee as Ephraim and Manasseh !'

Even the callous Levi felt the breath of sanctity in the air, and had a vague, restful sense of his Sabbath angel hovering about

and causing him to cast two shadows on the wall, while his evil
angel shivered impotent on the doorstep.

Then Reb Shemuel repeated three times a series of sentences
commencing : 'Peace be unto you, ye ministering angels,' and
thereupon the wonderful picture of an ideal woman from Proverbs,
looking affectionately at Simcha the while : 'A woman of worth,
whoso findeth her, her price is far above rubies.   The heart of her
husband trusteth in her. . . . Good and not evil will she do him
all the days of her life. . . . She riseth while it is yet night, giveth
food to her household and a task to her maidens. . . . She putteth
her own hands to the spindle. . . . She stretcheth out her hand
to the poor. . . . Strength and honour are her clothing, and she
looketh forth smilingly to the morrow.   She openeth her mouth
with wisdom, and the law of kindness is on her tongue.   She
looketh well to the ways of her household, and eateth not the
bread of idleness. . . . Deceitful is favour, and vain is beauty ;
but the woman that feareth the Lord, *she* shall be praised.'

Then, washing his hands with the due benediction, he filled the
goblet with wine, and while everyone reverently stood he 'made
Kiddush,' in a traditional joyous recitative :

'". . . Blessed art Thou, O Lord our God !   King of the universe !   Creator of the fruit of the vine !   who doth sanctify us with
His commandments and hath delight in us.   Thou hast chosen and
sanctified us above all peoples, and with love and favour hast made
us to inherit Thy holy Sabbath. . . ."'

And all the household, and the hungry Pole, answered 'Amen,'
each sipping of the cup in due gradation, then eating a special
morsel of bread cut by the father and dipped in salt ; after which
the good wife served the fish, and cups and saucers clattered and
knives and forks rattled.   And after a few mouthfuls the Pole knew
himself a prince in Israel, and felt he must forthwith make choice
of a maiden to grace his royal Sabbath board.   Soup followed the
fish ; it was not served direct from the saucepan, but transferred
by way of a large tureen, since any creeping thing that might have
got into the soup would have rendered the plateful in which it
appeared not legally potable, whereas, if it were detected in the
large tureen its polluting powers would be dissipated by being
diffused over such a large mass of fluid.   For like religious reasons,
another feature of the etiquette of the modern fashionable table
had been anticipated by many centuries—the eaters washed their
hands in a little bowl of water after the meal.   The *Pullack* was
thus kept, by main religious force, in touch with a liquid with
which he had no external sympathy.

When supper was over grace was chanted, and then the
Zemiroth were sung—songs summing up, in light and jingling
metre, the very essence of holy joyousness—neither riotous nor
ascetic : the note of spiritualised common-sense which has been
the key-note of historical Judaism.   For to feel 'the delight of
Sabbath' is a duty, and to take three meals thereon a religious

obligation—the sanctification of the sensuous by a creed to which everything is holy. The Sabbath is the hub of the Jew's universe ; to protract it is a virtue, to love it a liberal education. It cancels all mourning—even for Jerusalem ; the candles may gutter out at their own greasy will, unsnuffed, untended—is not Sabbath its own self-sufficient light?

> ' This is the sanctified rest day ;
> Happy the man who observes it,
> Thinks of it over the wine-cup,
> Feeling no pang at his heart-strings
> For that his purse-strings are empty ;
> Joyous, and if he must borrow,
> God will repay the good lender.
> Meat, wine, and fish in profusion—
> See no delight is deficient.
> Let but the table be spread well,
> Angels of God answer "Amen!"
> So when a soul is in dolour,
> Cometh the sweet restful Sabbath,
> Singing and joy in its footsteps ;
> Rapidly floweth Sambatyon,
> Till that, of God's love the symbol,
> Sabbath, the holy, the peaceful,
> Husheth its turbulent waters.
>
> Bless Him, O constant companions,
> Rock from whose stores we have eaten,
> Eaten have we and have left, too,
> Just as the Lord hath commanded,
> Father and Shepherd and Feeder,
> His is the bread we have eaten,
> His is the wine we have drunken,
> Wherefore with lips let us praise Him,
> Lord of the land of our fathers,
> Gratefully, ceaselessly chaunting,
> "None like Jehovah is holy."
>
> Light and rejoicing to Israel.
> Sabbath, the soother of sorrows,
> Comfort of down-trodden Israel,
> Healing the hearts that were broken !
> Banish despair ! Here is Hope come !
> What ! A soul crushed ? Lo, a stronger
> Bringeth the balsamous Sabbath.
> Build, oh, rebuild Thou, Thy Temple ;
> Fill again Zion, Thy city.
> Clad with delight will we go there,
> Other and new songs to sing there,
> Merciful One and All-Holy,
> Praisèd for ever and ever.'

During the meal the *Pullack* spoke with his host about the persecution in the land whence he had come—the bright spot in his picture being the fidelity of his brethren under trial, only a minority deserting, and those already tainted with Epicureanism—

students wishful of University distinction and such like. Orthodox Jews are rather surprised when men of (secular) education remain in the fold.

Hannah took advantage of a pause in their conversation to say in German :

'I am so glad, father, thou didst not bring that man home.'

'What man ?' said Reb Shemuel.

'The dirty monkey-faced little man who talks so much.'

The Reb considered.

'I know none such.'

'Pinchas she means,' said her mother—'the poet !'

Reb Shemuel looked at her gravely. This did not sound promising.

'Why dost thou speak so harshly of thy fellow-creatures ?' he said. 'The man is a scholar and a poet, such as we have too few in Israel.'

'We have too many *Schnorrers* in Israel already,' retorted Hannah.

'Sh !' whispered Reb Shemuel, reddening and indicating his guest with a slight movement of the eye.

Hannah bit her lip in self-humiliation, and hastened to load the lucky Pole's plate with an extra piece of fish.

'He has written me a letter,' she went on.

'He has told me so,' he answered. 'He loves thee with a great love.'

What nonsense, Shemuel !' broke in Simcha, setting down her coffee-cup with workaday violence. 'The idea of a man who has not a penny to bless himself with marrying our Hannah ! They would be on the Board of Guardians in a month.'

'Money is not everything. Wisdom and learning outweigh much. And, as the Midrash says : "As a scarlet ribbon becometh a black horse, so poverty becometh the daughter of Jacob." The world stands on the Torah, not on gold ; as it is written : "Better is the Law of Thy mouth to me than thousands of gold or silver." He is greater than I, for he studies the law for nothing, like the fathers of the Mishna, while I am paid a salary.'

'Methinks thou art little inferior,' said Simcha, 'for thou retainest little enough thereof. Let Pinchas get nothing for himself, 'tis his affair ; but if he wants my Hannah he must get something for her. Were the fathers of the Mishna also fathers of families ?'

'Certainly, is it not a command ? "Be fruitful and multiply."'

'And how did their families live ?'

'Many of our sages were artisans.'

'Aha !' snorted Simcha triumphantly.

'And says not the Talmud,' put in the Pole, as if he were on the family council, '"Flay a carcass in the streets rather than be under an obligation"?' This with supreme unconsciousness of any personal application. 'Yea, and said not Rabban Gamliel, the son of Rabbi Judah, the prince, "It is commendable to join the study of the law with worldly employment"? Did not Moses our teacher keep sheep ?'

'Truth,' replied the host. 'I agree with Maimonides that man should first secure a living, then prepare a residence, and after that seek a wife, and that they are fools who invert the order. But Pinchas works also with his pen. He writes articles in the papers. But the great thing, Hannah, is that he loves the Law.'

'H'm,' said Hannah. 'Let him marry the Law, then.'

'He is in a hurry,' said Reb Shemuel, with a flash of irreverent facetiousness. 'And he cannot become the Bridegroom of the Law till *Simchath Torah*.'

All laughed. The Bridegroom of the Law is the temporary title of the Jew who enjoys the distinction of being 'called up' to the public reading of the last fragment of the Pentateuch, which is got through once a year.

Under the encouragement of the laughter, the Rabbi added :

'But he will know much more of his bride than the majority of the Law's bridegrooms.'

Hannah took advantage of her father's pleasure in the effect of his jokes to show him Pinchas's epistle, which he deciphered laboriously. It commenced :

> H ebrew Hebe,
> A ll-fair Maid,
> N ext to Heaven
> N ightly laid,
> A h, I love you,
> H alf afraid.

The Pole, looking a different being from the wretch who had come empty, departed invoking peace on the household ; Simcha went into the kitchen to superintend the removal of the crockery thither, Levi slipped out to pay his respects to Esther Ansell, for the evening was yet young, and father and daughter were left alone.

Reb Shemuel was already poring over a Pentateuch in his Friday night duty of reading the portion twice in Hebrew and once in Chaldaic.

Hannah sat opposite him, studying the kindly furrowed face, the massive head set on rounded shoulders, the shaggy eyebrows, the long, whitening beard moving with the mumble of the pious lips, the brown peering eyes held close to the sacred tome, the high forehead crowned with the black skull-cap.

She felt a moisture gathering under her eye-lids as she looked at him.

'Father,' she said at last, in a gentle voice.

'Did you call me, Hannah ? ' he asked, looking up.

'Yes, dear. About this man, Pinchas.'

'Yes, Hannah.'

'I am sorry I spoke harshly of him.'

'Ah, that is right, my daughter. If he is poor and ill-clad we we must only honour him the more. Wisdom and learning must be respected even if they appear in rags. Abraham entertained God's messengers though they came as weary travellers.'

'I know, father. It is not because of his appearance that I do not like him. If he is really a scholar and a poet, I will try to admire him as you do.'

'Now you speak like a true daughter of Israel.'

'But about my marrying him—you are not really in earnest?'

'*He* is,' said Reb Shemuel evasively.

'Ah, I knew you were not,' she said, catching the lurking twinkle in his eye. 'You know I could never marry a man like that.'

'Your mother could,' said the Reb.

'Dear old goose!' she said, leaning across to pull his beard. 'You are not a bit like that; you know a thousand times more, you know you do.'

The old Rabbi held up his hands in comic deprecation.

'Yes, you do,' she persisted. 'Only you let him talk so much, you let everybody talk and bamboozle you.'

Reb Shemuel drew the hand that fondled his beard in his own, feeling the fresh warm skin with a puzzled look.

'The hands are the hands of Hannah,' he said; 'but the voice is the voice of Simcha.'

Hannah laughed merrily.

'All right, dear; I won't scold you any more. I'm so glad it didn't really enter your great, stupid, clever old head that I was likely to care for Pinchas.'

'My dear daughter, Pinchas wished to take you to wife, and I felt pleased. It is a union with a son of the Torah, who has also the pen of a ready writer. He asked me to tell you, and I did.'

'But you would not like me to marry any one I did not like?'

'God forbid! My little Hannah shall marry whomever she pleases.'

A wave of emotion passed over the girl's face.

'You don't mean that, father,' she said, shaking her head.

'True as the Torah. Why should I not?'

'Suppose,' she said slowly, 'I wanted to marry a Christian?'

Her heart beat painfully as she put the question.

Reb Shemuel laughed heartily.

'My Hannah would have made a good Talmudist. Of course I don't mean it in that sense.'

'Yes; but if I was to marry a very *link* Jew, you'd think it almost as bad.'

'No, no!' said the Reb, shaking his head. 'That's a different thing altogether. A Jew is a Jew, and a Christian a Christian.'

'But you can't always distinguish between them,' argued Hannah. 'There are Jews who behave as if they were Christians, except, of course, they don't believe in the Crucified One.'

Still the old Reb shook his head.

'The worst of Jews cannot put off his Judaism. His unborn soul undertook the Yoke of the Torah at Sinai.'

'Then you really wouldn't mind if I married a *link* Jew?'

He looked at her startled, a suspicion dawning in his eyes.

'I should mind,' he said slowly. 'But if you loved him he would become a good Jew.'

The simple conviction of his words moved her to tears, but she kept them back.

'But if he wouldn't?'

'I should pray. While there is life there is hope for the sinner in Israel.'

She fell back on her old question.

'And you would really not mind whom I married?'

'Follow your heart, my little one,' said Reb Shemuel. 'It is a good heart, and it will not lead you wrong.'

Hannah turned away to hide the tears that could no longer be stayed. Her father resumed his reading of the Law.

But he had got through very few verses ere he felt a soft warm arm round his neck, and a wet cheek laid close to his.

'Father, forgive me!' whispered the lips. 'I am so sorry. I thought—that I—that you—— Oh, father, father! I feel as if I had never known you before to-night!'

'What is it, my daughter?' said Reb Shemuel, stumbling into Yiddish in his anxiety. 'What hast thou done?'

'I have betrothed myself,' she answered, unwittingly adopting his dialect. 'I have betrothed myself without telling thee or mother.'

'To whom?' he asked anxiously.

'To a Jew,' she hastened to assure him. But he is neither a Talmud-sage nor pious. He is newly returned from the Cape.'

'Ah, they are a *link* lot!' muttered the Reb anxiously. 'Where didst thou first meet him?'

At the Club,' she answered. 'At the Purim ball—the night before Sam Levine came round here to be divorced from me.'

He wrinkled his great brow.

'Thy mother would have thee go,' he said. 'Thou didst not deserve I should divorce thee. What is his name?'

'David Brandon. He is not like other Jewish young men. I thought he was bad and did him wrong, and mocked at him when first he spoke to me, so that afterwards I felt tender towards him. His conversation is agreeable, for he thinks for himself; and deeming thou wouldst not hear of such a match, and that there was no danger, I met him at the Club several times in the evening, and—and—thou knowest the rest.'

She turned away her face, blushing, contrite, happy, anxious.

Her love-story was as simple as her telling of it. David Brandon was not the shadowy prince of her maiden dreams, nor was the passion exactly as she had imagined it; it was both stronger and stranger, and the sense of secrecy and impending opposition instilled into her love a poignant sweetness.

The Reb stroked her hair silently.

'I would not have said "Yea" so quick, father,' she went on, 'but David had to go to Germany to take a message to the aged

parents of his Cape chum, who died in the gold-fields. David had
promised the dying man to go personally as soon as he returned
to England,—I think it was a request for forgiveness and blessing,
—but after meeting me he delayed going, and when I learnt of it
I reproached him, but he said he could not tear himself away, and
he would not go till I had confessed I loved him. At last I said
if he would go home the moment I said it, and not bother about
getting me a ring or anything, but go off to Germany the first
thing the next morning, I would admit I loved him a little bit.
Thus did it occur. He went off last Wednesday. Oh, isn't it
cruel to think, father, that he should be going with love and joy
in his heart to the parents of his dead friend ? '

Her father's head was bent. She lifted it up by the chin and
looked pleadingly into the big brown eyes.

' Thou art not angry with me, father ? '

' No, Hannah. But thou shouldst have told me from the first.'

' I always meant to, father. But I feared to grieve thee.'

' Wherefore ? The man is a Jew. And thou lovest him, dost
thou not ? '

' As my life, father.'

He kissed her lips.

' It is enough, my Hannah. With thee to love him, he will
become pious. When a man has a good Jewish wife like my
beloved daughter, who will keep a good Jewish house, he cannot
be long among the sinners. The light of a true Jewish home will
lead his footsteps back to God.'

Hannah pressed her face to his in silence. She could not
speak. She had not strength to undeceive him further, to tell him
she had no care for trivial forms. Besides, in the flush of gratitude
and surprise at her father's tolerance, she felt stirrings of responsive tolerance to his religion. It was not the moment to analyse
her feelings or to enunciate her state of mind regarding religion.
She simply let herself sink in the sweet sense of restored confidence and love, her head resting against his.

Presently Reb Shemuel put his hands on her head and murmured again :

' May God make thee as Sarah, Rebecca, Rachel, and Leah ! '
Then he added : ' Go now, my daughter, and make glad the heart
of thy mother.'

Hannah suspected a shade of satire in the words, but was not
sure.

*   *   *   *   *   *   *

The roaring Sambatyon of life was at rest in the Ghetto ; on
thousands of squalid homes the light of Sinai shone. The
Sabbath angels whispered words of hope and comfort to the footsore hawker and the aching machinist, and refreshed their parched
souls with celestial anodyne and made them kings of the hour,
with leisure to dream of the golden chairs that awaited them in
Paradise.

The Ghetto welcomed the Sabbath Bribe with proud song and humble feast, and sped her parting with optimistic symbolisms of fire and wine, of spice and light and shadow. All around, their neighbours sought distraction in the blazing public-houses, and their tipsy bellowings resounded through the streets and mingled with the Hebrew hymns. Here and there the voice of a beaten woman rose on the air. But no Son of the Covenant was among the revellers or the wife-beaters ; the Jews remained a chosen race, a peculiar people, faulty enough, but redeemed at least from the grosser vices—a little human islet won from the waters of animalism by the genius of ancient engineers. For while the genius of the Greek or the Roman, the Egyptian or the Phœni-cian, survives but in word and stone, the Hebrew word alone was made flesh.

CHAPTER XIX

WITH THE STRIKERS

'IGNORANT donkey-heads !' cried Pinchas next Friday morn-ing. 'Him dey make a Rabbi, and give him the right of answer-ing questions, and he know no more of Judaism'—the patriotic poet paused to take a bite out of his ham sandwich—'than a cow of Sunday. I lof his daughter, and I tell him so, and he tells me she lof another. But I haf held him up on de point of my pen to de contempt of posterity. I haf written an acrostic on him ; it is terrible. Her vill I shoot.'

'Ah, they are a bad lot, these Rabbis !' said Simon Wolf, sipping his sherry.

The conversation took place in English, and the two men were seated in a small private room in a public-house, awaiting the advent of the strike committee.

'They are like de rest of the community ; I vash my hands of dem,' said the poet, waving his cigar in a fiery crescent.

'I have long since washed my hands of them,' said Simon Wolf, though the fact was not obvious. 'We can trust neither our Rabbis nor our philanthropists. The Rabbis, engrossed in the hypocritical endeavour to galvanise the corpse of Judaism into a vitality that shall last at least their own lifetime, have neither time nor thought for the great labour question. Our philanthro-pists do but scratch the surface. They give the working man with their right hand what they have stolen from him with the left.'

Simon Wolf was the great Jewish labour-leader. Most of his cronies were rampant atheists, disgusted with the commer-cialism of the believers. They were clever young artisans from Russia and Poland with a smattering of education, a feverish re-ceptiveness for all the iconoclastic ideas that were in the London air, a hatred of capitalism and strong social sympathies. They wrote vigorous Jargon for the *Friend of Labour,* and compassed the extreme proverbial limits of impiety by 'eating pork on the Day of Atonement.' This was done partly to vindicate their religious opinions, whose correctness was demonstrated by the non-appearance of thunderbolts, partly to show that nothing one way or the other was to be expected from Providence or its professors.

'The only way for our poor brethren to be saved from their slavery,' went on Simon Wolf, 'is for them to combine against the sweaters, and to let the West-End Jews go and hang themselves.'

'Ah, that is mine policee!' said Pinchas; 'that was mine policee ven I founded de Holy Land League. Help yourselves, and Pinchas vill help you. You muz combine, and den I vill be de Moses to lead you out of de land of bondage. *Nein,* I vill be more than Moses, for he had not de gift of eloquence.'

'And he was the meekest man that ever lived,' added Wolf.

'Yes, he was a fool-man,' said Pinchas imperturbably. 'I agree with Goethe—"*Nur Lumpen sind bescheiden*" : only clods are modaist. I am not modaist. Is de Almighty modaist ? I know, I feel vat I am, vat I can do.'

'Look here, Pinchas, you 're a very clever fellow, I know, and I 'm very glad to have you with us ; but, remember, I have organised this movement for years, planned it out as I sat toiling in Belcovitch's machine-room, written on it till I 've got the cramp, spoken on it till I was hoarse, given evidence before innumerable Commissions ; it is I who have stirred up the East-End Jews and sent the echo of their cry into Parliament, and I will not be interfered with ; do you hear ?'

'Yes, I hear. Vy you not listen to me ? You no understand vat I mean.'

'Oh, I understand you well enough. You want to oust me from my position.'

'Me ? me ?' repeated the poet in an injured and astonished tone ; 'vy, midout you de movement would crumble like a mummy in the air ; be not such a fool-man ! To everybody I haf said : "Ah, dat Simon Wolf he is a great man, a vair great man ; he is de only man among de English Jews who can save de East End ; it is he that should be member for Vitechapel, not that fool-man, Gideon." Be not such a fool-man. Haf anoder glaz sherry and some more ham sandwiches.'

The poet had a simple, childlike delight in occasionally assuming the host.

'Very well, so long as I have your assurance,' said the mollified labour-leader, mumbling the conclusion of the sentence into his wine-glass ; 'but you know how it is. After I have worked the thing for years, I don't want to see a drone romp in and take the credit.'

'Yes, "*sic vos non vobis,*" as the Talmud says. Do you know, I haf proved that Virgil stole all his ideas from the Talmud.

'First there was Black, and then there was Cohen; now Gideon, M.P., sees he can get some advertisement out of it in the press, he wants to preside at the meetings. Members of Parliament are a bad lot.'

'Yes, but dey shall not take de credit from you. I vill write and expose dem; the world shall know vat humbugs dey are; how de whole wealthy West End stood idly by with her hands in de working men's pockets while you vere building up de great organisation. You know all de Jargon-papers jump at vat I write; dey sign my name in vair large type—Melchitzedek Pinchas— under everyting, and I am so pleased with deir homage I do not ask for payment, for dey are vair poor. By dis time I am famous everyvere; my name has been in de evening papers, and ven I write about you to de *Times* you will become as famous as me. And den you vill write about me; ve vill put up for Vitechapel at the elections; ve vill both become membairs of Parliament, I and you—eh?'

'I'm afraid there's not much chance of that,' sighed Simon Wolf.

'Vy not? Dere are two seats. Vy should you not haf de oder?'

'Ain't you forgetting about election expenses, Pinchas?'

'*Nein!*' repeated the poet emphatically. 'I forgets noding. Ve vill start a fund.'

'We can't start funds for ourselves.'

'Be not a fool-man! of course not; you for me, I for you.'

'You won't get much,' said Simon, laughing ruefully at the idea.

'Tink not? P'raps not. But *you* vill for me. Ven I am in Parliament de load vill be easier for us both. Besides, I vill go to de Continent soon to give avay de rest of de copies of my book. I expect to make tousands of pounds by it, for dey know how to honour scholars and poets abroad. Dere dey haf not stupid-head stockbrokers like Gideon, M.P., ministers like the Reverend Elkan Benjamin, who keep four mistresses, and Rabbis like Reb Shemuel, with long beards outside and emptiness within, who sell deir daughters.'

'I don't want to look so far ahead,' said Simon Wolf. 'At present, what we have to do is to carry this strike through. Once we get our demands from the masters, a powerful blow will have been struck for the emancipation of ten thousand working men. They will have more money and more leisure, a little less of hell and a little more of heaven. The coming Passover would, indeed, be an appropriate festival even for the most heterodox among them if we could strike off their chains in the interim. But it seems impossible to get unity among them; a large section appears to mistrust me, though I swear to you, Pinchas, I am actuated by nothing but an unselfish desire for their good. May this morsel of sandwich choke me if I have ever been swayed by anything but sympathy with their wrongs. And yet you saw that malicious pamphlet that was circulated against me in Yiddish— silly, illiterate scribble !'

'Oh no !' said Pinchas ; 'it was vair beautiful—sharp as de sting of de hornet. But vat can you expect ? Christ suffered ; all great benefactors suffer. Am *I* happy ? But it is only your own foolishness dat you must dank if dere is dissension in de camp. The *Gemorah* says ve muz be vize, *chocham*, ve muz haf tact. See vat you haf done ! You haf frighten avay de ortodox fool-men. Dey are oppressed, dey sweat, but dey tink deir God make dem sweat. Vy you tell dem no ? Vat mattairs ? Free them from hunger and tirst first, den freedom from deir fool-superstitions vill come of itself. Jeshurun vax fat and kick. Hey ? You go de wrong vay.'

'Do you mean I 'm to pretend to be *froom* ?' said Simon Wolf.

'And ven ? Vat mattairs ? You are a fool, man. To get to de goal one muz go crooked vays. Ah, you haf no stadesmanship. You frightem dem. You lead processions vid bands and banners on Shabbos to de *Shools*. Many who vould be glad to be delivered by you, tremble for de heavenly lightning. Dey go not in de procession. Many go when deir head is on fire, afterwards dey take fright and beat deir breasts. Vat vill happen ? De ortodox are de majority ; in time dere vill come a leader who vill be or pretend to be ortodox as vell as Socialist. Den vat become of you ? You are left vid von, two, tree ateists, not enough to make *Minyan*. No, ve muz be *chocham* ; ve muz take de men as ve find dem. God has made two classes of men—vise-men and fool-men. Dere is one vise-man to a million fool-men, and he sits on deir head and dey support him. If dese fool-men vant to go to *Shool* and to fast on *Yom Kippur*, vat for you make a feast of pig and shock dem, so dey not believe in your Socialism ? Ven you vant to eat pig, you do it here, like ve do now, in private. In public ve spit out ven ve see pig. Ah, you are a fool-man ! I am a stadesman, a politician. I vill be de Machiavelli of de movement.'

'Ah, Pinchas, you are a devil of a chap, said Wolf, laughing. 'And yet you say you are the poet of patriotism and Palestine !'

'Vy not ? Vy should ve lif here in captivity ? Vy ve shall not haf our own State and our own President, a man who combine deep politic vid knowledge of Hebrew literature and de pen of a poet ? No, let us fight to get back our country ; ve vill not hang our harps on de villows of Babylon and weep ; ve vill take our swords vid Ezra and Judas Maccabæus and——'

'One thing at a time, Pinchas,' said Simon Wolf. 'At present we have to consider how to distribute these food-tickets. The commitee-men are late ; I wonder if there has been any fighting at the centres, where they have been addressing meetings.'

'Ah, dat is anoder point,' said Pinchas. 'Vy you no let me address meetings, not de little ones in de street, but de great ones in de hall of de club ? Dere my vords vould rush like de moundain dorrents, sveeping avay de corruptions. But you let all dese fool-men talk. You knew, Simon, I and you are de only two persons in de East End who speak Ainglish properly.'

'I know. But these speeches must be in Yiddish.'

'*Gewiss.* But who speak her like me and you? You muz gif me a speech to-night.'

'I can't—really not,' said Simon. The programme's arranged. You know they're all jealous of me already. I dare not leave one out.'

'Ah, no! do not say dat!' said Pinchas, laying his finger pleadingly on the side of his nose.

'I must.'

'You tear my heart in two. I lof you like a broder, almost like a voman. Just von!' There was an appealing smile in his eye.

'I cannot. I shall have a hornets' nest about my ears.'

'Von leedle von, Simon Wolf?' Again his finger was on his nose.

'It is impossible.'

'You haf not considair how my Yiddish shall make kindle every heart, strike tears from every eye, as Moses did from de rock.'

'I have. I know. But what am I to do?'

'Jus dis leedle favour, and I vill be gradeful to you all mine life.'

'You know I would if I could.'

Pinchas's finger was laid more insistently on his nose.

'Just dis vonce. Grant me dis, and I vill nevair ask anyding of you in all my life.'

'No, no! Don't bother, Pinchas. Go away now,' said Wolf getting annoyed. I have lots to do!'

'I vill never gif you mine ideas again!' said the poet, flashing up, and he went out and banged the door.

The labour-leader settled to his papers with a sigh of relief.

The relief was transient. A moment afterwards the door was slightly opened, and Pinchas's head was protruded through the aperture. The poet wore his most endearing smile; the finger was laid coaxingly against the nose.

'Just von leedle speech, Simon. Dink how I lofe you.'

'Oh, well, go away! I'll see,' replied Wolf, laughing amid all his annoyance.

The poet rushed in and kissed the hem of Wolf's coat.

'Oh, you be a great man!' he said. Then he walked out, closing the door gently. A moment afterwards a vision of the dusky head, with the carneying smile and the finger on the nose, reappeared.

'You von't forget your promise?' said the head.

'No, no. Go to the devil! I won't forget.'

Pinchas walked home through streets thronged with excited strikers discussing the situation with Oriental exuberance of gesture with any one who would listen. The demands of these poor slop-hands (who could only count on six hours out of the twenty-four for themselves, and who, by the help of their wives and little ones in finishing, might earn a pound a week) were moderate enough—

hours from eight to eight, with an hour for dinner and half an hour for tea, two shillings from the Government contractors for making a policeman's great-coat instead of one and ninepence halfpenny, and so on and so on.   Their intentions were strictly peaceful. Every face was stamped with the marks of intellect and ill-health, the hue of a muddy pallor relieved by the flash of eyes and teeth. Their shoulders stooped, their chests were narrow, their arms flabby.   They came in their hundreds to the hall at night.   It was square-shaped with a stage and galleries, for a Jargon-company sometimes thrilled the Ghetto with tragedy and tickled it with farce. Both species were playing to-night, and in Jargon to boot.   In real life you always get your drama mixed, and the sock of comedy galls the buskin of tragedy.   It was an episode in the pitiful tussle of hunger and greed, yet its humours were grotesque enough.

Full as the hall was, it was not crowded, for it was Friday night, and a large contingent of strikers refused to desecrate the Sabbath by attending the meeting.   But these were the zealots—Moses Ansell among them, for he, too, had struck.   Having been out of work already, he had nothing to lose by augmenting the numerical importance of the agitation.   The moderately pious argued that there was no financial business to transact, and attendance could hardly come under the denomination of work.   It was rather analogous to attendance at a lecture ; they would simply have to listen to speeches.   Besides, it would be but a black Sabbath at home with a barren larder, and they had already been to synagogue. Thus degenerates ancient piety in the stress of modern social problems.   Some of the men had not even changed their everyday face for their Sabbath countenance by washing it.   Some wore collars and shiny threadbare garments of dignified origin ; others were unaffectedly poverty-stricken with dingy shirt-cuffs peeping out of frayed sleeve-edges, and unhealthily coloured scarves folded complexly round their necks.   A minority belonged to the free-thinking party, but the majority only availed themselves of Wolf's services because they were indispensable.   For the moment he was the only possible leader, and they were sufficiently Jesuitic to use the devil himself for good ends.

Though Wolf would not give up a Friday night meeting, especially valuable as permitting of the attendance of tailors who had not yet struck, Pinchas's politic advice had not failed to make an impression.   Like so many reformers who have started with blatant atheism, he was beginning to see the insignificance of irreligious dissent as compared with the solution of the social problem, and Pinchas's seed had fallen on ready soil.   As a labour-leader pure and simple, he could count upon a far larger following than as a preacher of militant impiety.   He resolved to keep his atheism in the background for the future, and devote himself to the enfranchisement of the body before tampering with the soul.   He was too proud ever to acknowledge his indebtedness to the poet's suggestion, but he felt grateful to him all the same.

'My brothers,' he said in Yiddish, when his turn came to speak, 'it pains me much to note how disunited we are. The capitalists, the Belcovitches, would rejoice if they but knew all that is going on. Have we not enemies enough that we must quarrel and split up into little factions among ourselves?' (Hear, hear.) 'How can we hope to succeed unless we are thoroughly organised? It has come to my ears that there are men who insinuate things even about me, and before I go on further to-night I wish to put this question to you.'

He paused and there was a breathless silence. The orator threw his chest forwards and, gazing fearlessly at the assembly, cried in a stentorian voice.

'*Sind sie zufrieden mit ihrer chairman?*' (Are you satisfied with your chairman?)

His audacity made an impression. The discontented cowered timidly in their places.

'Yes,' rolled back from the assembly, proud of its English monosyllables.

'*Nein,*' cried a solitary voice from the topmost gallery.

Instantly the assembly was on its legs, eyeing the dissentient angrily. 'Get down! Go on the platform!' mingled with cries of 'Order!' from the chairman, who in vain summoned him on to the stage. The dissentient waved a roll of paper violently and refused to modify his standpoint. He was evidently speaking, for his jaws were making movements, which in the din and up-roar could not rise above grimaces. There was a battered high hat on the back of his head, and his hair was uncombed and his face unwashed. At last silence was restored and the tirade became audible.

'Cursed sweaters! capitalists! stealing men's brains! leaving us to rot and starve in darkness and filth. Curse them! Curse them!' The speaker's voice rose to a hysterical scream as he rambled on.

Some of the men knew him, and soon there flew from lip to lip: 'Oh, it's only *meshuggene Dovid.*'

Mad Davy was a gifted Russian university student, who had been mixed up with Nihilistic conspiracies, and had fled to England, where the struggle to find employ for his clerical talents had addled his brain. He had a gift for chess and mechanical invention, and in the early days had saved himself from starvation by the sale of some ingenious patents to a swaggering co-religionist who owned racehorses and a music-hall, but he sank into squaring the circle and inventing perpetual motion. He lived now on the casual crumbs of indigent neighbours, for the charitable organisations had marked him 'dangerous.' He was a man of infinite loquacity, with an intense jealousy of Simon Wolf, or any such uninstructed person who assumed to lead the populace; but when the assembly accorded him his hearing he forgot the occasion of his rising, in a burst of passionate invective against society.

When the irrelevancy of his remarks became apparent he was rudely howled down and his neighbours pulled him into his seat, where he gibbered and mowed inaudibly.

Wolf continued his address :

'*Sind sie zufrieden mit ihrer secretary ?*'

This time there was no dissent. The 'Yes' came like thunder.

'*Sind sie zufrieden mit ihrer treasurer ?*'

Yeas and nays mingled. The question of the retention of the functionary was put to the vote. But there was much confusion, for the East End Jew is only slowly becoming a political animal. The ayes had it, but Wolf was not yet satisfied with the satisfaction of the gathering. He repeated the entire batch of questions in a new formula, so as to drive them home.

'*Hot aner etwas zu sagen gegen mir ?*' Which is Yiddish for, 'Has any one anything to say against me?

'No !' came in a vehement roar.

'*Hot aner etwas zu sagen gegen dem secretary ?*'

'No !'

'*Hot aner etwas zu sagen gegen dem treasurer ?*'

'No !'

Having thus shown his grasp of logical exhaustiveness in a manner unduly exhausting to the more intelligent, Wolf consented to resume his oration. He had scored a victory, and triumph lent him added eloquence. When he ceased he left his audience in a frenzy of resolution and loyalty. In the flush of conscious power and freshly added influence, he found a niche for Pinchas's oratory.

'Brethren in exile,' said the poet in his best Yiddish.

Pinchas spoke German, which is an outlandish form of Yiddish and scarce understanded of the people, so that to be intelligible he had to divest himself of sundry inflections and to throw gender to the winds, and to say 'wet' for 'wird' and mix hybrid Hebrew and ill-pronounced English with his vocabulary. There was some cheering as Pinchas tossed his dishevelled locks and addressed the gathering, for everybody to whom he had ever spoken knew that he was a wise and learned man and a great singer in Israel.

'Brethren in exile,' said the poet, 'the hour has come for laying the sweaters low. Singly we are sand-grains, together we are the simoom. Our great teacher Moses was the first Socialist. The legislation of the Old Testament, the land laws, the jubilee regulations, the tender care for the poor, the subordination of the rights of property to the interests of the working man, all this is pure Socialism !'

The poet paused for the cheers, which came in a mighty volume. Few of those present knew what Socialism was, but all knew the word as a shibboleth of salvation from sweaters. Socialism meant shorter hours and higher wages, and was obtainable by marching with banners and brass bands—what need to inquire further?

'In short,' pursued the poet, 'Socialism is Judaism, and Judaism is Socialism, and Karl Marx and Lassalle, the founders of Socialism, were Jews. Judaism does not bother with the next world ; it says : " Eat, drink, and be satisfied, and thank the Lord thy God, who brought thee out of Egypt from the land of bondage." But we have nothing to eat, we have nothing to drink, we have nothing to be satisfied with, we are still in the land of bondage.' (Cheers.) ' My brothers how can we keep Judaism in a land where there is no Socialism? We must become better Jews, we must bring on Socialism, for the period of Socialism on earth and of peace and plenty and brotherly love is what all our prophets and great teachers meant by Messiah-times.'

A little murmur of dissent rose here and there, but Pinchas went on :

'When Hillel the Great summed up the law to the would-be proselyte while standing on one leg, how did he express it ? " Do not unto others what you would not have others do unto you ?" This is Socialism in a nutshell. Do not keep your riches for yourself ; spread them abroad. Do not fatten on the labour of the poor, but share it. Do not eat the food others have earnt, but earn your own. Yes, brothers, the only true Jews in England are the Socialists. Phylacteries, praying-shawls—all nonsense ! Work for Socialism—that pleases the Almighty. The Messiah will be a Socialist.'

There were mingled sounds, men asking each other dubiously, ' What says he ? ' They began to sniff brimstone. Wolf, shifting uneasily on his chair, kicked the poet's leg in reminder of his own warning. But Pinchas's head was touching the stars again. Mundane considerations were left behind somewhere in the depths of space below his feet.

' But how is the Messiah to redeem his people ? ' he asked. ' Not nowadays by the sword, but by the tongue. He will plead the cause of Judaism, the cause of Socialism, in Parliament. He will not come with mock miracle like Bar Cochba or Zevi. At the General Election, brothers, I will stand as the candidate for Whitechapel. I, a poor man, one of yourselves, will take my stand in that mighty assembly and touch the hearts of the legislators. They shall bend before my oratory as the bulrushes of the Nile when the wind passes. They will make me Prime Minister like Lord Beaconsfield, only he was no true lover of his people—he was not the Messiah. To hell with the rich bankers and the stockbrokers, we want them not. We will free ourselves.'

The extraordinary vigour of the poet's language and gestures told. Only half comprehending, the majority stamped and huzzahed. Pinchas swelled visibly. His slim lithe form, five and a quarter feet high, towered over the assembly. His complexion was as burnished copper ; his eyes flashed flame.

' Yes, brethren,' he resumed, ' these Anglo-Jewish swine trample unheeding on the pearls of poetry and scholarship. They choose for ministers men with four mistresses ; for Chief Rabbis hypo-

crites who cannot even write the Holy Tongue grammatically ; for
Dayanim men who sell their daughters to the rich ; for members
of Parliament stockbrokers who cannot speak English ; for philan
thropists greengrocers who embezzle funds.   Let us have nothing
to do with these swine—Moses our teacher forbade it.' (Laughter.
' I will be the member for Whitechapel.   See, my name Melchit
zedek Pinchas already makes M.P.—it was foreordained.   I
every letter of the Torah has its special meaning, and none was
put by chance, why should the finger of Heaven not have written
my name thus : M.P.—Melchitzedek Pinchas ?   Ah ! our brother
Wolf speaks truth ; wisdom issues from his lips.   Put aside your
petty quarrels, and unite in working for my election to Parliament
Thus, and thus only, shall you be redeemed from bondage, made
from beasts of burden into men, from slaves to citizens, from false
Jews to true Jews.   Thus, and thus only, shall you eat, drink, and
be satisfied, and thank me for bringing you out of the land of
bondage.   Thus, and thus only, shall Judaism cover the world as
the waters cover the sea.'
    The fervid peroration overbalanced the audience, and from all
sides except the platform applause warmed the poet's ears.   He
resumed his seat, and as he did so automatically drew out a
match and a cigar, and lit the one with the other.   Instantly the
applause dwindled, died ; there was a moment of astonished
silence, then a roar of execration.   The bulk of the audience, as
Pinchas, sober, had been shrewd enough to see, was still orthodox
This public profanation of the Sabbath by smoking was intoler
able.   How should the God of Israel aid the spread of Socialism
and the shorter hours movement, and the rise of prices a penny on
a coat, if such devil's incense were borne to His nostrils ?   Their
vague admiration of Pinchas changed into definite distrust
' *Epikouros, Epikouros, Meshumad !*' resounded from all sides
The poet looked wonderingly about him, failing to grasp the situa
tion.   Simon Wolf saw his opportunity.   With an angry jerk he
knocked the glowing cigar from between the poet's teeth.   There
was a yell of delight and approbation.
    Wolf jumped to his feet.   ' Brothers,' he roared, ' you know I
am not *froom* ; but I will not have anybody else's feelings trampled
upon.'   So saying, he ground the cigar under his heel.
    Immediately an abortive blow from the poet's puny arm swished
the air.   Pinchas was roused, the veins on his forehead swelled,
his heart thumped rapidly in his bosom.   Wolf shook his knobby
fist laughingly at the poet, who made no further effort to use any
other weapon of offence but his tongue.
    ' Hypocrite !' he shrieked.   ' Liar !   Machiavelli !   Child of the
separation !   A black year on thee !   An evil spirit in thy bones,
and in the bones of thy father and mother !   Thy father was a
proselyte, and thy mother an abomination.   The curses of Deu
teronomy light on thee !   Mayst thou become covered with boils
like Job !   And you,' he added, turning on the audience, ' pack of

Men-of-the-Earth! stupid animals! how much longer will you bend your neck to the yoke of superstition, while your bellies are empty? Who says I shall not smoke? Was tobacco known to Moses our teacher? If so, he would have enjoyed it on the Shabbos—he was a wise man like me. Did the Rabbis know of it? No, fortunately, else they were so stupid they would have forbidden it. You are all so ignorant that you think not of these things. Can any one show me where it stands that we must not smoke on Shabbos? Is not Shabbos a day of rest, and how can we rest if we smoke not? I believe, with the Baalshem, that God is more pleased when I smoke my cigar than at the prayers of all the stupid Rabbis. How dare you rob me of my cigar—is that keeping Shabbos?'

He turned back to Wolf, and tried to push his foot from off the cigar. There was a brief struggle. A dozen men leapt on the platform, and dragged the poet away from his convulsive clasp of the labour-leader's leg. A few opponents of Wolf on the platform cried, 'Let the man alone; give him his cigar!' and thrust themselves amongst the invaders. The hall was in tumult. From the gallery the voice of Mad Davy resounded again:

'Cursed sweaters! stealing men's brains! darkness and filth! Curse them! Blow them up, as we blew up Alexander! Curse them!'

Pinchas was carried, shrieking hysterically, and striving to bite the arms of his bearers, through the tumultuous crowd, amid a little ineffective opposition, and deposited outside the door.

Wolf made another speech, sealing the impression he had made. Then the poor narrow-chested men went home through the cold air to recite the Song of Solomon in their stuffy hovels and back-rooms and garrets. 'Behold, thou art fair, my love,' they intoned in a strange chant. 'Behold, thou art fair; thou hast doves' eyes. Behold, thou art fair, my beloved, yea, pleasant; also our couch is green. The beams of our house are cedar, and our rafters are fir. . . . For, lo, the winter is past, the rain is over and gone. The flowers appear upon the earth; the time of the singing of birds is come, and the voice of the turtle is heard in our land. . . . Thy plants are an orchard of pomegranates, with pleasant fruits, calamus, cinnamon, with all trees of frankincense; myrrh and aloe, with all the chief spices; a fountain of gardens, a well of living waters and streams from Lebanon. . . . Awake, O north wind, and come, thou south, blow upon my garden, that the spices thereof may flow out.'

CHAPTER XX

THE HOPE EXTINCT

THE strike came to an end soon after. To the delight of Melchitzedek Pinchas, Gideon, M.P., intervened at the eleventh hour, unceremoniously elbowing Simon Wolf out of his central position

A compromise was arranged, and jubilance and tranquillity reigned for some months, till the corruptions of competitive human nature brought back the old state of things, for employers have quite a diplomatic reverence for treaties and the brotherly love of employés breaks down under the strain of supporting families. Rather to his own surprise, Moses Ansell found himself in work at least three days a week, the other three being spent in hanging round the workshop waiting for it. It is an uncertain trade, is the manufacture of slops, which was all Moses was fitted for, but if you are not at hand you may miss the ' work' when it does come.

It never rains but it pours, and so more luck came to the garret of No. 1 Royal Street. Esther won five pounds at school. I was the Henry Goldsmith prize, a new annual prize for general knowledge instituted by a lady named Mrs. Henry Goldsmith, who had just joined the committee, and the semi-divine person herself, a surpassingly beautiful, radiant being, like a princess in a fairy tale, personally congratulated her upon her success. The money was not available for a year, but the neighbours hastened to congratulate the family on its rise to wealth. Even Levi Jacobs's visits became more frequent, though this could scarcely be ascribed to mercenary motives.

The Belcovitches recognised their improved status so far as to send to borrow some salt; for the colony of No. 1 Royal Street carried on an extensive system of mutual accommodation, coals, potatoes, chunks of bread, sauce-pans, needles, wood-choppers, all passing daily to and fro. Even garments and jewellery were lent on great occasions, and when that dear old soul Mrs. Simons went to a wedding, she was decked out in contributions from a dozen wardrobes. The Ansells themselves were too proud to borrow, though they were not above lending.

It was early morning, and Moses in his big phylacteries was droning his orisons. His mother had had an attack of spasms, and so he was praying at home to be at hand in case of need. Everybody was up, and Moses was superintending the household even while he was gabbling psalms. He never minded breaking off his intercourse with Heaven to discuss domestic affairs, for he was on free-and-easy terms with the powers that be, and there was scarce a prayer in the liturgy which he would not interrupt to reprimand Solomon for lack of absorption in the same. The exception was the *Amidah*, or Eighteen Blessings, so called because there are twenty-two. This section must be said standing and inaudibly, and when Moses was engaged upon it a message from an earthly monarch would have extorted no reply from him. There were other sacred silences which Moses would not break save of dire necessity, and then only by talking Hebrew; but the *Amidah* was the silence of silences. This was why the utterly unprecedented arrival of a telegraph boy did not move him. Nor even Esther's cry of alarm when she opened the telegram had any visible effect upon him, though in reality he whispered off his prayer at a record-beating rate, and duly danced three times on his toes with spasmodic celerity at the finale.

'Father,' said Esther, the never-before received species of letter trembling in her hand, 'we must go at once to see Benjy. He is very ill.'

'Has he written to say so?'

'No; this is a telegram. I have read of such. Oh, perhaps he is dead! It is always so in books. They break the news by saying the dead are still alive.

Her tones died away in a sob. The children clustered round her; Rachel and Solomon fought for the telegram in their anxiety to read it. Ikey and Sarah stood grave and interested. The sick grandmother sat up in bed excited.

'He never showed me his "four-corners,"' she moaned. 'Perhaps he did not wear the fringes at all.'

'Father, dost thou hear?' said Esther, for Moses Ansell was fingering the russet envelope with a dazed air 'We must go to the Orphanage at once.'

'Read it! What stands in the letter?' said Moses Ansell.

She took the message from the hands of Solomon.

'It stands: "Come up at once. Your son Benjamin very ill."'

'Tu! tu! tu!' clucked Moses. 'The poor child! But how can we go up? Thou canst not walk there. It will take *me* more than three hours.'

His praying-shawl slid from his shoulders in his agitation.

'Thou must not walk, either!' cried Esther excitedly. 'We must get to him at once! Who knows if he will be alive when we come? We must go by train from London Bridge the way Benjy came that Sunday. Oh, my poor Benjy!'

'Give me back the paper, Esther,' interrupted Solomon, taking it from her limp hand. 'The boys have never seen a telegram.'

'But we cannot spare the money,' urged Moses helplessly. 'We have just enough money to get along with to-day. Solomon, go on with thy prayers; thou seizest every excuse to interrupt them. Rachel, go away from him; thou art also a disturbing Satan to him. I do not wonder his teacher flogged him black and blue yesterday; he is a stubborn and rebellious son who should be stoned, according to Deuteronomy.

'We must do without dinner,' said Esther impulsively.

'Sarah sat down on the floor and howled, 'Woe is me! woe is me!'

'I didden touch 'er,' cried Ikey in indignant bewilderment.

''Tain't Ikey!' sobbed Sarah. 'Little Tharah wants 'er dinner.'

'Thou hearest?' said Moses pitifully. 'How can we spare the money?'

'How much is it?' asked Esther.

It will be a shilling each there and back,' replied Moses, who from his long periods of peregrination was a connoisseur in fares

'How can we afford it when I lose a morning's work into the bargain?'

'No, what talkest thou?' said Esther. 'Thou art looking a few months ahead—thou deemest, perhaps, I am already twelve. It will only be sixpence for me.'

Moses did not disclaim the implied compliment to his rigid honesty, but answered:

'Where is my head? Of course, thou goest half-price. But even so, where is the eighteenpence to come from?'

'But it is not eighteenpence!' ejaculated Esther with a new inspiration. Necessity was sharpening her wits to extraordinary acuteness. 'We need not take return-tickets. We can walk back.'

'But we cannot be so long away from the mother—both of us,' said Moses. 'She, too, is ill. And how will the children do without thee? I will go by myself.'

'No; I must see Benjy!' Esther cried.

'Be not so stiff-necked, Esther! Besides, it stands in the letter that I am to come—they do not ask thee. Who knows that the great people will not be angry if I bring thee with me? I dare say Benjamin will soon be better. He cannot have been ill long.'

'But quick, then, father, quick!' cried Esther, yielding to the complex difficulties of the position. 'Go at once!'

'Immediately, Esther. Wait only till I have finished my prayers. I am nearly done.'

'No! no!' cried Esther, agonised. 'Thou prayest so much, God will let thee off a little bit, just for once. Thou must go at once, and ride both ways—else how shall we know what has happened? I will pawn my new prize, and that will give thee money enough.'

'Good!' said Moses. 'While thou art pledging the book, I shall have time to finish praying.' He hitched up his *Talith*, and commenced to gabble off: '"Happy are those who dwell in Thy house; ever shall they praise Thee—Selah,"' and was already saying, '"And a Redeemer shall come unto Zion,"' by the time Esther rushed out through the door with the pledge. It was a gaudily-bound volume, called *Treasures of Science*; and Esther knew it almost by heart, having read it twice from gilt cover to gilt cover. All the same, she would miss it sorely.

The pawnbroker lived only round the corner, for, like the publican, he springs up wherever the conditions are favourable. He was a Christian. By a curious anomaly the Ghetto does not supply its own pawnbrokers, but sends them out to the provinces or the West End. Perhaps the business instinct dreads the solicitation of the racial.

Esther's pawnbroker was a rubicund, portly man. He knew the fortunes of a hundred families by the things left with him or taken back. It was on his stuffy shelves that poor Benjamin's coat had lain compressed and packed away, when it might have had a beautiful airing in the grounds of the Crystal Palace. It was from his stuffy shelves that Esther's mother had redeemed it, a day after the fair—soon to be herself compressed and packed away in a pauper's coffin, awaiting in silence whatsoever Redemption might be. The 'best coat' itself had long since been sold to a ragman; for Solomon, upon whose back it devolved when Benjamin was so happily translated, could never be got to keep a best coat longer than a year, and when a best coat is degraded to everyday wear its attrition is much more than six times as rapid.

'Good-mornen, my little dear,' said the rubicund man. 'You're early this mornen.' The apprentice had, indeed, only just taken down the shutters. 'What can I do for you to-day? You look pale, my dear; what's the matter?'

'I have a bran-new seven-and-sixpenny book,' she answered hurriedly, passing it to him.

He turned instinctively to the fly-leaf.

'Bran-new book!' he said contemptuously. '"Esther Ansell—for improvement"! When a book's spiled like that, what can you expect for it?'

'Why, it's the inscription that makes it valuable,' said Esther tearfully.

'Maybe,' said the rubicund man gruffly. 'But d' yer suppose I should just find a buyer named Esther Ansell? Do you suppose everybody in the world's named Esther Ansell, or is capable of improvement?'

'No,' breathed Esther dolefully. 'But I shall take it out myself soon.'

'In this world,' said the rubicund man, shaking his head sceptically, 'there ain't never no knowing. Well, how much d' yer want?'

'I only want a shilling,' said Esther, 'and threepence,' she added as a happy thought.

'All right,' said the rubicund man, softened; I won't 'aggle this mornen. You look quite knocked up. Here you are!'

And Esther darted out of the shop, with the money clasped tightly in her palm.

Moses had folded his phylacteries with pious primness, and put them away in a little bag, and he was hastily swallowing a cup of coffee.

'Here is the shilling,' she cried, 'and twopence extra for the 'bus to London Bridge. Quick!'

She put the ticket away carefully among its companions, in a discoloured leather purse her father had once picked up in the street, and hurried him off. When his step ceased on the stairs, she yearned to run after him and go with him; but Ikey was clamouring for breakfast, and the children had to run off to school. She remained at home herself, for the grandmother groaned heavily. When the other children had gone off, she tidied up the vacant bed and smoothed the old woman's pillows. Suddenly Benjamin's reluctance to have his father exhibited before his new companions recurred to her. She hoped Moses would not be needlessly obtrusive, and felt that if she had gone with him she might have supplied tact in this direction. She reproached herself for not having made him a bit more presentable. She should have spared another halfpenny for a new collar, and seen that he was washed. But in the rush and alarm all thoughts of propriety had been submerged.

Then her thoughts went off at a tangent, and she saw her classroom, where new things were being taught, and new marks gained. It galled her to think she was missing both.

She felt so lonely in the company of her grandmother, she could have gone downstairs and cried on Dutch Debby's musty lap. Then she strove to picture the room where Benjy was lying, but her imagination lacked the data. She would not let herself think the brilliant Benjamin was dead, that he would be sewn up in a shroud just like his poor mother, who had no literary talent whatever; but she wondered whether he was groaning like the grandmother. And so, half distracted, pricking up her ears at the slightest creak on the stairs, Esther waited for news of her Benjy. The hours dragged on and on, and the children coming home at one found dinner ready, but Esther still waiting. A dusty sunbeam streamed in through the garret window as though to give her hope.

Benjamin had been beguiled from his books into an unaccustomed game of ball in the cold March air. He had taken off his jacket, and had got very hot with his unwonted exertions. A reactionary chill followed. Benjamin had a slight cold, which, being ignored, developed rapidly into a heavy one, still without inducing the energetic lad to ask to be put upon the sick-list. Was not the publishing day of *Our Own* at hand?

The cold became graver with the same rapidity, and almost as soon as the boy had made complaint he was in a high fever, and the official doctor declared that pneumonia had set in. In the night Benjamin was delirious, and the nurse summoned the doctor, and next morning his condition was so critical that his father was telegraphed for. There was little to be done by science; all depended on the patient's constitution. Alas! the four years of plenty and country breezes had not counteracted the eight and three-quarter years of privation and foul air, especially in a lad more intent on emulating Dickens and Thackeray than on profiting by the advantages of his situation.

When Moses arrived, he found his boy tossing restlessly in a little bed, in a private little room away from the great dormitories. The 'matron,' a sweet-faced young lady, was bending tenderly over him, and a nurse sat at the bedside. The doctor stood, waiting, at the foot of the bed. Moses took his boy's hand. The matron silently stepped aside. Benjamin stared at him with wide, unrecognising eyes.

'*Nu*—how goes it, Benjamin?' cried Moses, in Yiddish, with mock heartiness.

'Thank you, Old Four-Eyes. It's very good of you to come. I always said there musn't be any hits at you in the paper. I always told the fellows you were a very decent chap.'

'What says he?' asked Moses, turning to the company. 'I cannot understand English.'

They could not understand his own question; but the matron guessed it. She tapped her forehead and shook her head for reply. Benjamin closed his eyes, and there was silence. Presently he opened them and looked straight at his father. A deeper crimson mantled on the flushed cheek, as Benjamin beheld the dingy, stooping being to whom he owed birth. Moses wore a dirty red scarf below his untrimmed beard; his clothes were greasy, his face had not yet been washed, and, for a climax, he had not removed his hat, which other considerations than those of etiquette should have impelled him to keep out of sight.

'I thought you were Old Four-Eyes,' the boy murmured in confusion. 'Wasn't he here just now?'

'Go and fetch Mr. Coleman,' said the matron to the nurse, half smiling through tears at her own knowledge of the teacher's nickname, and wondering what endearing term she was herself known by.

'Cheer up, Benjamin!' said his father, seeing his boy had become sensible of his presence. 'Thou wilt be all right soon. Thou hast been much worse than this.'

'What does he say?' asked Benjamin, turning his eyes towards the matron.

'He says he is sorry to see you so bad,' said the matron at a venture.

'But I shall be up soon, won't I? I can't have *Our Own* delayed,' whispered Benjamin.

'Don't worry about *Our Own*, my poor boy,' murmured the matron, pressing his forehead. Moses respectfully made way for her.

'What says he?' he asked. The matron repeated the words, but Moses could not understand the English.

Old Four-Eyes arrived—a mild, spectacled young man. He looked at the doctor, and the doctor's eye told him all.

'Ah, Mr. Coleman,' said Benjamin with joyous huskiness, 'you'll see that *Our Own* comes out this week as usual. Tell Jack Simmonds he must not forget to rule black lines round the page containing Bruno's epitaph. Bony-nose—I—I mean Mr. Bernstein—wrote it for us in dog-Latin. Isn't it a lark? Thick black lines, tell him. He was a good dog, and only bit one boy in his life.'

'All right; I'll see to it,' Old Four-Eyes assured him with answering huskiness.

'What says he?' helplessly inquired Moses, addressing himself to the new-comer.

'Isn't it a sad case, Mr. Coleman?' said the matron in a low tone. 'They can't understand each other.'

'You ought to keep an interpreter on the premises,' said the doctor, blowing his nose. Coleman struggled with himself. He knew the jargon to perfection, for his parents spoke it still, but he had always posed as being ignorant of it.

'Tell my father to go home, and not to bother; I'm all right—only a little weak,' whispered Benjamin.

Coleman was deeply perturbed. He was wondering whether he should plead guilty to a little knowledge, when a change of expression came over the wan face on the pillow. The doctor came and felt the boy's pulse.

'No; I don't want to hear that *Maaseh* !' cried Benjamin. 'Tell me about the Sambatyon, father, which refuses to flow on Shabbos.'

He spoke Yiddish, grown a child again. Moses's face lit up with joy. His eldest-born had returned to intelligibility. There was hope still, then. A sudden burst of sunshine flooded the room. In London the sun would not break through the clouds for some hours. Moses leaned over the pillow, his face working with blended emotions. He let a hot tear fall on his boy's upturned face.

'Hush, hush, my little Benjamin, don't cry!' said Benjamin, and began to sing in his mother's jargon :

> ' " *Sleep, little father, sleep ;*
> *Thy father shall be a Rav :*
> *Thy mother shall bring little apples ;*
> *Blessings on thy little head !"* '

Moses saw his dead Gittel lulling his boy to sleep. Blinded by his tears, he did not see that they were falling thick upon the little white face.

'Nay, dry thy tears, I tell thee, my little Benjamin !' said Benjamin in tones more tender and soothing, and launched into the strange wailing melody :

> ' " *Alas, woe is me !*
> *How wretched to be*
> *Driven away and banished,*
> *Yet so young, from thee !"* '

'And Joseph's mother called to him from the grave. Be comforted, my son ; a great future shall be thine.'

'The end is near,' Old Four-Eyes whispered to the father in jargon.

Moses trembled from head to foot. 'My poor lamb ! My poor Benjamin !' he wailed. 'I thought thou wouldst say *Kaddish* after me, not I for thee ! Then he began to recite quietly the Hebrew prayers. The hat he should have removed was appropriate enough now.

Benjamin sat up excitedly in bed.

'There's mother, Esther !' he cried in English, ' coming back with my coat. But what's the use of it now ?'

His head fell back again. Presently a look of yearning came over the face so full of boyish beauty.

'Esther,' he said, 'wouldn't you like to be in the green country to-day? Look how the sun shines!'

It shone indeed, with deceptive warmth, bathing in gold the green country that stretched beyond, and dazzling the eyes of the dying boy. The birds twittered outside the window.

'Esther,' he said wistfully, 'do you think there'll be another funeral soon?'

The matron burst into tears and turned away.

'Benjamin,' cried the father frantically, thinking the end had come, 'say the *Shemang*.'

The boy stared at him, a clearer look in his eyes.

'Say the *Shemang*!' said Moses peremptorily.

The word *Shemang*, the old authoritative tone, penetrated the consciousness of the dying boy.

'Yes, father, I was just going to,' he grumbled submissively.

They repeated the last declaration of the dying Israelite together. It was in Hebrew. ' "Hear, O Israel, the Lord our God, the Lord is One." ' Both understood that.

Benjamin lingered on a few more minutes, and died in a painless torpor.

'He is dead,' said the doctor.

'Blessed be the True Judge,' said Moses. He rent his coat and closed the staring eyes. Then he went to the toilette-table and turned the looking-glass to the wall, and opened the window and emptied the jug of water upon the green sunlit grass.

CHAPTER XXI

THE JARGON PLAYERS

'No, don't stop me, Pinchas!' said Gabriel Hamburg. 'I'm packing up, and I shall spend my Passover in Stockholm. The Chief Rabbi there has discovered a manuscript which I am anxious to see, and as I have saved up a little money, I shall speed thither.'

'Ah, he pays well, that boy-fool, Raphael Leon,' said Pinchas, emitting a lazy ring of smoke. They spoke in German.

'What do you mean?' cried Gabriel, flushing angrily. 'Do you mean, perhaps, that *you* have been getting money out of him?'

'Precisely. That is what I *do* mean,' said the poet naïvely. 'What else?'

'Well, don't let me hear you call him a fool. He *is* one to send you money, but then it is for others to call him so. That boy will be a great man in Israel. The son of rich English Jews

—a Harrow boy—yet he already writes Hebrew almost grammatically.'

Pinchas was aware of this fact; had he not written to the lad (in response to a crude Hebrew eulogium and a crisp Bank of England note): 'I and thou are the only two people in England who write the Holy Tongue grammatically?'

To Hamburg he replied now: 'It is true; soon he will vie with me and you.'

The old scholar took snuff impatiently.   The humours of Pinchas were beginning to pall upon him.

'Good-bye,' he said again.

'No, wait yet a little,' said Pinchas, buttonholing him resolutely. 'I want to show you my acrostic on Simon Wolf—ah! I will shoot him, the miserable labour-leader, the wretch who embezzles the money of the Socialist fools who trust him.   Aha! it will sting like Juvenal, that acrostic.'

'I haven't time,' said the gentle savant, beginning to lose his temper.

'Well, have I time?   I have to compose a three-act comedy by to-morrow at noon.   I expect I shall have to sit up all night to get it done in time.'   Then, anxious to complete the conciliation of the old snuff-and-pepper-box, as he mentally christened him for his next acrostic, he added: 'If there is anything in this manuscript that you cannot decipher or understand, a letter to me, care of Reb Shemuel, will always find me.   Somehow, I have a special genius for filling up lacunæ in manuscripts.   You remember the famous discovery that I made by rewriting the six lines torn out of the first page of that Midrash I discovered in Cyprus?'

'Yes; those six lines proved it thoroughly,' sneered the savant.

'Aha, you see,' said the poet, a gratified childish smile pervading his dusky features.   'But I must tell you of this comedy: it will be a satirical picture (in the style of Molière, only sharper) of Anglo-Jewish society.   The Rev. Elkan Benjamin, with his four mistresses, they will be all there; and Gideon, the Man-of-the-Earth M.P.—ah, it will be terrible!   If I could only get them to see it performed they should have free passes!'

'No, shoot them first; it would be more merciful.   But where is this comedy to be played?' asked Hamburg curiously.

'At the Jargon Theatre, the great theatre in Princes' Street, the only real national theatre in England.   The English stage—Drury Lane—pooh!   It is not in harmony with the people; it does not express them.'

Hamburg could not help smiling.   He knew the wretched little hall, since tragically famous for a massacre of innocents, victims to the fatal cry of 'Fire!'—more deadly than fiercest flame.

'But how will your audience understand it?' he asked.

'Aha!' said the poet, laying his finger on his nose and grinning, 'they will understand.   They know the corruptions of our society. All this conspiracy to crush me, to hound me out of England, so that ignoramuses may prosper and hypocrites wax fat—do you think it is not the talk of the Ghetto ? What ! shall it be the talk of Berlin, of Constantinople, of Mogadore, of Jerusalem, of Paris, and here it shall not be known ? Besides the leading actress will speak a prologue. Ah, she is beautiful : beautiful as Lilith, as the Queen of Sheba, as Cleopatra ! And how she acts ! She and Rachel—both Jewesses ! Think of it ! Ah, we are a great people ! If I could tell you the secrets of her eyes as she looks at me ; but no, you are dry as dust, a creature of prose ! And there will be an orchestra, too, for Pesach Weingott has promised to play the overture on his fiddle. How he stirs the soul ! It is like David playing before Saul.'

'Yes, but it won't be javelins the people will throw,' murmured Hamburg, adding aloud : 'I suppose you have written the music of this overture.'

'No, I cannot write music,' said Pinchas.

'Good heavens ! you don't say so ?' gasped Gabriel Hamburg. 'Let that be my last recollection of you. No ; don't say another word ! Don't spoil it ! Good-bye.' And he tore himself away, leaving the poet bewildered.

'Mad, mad !' said Pinchas, tapping his brow significantly. 'Mad, the old snuff-and-pepper-box !' He smiled at the recollection of his latest phrase. 'These scholars stagnate so ; they see not enough of the women. Ha ! I will go and see my actress.'

He threw out his chest, puffed out a volume of smoke, and took his way to Petticoat Lane. The compatriot of Rachel was wrapping up a scrag of mutton. She was a butcher's daughter, and did not even wield the chopper as Mrs. Siddons is reputed to have flourished the domestic table-knife. She was a simple, amiable girl, who had stepped into the position of lead in the stock Jargon company as a way of eking out her pocket-money, and because there was no one else who wanted the post. She was rather plain except when be-rouged and be-pencilled. The company included several tailors and tailoresses of talent, and the low comedian was a Dutchman who sold herrings. They all had the gift of improvisation more developed than memory, and con · sequently availed themselves of the faculty that worked easier. The repertory was written by goodness knew whom, and was very extensive. It embraced all the species enumerated by Polonius, including comic opera, which was not known to the Danish saw-monger. There was nothing the company would not have undertaken to play, or have come out of without a fair measure of success. Some of the plays were on Biblical subjects, but only a minority. There were also plays in rhyme, though Yiddish knows not blank verse.

Melchitzedek accosted his interpretress and made sheep's-eyes at her. But an actress who serves in a butcher's shop is doubly accustomed to such, and, being busy, the girl paid no attention to the poet, though the poet was paying marked attention to her.

'Kiss me, thou beauteous one, the gems of whose crown are footlights,' said the poet, when the custom ebbed for a moment.

'If thou comest near me,' said the actress, whirling the chopper, I'll chop thy ugly little head off.'

'Unless thou lendest me thy lips thou shalt not play in my comedy,' cried Pinchas angrily.

'*My* trouble!' said the leading lady, shrugging her shoulders.

Pinchas made several reappearances outside the open shop, with his insinuative finger on his nose, and his insinuative smile on his face, but in the end went away with a flea in his ear and hunted up the actor-manager, the only person who made any money to speak of out of the performances. That gentleman had not yet consented to produce the play that Pinchas had ready in manuscript, and which had been coveted by all the great theatres in the world, but which he, Pinchas, had reserved for the use of the only actor in Europe. The result of this interview was that the actor-manager yielded to Pinchas's solicitations, backed by frequent applications of poetic finger to poetic nose.

'But,' said the actor-manager with a sudden recollection, 'how about the besom?'

'The besom?' repeated Pinchas, nonplussed for once.

'Yes; thou sayest thou hast seen all the plays I have produced. Hast thou not noticed that I have a besom in all my plays?'

'Aha! Yes, I remember,' said Pinchas.

'An old garden-besom it is,' said the actor-manager. 'And it is the cause of all my luck.' He took up a house-broom that stood in the corner. 'In comedy I sweep the floor with it, so, and the people grin; in comic opera I beat time with it as I sing, so, and the people laugh; in farce I beat my mother-in-law with it, so, and the people roar; in tragedy I lean upon it, so, and the people thrill; in melodrama I sweep away the snow with it, so, and the people burst into tears. Usually I have my plays written beforehand, and the authors are aware of the besom. Dost thou think,' he concluded doubtfully, 'that thou hast sufficient ingenuity to work in the besom now that the play is written?'

Pinchas put his finger to his nose and smiled reassuringly.

'It shall be all besom,' he said.

'And when wilt thou read it to me?'

'Will to-morrow this time suit thee?'

'As honey a bear.'

'Good then!' said Pinchas. 'I shall not fail.'

The door closed upon him; in another moment it re-opened a bit and he thrust his grinning face through the aperture.

'Ten per cent. of the receipts!' he said with his cajoling digito-nasal gesture.

'Certainly,' rejoined the actor-manager briskly. 'After paying the expenses, ten per cent. of the receipts.'

'Thou wilt not forget?'

'I shall not forget.'

Pinchas strode forth into the street and lit a new cigar in his exultation. How lucky the play was not yet written ! Now he would be able to make it all turn round the axis of the besom. 'It shall be all besom !' His own phrase rang in his ears like voluptuous marriage bells. Yes, it should indeed be all besom ; with that besom he would sweep all his enemies—all the foul conspirators —in one clean sweep down, down to Sheol. He would sweep them along the floor with it, so, and grin ; he would beat time to their yells of agony, so, and laugh ; he would beat them over the heads, so, and roar ; he would lean upon it in statuesque great-ness, so, and thrill ; he would sweep away their remains with it, so, and weep for joy of countermining and quelling the long per-secution.

All night he wrote the play at railway speed, like a night express, puffing out volumes of smoke as he panted along. ' I dip my pen in their blood,' he said from time to time, and threw back his head and laughed aloud in the silence of the small-hours.

Pinchas had a good deal to do to explain the next day to the actor-manager where the fun came in. 'Thou dost not grasp all the allusions, the backhanded slaps, the hidden poniards—perhaps not,' the author acknowledged. 'But the great heart of the people —it will understand.'

The actor-manager was unconvinced, but he admitted there was a good deal of besom, and in consideration of the poet bating his terms to five per cent. of the receipts he agreed to give it a chance. The piece was billed widely in several streets under the title of ' The Hornet of Judah,' and the name of Melchitzedek Pinchas appeared in letters of the size stipulated by the finger on the nose.

But the leading actress threw up her part at the last moment, disgusted by the poet's amorous advances ; Pinchas volunteered to play the part himself, and, although his offer was rejected, he attired himself in skirts and streaked his complexion with red and white to replace the promoted second actress, and shaved off his beard.

But in spite of this heroic sacrifice the gods were unpropitious. They chaffed the poet in polished Yiddish throughout the first two acts. There was only a sprinkling of audience (most of it paper) in the dimly-lit hall, for the fame of the great writer had not yet spread from Berlin, Mogadore, Constantinople, and the rest of the universe.

No one could make head or tail of the piece, with its incessant play of occult satire against clergymen with four mistresses, Rabbis who sold their daughters, stockbrokers ignorant of Hebrew and destitute of English, greengrocers blowing Messianic and their own trumpets, labour-leaders embezzling funds, and the like. In vain the actor-manager swept the floor with the besom, beat time with the besom, beat his mother-in-law with the besom, leaned on the besom, swept bits of white paper with the bosom. The hall, empty of its usual crowd, was fuller of derisive laughter. At last the spectators tired of laughter, and the rafters re-echoed with hoots. At the end of the second act Melchitzedek Pinchas addressed the audience from the stage, in his ample petticoats, his brow streaming with paint and perspiration. He spoke of the great English conspiracy, and expressed his grief and astonishment at finding it had infected the entire Ghetto.

There was no third act. It was the poet's first, and last, appearance on any stage.

CHAPTER XXII

'FOR AULD LANG SYNE, MY DEAR'

THE learned say that Passover was a Spring Festival even before it was associated with the Redemption from Egypt, but there is not much nature to worship in the Ghetto, and the historical elements of the Festival swamp all the others. Passover still remains the most picturesque of the 'Three Festivals,' with its entire transmogrification of things culinary, its thorough taboo of leaven. The audacious archæologist of the thirtieth century may trace back the origin of the Festival to the spring-cleaning, the annual revel of the English housewife, for it is now that the Ghetto whitewashes itself, and scrubs itself, and paints itself, and pranks itself, and purifies its pans in a baptism of fire. Now, too, the publican gets unto himself a white sheet, and suspends it at his door, and proclaims that he sells *Kosher rum* by permission of the Chief Rabbi. Now the confectioner exchanges his 'stuffed monkeys,' and his bolas, and his jam-puffs, and his cheese-cakes, for unleavened 'palavas,' and worsted balls, and almond cakes. Time was when the Passover dietary was restricted to fruit and meat and vegetables, but year by year the circle is expanding, and it should not be beyond the reach of ingenuity to make bread itself Passoverian. It is now that the pious shopkeeper whose store is tainted with leaven sells his business to a friendly Christian, buying it back at the conclusion of the Festival. Now the Shalotten Shammos is busy from morning to night filling up charity-forms, artistically multiplying the poor man's children and dividing his rooms. Now is holocaust made of a people's breadcrumbs, and now is the national salutation changed to 'How do the *Motsos* agree with you?' half of the race growing facetious, and the other half finical, over the spotted Passover cakes.

It was on the evening preceding the opening of Passover that Esther Ansell set forth to purchase a shilling's-worth of fish in Petticoat Lane, involuntarily storing up in her mind vivid impressions of the bustling scene. It is one of the compensations of poverty that it allows no time for mourning.   Daily duty is the poor man's nepenthe.

Esther and her father were the only two members of the family upon whom the death of Benjamin made a deep impression.   He had been so long away from home that he was the merest shadow to the rest.   But Moses bore the loss with resignation, his emotions discharging themselves in the daily *Kaddish*.   Blent with his personal grief was a sorrow for the commentaries lost to Hebrew literature by his boy's premature transference to Paradise. Esther's grief was more bitter and defiant.   All the children were delicate, but it was the first time death had taken one.   The meaningless tragedy of Benjamin's end shook the child's soul to its depths.   Poor lad !   How horrible to be lying cold and ghastly beneath the winter snow !   What had been the use of all his long preparations to write great novels ?   The name of Ansell would now become ingloriously extinct.   She wondered whether *Our Own* would collapse, and secretly felt it must.   And then what of the hopes of worldly wealth she had built on Benjamin's genius ? Alas ! the emancipation of the Ansells from the yoke of poverty was clearly postponed.   To her, and her alone, must the family now look for deliverance.   Well, she would take up the mantle of the dead boy and fill it as best she might.   She clenched her little hands in iron determination.   Moses Ansell knew nothing either of her doubts or her ambitions.   Work was still plentiful three days a week, and he was unconscious he was not supporting his family in comparative affluence.   But even with Esther the incessant grind of school-life and quasi-motherhood speedily rubbed away the sharper edges of sorrow, though the custom prohibiting obvious pleasures during the year of mourning went in no danger of transgression, for poor little Esther gadded neither to children's balls nor to theatres.   Her thoughts were full of the prospects of piscine bargains as she pushed her way through a crowd so closely wedged, and lit up by such a glare of gas from the shops and such streamers of flame from the barrows, that the cold wind of early April lost its sting.

Two opposing currents of heavy laden pedestrians were endeavouring in their progress to occupy the same strip of pavement at the same moment, and the laws of space kept them blocked till they yielded to its remorseless conditions.   Rich and poor elbowed one another ; ladies in satins and furs were jammed against wretched-looking foreign women with their heads swathed in dirty handkerchiefs ; rough, red-faced English betting-men struggled good-humouredly with their greasy kindred from over the North Sea ; and a sprinkling of Christian yokels surveyed the Jewish hucksters and chapmen with amused superiority.

For this was the night of nights, when the purchases were made for the Festival, and great ladies of the West, leaving behind their daughters who played the piano and had a subscription at Mudie's, came down again to the beloved Lane to throw off the veneer of

refinement, and plunge gloveless hands in barrels where pickled
cucumbers weltered in their own *Russel*, and to pick fat juicy olives
from the rich-heaped tubs.   Ah me! what tragi-comedy lay behind
the transient happiness of these sensuous faces, laughing and
munching with the shamelessness of school-girls ! For to-night
they need not hanker in silence after the flesh-pots of Egypt.   To-
night they could laugh and talk over *Olov Hasholom* times—
' Peace be upon him !' times—with their old cronies, and loosen
the stays of social ambition, even while they dazzled the Ghetto
with the splendours of their get-up and the halo of the West End
whence they came.   It was a scene without parallel in the history
of the world—this phantasmagoria of grubs and butterflies, met
together for auld lang syne in their beloved hatching-place.   Such
violent contrasts of wealth and poverty as might be looked for in
romantic goldfields or in unsettled countries were evolved quite
naturally amid a colourless civilisation by a people with an incurable talent for the picturesque.

' Hullo ! Can that be you, Betsy?' some grizzled, shabby old
man would observe in innocent delight to Mrs. Arthur Montmorenci. ' Why, so it is ; I never would have believed my eyes !
Lord, what a fine woman you've grown ! And so you're little
Betsy who used to bring her father's coffee in a brown jug when
he and I stood side by side in the Lane ?   He used to sell slippers
next to my cutlery stall for eleven years.   Dear, dear, how time
flies, to be sure !'

Then Betsy Montmorenci's creamy face would grow scarlet
under the gas-jets, and she would glower and draw her sables
round her and look round involuntarily, to see if any Kensington
friends were within ear-shot.

Another Betsy Montmorenci would feel Bohemian for this occasion only, and would receive old acquaintances' greetings effusively,
and pass the old phrases and by-words with a strange sense
of stolen sweets ; while yet a third Betsy Montmorenci—a finer
spirit this, and worthier of the name—would cry to a Betsy Jacobs:
' Is that you, Betsy ? How *are* you? How *are* you? I'm so
glad to see you.   Won't you come and treat me to a cup of chocolate at Bonn's, just to show you haven't forgot *Olov Hasholom*
times ?'

And then, having thus thrown the responsibility of stand-offish-
ness on the poorer Betsy, the Montmorenci would launch into
recollections of those good old ' Peace be upon him !' times till the
grub forgot the splendours of the butterfly in a joyous resurrection
of ancient scandals.   But few of the Montmorencis, whatever their
species, left the Ghetto without pressing bits of gold into half-
reluctant palms in shabby back rooms where old friends or poor
relatives mouldered.

Overhead the stars burned silently, but no one looked up at
them.   Under foot lay the thick black veil of mud which the Lane
never lifted, but none looked down on it.   It was impossible

to think of aught but humanity in the bustle and confusion, in the
cram and crush, in the wedge and the jam, in the squeezing and
shouting, in the hubbub and medley—such a jolly, rampant,
screaming, fighting, maddening, jostling, polyglot, quarrelling,
laughing broth of a Vanity Fair! Mendicants, vendors, buyers,
gossips, showmen, all swelled the roar.

'Here's your cakes! all *Yontovdik* (for the festival)! *Yontovdik*——'

'Braces, best braces; all——'

'*Yontovdik*, only one shilling——'

'It's the Rav's orders, mum; all legs of mutton must be porged,
or my license ——'

'Cowcumbers! cowcumbers!'

'Now's your chance!'

'The best trousers, gentlemen. Corst me as sure as I stand——'

'On your own head, you old——'

'*Arbah Kanfus* (four-corners)! *Arbah*——'

'My old man's been under an operation——'

'Hokey-pokey! *Yontovdik!* Hokey——'

'Get out of the way, can't you!'

'By your life and mine, Betsy——'

'Gord blesh you, mishter! a toisand yer shall ye live!'

'Eat the best *Motsos*! Only fourpence——'

'The bones must go with, marm. I've cut it as lean as possible.'

'*Charoises!* (a sweet mixture), *Charoises! Moroire!* (bitter
herb), *Chraine!* (horse radish), *Pesachdik!* (for Passover.)'

'Come and have a glass of old Tom along o' me, sonny!'

'Fine plaice! Here y' are! Hi! where's yer pluck? S'elp
me——'

'Bob! *Yontovdik! Yontovdik!* only a bob!'

'Chuck steak and half a pound of fat!'

'A slap in the eye if you——'

'Gord bless you! Remember me to Jacob.'

'*Shaink* (spare) meer a 'apenny, missis *lieben*, missis *croin*
(dear)——'

'An unnatural death on you, you——'

'Lord, Sal, how you've altered!'

'Ladies, here you are!'

'I give you my word, sir, the fish will be home before you.'

'Painted in the best style for a tanner!'

'A spoonge, mister?'

'I'll cut a slice of this melon for you for——'

'She's dead, poor thing! peace be upon him!'

'*Yontovdik!* Three bob for one purse containing——'

'The real live tattooed Hindian, born in the Hafrican Harchi-
pellygo! Walk up!'

'This way for the dwarf that will speak, dance, and sing!'

'Tree lemons a penny! Tree lemons——'

'A *Shtibbur* (penny) for a poor blind man!'

' *Yontovdik! Yontovdik! Yontovdik! Yontovdik!* '

And in this last roar, common to so many of the mongers, the whole Babel would often blend for a moment and be swallowed up, re-emerging anon in its broken multiplicity.

Everybody Esther knew was in the crowd ; she met them all sooner or later. In Wentworth Street, amid dead cabbage-leaves and mud and refuse and orts and offal, stood the woe-begone Meckish, offering his puny sponges and wooing the charitable with grinning grimaces, tempered by epileptic fits at judicious intervals. A few inches off, his wife in costly sealskin jacket purchased salmon with a Maida Vale manner. Compressed in a corner was Shosshi Shmendrik, his coat-tails yellow with the yolks of dissolving eggs from a bag in his pocket. He asked her frantically if she had seen a boy whom he had hired to carry home his cod-fish and his fowls, and explained that his missus was busy in the shop, and had delegated to him the domestic duties. It is probable that if Mrs. Shmendrik, formerly the Widow Finkelstein, ever received these dainties, she found her good man had purchased fish artificially inflated with air and fowls fattened with brown paper. Hearty Sam Abrahams, the bass chorister, whose genial countenance spread sunshine for yards around, stopped her and gave her a penny. Further on she met her teacher, Miss Miriam Hyams, and curtseyed to her, for Esther was not of those who jeeringly called 'teacher' and 'master,' according to sex, after her superiors till the victims longed for Elisha's influence over bears. Later on she was shocked to see her teacher's brother piloting bonnie Bessie Sugarman through the thick of the ferment. Crushed between two barrows she found Mrs. Belcovitch and Fanny, who were shopping together, attended by Pesach Weingott, all carrying piles of purchases.

' Esther, if you should see my Becky in the crowd, tell her where I am,' said Mrs. Belcovitch. ' She is with one of her chosen young men. I am so feeble I can hardly crawl around, and my Becky ought to carry home the cabbages. She has well-matched legs, not one a thick one and one a thin one.'

Around the fishmongers the press was great. The fish trade was almost monopolised by English Jews, blonde, healthy-looking fellows with brawny bare arms, who were approached with dread by all but the bravest foreign Jewesses ; their scale of prices and politeness varied with the status of the buyer. Esther, who had an observant eye and ear for such things, often found amusement standing unobtrusively by. To-night there was the usual comedy awaiting her enjoyment. A well-dressed dame came up to ' Uncle Abe's stall, where half a dozen lots of fishy miscellanea were spread out.

' Good-evening, madam. Cold night, but fine. That lot ? Well, you 're an old customer, and fish are cheap to-day, so I can let you have 'em for a sovereign. Eighteen ? Well, it 's hard, but —boy ! take the lady's fish. Thank you. Good-evening.'

'How much that?' said a neatly-dressed woman, pointing to a precisely similar lot.

'Can't take less than nine bob. Fish are dear to-day. You won't get anything cheaper in the Lane ; by G— you won't ! Five shillings ! By my life and by my children's life, they cost me more than that. So sure as I stand here, I paid—well, come, gi 's seven and six and they 're yours. You can't afford more than five ? Well, 'old up your apron, old gal. I 'll make it up out of the rich. By your life and mine, you 've got a *Metsiah* (bargain) there.'

Here old Mrs. Shmendrik, Shosshi's mother, came up, a rich Paisley shawl over her head in lieu of a bonnet. Lane women who went out without bonnets were on the same plane as Lane men who went out without collars.

One of the terrors of the English fishmongers was that they required the customer to speak English, thus fulfilling an important educative function in the community. They allowed a certain percentage of jargon-words, for they themselves took licenses in this direction, but they professed not to understand pure Yiddish.

'Abraham, 'ow mosh for dees lot?' said old Mrs. Shmendrik, turning over a third similar heap and feeling the fish all over.

'Paws off !' said Abraham roughly. 'Look here ! I know the tricks of you Polakinties. I 'll name you the lowest price, and won't stand a farthing's bating. I 'll lose by you, but you ain't going to worry me. Eight bob ! There !'

'Avroomkely (dear little Abraham), take lebbenpence !'

'Elevenpence ! By G—!' cried Uncle Abe, desperately tearing his hair. 'I knew it !' And, seizing a huge plaice by the tail, he whirled it round and struck Mrs. Shmendrik full in the face, shouting, 'Take that, you old witch ! Sling your hook or I 'll murder you !'

'Thou dog !' shrieked Mrs. Shmendrik, falling back on the more copious resources of her native idiom. 'A black year on thee ! Mayst thou swell and die ! May the hand that struck me rot away ! Mayst thou be burnt alive ! Thy father was a *Gonof*, and thou art a *Gonof*, and thy whole family are *Gonovim*. May Pharaoh's ten plagues——'

There was little malice at the back of it all, the mere imaginative exuberance of a race whose early poetry consisted in saying things twice over.

Uncle Abraham menacingly caught up the plaice, crying :

'May I be struck dead on the spot, if you ain't gone in one second I won't answer for the consequences ! Now, then, clear off !'

'Come, Avroomkely,' said Mrs. Shmendrik, dropping suddenly from invective to insinuativeness. 'Take fourteen pence. Hear, my son ? Fourteen *Shtibbur*'s a lot of *Gelt*.'

'Are you a-going ?' cried Abraham in a terrible rage. 'Ten bob 's my price now.'

'Avroomkely, *noo zoog* (say now)—fourteen pence 'apenny ! I am a poor vooman. Here, fifteen pence !'

Abraham seized her by the shoulders and pushed her towards the wall, where she cursed picturesquely. Esther thought it was a bad time to attempt to get her own shilling's-worth. She fought her way towards another fishmonger.

There was a kindly, weather-beaten old fellow with whom Esther had often chaffered job lots when fortune smiled on the Ansells. Him, to her joy, Esther perceived. She saw a stack of gurnards on his improvised slab, and in imagination smelt herself frying them. Then a great shock as of a sudden icy douche traversed her frame, her heart seemed to stand still. For when she put her hand to her pocket to get her purse, she found but a thimble and a slate pencil and a cotton handkerchief. It was some minutes before she could or would realise the truth that the four and seven-pence halfpenny on which so much depended was gone ! Groceries and unleavened cakes charity had given, raisin wine had been preparing for days, but fish and meat and all the minor accessories of a well-ordered Passover table—these were the prey of the pickpocket. A blank sense of desolation overcame the child, infinitely more horrible than that which she felt when she spilt the soup ; the gurnards she could have touched with her finger seemed far off, inaccessible : in a moment more they and all things were blotted out by a hot rush of tears, and she was jostled as in a dream hither and thither by the double stream of crowd. Nothing since the death of Benjamin had given her so poignant a sense of the hollowness and uncertainty of existence. What would her father say, whose triumphant conviction that Providence had provided for his Passover was to be so rudely dispelled at the eleventh hour ? Poor Moses ! He had been so proud of having earned enough money to make a good *Yomtov*, and was more convinced than ever that, given a little capital to start with, he could build up a colossal business. And now she would have to go home and ' spoil everybody's *Yomtov*,' and see the sour faces of her little ones round a barren *Seder* table. Oh, it was terrible, and the child wept piteously, unheeded in the block, unheard amid the Babel !

CHAPTER XXIII

THE DEAD MONKEY

An old *Maaseh* the grandmother had told her came back to her fevered brain :

In a town in Russia lived an old Jew, who earned scarce enough to eat, and half of what he did earn was stolen from him in bribes to the officials to let him be. Persecuted and spat upon, he yet trusted in his God, and praised His name. And it came on towards Passover, and the winter was severe, and the Jew was nigh starving, and his wife had made no preparations for the Festival. And in the bitterness of her soul she derided her husband's faith, and made mock of him ; but he said, ' Have patience, my wife ! Our *Seder* board shall be spread as in the days of yore and as in former years.' But the Festival drew nearer and nearer, and there was nothing in the house. And the wife taunted her husband yet further, saying, ' Dost thou think that Elijah the prophet will call upon thee, or that the Messiah will come ? ' But he answered, ' Elijah the prophet walketh the earth, never having died ; who knows but that he will cast an eye my way ? ' Whereat his wife laughed outright. And the day wore on to within a few hours of Passover, and the larder was still empty of provender, and the old Jew still full of faith. Now, it befell that the governor of the city, a hard and cruel man, sat counting out piles of gold into packets for the payment of the salaries of the officials, and at his side sat his pet monkey ; and as he heaped up the pieces, so his monkey imitated him, making little packets of its own, to the amusement of the governor. And when the governor could not pick up a piece easily he moistened his forefinger, putting it to his mouth, whereupon the monkey followed suit each time ; only, deeming its master was devouring the gold, it swallowed a coin every time he put his finger to his lips. So that of a sudden it was taken ill and died. And one of his men said, ' Lo, the creature is dead. What shall we do with it ? ' And the governor was sorely vexed in spirit, because he could not make his accounts straight, and he answered gruffly : ' Trouble me not ! Throw it into the house of the old Jew down the street.' So the man took the carcase and threw it with thunderous violence into the passage of the Jew's house, and ran off as hard as he could. And the good wife went bustling out in alarm, and saw a carcase hanging over an iron bucket that stood in the passage. And she knew that it was the act of a Christian, and she took up the carrion to bury it, when, lo ! a rain of gold pieces came from the stomach, ripped up by the sharp rim of the vessel. And she called to her husband : ' Hasten ! See what Elijah the prophet hath sent us.' And she scurried into the market-place and bought wine and unleavened bread and bitter herbs, and all things necessary for the *Seder* table, and a little fish therewith, which might be hastily cooked before the Festival came in ; and the old couple were happy and gave the monkey honourable burial, and sang blithely of the deliverance at the Red Sea, and filled Elijah's goblet to the brim till the wine ran over upon the white cloth.

Esther gave a scornful little sniff as the thought of this happy *dénouement* flashed upon her. No miracle like that would happen to her or hers ; nobody was likely to leave a dead monkey on the stairs of the garret—hardly even the ' stuffed monkey ' of contemporary confectionery. And then her queer little brain forgot its grief in sudden speculations as to what she would think if her

four and sevenpence halfpenny came back. She had never yet
doubted the existence of the Unseen Power; only its working
seemed so incomprehensibly indifferent to human joys and sorrows.
Would she believe that her father was right in holding that a
special Providence watched over him? The spirit of her brother
Solomon came upon her, and she felt that she would. Speculation
had checked her sobs; she dried her tears in stony scepticism,
and, looking up, saw Malka's gipsy-like face bending over her,
breathing peppermint.

'What, weepest thou, Esther?' she said, not unkindly. 'I did
not know thou wast a gusher with the eyes.'

'I've lost my purse,' sobbed Esther, softened afresh by the sight
of a friendly face.

'Ah, thou *Schlemihl*! Thou art like thy father. How much
was in it?'

'Four and sevenpence halfpenny!' sobbed Esther.

'Tu, tu, tu, tu, tu!' ejaculated Malka in horror. 'Thou art the
ruin of thy father!' Then, turning to the fishmonger, with whom
she had just completed a purchase, she counted out thirty-five
shillings into his hand. 'Here, Esther,' she said, 'thou shalt carry
my fish, and I will give thee a shilling.'

A small slimy boy who stood expectant by scowled at Esther as
she painfully lifted the heavy basket and followed in the wake of
her relative, whose heart was swelling with self-approbation.

Fortunately, Zachariah Square was near, and Esther soon
received her shilling, with a proportionate sense of Providence.
The fish was deposited at Milly's house, which was brightly
illuminated, and seemed to poor Esther a magnificent palace of
light and luxury. Malka's own house, diagonally across the
Square, was dark and gloomy. The two families being at peace,
Milly's house was the headquarters of the clan and the clothes-
brush. Everybody was home for *Yomtov*. Malka's husband,
Michael, and Milly's husband, Ephraim, were sitting at the table
smoking big cigars, and playing loo with Sam Levine and David
Brandon, who had been seduced into making a fourth. The two
young husbands had but that day returned from the country; for
you cannot get unleavened bread at commercial hotels, and David,
in spite of a stormy crossing, had arrived from Germany an hour
earlier than he had expected, and, not knowing what to do with
himself, had been surveying the humours of the Festival Fair, till
Sam met him and dragged him round to Zachariah Square. It
was too late to call that night on Hannah, to be introduced to her
parents, especially as he had wired he would come the next day.
There was no chance of Hannah being at the Club; it was too
busy a night for all angels of the hearth; even to-morrow, the eve
of the Festival, would be an awkward time for a young man to thrust
his love-affairs upon a household given over to the more important
matters of dietary preparation. Still, David could not consent to
live another whole day without seeing the light of his eyes.

THE DEAD MONKEY 211

Leah, inwardly projecting an orgie of comic operas and dances, was assisting Milly in the kitchen. Both young women were covered with flour and oil and grease, and their coarse handsome faces were flushed, for they had been busy all day drawing fowls, stewing prunes and pippins, gutting fish, melting fat, changing the crockery, and doing the thousand and one things necessitated by gratitude for the discomfiture of Pharaoh at the Red Sea.

Ezekiel slumbered upstairs in his crib.

'Mother,' said Michael, pulling pensively at his whisker as he looked at his card, 'this is Mr. Brandon—a friend of Sam's. Don't get up, Brandon ; we don't make ceremonies here. Turn up yours —ah, the nine of trumps !'

'Lucky men !' said Malka, with Festival flippancy. 'While I must hurry off my supper, so as to buy the fish, and Milly and Leah must sweat in the kitchen, you can squat yourselves down and play cards.'

'Yes,' laughed Sam, looking up, and adding in Hebrew: '"Blessed art Thou, O Lord, who hath not made me a woman."'

'Now, now,' said David, putting his hand jocosely across the young man's mouth. 'No more Hebrew. Remember what happened last time. Perhaps there's some mysterious significance even in that, and you'll find yourself let in for something before you know where you are.'

'You're not going to prevent me talking the language of my fathers,' gurgled Sam, bursting into a merry operatic whistle when the pressure was removed.

'Milly ! Leah !' cried Malka. 'Come and look at my fish ! Such a *Metsiah* (bargain) ! See, they're alive yet !'

'They *are* beauties, mother !' said Leah, entering with her sleeves half tucked up, showing the finely-moulded white arms in curious juxtaposition with the coarse red hands.

'Oh, mother, they're alive !' said Milly, peering over her sister's shoulder.

Both knew by bitter experience that their mother considered herself a connoisseur in the purchase of fish.

'And how much do you think I gave for them?' went on Malka triumphantly.

'Two pounds ten,' said Milly.

Malka's eyes twinkled, and she shook her head.

'Two pounds fifteen,' said Leah, with the air of hitting it now.

Still Malka shook her head.

'Here, Michael, what do you think I gave for all this lot?'

'Diamonds !' said Michael.

'Be not a fool, Michael!' said Malka sternly. 'Look here a minute.'

'Eh ? Oh !' said Michael, looking up from his cards. 'Don't bother, mother. My game !'

'Michael,' thundered Malka, 'will you look at this fish ? How much do you think I gave for this splendid lot ? Here, look at 'em alive yet !'

' H'm—ha !' said Michael, taking his complex corkscrew combination out of his pocket and putting it back again. 'Three guineas?'

' Three guineas !' laughed Malka in good-humoured scorn. ' Lucky I don't let *you* do my marketing !'

' Yes, he 'd be a nice fishy customer !' said Sam Levine with a guffaw.

' Ephraim, what think you I got this fish for ? Cheap now, you know.'

' I don't know, mother,' replied the twinkling-eyed Pole obediently. ' Three pounds, perhaps, if you got it cheap.'

Samuel and David, duly appealed to, reduced the amount to two pounds five and two pounds respectively. Then, having got everybody's attention fixed upon her, she exclaimed :

' Thirty shillings !'

She could not resist nibbling off the five shillings. Everybody drew a long breath.

' Tu, tu !' they ejaculated in chorus. ' What a *Metsiah* !'

' Sam,' said Ephraim immediately afterwards, '*you* turned up the ace.'

Milly and Leah went back into the kitchen.

It was rather too quick a relapse into the common things of life, and made Malka suspect the admiration was but superficial. She turned with a spice of ill-humour, and saw Esther still standing timidly behind her. Her face flushed, for she knew the child had overheard her in a lie.

' What art thou waiting about for ?' she said roughly in Yiddish. ' *Na* ! there 's a peppermint.'

' I thought you might want me for something else,' said Esther, blushing, but accepting the peppermint for Ikey. 'And I—I——'

' Well, speak up ; I won't bite thee.' Malka continued to talk in Yiddish, though the child answered her in English.

' I—I—nothing,' said Esther, turning away.

' Here, turn thy face round, child,' said Malka, putting her hand on the girl's forcibly-averted head. ' Be not so sullen ; thy mother was like that : she 'd want to bite my head off if I hinted thy father was not the man for her, and then she 'd *schmull* and sulk for a week after. Thank God, we have no one like that in this house. I couldn't live for a day with people with such nasty tempers. Her temper worried her into the grave, though, if thy father had not brought his mother over from Poland, my poor cousin might have carried home my fish to-night instead of thee. Poor Gittel— peace be upon him ! Come, tell me what ails thee, or thy dead mother will be cross with thee.'

Esther turned her head, and murmured : ' I thought you might lend me the three and sevenpence halfpenny !'

' Lend thee !' exclaimed Malka. ' Why, how canst thou ever repay it ?'

' Oh yes,' affirmed Esther earnestly. ' I have lots of money in the bank.'

'Eh! what?   In the bank?' gasped Malka.

'Yes; I won five pounds in school, and I'll pay you out of that.'

'Thy father never told me that!' said Malka.   'He kept that dark.   Ah, he is a regular *Schnorrer*!'

'My father hasn't seen you since,' retorted Esther hotly.   'If you had come round when he was sitting *Shivah* for Benjamin—peace be upon him!—you would have known.'

Malka got as red as fire.   Moses had sent Solomon round to inform the *Mishpochah* of his affliction, but at a period when the most casual acquaintance thinks it his duty to call (armed with hard-boiled eggs, a pound of sugar, or an ounce of tea) on the mourners condemned to sit on the floor for a week, no representative of the 'Family' had made an appearance.   Moses took it meekly enough, but his mother insisted that such a slight from Zachariah Square would never have been received if he had married another woman, and Esther for once agreed with her grandmother's sentiments, if not with her Hibernian expression of them.

But that the child should now dare to twit the head of the Family with bad behaviour was intolerable to Malka, the more so as she had no defence.

'Thou impudent of face!' she cried sharply.   'Dost thou forget whom thou talkest to?'

'No,' retorted Esther.   'You are my father's cousin; that is why you ought to have come to see him.'

'I am not thy father's cousin, God forbid!' cried Malka.   'I was thy mother's cousin—God have mercy on her!—and I wonder not you drove her into the grave between the lot of you.   I am no relative of any of you, thank God! and from this day forwards I wash my hands of the lot of you, you ungrateful pack!   Let thy father send you all into the streets with matches; not another thing will I do for you.'

'Ungrateful!' said Esther hotly.   'Why, what have you ever done for us?   When my poor mother was alive, you made her scrub your floors and clean your windows, as if she was an Irishwoman.'

'Impudent of face!' cried Malka, almost choking with rage.   'What have I done for you?   Why—why—I—I, shameless hussy!   And this is what Judaism's coming to in England!   This is the manners and religion they teach thee at thy school, eh?   What have I—— Impudent of face!   At this very moment thou holdest one of my shillings in thy hand!'

'Take it!' said Esther, and threw the coin passionately to the floor, where it rolled about pleasantly for a terrible minute of human silence.   The smoke-wreathed card-players looked up at last.

'Eh? Eh?   What's this, my little girl?' said Michael genially.   'What makes you so naughty?'

A hysterical fit of sobbing was the only reply.   In the bitterness of that moment Esther hated the whole world.

'Don't cry like that ! Don't !' said David Brandon kindly.

Esther, her little shoulders heaving convulsively, put her hand on the latch.

'What's the matter with the girl, mother?' said Michael.

'She's *meshuggah*,' said Malka—'raving mad !' Her face was white, and she spoke as if in self-defence. 'She's such a *Schlemihl* that she lost her purse in the Lane, and I found her gushing with the eyes, and I let her carry home my fish, and gave her a shilling and a peppermint, and thou seest how she turns on me—thou seest ?'

'Poor little thing !' said David impulsively. 'Here, come here, my child !'

Esther refused to budge.

'Come here,' he repeated gently. 'See, I will make up the loss to you ! Take the pool ; I've just won it, so I shan't miss it.'

Esther sobbed louder, but she did not move.

David rose, emptied the heap of silver into his palm, walked over to Esther and pushed it into her pocket. Michael got up and added half a crown to it, and the other two men followed suit. Then David opened the door, put her outside gently, and said :

'There ! run away, my little dear, and be more careful of pick-pockets.'

All this while Malka had stood frozen to the stony dignity of a dingy terra-cotta statue. But ere the door could close again on the child, she darted forward and seized her by the collar of her frock.

'Give me that money !' she cried.

Half hypnotised by the irate swarthy face, Esther made no re-sistance while Malka rifled her pocket, less dexterously than the first operator. Malka counted out the coins.

'Seventeen and sixpence,' she announced in terrible tones. 'How darest thou take all this money from strangers, and perfect strangers ! Do my children think to shame me before my own relative ?' And throwing the money violently into the plate, she took out a gold coin and pressed it into the bewildered child's hand.

'There,' she shouted, 'hold that tight ! It is a sovereign ; and if ever I catch thee taking money from any one in this house but thy mother's own cousin, I'll wash my hands of thee for ever. Go now, go on ; I can't afford any more, so it's useless waiting. Good-night ; and tell thy father I wish him a happy *Yomtov*, and I hope he'll lose no more children.'

She hustled the child into the Square and banged the door upon her, and Esther went about her mammoth marketing half dazed, with an undercurrent of happiness, vaguely apologetic towards her father and his Providence.

Malka stooped down, picked up the clothes-brush from under the side-table, and strode silently and diagonally across the Square

There was a moment's dread silence ; the thunderbolt had fallen the Festival felicity of two households trembled in the balance Michael muttered impatiently, and went out on his wife's track.

'He's an awful fool,' said Ephraim; 'I should make her pay for her tantrums.'

The card-party broke up in confusion. David Brandon took his leave, and strolled about aimlessly under the stars, his soul blissful with the sense of a good deed that had only superficially miscarried. His feet took him to Hannah's house. All the windows were lit up. His heart began to ache at the thought that his bright, radiant girl was beyond that door-step he had never crossed. He pictured the love-light in her eyes, for surely she was dreaming of him as he of her. He took out his watch; the time was twenty to nine. After all, would it be so outrageous to call? He went away twice. The third time, defying the *convenances*, he knocked at the door, his heart beating almost as loudly.

CHAPTER XXIV

THE SHADOW OF RELIGION

THE little servant-girl who opened the door for him looked relieved at the sight of him, for it might have been the Rebbitzin returning from the Lane with heaps of supplies and an accumulation of ill-humour. She showed him into the study, and in a few moments Hannah hurried in with a big apron and a general flavour of the kitchen.

'How dare you come to-night!' she began, but the sentence died on his lips.

'How hot your face is!' he said, dinting the flesh fondly with his finger. 'I see my little girl is glad to have me back.'

'It's not that; it's the fire. I'm frying fish for *Yomtov*,' she said with a happy laugh.

'And yet you say you're not a good Jewess,' he laughed back.

'You had no right to come and catch me like this,' she pouted, 'all greasy and dishevelled. I'm not made up to receive visitors.'

'Call me a visitor?' he grumbled. 'Judging by your appearance, I should say you were always made up. Why, you're perfectly radiant.'

Then the talk became less intelligible. The first symptom of returning rationality was her inquiry:

'What sort of a journey did you have back?'

'The sea was rough, but I'm a good sailor.'

'And the poor fellow's father and mother?'

'I wrote you about them.'

'So you did, but only just a line.'

'Oh, don't let us talk about the subject just now, dear; it's too painful.   Come, let me kiss that little woe-begone look out of your eyes.   There ! now another : that was only for the right eye, this is for the left.   But where 's your mother ? '

' Oh, you innocent !' she replied ; 'as if you hadn't watched her go out of the house ! '

''Pon my honour not,' he said, smiling.   ' Why should I now ? Am I not the accepted son-in-law of the house, you silly, timid little thing !   What a happy thought it was of yours to let the cat out of the bag!   Come, let me give you another kiss for it !   Oh, I really must!   You deserve it, and whatever it costs me you shall be rewarded.   There !   Now then, where 's the old man ?   I have to receive his blessing, I know, and I want to get it over.'

' It's worth having, I can tell you, so speak more respectfully,' said Hannah, more than half in earnest.

' *You* are the best blessing he can give me, and that 's worth— well, I wouldn't venture to price it.'

' It's not your line, eh ? '

' I don't know ; I have done a good deal in gems ; but where *is* the Rabbi ? '

' Up in the bedrooms gathering the *Chomutz.*   You know he won't trust anybody else.   He creeps under all the beds, hunting with a candle for stray crumbs, and looks in all the wardrobes and the pockets of all my dresses.   Luckily I don't keep your letters there.   I hope he won't set something alight ; he did once.   And one year—oh, it was so funny !—after he had ransacked every hole and corner of the house, imagine his horror in the middle of Pass-over to find a crumb of bread audaciously planted—where do you suppose ?   In his Passover Prayer-Book.   But, oh !'—with a little scream—' you naughty boy !   I quite forgot.'   She took him by the shoulders and peered along his coat.   ' Have you brought any crumbs with you ?   This room's *Pesachdik* already.'

He looked dubious.

She pushed him towards the door.   ' Go out and give yourself a good shaking on the door-step, or else we shall have to clean out the room all over again.'

' Don't !' he protested.   ' I might shake out that.'

' What ? '

' The ring.'

She uttered a little pleased sigh.

' Oh, have you brought that ? '

' Yes, I got it while I was away.   You know, I believe the reason you sent me trooping to the Continent in such haste was you wanted to ensure your engagement ring being "made in Ger-many."   It 's had a stormy passage to England, has that ring.   I suppose the advantage of buying rings in Germany is that you 're certain not to get Paris diamonds in them—they are so intensely patriotic, the Germans.   That was your idea wasn't it, Hannah ? '

' Oh, show it me !   Don't talk so much,' she said, smiling.

'No,' he said teasingly ; 'no more accidents for me ! I 'll wait to make sure, till your father and mother have taken me to their arms. Rabbinical law is so full of pitfalls ; I might touch your finger this or that way, and then we should be married. And then if your parents said " No " after all——'

'We should have to make the best of a bad job,' she finished up laughingly.

'All very well,' he went on in his fun ; 'but it would be a pretty kettle of fish.'

'Heavens !' she cried, so it will be ; they will be charred to ashes.' And, turning tail, she fled to the kitchen, pursued by her lover. There, dead to the surprise of the servant, David Brandon fed his eyes on the fair incarnation of Jewish domesticity, type of the vestal virgins of Israel, ministresses at the hearth. It was a very homely kitchen, the dressers glittering with speckless utensils, and the deep-red glow of the coal, over which the pieces of fish spluttered and crackled in their bath of oil, filling the room with a sense of deep peace and cosy comfort. David's imagination transferred the kitchen to his future home, and he was almost dazzled by the thought of actually inhabiting such a fairyland alone with Hannah. He had knocked about a great deal, not always innocently, but deep down in his heart was the instinct of well-ordered life. His past seemed joyless folly and chill emptiness. He felt his eyes growing humid as he looked at the frank-souled girl who had given herself to him. He was not humble ; but for a moment he found himself wondering how he deserved the trust, and there was reverence in the touch with which he caressed her hair. In another moment the frying was complete, and the contents of the pan were neatly added to the dish. Then the voice of Reb Shemuel crying for Hannah came down the kitchen stairs, and the lovers returned to upper world. The Reb had a tiny harvest of crumbs in a brown paper, and wanted Hannah to stow it away safely till the morning, when, to make assurance doubly sure, a final expedition in search of leaven would be undertaken. Hannah received the packet, and in return presented her betrothed.

Reb Shemuel had not, of course, expected him till the next morning, but he welcomed him as heartily as Hannah could desire.

'The Most High bless you !' he said in his charming foreign accents. 'May you make my Hannah as good a husband as she will make you a wife !'

'Trust me, Reb Shemuel,' said David, grasping his great hand warmly.

'Hannah says you 're a sinner in Israel,' said the Reb, smiling playfully, though there was a touch of anxiety in the tones. 'But I suppose you will keep a *kosher* house.'

'Make your mind easy, sir,' said David heartily. 'We must, if it 's only to have the pleasure of your dining with us sometimes.'

The old man patted him gently on the shoulder.

'Ah, you will soon become a good Jew,' he said. 'My Hannah will teach you, God bless her!' Reb Shemuel's voice was a bit husky. He bent down and kissed Hannah's forehead. 'I was a bit *link* myself before I married my Simcha,' he added encouragingly.

'No, no, not you,' said David, smiling in response to the twinkle in the Reb's eye. 'I warrant *you* never skipped a *Mitzvah* even as a bachelor.'

'Oh yes, I did,' replied the Reb, letting the twinkle develop to a broad smile, 'for when I was a bachelor I hadn't fulfilled the precept to marry, don't you see?'

'Is marriage a *Mitzvah*, then?' inquired David, amused.

'Certainly. In our holy religion everything a man ought to do is a *Mitzvah*, even if it is pleasant.'

'Oh, then even I must have laid up some good deeds,' laughed David, 'for I have always enjoyed myself. Really, it isn't such a bad religion, after all.'

'Bad religion!' echoed Reb Shemuel genially. 'Wait till you've tried it. You've never had a proper training, that's clear. Are your parents alive?'

'No, they both died when I was a child,' said David, becoming serious.

'I thought so,' said Reb Shemuel. 'Fortunately my Hannah's didn't.' He smiled at the humour of the phrase, and Hannah took his hand and pressed it tenderly. 'Ah, it will be all right,' said the Reb with a characteristic burst of optimism. 'God is good; you have a sound Jewish heart at bottom, David, my son. Hannah get the *yomtovdik* wine. We will drink a glass for *Mazzoltov*, and I hope your mother will be back in time to join in.'

Hannah ran into the kitchen, feeling happier than she had ever been in her life. She wept a little, and laughed a little, and loitered a little to recover her composure and allow the two men to get to know each other a little.

'How is your Hannah's late husband?' inquired the Reb, with almost a wink, for everything combined to make him jolly as a sand-boy. 'I understand he is a friend of yours.'

'We used to be schoolboys together, that is all. Though, strangely enough, I've just spent an hour with him. He is very well,' answered David, smiling. 'He is about to marry again.'

'His first love, of course?' said the Reb.

'Yes; people always come back to that,' said David, laughing.

'That's right, that's right!' said the Reb. 'I am glad there was no unpleasantness.'

'Unpleasantness? No, how could there be? Leah knew it was only a joke. All's well that ends well, and we may perhaps all get married on the same day and risk another mix-up. Ha! ha! ha!'

'Is it your wish to marry soon, then?'

'Yes ; there are too many long engagements among our people : they often go off.'

'Then I suppose you have the means ?'

'Oh yes, I can show you my——'

The old man waved his hand.

'I don't want to see anything ; my girl must be supported decently, that is all I ask.   What do you do for a living ?'

'I have made a little money at the Cape, and now I think of going into business.'

'What business ?'

'I haven't settled.'

'You won't open on Shabbos ?' said the Reb anxiously.

David hesitated a second.   In some businesses Saturday is the best day ; still, he felt that he was not quite radical enough to break the Sabbath deliberately, and since he had contemplated settling down his religion had become rather more real to him. Besides, he must sacrifice something for Hannah's sake.

'Have no fear, sir,' he said cheerfully.

Reb Shemuel gripped his hand in grateful silence.

'You mustn't think me quite a lost soul,' pursued David after a moment of emotion.   'You don't remember me, but I had lots of blessings and halfpence from you when I was a lad.   I dare say I valued the latter more in those days.' He smiled to hide his emotion.

Reb Shemuel was beaming.   'Did you really ?' he inquired.   'I don't remember you.   But, then, I have blessed so many little children.   Of course you 'll come to the *Seder* to-morrow evening, and taste some of Hannah's cookery.   You 're one of the family now, you know.'

'I shall be delighted to have the privilege of having *Seder* with you,' replied David, his heart going out more and more to the fatherly old man.

'What *Shool* will you be going to for Passover ?   I can get you a seat in mine if you haven't arranged.'

'Thank you, but I promised Mr. Birnbaum to come to the little synagogue of which he is President.   It seems they have a scarcity of *Cohenim,* and they want me to bless the congregation, I suppose.'

'What !' cried Reb Shemuel excitedly, 'are you a *Cohen* ?'

'Of course I am.   Why, they got me to bless them in the Transvaal last Atonement.   So you see I 'm anything but a sinner in Israel.'   He laughed, but his laugh ended abruptly.   Reb Shemuel's face had grown white.   His hands were trembling.

'What is the matter ?   You are ill,' cried David.

The old man shook his head.   Then he struck his brow with his fist.   '*Ach Gott* !' he cried.   'Why did I not think of finding out before ?   But thank God I know it in time !'

'Finding out what ?' said David, fearing the old man's reason was giving way.

'My daughter cannot marry you,' said Reb Shemuel in hushed, quavering tones.

'Eh? What?' said David blankly.

'It is impossible.'

'What are you talking about, Reb Shemuel?'

'You are a *Cohen*. Hannah cannot marry a *Cohen*.'

'Not marry a *Cohen*? Why, I thought they were Israel' aristocracy.'

'That is why. A *Cohen* cannot marry a divorced woman.'

The fit of trembling passed from the old Reb to the young man His heart pulsed as with the stroke of a mighty piston. Withou comprehending, Hannah's prior misadventure gave him a horribl foreboding of critical complications.

'Do you mean to say I can't marry Hannah?' he asked almos in a whisper.

'Such is the law. A woman who has had *Gett* may not marry Cohen.'

'But you surely wouldn't call Hannah a divorced woman?' h cried hoarsely.

'How shall I not? Did not the House of Judgment authoris the divorce?'

'Great God!' exclaimed David. 'Then Sam has ruined ou lives.' He stood a moment in dazed horror, striving to grasp th terrible tangle. Then he burst forth: 'This is some of you cursed Rabbinical laws; it is not Judaism, it is not true Judaism God never made any such law.'

'Hush!' said Reb Shemuel sternly. 'It is the holy Torah. I is not even the Rabbis, of whom you speak like an Epicurean. I is in Leviticus xxi. 7: '"*Neither shall they take a woman pu away from her husband; for he is holy unto his God. Thou shal sanctify him, therefore; for he offereth the bread of thy God; h shall be holy unto thee, for I the Lord which sanctify you ar holy.*"'

For an instant David was overwhelmed by the quotation; th Bible was still a sacred book to him. Then he cried indignantly

'But God never meant it to apply to a case like this!'

'We must obey God's law,' said Reb Shemuel.

'Then it is the devil's law!' shouted David, losing all control c himself.

The Reb's face grew dark as night. There was a moment o dread silence.

'Here you are, father,' said Hannah, returning with the wine an some glasses which she had carefully dusted. Then she pause and gave a little cry, nearly losing her hold of the tray. 'What' the matter? What has happened?' she asked anxiously.

'Take away the wine—we shall drink nobody's health to night cried David brutally.

'My God!' said Hannah, all the hue of happiness dying out o her cheek. She threw down the tray on the table, and ran to he father's arms. 'What is it? oh, what is it, father?' she cried 'You haven't had a quarrel?'

The old man was silent.   The girl looked appealingly from one
o the other.

'No ; it 's worse than that,' said David in cold, harsh tones.
You remember your marriage in fun to Sam ? '

'Yes ! Merciful Heavens ! I guess it ! There was something
ıot valid in the *Gett*, after all.'

Her anguish at the thought of losing him was so apparent that
ıe softened a little.

'No, not that,' he said more gently.   'But this blessed religion
ıf ours reckons you a divorced woman, and so you can't marry me,
ıecause I 'm a *Cohen*.'

'Can't marry you because you 're a *Cohen* !' repeated Hannah,
lazed in her turn.

'We must obey the Torah,' said Reb Shemuel again in low,
ıolemn tones.   'It is your friend Levine who has erred, not the
ſorah.'

'The Torah cannot visit a mere bit of fun so cruelly,' protested
ɔavid.   'And on the innocent, too.'

'Sacred things should not be jested with,' said the old man in
ıtern tones that yet quavered with sympathy and pity.   'On his
ıead is the sin ; on his head is the responsibility.'

'Father !' cried Hannah in piercing tones, 'can nothing be done ? '

The old man shook his head sadly.

The poor pretty face was pallid, with a pain too deep for tears.
ſhe shock was too sudden, too terrible.   She sank helplessly into
ı chair.

'Something must be done—something shall be done !' thundered
ɔavid.   'I will appeal to the Chief Rabbi.'

'And what can he do ?   Can he go behind the Torah ?' said Reb
ſhemuel pitifully.

'I won't ask him to.   But if he has a grain of common-sense he
vill see that our case is an exception, and cannot come under the
ʌaw.'

'The Law knows no exceptions,' said Reb Shemuel gently,
ıuoting in Hebrew : ' " The Law of God is perfect, enlightening
ſhe eyes." Be patient, my dear children, in your affliction.   It is
ſhe will of God.   The Lord giveth, and the Lord taketh away.
ɜless ye the name of the Lord ! '

'Not I !' said David harshly.   'But look to Hannah ! She has
ſainted.'

'No, I am all right,' said Hannah wearily, opening the eyes she
ıad closed.   'Do not make so certain, father.   Look at your
ıooks again.   Perhaps they do make an exception in such a case.'

The Reb shook his head hopelessly.

'Do not expect that,' he said.   'Believe me, my Hannah, if
ſhere were a gleam of hope, I would not hide it from you.   Be a
ſood girl, dear, and bear your trouble like a true Jewish maiden.
ɟave faith in God, my child.   He doth all things for the best.
ɔome, now, rouse yourself.   Tell David you will always be a friend,

and that your father will love him as though he were indeed his
son.'

He moved towards her, and touched her tenderly. He felt a
violent spasm traversing his bosom.

'I can't, father,' she cried in a choking voice. 'I can't. Don'
ask me.'

David leaned against the manuscript-littered table in stony
silence. The stern granite faces of the old Continental Rabbis
seemed to frown down on him from the walls, and he returned the
frown with interest. His heart was full of bitterness, contempt,
revolt. What a pack of knavish bigots they must all have been.
Reb Shemuel bent down and took his daughter's head in his
trembling palms. The eyes were closed again ; the chest heaved
painfully with silent sobs.

'Do you love him so much, Hannah ?' whispered the old man.

Her sobs answered, growing loud at last.

'But you love your religion more, my child?' he murmured
anxiously. 'That will bring you peace.'

Her sobs gave him no assurance. Presently the contagion of
sobbing took him too.

'O God ! God !' he moaned. 'What sin have I committed
that Thou shouldst punish my child thus?'

'Don't blame God !' burst forth David at last. 'It's your own
foolish bigotry. Is it not enough your daughter doesn't ask to
marry a Christian? Be thankful, old man, for that ; and put
away all this antiquated superstition. We're living in the nineteenth century.'

'And what if we are !' said Reb Shemuel, blazing up in turn.
'The Torah is eternal. Thank God for your youth, and your
health and strength, and do not blaspheme Him because you
cannot have all the desire of your heart or the inclination of your
eyes.'

'Desire of my heart !' retorted David. 'Do you imagine I am
only thinking of my own suffering? Look at your daughter and
think of what you are doing to her, and beware before it is too late.'

'Is it in my hand to do or to forbear?' asked the old man. 'I
is the Torah. Am I responsible for that?'

'Yes,' said David, out of mere revolt. Then, seeking to justify
himself, his face lit up with sudden inspiration. 'Who need ever
know? The Maggid is dead. Old Hyams has gone to America.
So Hannah has told me. It's a thousand to one Leah's people
never heard of the law in Leviticus. If they had, it's another
thousand to one against their putting two and two together. It
requires a Talmudist like you to even dream of reckoning Hannah
as an ordinary divorced woman. If they did, it's a third thousand
to one against their telling anybody. There is no need for you to
perform the ceremony yourself. Let her be married by some
other minister—by the Chief Rabbi himself ; and, to make
assurance doubly sure, I'll not mention that I'm a *Cohen*.'

The words poured forth like a torrent, overwhelming the Reb for a moment. Hannah leapt up with a hysterical cry of joy:

'Yes, yes, father; it will be all right, after all. Nobody knows. Oh, thank God! thank God!'

There was a moment of tense silence. Then the old man's voice rose slowly and painfully.

'Thank God!' he repeated. 'Do you dare mention the Name, even when you propose to profane it? Do you ask me—your father, Reb Shemuel—to consent to such a Profanation of the Name?'

'And why not?' said David angrily. 'Whom else has a daughter the right to ask mercy from, if not her father?'

'God have mercy on me!' groaned the old Reb, covering his face with his hands.

'Come, come!' said David impatiently. 'Be sensible. It's nothing unworthy of you at all. Hannah was never really married, so cannot be really divorced. We only ask you to obey the spirit of the Torah, instead of the letter.'

The old man shook his hand, unwavering. His cheeks were white and wet, but his expression was stern and solemn.

'Just think!' went on David passionately. 'What am I better than another Jew—than yourself, for instance—that I shouldn't marry a divorced woman?'

'It is the Law. You are a *Cohen*—a priest.'

'A priest—ha! ha! ha!' laughed David bitterly. 'A priest—in the nineteenth century! When the Temple has been destroyed these two thousand years!'

'It will be rebuilt, please God,' said Reb Shemuel. 'We must be ready for it.'

'Oh yes, I'll be ready; ha! ha! ha! A priest! Holy unto the Lord! I a priest? ha! ha! ha! Do you know what my holiness consists in?' In eating *tripha* meat, and going to *Shool* a few times a year. And I, *I* am too holy to marry *your* daughter! Oh, it is rich!'

He ended in uncontrollable mirth, slapping his knee in ghastly enjoyment. His laughter rang terrible. Reb Shemuel trembled from head to foot. Hannah's cheek was drawn and white. She seemed overwrought beyond endurance. There followed a silence only less terrible than David's laughter.

'A *Cohen*!' burst forth David again; 'a holy *Cohen* up to date! Do you know what the boys say about us priests when we're blessing you common people? They say that if you look on us once during that sacred function you'll get blind, and if you look on us a second time you'll die. A nice reverent joke that, eh? Ha! ha! ha! you're blind already, Reb Shemuel. Beware you don't look at me again, or I'll commence to bless you. Ha! ha! ha! ha!' Again the terrible silence. 'Ah well,' David resumed, his bitterness welling forth in irony. 'And so the first sacrifice the priest is called upon to make is that of your daughter. But I

won't, Reb Shemuel, mark my words ; I won't, not till she offers
her own throat to the knife. If she and I are parted, on you and
you alone the guilt must rest. *You* will have to perform the sacrifice.'

'What God wishes me to do I will do,' said the old man in a
broken voice. 'What is it to that which our ancestors suffered for
the glory of the Name?'

'Yes ; but it seems you suffer by proxy,' retorted David savagely.

'My God? Do you think I would not die to make Hannah
happy?' faltered the old man. 'But God has laid the burden on
her, and I can only help her to bear it. And now, sir, I must beg
you to go ; you do but distress my child.'

'What say you, Hannah? Do you wish me to go?'

'Yes. What is the use—now?' breathed Hannah through white,
quivering lips.

'My child !' said the old man pitifully.

He strained her to his breast.

'All right,' said David in strange harsh tones, scarcely recog-
nisable as his. 'I see you are your father's daughter.' He took
his hat and turned his back upon the tragic embrace.

'David !' She called his name in an agonised, hoarse voice ;
she held her arms towards him. He did not turn round. 'David !'
Her voice rose to a shriek. 'You will not leave me ?'

He faced her exultant.

'Ah, you will come with me? You will be my wife?'

'No—no—not now, not now. I cannot answer you now. Let
me think. Good-bye, dearest, good bye !'

She burst out weeping. David took her in his arms and kissed
her passionately. Then he went out hurriedly.

Hannah wept on, her father holding her hand in piteous silence.

'Oh, it is cruel—your religion !' she sobbed ; 'cruel, cruel !'

'Hannah ! Shemuel ! where are you?' suddenly came the excited voice of Simcha from the passage. 'Come and look at the
lovely fowls I've bought—and such *Metsiahs*. They're worth
double. Oh, what a beautiful *Yomtov* we shall have !'

CHAPTER XXV

SEDER NIGHT.

' Prosaic miles of street stretch all around,
Astir with restless, hurried life, and spanned
By arches that with thund'rous trains resound,
And throbbing wires that galvanise the land ;
Gin palaces in tawdry splendour stand ;
The newsboys shriek of mangled bodies found
The last burlesque is playing in the Strand—
In modern prose, all poetry seems drowned.

Yet in ten thousand homes this April night
An ancient people celebrates its birth
To Freedom, with a reverential mirth,
With customs quaint and many a hoary rite,
Waiting until, its tarnished glories bright,
Its God shall be the God of all the Earth.'

To an imaginative child like Esther, Seder Night was a charmed time. The strange symbolic dishes—the bitter herbs and the sweet mixture of apples, almonds, spices and wine ; the roasted bone and the lamb ; the salt water and the four cups of raisin wine ; the great round unleavened cakes, with their mottled surfaces, some specially thick and sacred ; the special Hebrew melodies and verses, with their jingle of rhymes and assonances ; the quaint ceremonial, with its striking moments, as when the finger was dipped in the wine and the drops sprinkled over the shoulder in repudiation of the ten plagues of Egypt cabbalistically magnified to two hundred and fifty—all this penetrated deep into her consciousness and made the recurrence of every Passover coincide with a rush of pleasant anticipations and a sense of the special privilege of being born a happy Jewish child. Vaguely, indeed, did she co-ordinate the celebration with the history enshrined in it or with the prospective history of her race. It was like a tale out of the fairy-books, this miraculous deliverance of her forefathers in the dim haze of antiquity—true enough, but not more definitely realised on that account. And yet, not easily dissoluble links were being forged with her race, which has anticipated Positivism in vitalising history by making it religion.

The *Motsos* that Esther ate were not dainty—they were coarse, of the quality called ' seconds,' for even the unleavened bread of charity is not necessarily delicate eating—but few things melted sweeter on the palate than a segment of a *Motso* dipped in cheap raisin wine ; the unconventionality of the food made life less common, more picturesque. Simple Ghetto children, into whose existence the ceaseless round of fast and feast, of prohibited and enjoined pleasures, of varying species of food, brought change and relief ! Imprisoned in the area of a few narrow streets, unlovely and sombre, muddy and ill-smelling, immured in dreary houses and surrounded with mean and depressing sights and sounds, the spirit of childhood took radiance and colour from its own inner light, and the alchemy of youth could still transmute its lead to gold. No little princess in the courts of fairyland could feel a fresher interest and pleasure in life than Esther sitting at the *Seder* table, where her father—no longer a slave in Egypt—leaned royally upon two chairs, supplied with pillows as the *Din* prescribes. Not even the monarch's prime minister could have had a meaner opinion of Pharaoh than Moses Ansell in this symbolically sybaritic attitude. A live dog is better than a dead lion, as a great teacher in Israel had said. How much better, then, a live lion than a dead dog ? Pharaoh, for all his purple and fine linen and his treasure cities, was at the bottom of the Red Sea, smitten with two hundred and fifty plagues, and even if, as tradition asserted, he had been made to live on and on to be King of Nineveh, and to give ear to the warnings of Jonah, prophet and whale-explorer, even so he was but dust and ashes for other sinners to cover themselves withal ; but he, Moses Ansell, was the honoured master of his household, enjoying a foretaste of the lollings of the righteous in Paradise ; nay, more, dispensing hospitality to the poor and the hungry. Little fleas have lesser fleas, and Moses Ansell had never fallen so low but that, on this night of nights, when the slave sits with the master on equal terms, he could manage to entertain a Passover guest, usually some newly-arrived *Greener*, or some nondescript waif and stray returned to Judaism for the occasion and accepting a seat at the board in that spirit of *camaraderie* which is one of the most delightful features of the Jewish pauper. *Seder* was a ceremonial to be taken in none too solemn and sober a spirit, and there was an abundance of unreproved giggling throughout from the little ones, especially in those happy days when mother was alive and tried to steal the *A'ikoman*, or *Motso* specially laid aside for the final morsel, only to be surrendered to father when he promised to grant her whatever she wished. Alas ! it is to be feared Mrs. Ansell's wishes did not soar high. There was more giggling when the youngest talking son—it was poor Benjamin in Esther's earliest recollections—opened the ball by inquiring in a peculiarly pitched incantation, and with an air of blank ignorance, why this night differed from all other nights—in view of the various astonishing peculiarities of food and behaviour (enumerated in detail) visible to his vision. To which Moses and the *Bube* and the rest of the company, including the questioner, invariably replied in corresponding sing-song : 'Slaves have we been in Egypt,' proceeding to recount at great length, stopping for refreshment in the middle, the never-cloying tale of the great deliverance, with irrelevant digressions concerning Haman and Daniel and the wise men of Bona Berak, the whole of this most ancient of the world's extant domestic rituals terminating with an allegorical ballad like the 'house that Jack built,' concerning a kid that was eaten by a cat, which was bitten by a dog, which was beaten by a stick, which was burnt by a fire, which was quenched by some water, which was drunk by an ox, which was slaughtered by a slaughterer, who was slain by the Angel of Death, who was slain by the Holy One—blessed be He !

In wealthy houses this *Hagadah* was read from manuscripts with rich illuminations—the one development of pictorial art among the Jews—but the Ansells had wretchedly printed little books containing quaint but unintentionally comic woodcuts, pre-Raphaelite in perspective and ludicrous in draughtsmanship, depicting the miracles of the redemption, Moses burying the Egyptian, and sundry other passages of the text. In one a king was playing in the Temple to an exploding bomb intended to represent the Shechinah, or Divine glory. In another, Sarah, attired in a matronly cap and fashionable jacket and skirt, was standing behind the door of the tent, a solid detached villa, on the brink of a lake whereon ships and gondolas floated, what time Abraham welcomed the three celestial messengers, unobtrusively disguised with heavy pinions.

What delight as the quaffing of each of the four cups of wine loomed in sight ; what disappointment and mutual bantering when the cup had merely to be raised in the hand ; what chaff of the greedy Solomon, who was careful not to throw away a drop during the digital manœuvres when the wine must be jerked from the cup at the mention of each plague ! And what a solemn moment was that when the tallest goblet was filled to the brim for the delectation of the prophet Elijah, and the door thrown open for his entry. Could one not almost hear the rustling of the prophet's spirit through the room ? And what though the level of the wine subsided not a barley-corn ? Elijah, though there was no difficulty in his being in all parts of the world simultaneously, could hardly compass the greater miracle of emptying so many million goblets. Historians have traced this custom of opening the door to the necessity of asking the world to look in and see for itself that no blood of Christian child figured in the ceremonial, and for once science has illumined naïve superstition with a tragic glow more poetic still. For the London Ghetto persecution had dwindled to an occasional bellowing through the keyhole, as the local rowdies heard the unaccustomed melodies trolled forth from jocund lungs, and then the singers would stop for a moment, startled, and some one would say : 'Oh, it 's only a Christian rough,' and take up the thread of song.

And, then, when the *Afikoman* had been eaten, and the last cup of wine drunk, and it was time to go to bed, what a sweet sense of sanctity and security still reigned ! No need to say your prayers to-night, beseeching the guardian of Israel, who neither slumbereth nor sleepeth, to watch over you, and chase away the evil spirits. The angels are with you, Gabriel on your right, and Raphael on your left, and Michael behind you.

All about the Ghetto the light of the Passover rested, transfiguring the dreary rooms and illumining the drab lives.

Dutch Debby sat beside Mrs. Simons at the table of that good soul's married daughter, the same who had suckled little Sarah. Esther's frequent eulogiums had secured the poor lonely narrow-chested seamstress this enormous concession and privilege. Bobby squatted on the mat in the passage ready to challenge Elijah. At this table there were two pieces of fried fish, sent to Mrs. Simons by Esther Ansell. They represented the greatest revenge of Esther's life, and she felt remorseful towards Malka, remembering to whose gold she owed this proud moment. She made up her mind to write her a letter of apology in her best hand.

At the Belcovitches' the ceremonial was long, for the master of it insisted on translating the Hebrew into Jargon, phrase by phrase ; but no one found it tedious, especially after supper. Pesach was there, hand-in-hand with Fanny, their wedding very near now; and Becky lolled royally in all her glory, aggressive of ringlet, insolently unattached, a conscious beacon of bedazzlement to the pauper Pullack we last met at Reb Shemuel's Sabbath table; and there, too, was Chayah, she of the ill-matched legs. Be sure that Malka had returned the clothes-brush, and was throned in complacent majesty at Milly's table, and that Sugarman the Shadchan forgave his monocular consort her lack of a fourth uncle, while Joseph Strelitski, dreamer of dreams, rich with commissions from 'Passover' cigars, brooded on the Great Exodus. Nor could the Shalotten Shammos be other than beaming, ordering the complex ceremonial with none to contradict; nor Karlkammer be otherwhere than in the seven hundred and seventy-seventh heaven, which, calculated by *Gematriyah*, can easily be reduced to the seventh.

Shosshi Shmendrik did not fail to explain the deliverance to the ex-widow Finkelstein, nor Guedalyah the Greengrocer omit to hold his annual revel at the head of half a hundred merry 'pauper aliens.' Christian roughs might bawl derisively in the street, especially when doors were opened for Elijah, but hard words break no bones, and the Ghetto was uplifted above insult.

$$* \qquad * \qquad * \qquad * \qquad *$$

Melchitzedek Pinchas was the Passover guest at Reb Shemuel's table, for the reek of his Sabbath cigar had not penetrated to the old man's nostrils. It was a great night for Pinchas, wrought up to fervid nationalistic aspirations by the memory of the Egyptian deliverance, which he yet regarded as mythical in its details. It was a terrible night for Hannah, sitting opposite to him, under the fire of his poetic regard. She was pale and rigid, moving and speaking mechanically. Her father glanced towards her every now and again compassionately, but with trust that the worst was over. Her mother realised the crisis much less keenly than he, not having been in the heart of the storm. She had never even seen her intended son-in-law, except through the lens of a camera. She was sorry, that was all. Now that Hannah had broken the ice, and encouraged one young man, there was hope for the others.

Hannah's state of mind was divined by neither parent. Love itself is blind in those tragic silences which divide souls.

All night after that agonising scene she did not sleep; the feverish activity of her mind rendered sleep impossible, and unerring instinct told her that David was awake also, that they two, amid the silence of a sleeping city, wrestled in the darkness with the same terrible problem, and were never so much at one as in this, their separation. A letter came for her in the morning. It was unstamped, and had evidently been dropped into the letter-box by David's hand. It appointed an interview at ten o'clock at a corner of the Ruins; of course he could not come to the house. Hannah went out with a little basket to make some purchases. There was a cheery hum of life about the Ghetto, a pleasant Festival bustle; the air resounded with the raucous clucking of innumerable fowls on their way to the feather-littered, blood-stained shambles, where professional cut-throats wielded sacred knives ; boys armed with little braziers of glowing coal ran about the Ruins, offering half-penny pyres for the immolation of the last crumbs of leaven. Nobody paid the slightest attention to the two tragic figures, whose lives turned on the brief moments of conversation snatched in the thick of the hurrying crowd.

David's clouded face lightened a little as he saw Hannah advancing towards him.

' I knew you would come,' he said, taking her hand for a moment. His palm burnt ; hers was cold and limp. The stress of a great tempest of emotion had driven the blood from her face and limbs, but inwardly she was on fire. As they looked, each read revolt in the other's eyes.

' Let us walk on,' he said.

They moved slowly forwards. The ground was slippery and muddy under foot. The sky was gray. But the gaiety of the crowd neutralised the dull squalor of the scene.

' Well ? ' he said in a low tone.

' I thought you had something to propose,' she murmured.

' Let me carry your basket.'

' No, no ; go on. What have you determined ? '

' Not to give you up, Hannah, while I live.'

'Ah !' she said quietly. ' I have thought it all over, too, and I shall not leave you. But our marriage by Jewish law is impossible ; we could not marry at any synagogue without my father's know-ledge, and he would at once inform the authorities of the bar to our union.'

' I know, dear. But let us go to America, where no one will know. There we shall find plenty of Rabbis to marry us. There is nothing to tie me to this country. I can start my business in America just as well as here. Your parents, too, will think more kindly of you when you are across the seas. Forgiveness is easier at a distance. What do you say, dear ? '

She shook her head.

' Why should we be married in a synagogue ? ' she asked.

' Why ? ' repeated he, puzzled.

' Yes, why ? '

' Because we are Jews.'

' You would use Jewish forms to outwit Jewish laws ? ' she asked quietly.

' No, no. Why should you put it that way ? I don't doubt the Bible is all right in making the laws it does ; after the first heat of my anger was over, I saw the whole thing in its proper bearings. Those laws about priests were only intended for the days when we had a Temple, and in any case they cannot apply to a merely farci-cal divorce like yours. It is these old fools—I beg your pardon —it is these fanatical Rabbis who insist on giving them a rigidity God never meant them to have, just as they still make a fuss about *kosher* meat.   In America they are less strict ; besides, they won't know I am a *Cohen*.'

'No, David,' said Hannah firmly.   'There must be no more deceit.   What need have we to seek the sanction of any Rabbi ? If Jewish law cannot marry us without our hiding something, then I will have nothing to do with Jewish law.   You know my opinions ; I haven't gone so deeply into religious questions as you have——'

'Don't be sarcastic,' he interrupted.

'I have always been sick to death of this eternal ceremony, this endless coil of laws winding round us and cramping our lives at every turn ; and now it has become too oppressive to be borne any longer.   Why should we let it ruin our lives ?   And why, if we determine to break from it shall we pretend to keep to it ?   What do you care for Judaism ?   You eat *Triphas*, you smoke on Shabbos when you want to——'

'Yes, I know ; perhaps I'm wrong.   But everybody does it nowadays.   When I was a boy nobody dared be seen riding in a 'bus on Shabbos ; now you meet lots.   But all that is only old-fashioned Judaism.   There must be a God, else we shouldn't be here, and it's impossible to believe that Jesus was He.   A man must have some religion, and there isn't anything better.   But that's neither here nor there.   If you don't care for my plan,' he concluded anxiously, 'what's yours ?'

'Let us be married honestly by a registrar.'

'Any way you like, dear,' he said readily, 'so long as we are married—and quickly.'

'As quickly as you like.'

He seized her disengaged hand and pressed it passionately.

'That's my own darling Hannah !   Oh, if you could realise what I felt last night when you seemed to be drifting away from me !'

There was an interval of silence, each thinking excitedly.   Then David said :

'But have you the courage to do this and remain in London ?'

'I have courage for anything.   But, as you say, it might be better to travel.   It will be less of a break if we break away altogether—change everything at once.   It sounds contradictory, but you understand what I mean.'

'Perfectly.   It is difficult to live a new life with all the old things round you.   Besides, why should we give our friends the chance to cold-shoulder us ?   They will find all sorts of malicious reasons why we were not married in a *Shool*, and, if they hit on the true one, they may even regard our marriage as illegal.   Let us go to America, as I proposed.'

'Very well.   Do we go direct from London ?'

'No, from Liverpool.'

'Then we can be married at Liverpool before sailing.'

'A good idea.   But when do we start ?'

'At once—to-night.   The sooner the better.

He looked at her quickly.

'Do you mean it?' he said. His heart beat violently, as if it would burst. Waves of dazzling colour swam before his eyes.

'I mean it,' she said gravely and quietly. 'Do you think I could face my father and mother, knowing I was about to wound them to the heart? Each day of delay would be torture to me. Oh, why is religion such a curse?' She paused, overwhelmed for a moment by the emotion she had been suppressing. She resumed, in the same quiet manner : 'Yes, we must break away at once. We have kept our last Passover. We shall have to eat leavened food—it will be a decisive break. Take me to Liverpool, David, this very day. You are my chosen husband—I trust in you.'

She looked at him frankly with her dark eyes, that stood out in lustrous relief against the pale skin. He gazed into those eyes, and a flash as from the inner heaven of purity pierced his soul.

'Thank you, dearest,' he said in a voice with tears in it.

They walked on silently. Speech was as superfluous as it was inadequate. When they spoke again, their voices were calm ; the peace that comes of resolute decision was theirs at last, and each was full of the joy of daring greatly for the sake of their mutual love. Petty as their departure from convention might seem to the stranger, to them it loomed as a violent breach with all the traditions of the Ghetto and their past lives ; they were venturing forth into untrodden paths, holding each other's hand.

Jostling the loquacious crowd in the unsavoury byways of the Ghetto, in the gray chillness of a cloudy morning, Hannah seemed to herself to walk in enchanted gardens, breathing the scent of love's own roses mingled with the keen salt air that blew in from the sea of liberty. A fresh, new, blessed life was opening before her ; the clogging vapours of the past were rolling away at last ; the unreasoning, instinctive rebellion, bred of ennui and brooding dissatisfaction with the conditions of her existence and with the people about her, had by a curious series of accidents been hastened to its acutest development ; thought had at last fermented into active resolution ; and the anticipation of action flooded her soul with peace and joy in which all recollection of outside humanity was submerged.

'What time can you be ready by?' he said before they parted.

'Any time,' she answered. 'I can take nothing with me—I dare not pack anything. I suppose I can get necessaries in Liverpool. I have merely my hat and cloak to put on.'

'But that will be enough,' he said ardently. 'I want but you.'

'I know it, dear,' she answered gently. 'If you were as other Jewish young men I could not give up all else for you.'

'You shall never regret it, Hannah,' he said, moved to his depths, as the full extent of her sacrifice for love dawned upon him. He was a vagabond on the face of the earth, but she was tearing herself away from deep roots in the soil of home, as well as from the conventions of her circle and her sex. Once again he trembled with a sense of unworthiness, a sudden anxious doubt if he were noble enough to repay her trust. Mastering his emotion, he went on: 'I reckon my packing and arrangements for leaving the country will take me all day at least. I must see my bankers, if nobody else. I shan't take leave of anybody—that would arouse suspicion. I will be at the corner of your street with a cab at nine, and we'll catch the ten o'clock express from Euston. If we missed that, we should have to wait till midnight. It will be dark ; no one is likely to notice me. I will get a dressing-case for you, and anything else I can think of, and add it to my luggage.'

'Very well,' she said simply.

They did not kiss ; she gave him her hand, and, with a sudden inspiration, he slipped the ring he had brought the day before on her finger. The tears came into her eyes as she saw what he had done. They looked at each other through a mist, feeling bound beyond human intervention.

'Good-bye,' she faltered.

'Good-bye,' he said. 'At nine.'

'At nine,' she breathed, and hurried off without looking behind.

It was a hard day, the minutes crawling reluctantly into the hours, the hours dragging themselves wearily on towards the night. It was typical April weather—squalls and sunshine in capricious succession. When it drew towards dusk, she put on her best clothes for the Festival, stuffing a few precious mementoes into her pockets, and wearing her father's portrait next to her lover's at her breast. She hung a travelling-cloak and a hat on a peg near the hall-door, ready to hand as she left the house. Of little use was she in the kitchen that day, but her mother was tender to her as knowing her sorrow. Time after time Hannah ascended to her bedroom to take a last look at the things she had grown so tired of—the little iron bed, the wardrobe, the framed lithographs, the jug and basin with their floral designs. All things seemed strangely dear now she was seeing them for the last time. Hannah turned over everything—even the little curling-iron, and the card-board box full of tags and rags of ribbon and chiffon and lace and crushed artificial flowers, and the fans with broken sticks, and the stays with broken ribs, and the petticoats with dingy frills, and the twelve-button ball-gloves with dirty fingers, and the soiled pink wraps. Some of her books, especially her school-prizes, she would have liked to take with her, but that could not be. She went over the rest of the house, too, from top to bottom. It weakened her, but she could not conquer the impulse of farewell. Finally, she wrote a letter to her parents, and hid it under her looking-glass, knowing they would search her room for traces of her. She looked curiously at herself as she did so ; the colour had not returned to her cheeks. She knew she was pretty, and always strove to look nice for the mere pleasure of the thing. All her instincts were æsthetic. Now she had the air of a saint wrought up to spiritual exaltation. She was almost frightened by the vision. She had seen her face frowning, weeping, overcast with gloom ; never with an expression so fateful. It seemed as if her resolution was writ large upon every feature for all to read.

In the evening she accompanied her father to *Shool*. She did not often go in the evening, and the thought of going only suddenly occurred to her. Heaven alone knew if she would ever enter a synagogue again ; the visit would be part of her systematic farewell. Reb Shemuel took it as a symptom of resignation to the will of God, and he laid his hand lightly on her head in silent blessing, his eyes uplifted gratefully to heaven. Too late Hannah felt the misconception, and was remorseful. For the Festival occasion Reb Shemuel elected to worship at the Great Synagogue : Hannah, seated among the sparse occupants of the ladies' gallery and mechanically fingering a *Machzor*, looked down for the last time on the crowded auditorium, where the men sat in high hats and holiday garments. Tall wax-candles twinkled everywhere—in great gilt chandeliers depending from the ceiling, in sconces stuck about the window-ledges, in candelabra branching from the walls. There was an air of holy joy about the solemn old structure, with its massive pillars, its small side-windows, its high ornate roof and skylights, and its gilt-lettered tablets to the memory of pious donors.

The congregation gave the responses with joyous unction. Some of the worshippers tempered their devotion by petty gossip; and the beadle marshalled the men in low hats within the iron railings, sonorously sounding his automatic Amens. But to-night Hannah had no eye for the humours that were wont to awaken her scornful amusement ; a real emotion possessed her—the same emotion of farewell which she had experienced in her own bedroom. Her eyes wandered towards the Ark, surmounted by the stone tablets of the Decalogue, and the sad dark orbs filled with the brooding light of childish reminiscence. Once when she was a little girl her father told her that on Passover night an angel sometimes came out of the doors of the Ark from among the scrolls of the Law. For years she looked out for that angel, keeping her eyes patiently fixed on the curtain. At last she gave him up, concluding her vision was insufficiently purified, or that he was exhibiting at other synagogues. To-night her childish fancy recurred to her ; she found herself involuntarily looking towards the Ark and half expectant of the angel.

She had not thought of the *Seder* service she would have to partially sit through, when she made her appointment with David in the morning, but when during the day it occurred to her, a cynical smile traversed her lips. How apposite it was ! To-night would mark *her* exodus from slavery. Like her ancestors leaving Egypt, she too would partake of a meal in haste, staff in hand, ready for the journey. With what stout heart would she set forth —she, too, towards the promised land ! Thus had she thought some hours since, but her mood was changed now. The nearer the *Seder* approached, the more she shrank from the family ceremonial. A panic terror almost seized her now, in the synagogue, when the picture of the domestic interior flashed again before her mental vision ; she felt like flying into the street, on towards her lover, without ever looking behind.

Oh, why could David not have fixed the hour earlier, so as to spare her an ordeal so trying to the nerves ? The black-stoled choir was singing sweetly ; Hannah banished her foolish flutter of alarm by joining in, quietly, for congregational singing was regarded rather as an intrusion on the privileges of the choir, and calculated to put the singers out in their elaborate four-part fugues unaided by an organ.

'"With everlasting love hast Thou loved the house of Israel, Thy people,"' she sang : '"a Law and commandments, statutes and judgments, hast Thou taught us. Therefore, O Lord our God, when we lie down and when we rise up we will meditate on Thy statutes ; yea, we will rejoice in the words of Thy Law and in Thy commandments for ever, for they are our life and the length of our days, and we will meditate on them day and night. And mayest Thou never take away Thy love from us. Blessed art Thou, O Lord, who lovest Thy people Israel."'

Hannah scanned the English version of the Hebrew in her *Machzor* as she sang. Though she could translate every word, the meaning of what she sang was never completely conceived by her consciousness. The power of song over the soul depends but little on the words. Now the words seemed fateful, pregnant with special message. Her eyes were misty when the fugues were over. Again she looked towards the Ark, with its beautifully embroidered curtain, behind which were the precious scrolls, with their silken swathes and their golden bells and shields and pomegranates. Ah, if the angel would come out now ! If only the dazzling vision gleamed for a moment on the white steps ! Oh, why did he not come and save her ?

Save her ? From what ? She asked herself the question fiercely, in defiance of the still, small voice. What wrong had she ever done that she so young and gentle should be forced to make so cruel a choice between the old and the new ? This was the synagogue she should have been married in, stepping gloriously and honourably under the canopy amid the pleasant excitement of a congratulatory company. And now she was being driven to exile and the chillness of secret nuptials. No, no ; she did not want to be saved, in the sense of being kept in the fold ; it was the creed that was culpable, not she.

The service drew to an end. The choir sang the final hymn, the *Chazan* giving the last verse at great length, and with many musical flourishes.

'"The dead will God quicken in the abundance of His loving-kindness. Blessed for evermore be His glorious name."'

There was a clattering of reading-flaps and seat-lids, and the congregation poured out amid the buzz of mutual 'Good-*Yomtov's*.' Hannah rejoined her father, the sense of injury and revolt still surging in her breast. In the fresh starlit air, stepping along the wet gleaming pavements, she shook off the last influences of the synagogue ; all her thoughts converged on the meeting with David, on the wild flight northwards while good Jews were sleeping off the supper in celebration of their Redemption ; her blood coursed quickly through her veins, she was in a fever of impatience for the hour to come.

And thus it was that she sat at the *Seder* table, as in a dream, with images of desperate adventure flitting in her brain. The face of her lover floated before her eyes, close, close to her own, as it should have been to-night, had there been justice in heaven. Now and again the scene about her flashed in upon her consciousness, piercing her to the heart. When Levi asked the introductory question, it set her wondering what would become of him. Would manhood bring enfranchisement to him as womanhood was doing to her ? What sort of life would he lead the poor Reb and his wife ? The omens were scarcely auspicious. But a man's charter is so much wider than a woman's, and Levi might do much without paining them as she would pain them. Poor father ! The white hairs were predominating in his beard ; she had never noticed before how old he was getting. And mother—her face was quite wrinkled. Ah, well, we must all grow old. What a curious man Melchitzedek Pinchas was, singing so heartily the wonderful story ! Judaism certainly produced some curious types. A smile crossed her face as she thought of herself as his bride.

At supper she strove to eat a little, knowing she would need it. In bringing some plates from the kitchen, she looked at her hat and cloak carefully hung up on the peg in the hall nearest the street door. It would take but a second to slip them on. She nodded her head towards them, as who should say, 'Yes, we shall meet again very soon.' During the meal she found herself listening to the poet's monologues, delivered in his high-pitched, creaking voice.

Melchitzedek Pinchas had much to say about a certain actor-manager who had spoiled the greatest Jargon-play of the century, and a certain labour-leader who, out of the funds of his gulls, had subsidised the audience to stay away, and (though here the Reb cut him short for Hannah's sake) a certain leading lady, one of the quartette of mistresses of a certain clergyman, who had been beguiled by her paramour into joining the great English conspiracy to hound down Melchitzedek Pinchas, all of whom he would shoot presently, and had in the meantime enshrined like dead flies in the amber of immortal acrostics. The wind began to shake the shutters as they finished supper, and presently the rain began to patter afresh against the panes. Reb Shemuel distributed the pieces of *Afikoman* with a happy sigh, and lolling on his pillows and almost forgetting his family troubles in the sense of Israel's blessedness, began to chant the grace like the saints in the Psalm who sing aloud on their couches. The little Dutch clock on the mantelpiece began to strike. Hannah did not move. Pale and trembling, she sat riveted to her chair. One—two—three—four—five—six—seven —eight. She counted the strokes : as if to count them was the

only means of telling the hour ! as if her eyes had not been following the hands creeping, creeping ! She had a mad hope the
striking would cease with the eight, and there would be still time to
think. *Nine!* She waited, her ear longing for the tenth stroke.
If it were only ten o'clock, it would be too late. The danger would
be over. She sat, mechanically watching the hands. They crept
on. It was five minutes past the hour. She felt sure that David
was already at the corner of the street, getting wet and a little impatient. She half rose from her chair. It was not a nice night for
an elopement. She sank back into her seat. Perhaps they had
best wait till to-morrow night. She would go and tell David so.
But then, he would not mind the weather ; once they had met he
would bundle her into the cab and they would roll off, leaving the
old world irrevocably behind. She sat in a paralysis of volition—
rigid on her chair, magnetised by the warm comfortable room, the
old familiar furniture, the Passover table, with its white tablecloth
and its decanters and wine glasses, the faces of her father and
mother eloquent with the appeal of a thousand memories. The
clock ticked out loudly, fiercely, like a summoning drum ; the rain
beat an impatient tattoo on the window-panes : the wind rattled
the doors and casements. ' Go forth, go forth !' they called ; ' go
forth where your lover waits you, to bear you off into the new and the
unknown.' And the louder they called the louder Reb Shemuel
trolled his hilarious grace : ' " May He who maketh peace in the
high heavens bestow peace upon us, and upon all Israel, and say
ye Amen." '

The hands of the clock crept on. It was half-past nine. Hannah
sat lethargic, numb, unable to think, her strung-up nerves grown
flaccid, her eyes full of bitter-sweet tears, her soul floating along as
in a trance on the waves of familiar melody. Suddenly she became
aware that the others had risen, and that her father was motioning
to her. Instinctively she understood ; rose automatically, and went
to the door ; then a great shock of returning recollection whelmed
her soul. She stood rooted to the floor. Her father had filled
Elijah's goblet with wine, and it was her annual privilege to open
the door for the prophet's entry. Intuitively she knew that David
was pacing madly in front of the house, not daring to make known
his presence, and perhaps cursing her cowardice. A chill terror
seized her. She was afraid to face him ; his will was strong and
mighty, her fevered imagination figured it as the wash of a great
ocean breaking on the doorstep, threatening to sweep her off into
the roaring whirlpool of doom. She threw the door of the room
wide, and paused as if her duty were done.

' *Nu, nu,*' muttered Reb Shemuel, indicating the outer door.

It was so near that he always had that opened, too.

Hannah tottered forwards through the few feet of hall. The cloak
and hat on the peg nodded to her sardonically. A wild thrill of
answering defiance shot through her ; she stretched out her hand
towards them. ' Fly, fly ! it is your last chance,' said the blood
throbbing in her ears. But her hand dropped to her side, and in

that brief instant of terrible illumination Hannah saw down the whole long vista of her future life stretching straight and unlovely between great blank walls, on, on to a solitary grave ; knew that the strength had been denied her to diverge to the right or the left, that for her there would be neither Exodus nor Redemption. Strong in the conviction of her weakness, she noisily threw open the street-door. The face of David, sallow and ghastly, loomed upon her in the darkness. Great drops of rain fell from his hat and ran down his cheeks like tears. His clothes seemed soaked with rain.

' At last ! ' he exclaimed, in a hoarse, glad whisper. ' What has kept you ? '

' *Boruch Habo !* ' (Welcome art thou who arrivest !) came the voice of Reb Shemuel from within, greeting the prophet.

' Hush ! ' said Hannah. ' Listen a moment.'

The sing-song undulations of the old Rabbi's voice mingled harshly with the wail of the wind. ' " *Pour out Thy wrath on the heathen who acknowledge Thee not, and upon the kingdoms which invoke not Thy name : for they have devoured Jacob and laid waste his Temple. Pour out thy indignation upon them, and cause Thy fierce anger to overtake them. Pursue them in wrath, and destroy them from under the heavens of the Lord.*" '

' Quick, Hannah ! ' whispered David. ' We can't wait a moment more. Put on your things. We shall miss the train.'

A sudden inspiration came to her. For answer she drew his ring out of her pocket, and slipped it into his hand.

' Good-bye ! ' she murmured in a strange, hollow voice ; and slammed the street door in his face.

' Hannah ! '

His startled cry of agony and despair penetrated the woodwork, muffled to an inarticulate shriek. He rattled the door violently in unreasoning frenzy.

' Who 's that ? ' What 's that noise ? ' asked the Rebbitzin.

' Only some Christian rough shouting in the street,' answered Hannah.

It was truer than she knew.

*   *   *   *   *   *

The rain fell faster, the wind grew shriller, but the Children of the Ghetto basked by their firesides in faith and hope and content-ment. Hunted from shore to shore through the ages, they had found the national aspiration—Peace—in a country where Passover came without menace of blood. In the garret of No. 1 Royal Street little Esther Ansell sat brooding, her heart full of a vague tender poetry, and penetrated by the beauties of Judaism, which, please God, she would always cling to, her childish vision looking forward hopefully to the larger life that the years would bring.

END OF BOOK I.

BOOK II

THE GRANDCHILDREN OF THE GHETTO

CHAPTER I

THE CHRISTMAS DINNER

DAINTILY-EMBROIDERED napery, beautiful porcelain, Queen Anne silver, exotic flowers, glittering glass, soft rosy light, creamy expanses of shirt front, elegant low-necked dresses—all the conventional accompaniments of Occidental gastronomy.

It was not a large party. Mrs Henry Goldsmith professed to collect guests on artistic principles, as she did *bric-à-brac*, and with an eye to general conversation. The elements of the social salad were sufficiently incongruous to night, yet all the ingredients were Jewish.

For the history of the Grandchildren of the Ghetto, which is mainly a history of the middle classes, is mainly a history of isolation. 'The Upper Ten' is a literal phrase in Judah, whose aristocracy just about suffices for a synagogue quorum. Great majestic luminaries, each with its satellites, they swim serenely in the golden heavens. And the middle classes look up in worship, and the lower classes in supplication. 'The Upper Ten' have no spirit of exclusiveness ; they are willing to entertain royalty, rank, and the arts with a catholic hospitality that is only Eastern in its magnificence, while some of them remain Jews only for fear of being considered snobs by society. But the middle-class Jew has been more jealous of his caste, and for caste reasons. To exchange hospitalities with the Christain when you cannot eat his dinners were to get the worst of the bargain ; to invite his sons to your house when they cannot marry your daughters were to solicit awkward complications. In business, in civic affairs, in politics, the Jew has mixed freely with his fellow-citizens ; but indiscriminate social relations only become possible through a religious decadence which they in turn accelerate. A Christian in a company of middle-class Jews is like a lion in a den of Daniels. They show him deference and their prophetic side.

Mrs. Henry Goldsmith was of the upper middle classes, and her husband was the financial representative of the Kensington Synagogue at the United Council ; but her swan-like neck was still bowed beneath the yoke of North London, not to say provincial, Judaism. So to-night there were none of those external indications of Christmas which are so frequent at 'good' Jewish houses —no plum-pudding, snapdragon, mistletoe, not even a Christmas-tree. For Mrs. Henry Goldsmith did not countenance these co-quettings with Christianity. She would have told you that the incidence of her dinner on Christmas Eve was merely an accident, though a lucky accident, in so far as Christmas found Jews perforce at leisure for social gatherings. What she was celebrating was the Feast of Chanukah—of the re-dedication of the Temple after the pollutions of Antiochus Epiphanes—and the memory of the national hero, Judas Maccabæus. Christmas crackers· would have been incompatible with the Chanukah candles which the housekeeper, Mary O'Reilly, forced her master to light, and would have shocked that devout old dame. For Mary O'Reilly, as good a soul as she was a Catholic, had lived all her life with Jews, assisting while yet a girl in the kitchen of Henry Goldsmith's father, who was a pattern of ancient piety and a prop of the Great Synagogue. When the father died, Mary, with all the other family belongings, passed into the hands of the son, who came up to London from a provincial town, and, with a grateful recollection of her motherliness, domiciled her in his own establish-ment. Mary knew all the ritual laws and ceremonies far better than her new mistress, who, although a native of the provincial town in which Mr. Henry Goldsmith had established a thriving business, had received her education at a Brussels boarding-school. Mary knew exactly how long to keep the meat in salt, and the heinousness of frying steaks in butter. She knew that the fire must not be poked on the Sabbath, nor the gas lit or extinguished, and that her master must not smoke till three stars appeared in the sky. She knew when the family must fast, and when and how it must feast. She knew all the Hebrew and Jargon expressions which her employers studiously boycotted, and she was the only member of the household who used them habitually in her inter-course with the other members. Too late the Henry Goldsmiths awoke to the consciousness of her tyranny, which did not permit them to be irreligious even in private. In the fierce light which beats upon a provincial town with only one synagogue, they had been compelled to conform outwardly with many galling restric-tions, and they had sub-consciously looked forward to emancipation in the mighty Metropolis. But Mary had such implicit faith in their piety, and was so zealous in the practice of her own faith, that they had not the courage to confess that they scarcely cared a pin about a good deal of that for which she was so solicitous. They hesitated to admit that they did not respect their religion (or what she thought was their religion) as much as she did hers. It would have equally lowered them in her eyes to admit that their religion was not so good as hers, besides being disrespectful to the cherished memory of her ancient master. At first they had deferred to Mary's Jewish prejudices out of good-nature and care-lessness, but every day strengthened her hold upon them ; every act of obedience to the ritual law was a tacit acknowledgment of its sanctity, which made it more and more difficult to disavow its obligation.   The dread of shocking Mary came to dominate their lives, and the fashionable house near Kensington Gardens was still a veritable centre of true Jewish orthodoxy, with little to make old Aaron Goldsmith turn in his grave.

It is probable, though, that Mrs. Henry Goldsmith would have kept a *kosher* table even if Mary had never been born.   Many of their acquaintance and relatives were of an orthodox turn.   A *kosher* dinner could be eaten even by the heterodox, whereas a *tripha* dinner choked off the orthodox.   Thus it came about that even the Rabbinate might safely stoke its spiritual fires at Mrs. Henry Goldsmith's.

Hence, too, the prevalent craving for a certain author's blood could not be gratified at Mrs. Henry Goldsmith's Chanukah dinner.   Besides, nobody knew where to lay hands upon Edward Armitage, the author in question, whose opprobrious production, *Mordecai Josephs*, had scandalised West End Judaism.

'Why didn't he describe our circle?' asked the hostess, an angry fire in her beautiful eyes.   'It would have at least corrected the picture.   As it is, the public will fancy that we are all daubed with the same brush—that we have no thought in life beyond dress, money and solo-whist.'

'He probably painted the life he knew,' said Sidney Graham, in defence.

'Then I am sorry for him,' retorted Mrs. Goldsmith.   'It's a great pity he had such detestable acquaintances.   Of course, he has cut himself off from the possibility of any better now.'

The wavering flush on her lovely face darkened with disinterested indignation, and her beautiful bosom heaved with judicial grief.

'I should hope so,' put in Miss Cissy Levine sharply.   She was a pale, bent woman, with spectacles, who believed in the mission of Israel, and wrote domestic novels to prove that she had no sense of humour.   'No one has a right to foul his own nest.   Are there not plenty of subjects for the Jew's pen without his attacking his own people?   The calumniator of his race should be ostracised from decent society.'

'As according to him there is none,' laughed Sidney Graham, 'I cannot see where the punishment comes in.'

'Oh, he may say so in that book,' said Mrs. Montagu Samuels, an amiable, loose-thinking lady of florid complexion, who dabbled exasperatingly in her husband's philanthropic concerns from a vague idea that the wife of a committee-man is a committee-woman.   'But he knows better.'

'Yes, indeed,' said Mr. Montagu Samuels.   'The rascal has only written it to make money.   He knows it's all exaggeration and distortion.   But anything spicy pays nowadays.'

'As a West Indian merchant, he ought to know,' murmured Sidney Graham to his charming cousin, Adelaide Leon.

The girl's soft eyes twinkled as she surveyed the serious little City magnate with his placid spouse. Montagu Samuels was narrow-minded and narrow-chested, and managed to be pompous on a meagre allowance of body. He was earnest and charitable (except in religious wrangles, when he was earnest and uncharitable), and knew himself a pillar of the community, an exemplar to the drones and sluggards who shirked their share of public burdens and were callous to the dazzlement of communal honours.

'Of course it was written for money, Monty,' his brother, Percy Saville, the stockbroker, reminded him. 'What else do authors write for? It's the way they earn their living.'

Strangers found difficulty in understanding the fraternal relation of Percy Saville and Montagu Samuels, and did not readily grasp that Percy Saville was an Anglican version of Pizer Samuels, more in tune with the handsome, well-dressed personality it denoted. Montagu had stuck loyally to his colours, but Pizer had drooped under the burden of carrying his patronymic through the theatrical and artistic circles he favoured after business hours. Of such is the brotherhood of Israel.

'The whole book's written with gall,' went on Percy Saville emphatically. 'I suppose the man couldn't get into good Jewish houses, and he's revenged himself by slandering them.'

'Then he ought to have got into good Jewish houses,' said Sidney. 'The man has talent, nobody can deny that, and if he couldn't get into good Jewish society because he didn't have money enough, isn't that proof enough his picture is true?'

'I don't deny that there are people among us who make money the one Open Sesame to their houses,' said Mrs. Henry Goldsmith magnanimously.

'Deny it, indeed! Money is the Open Sesame to everything,' rejoined Sidney Graham, delightedly scenting an opening for a screed. He liked to talk bombshells, and did not often get pillars of the community to shatter. 'Money manages the schools and the charities and the synagogues, and indirectly controls the press. A small body of persons—always the same—sits on all councils, on all boards! Why? Because they pay the piper.'

'Well, sir, and is not that a good reason?' asked Montagu Samuels. 'The community is to be congratulated on having a few public-spirited men left in days when there are wealthy German Jews in our midst who not only disavow Judaism, but refuse to support its institutions. But, Mr. Graham, I would join issue with you. The men you allude to are elected, not because they are rich, but because they are good men of business, and most of the work to be done is financial.'

'Exactly,' said Sidney Graham in sinister agreement. 'I have always maintained that the United Synagogue could be run as a joint-stock company for the sake of a dividend, and that there wouldn't be an atom of difference in the discussions if the councillors were directors. I do believe the pillars of the community figure the Millennium as a time when every Jew shall have enough to eat, a place to worship in, and a place to be buried in. Their State Church is simply a financial system, to which the doctrines of Judaism happen to be tacked on. How many of the councillors believe in their established religion ? Why, the very beadles of their synagogues are prone to surreptitious shrimps and unobtrusive oysters ! Then take that institution for supplying *kosher* meat. I am sure there are lots of its committee who never inquire into the necrologies of their own chops and steaks, and who regard kitchen Judaism as obsolete ; but, all the same, they look after the finances with almost fanatical zeal. Finance fascinates them. Long after Judaism has ceased to exist, excellent gentlemen will be found regulating its finances.'

There was that smile on the faces of the graver members of the party which arises from reluctance to take a dangerous speaker seriously.

Sidney Graham was one of those favourites of society who are allowed Touchstone's licence. He had just as little wish to reform, and just as much wish to abuse, society as society has to be reformed and abused. He was a dark, bright-eyed young artist with a silky moustache. He had lived much in Paris, where he studied impressionism and perfected his natural talent for causerie, and his inborn preference for the hedonistic view of life. Fortunately he had plenty of money, for he was a cousin of Raphael Leon on the mother's side, and the remotest twigs of the Leon genealogical tree bear apples of gold. His real name was Abrahams, which is a shade too Semitic. Sidney was the black sheep of the family—good-natured to the core, and artistic to the finger-tips, he was an avowed infidel in a world where avowal is the unpardonable sin. He did not even pretend to fast on the Day of Atonement. Still, Sidney Graham was a good deal talked of in artistic circles, his name was often in the newspapers and so more orthodox people than Mrs. Henry Goldsmith were not averse from having him at their table, though they would have shrunk from being seen at his. Even Cousin Addie, who had a charming religious cast of mind, liked to be with him, though she ascribed this to family piety—for there is a wonderful solidarity about many Jewish families, the richer members of which assemble loyally at one another's births, marriages, funerals, and card parties, often to the entire exclusion of outsiders. An ordinary well-regulated family (so prolific is the stream of life) will include in its bosom ample elements for every occasion.

' Really, Mr. Graham, I think you are wrong about the *kosher* meat,' said Mr. Henry Goldsmith. ' Our statistics show no falling off in the number of bullocks killed, while there is a rise of two per cent. in the sheep slaughtered. No, Judaism is in a far more healthy condition than pessimists imagine. So far from sacrificing our ancient faith, we are learning to see how tuberculosis lurks in the lungs of unexamined carcases and is communicated to the consumer.   As for the members of the *Shechitah* Board not eating *Kosher*, look at me.'

The only person who looked at the host was the hostess.   Her look was one of approval—it could not be of æsthetic approval, like the look Percy Saville devoted to herself, for her husband was a cadaverous little man with prominent ears and teeth.

'And if Mr. Graham should ever join us on the Council of the United Synagogue,' added Montagu Samuels, addressing the table generally, 'he will discover that there is no communal problem with which we do not loyally grapple.'

'No, thank you,' said Sidney with a shudder.   'When I visit Raphael, I sometimes pick up a Jewish paper and amuse myself by reading the debates of your public bodies.   I understand most of your verbiage is edited away,' he looked Montagu Samuels full in the face, with audacious *naïveté*; 'but there is enough left to show that our monotonous group of public men consists of narrow-minded mediocrities.   The chief public work they appear to do, outside finance, is, when public exams. fall on Sabbaths or holidays, getting special dates for Jewish candidates, to whom these examinations are the avenues to atheism.   They never see the joke.   How can they?   Why, they take even themselves seriously.'

'Oh, come !' said Miss Cissy Levine indignantly.   'You often see "laughter" in the reports.'

'That must mean the speaker was laughing,' explained Sidney, 'for you never see anything to make the audience laugh.   I appeal to Mr. Montagu Samuels.'

'It is useless discussing a subject with a man who admittedly speaks without knowledge,' replied that gentleman with dignity.

'Well, how do you expect me to get the knowledge ?' grumbled Sidney.   'You exclude the public from your gatherings—I suppose to prevent them rubbing shoulders with the swells, the privilege of being snubbed by whom is the reward of public service.   Wonderfully practical idea that—to utilise snobbery as a communal force ! The United Synagogue is founded on it.   Your community coheres through it.'

'There you are scarcely fair,' said the hostess with a charming smile of reproof.   'Of course there are snobs amongst us, but is it not the same in all sects ?'

'Emphatically not,' said Sidney.   'If one of our swells sticks to a shred of Judaism, people seem to think the God of Judah should be thankful ; and if he goes to synagogue once or twice a year, it is regarded as a particular condescension to the Creator.'

'The mental attitude you caricature is not so snobbish as it seems,' said Raphael Leon, breaking into the conversation for the first time.   'The temptations to the wealthy and the honoured to desert their struggling brethren are manifold, and sad experience has made our race accustomed to the loss of its brightest sons.'

'Thanks for the compliment fair coz,' said Sidney, not without a complacent cynical pleasure in the knowledge that Raphael spoke truly, that he owed his own immunity from the obligations of the faith to his artistic success, and that the outside world was disposed to accord him a larger charter of morality on the same grounds. 'But if you can only deny nasty facts by accounting for them, I dare say Mr. Armitage's book will afford you ample opportunities for explanation. Or have Jews the brazenness to assert it is all invention?'

'No; no one would do that,' said Percy Saville, who had just done it. 'Certainly, there is a good deal of truth in the sketch of the ostentatious, over-dressed Johnsons, who, as everybody knows, are meant for the Jonases.'

'Oh yes,' said Mrs. Henry Goldsmith. 'And it's quite evident that the stockbroker who drops half his *h's*, and all his poor acquaintances, and believes in one Lord, is no other than Joel Friedman.'

'And the house where people drive up in broughams for supper and solo-whist after the theatre is the Davises', in Maida Vale,' said Miss Cissy Levine.

'Yes, the book's true enough,' began Mrs. Montagu Samuels. She stopped suddenly, catching her husband's eye, and the colour heightened on her florid cheek. 'What I say is,' she concluded awkwardly, 'he ought to have come among us, and shown the world a picture of the cultured Jews.'

'Quite so, quite so!' said the hostess. Then turning to the tall, thoughtful-looking young man who had hitherto contributed but one remark to the conversation, she said, half in sly malice, half to draw him out: 'Now you, Mr. Leon, whose culture is certified by our leading University, what do you think of this latest portrait of the Jew?'

'I don't know; I haven't read it,' replied Raphael apologetically.

'No more have I,' murmured the table generally.

'I wouldn't touch it with a pitchfork,' said Miss Cissy Levine.

'I think it's a shame they circulate it at the libraries,' said Mrs. Montagu Samuels. 'I just glanced over it at Mrs. Hugh Marston's house. It's vile. There are actually Jargon words in it. Such vulgarity!'

'Shameful!' murmured Percy Saville; 'Mr. Lazarus was telling me about it. It's plain treachery and disloyalty, this putting of weapons into the hands of our enemies. Of course we have our faults, but we should be told of them privately or from the pulpit.'   •

'That would be just as efficacious,' said Sidney admiringly.

'More efficacious,' said Percy Saville unsuspiciously. 'A preacher speaks with authority, but this penny-a-liner——'

'With truth?' queried Sidney.

Saville stopped, disgusted, and the hostess answered Sidney half coaxingly.

'Oh, I am sure you can't think that. The book is so one-sided.

Not a word about our generosity, our hospitality, our domesticity
—the thousand and one good traits all the world allows us.'

'Of course not ; since all the world allows them, it was unneces-
sary,' said Sidney.

'I wonder the Chief Rabbi doesn't stop it,' said Mrs. Montagu
Samuels.

'My dear, how can he?' inquired her husband. 'He has no
control over the publishing trade.'

'He ought to talk to the man,' persisted Mrs. Samuels.

'But we don't even know who he is,' said Percy Saville ; 'probably
"Edward Armitage" is only a *nom de plume.* You'd be surprised
to learn the real names of some of the literary celebrities I meet
about.'

'Oh, if he's a Jew you may be sure it isn't his real name,' laughed
Sidney. It was characteristic of him that he never spared a shot,
even when himself hurt by the kick of the gun. Percy coloured
slightly, unmollified by being in the same boat with the satirist.

'I have never seen the name in the subscription lists,' said the
hostess with ready tact.

'There is an Armitage who subscribes two guineas a year to the
Board of Guardians,' said Mrs. Montagu Samuels. 'But his
Christian name is George.'

'"Christian" name is distinctly good for "George,"' murmured
Sidney.

'There was an Armitage who sent a cheque to the Russian Fund,'
said Mr. Henry Goldsmith ; 'but that can't be an author : it was
quite a large cheque !'

'I am sure I have seen Armitage among the Births, Marriages,
and Deaths,' said Miss Cissy Levine.

'How well read they all are in the national literature !' Sidney
murmured to Addie.

Indeed, the sectarian advertisements served to knit the race together, counteracting the unravelling induced by the fashionable
dispersion of Israel, and waxing the more important as the other
links, the old traditional jokes, bywords, ceremonies, card-games,
prejudices, and tunes, which are more important than laws and
more cementatory than ideals, were disappearing before the over-
zealousness of a parvenu refinement that had not yet attained
to self-confidence. The Anglo-Saxon stolidity of the West-End
synagogue service, on week days entirely given over to paid
praying-men, was a typical expression of the universal tendency to
exchange the picturesque primitiveness of the Orient for the sobrie-
ties of fashionable civilisation. When Jeshurun waxed fat, he did
not always kick, but he yearned to approximate as much as possible to John Bull without merging in him ; to sink himself and
yet not be absorbed—not to be, and yet to be. The attempt to
realise the asymptote in human mathematics was not quite successful, too near an approach to John Bull generally assimilating
Jeshurun away. For such is the nature of Jeshurun. Enfranchise

him, give him his own way, and you make a new man of him; persecute him, and he is himself again.

'But if nobody has read the man's book,' Raphael Leon ventured to interrupt at last, 'is it quite fair to assume his book isn't fit to read?'

The shy dark little girl he had taken down to dinner darted an appreciative glance at her neighbour. It was in accordance with Raphael's usual anxiety to give the devil his due that he should be unwilling to condemn even the writer of an anti-Semitic novel unheard. But, then, it was an open secret in the family that Raphael was mad. They did their best to hush it up, but among themselves they pitied him behind his back. Even Sidney considered his cousin Raphael pushed a dubious virtue too far, in treating people's very prejudices with the deference due to earnest, reasoned opinions.

'But we know enough of the book to know we are badly treated,' protested the hostess.

'We have always been badly treated in literature,' said Raphael. 'We are made either angels or devils. On the one hand, Lessing and George Eliot ; on the other, the stock dramatist and novelist, with their low-comedy villain.'

'Oh !' said Mrs. Goldsmith doubtfully, for she could not quite think Raphael had become infected by his cousin's propensity for paradox. 'Do you think George Eliot and Lessing didn't understand the Jewish character?'

'They are the only writers who have ever understood it,' affirmed Miss Cissy Levine emphatically.

A little scornful smile played for a second about the mouth of the dark little girl.

'Stop a moment,' said Sidney. 'I've been so busy doing justice to this delicious asparagus that I have allowed Raphael to imagine nobody here has read *Mordecai Josephs*. I have, and I say there is more actuality in it than in *Daniel Deronda* and *Nathan der Weise* put together. It is a crude production, all the same ; the writer's artistic gift seems handicapped by a dead weight of moral platitudes and high falutin, and even mysticism. He not only presents his characters, but moralises over them—actually cares whether they are good or bad, and has yearnings after the indefinable. It is all very young. Instead of being satisfied that Judæa gives him characters that are interesting, he actually laments their lack of culture. Still, what he has done is good enough to make one hope his artistic instinct will shake off his moral.'

'Oh, Sidney, what are you saying?' murmured Addie.

'It's all right, little girl. You don't understand Greek.'

'It's not Greek,' put in Raphael. 'In Greek art beauty of soul and beauty of form are one. It's French you are talking, though the ignorant ateliers where you picked it up flatter themselves it's Greek.'

'It's Greek to Addie, anyhow,' laughed Sidney. 'But that's what makes the anti-Semitic chapters so unsatisfactory.'

'We all felt their unsatisfactoriness, if we could not analyse it so cleverly,' said the hostess.

'We all felt it,' said Mrs. Montagu Samuels.

'Yes, that's it,' said Sidney blandly. 'I could have forgiven the rose-colour of the picture if it had been more artistically painted.'

'Rose-colour!' gasped Mrs. Henry Goldsmith.

Rose-colour indeed! Not even Sidney's authority could persuade the table into that.

Poor rich Jews! The upper middle classes had every excuse for being angry. They knew they were excellent persons, well educated and well travelled, interested in charities (both Jewish and Christian), people's concerts, district-visiting, new novels, magazines, reading circles, operas, symphonies, politics, volunteer regiments, Show Sunday and Corporation banquets; that they had sons at Rugby and Oxford, and daughters who played and painted and sang, and homes that were bright oases of optimism in a jaded society; that they were good Liberals and Tories, supplementing their duties as Englishmen with a solicitude for the best interests of Judaism; that they left no stone unturned to emancipate themselves from the secular thraldom of prejudice; and they felt it very hard that a little vulgar section should always be chosen by their own novelists, and their efforts to raise the tone of Jewish society passed by.

Sidney, whose conversation always had the air of aloofness from the race, so that his own foibles often came under the lash of his sarcasm, proceeded to justify his assertion of the rose-colour picture in *Mordecai Josephs.* He denied that modern English Jews had any religion whatever, claiming that their faith consisted of forms that had to be kept up in public, but which they were too shrewd and cute to believe in or to practise in private, though every one might believe every one else did; that they looked upon due payment of their synagogue bills as discharging all their obligations to Heaven; that the preachers secretly despised the old formulas, and that the Rabbinate declared its intention of dying for Judaism only as a way of living by it; that the body politic was dead and rotten with hypocrisy, though the augurs said it was alive and well. He admitted that the same was true of Christianity. Raphael reminded him that a number of Jews had drifted quite openly from the traditional teaching, that thousands of well-ordered households found inspiration and spiritual satisfaction in every form of it, and that hypocrisy was too crude a word for the complex motives of those who obeyed it without inner conviction.

'For instance,' said he, 'a gentleman said to me the other day— I was much touched by the expression—" I believe with my father's heart."'

'It is a good epigram,' said Sidney, impressed. 'But what is to be said of a rich community which recruits its clergy from the lowest classes? The method of election by competitive performance—common as it is, among poor Dissenters—emphasises the subjection of the shepherd to his flock. You catch your ministers young—when they are saturated with suppressed scepticism—and bribe them with small salaries that seem affluence to the sons of poor immigrants. That the ministry is not an honourable profession may be seen from the anxiety of the minister to raise his children in the social scale by bringing them up to some other line of business.'

'That is true,' said Raphael gravely. 'Our wealthy families must be induced to devote a son each to the synagogue.'

'I wish they would,' said Sidney. 'At present every second man is a lawyer. We ought to have more officers and doctors, too. I like those old Jews who smote the Philistines hip and thigh—it is not good for a race to run all to brain—I suppose, though, we had to develop cunning to survive at all. There was an enlightened minister whose Friday evenings I used to go to when a youth—delightful talk we had there, too ; you know whom I mean. Well, one of his sons is a solicitor, and the other a stockbroker. The rich men he preached to helped to place his sons. He was a charming man, but imagine him preaching to them the truths in *Mordecai Josephs*, as Mr. Saville suggested.'

'*Our* minister lets us have it hot enough, though,' said Mr. Henry Goldsmith, with a guffaw.

His wife hastened to obliterate the unrefined expression.

'Mr. Strelitski is a wonderfully eloquent young man, so quiet and reserved in society, but like an ancient prophet in the pulpit.'

'Yes, we were very lucky to get him,' said Mr. Henry Goldsmith. The little dark girl shuddered.

'What is the matter?' asked Raphael softly.

'I don't know. I don't like the Rev. Joseph Strelitski. He is eloquent, but his dogmatism irritates me. I don't believe he is sincere. He doesn't like me, either.'

'Oh, you 're both wrong,' he said in concern.

'Strelitski is a draw, I admit,' said Mr. Montagu Samuels, who was the President of a rival synagogue. 'But Rosenbaum is a good pull-down on the other side, eh ?'

Mr. Henry Goldsmith groaned. The second minister of the Kensington synagogue was the scandal of the community. He wasn't expected to preach, and he didn't practise.

'I 've heard of that man,' said Sidney, laughing. 'He 's a bit of a gambler and a spendthrift, isn't he ? Why do you keep him on ?'

'He has a fine voice, you see,' said Mr. Goldsmith. 'That makes a Rosenbaum faction at once. Then he has a wife and family ; that makes another.'

'Strelitski isn't married, is he ?' asked Sidney.

'No,' said Mr. Goldsmith ; 'not yet. The congregation expect

im to, though. I don't care to give him the hint myself, he is a
ittle queer sometimes.'

'He owes it to his position,' said Miss Cissy Levine.

'That is what we think,' said Mrs. Henry Goldsmith, with the
majestic manner that suited her opulent beauty.

'I wish we had him in our synagogue,' said Raphael. 'Michaels
s a well-meaning, worthy man, but he is dreadfully dull.'

'Poor Raphael!' said Sidney. 'Why did you abolish the old
style of minister who had to slaughter the sheep? Now the
minister reserves all his powers of destruction for his own flock.'

'I have given him endless hints to preach only once a month,'
said Mr. Montagu Samuels dolefully. 'But every Saturday our
hearts sink as we see him walk to the pulpit.'

'You see, Addie, how a sense of duty makes a man criminal,'
said Sidney. 'Isn't Michaels the minister who defends orthodoxy
in a way that makes the orthodox rage over his unconscious
heresies, while the heterodox enjoy themselves by looking out for
his historical and grammatical blunders?'

'Poor man! he works hard,' said Raphael gently. 'Let him be.
Over the dessert the conversation turned by way of the Rev.
Strelitski's marriage to the growing willingness of the younger
generation to marry out of Judaism. The table discerned in intermarriage the beginning of the end.

'But why postpone the inevitable?' asked Sidney calmly.
'What is this mania for keeping up an effete-ism? Are we to
cripple our lives for the sake of a word? It's all romantic fudge,
the idea of perpetual isolation. You get into little cliques, and
mistake narrow-mindedness for fidelity to an ideal. I can live for
months and forget there are such beings as Jews in the world. I
have floated down the Nile in a *dahabiya* while you were beating
your breasts in the synagogue, and the palm trees and the pelicans
knew nothing of your sacrosanct chronological crisis, your annual
epidemic of remorse.'

The table thrilled with horror, without, however, quite believing
in the speaker's wickedness. Addie looked troubled.

'A man and wife of different religions can never know true
happiness,' said the hostess.

'Granted,' retorted Sidney. 'But why shouldn't Jews without
Judaism marry Christians without Christianity? Must a Jew
needs have a Jewess to help him break the Law?'

'Intermarriage must not be tolerated,' said Raphael. 'It would
hurt us less if we had a country. Lacking that, we must preserve
our human boundaries.'

'You have good phrases sometimes,' admitted Sidney. 'But
why must we preserve any boundaries? Why must we exist at all
as a separate people?'

'To fulfil the mission of Israel,' said Mr. Montagu Samuels solemnly.

'Ah,' what is that? That is one of the things nobody ever
seems able to tell me.'

'We are God's witnesses,' said Mrs. Henry Goldsmith, snipping off for herself a little bunch of hot-house grapes.

'False witnesses mostly, then,' said Sidney. A Christian friend of mine, an artist, fell in love with a girl and courted her regularly at her house for four years. Then he proposed ; she told him to ask her father, and he then learnt for the first time that the family was Jewish, and his suit could not therefore be entertained. Could a satirist have invented anything funnier? Whatever it was Jews have to bear witness to, these people had been bearing witness to so effectually that a constant visitor never heard a word of the evidence during four years. And this family is not an exception ; it is a type. Abroad the English Jew keeps his Judaism in the background, at home in the back kitchen. When he travels, his Judaism is not packed up among his *impedimenta*. He never obtrudes his creed, and even his Jewish newspaper is sent to him in a wrapper labelled something else. How's that for witnesses ? Mind you, I'm not blaming the men, being one of 'em. They may be the best fellows going, honourable, high-minded, generous —why expect them to be martyrs more than other Englishmen? Isn't life hard enough without inventing a new hardship? I declare there's no narrower creature in the world than your idealist ; he sets up a moral standard which suits his own line of business, and rails at men of the world for not conforming to it. God's witnesses, indeed ! I say nothing of those who are rather the devil's witnesses, but think of the host of Jews like myself who, whether they marry Christians or not, simply drop out, and whose absence of all religion escapes notice in the medley of creeds. We no more give evidence than those old Spanish Jews —Marannos they were called, weren't they?—who wore the Christian mask for generations. Practically many of us are Marannos still—I don't mean the Jews who are on the stage, and the press, and all that, but the Jews who have gone on believing. One Day of Atonement I amused myself by noting the pretexts on the shutters of shops that were closed in the Strand. "Our annual holiday," "Stock-taking day," "Our annual beanfeast," "Closed for repairs." '

'Well, it's something if they keep the Fast at all,' said Mr. Henry Goldsmith. 'It shows spirituality is not dead in them.'

'Spirituality !' sneered Sidney. 'Sheer superstition, rather. A dread of thunderbolts. Besides, fasting is a sensuous *attraction* But for the fasting, the Day of Atonement would have long since died out for these men. "Our annual beanfeast " ! There's witnesses for you ! '

'We cannot help it if we have false witnesses among us,' said Raphael Leon quietly. 'Our mission is to spread the truth of the Torah till the earth is filled with the knowledge of the Lord as the waters cover the sea.'

'But we don't spread it.'

We do. Christianity and Mohammedanism are offshoots of

Judaism; through them we have won the world from paganism, and taught it that God is one with the moral law.'

'Then we are somewhat in the position of an ancient school-master lagging superfluous in the schoolroom, where his whilom pupils are teaching.'

'By no means. Rather of one who stays on to protest against the false additions of his whilom pupils.'

'But we don't protest.'

'Our mere existence, since the Dispersion, is a protest,' urged Raphael. 'When the stress of persecution lightens, we may protest more consciously. We cannot have been preserved in vain through so many centuries of horrors, through the invasions of the Goths and Huns, through the Crusades, through the Holy Roman Empire, through the times of Torquemada. It is not for nothing that a handful of Jews loom so large in the history of the world, that their past is bound up with every noble human effort, every high ideal, every development of science, literature, and art. The ancient faith that has united us so long must not be lost just as it is on the very eve of surviving the faiths that sprung from it, even as it has survived Egypt, Assyria, Rome, Greece, and the Moors. If any of us fancy we have lost it, let us keep together still. Who knows but that it will be born again in us, if we are only patient? Race affinity is a potent force, why be in a hurry to dissipate it? The Marannos you speak of were but maimed heroes, yet one day the olden flame burst through the layers of three generations of Christian profession and intermarriage, and a brilliant company of illustrious Spaniards threw up their positions and sailed away in voluntary exile to serve the God of Israel. We shall yet see a spiritual revival even among our brilliant English Jews who have hid their face from their own flesh.'

The dark little girl looked up into his face with ill-suppressed wonder.

'Have you done preaching at me, Raphael?' inquired Sidney. 'If so, pass me a banana.'

Raphael smiled sadly and obeyed.

'I'm afraid if I see much of Raphael I shall be converted to Judaism,' said Sidney, peeling the banana. 'I had better take a hansom to the Riviera at once. I intended to spend Christmas there; I never dreamt I should be talking theology in London.'

'Oh, I think Christmas in London is best,' said the hostess unguardedly.

'Oh, I don't know. Give me Brighton,' said the host.

'Well, yes, I suppose Brighton *is* pleasanter,' said Mr. Montagu Samuels.

'Oh, but so many Jews go there,' observed Percy Saville.

'Yes, that *is* the drawback,' said Mrs. Henry Goldsmith. 'Do you know, some years ago I discovered a delightful village in Devonshire, and took the household there in the summer. The very next year when I went down I found no less than two Jewish families temporarily located there. Of course I have never gone there since.'

'Yes, it's wonderful how Jews scent out all the nicest places,' agreed Mrs. Montagu Samuels. 'Five years ago you could escape them by not going to Ramsgate ; now even the Highlands are getting impossible.'

Thereupon the hostess rose and the ladies retired to the drawing-room, leaving the gentlemen to discuss coffee, cigars, and the paradoxes of Sidney, who, tired of religion, looked to dumb show plays for the salvation of dramatic literature.

There was a little milk-jug on the coffee-tray. It represented a victory over Mary O'Reilly. The late Aaron Goldsmith never took milk till six hours after meat, and it was with some trepidation that the present Mr. Goldsmith ordered it to be sent up one evening after dinner. He took an early opportunity of explaining apologetically to Mary that some of his guests were not so pious as himself, and hospitality demanded the concession.

Mr. Henry Goldsmith did not like his coffee black. His dinner table was hardly ever without a guest.

CHAPTER II

RAPHAEL LEON

WHEN the gentlemen joined the ladies, Raphael instinctively returned to his companion of the dinner-table. She had been singularly silent during the meal, but her manner had attracted him. Over his black coffee and cigarette, it struck him that she might have been unwell, and that he had been insufficiently attentive to the little duties of the table, and he hastened to ask if she had a headache.

'No, no,' she said with a grateful smile. 'At least, not more than usual.'

Her smile was full of pensive sweetness, which made her face beautiful. It was a face that would have been almost plain but for the soul behind. It was dark, with great earnest eyes. The profile was disappointing, the curves were not perfect, and there was a reminder of Polish origin in the lower jaw and the cheek bone. Seen from the front, the face fascinated again, in the Eastern glow of its colouring, in the flash of the white teeth, in the depths of the brooding eyes, in the strength of the features that yet softened to womanliest tenderness and charm when flooded by the sunshine of a smile. The figure was *petite* and graceful, set off by a simple, tight-fitting, high-necked dress of ivory silk draped with lace, with a spray of Neapolitan violets at the throat. They sat in a niche of the spacious and artistically furnished drawing

oom, in the soft light of the candles, talking quietly while Addie
played Chopin.

Mrs. Henry Goldsmith's æsthetic instincts had had full play in
the elaborate carelessness of the ensemble, and the result was a
triumph, a medley of Persian luxury and Persian grace, a dream
of somniferous couches and arm-chairs, rich tapestry, vases, fans,
engravings, books, bronzes, tiles, plaques, and flowers.   Mr. Henry
Goldsmith was himself a connoisseur in the arts, his own and his
father's fortunes having been built up in the curio and antique
business, though to old Aaron Goldsmith appreciation had meant
strictly pricing, despite his genius for detecting false Correggios
and sham Louis Quatorze cabinets.

'Do you suffer from headaches?' inquired Raphael solicitously.

'A little.   The doctor says I studied too much and worked too
hard when a little girl.   Such is the punishment of perseverance.
Life isn't like the copy-books.'

'Oh, but I wonder your parents let you over-exert yourself.'

'A melancholy smile played about the mobile lips.   'I brought
myself up,' she said.   'You look puzzled.   Oh, I know! Confess
you think I'm Miss Goldsmith!'

'Why—are—you not?' he stammered.

'No, my name is Ansell—Esther Ansell.'

'Pardon me.   I am so bad at remembering names in introductions.   But I've just come back from Oxford, and it's the first
time I've been to this house, and seeing you here without a cavalier
when we arrived, I thought you lived here.'

'You thought rightly; I do live here.'   She laughed gently at
his changing expression.

'I wonder Sidney never mentioned you to me,' he said.

'Do you mean Mr. Graham?' she said, with a slight blush.

'Yes; I know he visits here.'

'Oh, he is an artist.   He has eyes only for the beautiful.'
She spoke quickly, a little embarrassed.

'You wrong him ; his interests are wider than that.'

'Do you know, I am so glad you didn't pay me the obvious
compliment,' she said, recovering herself.   'It looked as if I were
fishing for it.   I'm so stupid.'

He looked at her blankly.

'*I*'m stupid,' he said, 'for I don't know what compliment I
missed paying.'

'If you regret it, I shall not think so well of you,' she said.   'You
know I've heard all about your brilliant success at Oxford.'

'They put all those petty little things in the Jewish papers, don't
they?'

'I read it in the *Times*,' retorted Esther.   'You took a double-
first and the prize for poetry, and a heap of other things ; but I
noticed the prize for poetry, because it is so rare to find a Jew
writing poetry.'

'Prize poetry is not poetry,' he reminded her.   'But considering

the Jewish Bible contains the finest poetry in the world, I do n
see why you should be surprised to find a Jew trying to write some

'Oh, you know what I mean,' answered Esther.   'What is th
use of talking about the old Jews? We seem to be a different rac
now.   Who cares for poetry?'

'Our poet's scroll reaches on uninterruptedly through the Midd
Ages.   The passing phenomenon of to-day must not blind us t
the real traits of our race,' said Raphael.

'Nor must we be blind to the passing phenomenon of to-day
retorted Esther.   We have no ideals now.'

'I see Sidney has been infecting you,' he said gently.

'No, no; I beg you will not think that,' she said, flushing almos
resentfully.   'I have thought these things, as the Scripture tells u
to meditate on the Law, day and night, sleeping and waking
standing up and sitting down.'

'You cannot have thought of them without prejudice, then,' h
answered, 'if you say we have no ideals.'

'I mean, we're not responsive to great poetry—to the messag
of a Browning, for instance.'

'I deny it.   Only a small percentage of his own race is respon
sive.   I would wager our percentage proportionally higher.   Bu
Browning's philosophy of religion is already ours—for hundreds o
years every Saturday night every Jew has been proclaiming th
view of life and Providence in "Pisgah Sights":

> '"All's lend and borrow,
> Good, see, wants evil,
> Joy demands sorrow,
> Angel weds devil."

What is this but the philosophy of our formula for ushering ou
the Sabbath and welcoming in the day of toil, accepting the hol
and the profane, the light and the darkness?'

'Is that in the Prayer-Book?' said Esther astonished.

'Yes, you see you are ignorant of our own ritual while admirin
everything non-Jewish.   Excuse me if I am frank, Miss Ansell, bu
there are many people among us who rave over Italian antiquitie
but can see nothing poetical in old Judaism.   They listen eagerl
to Dante, but despise David.'

'I shall certainly look up the liturgy,' said Esther.   'But tha
will not alter my opinion.   The Jew may say these fine things, bu
they are only a tune to him.   Yes, I begin to recall the passage i
Hebrew—I see my father making *Havdalah*—the melody goes i
my head like a sing-song.   But I never in my life thought of th
meaning.   As a little girl I always got my conscious religiou
inspiration out of the new Testament.   It sounds very shocking,
know.'

Undoubtedly you put your finger on an evil.   But there i
religious edification in common prayers and ceremonies even whe
divorced from meaning.   Remember the Latin prayers of th
Catholic poor.   Jews may be below Judaism, but are not all me

below their creed? If the race which gave the world the Bible knows it least——'

He stopped suddenly, for Addie was playing *pianissimo*, and although she was his sister, he did not like to put her out.

'It comes to this,' said Esther, when Chopin spoke louder : 'our Prayer-Book needs depolarisation, as Wendell Holmes says of the Bible.'

'Exactly,' assented Raphael. 'And what our people need is to make acquaintance with the treasure of our own literature. Why go to Browning for theism, when the words of his " Rabbi Ben Ezra " are but a synopsis of a famous Jewish argument?

> ' " I see the whole design,
> I, who saw Power, see now Love, perfect too.
> Perfect I call Thy plan,
> Thanks that I was a man !
> Maker, remaker, complete, I trust what Thou shalt do." '

It sounds like a bit of Bachja. That there is a Power outside us nobody denies ; that this Power works for our good and wisely is not so hard to grant when the facts of the soul are weighed with the facts of Nature. Power, Love, Wisdom—there you have a real trinity which makes up the Jewish God. And in this God we trust— incomprehensible as are His ways, unintelligible as is His essence. "Thy ways are not My ways, nor thy thoughts My thoughts." That comes into collision with no modern philosophies—we appeal to experience, and make no demands upon the faculty for believing things "because they are impossible." And we are proud and happy in that the dread Unknown God of the infinite universe has chosen our race as the medium by which to reveal His will to the world. We are sanctified to His service. History testifies that this has verily been our mission, that we have taught the world Religion as truly as Greece has taught Beauty and Science. Our miraculous survival through the cataclysms of ancient and modern dynasties is a proof that our mission is not yet over.'

The sonata came to an end. Percy Saville started a comic song, playing his own accompaniment. Fortunately, it was loud and rollicking.

'And do you really believe that we are sanctified to God's service?' said Esther, casting a melancholy glance at Percy's grimaces.

'Can there be any doubt of it? God made choice of one race to be messengers and apostles, martyrs at need to His truth. Happily the sacred duty is ours,' he said earnestly, utterly uncon- scious of the incongruity that struck Esther so keenly. And yet, of the two, he had by far the greater gift of humour. It did not destroy his idealism, but kept it in touch with things mundane. Esther's vision, though more penetrating, lacked this corrective of humour, which makes always for breadth of view. Perhaps it was because she was a woman that the trivial sordid details of life's comedy hurt her so acutely that she could scarce sit out the play patiently. Where Raphael would have admired the lute, Esther was troubled by the little rifts in it.

'But isn't that a narrow conception of God's revelation?' she asked.

'No. Why should God not teach through a great race as through a great man?

'And you really think that Judaism is not dead, intellectually speaking?'

'How can it die? Its truths are eternal, deep in human nature, and the constitution of things. Ah, I wish I could get you to see with the eyes of the great Rabbis and sages in Israel ; to look on this human life of ours, not with the pessimism of Christianity, but as a holy and precious gift, to be enjoyed heartily, yet spent in God's service—birth, marriage, death, all holy ; good, evil, alike holy. Nothing on God's earth common or purposeless ; everything chanting the great song of God's praise, "The morning stars singing together," as we say in the Dawn Service.'

As he spoke Esther's eyes filled with strange tears. Enthusiasm always infected her, and for a brief instant her sordid universe seemed to be transfigured to a sacred joyous reality, full of infinite potentialities of worthy work and noble pleasure. A thunder of applausive hands marked the end of Percy Saville's comic song. Mr. Montagu Samuels was beaming at his brother's grotesque drollery. There was an interval of general conversation, followed by a round game, in which Raphael and Esther had to take part. It was very dull, and they were glad to find themselves together again.

'Ah, yes,' said Esther sadly, resuming the conversation as if there had been no break ; 'but this is a Judaism of your own creation. The real Judaism is a religion of pots and pans. It does not call to the soul's depths like Christianity.'

'Again, it is a question of the point of view taken. From a practical, our ceremonialism is a training in self-conquest, while it links the generations, "bound each to each by natural piety," and unifies our atoms, dispersed to the four corners of the earth, as nothing else could. From a theoretical, it is but an extension of the principle I tried to show you. Eating, drinking, every act of life is holy, is sanctified by some relation to Heaven. We will not arbitrarily divorce some portions of life from religion, and say these are of the world, the flesh or the devil, any more than we will save up our religion for Sundays. There is no devil, no original sin, no need of salvation from it, no need of a mediator. Every Jew is in as direct relation with God as the Chief Rabbi. Christianity is an historical failure : its counsels of perfection, its command to turn the other cheek, a farce. When a modern spiritual genius, a Tolstoi, repeats it, all Christendom laughs as at a new freak of insanity. All practical honourable men are Jews at heart. Judaism has never tampered with human dignity, nor perverted the moral consciousness. Our housekeeper, a Christian, once said to my sister Addie : " I 'm so glad to see you do so much charity, miss. *I* need not, because I 'm saved already." Judaism is the true "religion of humanity." It does not seek to make men and women angels before their time. Our marriage service blesses the King of the Universe, who has created "joy and gladness, bridegroom and bride, mirth and exultation, pleasure and delight, love, brotherhood, peace and fellowship." '

' It is all very beautiful in theory,' said Esther ; ' but so is Christianity, which is also not to be charged with its historical caricatures, nor with its superiority to average human nature. As for the doctrine of original sin, it is the one thing that the science of heredity has demonstrated, with a difference. But do not be alarmed ; I do not call myself a Christian because I see some relation between the dogmas of Christianity and the truths of experience, nor even because '—here she smiled wistfully—' I should like to believe in Jesus. But you are less logical. When you said there was no devil, I felt sure I was right, that you belong to the modern schools that get rid of all the old beliefs, but cannot give up the old names. You know as well as I do that, take away the belief in hell—a real old-fashioned hell of fire and brimstone—even such Judaism as survives would freeze to death without that genial warmth.'

' I know nothing of the kind,' he said. ' And I am in no sense a modern. I am (to adopt a phrase which is to me tautologous) an orthodox Jew.'

Esther smiled.

' Forgive my smiling,' she said. ' I am thinking of the orthodox Jews I used to know, who used to bind their phylacteries on their arms and foreheads every morning.'

' I bind my phylacteries on my arm and forehead every morning,' he said simply.

' What !' gasped Esther. ' You, an Oxford man !'

' Yes,' he said gravely. ' Is it so astonishing to you ?'

' Yes, it is. You are the first educated Jew I have ever met who believed in that sort of thing.'

' Nonsense ?' he said inquiringly. ' There are hundreds like me.'

' She shook her head. ' There 's the Rev Joseph Strelitski. I suppose *he* does, but then he 's paid for it.'

' Oh, why will you sneer at Strelitski ?' he said, pained. ' He has a noble soul. It is to the privilege of his conversation that I owe my best understanding of Judaism.'

' Ah, I was wondering why the old arguments sounded so different, so much more convincing from your lips,' murmured Esther. ' Now I know : because he wears a white tie. That sets up all my bristles of contradiction when he opens his mouth.'

' But I wear a white tie, too,' said Raphael, his smile broadening in sympathy with the slow response on the girl's serious face.

' That 's not a trade-mark,' she protested. ' But forgive me, I didn't know Strelitski was a friend of yours. I won't say a word

against him any more.   His sermons really are above the average,
and he strives more than the others to make Judaism more spiritual.'

'More spiritual!' he repeated, the pained expression returning.
'Why, the very theory of Judaism has always been the spiritualisa-
tion of the material.'

'And the practice of Judaism has always been the materialisation
of the spiritual,' she answered.

He pondered the saying thoughtfully, his face growing sadder.

'You have lived among your books,' Esther went on.   'I have
lived among the brutal facts.   I was born in the Ghetto, and when
you talk of the mission of Israel, silent sardonic laughter goes
through me as I think of the squalor and the misery.'

'God works through human suffering.   His ways are large,' said
Raphael almost in a whisper.

'And wasteful,' said Esther.   'Spare me clerical platitudes à la
Strelitski.   I have seen so much.'

'And suffered much?' he asked gently.

She nodded, scarce perceptibly.

'Oh, if you only knew my life!'

'Tell it me,' he said.   His voice was soft and caressing.   His
frank soul seemed to pierce through all conventionalities, and to go
straight to hers.

'I cannot—not now,' she murmured.   'There is so much to tell.'

'Tell me a little,' he urged.

She began to speak of her history, scarce knowing why, forgetting he was a stranger.   Was it racial affinity, or was it merely the
spiritual affinity of souls that feel their identity through all differences of brain.

'What is the use?' she said.   'You with your childhood could
never realise mine.   My mother died when I was seven; my father
was a Russian pauper alien who rarely got work.   I had an elder brother
of brilliant promise.   He died before he was thirteen.   I had a lot
of brothers and sisters and a grandmother, and we all lived, half
starved, in a garret.'

Her eyes grew humid at the recollection; she saw the spacious
drawing-room and the dainty *bric à brac* through a mist.

'Poor child!' murmured Raphael.

'Strelitski, by the way, lived in our street then.   He sold cigars
on commission and earned an honest living; sometimes I used to
think that is why he never cares to meet my eye, he remembers
me and knows I remember him; at other times I thought he
knew that I saw through his professions of orthodoxy.   But as you
champion him, I suppose I must look for a more creditable reason
for his inability to look me straight in the face.   Well, I grew up,
I got on well at school, and about ten years ago I won a prize given
by Mrs. Henry Goldsmith, whose kindly interest I excited thenceforward.   At thirteen I became a teacher.   This had always been my
aspiration; when it was granted I was more unhappy than ever.   I
began to realise acutely that we were terribly poor.   I found it difficult

to dress so as to ensure the respect of my pupils and colleagues ; the work was unspeakably hard and unpleasant ; tiresome and hungry little girls had to be ground to suit the inspectors, and fell victims to the then prevalent competition among teachers for a high percentage of passes ; I had to teach Scripture history, and I didn't believe in it. None of us believed in it—the talking serpent, the Egyptian miracles, Samson, Jonah and the whale, and all that. Everything about me was sordid and unlovely. I yearned for a fuller, wider life, for larger knowledge. I hungered for the sun. In short I was intensely miserable. At home things went from bad to worse ; often I was the sole bread-winner, and my few shillings a week were our only income. My brother Solomon grew up, but could not get into a decent situation, because he must not work on the Sabbath. Oh, if you knew how young lives are cramped and shipwrecked at the start by this one curse of the Sabbath, you would not wish us to persevere in our isolation. It sent a mad thrill of indignation through me to find my father daily entreating the deaf heavens.'

He would not argue now. His eyes were moist.

' Go on,' he murmured.

' The rest is nothing. Mrs Henry Goldsmith stepped in as the *dea ex machinâ*. She had no children, and she took it into her head to adopt me. Naturally I was dazzled, though anxious about my brothers and sisters. But my father looked upon it as a god-send. Without consulting me, Mrs. Goldsmith arranged that he and the other children should be shipped to America ; she got him some work at a relative's in Chicago. I suppose she was afraid of having the family permanently hanging about the Terrace. At first I was grieved ; but when the pain of parting was over I found myself relieved to be rid of them, especially of my father. It sounds shocking, I know, but I can confess all my vanities now, for I have learnt all is vanity. I thought Paradise was opening before me ; I was educated by the best masters, and graduated at the London University. I travelled and saw the Continent, had my fill of sunshine and beauty. I have had many happy moments, realised many childish ambitions, but happiness is as far away as ever. My old school colleagues envy me ; yet I do not know whether I would not go back without regret.'

' Is there anything lacking in your life, then ? ' he asked gently.

' No ; I happen to be a nasty, discontented little thing—that is all,' she said, with a faint smile. ' Look on me as a psychological paradox, or a text for the preacher.'

' And do the Goldsmiths know of your discontent ? '

' Heaven forbid ! They have been so very kind to me. We get along very well together. I never discuss religion with them, only the services and the minister.'

' And your relatives ? '

' Oh, they are all well and happy. Solomon has a store in Detroit. He is only nineteen, and dreadfully enterprising. Father is a pillar of a Chicago *Chevrah*. He still talks Yiddish. He has escaped learning American just as he escaped learning English. I buy him a queer old Hebrew book sometimes with my pocket-money, and he is happy. One little sister is a typewriter, and the other is just out of school and does the house-work. I suppose I shall go out and see them all some day.'

'What became of the grandmother you mentioned?'

'She had a charity funeral a year before the miracle happened. She was very weak and ill, and the charity doctor warned her that she must not fast on the day of Atonement. But she wouldn't even moisten her parched lips with a drop of cold water. And so she died, exhorting my father with her last breath to beware of Mrs. Simons (a good-hearted widow who was very kind to us), and to marry a pious Polish woman.'

'And did he?'

'No, I am still stepmotherless. Your white tie's gone wrong. It's all on one side.'

'It generally is,' said Raphael, fumbling perfunctorily at the little bow.

'Let me put it straight. There! And now you know all about me, I hope you are going to repay my confidences in kind.'

'I am afraid I cannot oblige with anything so romantic,' he said, smiling. 'I was born of rich but honest parents, of a family settled in England for three generations, and went to Harrow and Oxford in due course. That is all. I saw a little of the Ghetto, though, when I was a boy. I had some correspondence on Hebrew literature with a great Jewish scholar, Gabriel Hamburg (he lives in Stockholm now), and one day when I was up from Harrow I went to see him. By good fortune I assisted at the foundation of the Holy Land League, now presided over by Gideon, the member for Whitechapel. I was moved to tears by the en-thusiasm. It was there I made the acquaintance of Strelitski. He spoke as if inspired. I also met a poverty-stricken poet, Melchi-tzedek Pinchas, who afterwards sent me his work, *Metatoron's Flames* to Harrow. A real neglected genius. Now, there's the man to bear in mind when one speaks of Jews and poetry! After that night I kept up a regular intercourse with the Ghetto, and have been there several times lately.'

'But surely you don't also long to return to Palestine?'

'I do. Why should we not have our own country?'

'It would be too chaotic. Fancy all the Ghettos of the world amalgamating! Everybody would want to be ambassador at Paris, as the old joke says.'

'It would be a problem for the statesmen among us. Dissenters, Churchmen, atheists, slum-savages, clodhoppers, philosophers, aristocrats—make up Protestant England. It is the popular ignorance of the fact that Jews are as diverse as Protestants that makes such novels as we were discussing at dinner harmful.'

'But is the author to blame for that? He does not claim to

present the whole truth, but a facet. English society lionised Thackeray for his pictures of it. Good heavens ! do Jews suppose they alone are free from the snobbery, hypocrisy and vulgarity that have shadowed every society that has ever existed ?'

'In no work of art can the spectator be left out of account,' he urged. 'In a world full of smouldering prejudices a scrap of paper may start the bonfire. English society can afford to laugh where Jewish society must weep. That is why our papers are always so effusively grateful for Christian compliments. You see, it is quite true that the author paints not the Jew, but bad Jews ; but, in the absence of paintings of good Jews, bad Jews are taken as identical with Jews.'

'Oh, then you agree with the others about the book ? ' she said, in a disappointed tone.

'I haven't read it ; I am speaking generally. Have you ?'

'Yes.'

'And what do you think of it ? I don't remember your express-ing an opinion at table.'

She pondered an instant.

'I thought highly of it, and agreed with every word of it——'

She paused. He looked expectantly into the dark intense face ; he saw it was charged with further speech.

'Till I met you,' she concluded abruptly.

A wave of emotion passed over his face.

'You don't mean that ? ' he murmured.

'Yes, I do. You have shown me new lights.'

'I thought I was speaking platitudes,' he said simply. 'It would be nearer the truth to say you have given *me* new lights.'

The little face flushed with pleasure, the dark skin shining, the eyes sparkling. Esther looked quite pretty.

'How is that possible ? ' she said. 'You have read and thought twice as much as I.'

'Then you must be indeed poorly off,' he said, smiling. 'But I am really glad we met. I have been asked to edit a new Jewish paper, and our talk has made me see more clearly the lines on which it must be run if it is to do any good. I am awfully indebted to you.'

'A new Jewish paper?' she said, deeply interested. 'We have so many already. What is its *raison d'être* ? '

'To convert you,' he said, smiling, but with a ring of seriousness in the words.

'Isn't that like a steam-hammer cracking a nut, or Hoti burning down his house to roast a pig ? And suppose I refuse to take in the new Jewish paper ? Will it suspend publication ? '

He laughed.

'What 's this about a new Jewish paper ? ' said Mrs. Goldsmith, suddenly appearing in front of them with her large genial smile. 'Is that what you two have been plotting ? I notice you 've laid your heads together all the evening. Ah well, birds of a feather flock together. Do you know my little Esther took the scholarship for logic at London? I wanted her to proceed to the M.A. at once, but the doctor said she must have a rest.' She laid her hand affectionately on the girl's hair.

Esther looked embarrassed.

'And so she is still a Bachelor?' said Raphael, smiling, but evidently impressed.

'Yes, but not for long, I hope,' returned Mrs Goldsmith. 'Come, darling, everybody's dying to hear one of your little songs.'

'The dying is premature,' said Esther. 'You know I only sing for my own amusement.'

'Sing for mine, then,' pleaded Raphael.

'To make you laugh?' queried Esther. 'I know you'll laugh at the way I play the accompaniment. One's fingers have to be used to it from childhood——'

Her eyes finished the sentence, 'and you know what mine was.'

The look seemed to seal their secret sympathy.

She went to the piano and sang in a thin but trained soprano. The song was a ballad with a quaint air full of sadness and heart-break. To Raphael, who had never heard the psalmic wails of the Sons of the Covenant or the Polish ditties of Fanny Belcovitch, it seemed also full of originality. He wished to lose himself in the sweet melancholy, but Mrs. Goldsmith, who had taken Esther's seat at his side, would not let him.

'Her own composition, words and music,' she whispered. 'I wanted her to publish it, but she is so shy and retiring. Who would think she was the child of a pauper immigrant, a rough jewel one has picked up and polished? If you really are going to start a new Jewish paper, she might be of use to you. And then there is Miss Cissy Levine: you have read her novels, of course? Sweetly pretty. Do you know, I think we are badly in want of a new paper, and you are the only man in the community who could give it us. We want educating, we poor people, we know so little of our faith and our literature.'

'I am so glad you feel the want of it,' whispered Raphael, forgetting Esther in his pleasure at finding a soul yearning for the light.

'Intensely. I suppose it will be advanced?'

Raphael looked at her a moment a little bewildered.

'No, it will be orthodox. It is the orthodox party that supplies the funds.'

A flash of light leapt into Mrs. Goldsmith's eyes.

'I am so glad it is not as I feared,' she said. 'The rival party has hitherto monopolised the press, and I was afraid that, like most of our young men of talent, you would give it that tendency. Now at last we poor orthodox will have a voice. It will be written in English?'

'As far as I can,' he said, smiling.

'No, you know what I mean. I thought the majority of the orthodox couldn't read English, and that they have their jargon papers. Will you be able to get a circulation?'

'There are thousands of families in the East End now among whom English is read, if not written. The evening papers sell as well there as anywhere else in London.'

'Bravo!' murmured Mrs. Goldsmith, clapping her hands.

Esther had finished her song. Raphael awoke to the remembrance of her. But she did not come to him again, sitting down instead on a lounge near the piano, where Sidney bantered Addie with his most paradoxical persiflage.

Raphael looked at her. Her expression was abstracted; her eyes had an inward look. He hoped her headache had not got worse. She did not look at all pretty now. She seemed a frail little creature with a sad, thoughtful face and an air of being alone in the midst of a merry company. Poor little thing! He felt as if he had known her for years. She seemed curiously out of harmony with all these people. He doubted even his own capacity to commune with her inmost soul. He wished he could be of service to her, could do anything for her that might lighten her gloom and turn her morbid thoughts in healthier directions.

The butler brought in some claret negus. It was the break-up signal. Raphael drank his negus with a pleasant sense of arming himself against the cold air. He wanted to walk home smoking his pipe, which he always carried in his overcoat. He clasped Esther's hand with a cordial smile of farewell.

'We shall meet again soon, I trust,' he said.

'I hope so,' said Esther. 'Put me down as a subscriber to that paper.'

'Thank you,' he said; 'I won't forget.'

'What's that?' said Sidney, pricking up his ears, 'doubled your circulation already?'

Sidney put Cousin Addie into a hansom, as she did not care to walk, and got in beside her.

'My feet are tired,' she said; 'I danced a lot last night, and was out a lot this afternoon. It's all very well for Raphael, who doesn't know whether he's walking on his head or his heels. Here, put your collar up, Raphael; not like that, it's all crumpled. Haven't you got a handkerchief to put round your throat? Where's that one I gave you? Lend him yours, Sidney.'

'You don't mind if *I* catch my death of cold. I've got to go on to a Christmas dance when I deposit you on your doorstep,' grumbled Sidney. 'Catch! There, you duffer! It's gone into the mud. Sure you won't jump in? Plenty of room. Addie can sit on my knee. Well, ta-ta! Merry Christmas!'

Raphael lit his pipe and strode off with long ungainly strides. It was a clear, frosty night, and the moonlight glistened on the silent spaces of street and square.

'Go to bed, my dear,' said Mrs. Goldsmith, returning to the lounge where Esther still sat brooding. 'You look quite worn out.'

Left alone, Mrs. Goldsmith smiled pleasantly at Mr. Goldsmith, who, uncertain of how he had behaved himself, always waited anxiously for the verdict. He was pleased to find it was 'Not guilty' this time.

'I think that went off very well,' she said. She was looking very lovely to-night, the low bodice emphasising the voluptuous outlines of the bust.

'Splendidly!' he returned. He stood with his coat-tails to the fire, his coarse-grained face beaming like an extra lamp. 'The people and those croquettes were A 1. The way Mary's picked up French cookery is wonderful.'

'Yes, especially considering she denies herself butter. But I'm not thinking of that, nor of our guests.' He looked at her, wondering. 'Henry,' she continued impressively, 'how would you like to get into Parliament?'

'Eh, Parliament? Me?' he stammered.

'Yes, why not? I've always had it in my eye.'

His face grew gloomy.

'It is not practicable,' he said, shaking the head with the prominent teeth and ears.

'Not practicable!' she echoed sharply. 'Just think of what you've achieved already, and don't tell me you're going to stop now. Not practicable, indeed! Why, that's the very word you used years ago in the provinces when I said you ought to be President. You said old Winkelstein had been in the position too long to be ousted. And yet I felt certain your superior English would tell in the long-run in such a miserable congregation of foreigners, and when Winkelstein had made that delicious blunder about the "university" of the Exodus instead of the "anniversary" and I went about laughing over it in all the best circles, the poor man's day was over. And when we came to London, and seemed to fall again to the bottom of the ladder because our greatness was swallowed up in the vastness, didn't you despair then? Didn't you tell me that we should never rise to the surface?'

'It didn't seem probable, did it?' he murmured in self-defence.

'Of course not. That's just my point. Your getting into the House of Commons doesn't seem probable now. But in those days your getting merely to know M.P.'s was equally improbable. The synagogal dignities were all filled up by old hands; there was no way of getting on the Council and meeting our magnates.'

'Yes, but your solution of that difficulty won't do here. I had not much difficulty in persuading the United Synagogue that a new synagogue was a crying want in Kensington, but I could hardly persuade the Government that a new constituency is a crying want in London.'

He spoke pettishly; his ambition always required rousing, and was easily daunted.

'No, but somebody's going to start a new something else, Henry,' said Mrs. Goldsmith with enigmatic cheerfulness. 'Trust in me; think of what we have done in less than a dozen years at comparatively trifling cost, thanks to that happy idea of a new synagogue

—you, the representative of the Kensington synagogue, with a "Sir" for a colleague and a congregation that from exceptionally small beginnings has sprung up to be the most fashionable in London ; likewise a member of the Council of the Anglo-Jewish Association and an honorary officer of the *Shechitah* Board ; I, connected with several first-class charities, on the committee of our leading school, and acknowledged discoverer of a girl who gives promise of doing something notable in literature or music. We have a reputation for wealth, culture, and hospitality, and it is quite two years since we shook off the last of the Maida Vale lot, who are so graphically painted in that novel of Mr. Armitage's. Who are our guests now ? Take to-night's. A celebrated artist, a brilliant young Oxford man, both scions of the same wealthy and well-considered family ; an authoress of repute, who dedicates her books (by permission) to the very first families of the community ; and, lastly, the Montagu Samuels, with the brother, Percy Saville, who go only to the best houses. Is there any other house, where the company is so exclusively Jewish, that could boast of a better gathering?'

'I don't say anything against the company,' said her husband awkwardly ; 'it's better than we got in the provinces. But your company isn't your constituency. What constituency would have me?

'Certainly no ordinary constituency would have you,' admitted his wife frankly. 'I am thinking of Whitechapel.'

'But Gideon represents Whitechapel.'

'Certainly ; as Sidney Graham says, he represents it very well. But he has made himself unpopular ; his name has appeared in print as a guest at City banquets, where the food can't be *kosher.* He has alienated a goodly proportion of the Jewish vote.'

'Well?' said Mr. Goldsmith, still wonderingly.

'Now is the time to bid for his shoes. Raphael Leon is about to establish a new Jewish paper. I was mistaken about that young man. You remember my telling you I had heard he was eccentric, and despite his brilliant career a little touched on religious matters. I naturally supposed his case was like that of one or two other Jewish young men we know, and that he yearned for spirituality, and his remarks at table rather confirmed the impression. But he is worse than that—and I nearly put my foot in it— his craziness is on the score of orthodoxy. Fancy that !—a man who has been to Harrow and Oxford longing for a gaberdine and side-curls ! Well, well, live and learn ! What a sad trial for his parents !'

She paused musing.

'But, Rosetta, what has Raphael Leon to do with my getting into Parliament ?'

'Don't be stupid, Henry ! Haven't I explained to you that Leon is going to start an orthodox paper which will be circulated among your future constituents ? It's extremely fortunate that we have always kept to our religion. We have a widespread reputation for orthodoxy. We are friends with Leon, and we can get Esther to

write for the paper (I could see he was rather struck by her).
Through this paper we can keep you and your orthodoxy constantly
before the constituency. The poor people are quite fascinated by
the idea of rich Jews like us keeping a strictly *kosher* table, but the
image of a Member of Parliament with phylacteries on his forehead
will simply intoxicate them.'

She smiled herself at the image—the smile that always intoxicated Percy Saville.

'You're a wonderful woman, Rosetta,' said Henry, smiling in
response with admiring affection and making his incisors more
prominent. He drew her head down to him and kissed her lips.

She returned his kiss lingeringly, and they had a flash of that
happiness which is born of mutual fidelity and trust.

'Can I do anything for you, mum, afore I go to bed?' said stout
old Mary O'Reilly, appearing at the door.

Mary was a privileged person, unappalled even by the butler.
Having no relatives, she never took a holiday, and never went out,
except to chapel.

'No, Mary, thank you. The dinner was excellent. Good-night,
and merry Christmas!'

'Same to you, mum'; and as the unconscious instrument of
Henry Goldsmith's candidature turned away, the Christmas bells
broke merrily upon the night. The peals fell upon the ears of
Raphael Leon, still striding along, casting a gaunt shadow on the
hoar-frosted pavement, but he marked them not : upon Addie, sitting by her bedroom mirror thinking of Sidney speeding to the
Christmas dance ; upon Esther turning restlessly on the luxurious
eider-down, oppressed by panoramic pictures of the martyrdom of
her race. Lying between sleep and waking, especially when her
brain had been excited, she had the faculty of seeing wonderful
vivid visions, indistinguishable from realities. The martyrs who
mounted the scaffold and the stake all had the face of Raphael.

'The mission of Israel' buzzed through her brain. Oh, the irony
of history ! Here was another life going to be wasted on an illusory
dream. The figures of Raphael and her father suddenly came into
grotesque juxtaposition. A bitter smile passed across her face.

The Christmas bells rang on, proclaiming peace in the name of
Him who came to bring a sword into the world.

'Surely,' she thought, 'the people of Christ has been the Christ
of peoples.'

And then she sobbed meaninglessly in the darkness.

CHAPTER III

'THE FLAG OF JUDAH'

THE call to edit the new Jewish paper seemed to Raphael the
voice of Providence. It came just when he was hesitating about
his future, divided between the attractions of the ministry, pure

Hebrew scholarship, and philanthrophy. The idea of a paper destroyed these conflicting claims by comprehending them all. A paper would be at once a pulpit, a medium for organising effective human service, and an incentive to serious study in the preparation of scholarly articles.

The paper was to be the property of the Co-operative Kosher Society, an association originally founded to supply unimpeachable Passover cakes. It was suspected by the pious that there was a taint of heresy in the flour used by the ordinary bakers, and it was remarked that the Rabbinate itself imported its *Motsos* from abroad. Successful in its first object, the Co-operative Kosher Society extended its operations to more perennial commodities, and sought to save Judaism from dubious cheese and butter, as well as to provide public baths for women in accordance with the precepts of Leviticus.

But these ideals were not so easy to achieve, and so gradually the idea of a paper to preach them to a godless age formed itself. The members of the Society met in Aaron Schlesinger's back office to consider them. Schlesinger was a cigar-merchant, and the discussions of the Society were invariably obscured by gratuitous smoke. Schlesinger's junior partner, Lewis De Haan, who also had a separate business as a surveyor, was the soul of the Society, and talked a great deal. He was a stalwart old man, with a fine imagination and figure, boundless optimism, a big biceps, a long venerable white beard, a keen sense of humour, and a versatility which enabled him to turn from the price of real estate to the elucidation of a Talmudical difficulty, and from the consignment of cigars to the organisation of apostolic movements. Among the leading spirits were our old friends Karlkammer the red-haired zealot, Sugarman the Shadchan, and Guedalyah the Greengrocer, together with Gradkoski the scholar, fancy goods merchant, and man of the world. A furniture-dealer, who was always failing, was also an important personage ; while Ebenezer Sugarman, a young man who had once translated a romance from the Dutch, acted as secretary. Melchitzedek Pinchas invariably turned up at the meetings, and smoked Schlesinger's cigars. He was not a member ; he had not qualified himself by taking ten-pound shares (far from fully paid up), but nobody liked to eject him, and no hint less strong than a physical would have moved the poet.

All the members of the council of the Co-operative Kosher Society spoke English volubly, and more or less grammatically, but none had sufficient confidence in the others to propose one of them for editor, though it is possible that none would have shrunk from having a shot. Diffidence is not a mark of the Jew. The claims of Ebenezer Sugarman and of Melchitzedek Pinchas were put forth most vehemently by Ebenezer and Melchitzedek respectively, and their mutual accusations of incompetence enlivened Mr. Schlesinger's back office.

'He ain't able to spell the commonest English words,' said

Ebenezer, with a contemptuous guffaw that sounded like the croak of a raven.

The young littérateur, the sumptuousness of whose *Bar-mitzvah* party was still a memory with his father, had lank black hair, with a long nose that supported blue spectacles.

' What does he know of the Holy Tongue ? ' croaked Melchitzedek witheringly, adding in a confidential whisper to the cigar-merchant, ' I and you, Schlesinger, are the only two men in England who can write the Holy Tongue grammatically.'

The little poet was as insinuative and volcanic (by turns) as ever. His beard was, however, better trimmed, and his complexion healthier, aud he looked younger than ten years ago. His clothes were quite spruce. For several years he had travelled about the Continent, mainly at Raphael's expense. He said his ideas came better in touring and at a distance from the unappreciative English Jewry. It was a pity, for with his linguistic genius his English would have been immaculate by this time. As it was, there was a considerable improvement in his writing, if not so much in his accent.

' What do I know of the Holy Tongue ! ' repeated Ebenezer scornfully. ' Hold yours ! '

The committee laughed, but Schlesinger, who was a serious man, said :

' Business, gentlemen, business ! '

' Come, then ! I'll challenge you to translate a page of *Metatoron's Flames*,' said Pinchas, skipping about the office like a sprightly grasshopper. ' You know no more than the Reverend Joseph Strelitski, vith his vite tie and his princely income.'

De Haan seized the poet by the collar, swung him off his feet, and tucked him up in the coal-scuttle.

' Yah ! ' croaked Ebenezer. ' Here's a fine editor. Ho ! ho ! ho ! '

' We cannot have either of them. It's the only way to keep them quiet,' said the furniture-dealer who was always failing.

Ebenezer's face fell and his voice rose.

' I don't see why I should be sacrificed to '*im*. There ain't a man in England who can write English better than me. Why, everybody says so. Look at the success of my book, *The Old Burgomaster*, the best Dutch novel ever written. The *St. Pancras Press* said it reminded them of Lord Lytton—it did indeed. I can show you the paper. I can give you one each if you like. And, then, it ain't as if I didn't know 'Ebrew, too. Even if I was in doubt about anything, I could always go to my father. You give me this paper to manage, and I'll make your fortunes for you in a twelvemonth ; I will, as sure as I stand here.'

Pinchas had made spluttering interruptions as frequently as he could in resistance of De Haan's brawny hairy hand, which was pressed against his nose and mouth to keep him down in the coal-scuttle, but now he exploded with a force that shook off the hand like a bottle of soda-water expelling its cork.

'You Man-of-the-Earth,' he cried, sitting up in the coal-scuttle, 'you are not even orthodox. Here, my dear gentlemen, is the very position created by Heaven for me, in this disgraceful country vhere genius starves. Here at last you have the opportunity of covering yourself vid eternal glory. Have I not given you the idea of starting this paper? And vas I not born to be a Rédacteur, a editor, as you call it? Into the paper I vill pour all the fires of my song.'

'Yes, burn it up,' croaked Ebenezer.

'I vill lead the Freethinkers and the Reformers back into the fold. I vill be Elijah, and my vings shall be quill pens. I vill save Judaism.'

He started up, swelling, but De Haan caught him by his waist-band, and readjusted him in the coal-scuttle.

'Here, take another cigar, Pinchas,' he said, passing Schlesinger's private box as if with a twinge of remorse for his treatment of one he admired as a poet, though he could not take him seriously as a man.

The discussion proceeded; the furniture-dealer's counsel was followed. It was definitely decided to let the two candidates neutralise each other.

'Vat vill you give me if I find you a Rédacteur?' suddenly asked Pinchas. 'I give up my editorial seat——'

'Editorial coal-scuttle,' growled Ebenezer.

'Pooh! I find you a first-class Rédacteur, who vill not vant a big salary; perhaps he vill do it for nothing. How much commission vill you give me?'

'Ten shillings on every pound if he does not want a big salary,' said De Haan instantly, 'and twelve and sixpence on every pound if he does it for nothing.'

And Pinchas, who was easily bamboozled when finance became complex, went out to find Raphael.

Thus, at the next meeting, the poet produced Raphael in triumph, and Gradkoski, who loved a reputation for sagacity, turned a little green with disgust at his own forgetfulness. Gradkoski was among those founders of the Holy Land League with whom Raphael had kept up relations, and he could not deny that the young enthusiast was the ideal man for the post. De Haan, who was busy directing the clerks to write out ten thousand wrappers for the first number, and who had never heard of Raphael before, held a whispered confabulation with Gradkoski and Schlesinger, and in a few moments Raphael was rescued from obscurity, and appointed to the editorship of *The Flag of Judah* at a salary of nothing a year. De Haan immediately conceived a vast contemptuous admiration of the man.

'You von't forget me,' whispered Pinchas, buttonholing the editor at the first opportunity, and placing his forefinger insinuatively alongside his nose. 'You vill remember that I expect a commission on your salary.'

Raphael smiled good-naturedly, and, turning to De Haan, said : 'But do you think there is any hope of a circulation?'

'A circulation, sir, a circulation!' repeated De Haan. 'Why, we shall not be able to print fast enough. There are seventy thousand orthodox Jews in London alone.'

'And besides,' added Gradkoski, in a corroboration strongly like a contradiction, 'we shall not have to rely on the circulation. Newspapers depend on their advertisements.'

'Do they?' said Raphael helplessly.

'Of course,' said Gradkoski, with his air of worldly wisdom. 'And don't you see, being a religious paper, we are bound to get all the communal advertisements. Why, we get the Co-operative Kosher Society to start with.'

'Yes, but we ain't going to pay for that,' said Sugarman the Shadchan.

'That doesn't matter,' said De Haan. 'It'll look well. We can fill up a whole page with it. You know what Jews are ; they won't ask, "Is this paper wanted?" they'll balance it in their hand, as if weighing up the value of the advertisements, and ask, " Does it pay?" But it *will* pay ! it must pay ! With you at the head of it, Mr. Leon, a man whose fame and piety are known and respected wherever a *Mezuzah* adorns a doorpost : a man who is in sympathy with the East End, and has the ear of the West ; a man who will preach the purest Judaism in the best English—with such a man at the head of it we shall be able to ask bigger prices for advertisements than the existing Jewish papers.'

Raphael left the office in a transport of enthusiasm, full of Messianic emotions.

At the next meeting he announced that he was afraid he could not undertake the charge of the paper. Amid universal consternation, tempered by the exultation of Ebenezer, he explained that he had been thinking it over, and did not see how it could be done. He said he had been carefully studying the existing communal organs, and saw that they dealt with many matters of which he knew nothing ; whilst he might be competent to form the taste of the community in religious and literary matters, it appeared that the community was chiefly excited about elections and charities.

'Moreover,' said he, 'I noticed that it is expected of these papers to publish obituaries of communal celebrities, for whose biographies no adequate materials are anywhere extant. It would scarcely be decent to obtrude upon the sacred grief of the bereaved relatives with a request for particulars.'

'Oh, that's all right,' laughed De Haan. 'I'm sure *my* wife would be glad to give you any information.'

'Of course, of course,' said Gradkoski soothingly. 'You will get the obituaries sent in of themselves by the relatives.'

Raphael's brow expressed surprise and incredulity.

'And, besides, we are not going to crack up the same people as the other papers,' said De Haan : 'otherwise we should not supply a want. We must dole out our praise and blame quite differently, and we must be very scrupulous to give only a little praise, so that it shall be valued the more.'

He stroked his white beard tranquilly.

'But how about meetings?' urged Raphael; 'I find that sometimes two take place at once. I can go to one, but I can't be at both.'

'Oh, that will be all right,' said De Haan airily. 'We will leave out one, and people will think it is unimportant. We are bringing out a paper for our own ends—not to report the speeches of busybodies.'

Raphael was already exhibiting a conscientiousness which must be nipped in the bud. Seeing him silenced, Ebenezer burst forth anxiously :

'But Mr. Leon is right. There must be a sub-editor.'

'Certainly there must be a sub-editor,' cried Pinchas eagerly.

'Very well, then,' said De Haan, struck with a sudden thought ; 'it is true Mr. Leon cannot do all the work. I know a young fellow who'll be just the very thing. He'll come for a pound a week.'

'But I 'll come for a pound a week,' said Ebenezer.

'Yes, but you won't get it,' said Schlesinger impatiently.

'*Sha*, Ebenezer !' said old Sugarman imperiously.

De Haan thereupon hunted up a young gentleman who dwelt in his mind as 'Little Sampson,' and straightway secured him at the price named. He was a lively young Bohemian, born in Australia, who had served an apprenticeship on the Anglo-Jewish press, worked his way up into the larger journalistic world without, and was now engaged in organising a comic-opera touring company, and in drifting back again into Jewish journalism. This young gentleman, who always wore long curling locks, an eyeglass, and a romantic cloak which covered a multitude of shabbinesses, fully allayed Raphael's fears as to the difficulties of editorship,

'Obituaries !' he said scornfully ; 'you rely on me for that. The people who are worth chronicling are sure to have lived in the back numbers of our contemporaries, and I can always hunt them up in the Museum. As for the people who are not, their families will send them in, and your only trouble will be to conciliate the families of those you ignore.

'But about all those meetings?' said Raphael.

'I 'll go to some,' said the sub-editor goodnaturedly, 'whenever they don't interfere with the rehearsals of my opera. You know, of course, I am bringing out a comic opera, composed by myself. Some lovely tunes in it ! One goes like this : "Ta-ra-ra-ta, ta-dee-dum-dee." That 'll knock 'em. Well, as I was saying, I 'll help you as much as I can find time for. You rely on me for that.'

'Yes,' said poor Raphael, with a sickly smile ; 'but suppose neither of us goes to some important meeting.'

' No harm done. God bless you ! I know the styles of all our chief speakers—ahem, ha !—pauperisation of the East End, ha !—I would emphatically say that this scheme—ahem!—his lordship's untiring zeal for—hum !—the welfare of—and so on.   Ta-dee-dum-da, ta-ra, rum-dee.   They always send on the agenda before-hand.   That's all I want, and I'll lay you twenty to one I'll turn out as good a report as any of our rivals.   You rely on me for *that*.   I know exactly how debates go.   At the worst I can always swop with another reporter—a prize distribution for an obituary : or a funeral for a concert.'

' And do yon really think we two between us can fill up the paper every week ?' said Raphael doubtfully.

Little Sampson broke into a shriek of laughter, dropped his eyeglass, and collapsed helplessly into the coal-scuttle.   The committee-men looked up from their confabulations in astonishment.

' Fill up the paper !   Ho, ho, ho !' roared Little Sampson, still doubled up.   'Evidently *you've* never had anything to do with papers.   Why, the reports of London and provincial sermons alone would fill three papers a week.'

' Yes ; but how are we to get these reports, especially from the provinces ?'

' How ?   Ho, ho, ho !' and for some time Little Sampson was physically incapable of speech.   'Don't you know,' he gasped, ' that the ministers always send up their own sermons, pages upon pages of foolscap ?'

' Indeed ?' murmured Raphael.

' What, haven't you noticed all Jewish sermons are "eloquent"?'

' They write that themselves ?'

' Of course ; sometimes they put "able," and sometimes "learned," but as a rule they prefer to be "eloquent."   The run on that epithet is tremendous.   Ta-dee-dum-da.   In holiday seasons they are also very fond of "enthralling the audience," and of "melting them to tears " ; but this is chiefly during the Ten Days of Repentance, or when a boy is *Bar-mitzvah*.   Then think of the people who send in accounts of the oranges they gave away to Distressed Widows, or of the prizes won by their children at fourth-rate schools, or of the silver pointers they present to the synagogue.   Whenever a reader sends a letter to an evening paper, he will want you to quote it, and if he writes a paragraph in the obscurest leaflet, he will want you to note it as "Literary Intelligence."   Why, my dear fellow, your chief task will be to cut down.   Ta-ra-ra-ta !   Any Jewish paper could be entirely supported by voluntary contributions—as, for the matter of that, could any newspaper in the world.'   He got up and shook the coal-dust languidly from his cloak.

' Besides, we shall all be helping you with articles,' said De Haan encouragingly.

' Yes, we shall all be helping you,' said Ebenezer.

'I vill give you from the Pierian Spring—bucketsful,' said Pinchas in a flush of generosity.

'Thank you, I shall be much obliged,' said Raphael heartily ; 'for I don't quite see the use of a paper filled up as Mr. Sampson suggests.' He flung his arms out and drew them in again. It was a way he had when in earnest. 'Then, I should like to have some foreign news. Where's that to come from?'

'You rely on me for *that*,' said Little Sampson cheerfully. 'I will write at once to all the chief Jewish papers in the world, French, German, Dutch, Italian, Hebrew, and American, asking them to exchange with us. There is never any dearth of foreign news. I translate a thing from the Italian *Vessillo Israelitico* and the *Israelitische Nieuwsbode* of Amsterdam copies it from us ; *Der Israelit* then translates it into German, whence it gets into Hebrew, in *Hamagid*, thence into *L'Univers Israélite* of Paris, and thence into the *American Hebrew*. When I see it in American, not having to translate it, it strikes me as fresh, and so I transfer it bodily to our columns, whence it gets translated into Italian, and so the merry-go-round goes eternally on. Ta-dee-rum-day. You rely on me for your foreign news. Why, I can get you foreign telegrams if you'll only allow me to stick "Trieste, December 21," or things of that sort at the top. Ti-tum, tee-ti.' He went on humming a sprightly air, then suddenly interrupting himself, he said, 'But have you got an advertisement canvasser, Mr. De Haan?'

'No, not yet,' said De Haan, turning round. The committee had resolved itself into animated groups, dotted about the office, each group marked by a smoke-drift. The clerks were still writing the ten thousand wrappers, swearing inaudibly.

'Well, when are you going to get him?'

'Oh, we shall have advertisements rolling in of themselves,' said De Haan with a magnificent sweep of the arm. 'And we shall all assist in that department. Help yourself to another cigar, Sampson.' And he passed Schlesinger's box. Raphael and Karlkammer were the only two men in the room not smoking cigars— Raphael because he preferred his pipe, and Karlkammer for some more mystic reason.

'We must not ignore Cabbalah,' the zealot's voice was heard to observe.

'You can't get advertisements by Cabbalah,' dryly interrupted Guedalyah the Greengrocer, a practical man, as everybody knew.

'No, indeed,' protested Sampson. 'The advertisement canvasser is a more important man than the editor.'

Ebenezer pricked up his ears.

'I thought *you* undertook to do some canvassing for your money,' said De Haan.

'So I will, so I will ; rely on me for that. I shouldn't be surprised if I get the capitalists who are backing up my opera to give you the advertisements of the tour, and I'll do all I can in

my spare time. But I feel sure you'll want another man—only
you must pay him well and give him a good commission. It'll pay
you best in the long run to have a good man, there are so many
seedy duffers about,' said Little Sampson, drawing his faded cloak
loftily around him. 'You want an eloquent, persuasive man, with
a gift of the gab——'

'Didn't I tell you so?' interrupted Pinchas, putting his finger to
his nose. 'I vill go to the advertisers and speak burning words
to them. I vill——'

'Garn! They'd kick you out!' croaked Ebenezer. 'They'll
only listen to an Englishman.' His coarse-featured face glistened
with spite.

'My Ebenezer has a good appearance,' said old Sugarman,
'and his English is fine, and dat is half de battle.'

Schlesinger, appealed to, intimated that Ebenezer might try,
but that they could not well spare him any percentage at the start.
After much haggling, Ebenezer consented to waive his commission
if the committee would consent to allow an original tale of his to
appear in the paper.

The stipulation having been agreed to, he capered joyously about
the office, and winked periodically at Pinchas from behind the
battery of his blue spectacles. The poet was, however, rapt in a
discussion as to the best printer. The committee were for having
Gluck, who had done odd jobs for most of them ; but Pinchas
launched into a narrative of how, when he edited a great organ in
Buda-Pesth, he had effected vast economies by starting a little
printing-office of his own in connection with the paper.

'You vill set up a little establishment,' he said. 'I vill manage
it for a few pounds a veek. Then I vill not only print your paper
—I vill get you large profits from extra printing. Vith a man of
great business talent at the head of it——'

De Haan made a threatening movement, and Pinchas edged
away from the proximity of the coal-scuttle.

'Gluck's our printer!' said De Haan peremptorily. 'He has
Hebrew type. We shall want a lot of that. We must have a lot
of Hebrew quotations—not spell Hebrew words in English like the
other papers. And the Hebrew date must come before the English.
The public must see at once that our principles are superior.
Besides, Gluck's a Jew, which will save us from the danger of
having any of the printing done on Saturdays.'

'But shan't we want a publisher?' asked Sampson.

'That's vat I say,' cried Pinchas. 'If I set up this office, I can
be your publisher, too. Ve must do things business-like.'

'Nonsense, nonsense! We are our own publishers,' said De
Haan. 'Our clerks will send out the invoices and the subscription
copies, and an extra office-boy can sell the papers across the counter.'

Sampson smiled in his sleeve.

'All right. That will do—for the first number,' he said cordially.
'Ta-ra-ra-ta.'

'Now then, Mr. Leon, everything is settled,' said De Haan, stroking his beard briskly. ' I think I'll ask you to help us to draw up the posters. We shall cover all London, sir—all London.'

'But wouldn't that be wasting money?' said Raphael.

'Oh, we're going to do the thing properly. I don't believe in meanness.'

'It'll be enough if we cover the East End,' said Schlesinger dryly.

'Quite so. The East End *is* London, as far as we are concerned,' said De Haan readily.

Raphael took the pen and the paper which De Haan tendered him, and wrote ' *The Flag of Judah* ' the title having been fixed at their first interview.

'The only orthodox paper!' dictated De Haan. 'Largest circulation of any Jewish paper in the world!'

'No, how can we say that?' said Raphael, pausing.

'No, of course not,' said De Haan. 'I was thinking of the subsequent posters. Look out for the first number—on Friday, January 1st! The best Jewish writers! The truest Jewish teachings! Latest Jewish news, and finest Jewish stories! Every Friday, twopence.'

'Twopence?' echoed Raphael looking up. 'I thought you wanted to appeal to the masses. I should say it must be a penny.'

'It *will* be a penny,' said De Haan oracularly.

'We have thought it all over,' interposed Gradkoski. 'The first number will be bought up out of curiosity whether at a penny or at twopence. The second will go almost as well, for people will be anxious to see how it compares with the first. In that number we shall announce that, owing to the enormous success, we have been able to reduce it to a penny. Meantime, we make all the extra pennies.'

'I see,' said Raphael dubiously.

'We must have *Chochmah*,' said De Haan. 'Our sages recommend that.'

Raphael still had his doubts, but he had also a painful sense of his lack of the ' practical wisdom' recommended by the sages cited. He thought these men were probably in the right. Even religion could not be pushed on the masses without business methods—and so long as they were in earnest about the doctrines to be preached, he could even feel a dim admiration for their superior shrewdness in executing a task in which he himself would have hopelessly broken down. Raphael's mind was large, and larger by being conscious of its cloistral limitations. And the men were in earnest; not even their most intimate friends could call this into question.

'We are going to save London,' De Haan put it in one of his dithyrambic moments. 'Orthodoxy has too long been voiceless, and yet it is five-sixths of Judea. A small minority has had all the say. We must redress the balance. We must plead the cause of the People against the Few.'

Raphael's breast throbbed with similar hopes. His Messianic emotions resurged. Sugarman's solicitous request that he should buy a Hamburg lottery ticket scarcely penetrated his consciousness. Carrying the copy of the poster, he accompanied De Haan to Gluck's. It was a small shop in a back street, with Jargon papers and handbills in the window, and a pervasive heavy oleaginous odour. A hand-press occupied the centre of the interior, the back of which was partitioned off, and marked 'private.' Gluck came forward, grinning welcome. He wore an unkempt beard and a dusky apron.

'Can you undertake to print an eight-page paper?' inquired De Haan.

'If I can print at all, I can print anything,' responded Gluck reproachfully. 'How many shall you want?'

'It's the orthodox paper we've been planning so long,' said De Haan evasively.

Gluck nodded his head.

'There are seventy thousand orthodox Jews in London alone,' said De Haan with rotund enunciation. 'So you see what you may have to print. It'll be worth your while to do it extra cheap.'

Gluck agreed readily, naming a low figure. After half an hour's discussion it was reduced by ten per cent.

'Good-bye, then,' said De Haan. 'So let it stand. We shall start with a thousand copies of the first number, but where we shall end, the Holy One—blessed be He!—alone knows. I will now leave you and the editor to talk over the rest. To-day's Monday. We must have the first number out by Friday week. Can you do that, Mr. Leon?'

'Oh, that will be ample,' said Raphael, shooting out his arms.

He did not remain of that opinion. Never had he gone through such an awful, anxious time, not even in his preparations for the stiffest exams. He worked sixteen hours a day at the paper. The only evening he allowed himself off was when he dined with Mrs. Henry Goldsmith and met Esther. First numbers invariably take twice as long to produce as second numbers, even in the best regulated establishments. All sorts of mysterious sticks and leads and founts and formes are found wanting at the eleventh hour. As a substitute for gray hair-dye, there is nothing in the market to compete with the production of first numbers. But in Gluck's establishment these difficulties were multiplied by a hundred. Gluck spent a great deal of time in going round the corner to get something from a brother printer. It took an enormous time to get a proof of any article out of Gluck.

'My men are so careful,' Gluck explained. 'They don't like to pass anything till it's free from typos.'

The men must have been highly disappointed, for the proofs were invariably returned bristling with corrections and having a highly hieroglyphic appearance. Then Gluck would go in and slang his men. He kept them behind the partition painted 'Private.

The fatal Friday drew nearer and nearer. By Thursday not a single page had been made up. Still Gluck pointed out that there were only eight, and the day was long. Raphael had not the least idea in the world how to make up a paper, but about eleven Little Sampson kindly strolled into Gluck's and explained to his editor his own method of pasting the proofs on sheets of paper of the size of the pages. He even made up one page himself to a blithe vocal accompaniment. When the busy composer and acting-manager hurried off to conduct a rehearsal, Raphael expressed his gratitude warmly. The hours flew; the paper evolved as by geologic stages. As the fateful day wore on, Gluck was scarcely visible for a moment. Raphael was left alone eating his heart out in the shop, and solacing himself with huge whiffs of smoke. At immense intervals Gluck appeared from behind the partition bearing a page or a galley-slip. He said his men could not be trusted to do their work unless he was present. Raphael replied that he had not seen the compositors come through the shop to get their dinners, and he hoped Gluck would not find it necessary to cut off their meal-times. Gluck reassured him on this point; he said his men were so loyal that they preferred to bring their food with them rather than have the paper delayed. Later on he casually mentioned that there was a back entrance. He would not allow Raphael to talk to his workmen personally, arguing that it spoiled their discipline. By eleven o'clock at night seven pages had been pulled and corrected, but the eighth page was not forthcoming. The *Flag* had to be machined, dried, folded, and a number of copies put into wrappers and posted by three in the morning. The situation looked desperate. At a quarter to twelve Gluck explained that a column of matter already set up had been 'pied' by a careless compositor. It happened to be the column containing the latest news, and Raphael had not even seen a proof of it. Still, Gluck conjured him not to trouble further; he would give his reader strict injunctions not to miss the slightest error. Raphael had already seen and passed the first column of this page, let him leave it to Gluck to attend to this second column; all would be well without his remaining later, and he would receive a copy of the *Flag* by the first post. The poor editor, whose head was splitting, weakly yielded; he just caught the midnight train to the West End, and he went to bed feeling happy and hopeful.

At seven o'clock the next morning the whole Leon household was roused by a thunderous double rat-tat at the door. Addie was even heard to scream. A housemaid knocked at Raphael's door and pushed a telegram under it. Raphael jumped out of bed, and read:

'Third of column more matter wanted. Come at once.— GLUCK.'

'How can that be?' he asked himself in consternation. 'If

the latest news made a column when it was first set up before the accident, how can it make less now?'

He dashed up to Gluck's office in a hansom and put the conundrum to him.

'You see we had no time to distribute the "pie," and we had no more type of that kind, so we had to reset it smaller,' answered Gluck glibly.

His eyes were bloodshot; his face was haggard. The door of the private compartment stood open.

'Your men are not come yet, I suppose,' said Raphael.

'No,' said Gluck. 'They didn't go away till two, poor fellows. Is that the copy?' he asked, as Raphael handed him a couple of slips he had distractedly scribbled in the cab under the heading of 'Talmudic Tales.' 'Thank you; it's just about the size. I shall have to set it myself.'

'But won't we be terribly late?' said poor Raphael.

'We shall be out to-day,' responded Gluck cheerfully. 'We shall be in time for the Sabbath, and that's the important thing. Don't you see they're half printed already?' He indicated a huge pile of sheets. Raphael examined them with beating heart. 'We've only got to print 'em on the other side and the thing's done,' said Gluck.

'Where are your machines?'

'There,' said Gluck, pointing.

'That hand-press!' cried Raphael, astonished. 'Do you mean to say you print them all with your own hand?'

'Why not?' said the dauntless Gluck. 'I shall wrap them up for the post, too.' And he shut himself up with the last of the 'copy.'

Raphael, having exhausted his interest in the half-paper, fell to striding about the little shop, when who should come in but Pinchas, smoking a cigar of the Schlesinger brand!

'Ah, my prince of Rédacteurs,' said Pinchas, darting at Raphael's hand and kissing it. 'Did I not say you vould produce the finest paper in the kingdom? But vy have I not my copy by post? You must not listen to Ebenezer ven he says I must not be on the free list, the blackguard!'

Raphael explained to the incredulous poet that Ebenezer had not said anything of the kind. Suddenly Pinchas's eye caught sight of the sheets. He swooped down upon them like a hawk. Then he uttered a shriek of grief.

'Vere's my poem, my great poesie?'

Raphael looked embarrassed.

'This is only half the paper,' he said evasively.

'Ha, then it vill appear in the other half, *hein*?' he said, with hope tempered by a terrible suspicion.

'N-n-o,' stammered Raphael timidly.

'No?' shrieked Pinchas.

'You see—the—the fact is, it wouldn't scan. Your Hebrew

poetry is perfect, but English poetry is made rather differently, and I 've been too busy to correct it.'

'But it is exactly like Lord Byron's !' shrieked Pinchas. 'Mein Gott ! All night I lie avake, vaiting for the post. At eight o'clock the post comes, but the *Flag of Judah* she vaves not. I rush round here, and now my beautiful poem vill not appear !' He seized the sheet again, then cried fiercely : 'You have a tale, " The waters of Babylon," by Ebenezer the fool-boy, but my poesie have you not. *Gott in Himmel !'* He tore the sheet frantically across, and rushed from the shop. In five minutes he reappeared. Raphael was absorbed in reading the last proof. Pinchas plucked timidly at his coat-tails. 'You vill put it in next veek ?' he said winningly.

'I dare say,' said Raphael gently.

'Ah, promise me ! I vill love you like a brother. I vill be grateful to you for ever and ever. I vill never ask another favour of you in all my life. Ve are already like brothers—*hein ?*—I and you, the only two men——'

'Yes, yes,' interrupted Raphael. 'It shall appear next week.'

'God bless you !' said Pinchas, kissing Raphael's coat-tails passionately and rushing without.

Looking up accidently some minutes afterwards, Raphael was astonished to see the poet's grinning head thrust through the half-open door with a finger laid insinuatingly on the side of the nose. The head was fixed there as if petrified, waiting to catch the editor's eye.

The first number of *The Flag of Judah* appeared early in the afternoon.

CHAPTER IV

THE TROUBLES OF AN EDITOR

THE new organ did not create a profound impression. By the rival party it was mildly derided, though many fair-minded persons were impressed by the rather unusual combination of rigid ortho-doxy with a high spiritual tone, and Raphael's conception of Judaism as outlined in his first leader, his view of it as a happy human compromise between an empty, unpractical spiritualism and a choked-up, over-practical formalism, avoiding the opposite extremes of its offshoots, Christianity and Mohammedanism, was novel to many of his readers, unaccustomed to think about their faith. Dissatisfied as Raphael was with the number, he felt he had fluttered some of the dove-cotes at least. Several people of taste congratulated him during Saturday and Sunday ; it was with a continuance of Messianic emotions and with agreeable anticipations that he repaired on Monday morning to the little den which had been inexpensively fitted up for him above the offices of Messrs. Schlesinger and De Haan. To his surprise he found it crammed with the committee, all gathered round Little Sampson, who, with flushed face and cloak tragically folded, was expostulating at the top of his voice. Pinchas stood at the back in silent amusement. As Raphael entered jauntily, a change came over the company : a low premonitory roar issued from a dozen lips, the lowering faces turned quickly towards him. Involuntarily Raphael started back in alarm, then stood rooted to the threshold. There was a dread ominous silence. Then the storm burst.

'*Du Shaigatz! Du Pasha Yisroile!*' came from all quarters of the compass.

To be called a graceless Gentile and a sinner in Israel is not pleasant to a pious Jew ; but all Raphael's minor sensations were swallowed up in a great wonderment.

'We are ruined!' moaned the furniture-dealer who was always failing.

'You have ruined us!' came the chorus from the thick, sensuous lips, and swarthy fists were shaken threateningly.

Sugarman's hairy paw was almost against his face. Raphael turned cold, then a rush of red-hot blood flooded his veins. He put out his good right hand, and smote the nearest fist aside. Sugarman blenched and skipped back, and the line of fists wavered.

'Don't be fools, gentlemen,' said De Haan, his keen sense of humour asserting itself. 'Let Mr. Leon sit down.'

Raphael, still dazed, took his seat on the editorial chair.

'Now what can I do for you?' he said courteously.

The fists drooped at his calm.

'Do for us?' said Schlesinger dryly. 'You've done for the paper. It's not worth twopence.'

'Well, bring it out at a penny at once, then,' laughed Little Sampson, reinforced by the arrival of his editor.

Guedalyah the Greengrocer glowered at him.

'I am very sorry, gentlemen, I have not been able to satisfy you,' said Raphael ; 'but in a first number one can't do much.'

'Can't they?' said De Haan. 'You've done so much damage to orthodoxy that we don't know whether to go on with the paper.'

'You're joking,' murmured Raphael.

'I wish I was,' laughed De Haan bitterly.

'But you astonish me,' persisted Raphael. 'Would you be so good as to point out where I have gone wrong?'

'With pleasure, or rather with pain,' said De Haan.

Each of the committee drew a tattered copy from his pocket, and followed De Haan's demonstration with a murmured accompaniment of lamentation.

'The paper was founded to inculcate the inspection of cheese, the better supervision of the sale of meat, the construction of adies' baths, and all the principles of true Judaism,' said De Haan gloomily. 'And there's not one word about these things, but a great deal about spirituality and the significance of the ritual. But I will begin at the beginning. Page 1.'

'But that's advertisements,' muttered Raphael.

'The part surest to be read! The very first line of the paper is simply shocking. It reads:

'"DEATH.

'"On the 29th ult., at 22 Buckley Street, the Rev. Abraham Barnett, in his fifty-fourth——"'

'But death is always shocking. What's wrong about that?' interposed Little Sampson.

'Wrong!' repeated De Haan witheringly. 'Where did you get that from? That was never sent in.'

'No, of course not,' said the sub-editor; 'but we had to have at least one advertisement of that kind, just to show we should be pleased to advertise our readers' deaths. I looked in the daily papers to see if there were any births or marriages with Jewish names, but I couldn't find any, and that was the only Jewish-sounding death I could see.'

'But the Rev. Abraham Barnett was a *Meshumad*!' shrieked Sugarman the Shadchan.

Raphael turned pale. To have inserted an advertisement about an apostate missionary was indeed terrible; but Little Sampson's audacity did not desert him.

'I thought the orthodox party would be pleased to hear of the death of a *Meshumad*,' he said suavely, screwing his eye-glass more tightly into its orbit, 'on the same principle that anti-Semites take in the Jewish papers to hear of the death of Jews.'

For a moment De Haan was staggered.

'That would be all very well,' he said. 'Let him be an atonement for us all; but then you've gone and put, "May his soul be bound up in the bundle of life!"'

It was true. The stock Hebrew equivalent for 'R.I.P.' glared from the page.

'Fortunately, that taking advertisement of *kosher* trousers comes just underneath,' said De Haan, 'and that may draw off the attention. On page 2 you actually say in a note that Rabbenu Bachja's great poem on Repentance should be incorporated in the ritual, and might advantageously replace the obscure *Piyut* by Kalir. But this is rank Reform; it's worse than the papers we came to supersede.'

'But surely you know it is only the printing-press that has stereotyped our liturgy; that for Maimonides and Ibn Ezra, for David Kimchi and Joseph Albo, the contents were fluid; that——'

'We don't deny that,' interrupted Schlesinger; 'but we can't have any more alterations nowadays. Who is there worthy to alter them? You?'

'Certainly not. I merely suggest.'

'You are playing into the hands of our enemies,' said De Haan, shaking his head. 'We must not let our readers even imagine that the Prayer-Book can be tampered with. It's the thin end of the wedge. To trim our liturgy is like trimming living flesh ; wherever you cut, the blood oozes. The four cubits of the *Halachah*, that is what is wanted, not changes in the liturgy. Once touch anything, and where are you to stop ? Our religion becomes a flux. Our old Judaism is like an old family mansion, where each generation has left a memorial, and where every room is hallowed with traditions of merrymaking and mourning. We do not want our fathers' home decorated in the latest style ; the next step will be removal to a new dwelling altogether. On page 3 you refer to the second Isaiah.'

'But I deny that there were two Isaiahs.'

'So you do ; but it is better for our readers not to hear of such impious theories. The space would be much better occupied in explaining the Portion for the week. The next leaderette has a flippant tone, which has excited unfavourable comment among some of the most important members of the Dalston synagogue. They object to humour in a religious paper. On page 4 you have deliberately missed an opportunity of puffing the Kosher Co-operative Society. Indeed, there is not a word throughout about our Society. But I like Mr. Henry Goldsmith's letter on this page though ; he is a good orthodox man, and he writes from a good address. It will show we are not only read in the East End. Pity he's such a Man-of-the-Earth, though. Yes, and that's good, the communication from the Rev. Joseph Strelitski. I think he's a bit of an *Epikouros* ; but it looks as if the whole of the Kensington synagogue was with us. I understand he is a friend of yours ; it will be as well for you to continue friendly. Several of us here knew him well in *Olov Hasholom* times, but he is become so grand, and rarely shows himself at the Holy Land League meetings. He can help us a lot if he will.'

'Oh, I'm sure he will,' said Raphael.

'That's good,' said De Haan, caressing his white beard. Then, growing gloomy again, he went on : 'On page 5 you have a little article by Gabriel Hamburg, a well-known *Epikouros*.'

'Oh, but he is one of the greatest scholars in Europe !' broke in Raphael. 'I thought you'd be extra pleased to have it. He sent it to me from Stockholm as a special favour !' He did not mention he had secretly paid for it. 'I know some of his views are heterodox, and I don't agree with half he says, but this article is perfectly harmless.'

'Well, let it pass : very few of our readers have ever heard of him. But on the same page you have a Latin quotation. I don't say there's anything wrong in that, but it smacks of Reform. Our readers don't understand it, and it looks as if our Hebrew were poor. The Mishnah contains texts suited for all purposes. We are in no need of Roman writers. On page 6 you speak of the Reform School as if it were to be reasoned with. Sir, if we mention these freethinkers at all, it must be in the strongest language. By worshipping bareheaded, and by seating the sexes together, they have defiled Judaism.'

'Stop a minute,' interrupted Raphael warmly. 'Who told you the Reformers do this?'

'Who told me, indeed? Why, it's common knowledge. That's how they've been going on for the last fifty years.'

'Everybody knows it,' said the committee in chorus.

'Has one of you ever been there?' said Raphael, rising in excitement.

'God forbid!' cried the chorus.

'Well I have, and it's a lie,' said Raphael. His arms whirled round to the discomfort of the committee.

'You ought not to have gone there,' said Schlesinger severely. 'Besides, will you deny they have the organ in their Sabbath services?'

'No, I won't!'

'Well, then,' said De Haan triumphantly, 'if they are capable of that, they are capable of any wickedness. Orthodox people can have nothing to do with them.'

'But orthodox immigrants take their money,' said Raphael.

'Their money is *kosher*; they are *tripha*,' said De Haan sententiously. 'Page 7—now we get to the most dreadful thing of all!'

A solemn silence fell on the room. Pinchas sniggered unobtrusively.

'You have a little article headed "Talmudic Tales." Why in heaven's name you couldn't have finished the column with bits of news I don't know. Satan himself must have put the thought into your head. Just at the end of the paper, too! For I can't reckon page 8, which is simply our own advertisement.'

'I thought it would be amusing,' said Raphael.

'Amusing! If you had simply told the tales, it might have been. But look how you introduce them! "These amusing tales occur in the fifth chapter of Baba Bathra, and are related by Rabbi Bar Bar Channah. Our readers will see that they are parables or allegories rather than actual facts."'

'But do you mean to say you look upon them as facts!' cried Raphael, sawing the air wildly, and pacing about on the toes of the committee.

'Surely!' said De Haan, while a low growl at his blasphemous doubts ran along the lips of the committee.

'Was it treacherously to undermine Judaism that you so eagerly offered to edit for nothing?' said the furniture-dealer who was always failing.

'But listen here!' cried Raphael exasperated.

' "Harmez, the son of Lilith, a demon, saddled two mules and

made them stand on opposite sides of the river Doneg. He then
jumped from the back of one to that of the other. He had, at the
time, a cup of wine in each hand, and as he jumped he threw the
wine from each cup into the other without spilling a drop,
although a hurricane was blowing at the time. When the king of
demons heard that Harmez had been thus showing off to mortals,
he slew him." Does any of you believe that?'

'Vould our sages—their memories for a blessing!—put anything
into the Talmud that vasn't true?' queried Sugarman. 'Ve know
there are demons because it stands that Solomon knew their
language.'

'But, then, what about this?' pursued Raphael. '"I saw a
frog which was as big as the district of Akra Hagronia. A sea-
monster came and swallowed the frog, and a raven came and ate
the sea-monster. The raven then went and perched on a tree.
Consider how strong that tree must have been. R. Papa Ben
Samuel remarks: Had I not been present, I should not have
believed it." Doesn't this appendix about Ben Samuel show
that it was never meant to be taken seriously?'

'It has some high meaning we do not understand in these
degenerate times,' said Guedalyah the Greengrocer. 'It is not
for our paper to weaken faith in the Talmud.'

'Hear, hear!' said De Haan, while '*Epikouros!*' rumbled
through the air like distant thunder.

'Didn't I say an Englishman could never master the Talmud!'
Sugarman asked in triumph.

This reminder of Raphael's congenital incompetence softened
their minds towards him, so that when he straightway resigned
his editorship, their self-constituted spokesman besought him to
remain. Perhaps they remembered, too, that he was cheap.

'But we must all edit the paper,' said De Haan enthusiastically,
when peace was re-established. 'We must have meetings every
day, and every article must be read aloud before it is printed.'

Little Sampson winked cynically, passing his hand pensively
through his thick tangled locks, but Raphael saw no objection to
the arrangement. As before, he felt his own impracticability
borne in upon him, and he decided to sacrifice himself for the
Cause as far as conscience permitted. Excessive as was the zeal
of these men, it was after all in the true groove. His annoyance
returned for a while, however, when Sugarman the Shadchan
seized the auspicious moment of restored amity to inquire insinuatingly if his sister was engaged. Pinchas and Little Sampson
went down the stairs quivering with noiseless laughter, which
became boisterous when they reached the street. Pinchas was in
high feather.

'The fool-men!' he said, as he led the sub-editor into a public-
house and regaled him on stout and sandwiches.

'They believe any *Narrischkeit*. I and you are the only two
sensible Jews in England. You vill see that my poesie goes

n next veek—promise me that! To your life!' Here they
touched glasses. 'Ah, it is beautiful poesie. Such high tragic
ideas! You vill kiss me when you read them.' He laughed in
childish light-heartedness. 'Perhaps I write you a comic opera
or your company—*hein*? Already I love you like a brother.
Another glass stout? Bring us two more, thou Hebe of the hops-
nectar. You have seen my comedy "The Hornet of Judah"?
No? Ah, she vas a great comedy, Sampson. All London talked
of her. She has been translated into every tongue. Perhaps I
play in your company. I am a great actor—*hein*? You know
not my forte is voman's parts—I make myself so lovely complexion
vith red paint, I fall in love vith me.' He sniggered over his
tout. 'The Rédacteur will not redact long, *hein*?' he said
presently. 'He is a fool-man. If he work for nothing they think
that is what he is worth. They are orthodox—he-he!'

'But he is orthodox too,' said Little Sampson.

'Yes,' replied Pinchas musingly. 'It is strange. It is vairy
strange. I cannot understand him. Never in all my experience
have I met another such man. There vas an Italian exile I
talked vith once in the island of Chios—his eyes were like Leon's,
soft vith a shining splendour like the stars vich are the eyes of
the angels of love. Ah, he is a good man, and he writes sharp—
he has ideas, not like an English Jew at all. I could throw my
arms round him sometimes. I love him like a brother.' His
voice softened. 'Another glass stout—ve vill drink to him.'

Raphael did not find the editing by committee feasible. The fric-
ion was incessant, the waete of time monstrous. The second number
cost him even more headaches than the first, and this although
the gallant Gluck, abandoning his single-handed emprise, fortified
himself with a real live compositor and had arranged for the paper
to be printed by machinery. The position was intolerable. It
put a touch of acid into his dulciferous mildness. Just before
going to press he was positively rude to Pinchas. It would seem
that Little Sampson, sheltering himself behind his capitalists, had
refused to give the poet a commission for a comic opera, and
Pinchas raved at Gideon, M.P., who he was sure was Sampson's
financial backer, and threatened to shoot him and danced mania-
cally about the office.

'I have written an attack on the Member for Vitechapel,' he
said, growing calmer, 'to hand him down to the execration of pos-
erity, and I have brought it to the *Flag*. It must go in this veek.'

'We have already your poem,' said Raphael.

'I know, but I do not grudge my work; I am not like your
money-making English Jews.'

'There is no room. The paper is full.'

'Leave out Ebenezer's tale—with the blue spectacles.'

'There is none. It was complete in one number.'

'Well, must you put in your leader?'

'Absolutely; please go away. I have this page to read.'

'But you can leave out some advertisements.'

'I must not. We have too few as it is.'

The poet put his finger alongside his nose, but Raphael wa‹ adamant.

'Do me this one favour,' he pleaded. 'I love you like a brothe‹ —just this one little thing ! I vill never ask another favour of yo‹ all my life.'

'I would not put it in even if there was room. Go away,' sai‹ Raphael almost roughly.

The unaccustomed accents gave Pinchas a salutary shock. H‹ borrowed two shillings and left, and Raphael was afraid to loo‹ up lest he should see his head wedged in the doorway. Soo‹ after, Gluck and his one compositor carried out the formes to b‹ machined. Little Sampson, arriving with a gay air on his lip‹ met them at the door.

On the Friday Raphael sat in the editorial chair utterly di‹ spirited—a battered wreck. The committee had just left him. ‹ heresy had crept into a bit of late news not inspected by then‹ and they declared that the paper was not worth twopence an‹ had better be stopped. The demand for this second number wa‹ moreover, rather poor, and each man felt his ten-pound shar‹ melting away, and resolved not to pay up the half yet unpaid. I‹ was Raphael's first real experience of men—after the enchante‹ towers of Oxford, where he had foregathered with dreamers.

His pipe hung listless in his mouth—an extinct volcano. Hi‹ first fit of distrust in human nature—nay, even in the purifyin‹ powers of orthodoxy—was racking him. Strangely enough, thi‹ wave of scepticism tossed up the thought of Esther Ansell, an‹ stranger still, on the top of this thought in walked Mr. Henr‹ Goldsmith. Raphael jumped up and welcomed his late hos‹ whose leathery countenance shone with the polish of a swee‹ smile. It appeared that the communal pillar had been passin‹ casually, and thought he'd look Raphael up.

'So you don't pull well together,' he said, when he had elicite‹ an outline of the situation from the editor.

'No, not altogether,' admitted Raphael.

'Do you think the paper 'll live ?'

'I can't say,' said Raphael, dropping limply into his chai‹ 'Even if it does, I don't know whether it will do much good if ru‹ on their lines ; for, although it is of great importance that we ge‹ *kosher* food and baths, I hardly think they go about it in the righ‹ spirit. I may be wrong. They are older men than I, and hav‹ seen more of actual life, and know the class we appeal to better.'

'No, no, you are not wrong,' said Mr. Goldsmith vehementl‹ 'I am myself dissatisfied with some of the committee's contribu‹ tions to this second number. It is a great opportunity to sav‹ English Judaism, but it is being frittered away.'

'I am afraid it is,' said Raphael, removing his empty pipe fror‹ his mouth, and staring at it blankly.

Mr. Goldsmith brought his fist down sharp on the soft litter that covered the editorial table.

'It shall not be frittered away !' he cried.   'No, not if I have to buy the paper !'

Raphael looked up eagerly.

'What do you say?' said Goldsmith.   'Shall I buy it up and let you work it on your lines?'

'I shall be very glad,' said Raphael, the Messianic look returning to his face.

'How much will they want for it?'

'Oh, I think they'll be glad to let you take it over.   They say it's not worth twopence, and I'm sure they haven't got the funds to carry it on,' replied Raphael, rising.   'I'll go down about it at once.   The committee have just been here, and I dare say they are still in Schlesinger's office.'

'No, no,' said Goldsmith, pushing him down into his seat.   'It will never do if people know I'm the proprietor.'

'Why not?'

'Oh, lots of reasons.   I'm not a man to brag.   If I want to do a good thing for Judaism, there's no reason for all the world to know it.   Then, again, from my position on all sorts of committees, I shall be able to influence the communal advertisements in a way I couldn't if people knew I had any connection with the paper. So, too, I shall be able to recommend it to my wealthy friends (as no doubt it will deserve to be recommended) without my praise being discounted.'

'Well, but, then, what am I to say to the committee?'

'Can't you say you want to buy it for yourself?   They know you can afford it.'

'But why *shouldn't* I buy it for myself?'

'Pooh !   Haven't you got better use for your money?'

It was true.   Raphael had designs more tangibly philanthropic for the five thousand pounds left him by his aunt.   And he was business-like enough to see that Mr. Goldsmith's money might as well be utilised for the good of Judaism.   He was not quite easy about the little fiction that would be necessary for the transaction, but the combined assurances of Mr. Goldsmith and his own common-sense that there was no real deception or harm involved in it ultimately prevailed.   Mr. Goldsmith left, promising to call again in an hour, and Raphael, full of new hopes, burst upon the committee.   But his first experience of bargaining was no happier than the rest of his worldly experiences.   When he professed his willingness to relieve them of the burden of carrying on the paper, they first stared, then laughed, then shook their fists.   As if they would leave him to corrupt the faith !   When they understood he was willing to pay something, the value of the *Flag of Judah* went up from less than twopence to more than two hundred pounds. Everybody was talking about it; its reputation was made ; they were going to print double next week.

CHILDREN OF THE GHETTO

'But it has not cost you forty pounds yet!' said the astonished Raphael.

'What are you saying? Look at the posters alone!' said Sugarman.

'But you don't look at it fairly,' argued De Haan, whose Talmudical studies had sharpened wits already super-subtle. 'Whatever it has cost us, it would have cost us much more if we had had to pay our editor, and it is very unfair of you to leave that out of account.'

Raphael was overwhelmed.

'It's taking away with the left hand what you gave us with the right,' added De Haan, with infinite sadness. 'I had thought better of you, Mr. Leon.'

'But you got a good many twopences back, murmured Raphael.

'It's the future profits that we're losing,' explained Schlesinger.

In the end Raphael agreed to give a hundred pounds, which made the members inwardly determine to pay up the residue on their shares at once. De Haan also extorted a condition that the *Flag* should continue to be the organ of the Kosher Co-operative Society for at least six months, doubtless perceiving that should the paper live and thrive over that period, it would not then pay the proprietor to alter its principles; by which bargain the Society secured for itself a sum of money, together with an organ gratis, for six months and, to all seeming, in perpetuity, for at bottom they knew well that Raphael's heart was sound. They were all on the free list, too, and they knew he would not trouble to remove them.

Mr. Henry Goldsmith, returning, was rather annoyed at the price, but did not care to repudiate his agent.

'Be economical,' he said. 'I will get you a better office and find a proper publisher and canvasser. But cut it as close as you can.'

Raphael's face beamed with joy.

'Oh, depend upon me,' he said.

'What is your own salary?' asked Goldsmith.

'Nothing,' said Raphael.

A flash passed across Goldsmith's face, then he considered a moment.

'I wish you would let it be a guinea,' he said. 'Quite nominal you know. Only I like to have things in proper form. And if ever you want to go, you know, you'll give me a month's notice and,' here he laughed genially, 'I'll do ditto when I want to get rid of you. Ha! ha! ha! Is that a bargain?'

Raphael smiled in reply, and the two men's hands met in a hearty clasp.

'Miss Ansell will help you, I know,' said Goldsmith cheerily 'that girl's got it in her, I can tell you. 'She'll take the shine out of some of our West-Enders. Do you know, I picked her out of the gutter, so to speak?'

'Yes, I know,' said Raphael. 'It was very good and discrimin-ating of you.   How is she?'

'She's all right ; come up and see her about doing something for you.   She goes to the Museum sometimes in the afternoons, but you'll always find her in on Sundays—or most Sundays.   Come up and dine with us again soon, will you?   Mrs. Goldsmith will be so pleased.'

'I will,' said Raphael fervently ; and when the door closed upon the communal pillar, he fell to striding feverishly about his little den.

His trust in human nature was restored, and the receding wave of scepticism bore off again the image of Esther Ansell.   Now to work for Judaism !

The sub-editor made his first appearance that day carolling joyously.

'Sampson,' said Raphael abruptly, 'your salary is raised by a guinea a week.'

The joyous song died away on Little Sampson's lips ; his eye-glass dropped ; he let himself fall backwards, impinging noiselessly upon a heap of 'returns' of number one.

CHAPTER V

A WOMAN'S GROWTH

THE sloppy Sunday afternoon, which was the first opportunity Raphael had of profiting by Mr. Henry Goldsmith's general invi-tation to call and see Esther, happened to be that selected by the worthy couple for a round of formal visits.

Esther was left at home with a headache, little expecting pleasanter company.   She hesitated about receiving Raphael, but on hearing that he had come to see her rather than her patrons, she smoothed her hair, put on a prettier frock, and went down into the drawing-room, where she found him striding restlessly in bespattered boots and moist overcoat.   When he became aware of her presence, he went towards her eagerly and shook her hand with jerky awkwardness.

'How are you?' he said heartily.

'Very well, thank you,' she replied automatically ; then a twinge as of reproach at the falsehood darted across her brow, and she added : 'A trifle of the usual headache.   I hope you are well?

'Quite, thank you,' he rejoined.

His face rather contradicted him ; it looked thin, pale, and weary.   Journalism writes lines on the healthiest countenance. Esther looked at him disapprovingly ; she had the woman's artistic instinct if not the artist's, and Raphael, with his damp overcoat, everlastingly crumpled at the collar, was not an æsthetic object.

Whether in her pretty moods or her plain, Esther was always neat and dainty. There was a bit of ruffled lace at her throat, and the heliotrope of her gown contrasted agreeably with the dark skin of the vivid face.

'Do take off your overcoat and dry yourself at the fire,' she said.

While he was disposing of it, she poked the fire into a big cheerful blaze, seating herself opposite him in a capacious arm-chair, where the flame picked her out in bright tints upon the dusky background of the great dim room.

'And how is the *Flag of Judah*?' she said.

'Still waving,' he replied. It is about that that I have come.'

'About that?' she said wonderingly. 'Oh, I see; you want to know if the one person it is written at has read it. Well, make your mind easy. I have. I have read it religiously—no I don't mean that—yes, I do; it's the appropriate word.'

'Really?'

He tried to penetrate behind the bantering tone.

'Yes, really. You put your side of the case eloquently and well. I look forward to Friday with interest. I hope the paper is selling.'

'So, so,' he said. 'It is uphill work. The Jewish public look on journalism as a branch of philanthropy, I fear, and Sidney suggests publishing our free list as a Jewish directory.'

She smiled.

'Mr. Graham is very amusing. Only he is too well aware of it. He has been here once since that dinner, and we discussed you. He says he can't understand how you came to be a cousin of his—even a second cousin. He says he is *l'homme qui rit*, and you are *l'homme qui prie*.'

'He has let that off on me already, supplemented by the explanation that every extensive Jewish family embraces a genius and a lunatic. He admits that he is the genius. The unfortunate part for me,' ended Raphael, laughing, 'is that he *is* a genius.'

'I saw two of his little things the other day at the Impressionist Exhibition in Piccadilly. They are very clever and dashing.'

'I am told he draws ballet-girls,' said Raphael moodily.

'Yes; he is a disciple of Degas.'

'You don't like that style of art?' he said, a shade of concern in his voice.

'I do not,' said Esther emphatically. 'I am a curious mixture. In art I have discovered in myself two conflicting tastes, and neither is for the modern realism, which I yet admire in literature. I like poetic pictures impregnated with vague romantic melancholy, and I like the white lucidity of classic statuary. I suppose the one taste is the offspring of temperament, the other of thought; for intellectually I admire the Greek ideals, and was glad to hear you correct Sidney's perversion of the adjective. I wonder,' she added reflectively, 'if one can worship the gods of the Greeks without believing in them.'

' But you wouldn't make a cult of Beauty ? '

' Not if you take Beauty in the narrow sense in which I should fancy your cousin uses the word. But, in a higher and broader sense, is it not the one fine thing in life which is a certainty, the one ideal which is not illusion ? '

' Nothing is illusion ' said Raphael earnestly. ' At least, not in your sense. Why should the Creator deceive us ? '

' Oh, well, don't let us get into metaphysics. We argue from different platforms,' she said. ' Tell me what you really came about in connection with the *Flag*.'

' Mr. Goldsmith was kind enough to suggest that you might write for it.'

' What ! ' exclaimed Esther, sitting upright in her armchair. ' I—I write for an orthodox paper ? '

' Yes ; why not ? '

' Do you mean I'm to take part in my own conversion ? '

' The paper is not entirely religious,' he reminded her.

' No, there are the advertisements,' she said slyly.

' Pardon me,' he said. ' We don't insert any advertisement contrary to the principles of orthodoxy. Not that we are much tempted.'

' You advertise soap,' she murmured.

' Oh, please don't you go in for those cheap sarcasms ! '

' Forgive me,' she said. Remember, my conceptions of orthodoxy are drawn mainly from the Ghetto, where cleanliness, so far from being next to godliness, is nowhere in the vicinity. But what can I do for you ? '

' I don't know. At present the staff—the *Flag*-staff, as Sidney calls it—consists of myself and a sub-editor, who take it in turn to translate the only regular outside contributor's articles into English.'

' Who's that ? '

' Melchitzedek Pinchas, the poet I told you of.'

' I suppose he writes in Hebrew ? '

' No ; if he did the translation would be plain-sailing enough. The trouble is that he will write in English. I must admit, though, he improves daily. Our correspondents, too, have the same weakness for the vernacular, and I grieve to add that when they do introduce a Hebrew word, they do not invariably spell it correctly.'

She smiled ; her smile was never so fascinating as by firelight.

Raphael rose and paced the room nervously, flinging out his arms in uncouth fashion to emphasise his speech.

' I was thinking you might introduce a secular department of some sort which would brighten up the paper. My articles are so plaguy dull.'

' Not so dull—for religious articles,' she assured him.

' Could you treat Jewish matters from a social standpoint—gossipy sort of thing ? '

She shook her head.

'I'm afraid to trust myself to write on Jewish subjects. I should be sure to tread on somebody's corns.'

'Oh, I have it!' he cried, bringing his arms in contact with a small Venetian vase, which Esther, with great presence of mind, just managed to catch ere it reached the ground.

'No, I have it!' she said, laughing. 'Do sit down, else nobody can answer for the consequences.'

She half pushed him into his chair, where he fell to warming his hands contemplatively.

'Well?' she said after a pause. 'I thought you had an idea.'

'Yes, yes,' he said, rousing himself. 'The subject we were just discussing—art.'

'But there is nothing Jewish about art.'

'All noble work has its religious aspects. Then there are Jewish artists.'

'Oh yes. Your contemporaries do notice their exhibits, and there seem to be more of them than the world ever hears of. But if I went to a gathering for you, how should I know which were Jews?'

'By their names, of course.'

'By no means of course. Some artistic Jews have forgotten their own names.'

'That's a dig at Sidney.'

'Really, I wasn't thinking of him for the moment,' she said a little sharply. 'However, in any case there's nothing worth doing till May, and that's some months ahead. I'll do the Academy for you, if you like.'

'Thank you. Won't Sidney stare if you pulverise him in the *Flag of Judah*? Some of the pictures have also Jewish subjects, you know.'

'Yes, but if I mistake not, they're invariably done by Christian artists.'

'Nearly always,' he admitted pensively. 'I wish we had a Jewish allegorical painter to express the high conceptions of our sages.'

'As he would probably not know what they are——' she murmured. Then, seeing him rise as if to go, she said: 'Won't you have a cup of tea?'

'No, don't trouble,' he answered.

'Oh yes, do!' she pleaded. 'Or else I shall think you're angry with me for not asking you before.' And she rang the bell.

She discovered, to her amusement, that Raphael took two pieces of sugar per cup, but that, if they were not inserted, he did not notice their absence. Over tea, too, Raphael had a new idea, this time fraught with peril to the Sèvres teapot.

'Why couldn't you write us a Jewish serial story?' he said suddenly. 'That would be a novelty in communal journalism.'

Esther looked startled by the proposition.

'How do you know I could?' she said after a silence.

'I don't know,' he replied. 'Only I fancy you could. Why not?' he said encouragingly. 'You don't know what you can do till you try. Besides, you write poetry.'

'The Jewish public doesn't like the looking-glass,' she answered him, shaking her head.

'Oh, you can't say that! They've only objected as yet to the distorting-mirror. You're thinking of the row over that man Armitage's book. Now, why not write an antidote to that book? There now, there's an idea for you!'

'It *is* an idea,' said Esther, with overt sarcasm. 'You think art can be degraded into an antidote.'

'Art is not a fetish,' he urged. 'What degradation is there in art teaching a noble lesson?'

'Ah, that is what you religious people will never understand,' she said scathingly. 'You want everything to preach.'

'Everything does preach something,' he retorted. 'Why not have the sermon good?'

'I consider the original sermon *was* good,' she said defiantly. 'It doesn't need an antidote.'

'How can you say that? Surely, merely as one who was born a Jewess, you wouldn't care for the sombre picture drawn by this Armitage to stand as a portrait of your people.'

She shrugged her shoulders—the ungraceful shrug of the Ghetto.

'Why not? It is one-sided, but it is true.'

'I don't deny that; probably the man was sincerely indignant at certain aspects. I am ready to allow he did not even see he was one-sided. But if *you* see it, why not show the world the other side of the shield?'

She put her hand wearily to her brow.

'Do not ask me,' she said. 'To have my work appreciated merely because the moral tickled the reader's vanity would be a mockery. The suffrages of the Jewish public—I might have valued them once; now I despise them.'

She sank further back on the chair, pale and silent.

'Why, what harm have they done you?' he asked.

'They are so stupid,' she said, with a gesture of distaste.

'That is a new charge against the Jews.'

'Look at the way they have denounced this Armitage, saying his book is vulgar and wretched and written for gain, and all because it does not flatter them.'

'Can you wonder at it? To say "you're another" may not be criticism, but it is human nature.'

Esther smiled sadly.

'I cannot make you out at all,' she said.

'Why? What is there strange about me?'

'You say such shrewd, humorous things sometimes—I wonder how you can remain orthodox.'

'Now I can't understand *you*,' he said, puzzled.

'Oh, well! Perhaps if you could, you wouldn't be orthodox. Let us remain mutual enigmas. And will you do me a favour?'

'With pleasure,' he said, his face lighting up.

'Don't mention Mr. Armitage's book to me again. I am sick of hearing about it.'

'So am I,' he said, rather disappointed. 'After that dinner I thought it only fair to read it ; and although I detect considerable crude power in it, still I am very sorry it was ever published. The presentation of Judaism is most ignorant. All the mystical yearnings of the heroine might have found as much satisfaction in the faith of her own race as they find expression in its poetry.'

He rose to go.

'Well, I am to take it for granted you will not write that antidote?'

'I'm afraid it would be impossible for me to undertake it,' she said, more mildly than before, and pressed her hand again to her brow.

'Pardon me,' he said, in much concern. 'I am too selfish. I forgot you are not well. How is your head feeling now?'

'About the same, thank you,' she said, forcing a grateful smile. 'You may rely on me for art, yes ; and music, too, if you like.'

'Thank you,' he said. 'You read a great deal, don't you?'

She nodded her head.

'Well, every week books are published of more or less direct Jewish interest ; I should be glad of notes about such, to brighten up the paper.'

'For anything strictly unorthodox you may count on me. If that antidote turns up, I shall not fail to cackle over it in your columns. By-the-bye, are you going to review the poison? Excuse so many mixed metaphors,' she added, with a rather forced laugh.

'No, I shan't say anything about it. Why give it an extra advertisement by slating it?'

'Slating,' she repeated, with a faint smile. 'I see you have mastered all the slang of your profession.'

'Ah, that's the influence of my sub-editor,' he said, smiling in return. 'Well, good-bye.'

'You're forgetting your overcoat,' she said ; and having smoothed out that crumpled collar, she accompanied him down the wide soft-carpeted staircase into the hall, with its rich bronzes and glistening statues.

'How are your people in America?' he bethought himself to ask on the way down.

'They are very well, thank you,' she said. 'I send my brother Solomon the *Flag of Judah*. He is also, I am afraid, one of the unregenerate. You see, I am doing my best to enlarge your congregation.'

He could not tell whether it was sarcasm or earnest.

'Well, good-bye,' he said, holding out his hand. 'Thank you for your promise.'

'Oh, that's not worth thanking me for,' she said, touching his long white fingers for an instant. 'Look at the glory of seeing myself in print. I hope you're not annoyed with me for refusing to contribute fiction?' she ended, growing suddenly remorseful at the moment of parting.

'Of course not. How could I be?'

'Couldn't your sister Adelaide do you a story?'

'Addie?' he repeated, laughing. 'Fancy Addie writing stories! Addie has no literary ability.'

'That's always the way with brothers, Solomon says——'

She paused suddenly.

'I don't remember for the moment that Solomon has any pro- verb on the subject,' he said, still amused at the idea of Addie as an authoress.

'I was thinking of something else. Good-bye. Remember me to your sister, please.'

'Certainly,' he said; then he exclaimed: 'Oh, what a blockhead I am! I forgot to remember her to you. She says she would be so pleased if you would come and have tea and a chat with her some day. I should like you and Addie to know each other.'

'Thanks, I will. I will write to her some day. Good-bye once more.'

He shook hands with her and fumbled at the door.

'Allow me,' she said, and opened it upon the gray dulness of the dripping street. 'When may I hope for the honour of another visit from a real live editor?'

'I don't know,' he said, smiling; 'I'm awfully busy. I have to read a paper on Ibn Ezra at Jews' College to-day fortnight.'

'Outsiders admitted?' she asked.

'The lectures are for outsiders,' he said, 'to spread the know- ledge of our literature—only they won't come. Have you never been to one?'

She shook her head.

'There!' he said. 'You complain of our want of culture, and you don't even know what's going on.'

She tried to take the reproof with a smile, but the corners of her mouth quivered.

He raised his hat and went down the steps.

She followed him a little way along the Terrace, with eyes grow- ing dim with tears she could not account for. She went back to the drawing-room and threw herself into the arm-chair where he had sat, and made her headache worse by thinking of all her un- happiness. The great room was filling with dusk, and in the twilight pictures gathered and dissolved. What girlish dreams and revolts had gone to make that unfortunate book, which, after endless boomerang-like returns from the publishers, had appeared —only to be denounced by Jewry, ignored by its journals, and scantily noticed by outside criticism. *Mordecai Josephs* had fallen almost still-born from the press; the sweet secret she had hoped to tell her patroness had turned bitter, like that other secret of her dead love for Sidney, in the reaction from which she had written most of her book. How fortunate, at least, that her love had flickered out—had proved but the ephemeral sentiment of a romantic girl for the first brilliant man she had met. Sidney had fascinated her by his verbal audacities in a world of narrow conventions ; he had for the moment laughed away spiritual aspirations and yearnings with a raillery that was almost like ozone to a young woman avid of martyrdom for the happiness of the world. How, indeed, could she have expected the handsome young artist to feel the magic that hovered about her talks with him, to know the thrill that lay in the formal hand-clasp, to be aware that he interpreted for her poems and pictures, and incarnated the undefined ideal of girlish day-dreams ? How could he ever have had other than an intellectual thought of her—how could any man, even the religious Raphael, sickly, ugly little thing that she was ? She got up and looked in the glass now to see herself thus, but the shadows had gathered too thickly. She snatched up a newspaper that lay on a couch, lit it, and held it before the glass. It flared up threateningly, and she beat it out—laughing hysterically and asking herself if she was mad. But she had seen the ugly little face—its expression frightened her. Yes, love was not for her ; she could only love a man of brilliancy and culture, and she was nothing but a Petticoat Lane girl, after all. Its coarseness, its vulgarity, underlay all her veneer. They had got into her book —everybody said so, Raphael said so. How dared she write disdainfully of Raphael's people ?—she, an upstart, an outsider !

She went to the library, lit the gas, got down a volume of Graetz's *History of the Jews*, which she had latterly taken to reading, and turned over its wonderful pages. Then she wandered restlessly back to the great dim drawing-room, and played amateurish fantasias on the melancholy Polish melodies of her childhood, till Mr. and Mrs. Henry Goldsmith returned. They had captured the Rev. Joseph Strelitski, and brought him back to dinner. Esther would have excused herself from the meal, but Mrs. Goldsmith insisted the minister would think her absence intentionally discourteous. In point of fact, Mrs. Goldsmith—like all Jewesses, a born matchmaker—was not disinclined to think of the popular preacher as a sort of adopted son-in law. She did not tell herself so, but she instinctively resented the idea of Esther marrying into the station of her patroness. Strelitski, though his position was one of distinction for a Jewish clergyman, was, like Esther, of humble origin. It would be a match which she could bless from her pedestal in genuine good-will towards both parties.

The fashionable minister was looking careworn and troubled. He had aged twice ten years since his outburst at the Holy Land League. The black curl hung disconsolately on his forehead. He sat at Esther's side, but rarely looking at her or addressing her, so that her taciturnity and scarcely-veiled dislike did not

noticeably increase his gloom. He rallied now and again out of
politeness to his hostess, flashing out a pregnant phrase or two.
But prosperity did not seem to have brought happiness to the
whilom poor Russian student, even though he had fought his way
to it unaided.

CHAPTER VI

COMEDY OR TRAGEDY?

THE weeks went on and Passover drew nigh. The recurrence
of the feast brought no thrill to Esther now. It was no longer a
charmed time, with strange things to eat and drink, and a comparative plenty of them—stranger still. Lack of appetite was the
chief dietary want now. Nobody had any best clothes to put on,
in a world where everything was for the best in the way of clothes.
Except for the speckled Passover cakes, there was hardly any
external symptom of the sacred Festival. While the Ghetto was
turning itself inside out, the Kensington Terrace was calm in the
dignity of continuous cleanliness. Nor did Henry Goldsmith
himself go prowling about the house in quest of vagrant crumbs.
Mary O'Reilly attended to all that, and the Goldsmiths had
implicit confidence in her fidelity to the traditions of their faith.
Wherefore the evening of the day before Passover, instead of being devoted to frying fish and provisioning, was free for more
secular occupations. Esther, for example, had arranged to go to
see the *début* of a new Hamlet, with Addie. Addie had asked her
to go, mentioning that Raphael, who was taking her, had suggested that she should bring her friend—for they had become
great friends, had Addie and Esther, ever since Esther had gone
to take that cup of tea, with the chat that is more essential than
milk or sugar.

The girls met or wrote every week. Raphael Esther never met
nor heard from directly. She found Addie a sweet, lovable girl,
full of frank simplicity and unquestioning piety. Though dazz-
lingly beautiful, she had none of the coquetry which Esther, with
a touch of jealousy, had been accustomed to associate with beauty,
and she had little of the petty malice of girlish gossip. Esther
summed her up as Raphael's heart without his head. It was
unfair, for Addie's own head was by no means despicable. But
Esther was not alone in taking eccentric opinions as the touchstone of intellectual vigour. Anyhow, she was distinctly happier
since Addie had come into her life, and she admired her as a
mountain torrent might admire a crystal pool, half envying her
happier temperament.

The Goldsmiths were just finishing dinner when the expected

ring came. To their surprise the ringer was Sidney. He was shown into the dining-room.

'Good-evening, all,' he said. 'I've come as a substitute for Raphael.'

Esther grew white.

'Why, what has happened to him?' she asked.

'Nothing. I had a wire to say he was unexpectedly detained in the City, and asking me to take Addie and to call for you.'

Esther turned from white to red. How rude of Raphael! How disappointing not to meet him after all! And did he think she could thus unceremoniously be handed over to somebody else? She was about to beg to be excused, when it struck her a refusal would look too pointed. Besides, she did not fear Sidney now. It would be a test of her indifference. So she murmured instead:

'What can detain him?'

'Charity, doubtless. Do you know that after he is fagged out with upholding the *Flag* from early morning till late eve, he devotes the later eve to gratuitous tuition, lecturing, and the like?'

'No,' said Esther, softened. 'I knew he came home late, but I thought he had to report communal meetings.'

'That too, But Addie tells me he never came home at all one night last week. He was sitting up with some wretched dying pauper.'

'He'll kill himself,' said Esther anxiously.

'People are right about him. He is quite hopeless,' said Percy Saville, the solitary guest, tapping his forehead significantly.

'Perhaps it is we who are hopeless,' said Esther sharply.

'I wish we were all as sensible,' said Mrs. Henry Goldsmith, turning on the unhappy stockbroker with her most superior air. 'Mr. Leon always reminds me of Judas Maccabæus.'

He shrank before the blaze of her mature beauty, the fulness of her charms revealed by her rich evening dress, her hair radiating strange subtle perfume. His eyes sought Mr. Goldsmith's for refuge and consolation.

'That is so,' said Mr. Goldsmith, rubbing his red chin. 'He is an excellent young man.'

'May I trouble you to put on your things at once, Miss Ansell?' said Sidney. 'I have left Addie in the carriage, and we are rather late. I believe it is usual for ladies to put on "things" even when in evening dress. I may mention that there is a bouquet for you in the carriage, and, however unworthy a substitute I may be for Raphael, I may at least claim he would have forgotten to bring you that.'

Esther smiled despite herself as she left the room to get her cloak. She was chagrined and disappointed, but she resolved not to inflict her ill-humour on her companions.

She had long since got used to carriages, and when they arrived at the theatre she took her seat in the box without heart-fluttering.

It was an old discovery now that boxes had no connection with oranges nor stalls with costers' barrows.

The house was brilliant. The orchestra was playing the overture.

'I wish Mr. Shakespeare would write a new play,' grumbled Sidney. 'All these revivals make him lazy—heavens! what his fees must tot up to ! If I were not sustained by the presence of you two girls, I should no more survive the fifth act than most of the characters. Why don't they brighten the piece up with ballet-girls ? '

'Yes, I suppose you blessed Mr. Leon when you got his tele-gram,' said Esther. 'What a bore it must be to you to be saddled with his duties ! '

'Awful ! ' admitted Sidney gravely. ' Besides, it interferes with my work.'

'Work ? ' said Addie. ' You know you only work by sunlight.'

'Yes, that's the best of my profession—in England. It gives you such opportunities of working—at other professions.'

'Why, what do you work at ? ' inquired Esther laughing.

'Well, there's amusement—the most difficult of all things to achieve ! Then there's poetry. You don't know what a dab I am at rondeaux and barcarolles. And I write music, too—lovely little serenades to my lady-loves, and reveries that are like dainty pastels.'

'All the talents ! ' said Addie, looking at him with a fond smile. 'But if you have any time to spare from the curling of your lovely silken moustache, which is entirely like a delicate pastel, will you kindly tell me what celebrities are present ? '

'Yes, do,' added Esther. 'I have only been to two first-nights, and then I had nobody to point out the lions.'

'Well, first of all I see a very celebrated painter in a box—a man who has improved considerably on the weak draughtsmanship displayed by Nature in her human figures, and the amateurishness of her glaring sunsets.'

'Who's that ! ' inquired Addie and Esther eagerly.

'I think he calls himself Sidney Graham ; but that, of course, is only a *nom de pinceau.*'

'Oh ! ' said the girls, with a reproachful smile.

'Do be serious,' said Esther. 'Who is that stout gentleman with the bald head ? ' She peered down curiously at the stalls through her opera-glass.

'What, the lion without the mane ? That's Tom Day, the dramatic critic of a dozen papers. A terrible Philistine ! Lucky for Shakespeare he didn't flourish in Elizabethan times ! '

He rattled on till the curtain rose, and the hushed audience settled down to the enjoyment of the tragedy.

'This looks as if it is going to be the true Hamlet,' said Esther, after the first act.

'What do you mean by the true Hamlet ? ' queried Sidney cynically.

'The Hamlet for whom life is at once too big and too little,' said Esther.

'And who was at once mad and sane,' laughed Sidney. 'The plain truth is that Shakespeare followed the old tale, and what you take for subtlety is but the blur of uncertain handling. Aha! you look shocked. Have I found your religion at last?'

'No; my reverence for our national bard is based on reason,' rejoined Esther seriously. 'To conceive Hamlet, the typical nineteenth-century intellect, in that bustling picturesque Elizabethan time was a creative feat bordering on the miraculous. And then look at the solemn, inexorable march of Destiny in his tragedies, awful as its advance in the Greek dramas. Just as the marvels of the old fairy-tales were an instinctive prevision of the miracles of modern science, so this idea of Destiny seems to me an instinctive anticipation of the formulas of modern science. What we want to-day is a dramatist who shall show us the great natural silent forces, working the weal and woe of human life through the illusions of consciousness and freewill.'

'What you want to-night, Miss Ansell, is black coffee,' said Sidney; 'and I'll tell the attendant to get you a cup, for I dragged you away from dinner before the crown and climax of the meal. I have always noticed myself that when I am interrupted in my meals all sorts of bugbears, scientific or otherwise, take possession of my mind.'

He called the attendant.

'Esther has the most nonsensical opinions,' said Addie gravely. 'As if people weren't responsible for their actions! Do good, and all shall be well with thee, is sound Bible teaching and sound common-sense.'

'Yes, but isn't it the Bible that says, "The fathers have eaten a sour grape, and the teeth of the children are set on edge"?' Esther retorted.

Addie looked perplexed. 'It sounds contradictory,' she said honestly.

'Not at all, Addie,' said Esther. 'The Bible is a literature, not a book. If you choose to bind Tennyson and Milton in one volume that doesn't make them a book. And you can't complain if you find contradictions in the text. Don't you think the sour grape text the truer, Mr. Graham?'

'Don't ask me, please. I'm prejudiced against anything that appears in the Bible.'

In his flippant way Sidney spoke the truth. He had an almost physical repugnance for his fathers' ways of looking at things.

'I think you're the two most wicked people in the world,' exclaimed Addie gravely.

'We are,' said Sidney lightly. 'I wonder you consent to sit in the same box with us. How you can find my company endurable I can never make out.'

Addie's lovely face flushed, and her lip quivered a little.

' It 's your friend who 's the wickeder of the two,' pursued Sidney, 'for she 's in earnest, and I 'm not. Life 's too short for us to take the world's troubles on our shoulders, not to speak of the unborn millions. A little light and joy, the flush of sunset or of a lovely woman's face, a fleeting strain of melody, the scent of a rose, the flavour of old wine, the flash of a jest, and ah, yes, a cup of coffee —here 's yours, Miss Ansell—that 's the most we can hope for in life. Let us start a religion with one commandment, "Enjoy thyself." '

' That religion has too many disciples already,' said Esther stirring her coffee.

' Then why not start it if you wish to reform the world ? ' asked Sidney. 'All religions survive merely by being broken. With only one commandment to break, everybody would jump at the chance. But so long as you tell people they musn't enjoy themselves, they will. It 's human nature, and you can't alter that by Act of Parliament or Confession of Faith. Christ ran amuck at human nature, and human nature celebrates his birthday with panto-mimes.'

' Christ understood human nature better than the modern young man,' said Esther scathingly, 'and the proof lies in the almost limitless impress he has left on history.'

' Oh, that was a fluke,' said Sidney lightly. ' His real influence is only superficial. Scratch the Christian and you find the pagan —spoiled.'

' He divined by genius what science is slowly finding out,' said Esther, ' when he said " Forgive them, for they know not what they do." '

Sidney laughed heartily. ' That seems to be your King Charles's head, seeing divinations of modern science in all the old ideas. Personally I honour him for discovering that the Sabbath was made for man and not man for the Sabbath. Strange he should have stopped half-way to the truth ! '

' What is the truth ? ' asked Addie curiously.

' Why, that morality was made for man, not man for morality,' said Sidney. ' That chimera of meaningless virtue which the Hebrew has brought into the world is the last monster left to slay. The Hebrew view of life is too one-sided. The Bible is a litera-ture without a laugh in it. Even Raphael thinks the great Radical of Galilee carried spirituality too far.'

' Yes, he thinks he would have been reconciled to the Jewish doctors, and would have understood them better,' said Addie, ' only he died so young.'

' That 's a good way of putting it,' said Sidney admiringly. ' One can see Raphael is my cousin, despite his religious aberrations. It opens up new historical vistas. Only it is just like Raphael to find excuses for everybody, and Judaism in everything. I am sure he considers the devil a good Jew at heart. If he admits any moral obliquity in him, he puts it down to the climate.'

This made Esther laugh outright, even while there were tears for Raphael in the laugh. Sidney's intellectual fascination reasserted itself over her ; there seemed something inspiring in standing with him on the free heights that left all the clogging vapours and fogs of moral problems somewhere below, where the sun shone and the clear wind blew, and talk was a game of bowls with Puritan ideals for nine-pins. He went on amusing her till the curtain rose, with a pretended theory of Mohammedology which he was working at. Just as for the Christian apologist the Old Testament was full of hints of the New, so he contended was the New Testament full of foreshadowings of the Koran, and he cited as a most convincing text, 'In heaven there shall be no marrying, nor giving in marriage.' He professed to think that Mohammedanism was the dark horse that would come to the front in the race of religions, and win in the West as it had won in the East.

'There's a man staring dreadfully at you, Esther,' said Addie, when the curtain fell on the second act.

'Nonsense,' said Esther, reluctantly returning from the realities of the play to the insipidities of actual life. 'Whoever it is, it must be at you.'

She looked affectionately at the great glorious creature at her side, tall and stately, with that winning gentleness of expression which spiritualises the most voluptuous beauty.

Addie wore pale sea green, and there were lilies of the valley at her bosom, and a diamond star in her hair. No man could admire her more than Esther, who felt quite vain of her friend's beauty, and happy to bask in its reflected sunshine. Sidney followed her glance, and his cousin's charms struck him with almost novel freshness. He was so much with Addie that he always took her for granted. The semi-unconscious liking he had for her society was based on other than physical traits. He let his eyes rest upon her for a moment in half-surprised appreciation, figuring her as half-bud, half-blossom. Really, if Addie had not been his cousin—and a Jewess ! She was not much of a cousin when he came to cipher it out, but, then she was a good deal of a Jewess.

'I'm sure it's you he's staring at,' persisted Addie.

'Don't be ridiculous !' persisted Esther. 'Which man do you mean ?'

'There ! The fifth row of stalls, the one, two, four, seven—the seventh man from the end. He's been looking at you all through, but now he's gone in for a good long stare. There ! next to that pretty girl in pink.'

'Do you mean the young man with the dyed carnation in his buttonhole and the crimson handkerchief in his bosom ?'

'Yes, that's the one. Do you know him ?'

'No,' said Esther, lowering her eyes and looking away. But when Addie informed her that the young man had renewed his attentions to the girl in pink, she levelled her opera-glass at him. Then she shook her head. 'There seems something familiar about his face, but I cannot for the life of me recall who it is.'

'The "something familiar about his face" is his nose,' said Addie laughing, 'for it is emphatically Jewish.'

'At that rate,' said Sidney, 'nearly half the theatre would be familiar, including a goodly proportion of the critics, and Hamlet and Ophelia themselves. But I know the fellow.'

'You do? Who is he?' asked the girls eagerly.

'I don't know. He's one of the mashers of the *Frivolity*. I'm another, and so we often meet. But we never speak as we pass by. To tell the truth, I resent him.'

'It's wonderful how fond Jews are of the theatre,' said Esther, 'and how they resent other Jews going.'

'Thank you,' said Sidney. 'But as I'm not a Jew the arrow glances off.'

'Not a Jew?' repeated Esther in amaze.

'No. Not in the current sense. I always deny I'm a Jew.'

'How do you justify that?' said Addie incredulously.

'Because it would be a lie to say I was. It would be to produce a false impression. The conception of a Jew in the mind of the average Christian is a mixture of Fagin, Shylock, Rothschild, and the caricatures of the American comic papers. I am certainly not like that, and I'm not going to tell a lie and say I am. In conversation always think of your audience. It takes two to make a truth. If an honest man told an old lady he was an atheist, that would be a lie, for to her it would mean he was a dissolute reprobate. To call myself Abrahams would be to live a daily lie. I am not a bit like the picture called up by Abrahams. Graham is a far truer expression of myself.'

'Extremely ingenious,' said Esther, smiling. 'But ought you not rather to utilise yourself for the correction of the portrait of Abrahams?'

Sidney shrugged his shoulders.

'Why should I subject myself to petty martyrdom for the sake of an outworn creed and a decaying sect?'

We are not decaying,' said Addie indignantly.

'Personally you are blossoming,' said Sidney with a mock bow. 'But nobody can deny that our recent religious history has been a series of dissolving views. Look at that young masher there, who is still ogling your fascinating friend, rather, I suspect, to the annoyance of the young lady in pink, and compare him with the old hard-shell Jew. When I was a lad named Abrahams, painfully training in the way I wasn't going to go, I got an insight into the lives of my ancestors. Think of the people who built up the Jewish Prayer-Book, who added line to line and precept to precept, and whose whole thought was intertwined with religion ; and then look at that young fellow with the dyed carnation and the crimson silk handkerchief, who probably drives a drag to the

Derby, and for aught I know runs a music-hall. It seems almost incredible he should come of that Puritan old stock!'

'Not at all,' said Esther. 'If you knew more of our history, you would see it is quite normal. We were always hankering after the gods of the heathen, and we always loved magnificence—remember our Temples. In every land we have produced great merchants and rulers, prime ministers, viziers, nobles. We built castles in Spain (solid ones) and palaces in Venice. We have had saints and sinners, free-livers and ascetics, martyrs and money-lenders. "Polarity" Graetz calls the self-contradiction which runs through our history. I figure the Jew as the eldest-born of Time, touching the Creation and reaching forward into the Future, the true *blasé* of the universe—the Wandering Jew who has been everywhere, seen everything, done everything, led everything, thought everything, and—suffered everything.'

'Bravo! Quite a bit of Beaconsfieldian fustian,' said Sidney, laughing, yet astonished. 'One would think you were anxious to assert yourself against the ancient peerage of this mushroom realm!'

'It is the bare historical truth,' said Esther quietly. 'We are so ignorant of our own history—can we wonder at the world's ignorance of it? Think of the part the Jew has played: Moses giving the world its morality, Jesus its religion, Isaiah its millennial visions, Spinoza its cosmic philosophy, Ricardo its political economy, Karl Marx and Lassalle its Socialism, Heine its loveliest poetry, Mendelssohn its most restful music, Rachel its supreme acting; and then think of the stock Jew of the American comic papers! There lies the real comedy, too deep for laughter.'

'Yes; but most of the Jews you mention were outcasts or apostates,' retorted Sidney. 'There lies the real tragedy, too deep for tears. Ah! Heine summed it up best: "Judaism is not a religion —it is a misfortune." But do you wonder at the intolerance of every nation towards its Jews? It is a form of homage. Tolerate them, and they spell "Success"—and patriotism is an ineradicable prejudice. Since when have you developed this extraordinary enthusiasm for Jewish history? I always thought you were an anti-Semite.'

Esther blushed, and meditatively sniffed at her bouquet, but fortunately the rise of the curtain relieved her of the necessity for a reply. It was only a temporary relief, however, for the quizzical young artist returned to the subject immediately the act was over.

I know you're in charge of the æsthetic department of the *Flag*,' he said. 'I had no idea you wrote the leaders.'

'Don't be absurd!' murmured Esther.

'I always told Addie Raphael could never write so eloquently —didn't I, Addie? Ah, I see you're blushing to find it fame, Miss Ansell.'

Esther laughed, though a bit annoyed.

'How can you suspect me of writing orthodox leaders?' she asked.

'Well, who else *is* there?' urged Sidney with mock *naïveté*. 'I went down there once and saw the shanty. The editorial sanctum was crowded. Poor Raphael was surrounded by the queerest-looking set of creatures I ever clapped eyes on. There was a quaint lunatic in a check suit, describing his apocalyptic visions; a dragoman with sore eyes and a grievance against the Board of Guardians; a venerable son of Jerusalem, with a most artistic white beard, who had covered the editorial table with carved nick-nacks in olive and sandalwood; an inventor who had squared the circle and the problem of perpetual motion, but could not support himself; a Roumanian exile with a scheme for fertilising Palestine; and a wild-eyed, hatchet-faced Hebrew poet who told me I was a famous patron of learning, and sent me his book soon after with a Hebrew inscription which I couldn't read, and a request for a cheque, which I didn't write. I thought I just capped the company of oddities, when in came a sallow, red-haired chap, with the extraordinary name of Karlkammer, and kicked up a deuce of a shine with Raphael for altering his letter. Raphael mildly hinted that the letter was written in such unintelligible English that he had to grapple with it for an hour before he could reduce it to the coherence demanded of print. But it was no use—it seems Raphael had made him say something heterodox he didn't mean, and he insisted on being allowed to reply to his own letter! He had brought the counterblast with him—six sheets of foolscap, with all the *t's* uncrossed—and insisted on signing it with his own name. I said: "Why not? Set a Karlkammer to answer to a Karlkammer." But Raphael said it would make the paper a laughing-stock, and between the dread of that and the consciousness of having done the man a wrong, he was quite unhappy. He treats all his visitors with angelic consideration, when in another newspaper office the very office-boy would snub them. Of course, nobody has a bit of consideration for him, or his time, or his purse.'

'Poor Raphael!' murmured Esther, smiling sadly at the grotesque images conjured up by Sidney's description.

'I go down there now whenever I want models,' concluded Sidney gravely.

'Well, it is only right to hear what these poor people have to say,' Addie observed. 'What is a paper for, except to right wrongs?'

'Primitive person!' said Sidney. 'A paper exists to make a profit.'

'Raphael's doesn't,' retorted Addie.

'Of course not,' laughed Sidney. 'It never will so long as there's a conscientious editor at the helm. Raphael flatters nobody, and reserves his praises for people with no control of the communal advertisements. Why, it quite preys upon his mind to think that he is linked to an advertisement canvasser with a gorgeous imagination, who goes about representing to the unwary Christian that the *Flag* has a circulation of fifteen hundred.'

'Dear me!' said Addie, a smile of humour lighting up her beautiful features.

'Yes,' said Sidney, 'I think he salves his conscience by an extra hour's slumming in the evening. Most religious folks do their moral book-keeping by double entry. Probably that's why he's not here to-night.'

'It's too bad!' said Addie, her face growing grave again. 'He comes home so late and so tired that he always falls asleep over his books.'

'I don't wonder,' laughed Sidney. 'Look what he reads! Once I found him nodding peacefully over Thomas à Kempis.'

'Oh, but he often reads that,' said Addie. 'When we wake him up and tell him to go to bed, he says indignantly he wasn't sleeping, but thinking, turns over a page and falls asleep again.'

They all laughed.

'Oh, he's a famous sleeper,' Addie continued. 'It's as difficult to get him out of bed as into it. He says himself he's an awful lounger, and used to idle away whole days before he invented time-tables. Now he has every hour cut and dried—he says his salvation lies in regular hours.'

'Addie, Addie, don't tell tales out of school! said Sidney.

'Why, what tales?' asked Addie, astonished. 'Isn't it rather to his credit that he has conquered his bad habits?'

'Undoubtedly; but it dissipates the poetry in which I am sure Miss Ansell was enshrouding him. It shears a man of his heroic proportions to hear he has to be dragged out of bed. These things should be kept in the family.'

Esther stared hard at the house. Her cheeks glowed as if the limelight man had turned his red rays on them. Sidney chuckled mentally over his insight. Addie smiled.

'Oh, nonsense! I'm sure Esther doesn't think less of him because he keeps a time-table.'

'You forget your friend has what you haven't—artistic instinct. It's ugly. A man should be a man, not a railway system. If I were you, Addie, I'd capture that time-table, erase "lecturing," and substitute "cricketing." Raphael would never know, and every afternoon, say at 2 P.M., he'd consult his time-table, and, seeing he had to cricket, he'd take up his stumps and walk to Regent's Park.'

'Yes, but he can't play cricket!' said Esther, laughing, and glad of the opportunity.

'Oh, can't he?' Sidney whistled. 'Don't insult him by telling him that. Why, he was in the Harrow eleven, and scored his century in the match with Eton—those long arms of his send the ball flying as if it were a drawing-room ornament.'

'Oh yes,' affirmed Addie. 'Even now cricket is his one temptation.'

Esther was silent. Her Raphael seemed toppling to pieces. The silence seemed to communicate itself to her companions. Addie broke it by sending Sidney to smoke a cigarette in the lobby.

'Or else I shall feel quite too selfish,' she said. 'I know you're just dying to talk to some sensible people.—Oh, I beg your pardon, Esther!'

The squire of dames smiled but hesitated.

'Yes, do go,' said Esther. 'There's six or seven minutes' more interval. This is the longest wait.'

'Ladies' will is my law,' said Sidney gallantly, and taking a cigarette-case from his cloak, which was hung on a peg at the back of the box, he strolled out. 'Perhaps,' he said, 'I shall skip some Shakespeare if I meet a congenial intellectual soul to gossip with.'

He had scarce been gone two minutes when there came a gentle tapping at the door, and the visitor being invited to come in, the girls were astonished to behold the young gentleman with the dyed carnation and the crimson silk handkerchief. He looked at Esther with an affable smile.

'Don't you remember me?' he said. The ring of his voice woke some far-off echo in her brain. But no recollection came to her.

'I remembered you almost at once,' he went on, in a half-reproachful tone, 'though I didn't care about coming up while you had another fellow in the box. Look at me carefully, Esther.'

The sound of her name on the stranger's lips set all the chords of memory vibrating—she looked again at the dark oval face with the aquiline nose, the glittering eyes, the neat black moustache, the close-shaved cheeks and chin, and in a flash the past resurged, and she murmured almost incredulously, 'Levi!'

The young man got rather red.

'Ye-e-s!' he stammered. 'Allow me to present you my card.'

He took it out of a little ivory case and handed it to her. It read: 'Mr. Leonard James.'

An amused smile flitted over Esther's face, passing into one of welcome. She was not at all displeased to see him.

'Addie,' she said, this is Mr. Leonard James, a friend I used to know in my girlhood.'

'Yes, we were boys together, as the song says,' said Leonard James, smiling facetiously.

Addie inclined her head in the stately fashion which accorded so well with her beauty, and resumed her investigation of the stalls. Presently she became absorbed in a tender reverie induced by the passionate waltz music, and she forgot all about Esther's strange visitor, whose words fell as insensibly on her ears as the ticking of a familiar clock. But to Esther Leonard James's conversation was full of interest. The two ugly ducklings of the back-pond had become to all appearance swans of the ornamental water, and it was natural that they should gabble of auld lang syne and the devious routes by which they had come together again.

'You see, I'm like you, Esther,' explained the young man; 'I'm not fitted for the narrow life which suits my father and mother and my sister. They've got no ideas beyond the house and religion,

and all that sort of thing. What do you think my father wanted
me to be? A minister! Think of it—ha! ha! ha! Me a
minister! I actually did go for a couple of terms to Jews' College.
Oh yes, you remember! Why, I was there when you were a
school teacher and got taken up by the swells. But our stroke of
fortune came soon after yours. Did you never hear of it? My!
you must have dropped all your old acquaintances if no one ever
told you that. Why, father came in for a couple of thousand
pounds! I thought I'd make you stare. Guess who from?'

'I give it up,' said Esther.

'Thank you. It was never yours to give,' said Leonard, laughing jovially at his wit. 'Old Steinwein—you remember his death.
It was in all the papers—the eccentric old buffer who was touched
in the upper story, and used to give so much time and money to
Jewish affairs, setting up lazy old Rabbis in Jerusalem to shake
themselves over their Talmuds. You remember his gifts to the
poor—six and sevenpence each, because he was seventy-nine years
old, and all that. Well, he used to send the pater a basket of
fruit every *Yomtov*; but he used to do that to every Rabbi all
round, and my old man had not the least idea he was the object of
special regard till the old chap pegged out. Ah, there's nothing
like Torah, after all.'

'You don't know what you may have lost through not becoming
a minister,' suggested Esther slyly.

'Ah, but I know what I've gained. Do you think I could stand
having my hands and feet tied — with phylacteries?' asked
Leonard, becoming vividly metaphoric in the intensity of his
repugnance to the galling bonds of orthodoxy. 'Now I do as I
like, go where I please, eat what I please. Just fancy not being
able to join fellows at supper because you mustn't eat oysters or
steak! Might as well go into a monastery at once. All very well
in ancient Jerusalem, where everybody was rowing in the same
boat. Have you ever tasted pork, Esther?'

'No,' said Esther, with a faint smile.

'I have,' said Leonard. 'I don't say it to boast, but I have had
it times without number. I didn't like it the first time—thought
it would choke me, you know ; but that soon wears off. Now I
breakfast off ham and eggs regularly. I go the whole hog you see.
Ha! ha! ha!'

'If I didn't see from your card you're not living at home, that
would have apprised me of it,' said Esther.

'Of course I couldn't live at home. Why, the guv'nor couldn't
bear to let me shave. Ha! ha! ha! Fancy a religion that makes
you keep your hair on unless you use a depilatory. I was articled
to a swell solicitor. The old man resisted a long time, but he gave
in at last and let me live near the office.'

'Ah, then I presume you came in for some of the two thousand,
despite your non-connection with Torah.'

'There isn't much left of it now,' said Leonard, laughing.

'What's two thousand in seven years in London? There were over four hundred guineas swallowed up by the premium and the fees and all that.'

'Well, let us hope it 'll all come back in costs.'

'Well, between you and me,' said Leonard seriously, 'I should be surprised if it does. You see, I haven't yet scraped through the Final—they're making the beastly exam. stiffer every year. No, it isn't to that quarter I look to recoup myself for the outlay on my education.

'No?' said Esther.

'No. Fact is—between you and me—I 'm going to be an actor.

'Oh!' said Esther.

'Yes. I 've played several times in private theatricals—you know we Jews have a knack for the stage ; you'd be surprised to know how many pros. are Jews. There 's heaps of money to be made nowadays on the boards. I 'm in with lots of 'em and ought to know. It 's the only profession where you don't want any train-ing, and these law books are as dry as the *Mishnah* the old man used to make me study. Why, they say to-night's Hamlet was in a counting-house four years ago.'

'I wish you success,' said Esther somewhat dubiously. 'And how is your sister Hannah? Is she married yet?'

'Married! Not she! She 's got no money, and you know what our Jewish young men are. Mother wanted her to have the two thousand pounds for a dowry, but fortunately Hannah had the sense to see that it 's the man that 's got to make his way in the world. Hannah is always certain of her bread-and-butter, which is a good deal in these hard times. Besides, she 's naturally grumpy, and she doesn't go out of her way to make herself agreeable to young men. It 's my belief she 'll die an old maid. Well, there 's no accounting for tastes.'

'And your mother and father?'

'They are all right, I believe. I shall see them to-morrow night —Passover, you know. I haven't missed a single *Seder* at home,' he said with conscious virtue. It 's an awful bore, you know. I often laugh to think of the chappies' faces if they could see me leaning on a pillow and gravely asking the old man why we eat Passover cakes.' He laughed now to think of it. 'But I never miss—they'd cut up rough, I expect, if I did.'

'Well, that 's something in your favour,' murmured Esther gravely.'

He looked at her sharply, suddenly suspecting that his auditor was not perfectly sympathetic. She smiled a little at the images passing through her mind, and Leonard, taking her remark for badinage, allowed his own features to relax to their original amiability.

'You 're not married, either, I suppose,' he remarked.

'No,' said Esther. 'I 'm like your sister Hannah,'

He shook his head sceptically.

'Ah, I expect you 'll be looking very high,' he said.

'Nonsence !' murmured Esther, playing with her bouquet.

A flash passed across his face, but he went on in the same tone.

'Ah, don't tell me ! Why shouldn't you ? Why, you 're looking perfectly charming to-night.'

'Please don't,' said Esther. 'Every girl looks perfectly charming when she 's nicely dressed. Who and what am I ? Nothing. Let us drop the subject.

'All right ; but you *must* have grand ideas, else you 'd have sometimes gone to see my people, as in the old days.'

'When did I visit your people ? You used to come and see me sometimes.' A shadow of a smile hovered about the tremulous lips. 'Believe me, I didn't consciously drop any of my old acquaintances. My life changed—my family went to America— later on I travelled. It is the currents of life, not their wills, that bear old acquaintances asunder.'

He seemed pleased with her sentiments, and was about to say something, but she added :

'The curtain 's going up. Hadn't you better go down to your friend ? She 's been looking up at us impatiently.'

'Oh no, don't bother about her,' said Leonard, reddening a little. 'She—she won't mind. She 's only—only an actress, you know. I have to keep in with the profession in case any opening should turn up. You never know. An actress may become a lessee at any moment. Hark ! The orchestra is striking up again—the scene isn't set yet. Of course I 'll go if you want me to !'

'No, stay by all means, if you want to,' murmured Esther. 'We have a chair unoccupied.'

'Do you expect that fellow Sidney Graham back ?'

'Yes, sooner or later. But how do you know his name ?' queried Esther in surprise.

'Everybody about town knows Sidney Graham, the artist. Why, we belong to the same club, the Flamingo, though he only turns up for the great glove-fights. Beastly cad, with all due respect to your friends, Esther. I was introduced to him once, but he stared at me next time so haughtily that I cut him dead. Do you know, ever since then I 've suspected he 's one of us ; perhaps you can tell me, Esther ? I dare say he 's no more Sidney Graham than I am.'

'Hush !' said Esther, glancing warningly towards Addie, who, however, betrayed no sign of attention.

'Sister ?' asked Leonard, lowering his voice to a whisper.

Esther shook her head.

'Cousin. But Mr. Graham is a friend of mine as well, and you mustn't talk of him like that.'

'Ripping fine girl !' murmured Leonard irrelevantly. 'Wonder at his taste !'

He took a long stare at the abstracted Addie.

'What do you mean ?' said Esther, her annoyance increasing.

Her old friend's tone jarred upon her.

'Well, I don't know what he could see in the girl he's engaged to.'

Esther's face became white. She looked anxiously towards the unconscious Addie.

'You are talking nonsense,' she said in a low, cautious tone. 'Mr. Graham is too fond of his liberty to engage himself to any girl.'

'Oho!' said Leonard, with a subdued whistle. 'I hope you're not sweet on him yourself.'

Esther gave an impatient gesture of denial. She resented Leonard's rapid resumption of his old familiarity.

'Then take care not to be,' he said. 'He's engaged privately to Miss Hannibal, a daughter of the M.P. Tom Sledge, the sub-editor of the *Cormorant* told me. You know they collect items about everybody, and publish them at what they call the psychological moment. Graham goes to the Hannibals' every Saturday afternoon. They're very strict people ; the father, you know, is a prominent Wesleyan, and she's not the sort of girl to be played with.'

'For Heaven's sake speak more softly !' said Esther, though the orchestra was playing *fortissimo* now, and they had spoken so quietly all along that Addie could scarcely have heard without a special effort. It can't be true. You are repeating mere idle gossip.'

'Why, they know everything at the *Cormorant*,' said Leonard indignantly. 'Do you suppose a man can take such a step as that without its getting known ? Why, I shall be chaffed—enviously—about you two to-morrow ! Many a thing the world little dreams of is an open secret in club smoking-rooms. Generally more discreditable than Graham's, which must be made public of itself sooner or later.'

To Esther's relief the curtain rose. Addie woke up and looked round, but seeing that Sidney had not returned, and that Esther was still in colloquy with the invader, she gave her attention to the stage. Esther could no longer bend her eye on the mimic tragedy ; her eyes rested pityingly upon Addie's face, and Leonard's eyes rested admiringly upon Esther's. Thus Sidney found the group, when he returned in the middle of the act, to his surprise and displeasure. He stood silently at the back of the box till the act was over. Leonard James was the first to perceive him; knowing he had been telling tales about him, he felt uneasy under his supercilious gaze. He bade Esther good-bye, asking and receiving permission to call upon her. When he was gone, constraint fell upon the party. Sidney was moody ; Addie pensive ; Esther full of stifled wrath and anxiety. At the close of the performance Sidney took down the girls' wrappings from the pegs. He helped Esther courteously, then hovered over his cousin with a solicitude that brought a look of calm happiness into Addie's face, and an expression of pain into Esther's. As they moved slowly along the crowded corridors, he allowed Addie to get a few paces in advance. It was his last opportunity of saying a word to Esther alone.

' If I were you, Miss Ansell, I wouldn't allow that cad to presume on any acquaintance he may have——'

All the latent irritation in Esther's breast burst into a flame at the idea of Sidney's constituting himself a judge. ' If I had not cultivated his acquaintance I should not have had the pleasure of congratulating you on your engagement,' she replied, almost in a whisper.

To Sidney it sounded like a shout. His colour heightened ; he was visibly taken aback.

' What are you talking about ? ' he murmured automatically.

'About your engagement to Miss Hannibal.'

' That blackguard told you ! ' he whispered angrily, half to himself. ' Well, what of it ? I am not bound to advertise it, am I ? It 's my private business, isn't it ? You don't expect me to hang a placard round my breast like those on concert-room chairs, " Engaged " ? '

' Certainly not,' said Esther. But you might have told your friends, so as to enable them to rejoice sympathetically.'

' You turn your sarcasm prettily,' he said mildly ; but the sympathetic rejoicing was just what I wanted to avoid. You know what a Jewish engagement is—how the news spreads like wild-fire from Piccadilly to Petticoat Lane, and the whole house of Israel gathers together to discuss the income and the prospects of the happy pair. I object to sympathetic rejoicing from the slums, especially as in this case it would probably be exchanged for curses. Miss Hannibal is a Christian, and for a Jew to embrace a Christian is, I believe, the next worst thing to his embracing Christianity, even when the Jew is a pagan.'

His wonted flippancy rang hollow. He paused suddenly, and stole a look at his companion's face in search of a smile, but it was pale and sorrowful. The flush on his own face deepened ; his features expressed internal conflict. He addressed a light word to Addie in front. They were nearing the portico ; it was raining outside, and a cold wind blew in to meet them. He bent his head down to the delicate little face at his side, and his tones were changed.

' Miss Ansell,' he said tremulously, ' if I have in any way misled you by my reticence, I beg you to believe it was unintentionally. The memory of the pleasant quarters of an hour we have spent together will always——'

' Good God ! ' said Esther hoarsely, her cheeks flaming, her ears tingling. To whom are you apologising ? ' He looked at her perplexed. ' Why have you not told Addie ? ' she forced herself to say.

In the press of the crowd, on the edge of the threshold, he stood still. Dazzled as by a flash of lightning, he gazed at his cousin—her beautifully poised head, covered with its fleecy white shawl, dominating the throng. The shawl became an aureole to his misty vision.

'Have you told her?' he whispered with answering hoarseness.

'No,' said Esther.

'Then don't tell her,' he whispered eagerly.

'I must. She must hear it soon. Such things must ooze out sooner or later.'

'Then let it be later. Promise me this.'

'No good can come of concealment.'

'Promise me—for a little while, till I give you leave.'

His pleading, handsome face was close to hers. She wondered how she could ever have cared for a creature so weak and pitiful.

'So be it,' she breathed.

'Miss Leon's carriage!' bawled the commissionaire. There was a confusion of rain-beaten umbrellas, gleaming carriage-lamps, zigzag reflections on the black pavements, and clattering omnibuses full inside. But the air was fresh.

'Don't go into the rain, Addie,' said Sidney, pressing forward anxiously. 'You're doing all my work to-night. Hullo! where did *you* spring from?'

It was Raphael who had elicited the exclamation. He suddenly loomed upon the party, bearing a decrepit, dripping umbrella.

'I thought I should be in time to catch you—and to apologise,' he said, turning to Esther.

'Don't mention it,' murmured Esther, his unexpected appearance completing her mental agitation.

'Hold the umbrella over the girls, you beggar!' said Sidney.

'Oh, I beg your pardon,' said Raphael, poking the rim against a policeman's helmet in his anxiety to obey.

'Don't mention it,' said Addie smiling.

'All right, sir,' growled the policeman good-humouredly.

Sidney laughed heartily.

'Quite a general amnesty,' he said. 'Ah! here's the carriage. Why didn't you get inside it out of the rain, or stand in the entrance? You're wringing wet!'

'I didn't think of it,' said Raphael. 'Besides, I've only been here a few minutes. The 'buses are so full when it rains. I had to walk all the way from Whitechapel.'

'You're incorrigible,' grumbled Sidney. 'As if you couldn't have taken a hanson?'

'Why waste money?' said Raphael. They got into the carriage. 'Well, did you enjoy yourselves?' he asked cheerfully.

'Oh yes; thoroughly,' said Sidney. 'Addie wasted two pocket-handkerchiefs over Ophelia—almost enough to pay for that hansom. Miss Ansell doted on the finger of destiny; and I chopped logic and swopped cigarettes with O'Donovan. I hope you enjoyed yourself equally.'

Raphael responded with a melancholy smile. He was seated opposite Esther, and ever and anon some flash of light from the street revealed clearly his sodden, almost shabby garments, and the weariness of his expression. He seemed quite out of harmony with the dainty pleasure party, but just on that account the more in harmony with Esther's old image, the heroic side of him growing only more lovable for the human alloy. She bent towards him at last, and said :

'I am sorry you were deprived of your evening's amusement. I hope the reason didn't add to the unpleasantness.'

'It was nothing,' he murmured awkwardly—'a little unexpected work. One can always go to the theatre.'

'Ah, I am afraid you overwork yourself too much. You musn't. Think of your own health.'

His look softened. He was in a harassed, sensitive state. The sympathy of her gentle accents, the concern upon the eager little face, seemed to flood his own soul with a self-compassion new to him.

'My health doesn't matter,' he faltered. There were sweet tears in his eyes, a colossal sense of gratitude at his heart. He had always meant to pity her and help her—it was sweeter to be pitied, though of course she could not help him. He had no need of help, and on second thoughts he wondered what room there was for pity.

'No, no ; don't talk like that,' said Esther. 'Think of your parents—and Addie.'

CHAPTER VII

WHAT THE YEARS BROUGHT

THE next morning Esther sat in Mrs. Henry Goldsmith's boudoir, filling up some invitation forms for her patroness, who often took advantage of her literary talent in this fashion. Mrs. Goldsmith herself lay back languidly upon a great easy-chair before an asbestos fire, and turned over the leaves of the new number of the *Acadæum*. Suddenly she uttered a little exclamation.

'What is it ?' said Esther.

'They've got a review here of that Jewish novel.'

'Have they ?' said Esther, glancing up eagerly. I'd given up looking for it.'

'You seem very interested in it,' said Mrs. Goldsmith with a little surprise.

'Yes, I—I wanted to know what they said about it,' explained Esther quickly ; 'one hears so many worthless opinions.'

'Well, I'm glad to see we were all right about it,' said Mrs. Goldsmith, whose eye had been running down the column. 'Listen here : " It is a disagreeable book at best, what might have been a powerful tragedy being disfigured by clumsy workmanship and sordid superfluous detail. The exaggerated unhealthy pessimism which the very young mistake for insight pervades the work, and there are some spiteful touches of observation which seem to point to a woman's hand. Some of the minor personages have the air of being sketched from life. The novel can scarcely be acceptable to the writer's circle. Readers, however, in search of the unusual will find new ground broken in this immature study of Jewish life." There, Esther, isn't that just what I've been saying in other words?'

'It's hardly worth bothering about the book now,' said Esther in lower tones; 'it's such a long time ago now since it came out. I don't know what's the good of reviewing it now. These literary papers always seem so cold and cruel to unknown writers.'

'Cruel! It isn't half what he deserves,' said Mrs. Goldsmith, 'or ought I to say she? Do you think there's anything, Esther, in that idea of its being a woman?'

'Really, dear, I'm sick to death of that book,' said Esther. 'These reviewers always try to be very clever and to see through brick walls. What does it matter if it's a he or a she?'

'It doesn't matter, but it makes it more disgraceful if it's a woman. A woman has no business to know the seamy side of human nature.'

At this instant, a domestic knocked and announced that Mr. Leonard James had called to see Miss Ansell. Annoyance, surprise, and relief struggled to express themselves on Esther's face.

'Is the gentleman waiting to see me?' she said.

'Yes, Miss, he's in the hall.' Esther turned to Mrs. Goldsmith. 'It's a young man I came across unexpectedly last night at the theatre. He's the son of Reb Shemuel, of whom you may have heard. I haven't met him since we were boy and girl together. He asked permission to call, but I didn't expect him so soon.'

'Oh, see him by all means, dear! He is probably anxious to talk over old times.'

'May I ask him up here?' said Esther.

'Not unless you particularly want to introduce him to me. I dare say he would rather have you to himself.'

There was a touch of superciliousness about her tone which Esther rather resented, although not particularly anxious for Levi's social recognition.

'Show him into the library,' she said to the servant. 'I will be down in a minute.'

She lingered a few minutes to finish up the invitations and exchange a few indifferent remarks with her companion, and then went down, wondering at Levi's precipitancy in renewing the acquaintance. She could not help thinking of the strangeness of life. That time yesterday she had not dreamt of Levi, and now she was about to see him for the second time, and seemed to know him as intimately as if they had never been parted.

Leonard James was pacing the carpet. His face was perturbed, though his stylishly-cut clothes were composed and immaculate. A cloak was thrown loosely across his shoulders. In his right hand he held a bouquet of spring flowers, which he transferred to his left in order to shake hands with her.

'Good-afternoon, Esther,' he said heartily. 'By Jove! you have got among tip-top people. I had no idea! Fancy you ordering Jeames de la Pluche about. And how happy you must be among all these books! I've brought you a bouquet. There, isn't it a beauty? I got it at Covent Garden this morning.'

'It's very kind of you,' murmured Esther, not so pleased as she might have been, considering her love of beautiful things. 'But you really ought not to waste your money like that.'

'What nonsense, Esther! Don't forget I'm not in the position my father was. I'm going to be a rich man. No, don't put it into a vase; put it in your own room, where it will remind you of me. Just smell those violets; they are awfully sweet and fresh. I flatter myself it's quite as swell and tasteful as the bouquet you had last night. Who gave you that, Esther?'

The 'Esther' mitigated the off-handedness of the question, but made the sentence jar doubly upon her ear. She might have brought herself to call him 'Levi' in exchange, but then she was not certain he would like it. 'Leonard' was impossible. So she forbore to call him by any name.

'I think Mr. Graham brought it. Won't you sit down?' she said indifferently.

'Thank you. I thought so. Luck that fellow's engaged! Do you know, Esther, I didn't sleep all night.'

'No?' said Esther. 'You seemed quite well when I saw you.'

'So I was, but seeing you again so unexpectedly excited me. You have been whirling in my brain ever since. I hadn't thought of you for years.'

'I hadn't thought of you,' Esther echoed frankly.

'No, I suppose not,' he said a little ruefully. 'But, anyhow, Fate has brought us together again. I recognised you the moment I set eyes on you, for all your grand clothes and your swell bouquets. I tell you I was just struck all of a heap. Of course I knew about your luck, but I hadn't realised it. There wasn't any one in the whole theatre who looked the lady more— 'pon honour! You'd have no cause to blush in the company of duchesses. In fact, I know a duchess or two who don't look near so refined. I was quite surprised. Do you know, if any one had told me you used to live up in a garret——'

'Oh, please don't recall unpleasant things,' interrupted Esther petulantly, a little shudder going through her, partly at the picture he called up, partly at his grating vulgarity. Her repulsion to him was growing. Why had he developed so disagreeably? She had not disliked him as a boy, and he certainly had not inherited his traits of coarseness from his father, whom she still conceived as a courtly old gentleman.

'Oh, well, if you don't like it, I won't. I see you're like me; I never think of the Ghetto if I can help it. Well, as I was saying, I haven't had a wink of sleep since I saw you. I lay tossing about, thinking all sorts of things, till I could stand it no longer, and I got up and dressed and walked about the streets, and strayed into Covent Garden Market, where the inspiration came upon me to get you this bouquet. For, of course, it was about you that I had been thinking——'

'About me?' said Esther, turning pale.

'Yes, of course. Don't make *Schnecks*; you know what I mean. I can't help using the old expression when I look at you; the past seems all come back again. They were happy days—weren't they, Esther?—when I used to come up to see you in Royal Street. I think you were a little sweet on me in those days, Esther, and I know I was regular mashed on you.'

He looked at her with a fond smile.

'I dare say you were a silly boy,' said Esther, colouring uneasily under his gaze. 'However, you needn't reproach yourself now.'

'Reproach myself, indeed! Never fear that. What I have been reproaching myself with all night is never having looked you up. Somehow, do you know, I kept asking myself whether I hadn't made a fool of myself lately, and I kept thinking things might have been different if——'

'Nonsense, nonsense!' interrupted Esther with an embarrassed laugh. 'You've been doing very well, learning to know the world, and studying law, and mixing with pleasant people.'

'Ah, Esther,' he said, shaking his head, 'it's very good of you to say that. I don't say I've done anything particularly foolish or out-of-the-way; but when a man is alone he sometimes gets a little reckless and wastes his time, and—you know what it is. I've been thinking if I had some one to keep me steady, some one I could respect, it would be the best thing that could happen to me.'

'Oh, but surely you ought to have sense enough to take care of yourself! And there is always your father. Why don't you see more of him?'

'Don't chaff a man when you see he's in earnest. You know what I mean. It's you I am thinking of.'

'Me? Oh, well, if you think my friendship can be of any use to you, I shall be delighted. Come and see me sometimes, and tell me of your struggles.'

'You know I don't mean that,' he said desperately. 'Couldn't we be more than friends? Couldn't we commence again— where we left off?'

'How do you mean?' she murmured.

'Why are you so cold to me?' he burst out. 'Why do you make it so hard for me to speak? You know I love you; that I fell in love with you all over again last night. I never really forgot you; you were always deep down in my breast. All that I said about steadying me wasn't a lie. I felt that, too. But the real thing I feel is the need of you. I want you to care for me as I care for you. You used to, Esther; you know you did.'

'I know nothing of the kind,' said Esther; 'and I can't understand why a young fellow like you wants to bother his head with such ideas. You've got to make your way in the world.'

'I know, I know; that's why I want you. I didn't tell you the exact truth last night, Esther, but I must really earn some money soon. All that two thousand is used up, and I only get along by squeezing some money out of the old man every now and again. Don't frown; he got a rise of screw three years ago, and can well afford it. Now, that's what I said to myself last night : if I were engaged, it would be an incentive to earning something.'

'For a Jewish young man you are fearfully unpractical,' said Esther, with a forced smile. 'Fancy proposing to a girl without even prospects of prospects.'

'Oh, but I *have* got prospects. I tell you I shall make no end of money on the stage.'

'Or no beginning,' she said, finding the facetious vein easiest.

'No fear. I know I've got as much talent as Bob Andrews (he admits it himself), and *he* draws his thirty quid a week.

'Wasn't that the man who appeared at the police-court the other day for being drunk and disorderly ?'

'Y-e-es,' admitted Leonard, a little disconcerted. 'He is a very good fellow, but he loses his head when he's in liquor.'

'I wonder you can care for society of that sort,' said Esther.

'Perhaps you're right. They're not a very refined lot. I tell you what, I'd like to go on the stage, but I'm not mad on it, and if you only say the word I'll give it up. There ! And I'll go on with my law studies, honour bright I will !'

'I should, if I were you,' she said.

'Yes, but I can't do it without encouragement. Won't you say "Yes"? Let's strike the bargain. I'll stick to law, and you'll stick to me.'

She shook her head.

'I am afraid I could not promise anything you mean. As I said before, I shall always be glad to see you. If you do well, no one will rejoice more than I.'

'Rejoice ! What's the good of that to me ? I want you to care for me ; I want to look forward to your being my wife.'

'Really I cannot take advantage of a moment of folly like this. You don't know what you're saying. You saw me last night after many years, and in your gladness at seeing an old friend you flare up and fancy you're in love with me. Why, who ever heard of such foolish haste ? Go back to your studies, and in a day or two you will find the flame sinking as rapidly as it leapt up.'

'No, no ! Nothing of the kind !' His voice was thicker, and there was real passion in it. She grew dearer to him as the hope of her love receded. 'I couldn't forget you. I care for you awfully. I realised last night that my feeling for you is quite unlike what I have ever felt towards any other girl. Don't say no! Don't send me away despairing. I can hardly realise that you have grown so strange and altered. Surely you oughtn't to put on any side with me. Remember the time we have had together.'

'I remember,' she said gently. 'But I do not want to marry any one ; indeed I don't.'

'Then, if there is no one else in your thoughts, why shouldn't it be me? There! I won't press you for an answer now. Only don't say it's out of the question.'

'I'm afraid I must.'

'No, you mustn't, Esther—you mustn't!' he exclaimed excitedly. 'Think of what it means for me! You are the only Jewish girl I shall ever care for ; and father would be pleased if I were to marry you. You know if I wanted to marry a *Shiksah* there'd be awful rows. Don't treat me as if I were some outsider with no claim upon you. I believe we should get on splendidly together, you and me. We've been through the same sort of thing in childhood ; we should understand each other, and be in sympathy with each other in a way I could never be with another girl, and I doubt if you could with another fellow.'

The words burst from him like a torrent, with excited, foreign-looking gestures. Esther's headache was coming on badly.

'What would be the use of my deceiving you?' she said gently. 'I don't think I shall ever marry. I'm sure I could never make you—or any one else—happy. Won't you let me be your friend?'

'Friend!' he echoed bitterly. 'I know what it is—I'm poor! I've got no money-bags to lay at your feet. You're like all the Jewish girls, after all. But I only ask you to wait—I shall have plenty of money by-and-by. Who knows what more luck my father might drop in for? There are lots of rich religious cranks. And then I'll work hard, honour bright I will!'

'Pray be reasonable,' said Esther quietly. 'You know you are talking at random. Yesterday this time you had no idea of such a thing. To-day you are all on fire. To-morrow you will forget all about it.'

'Never! Never!' he cried. 'Haven't I remembered you all these years? They talk of man's faithlessness and woman's faithfulness. It seems to me it's all the other way. Women are a deceptive lot.'

'You know you have no right whatever to talk like that to me!' said Esther, her sympathy beginning to pass over into annoyance. 'To-morrow you will be sorry. Hadn't you better go before you give yourself—and me—more cause for regret?'

'Ho! you are sending me away, are you?' he said in angry surprise.

'I am certainly suggesting it as the wisest course.'

'Oh, don't give me any of your fine phrases!' he said brutally.

'I see what it is—I've made a mistake. You're a stuck-up, conceited little thing! You think because you live in a grand house nobody is good enough for you! But what are you, after all? A *Schnorrer*—that's all! A *Schnorrer* living on the charity of strangers. If I mix with grand folks, it is as an independent man and an equal; but you, rather than marry any one who mightn't be able to give you carriages and footmen, you prefer to remain a *Schnorrer*!'

Esther was white, and her lips trembled.

'Now I must ask you to go,' she said.

'All right—don't flurry yourself!' he said savagely. 'You don't impress me with your airs. Try them on people who don't know what you were—a *Schnorrer's* daughter! Yes, your father was always a *Schnorrer*, and you are his child. It's in the blood. Ha! ha! ha! Moses Ansell's daughter! Moses Ansell's daughter—a pedlar, who went about the country with brass jewellery and stood in the Lane with lemons, and *schnorred* half-crowns of my father! You took jolly good care to ship him off to America, but, 'pon my honour! you can't expect others to forget him as quickly as you. It's a rich joke, you refusing me! You're not fit for me to wipe my shoes on. My mother never cared for me to go to your garret; she said I must mix with my equals, and goodness knew what disease I might pick up in the dirt. 'Pon my honour the old girl was right!'

'She *was* right!' Esther was stung into retorting. 'You must mix only with your equals. Please leave the room now, or else I shall.'

His face changed. His frenzy gave way to a momentary shock of consternation as he realised what he had done.

'No, no, Esther! I was mad; I didn't know what I was saying. I didn't mean it. Forget it.'

'I cannot. It was quite true,' she said bitterly. 'I am only a *Schnorrer's* daughter. Well, are you going, or must I?'

He muttered something inarticulate, then seized his hat sulkily, and went to the door without looking at her.

'You have forgotten something,' she said.

He turned; her forefinger pointed to the bouquet on the table. He had a fresh access of rage at the sight of it, jerked it contemptuously to the floor with a sweep of his hat, and stamped upon it. Then he rushed from the room, and an instant after she heard the hall-door slam.

She sank against the table sobbing nervously. It was her first proposal. A *Schnorrer*, and the daughter of a *Schnorrer*! Yes, that was what she was. And she had even repaid her benefactors with deception. What hopes could she yet cherish? In literature she was a failure; the critics gave her few gleams of encouragement, while all her acquaintances, from Raphael downwards, would turn and rend her, should she dare declare herself. Nay, she was ashamed of herself for the mischief she had wrought. No one in the world cared for her; she was quite alone. The only man in whose breast she could excite love or the semblance of it was a contemptible cad. And who was she that she should venture to hope for love? She figured herself as an item in a catalogue—'A little, ugly, low-spirited, absolutely penniless young woman, subject to nervous headaches.' Her sobs were interrupted by a ghastly burst of self-mockery. Yes, Levi was right! She ought to think herself lucky to get him. Again, she asked herself, what had existence to offer her? Gradually her sobs ceased; she remembered to-night would be *Seder* night, and her thoughts, so violently turned Ghetto-wards, went back to that night, soon after poor Benjamin's death, when she sat before the garret-fire striving to picture the larger life of the Future.

Well, this was the Future!

CHAPTER VIII

THE ENDS OF A GENERATION

THE same evening Leonard James sat in the stalls of the Colosseum Music-Hall, sipping champagne and smoking a cheroot. He had not been to his chambers (which were only round the corner) since the hapless interview with Esther, wandering about in the streets and the clubs in a spirit compounded of outraged dignity, remorse, and recklessness. All men must dine; and dinner at the Flamingo Club soothed his wounded soul and left only the recklessness, which is a sensation not lacking in agreeableness. Through the rosy mists of the Burgundy there began to surge up other faces than that cold, pallid little face which had hovered before him all the afternoon like a tantalising phantom; at the Chartreuse stage he began to wonder what hallucination, what aberration of sense, had overcome him that he should have been stirred to his depths and distressed so hugely. Warmer faces were these that swam before him, faces fuller of the joy of life. The devil take all stuck-up little saints!

About eleven o'clock, when the great ballet of 'Venetia' was over, Leonard hurried round to the stage-door, saluted the door-keeper with a friendly smile and a sixpence, and sent in his card to Miss Gladys Wynne, on the chance that she might have no supper engagement. Miss Wynne was only a humble *coryphée*, but the admirers of her talent were numerous, and Leonard counted himself fortunate in that she was able to afford him the privilege of her society to-night. She came out to him in a red fur-lined cloak, for the air was keen. She was a majestic being, with a florid complexion not entirely artificial, big blue eyes, and teeth of that whiteness which is the practical equivalent of a sense of humour in evoking the possessor's smiles. They drove to a restaurant a few hundred yards distant, for Miss Wynne detested using her feet except to dance with. It was a fashionable restaurant, where the prices obligingly rose after ten, to accommodate the purses of the supper *clientèle*. Miss Wynne always drank champagne, except when alone, and in politeness Leonard had to imbibe more of this frothy compound. He knew he would have to pay for the day's extravagance by a week of comparative abstemiousness, but recklessness generally meant magnificence with him. They occupied a cosy little corner behind a screen, and Miss Wynne bubbled over with laughter like an animated champagne-bottle. One or two of his acquaintances espied him and winked genially, and Leonard had the satisfaction of feeling that he was not dissipating his money without purchasing enhanced reputation. He had not felt in gayer spirits for months than when, with Gladys Wynne on his arm and a cigarette in his mouth, he sauntered out of the brilliantly-lit restaurant into the feverish dusk of the midnight street, shot with points of fire.

'Hansom, sir?'

'*Levi!*'

A great cry of anguish rent the air. Leonard's cheeks burnt. Involuntarily he looked round. Then his heart stood still. There, a few yards from him, rooted to the pavement, with stony, staring face, was Reb Shemuel. The old man wore an unbrushed high hat and an uncouth, unbuttoned overcoat. His hair and beard were quite white now, and the strong countenance, lined with countless wrinkles, was distorted with pain and astonishment. He looked a cross between an ancient prophet and a shabby street-lunatic. The unprecedented absence of the son from the *Seder* ceremonial had filled the Reb's household with the gravest alarm. Nothing short of death or mortal sickness could be keeping the boy away. It was long before the Reb could bring himself to commence the *Agadah* without his son to ask the time-honoured opening question, and when he did, he paused every minute to listen to footsteps or the voice of the wind without. The joyous holiness of the Festival was troubled; a black cloud overshadowed the shining table-cloth; at supper the food choked him. But *Seder* was over, and yet no sign of the missing guest, no word of explanation. In poignant anxiety the old man walked the three miles that lay between him and tidings of the beloved son. At his chambers he learnt that their occupant had not been in all day. Another thing he learnt there, too; for the *Mezuzah* which he had fixed up on the door-post when his boy moved in had been taken down, and it filled his mind with a dread suspicion that Levi had not been eating at the *kosher* restaurant in Hatton Garden, as he had faithfully vowed to do. But even this terrible thought was swallowed up in the fear that some accident had happened to him. He haunted the house for an hour, filling up the intervals of fruitless inquiry with little random walks round the neighbourhood, determined not to return home to his wife without news of their child. The restless life of the great twinkling streets was almost a novelty to him ; it was rarely his perambulations in London extended outside the Ghetto, and the radius of his life was proportionately narrow, with the intensity that narrowness forces on a big soul. The streets dazzled him ; he looked blinkingly hither and thither in the despairing hope of finding his boy. His lips moved in silent prayer ; he raised his eyes beseechingly to the cold glittering heavens. Then all at once, as the clocks pointed to midnight, he found him. Found him coming out of an unclean place, where he had violated the Passover. Found him—fit climax of horror—with the 'strange woman' of the *Proverbs*, for whom the faithful Jew has a hereditary hatred.

His son—his, Reb Shemuel's ! He, the servant of the Most High, the teacher of the Faith to reverential thousands, had brought a son into the world to profane the Name ! Verily, his gray hairs would go down with sorrow to a speedy grave ! And the sin was half his own ; he had weakly abandoned his boy in the midst of a great city. For one awful instant, that seemed an eternity, the old man and the young faced each other across the chasm which divided their lives. To the son the shock was scarcely less violent than to the father. The *Seder*, which the day's unwonted excitement had clean swept out of his mind, recurred to him in a flash, and by the light of it he understood the puzzle of his father's appearance. The thought of explaining rushed up only to be dismissed. The door of the restaurant had not yet ceased swinging behind him ; there was too much to explain. He felt that all was over between him and his father. It was unpleasant, terrible even, for it meant the annihilation of his resources. But though he still had an almost physical fear of the old man, far more terrible even than the presence of his father was the presence of Miss Gladys Wynne. To explain, to brazen it out—either course was equally impossible. He was not a brave man, but at that moment he felt death were preferable to allowing her to be the witness of such a scene as must ensue. His resolution was taken within a few brief seconds of the tragic *rencontre*. With wonderful self-possession, he nodded to the cabman who had put the question, and whose vehicle was drawn up opposite the restaurant. Hastily he helped the unconscious Gladys into the hansom. He was putting his foot on the step himself, when Reb Shemuel's paralysis relaxed suddenly. Outraged by this final pollution of the Festival, he ran forward and laid his hand on Levi's shoulder. His face was ashen, his heart thumped painfully ; the hand on Levi's cloak shook as with palsy.

Levi winced ; the old awe was upon him. Through a blinding whirl he saw Gladys staring wonderingly at the queer-looking intruder. He gathered all his mental strength together with a mighty effort, shook off the great trembling hand, and leapt into the hansom.

'Drive on !' came in strange guttural tones from his parched throat.

The driver lashed the horse ; a rough jostled the old man aside and slammed the door to ; Leonard mechanically threw him a coin ; the hansom glided away.

'Who was that, Leonard?' said Miss Wynne curiously.

'Nobody ; only an old Jew who supplies me with cash.'

Gladys laughed merrily—a rippling, musical laugh. She knew the sort of person.

CHAPTER IX

THE 'FLAG' FLUTTERS

THE *Flag of Judah*, price one penny, largest circulation of any Jewish organ, continued to flutter, defying the battle, the breeze, and its communal contemporaries. At Passover there had been an illusive augmentation of advertisements proclaiming the virtues of unleavened everything. With the end of the Festival most of these fell out, staying as short a time as the daffodils. Raphael was in despair at the meagre attenuated appearance of the erst prosperous-looking pages. The weekly loss on the paper weighed on his conscience.

'We shall never succeed,' said the sub-editor, shaking his romantic hair, 'till we run it for the Upper Ten. These ten people can make the paper, just as they are now killing it by refusing their countenance.'

'But they must surely reckon with us sooner or later,' said Raphael.

'It will be a long reckoning, I fear ; you take my advice, and put in more butter. It 'll be *kosher* butter, coming from us.'

The little Bohemian laughed as heartily as his eyeglass permitted.

'No ; we must stick to our guns. After all, we have had some very good things lately. Those articles of Pinchas's are not bad, either.'

'They 're so beastly egotistical. Still, his English is improving, and his theories are ingenious, and far more interesting than those terribly dull long letters of Goldsmith, which you will put in.'

Raphael flushed a little, and began to walk up and down the new and superior sanctum with his ungainly strides, puffing furiously at his pipe. The appearance of the room was less bare ; the floor was carpeted with old newspapers and scraps of letters. A huge picture of an Atlantic liner, the gift of a steamship company, leaned cumbrously against a wall.

'Still, all our literary excellencies,' pursued Sampson, 'are outweighed by our shortcomings in getting births, marriages, and deaths. We are gravelled for lack of that sort of matter. What is the use of your elaborate essay on the Septuagint, when the public is dying to hear who 's dead?'

'Yes, I am afraid it is so,' said Raphael, emitting a huge volume of smoke.

'I'm sure it is so. If you would only give me a freer hand I feel sure I could work up that column. We can, at least, make a better show. I would avoid the danger of discovery by shifting the scene to foreign parts. I could marry some people in Bombay, and kill some in Cape Town, redressing the balance by bringing others into existence at Cairo and Cincinnati. Our contemporaries would score off us in local interest, but we should take the shine out of them in cosmopolitanism.'

'No, no; remember that *Meshumad*,' said Raphael, smiling.

'He was real; if you had allowed me to invent a corpse we should have been saved that contretemps. We have one death this week, fortunately, and I am sure to fish out another in the daily papers. But we haven't had a birth for three weeks running; it's just ruining our reputation. Everybody knows that the orthodox are a fertile lot, and it looks as if we hadn't got the support even of our own party. Ta-ra-ra-ta! Now, you must really let me have a birth. I give you my word nobody'll suspect it isn't genuine. Come now! How's this?'

He scribbled on a piece of paper and handed it to Raphael, who read:

'BIRTH.

'On the 15th inst., at 17 East Stuart Lane, Kennington, the wife of Joseph Samuels of a son.'

'There!' said Sampson proudly. 'Who would believe the little beggar had no existence? Nobody lives in Kennington, and that East Stuart Lane is a master-stroke. You might suspect Stuart Lane, but nobody would ever dream there's no such place as *East* Stuart Lane. Don't say the little chap must die; I begin to take quite a paternal interest in him. May I announce him? Don't be too scrupulous. Who'll be a penny the worse for it?'

He began to chirp, with bird-like trills of melody.

Raphael hesitated; his moral fibre had been weakened. It is impossible to touch print and not be defiled.

Suddenly Sampson ceased to whistle, and smote his head with his chubby fist.

'Ass that I am!' he exclaimed.

'What new reason have you discovered to think so?' said Raphael.

'Why, we dare not create boys. We shall be found out; boys must be circumcised, and some of the periphrastically styled "Initiators into the Abrahamic Covenant" may spot us. It was a girl that Mrs. Joseph Samuels was guilty of.'

He amended the sex.

Raphael laughed heartily.

'Put it by—there's another day yet—we shall see.'

'Very well,' said Sampson resignedly. 'Perhaps by to-morrow we shall be in luck, and able to sing "Unto us a child is born, unto us a son is given." By the way, did you see the letter complaining of our using that quotation on the ground it was from the New Testament?'

'Yes,' said Raphael, smiling. 'Of course the man doesn't know his Old Testament, but I trace his misconception to his having heard Handel's *Messiah*. I wonder he doesn't find fault with the Morning Service for containing the Lord's prayer, or with Moses for saying, "Thou shalt love thy neighbour as thyself."'

'Still, that's the sort of man newspapers have to cater for,' said the sub-editor. 'And we don't. We have cut down our Provincial Notes to a column. My idea would be to make two pages of them, not cutting out any of the people's names and leaving in more of the adjectives. Every man's name we mention means at least one copy sold. Why can't we drag in a couple of thousand names every week?'

'That would make our circulation altogether nominal,' laughed Raphael, not taking the suggestion seriously.

Little Sampson was not only the Mephistopheles of the office, debauching his editor's guileless mind with all the wily ways of the old journalistic hand ; he was of real use in protecting Raphael against the thousand and one pitfalls that make the editorial chair as perilous to the occupant as Sweeney Todd's ; against the people who tried to get libels inserted as news or as advertisements, against the self-puffers and the axe-grinders. He also taught Raphael how to commence interesting correspondence and how to close awkward. The *Flag* played a part in many violent discussions. Little Sampson was great in inventing communal crises, and in getting the public to believe it was excited. He also won a great victory over the other party every three weeks ; Raphael did not wish to have so many of these victories, but Little Sampson pointed out that if he did not have them the rival newspaper would annex them. One of the earliest sensations of the *Flag* was a correspondence exposing the misdeeds of some communal officials, but in the end the very persons who made the allegations ate humble pie. Evidently official pressure had been brought to bear, for red tape rampant might have been the heraldic device of Jewish officialdom. In no department did Jews exhibit more strikingly their marvellous powers of assimilation to their neighbours.

Among the discussions which rent the body politic was the question of building a huge synagogue for the poor. The *Flag* said it would only concentrate them, and its word prevailed. There were also the grave questions of English and harmoniums in the synagogue, of the confirmation of girls and their utilisation in the choir. The Rabbinate, whose grave difficulties in reconciling all parties to its rule were augmented by the existence of the *Flag*, pronounced it heinous to introduce English excerpts into

the liturgy ; if, however, they were not read from the central platform, they were legitimate ; harmoniums were permissible, but
only during special services, and an organisation of mixed voices
was allowable, but not a mixed choir ; children might be confirmed, but the word 'confirmation' should be avoided. Poor
Rabbinate ! The politics of the little community were extremely
complex. What with rabid zealots yearning for the piety of the
good old times, spiritually-minded ministers working with uncomfortable earnestness for a larger Judaism, radicals dropping out,
moderates clamouring for quiet, and schismatics organising new
and tiresome movements, the Rabbinate could scarcely do aught
else than emit sonorous platitudes and remain in office.

And beneath all these surface ruffles was the steady silent drift
of the new generation away from the old landmarks. The synagogue did not attract ; it spoke Hebrew to those whose mother-
tongue was English, its appeal was made through channels which
conveyed nothing to them, it was out of touch with their real lives,
its liturgy prayed for the restoration of sacrifices which they did
not want and for the welfare of Babylonian colleges that had
ceased to exist. The old generation merely believed its beliefs ;
if the new as much as professed them, it was only by virtue of the
old home associations and the inertia of indifference. Practically
it was without religion. The Reform Synagogue, though a centre
of culture and prosperity, was cold, crude, and devoid of magnet-
ism. Half a century of stagnant reform and restless dissolution
had left orthodoxy still the established doxy. For as orthodoxy
evaporated in England, it was replaced by fresh streams from
Russia, to be evaporated and replaced in turn, England acting as
an automatic distillery. Thus the Rabbinate still reigned, though
it scarcely governed either the East End or the West. For the
East End formed a Federation of the smaller synagogues to
oppose the dominance of the United Synagogue, importing a
minister of superior orthodoxy from the Continent, and the *Flag*
had powerful leaders on the great struggle between plutocracy and
democracy, and the voice of Mr. Henry Goldsmith was heard on
behalf of Whitechapel. And the West, in so far as it had spiritual
aspirations, fed them on non-Jewish literature and the higher
thought of the age. The finer spirits, indeed, were groping for a
purpose and a destiny, doubtful even if the racial isolation they
perpetuated were not an anachronism. While the community had
been battling for civil and religious liberty, there had been a uni-
fying, almost spiritualising, influence in the sense of common
injustice, and the question *Cui bono* had been postponed. Drown-
ing men do not ask if life is worth living. Later the Russian per-
secutions came to interfere again with national introspection,
sending a powerful wave of racial sympathy round the earth. In
England a backwash of the wave left the Asmonean society,
wherein, for the first time in history, Jews gathered with nothing
in common save blood—artists, lawyers, writers, doctors—men

who in pre-emancipation times might have become Christians like Heine, but who now formed an effective protest against the popular conceptions of the Jew, and a valuable antidote to the disproportionate notoriety achieved by less creditable types. At the Asmonean society, brilliant free-lances, each thinking himself a solitary exception to a race of bigots, met one another in mutual astonishment. Raphael alienated several readers by uncompromising approval of this characteristically modern movement. Another symptom of the new intensity of national brotherhood was the attempt towards amalgamating the Spanish and German communities, but brotherhood broke down under the disparity of revenue, the rich Spanish sect displaying once again the exclusiveness which has marked its history.

Amid these internal problems, the unspeakable immigrant was an added thorn. Very often the victim of Continental persecution was assisted on to America, but the idea that he was hurtful to native labour rankled in the minds of Englishmen, and the Jewish leaders were anxious to remove it, all but proving him a boon. In despair it was sought to anglicise him by discourses in Yiddish. With the poor alien question was connected the return to Palestine. The Holy Land League still pinned its faith to Zion, and the *Flag* was with it to the extent of preferring the ancient fatherland, as the scene of agricultural experiments, to the South American soils selected by other schemes. It was generally felt that the redemption of Judaism lay largely in a return to the land, after several centuries of less primitive and more degrading occupations. When South America was chosen, Strelitski was the first to counsel the League to co-operate in the experiment, on the principle that half a loaf is better than no bread. But for the orthodox the difficulties of regeneration by the spade were enchanced by the Sabbatical Year Institute of the Pentateuch, ordaining that land must lie fallow in the seventh year. It happened that this septennial holiday was just going on, and the faithful Palestine farmers were starving in voluntary martyrdom. The *Flag* raised a subscription for their benefit. Raphael wished to head the list with twenty pounds, but on the advice of Little Sampson he broke it up into a variety of small amounts spread over several weeks, and attached to imaginary names and initials. Seeing so many other readers contributing, few readers felt called upon to tax themselves. The *Flag* received the ornate thanks of a pleiad of Palestine Rabbis for its contribution of twenty-five guineas, two of which were from Mr. Henry Goldsmith. Gideon, the member for Whitechapel, remained callous to the sufferings of his brethren in the Holy Land. In daily contact with so many diverse interests Raphael's mind widened as imperceptibly as the body grows. He learnt the manners of many men and committees—admired the genuine goodness of some of the Jewish philanthropists and the fluent oratory of all, even while he realised the pettiness of their outlook and their reluctance to face facts. They were timorous, with a dread of decisive action and definitive speech suggesting the deferential, deprecatory corporeal wrigglings of the mediæval Jew. They seemed to keep strict ward over the technical privileges of the different bodies they belong to, and in their capacity of members of the Fiddle-de-dee to quarrel with themselves as members of the Fiddle-de-dum, and to pass votes of condolence or congratulation twice over as members of both. But the more he saw of his race the more he marvelled at the omnipresent ability, being tempted at times to allow truth to the view that Judaism was a successful sociological experiment, the moral and physical training of a chosen race whose very dietary had been religiously regulated.

And even the revelations of the seamy side of human character, which thrust themselves upon the most purblind of editors, were blessings in disguise. The office of the *Flag* was a forcing house for Raphael; many latent thoughts developed into extraordinary maturity. A month of the *Flag* was equal to a year of experience in the outside world. And not even Little Sampson himself was keener to appreciate the humours of the office, when no principle was involved; though what made the sub-editor roar with laughter often made the editor miserable for the day. For compensation Raphael had felicities from which Little Sampson was cut off; gladdened by revelations of earnestness and piety in letters that were merely bad English to the sub-editor.

A thing that set them both laughing occurred on the top of their conversation about the reader who objected to quotations from the Old Testament. A package of four old *Flags* arrived, accompanied by a letter. This was the letter:

'DEAR SIR,
        'Your man called upon me last night, asking for payment for four advertisements of my Passover groceries. But I have changed my mind about them and do not want them, and therefore beg to return the four numbers sent me. You will see I have not opened them or soiled them in any way, so please cancel the claim in your books.
                'Yours truly,
                        'ISAAC WOLLBERG.'

'He evidently thinks the vouchers sent him *are* the advertisements,' screamed Little Sampson.

'But if he is as ignorant as all that, how could he have written the letter?' asked Raphael.

'Oh, it was probably written for him for twopence by the Shalotten Shammos, the begging-letter writer.'

'This is almost as funny as Karlkammer,' said Raphael.

Karlkammer had sent in a long essay on the 'Sabbatical Year Question,' which Raphael had revised and published, with Karlkammer's title at the head and Karlkammer's name at the foot.

Yet, owing to the few rearrangements and inversions of sentences, Karlkammer never indentified it as his own, and was perpetually calling to inquire when his article would appear. He brought with him fresh manuscripts of the article as originally written. He was not the only caller. Raphael was much pestered by visitors on kindly counsel bent or stern exhortation. The sternest were those who had never yet paid their subscriptions. De Haan also kept up proprietorial rights of interference. In private life Raphael suffered much from pillars of the Montagu Samuels type, who accused him of flippancy, and no communal crisis invented by Little Sampson ever equalled the pother and commotion that arose when Raphael incautiously allowed him to burlesque the notorious *Mordecai Josephs* by comically exaggerating its exaggerations. The community took it seriously as an attack upon the race. Mr. and Mrs. Henry Goldsmith were scandalised, and Raphael had to shield Little Sampson by accepting the whole responsibility for its appearance.

'Talking of Karlkammer's article, are you ever going to use up Herman's scientific paper?' asked Little Sampson.

'I'm afraid so,' said Raphael, 'I don't know how we can get out of it. But his eternal *kosher* meat sticks in my throat. We are Jews for the love of God, not to be saved from consumption bacilli. But I won't use it to-morrow ; we have Miss Cissy Levine's tale. It's not half bad. What a pity she has the expenses of her books paid ! If she had to achieve publication by merit, her style might be less slipshod.'

'I wish some rich Jew would pay the expenses of my opera tour,' said Little Sampson ruefully. 'My style of doing the thing would be improved. The people who are backing me up are awfully stingy. Actually buying up battered old helmets for my chorus of Amazons.'

Intermittently the question of the sub-editor's departure for the provinces came up ; it was only second in frequency to his 'victories.' About once a month the preparations for the tour were complete, and he would go about in a heyday of jubilant vocalisation ; then his comic *prima donna* would fall ill or elope, his conductor would get drunk, his chorus would strike, and Little Sampson would continue to sub-edit the *Flag of Judah*.

Pinchas unceremoniously turned the handle of the door and came in. The sub-editor immediately hurried out to get a cup of tea. Pinchas had fastened upon him the responsibility for the omission of an article last week, and had come to believe that he was in league with rival Continental scholars to keep Melchitzedek Pinchas's effusions out of print, and so Little Sampson dared not face the angry savant. Raphael, thus deserted, cowered in his chair. He did not fear death, but he feared Pinchas, and had fallen into the cowardly habit of bribing him lavishly not to fill the paper. Fortunately the poet was in high feather.

'Don't forget the announcement that I lecture at the Club on

Sunday. You see all the efforts of Reb Shemuel, of the Rev. Joseph Strelitski, of the Chief Rabbi, of Ebenezer vid his blue spectacles, of Sampson, of all the phalanx of English Men-of-the Earth, they all fail. Ah, I am a great man.'

'I won't forget,' said Raphael wearily. 'The announcement is already in print.'

'Ah, I love you. You are the best man in the vorld. It is you who have championed me against those who are thirsting for my blood. And now I vill tell you joyful news. There is a maiden coming up to see you ; she is asking in the publisher's office. Oh, such a lovely maiden !'

Pinchas grinned all over his face, and was like to dig his editor in the ribs.

'What maiden ?'

'I do not know, but vai-r-r-y beautiful. Aha, I vill go. Have you not been good to *me* ? But vy come not beaudiful maidens to *me* ?'

'No, no, you needn't go,' said Raphael, getting red.

Pinchas grinned, as one who knew better, and struck a match to rekindle a stump of cigar.

'No, no I go write my lecture ; oh, it vill be a great lecture. You vill announce it in the paper ? You vill not leave it out like Sampson left out my article last week ?'

He was at the door now, with his finger alongside his nose.

Raphael shook himself impatiently, and the poet threw the door wide and disappeared.

For a full minute Raphael dared not look towards the door, for fear of seeing the poet's cajoling head framed in the opening. When he did, he was transfixed to see Esther Ansell's there, regarding him pensively.

His heart beat painfully at the shock ; the room seemed flooded with sunlight.

'May I come in ?' she said, smiling.

CHAPTER X

ESTHER DEFIES THE UNIVERSE

ESTHER wore a neat black mantle, and looked taller and more womanly than usual in a pretty bonnet and a spotted veil. There was a flush of colour in her cheeks, her eyes sparkled. She had walked, in cold sunny weather, from the British Museum (where she was still supposed to be), and the wind had blown loose a little wisp of hair over the small shell-like ear. In her left hand she held a roll of manuscript—it contained her criticisms of the May Exhibitions. Whereby hung a tale.

In the dark days that followed the scene with Levi, Esther's

resolution had gradually formed. The position had become unten-
able. She could no longer remain a *Schnorrer*, abusing the bounty
of her benefactors into the bargain. She must leave the Goldsmiths,
and at once. That was imperative ; the second step could be
thought over when she had taken the first. And yet she postponed taking the first. Once she drifted out of her present sphere,
she could not answer for the future ; could not be certain, for instance, that she would be able to redeem her promise to Raphael
to sit in judgment upon the Academy and other picture galleries
that bloomed in May. At any rate, once she had severed connection with the Goldsmith circle she would not care to renew it, even
in the case of Raphael. No ; it was best to get this last duty off
her shoulders, then to say farewell to him and all the other human
constituents of her brief period of partial sunshine. Besides, the
personal delivery of the precious manuscript would afford her the
opportunity of this farewell to him. With his social remissness, it
was unlikely he would call soon upon the Goldsmiths, and she now
restricted her friendship with Addie to receiving Addie's visits, so
as to prepare for its dissolution.

Addie amused her by reading extracts from Sidney's letters, for
the brilliant young artist had suddenly gone off to Norway the
morning after the *début* of the new Hamlet. Esther felt that it
might be as well if she stayed on to see how the drama of these
two lives developed. These things she told herself in the reaction
from the first impulse of instant flight.

Raphael put down his pipe at the sight of her, and a frank smile
of welcome shone upon his flushed face.

' This is so kind of you ! ' he said. ' Who would have thought
of seeing you here ? I am so glad. I hope you are well. You
look better.' He was wringing her little gloved hand violently as
he spoke.

' I feel better, too, thank you. The air is so exhilarating. I 'm
glad to see you 're still in the land of the living. Addie has told
me of your debauches of work.'

' Addie is foolish. I never felt better. Come inside. Don't be
afraid of walking on the papers, they 're all old.'

' I always heard literary people were untidy, said Esther, smiling.
' *You* must be a regular genius.'

' Well, you see, we don't have many ladies coming here,' said
Raphael deprecatingly, ' though we have plenty of old women.'

' It 's evident you don't, else some of them would go down on
their hands and knees and never get up till this litter was tidied
up a bit.'

' Never mind that now, Miss Ansell. Sit down, won't you ?
You must be tired. Take the editorial chair—allow me a minute.'
He removed some books from it.

' Is that the way you sit on the books sent in for review ? ' She
sat down. ' Dear me ! it 's quite comfortable. You men like
comfort, even the most self-sacrificing. But where is your fighting

editor ? It would be awkward if an aggrieved reader came in and mistook me for the editor, wouldn't it ? It isn't safe for me to remain in this chair !'

'Oh yes, it is ! We've tackled our aggrieved readers for to-day,' he assured her.

She looked curiously round.

'Please pick up your pipe ; it's going out. I don't mind smoke —indeed I don't. Even if I did, I should be prepared to pay the penalty of bearding an editor in his den.'

Raphael resumed his pipe gratefully.

'I wonder, though, you don't set the place on fire,' Esther rattled on, 'with all this mass of inflammable matter about.'

'It is very dry, most of it,' he admitted with a smile.

'Why don't you have a real fire ? It must be quite cold sitting here all day. What's that great ugly picture over there ?'

'That steamer ? It's an advertisement.'

'Heavens ! what a decoration ! I should like to have the criticism of that picture. I've brought you those picture-galleries, you know : that's what I've come for.'

'Thank you ; that's very good of you ! I'll send it to the printers at once.'

He took the roll, and placed it in a pigeon-hole without taking his eyes off her face.

'Why don't you throw that awful staring thing away ?' she asked, contemplating the steamer with a morbid fascination ; 'and sweep away the old papers, and have a few little water-colours hung up, and put a vase of flowers on your desk. I wish I had the control of the office for a week.'

'I wish you had,' he said gallantly. 'I can't find time to think of those things. I am sure you are brightening it up already.'

The little blush on her cheek deepened. Compliment was unwonted with him ; and, indeed, he spoke as he felt. The sight of her seated so strangely and unexpectedly in his own humdrum sanctum, the imaginary picture of her beautifying it and evolving harmony out of the chaos with artistic touches of her dainty hands, filled him with pleasant, tender thoughts such as he had scarce known before. The common-place editorial chair seemed to have undergone consecration and poetic transformation. Surely the sunshine that streamed through the dusty window would for ever rest on it henceforwards. And yet the whole thing appeared fantastic and unreal.

'I hope you are speaking the truth,' replied Esther with a little laugh. 'You need brightening, you old dry-as-dust philanthropist, sitting poring over stupid manuscripts when you ought to be in the country enjoying the sunshine.' She spoke in airy accents, with an under-current of astonishment at her attack of high spirits on an occasion she had designed to be harrowing.

'Why, I haven't *looked* at your manuscript yet,' he retorted gaily, but as he spoke there flashed upon him a delectable vision of blue sea and waving pines with one fair wood-nymph flitting through the trees, luring him on from this musty cell of never-ending work to unknown ecstasies of youth and joyousness. The leafy avenues were bathed in sacred sunlight, and a low magic music thrilled through the quiet air. It was but the dream of a second—the dingy walls closed round him again ; the great ugly steamer, that never went anywhere, sailed on. But the wood-nymph did not vanish ; the sunbeam was still on the editorial chair, lighting up the little face with a celestial halo. And when she spoke again, it was as if the music that thrilled the visionary glades was a reality, too.

'It's all very well, your treating reproof as a jest,' she said more gravely. 'Can't you see that it's false economy to risk a break-down, even if you use yourself purely for others? You're looking far from well. You are overtaxing human strength. Come now, admit my sermon is just. Remember, I speak not as a Pharisee, but as one who made the mistake herself—a fellow-sinner.' She turned her dark eyes reproachfully upon him.

'I—I—don't sleep very well,' he admitted, 'but otherwise I assure you I feel all right.'

It was the second time she had manifested concern for his health. The blood coursed deliciously in his veins ; a thrill ran through his whole form. The gentle, anxious face seemed to grow angelic. Could she really care if his health gave way ? Again he felt a rush of self-pity that filled his eyes with tears. He was grateful to her for sharing his sense of the empty cheerlessless of his existence. He wondered why it had seemed so full and cheery just before.

'And you used to sleep so well,' said Esther slyly, remembering Addie's domestic revelations. 'My stupid manuscript should come in useful.'

'Oh, forgive my stupid joke !' he said remorsefully.

'Forgive mine !' she answered. Sleeplessness is too terrible to joke about. Again I speak as one who knows.'

'Oh, I'm sorry to hear that !' he said, his egoistic tenderness instantly transformed to compassionate solicitude.

'Never mind me—I am a woman and can take care of myself. Why don't you go over to Norway and join Mr. Graham ?'

'That's quite out of the question,' he said, puffing furiously at his pipe. 'I can't leave the paper.'

'Oh, men always say that ! Haven't you let your pipe out ? I don't see any smoke.'

He started and laughed. 'Yes, there's no more tobacco in it.' He laid it down.

'No, I insist on your going on, or else I shall feel uncomfortable. Where's your pouch ?'

He felt all over his pockets. 'It must be on the table.'

She rummaged among the mass of papers. 'Ha ! there are your scissors !' she said scornfully, turning them up. She found the pouch in time and handed it to him. ' I ought to have the management of this office for a day,' she remarked again.

' Well, fill my pipe for me,' he said, with an audacious inspiration. He felt an unreasoning impulse to touch her hand, to smooth her soft cheek with his fingers, and press her eyelids down over her dancing eyes. She filled the pipe, full measure and running over ; he took it by the stem, her warm gloved fingers grazing his chilly bare hand and suffusing him with a delicious thrill.

' Now you must crown your work,' he said. ' The matches are somewhere about.'

She hunted again, interpolating exclamations of reproof at the risk of fire.

' They're safety matches, I think,' he said. They proved to be wax vestas. She gave him a liquid glance of mute reproach that filled him with bliss as overbrimmingly as his pipe had been filled with bird's-eye ; then she struck a match, protecting the flame scientifically in the hollow of her little hand. Raphael had never imagined a wax vesta could be struck so charmingly. She tip-toed to reach the bowl in his mouth, but he bent his tall form and felt her breath upon his face. The volumes of smoke curled up triumphantly, and Esther's serious countenance relaxed in a smile of satisfaction. She resumed the conversation where it had been broken off by the idyllic interlude of the pipe.

' But if you can't leave London, there's plenty of recreation to be had in town. ' I'll wager you haven't yet been to see *Hamlet*, in lieu of the night you disappointed us.'

' Disappointed myself, you mean,' he said, with a retrospective consciousness of folly. ' No, to tell the truth, I haven't been out at all lately. Life is so short.'

' Then, why waste it ? '

' Oh, come, I can't admit I waste it,' he said, with a gentle smile that filled her with a penetrating emotion. ' You mustn't take such material views of life.' Almost in a whisper he quoted, ' " To him that hath the kingdom of God all things shall be added "' ; and went on, ' Socialism is, at least, as important as Shakespeare.'

' Socialism ! ' she repeated. ' Are you a Socialist, then ? '

' Of a kind,' he answered. ' Haven't you detected the cloven hoof in my leaders ? I'm not violent, you know ; don't be alarmed. But I have been doing a little mild propagandism lately in the evenings—Land Nationalisation and a few other things which would bring the world more in harmony with the Law of Moses.'

' What ! do you find Socialism, too, in orthodox Judaism ? '

' It requires no seeking.'

' Well, you're almost as bad as my father, who found everything in the Talmud. At this rate you will certainly convert me soon ; or, at least, I shall, like M. Jourdain, discover I've been orthodox all my life without knowing it.'

'I hope so,' he said gravely. 'But have you Socialistic sympathies?'

She hesitated. As a girl she had felt the crude Socialism which is the unreasoned instinct of ambitious poverty, the individual revolt mistaking itself for hatred of the general injustice. When the higher sphere has welcomed the Socialist, he sees he was but the exception to a contented class. Esther had gone through the second phase, and was in the throes of the third, to which only the few attain.

'I used to be a red-hot Socialist once!' she said. 'To-day I doubt whether too much stress is not laid on material conditions. High thinking is compatible with the plainest living. "The soul is its own place, and can make a heaven of hell, a hell of heaven." Let the people who wish to build themselves lordly treasure-houses do so, if they can afford it; but let us not degrade our ideals by envying them.'

The conversation had drifted into seriousness; Raphael's thoughts reverted to their normal intellectual cast; but he still watched with pleasure the play of her mobile features as she expounded her opinions.

'Ah, yes, that is a nice abstract theory,' he said. 'But what if the mechanism of competitive society works so that thousands don't get even the plainest living? You should just see the sights I have seen, then you would understand why for some time the improvement of the material condition of the masses must be the great problem. Of course, you won't suspect me of underrating the moral and religious considerations?'

Esther smiled almost imperceptibly. The idea of Raphael, who could not see two inches before his nose, telling *her* to examine the spectacle of human misery would have been distinctly amusing, even if her early life had been passed amongst the same scenes as his. It seemed a part of the irony of things and the paradox of fate that Raphael, who had never known cold or hunger, should be so keenly sensitive to the sufferings of others; while she, who had known both, had come to regard them with philosophical tolerance. Perhaps she was destined ere long to renew her acquaintance with them. Well, that would test her theories, at any rate.

'Who is taking material views of life now?' she asked.

'It is by perfect obedience to the Mosaic Law that the kingdom of God is to be brought about on earth,' he answered. 'And in spirit orthodox Judaism is, undoubtedly, akin to Socialism.' His enthusiasm set him pacing the room, as usual, his arms working like the sails of a windmill.

Esther shook her head.

'Well, give me Shakespeare!' she said. 'I had rather see *Hamlet* than a world of perfect prigs!' She laughed at the oddity of her own comparison, and added, still smiling, 'Once upon a time I used to think Shakespeare a fraud. But that was merely because he was an institution. It is a real treat to find one superstition that will stand analysis !'

'Perhaps you will find the Bible turn out like that,' he said hopefully.

'I *have* found it. Within the last few months I have read it right through again—Old and New. It is full of sublime truths, noble apophthegms, endless touches of nature, and great poetry. Our tiny race may well be proud of having given humanity its greatest, as well as its most widely-circulated, books. Why can't Judaism take a natural view of things and an honest pride in its genuine history, instead of building its synagogues on shifting sand ?'

'In Germany—later in America—the reconstruction of Judaism has been attempted in every possible way ; inspiration has been sought, not only in literature, but in archæology, and even in anthropology ; it is these which have proved the shifting sand. You see, your scepticism is not even original.' He smiled a little, serene in the largeness of his faith. His complacency grated upon her. She jumped up.

'We always seem to get into religion, you and I,' she said. 'I wonder why ! It is certain we shall never agree. Mosaism is magnificent, no doubt, but I cannot help feeling Mr. Graham is right when he points out its limitations. Where would the art of the world be if the Second Commandment had been obeyed ? Is there any such thing as an absolute system of morality ? How is it the Chinese have got on all these years without religion ? Why should Jews claim the patent in those moral ideas which you find just as well in all the great writers of antiquity ? Why——' She stopped suddenly, seeing his smile had broadened.

'Which of all these objections am I to answer ?' he asked merrily. 'Some I'm sure you don't mean.'

'I mean all those you can't answer. So please don't try. After all, you're not a professional explainer of the universe that I should heckle you thus.'

'Oh, but I set up to be,' he protested.

'No, you don't. You haven't called me a blasphemer once. I'd better go before you become really professional. I shall be late for dinner.'

'What nonsense ! It is only four o'clock,' he pleaded, consulting an old-fashioned silver watch.

'As late as that !' said Esther in horrified tones. 'Good-bye. Take care to go through my "copy" in case any heresies have filtered into it.'

'Your "copy" ? Did you give it me ?' he inquired.

'Of course I did. You took it from me. Where did you put it ? Oh, I hope you haven't mixed it up with those papers. It'll be a terrible task to find it !' cried Esther excitedly.

'I wonder if I could have put it in the pigeon-hole for copy,' he said. 'Yes ; what luck !'

Esther laughed heartily.

'You seem tremendously surprised to find anything in its right place.'

The moment of solemn parting had come, yet she found herself laughing on. Perhaps she was glad to find the farewell easier than she had foreseen. It had certainly been made easier by the theological passage of arms, which brought out all her latent antagonism to the prejudiced young pietist. Her hostility gave rather a scornful ring to the laugh, which ended with a suspicion of hysteria.

'What a lot of stuff you've written,' he said. 'I shall never be able to get this into one number.'

'I didn't intend you should. It's to be used in instalments, if it's good enough. I did it all in advance, because I'm going away.'

'Going away!' he cried, arresting himself in the midst of an inhalation of smoke. 'Where?'

'I don't know,' she said wearily.

He looked alarm and interrogation.

'I am going to leave the Goldsmiths,' she said. 'I haven't decided exactly what to do next.'

'I hope you haven't quarrelled with them.'

'No, no ; not at all. In fact, they don't even know I am going. I only tell you in confidence. Please don't say anything to anybody. Good-bye. I may not come across you again. So this may be a last good-bye.'

She extended her hand ; he took it mechanically.

'I have no right to pry into your confidence,' he said anxiously, 'but you make me very uneasy.' He did not let go her hand ; the warm touch quickened his sympathy. He felt he could not part with her, and let her drift into Heaven knew what. 'Won't you tell me your trouble?' he went on. 'I am sure it is some trouble. Perhaps I can help you. I should be so glad if you would give me the opportunity.'

The tears struggled to her eyes, but she did not speak. They stood in silence, with their hands still clasped, feeling very near to each other, and yet still so far apart.

'Cannot you trust me?' he asked. 'I know you are unhappy, but I had hoped you had grown cheerfuller of late. You told me so much at our first meeting, surely you might trust me yet a little farther.'

'I have told you enough,' she said at last. 'I cannot any longer eat the bread of charity ; I must go away and try to earn my own living.'

'But what will you do?'

'What do other girls do? Teaching, needlework, anything. Remember, I'm an experienced teacher, and a graduate to boot.'

Her pathetic smile lit up the face with tremulous tenderness.

'But you will be quite alone in the world,' he said, solicitude vibrating in every syllable.

'I am used to being quite alone in the world.'

The phrase threw a flash of light along the backward vista of her life with the Goldsmiths, and filled his soul with pity and yearning.

'But suppose you fail?'

'If I fail——' she repeated, and rounded off the sentence with a shrug.

It was the apathetic, indifferent shrug of Moses Ansell; only his was the shrug of faith in Providence, hers of despair. It filled Raphael's heart with deadly cold, and his soul with sinister forebodings. The pathos of her position seem to him intolerable.

'No, no, this must not be!' he cried, and his hand gripped hers fiercely, as if he were afraid of her being dragged away by main force.

He was terribly agitated; his whole being seemed to be undergoing profound and novel emotions. Their eyes met; in one and the same instant the knowledge broke upon her that she loved him, and that if she chose to play the woman he was hers and life a Paradisian dream. The sweetness of the thought intoxicated her, thrilled her veins with fire. But the next instant she was chilled as by a gray cold fog. The realities of things came back—a whirl of self-contemptuous thoughts blent with a hopeless sense of the harshness of life. Who was she, to aspire to such a match? Had her earlier day-dream left her no wiser than that? The *Schnorrer's* daughter setting her cap at the wealthy Oxford man, forsooth! What would people say? And what would they say if they knew how she had sought him out in his busy seclusion, to pitch a tale of woe and move him by his tenderness of heart to a pity he mistook momentarily for love? The image of Levi came back suddenly; she quivered, reading herself through his eyes. And yet would not his crude view be right—suppress the consciousness as she would in her maiden breast—had she not been urged hither by an irresistible impulse? Knowing what she felt now, she could not realise she had been ignorant of it when she set out. She was a deceitful, scheming little thing. Angry with herself, she averted her gaze from the eyes that hungered for her, though they were yet unlit by self-consciousness; she loosed her hand from his, and, as if the cessation of the contact restored her self-respect, some of her anger passed unreasonably towards him.

'What right have you to say it must not be?' she inquired haughtily. 'Do you think I can't take care of myself, that I need any one to protect me or to help me?'

'No—I—I—only mean——' he stammered in infinite distress, feeling himself somehow a blundering brute.

'Remember I am not like the girls you are used to meet. I have known the worst that life can offer. I can stand alone—yes, and face the whole world. Perhaps you don't know that I wrote *Mordecai Josephs*, the book you burlesqued so mercilessly !'

'*You* wrote it !'

'Yes, I. I am Edward Armitage. Did those initials never strike you? I wrote it, and I glory in it. Though all Jewry cry out the picture is false, I say it is true. So now you know the truth. Proclaim it to all Hyde Park and Maida Vale, tell it to all your narrow-minded friends and acquaintances, and let them turn and rend me. I can live without them or their praise. Too long they have cramped my soul. Now at last I am going to cut myself free—from them and from you and all your petty prejudices and interests. Good-bye for ever !'

She went out abruptly, leaving the room dark and Raphael shaken and dumfounded ; she went down the stairs and into the keen bright air with a fierce exultation at her heart, an intoxicating sense of freedom and defiance. It was over. She had vindicated herself to herself and to the imaginary critics. The last link that bound her to Jewry was snapped ; it was impossible it could ever be reforged. Raphael knew her in her true colours at last. She seemed to herself a Spinoza the race had cast out.

The editor of the *Flag of Judah* stood for some minutes as if petrified ; then he turned suddenly to the litter on his table and rummaged among it feverishly. At last, as with a happy recollection, he opened a drawer. What he sought was there. He started reading *Mordecai Josephs*, forgetting to close the drawer. Passage after passage suffused his eyes with tears ; a soft magic hovered about the nervous sentences; he read her eager little soul in every line. Now he understood. How blind he had been ! How could he have missed seeing ? Esther stared at him from every page. She was the heroine of her own book ; yes, and the hero, too, for he was but another side of herself translated into the masculine. The whole book was Esther, the whole Esther and nothing but Esther, for even the satirical descriptions were but the revolt of Esther's soul against mean and evil things. He turned to the great love scene of the book, and read on and on, fascinated, without getting further than the chapter.

CHAPTER XI

GOING HOME

No need to delay longer ; every need for instant flight. Esther had found courage to confess her crime against the community to Raphael ; there was no seething of the blood to nerve her to face Mrs. Henry Goldsmith. She retired to her own room soon after dinner on the plea (which was not a pretext) of a headache. Then she wrote :

'DEAR MRS. GOLDSMITH,

'When you read this I shall have left your house, never to return. It would be idle to attempt to explain my reasons. I could not hope to make you see through my eyes. Suffice it to say that I cannot any longer endure a life of dependence, and that I feel I have abused your favours by writing that Jewish novel of which you disapprove so vehemently. I never intended to keep the secret from you after publication. I thought the book would succeed and you would be pleased ; at the same time, I dimly felt that you might object to certain things and ask to have them altered, and I have always wanted to write my own ideas, and not other people's. With my temperament, I see now that it was a mistake to fetter myself by obligations to anybody ; but the mistake was made in my girlhood, when I knew little of the world and perhaps less of myself. Nevertheless, I wish you to believe, dear Mrs. Goldsmith, that all the blame for the unhappy situation which has arisen I put upon my own shoulders, and that I have nothing for you but the greatest affection and gratitude for all the kindnesses I have received at your hands. I beg you not to think that I make the slightest reproach against you ; on the contrary, I shall always henceforth reproach myself with the thought that I have made you so poor a return for your generosity and incessant thoughtfulness. But the sphere in which you move is too high for me ; I cannot assimilate with it, and I return, not without gladness, to the humble sphere whence you took me. With kindest regards and best wishes,

'I am,

'Yours ever gratefully,

'ESTHER ANSELL.'

There were tears in Esther's eyes when she finished, and she was penetrated with admiration of her own generosity in so freely admitting Mrs. Goldsmith's and in allowing that her patron got nothing out of the bargain. She was doubtful whether the sentence about the high sphere was satirical or serious. People do not know what they mean almost as often as they do not say it.

Esther put the letter into an envelope and placed it on the open writing-desk she kept on her dressing-table. She then packed a few toilette essentials in a little bag, together with some American photographs of her brother and sisters in various stages of adolescence. She was determined to go back empty-handed as she came, and was reluctant to carry off the few sovereigns of pocket-money in her purse, and hunted up a little gold locket she had received while yet a teacher in celebration of the marriage of a communal magnate's daughter. Thrown aside seven years ago, it now bade fair to be the corner-stone of the temple ; she had meditated pledging it and living on the proceeds till she found work, but when she realised its puny pretensions to cozen pawnbrokers, it flashed upon her that she could always repay Mrs.

Goldsmith the few pounds she was taking away. In a drawer there was a heap of manuscript carefully locked away ; she took it and looked through it hurriedly, contemptuously. Some of it was music, some poetry, the bulk prose. At last she threw it suddenly on the bright fire which good Mary O'Reilly had providentially provided in her room ; then, as it flared up, stricken with remorse, she tried to pluck the sheets from the flames ; only by scorching her fingers and raising blisters did she succeed, and then, with scornful resignation, she instantly threw them back again, warming her feverish hands merrily at the bonfire. Rapidly looking through all her drawers, lest perchance in some stray manuscript she should leave her soul naked behind her, she came upon a forgotten faded rose. The faint fragrance was charged with strange memories of Sidney. The handsome young artist had given it her in the earlier days of their acquaintanceship. To Esther tonight it seemed to belong to a period infinitely more remote than her childhood. When the shrivelled rose had been further crumpled into a little ball and then picked to bits, it only remained to inquire where to go ; what to do she could settle when there. She tried to collect her thoughts. Alas ! it was not so easy as collecting her luggage. For a long time she crouched on the fender and looked into the fire, seeing in it only fragmentary pictures of the last seven years—bits of scenery, great cathedral interiors arousing mysterious yearnings, petty incidents of travel, moments with Sidney, drawing-room episodes, strange passionate scenes with herself as single performer, long silent watches of study and aspiration—like the souls of the burnt manuscripts made visible. Even that very afternoon's scene with Raphael was part of the ' old unhappy far-off things ' that could only live henceforwards in fantastic arcades of glowing coal, out of all relation to future realities. Her new-born love for Raphael appeared as ancient and as arid as the girlish ambitions that had seemed on the point of blossoming when she was transplanted from the Ghetto. That, too, was in the flames—and should remain there.

At last she started up with a confused sense of wasted time, and began to undress mechanically, trying to concentrate her thoughts the while on the problem that faced her. But they wandered back to her first night in the fine house—when a separate bedroom was a new experience and she was afraid to sleep alone, though turned fifteen. But she was more afraid of appearing a great baby, and so no one in the world would ever know what the imaginative little creature had lived down.

In the middle of brushing her hair she ran to the door and locked it, from a sudden dread that she might oversleep herself and some one would come in and see the letter on the writing-desk. She had not solved the problem even by the time she got into bed ; the fire opposite the foot was burning down, but there was a red glow penetrating the dimness. She had forgotten to draw the blind, and she saw the clear stars shining peacefully in the sky. She looked and looked at them, and they led her thoughts away from the problem once more. She seemed to be lying in Victoria Park, looking up with innocent mystic rapture and restfulness at the brooding blue sky. The blood-and-thunder boys' story she had borrowed from Solomon had fallen from her hand and lay unheeded on the grass. Solomon was tossing a ball to Rachel which he had acquired by a colossal accumulation of buttons, and Isaac and Sarah were rolling and wrangling on the grass. Oh, why had she deserted them? What were they doing now, without her mother-care, out and away beyond the great seas ? For weeks together the thought of them had not once crossed her mind ; to-night she stretched her arms involuntarily towards her loved ones, not towards the shadowy figures of reality—scarcely less phantasmal than the dead Benjamin—but towards the childish figures of the past. What happy times they had had together in the dear old garret !

In her strange half-waking hallucination, her outstretched arms were clasped round little Sarah. She was putting her to bed, and the tiny thing was repeating after her—in broken Hebrew—the children's night prayer, ' Suffer me to lie down in peace, and let me rise up in peace. Hear, O Israel, the Lord our God, the Lord is one,' with its unauthorised appendix in baby-English, ' Dod teep me and mate me a dood dirl orways.'

She woke to full consciousness with a start ; her arms chilled, her face wet. But the problem was solved.

She would go back to them—back to her true home, where loving faces waited to welcome her, where hearts were open and life was simple and the weary brain could find rest from the stress and struggle of obstinate questionings of destiny. Life was so simple at bottom ; it was she that was so perversely complex. She would go back to her father, whose naïve, devout face swam glorified upon a sea of tears ; yea, and back to her father's primitive faith like a tired lost child that spies its home at last. The quaint, monotonous cadence of her father's prayers rang pathetically in her ears, and a great light—the light that Raphael had shown her—seemed to blend mystically with the once meaningless sounds. Yea, all things were from Him who created light and darkness, good and evil. She felt her cares falling from her, her soul absorbing itself in the sense of a Divine love—awful, profound, immeasurable—underlying and transcending all things, incomprehensibly satisfying the soul and justifying and explaining the universe. The infinite fret and fume of life seemed like the petulance of an infant in the presence of this restful tenderness diffused through the great spaces. How holy the stars seemed up there in the quiet sky, like so many Sabbath lights shedding visible consecration and blessing !

Yes, she would go back to her loved ones—back from this dainty room, with its white laces and perfumed draperies, back if need be to a Ghetto garret. And in the ecstasy of her abandonment of all worldly things, a great peace fell upon her soul.

In the morning the nostalgia of the Ghetto was still upon her, blent with a passion of martyrdom that made her yearn for a lower social depth than was really necessary. But the more human aspects of the situation were paramount in the gray chillness of a bleak May dawn. Her resolution to cross the Atlantic forthwith seemed a little hasty, and though she did not flinch from it, she was not sorry to remember she had not money enough for the journey. She must perforce stay in London till she had earned it ; meantime she would go back to the districts and the people she knew so well, and accustom herself again to the old ways, the old simplicities of existence.

She dressed herself in her plainest apparel, though she could not help her spring bonnet being pretty. She hesitated between a hat and a bonnet, but decided that her solitary position demanded as womanly an appearance as possible. Do what she would, she could not prevent herself looking exquisitely refined, and the excitement of adventure had lent that touch of colour to her face which made it fascinating. About seven o'clock she left her room noiselessly and descended the stairs cautiously, holding her little black bag in her hand.

'Och, be the holy mother, Miss Esther, phwat a turn ye gave me !' said Mary O'Reilly, emerging unexpectedly from the dining-room and meeting her at the foot of the stairs. 'Phwat's the matther?'

'I'm going out, Mary,' she said, her heart beating violently.

'Sure, an' it's rale purty ye look, Miss Esther ; but it's divil a bit the marnin' for a walk. It looks a raw kind of a day, as if the weather was sorry for bein' so bright yesterday.'

'Oh, but I must go, Mary !'

'Ah, the saints bliss your kind heart !' said Mary, catching sight of the bag. 'Sure, then, it's a charity irrand you're bent on. I mind me how my blissed old masther, Mr. Goldsmith's father—*Olov Hasholom*—who's gone to glory, used to walk to *Shool* in all winds and weathers : sometimes it was five o'clock of a winter's marnin', and I used to git up and make him an iligant cup of coffee before he went to *Selichoth* ; he niver would take milk and sugar in it, becaz that would be atin' belike, poor dear old ginthleman ! Ah, the Holy Vargin be kind to him !'

'And may she be kind to you, Mary !' said Esther. And she impulsively pressed her lips to the old woman's seamed and wrinkled cheek, to the astonishment of the guardian of Judaism. Virtue was its own reward ; for Esther profited by the moment of the loquacious creature's breathlessness to escape. She opened the hall door and passed into the silent street, whose cold pavements seemed to reflect the bleak stony tints of the sky.

For the first few minutes she walked hastily, almost at a run. Then her pace slackened, she told herself there was no hurry, and

she shook her head when a cabman interrogated her. The omnibuses were not running yet. When they commenced, she would
take one to Whitechapel. The signs of awakening labour stirred
her with new emotions—the early milkman with his cans, casual
artisans with their tools, a grimy sweep, a work-girl with a paper
lunch package, an apprentice whistling. Great sleeping houses
lined her path like gorged monsters drowsing vuluptuously. The
world she was leaving behind her grew alien and repulsive, her
heart went out to the patient world of toil. What had she been
doing all these years—amid her books and her music and her
rose-leaves—aloof from realities?

The first 'bus overtook her half-way, and bore her back to the
Ghetto.

The Ghetto was all astir, for it was half-past eight of a workaday
morning. But Esther had not walked a hundred yards before
her breast was heavy with inauspicious emotions. The well-known
street she had entered was strangely broadened. Instead of the
dirty picturesque houses rose an appalling series of artisans'
dwellings, monotonous brick barracks, whose dead, dull prose
weighed upon the spirits. But, as in revenge, other streets,
unaltered, seemed incredibly narrow. Was it possible it could
have taken even her childish feet six strides to cross them, as she
plainly remembered? And they seemed so unspeakably sordid
and squalid. Could she ever really have walked them with light
heart, unconscious of the ugliness? Did the gray atmosphere
that overhung them ever lift, or was it their natural and appropriate mantle? Surely the sun could never shine upon these
slimy pavements, kissing them to warmth and life.

Great magic shops where all things were to be had—peppermints
and cotton, china-faced dolls and lemons—had dwindled into the
front windows of tiny private dwelling-houses; the black-wigged
crones, the greasy, shambling men, were uglier and greasier than
she had ever conceived them. They seemed caricatures of
humanity—scarecrows in battered hats or draggled skirts. But
gradually, as the scene grew upon her, she perceived that, in spite
of the 'model dwellings' builder, it was essentially unchanged.
No vestige of improvement had come over Wentworth Street—the
narrow noisy market street, where serried barrows flanked the
reeking roadway exactly as of old, and where Esther trod on mud
and refuse and babies. Babies! they were everywhere; at the
breasts of unwashed women, on the knees of grandfathers smoking
pipes; playing under the barrows, sprawling in the gutters and
the alleys. All the babies' faces were sickly and dirty, with
pathetic childish prettinesses asserting themselves against the
neglect and the sallowness. One female mite in a dingy tattered
frock sat in an orange box, surveying the bustling scene with a
preternaturally grave expression, and realising literally Esther's
early conception of the theatre.

There was a sense of blankness in the wanderer's heart, of unfamiliarity in the midst of familiarity. What had she in common with all this mean wretchedness, with this semi-barbarous breed of beings? The more she looked, the more her heart sank. There was no flaunting vice, no rowdiness, no drunkenness, only the squalor of an Oriental city without its quaintness and colour. She studied the posters and the shop-windows, and caught old snatches of gossip from the groups in the butchers' shop. All seemed as of yore. And yet here and there the hand of Time had traced new inscriptions. For Baruch Emanuel the hand of Time had written a new placard. It was a mixture of German, bad English and Cockneyese, phonetically spelt in Hebrew letters.

' Mens Solens Und Eelen .	.	.	2/6
Lydies Deeto .	.	.	1/6
Kindersche Deeto	.	.	1/6
Hier wird gemacht			
Aller Hant Sleepers			
Fur Trebbelers			
Zu De Billigsten Preissen.'			

Baruch Emanuel had prospered since the days when he wanted ' lasters and riveters ' without being able to afford them. He no longer gratuitously advertised *Mordecai Schwartz* in envious emulation, for he had several establishments, and owned five two-story houses, and was treasurer of his little synagogue, and spoke of Socialists as an inferior variety of Atheists. Not that all this bourgeoning was to be counted to leather, for Baruch had developed enterprises in all directions, having all the versatility of Moses Ansell without his catholic capacity for failure.

The hand of Time had also constructed a ' working-men's Métropole' almost opposite Baruch Emanuel's shop, and papered its outside walls with moral pictorial posters, headed ' Where have you been to, Thomas Brown ?' ' Mike and his moke,' and so on. Here single-bedded cabins could be had as low as fourpence a night. From the journals in a tobacconist's window Esther gathered that the reading public had increased, for there were importations from New York, both in Jargon and in pure Hebrew, and from a large poster in Yiddish and English, announcing a public meeting, she learnt of the existence of an offshoot of the Holy Land League—' The Flowers of Zion Society'—' established by East End youths for the study of Hebrew and the propagation of the Jewish National Idea.' Side by side with this, as if in ironic illustration of the other side of the life of the Ghetto, was a seeming royal proclamation, headed ' V. R.,' informing the public that by order of the Secretary of State for War a sale of wrought and cast iron, zinc, canvas, tools, and leather, would take place at the Royal Arsenal, Woolwich.

As she wandered on, the great school-bell began to ring ; involuntarily she quickened her step and joined the chattering children's procession. She could have fancied the last ten years a dream. Were they, indeed, other children, or were they not the same that jostled her when she picked her way through this very slush in her clumsy masculine boots? Surely those little girls in lilac print frocks were her class-mates! It was hard to realise that Time's wheel had been whirling on fashioning her to a woman; that, while she had been living and learning, and seeing the manners of men and cities, the Ghetto, unaffected by her experiences, had gone on in the same narrow rut. A new genera-tion of children had arisen to suffer and sport in room of the old, and that was all. The thought overwhelmed her, gave her a new and poignant sense of brute, blind forces; she seemed to catch in this familiar scene of childhood the secret of the gray atmosphere of her spirit. It was here she had, all insensibly, absorbed those heavy vapours that formed the background of her being, a per-manent sombre canvas behind all the iridescent colours of joyous emotion. *What* had she in common with all this mean wretched-ness? Why, everything. This it was with which her soul had intangible affinities, not the glory of sun and sea and forest, 'the palms and temples of the South.'

The heavy vibrations of the bell ceased; the street cleared; Esther turned back and walked instinctively homewards to Royal Street. Her soul was full of the sense of the futility of life; yet the sight of the great shabby house could still give her a chill. Outside the door a wizened old woman, with a chronic sniff, had established a stall for wizened old apples; but Esther passed her by heedless of her stare, and ascended the two miry steps that led to the mud-carpeted passage.

The apple-woman took her for a philanthropist paying a surprise visit to one of the families of the house, and resented her as a spy. She was discussing the meanness of the thing with the pickled-herring dealer next door, while Esther was mounting the dark stairs with the confidence of old habit. She was making automati-cally for the garret, like a somnambulist, with no definite object, morbidly drawn towards the old home. The unchanging musty smells that clung to the staircase flew to greet her nostrils, and at once a host of sleeping memories started to life, besieging her and pressing upon her on every side. After a tumultuous intolerable moment, a childish figure seemed to break from the gloom ahead —the figure of a little girl, with a grave face and candid eyes—a dutiful, obedient, shabby little girl, so anxious to please her school-mistress, so full of craving to learn and to be good and to be loved by God, so audaciously ambitious of becoming a teacher, and so confident of being a good Jewess always. Satchel in hand, the little girl sped up the stairs swiftly, despite her cumbrous, slatternly boots; and Esther, holding her bag, followed her more slowly, as if she feared to contaminate her by the touch of one so weary-worldly-wise, so full of revolt and despair.

All at once Esther sidled timidly towards the balustrade with an instinctive movement, holding her bag out protectingly. The

figure vanished, and Esther awoke to the knowledge that 'Bobby'
was not at his post. Then with a flash came the recollection of
Bobby's mistress—the pale, unfortunate young seamstress she had
so unconscionably neglected. She wondered if she were alive or
dead. A waft of sickly odours surged from below. Esther felt a
deadly faintness coming over her; she had walked far, and nothing
had yet passed her lips since yesterday's dinner, and at this
moment, too, an overwhelming terrifying feeling of loneliness
pressed like an icy hand upon her heart. She felt that in another
instant she must swoon, there, upon the foul landing. She sank
against the door, beating passionately at the panels. It was opened
from within; she had just strength enough to clutch the door-post
so as not to fall. A thin, careworn woman swam uncertainly before
her eyes. Esther could not recognise her, but the plain iron bed,
almost corresponding in area with that of the room, was as of old;
and so was the little round table, with a teapot and a cup and
saucer, and half a loaf standing out amid a litter of sewing, as if
the owner had been interrupted in the middle of breakfast. Stay!
what was that journal resting against the half-loaf as for perusal
during the meal? Was it not the *London Journal*? Again she
looked, but with more confidence, at the woman's face. A wave
of curiosity, of astonishment at the stylishly-dressed visitor,
passed over it, but in the curves of the mouth, in the movement of
the eyebrows, Esther renewed indescribably subtle memories.

'Debby!' she cried hysterically. A great flood of joy swamped
her soul. She was not alone in the world, after all! Dutch
Debby uttered a little startled scream. 'I've come back, Debby,
I've come back!' and the next moment the brilliant girl-graduate
fell fainting into the seamstress's arms.

CHAPTER XII

A SHEAF OF SEQUELS

WITHIN half an hour Esther was smiling pallidly, and drinking
tea out of Debby's own cup, to Debby's unlimited satisfaction.
Debby had no spare cup, but she had a spare chair without a
back, and Esther was of course seated on the other. Her bonnet
and cloak were on the bed.

'And where is Bobby?' inquired the young lady visitor.

Debby's joyous face clouded.

'Bobby is dead,' she said softly; 'he died four years ago come
next *Shevuos*.'

'I'm so sorry,' said Esther, pausing in her tea-drinking with a
pang of genuine emotion. 'At first I was afraid of him, but that
was before I knew him.'

'There never beat a kinder heart on God's earth,' said Debby emphatically ; 'he wouldn't hurt a fly.'

Esther had often seen him snapping at flies, but she could not smile.

'I buried him secretly in the back-yard,' Debby confessed ; 'see ! there, where the paving-stone is loose !'

Esther gratified her by looking through the little back window into the sloppy enclosure where washing hung.   She noticed a cat sauntering quietly over the spot without any of the satisfaction it might have felt had it known it was walking over the grave of a hereditary enemy.

'So I don't feel as if he was far away,' said Debby.   'I can always look out and picture him squatting above the stone instead of beneath it.'

'But didn't you get another ?'

'Oh, how can you talk so heartlessly !'

'Forgive me, dear ! of course you couldn't replace him.   And haven't you had any other friends ?'

'Who would make friends with me, Miss Ansell ?' Debby asked quietly.

'I shall "make out friends" with you, Debby, if you call me that,' said Esther, half laughing, half crying.   'What was it we used to say in school ?   I forget, but I know we used to wet our little fingers in our mouths and jerk them abruptly towards the other party ; that's what I shall have to do with you.'

'Oh well, Esther, don't be cross !   But you do look such a real lady.   I always said you would grow up clever, didn't I, though ?'

'You did, dear, you did.   I can never forgive myself for not having looked you up.'

'Oh, but you had so much to do, I have no doubt !' said Debby magnanimously, though she was not a little curious to hear all Esther's wonderful adventures, and to gather more about the reasons of the girl's mysterious return than had yet been vouch-safed her.   All she had dared to ask was about the family in America.

'Still, it was wrong of me,' said Esther, in a tone that brooked no protest.   'Suppose you had been in want and I could have helped you ?'

'Oh, but you know I never take any help !' said Debby stiffly.

'I didn't know that,' said Esther, touched.   'Have you never taken soup at the Kitchen !'

'I wouldn't dream of such a thing.   Do you ever remember me going to the Board of Guardians ?   I wouldn't go there to be bullied, not if I were starving.   It's only the cadgers who don't want it who get relief.   But, thank God, in the worst seasons I have always been able to earn a crust and a cup of tea.   You see, I am only a small family,' concluded Debby with a sad smile, 'and the less one has to do with other people the better.'

Esther started slightly, feeling a strange new kinship with this lonely soul.

'But surely you would have taken help of me?' she said.

Debby shook her head obstinately.

'Well, I'm not so proud,' said Esther with a tremulous smile, 'for, see, I have come to take help of you!'

Then the tears welled forth, and Debby with an impulsive movement pressed the little sobbing form against her faded bodice, bristling with pin-heads. Esther recovered herself in a moment and drank some more tea.

'Are the same people living here?' she said.

'Not altogether. The Belcovitches have gone up in the world; they live on the first floor now.'

'Not much of a rise that,' said Esther, smiling, for the Belcovitches had always lived on the third floor.

'Oh, they could have gone to a better street altogether,' explained Debby, 'only Mr. Belcovitch didn't like the expense of a van.'

'Then Sugarman the Shadchan must have moved too,' said Esther; 'he used to have the first floor.'

'Yes; he's got the third now. You see, people get tired of living in the same place. Then Ebenezer, who became very famous through writing a book—so he told me—went to live by himself, so they didn't want to be so grand. The back apartment at the top of the house you used once to inhabit,' Debby put it as delicately as she could, 'is vacant. The last family had the brokers in.'

'Are the Belcovitches all well? I remember Fanny married and went to Manchester before I left here.'

'Oh yes, they are all well!'

'What! even Mrs. Belcovitch?'

'She still takes medicine, but she seems just as strong as ever.'

'Becky married yet?'

'Oh no, but she has won two breach of promise cases.'

'She must be getting old.'

'She is a fine young woman, but the young men are afraid of her now.'

'Then they don't sit on the stairs in the morning any more?'

'No; young men seem so much less romantic nowadays,' said Debby, sighing; 'besides, there is one flight less now, and half the stairs face the street door. The next flight was so private——'

'I suppose I shall look in and see them all,' said Esther smiling; 'but tell me, is Mrs. Simons living here still?'

'No.'

'Where, then? I should like to see her; she was so very kind to little Sarah, you know. Nearly all our fried fish came from her.'

'She is dead; she died of cancer; she suffered a great deal.'

'Oh!' Esther put her cup down and sat back with face grown white. 'I am afraid to ask about any one else,' she said at last. 'I suppose the Sons of the Covenant are getting on all right; *they* can't be dead—at least, not all of them.'

'They have split up,' said Debby gravely, 'into two communities. Mr. Belcovitch and the Shalotten Shammos quarrelled about the sale of the *Mitzvahs* at the Rejoicing of the Law two years ago. As far as I could gather, the carrying of the smallest scroll of the Law was knocked down to the Shalotten Shammos for eighteen-pence, but Mr. Belcovitch, who had gone outside a moment, said he had bought up the privilege in advance, to present to Daniel Hyams, who was a visitor, and whose old father had just died in Jerusalem. There was nearly a free fight in the *Shool*. So the Shalotten Shammos seceded with nineteen followers and their wives and set up a rival *Chevrah* round the corner. The other twenty-five still come here. The deserters tried to take Greenberg the Chazan with them, but Greenberg wanted a stipulation that they wouldn't engage an extra Reader to do his work during the High Festivals ; he even offered to do it cheaper if they would let him do all the work, but they wouldn't consent. As a compromise, they proposed to replace him only on the Day of Atonement, as his voice was not agreeable enough for that. But Greenberg was obstinate. Now I believe there is a movement for the Sons of the Covenant to connect their *Chevrah* with the Federation of Minor Synagogues, but Mr. Belcovitch says he won't join the Federation unless the term " Minor " is omitted. He is a great politician now.'

'Ah ! I dare say he reads the *Flag of Judah*,' said Esther, laughing, though Debby recounted all this history quite seriously. 'Do you ever see that paper ? '

'I never heard of it before,' said Debby simply. ' Why should I waste money on new papers when I can always forget the *London Journal* sufficiently ? Perhaps Mr. Belcovitch buys it ; I have seen him with a Yiddish paper. The " hands " say that instead of breaking off suddenly in the middle of a speech, as of old, he sometimes stops pressing for five minutes together to denounce Gideon, the member for Whitechapel, and to say that Mr. Henry Goldsmith is the only possible saviour of Judaism in the House of Commons.'

'Ah, then he does read the *Flag of Judah* ! His English must have improved.'

'I was glad to hear him say that,' added Debby, when she had finished struggling with the fit of coughing brought on by too much monologue, ' because I thought it must be the husband of the lady who was so good to you. I never forgot her name.'

Esther took up the *London Journal* to hide her reddening cheeks.

' Oh, read some of it aloud,' cried Dutch Debby. It 'll be like old times.'

Esther hesitated, a little ashamed of such childish behaviour. But, deciding to fall in for a moment with the poor woman's humour, and glad to change the subject, she read :

' " Soft scents steeped the dainty conservatory in delicious drowsiness. Reclining on a blue silk couch, her wonderful beauty rather revealed than concealed by the soft clinging draperies she wore, Rosaline smiled bewitchingly at the poor young peer, who could not pluck up courage to utter the words of flame that were scorching his lips. The moon silvered the tropical palms, and from the brilliant ball-room were wafted the sweet penetrating strains of the ' Blue Danube' waltz."'

Dutch Debby heaved a great sigh of rapture.

'And you have seen such sights?' she said in awed admiration.

'I have been in brilliant ball-rooms and moonlit conservatories,' said Esther evasively. She did not care to rob Dutch Debby of her ideals by explaining that high life was not all passion and palm trees.

'I am so glad,' said Debby affectionately. 'I have often wished to myself, only a make-believe wish, you know, not a real wish, if you understand what I mean, for of course I know it's impossible. I sometimes sit at that window before going to bed and look at the moon as it silvers the swaying clothes-props, and I can easily imagine they are great tropical palms, especially when the organ is playing round the corner. Sometimes the moon shines straight down on Bobby's tombstone, and then I am glad. Ah, now you're smiling! I know you think me a crazy old thing.'

'Indeed, indeed, dear, I think you are the darlingest creature in the world!' and Esther jumped up and kissed her to hide her emotion. 'But I musn't waste your time,' she said briskly; 'I know you have your sewing to do. It's too long to tell you my story now ; suffice it to say, as the *London Journal* says, that I am going to take a lodging in the neighbourhood. Oh dear, don't make those great eyes ! I want to live in the East End.'

'You want to live here like a princess in disguise; I see.'

'No, you don't, you romantic old darling ! I want to live here like everybody else. I'm going to earn my own living.'

'Oh, but you can never live by yourself.'

'Why not? Now from romantic you become conventional. *You've* lived by yourself.'

'Oh, but I'm different !' said Debby, flushing.

'Nonsense, I'm just as good as you. But if you think it improper'—here Esther had a sudden idea—' come and live with me.'

'What, be your chaperon?' cried Debby in responsive excitement, then her voice dropped again. 'Oh no ! how could I ?'

'Yes, yes, you must,' said Esther eagerly.

'Debby's obstinate shake of the head repelled the idea.

'I couldn't leave Bobby,' she said. After a pause she asked timidly, 'Why not stay here?'

'Don't be ridiculous,' Esther answered. Then she examined the bed. ' Two couldn't sleep here,' she said.

'Oh yes, they could,' said Debby thoughtfully bisecting the blanket with her hand ; 'and the bed's quite clean, or I wouldn't venture to ask you. Maybe it's not so soft as you've been used to.'

Esther pondered ; she was fatigued, and she had undergone too many poignant emotions already to relish the hunt for a lodging. It was really lucky this haven offered itself.

' I 'll stay for to-night, anyhow,' she announced, while Debby's face lit up as with a bonfire of joy. ' To-morrow we 'll discuss matters further ; and now, dear, can I help you with your sewing ? '

' No, Esther, thank you kindly. You see, there 's only enough for one,' said Debby apologetically ; ' to-morrow there may be more. Besides you were never as clever with your needle as your pen. You always used to lose marks for needlework, and don't you remember how you herring-boned the tucks of those petticoats instead of feather-stitching them ? Ha, ha, ha ! I have often laughed at the recollection.'

' Oh, that was only absence of mind !' said Esther, tossing her head in affected indignation. ' If my work isn't good enough for you, I think I 'll go down and help Becky with her machine.'

She put on her bonnet, and not without curiosity descended a flight of stairs and knocked at a door which, from the steady whirr going on behind it, she judged to be that of the workroom.

' Art thou a man or a woman ? ' came in Yiddish the well-remembered tones of the valetudinarian lady.

' A woman,' answered Esther in German.

She was glad she had learned German ; it would be the best substitute for Yiddish in her new old life.

' *Herein !* ' said Mrs. Belcovitch with sentry-like brevity.

Esther turned the handle, and her surprise was not diminished when she found herself, not in the workroom, but in the invalid's bedroom. She almost stumbled over the pail of fresh water, the supply of which was always kept there. A coarse, bouncing, full-figured young woman with frizzly black hair paused with her foot on the treadle of her machine to stare at the new-comer. Mrs. Belcovitch, attired in a skirt and a nightcap, paused aghast in the act of combing out her wig, which hung over an edge of the back of a chair that served as a barber's block. Like the apple-woman, she fancied the apparition a lady philanthropist ; and though she had long ceased to take charity, the old instincts leapt out under the sudden shock.

' Becky, quick, rub my leg with liniment—the thick one,' she whispered in Yiddish.

' It 's only me—Esther Ansell !' cried the visitor.

' What ! Esther !' cried Mrs. Belcovitch ; ' Gott in Himmel !' and, throwing down the comb, she fell in excess of emotion upon Esther's neck. ' I have so often wanted to see you,' cried the sickly-looking little woman, who hadn't altered a wrinkle. ' Often have I said to my Becky, "Where is little Esther ? Gold one sees and silver one sees, but Esther sees one not." Is it not so, Becky ? Oh, how fine you look ! Why, I mistook you for a lady ! You are married—not ? Ah well, you 'll find wooers as thick as the street-dogs ! And how goes it with the father and the family in America ?'

' Excellently,' answered Esther. ' How are you, Becky ?'

Becky murmured something, and the two young women shook

hands. Esther had an olden awe of Becky, and Becky was now
a little impressed by Esther.

'I suppose Mr. Weingott is getting a good living now in Manchester?' Esther remarked cheerfully to Mrs. Belcovitch.

'No, he has a hard struggle,' answered his mother-in-law; 'but
I have seven grandchildren, God be thanked! and I expect an
eighth. If my poor lambkin had been alive now she would have
been a great-grandmother. My eldest grandchild, Hertzel, has a
talent for the fiddle. A gentleman is paying for his lessons, God
be thanked! I suppose you have heard I won four pounds on the
lotter*ee*. You see I have not tried thirty years for nothing. If I
only had my health, I should have little to grumble at. Yes, four
pounds; and what think you I have bought with it? You shall
see it inside. A cupboard with glass doors, such as we left behind
in Poland, and we have hung the shelves with pink paper and
made loops for silver forks to rest in; it makes me feel as if I had
just cut off my tresses. But then I look on my Becky, and I remember that—go thou inside, Becky, my life! Thou makest it
too hard for him. Give him a word while I speak with Esther.'

Becky made a grimace and shrugged her shoulders, but disappeared through the door that led to the real workshop.

'A fine maid,' said the mother, her eyes following the girl with
pride. 'No wonder she is so hard to please! She vexes him so
that he eats out his heart. He comes every morning with a bag
of cakes or an orange or a fat Dutch herring, and now she has
moved her machine to my bedroom, where he can't follow her, the
unhappy youth!'

'Who is it now?' inquired Esther in amusement.

'Shosshi Shmendrik.'

'Shosshi Shmendrik! Wasn't that the young man who married
the Widow Finkelstein?'

'Yes, a very honourable and seemly youth; but she preferred
her first husband,' said Mrs. Belcovitch, laughing, 'and followed
him only four years after Shosshi's marriage. Shosshi has now all
her money—a very seemly and honourable youth.'

'But will it come to anything?'

'It is already settled; Becky gave in two days ago. After all,
she will not always be young. The *Tenaim* will be held next
Sunday. Perhaps you would like to come to see the betrothal
contract signed. The Kovna Maggid will be here, and there will
be rum and cakes to the heart's desire. Becky has Shosshi in
great affection—they are just suited; only she likes to tease, poor
little thing! And then she is so shy. Go in and see them, and
the cupboard with glass doors.'

Esther pushed open the door, and Mrs. Belcovitch resumed her
loving manipulation of the wig.

The Belcovitch workshop was another of the landmarks of the
past that had undergone no change, despite the cupboard with
glass doors and the slight difference in the shape of the room.

The paper roses still bloomed in the corners of the mirror; the cotton-labels still adorned the wall around it; the master's new umbrella still stood unopened in a corner. The 'hands' were other—but, then, Mr. Belcovitch's hands were always changing. He never employed 'union men,' and his hirelings never stayed with him longer than they could help. One of the present batch, a bent, middle-aged man with a deeply-lined face, was Simon Wolf, long since thrown over by the Labour party he had created, and fallen lower and lower till he returned to the Belcovitch work-shop whence he sprang. Wolf, who had a wife and six children, was grateful to Mr. Belcovitch in a dumb, sullen way, remembering how that capitalist had figured in his red rhetoric, though it was an extra pang of martyrdom to have to listen deferentially to Belcovitch's numerous political and economical fallacies. He would have preferred the curter dogmatism of earlier days. Shosshi Shmendrik was chatting quite gaily with Becky, and held her finger-tips cavalierly in his coarse fist without obvious objection on her part. His face was still pimply, but it had lost its painful shyness and its readiness to blush without provocation. His bearing, too, was less clumsy and uncouth. Evidently to love the Widow Finkelstein had been a liberal education to him. Becky had broken the news of Esther's arrival to her father, as was evident from the odour of turpentine emanating from the opened bottle of rum on the central table. Mr. Belcovitch, whose hair was gray now, but who seemed to have as much stamina as ever, held out his left hand—the right was wielding the pressing-iron—without moving another muscle.

'*Nu*, it gladdens me to see you are better off than of old,' he said gravely in Yiddish.

'Thank you. I am glad to see you looking so fresh and healthy,' replied Esther in German.

'You were taken away to be educated, was it not?'

'Yes.'

'And how many tongues do you know?'

'Four or five,' said Esther smiling.

'Four or five!' repeated Mr. Belcovitch, so impressed that he stopped pressing. 'Then you can aspire to be a clerk! I know several firms where they have young women now.'

'Don't be ridiculous, father!' interposed Becky. 'Clerks aren't so grand nowadays as they used to be. Very likely she would turn up her nose at a clerkship.'

'I'm sure I wouldn't,' said Esther.

'There, thou hearest!' said Mr. Belcovitch, with angry satis-faction. 'It is thou who hast too many flies in thy nostrils. Thou wouldst throw over Shosshi if thou hadst thine own way. Thou art the only person in the world who listens not to me. Abroad my word decides great matters. Three times has my name been printed in the *Flag of Judah*. Little Esther had not such a father as thou, but never did she make mock of him.'

'Of course, everybody's better than me,' said Becky petulantly, as she snatched her fingers away from Shosshi.

'No ; thou art better than the whole world,' protested Shosshi Shmendrik, feeling for the fingers.

'Who spoke to thee?' demanded Belcovitch, incensed.

'Who spoke to thee ?' echoed Becky.

And when Shosshi, with empurpled pimples, cowered before both, father and daughter felt allies again, and peace was re-established at Shosshi's expense. But Esther's curiosity was satisfied. She seemed to see the whole future of this domestic group : Belcovitch accumulating gold-pieces, and Mrs. Belcovitch medicine-bottles, till they died and the lucky but hen-pecked Shosshi gathered up half the treasure on behalf of the buxom Becky. Refusing the glass of rum, she escaped.

The dinner, which Debby (under protest) did not pay for, con-sisted of viands from the beloved old cookshop, the potatoes and rice of childhood being supplemented by a square piece of baked meat, likewise knives and forks. Esther was anxious to experience again the magic taste and savour of the once-coveted delicacies. Alas ! the preliminary sniff failed to make her mouth water ; the first bite betrayed the inferiority of the potatoes used. Even so the unattainable tart of infancy mocks the moneyed but dyspeptic adult. But she concealed her disillusionment bravely.

'Do you know,' said Debby, pausing in her voluptuous scouring of the gravy-lined plate with a bit of bread, 'I can hardly believe my eyes. It seems a dream, that you are sitting at dinner with me. Pinch me, will you?'

'You have been pinched enough,' said Esther sadly. Which shows that one can pun with a heavy heart. This is one of the things Shakespeare knew and Dr. Johnson didn't.

In the afternoon Esther went round to Zachariah Square. She did not meet any of the old faces as she walked through the Ghetto, though a little crowd that blocked her way at one point turned out to be merely spectators of an epileptic performance by Meckish. Esther turned away in amused disgust. She wondered whether Mrs. Meckish still flaunted it in satins and heavy neck-laces, or whether Meckish had divorced her, or survived her, or something equally inconsiderate. Hard by the old Ruins (which she found 'ruined' by a railway) Esther was almost run over by an iron hoop driven by a boy with a long swarthy face that irresistibly recalled Malka's.

'Is your grandmother in town ?' she said at a venture.

'Y-e-s,' said the driver wonderingly. 'She is over in her own house.'

Esther did not hasten towards it.

'Your name's Ezekiel, isn't it?'

'Yes,' replied the boy ; and then Esther was sure it was the redeemed son of whom her father had told her.

'Are your mother and father well ?'

'Father's away travelling.' Ezekiel's tone was a little impatient ; his feet shuffled uneasily, itching to chase the flying hoop.

'How's your aunt—your aunt—I forget her name.'

'Aunt Leah? She's gone to Liverpool.'

'What for?'

'She lives there ; she has opened a branch store of granma's business. Who are you?' concluded Ezekiel candidly.

'You won't remember me,' said Esther. 'Tell me—your aunt is called Mrs. Levine, isn't she?'

'Oh yes ! but,' with a shade of contempt, 'she hasn't got any children.'

'How many brothers and sisters have *you* got?' said Esther with a little laugh.

'Heaps. Oh, but you won't see them if you go in ; they're in school, most of 'em.'

'And why aren't you at school?'

The redeemed son became scarlet.

'I've got a bad leg,' ran mechanically off his tongue. Then, administering a savage thwack to his hoop, he set out in pursuit of it. 'It's no good calling on mother?' he yelled back, turning his head unexpectedly. 'She ain't in.'

Esther walked into the Square, where the same big-headed babies were still rocking in swings suspended from the lintels, and and where the same ruddy-faced septuagenarians sat smoking short pipes and playing nap on trays in the sun. From several doorways came the reek of fish-frying. The houses looked ineffably petty and shabby. Esther wondered how she could ever have conceived this a region of opulence, still more how she could ever have located Malka and her family on the very outskirt of the semi-divine classes. But the semi-divine persons themselves had long since shrunk and dwindled.

She found Malka brooding over the fire ; on the side-table was the clothes-brush. The great events of a crowded decade of European history had left Malka's domestic interior untouched. The fall of dynasties, philosophies, and religions had not shaken one china dog from its place. She had not turned a hair of her wig : the black silk bodice might have been the same ; the gold chain at her bosom was. Time had written a few more lines on the tan-coloured equine face, but his influence had been only skin-deep. Everybody grows old ; few people grow. Malka was of the majority.

It was only with difficulty that she recollected Esther, and she was visibly impressed by the young lady's appearance.

'It's very good of you to come and see an old woman,' she said in her mixed dialect, which skipped irresponsibly from English to Yiddish and back again. It's more than my own *Kinder* do. I wonder they let you come across and see me.'

'I haven't been to see them yet,' Esther interrupted.

'Ah, that explains it,' said Malka with satisfaction. 'They'd have told you, "Don't go and see the old woman ; she's *meshuggah* ; she ought to be in the asylum. I bring children into the world, and buy them husbands and businesses and bedclothes, and this is my profit. The other day my Milly—the impudent face ! I would have boxed her ears if she hadn't been suckling Nathaniel ! Let her tell me again that ink isn't good for the wringworm, and my five fingers shall leave a mark on her face worse than any of Gabriel's ringworms. But I have washed my hands of her—she can go her way, and I 'll go mine. I 've taken an oath I 'll have nothing to do with her and her children—no, not if I live a thousand years. It 's all through Milly's ignorance she has had such heavy losses.'

'What ! Mr. Phillips's business been doing badly ? I 'm so sorry.'

'No, no ! my family never does bad business. It 's my Milly's children. She lost two. As for my Leah, God bless her ! she 's been more unfortunate still. I always said that old beggar-woman had the evil-eye ! I sent her to Liverpool with her Sam.'

'I know,' murmured Esther.

'But she is a good daughter. I wish I had a thousand such ! She writes to me every week, and my little Ezekiel writes back— English they learn them in that heathen school,' Malka interrupted herself sarcastically ; 'and it was I who had to learn him to begin a letter properly, with—" I write you these few lines, hoping to find you in good health as, thank God, it leaves me at present." He used to begin anyhow.'

She came to a stop, having tangled the thread of her discourse, and bethought herself of offering Esther a peppermint. But Esther refused, and bethought herself of inquiring after Mr. Birnbaum.

'My Michael is quite well, thank God !' said Malka, 'though he is still pigheaded in business matters ! He buys so badly, you know—gives a hundred pounds for what 's not worth twenty.'

'But you said business was all right ?'

'Ah, that 's different. Of course he sells at a good profit, thank God ! If I wanted to provoke Providence, 'I could keep my carriage like any of your grand West-End ladies. But that doesn't make him a good buyer. And the worst of it is he always thinks he has got a bargain. He won't listen to reason at all,' said Malka, shaking her head dolefully. 'He might be a child of mine instead of my husband. If God didn't send him such luck and blessing we might come to want bread, coal, and meat tickets ourselves, instead of giving them away. Do you know, I found out that Mrs. Isaacs, across the Square, only speculates her guinea in the drawings to give away the tickets she wins to her poor relations, so that she gets all the credit of charity and her name in the papers while saving the money she 'd have to give to her poor relations all the same. Nobody can say I give my tickets to my poor relations. You should just see how much my Michael vows away at *Shool* ! He 's been *Parnass* for the last twelve years straight off, all the members respect him so much ; it isn't often you see a business man with such fear of Heaven. Wait ! my Ezekiel will be *Bar-mitzvah* in a few years ; then you shall see what I will do for that *Shool*. You shall see what an example of *Yiddishkeit* I will give to a *link* generation. Mrs. Benjamin, of the Ruins, purified her knives and forks for Passover by sticking them between the boards of the floor. Would you believe, she didn't make them red-hot first ! I gave her a bit of my mind. She said she forgot. But not she ! She 's no cat's head. She 's a regular Christian, that 's what she is. I shouldn't wonder if she becomes one like that blackguard David Brandon. I always told my Milly he was not the sort of person to allow across the threshold. It was Sam Levine who brought him. You see what comes of having the son of a proselyte in the family. Some say Reb Shemuel's daughter narrowly escaped being engaged to him. But that story has a beard already. I suppose it 's the sight of you brings up *Olov Hasholom* times. Well, and how are you ?' she concluded abruptly, becoming suddenly conscious of imperfect courtesy.

' Oh, I 'm very well, thank you,' said Esther.

' Ah, that 's right. You 're looking very well, *imbeschreer*— quite a grand lady. I always knew you 'd be one some day. There was your poor mother—peace be upon him ! She went and married your father, though I warned her he was a *Schnorrer* and only wanted her because she had a rich Family ; he 'd have sent you out with matches if I hadn't stepped in. I remember saying to him, "That little Esther has Aristotle's head, let her learn all she can ; as sure as I stand here she will grow up to be a lady : I shall have no need to be ashamed of owning her for a cousin." He was not so pigheaded as your mother, and you see the result.'

She surveyed the result with an affectionate smile, feeling genuinely proud of her share in its production.

' If my Ezekiel were only a few years older !' she added musingly.

' Oh, but I am not a great lady,' said Esther, hastening to disclaim false pretensions to the hand of the hero of the hoop ; ' I 've left the Goldsmiths, and come back to live in the East End.'

' What !' said Malka, ' left the West End !'

Her swarthy face grew darker ; the skin about her black eyebrows was wrinkled with wrath.

' Are you *meshuggah* ?' she asked after an awful silence.   ' Or have you, perhaps, saved up a tidy sum of money ?'

Esther flushed and shook her head.

' Then it 's no use coming to me. I 'm not a rich woman, far from it, and I have been blessed with *Kinder* who are helpless without me. It 's as I always said to your father.   "Méshe," I said, "you 're a *Schnorrer*, and your children 'll grow up *Schnorrers*." '

Esther turned white, but the dwindling of Malka's semi-divinity had diminished the old woman's power of annoying her.

'I want to earn my own living,' she said, with a smile that was almost contemptuous. 'Do you call that being a *Schnorrer*?'

'Don't argue with me. You're just like your poor mother— peace be upon him!' cried the irate old woman. 'You God's fool! you were provided for in life, and you have no right to come upon the Family.'

'But isn't it *schnorring* to be dependent on strangers?' inquired Esther with bitter amusement.

'Don't stand there with your impudence-face!' cried Malka, her eyes blazing fire. 'You know as well as I do that a *Schnorrer* is a person you give sixpences to. When a rich family takes in a motherless girl like you and clothes her and feeds her, why, it's mocking Heaven to run away and want to earn your own living! Earn your living! Pooh! what living can you earn, you with your gloves? You're all by yourself in the world now—your father can't help you any more. He did enough for you when you were little, keeping you at school when you ought to have been out selling matches. You'll starve and come to me, that's what you'll do.'

'I may starve, but I'll never come to you,' said Esther, now really irritated by the truth in Malka's words. What living, indeed could she earn! She turned her back haughtily on the old woman, not without a recollection of a similar scene in her childhood. History was repeating itself on a smaller scale than seemed consistent with its dignity. When she got outside she saw Milly in conversation with a young lady at the door of her little house, diagonally opposite. Milly had noticed the strange visitor to her mother, for the rival camps carried on a system of espionage from behind their respective gauze blinds, and she had come to the door to catch a better glimpse of her when she left. Esther was passing through Zachariah Square without any intention of recognising Milly. The daughter's flaccid personality was not so attractive as the mother's; besides, a visit to her might be construed into a mean revenge on the old woman. But as if in response to a remark of Milly's, the young lady turned her face to look at Esther, and then Esther saw that it was Hannah Jacobs. She felt hot and uncomfortable, and half reluctant to renew acquaintance with Levi's family; but with another impulse she crossed over to the group and went through the inevitable formulæ. Then, refusing Milly's warm-hearted invitation to have a cup of tea, she shook hands and walked away.

'Wait a minute, Miss Ansell,' said Hannah. 'I'll come with you.'

Milly gave her a shilling with a facetious grimace, and she rejoined Esther.

'I'm collecting money for a poor family of *Greeners* just landed,' she said. 'They had a few roubles, but they fell among the usual sharks at the docks, and the cabman took all the rest of their money to drive them to the Lane. I left them all crying and rocking themselves to and fro in the street while I ran round to collect a little to get them a lodging.'

' Poor things,' said Esther.

'Ah, I can see you 've been away from Jews,' said Hannah, smiling. ' In the olden days you would have said *Achi nebbich.*'

' Should I ? ' said Esther smiling in return, and beginning to like Hannah. She had seen very little of her in those olden days, for Hannah had been an adult and well-to-do as long as Esther could remember ; it seemed amusing now to walk side by side with her in perfect equality and apparently little younger. For Hannah's appearance had not aged perceptibly, which was, perhaps, why Esther recognised her at once. She had not become angular like her mother, nor coarse and stout like other mothers. She remained slim and graceful, with a virginal charm of expression. But the pretty face had gained in refinement ; it looked earnest, almost spiritual, telling of suffering and patience, not unblent with peace.

Esther silently extracted half a crown from her purse and handed it to Hannah.

' I didn't mean to ask you, indeed I didn't,' said Hannah.

' Oh, I am glad you told me,' said Esther tremulously.

The idea of *her* giving charity, after the account of herself she had just heard, seemed ironical enough. She wished the transfer of the coin had taken place within eyeshot of Malka, then dismissed the thought as unworthy.

' You 'll come in and have a cup of tea with us, won't you, after we 've lodged the *Greeners* ? ' said Hannah. ' Now don't say no. It 'll brighten up my father to see Reb Moshé's little girl.'

Esther tacitly assented.

' I heard of all of you recently,' she said, when they had hurried on a little further. ' I met your brother at the theatre.'

Hannah's face lit up.

' How long was that ago ? ' she inquired anxiously.

' I remember exactly. It was the night before the first *Seder* night.'

' Was he well ? '

' Perfectly.'

' Oh, I am so glad.'

She told Esther of Levi's strange failure to appear at the annual family festival. ' My father went out to look for him. Our anxiety was intolerable. He did not return till half-past one in the morning. He was in a terrible state. "Well," we asked, " have you seen him ? " " I have seen him," he answered. " He is dead." '

Esther grew pallid. Was this the sequel to the strange episode in Mr. Henry Goldsmith's library ?

' Of course he wasn't really dead,' pursued Hannah to Esther's relief. ' My father would hardly speak a word more, but we gathered he had seen him doing something very dreadful, and that henceforth Levi would be dead to him. Since then we dare not speak his name. Please don't refer to him at tea. I went to his rooms on the sly a few days afterwards, but he had left then, and since then I haven't been able to hear anything of him. Sometimes I fancy he's gone off to the Cape.'

'More likely to the provinces with a band of strolling players. He told me he thought of throwing up the law for the boards, and I know you cannot make a beginning in London.'

'Do you think that's it?' said Hannah, looking relieved in her turn.

'I feel sure that's the explanation, if he's not in London. But what in Heaven's name can your father have seen him doing?'

'Nothing very dreadful, depend upon it,' said Hannah, a slight shade of bitterness crossing her wistful features. 'I know he's inclined to be wild, and he should never have been allowed to get the bit between his teeth ; but I dare say it was only some ceremonial crime Levi was caught committing.'

'Certainly ; that would be it,' said Esther. He confessed to me that he was very *link*. Judging by your tone, you seem rather inclined that way yourself,' she said, smiling and a little surprised.

'Do I?' I don't know,' said Hannah simply. 'Sometimes I think I'm very *froom*.'

'Surely you know what you are?' persisted Esther.

Hannah shook her head.

'Well, you know whether you believe in Judaism or not?'

'I don't know what I believe. I do everything a Jewess ought to do, I suppose. And yet, oh, I don't know.'

Esther's smile faded ; she looked at her companion with fresh interest. Hannah's face was full of brooding thought, and she had unconsciously come to a standstill.

'I wonder whether anybody understands herself,' she said reflectively. Do you?'

Esther flushed at the abrupt question without knowing why.

'I—I don't know,' she stammered.

'No, I don't think anybody does, quite,' Hannah answered. 'I feel sure I don't ; and yet—yes, I do. I must be a good Jewess ; I must believe my life.'

Somehow the tears came into her eyes ; her face had the look of a saint. Esther's eyes met hers in a strange subtle glance ; then their souls were knit. They walked on rapidly.

'Well, I do hope you'll hear from him soon,' said Esther.

'It's cruel of him not to write,' replied Hannah, knowing she meant Levi ; he might easily send me a line in a disguised hand. But then, as Miriam Hyams always says, brothers are so selfish.'

'Oh, how is Miss Hyams? I used to be in her class.'

'I could guess that from your still calling her Miss,' said Hannah with a gentle smile.

'Why, is she married?'

'No, no ; I don't mean that. She still lives with her brother and his wife ; he married Sugarman the Shadchan's daughter, you know.'

' Bessie, wasn't it ? '

' Yes ; they are a devoted couple, and I suspect Miriam is a little jealous ; but she seems to enjoy herself, any way. I don't think there is a piece at the theatres she can't tell you about, and she makes Daniel take her to all the dances going.'

' Is she still as pretty ? ' asked Esther. ' I know all her girls used to rave over her and throw her in the faces of girls with ugly teachers. She certainly knew how to dress.'

' She dresses better than ever,' said Hannah evasively.

' That sounds ominous,' observed Esther laughingly.

' Oh, she 's good-looking enough ! Her nose seems to have turned up more ; but perhaps that 's an optical illusion ; she talks so sarcastically nowadays that I seem to see it.' Hannah smiled a little. ' She doesn't think much of Jewish young men. By the way, are you engaged yet, Esther ? '

' What an idea ! ' murmured Esther, blushing beneath her spotted veil.

' Well, you 're very young,' said Hannah, glancing down at the smaller figure with a sweet matronly smile.

' I shall never marry,' Esther said in low tones.

' Don't be ridiculous, Esther ! There 's no happiness for a woman without it. You needn't talk like Miriam Hyams—at least, not yet. Oh yes, I know what you 're thinking——'

' No, I'm not,' faintly protested Esther.

' Yes, you are,' said Hannah, smiling at the paradoxical denial. ' But who 'd have *me* ? Ah, here are the *Greeners* ! ' and her smile softened to angelic tenderness.

It was a frouzy, unsightly group that sat on the pavement, surrounded by a semi-sympathetic crowd—the father in a long grimy coat ; the mother covered, as to her head, with a shawl, which also contained the baby. But the elders were *naïvely* childish, and the children uncannily elderly ; and something in Esther's breast seemed to stir with a strange sense of kinship. The race instinct awoke to consciousness of itself. Dulled by contact with cultured Jews, transformed almost to repulsion by the spectacle of the coarsely prosperous, it leapt into life at the appeal of squalor and misery. In the morning the Ghetto had simply chilled her ; her heart had turned to it as to a haven, and the reality was dismal. Now that the first ugliness had worn off, she felt her heart warming. Her eyes moistened. She thrilled from head to foot with the sense of a mission—of a niche in the temple of human service which she had been predestined to fill. Who could comprehend as she these stunted souls, limited in all save suffering ? Happiness was not for her ; but service remained. Penetrated by the new emotion, she seemed to herself to have found the key to Hannah's holy calm.

With the money now in hand, the two girls sought a lodging for the poor waifs. Esther suddenly remembered the empty back-garret in No. 1 Royal Street, and here, after due negotiations with the pickled-herring dealer next door, the family was installed. Esther's emotions at the sight of the old place were poignant ; happily the bustle of installation, of laying down a couple of mattresses, of borrowing Dutch Debby's tea-things, and of getting ready a meal, alloyed their intensity. That little figure with the masculine boots showed itself but by fits and flashes. But the strangeness of the episode formed the undercurrent of all her thoughts ; it seemed to carry to a climax the irony of her initial gift to Hannah.

Escaping from the blessings of the *Greeners*, she accompanied her new friend to Reb Shemuel's. She was shocked to see the change in the venerable old man ; he looked quite broken-up. But he was chivalrous as of yore ; the vein of quiet humour was still there, though his voice was charged with gentle melancholy. The Rebbitzin's nose had grown sharper than ever ; her soul seemed to have fed on vinegar. Even in the presence of a stranger, the Rebbitzin could not quite conceal her dominant thought. It hardly needed a woman to divine how it fretted Mrs. Jacobs that Hannah was an old maid ; it needed a woman like Esther to divine that Hannah's renunciation was voluntary ; though even Esther could not divine her history, nor understand that her mother's daily nagging was the greater because the pettier part of her martyrdom.

They all jumbled themselves into grotesque combinations, the things of to-day and the things of endless yesterdays, as Esther slept in the narrow little bed next to Dutch Debby, who squeezed herself into the wall, pretending to revel in exuberant spaciousness. It was long before she could get to sleep. The excitement of the day had brought on her headache ; she was depressed by restriking the courses of so many narrow lives ; the glow of her new-found mission had already faded in the thought that she was herself a pauper, and she wished she had let the dead past lie in its halo, not peered into the crude face of reality. But at bottom she felt a subtle melancholy joy in understanding herself at last, despite Hannah's scepticism, in penetrating the secret of her pessimism, in knowing herself a Child of the Ghetto.

And yet Pesach Weingott played the fiddle merrily enough when she went to Becky's engagement-party in her dreams, and galoped with Shosshi Shmendrik, disregarding the terrible eyes of the bride to be ; when Hannah, wearing an aureole like a bridal veil, paired off with Meckish, frothing at the mouth with soap, and Mrs. Belcovitch, whirling a medicine bottle, went down the middle on a pair of huge stilts, one a thick one and one a thin one, while Malka spun round like a teetotum, throwing Ezekiel in long-clothes through a hoop ; what time Moses Ansell waltzed superbly with the dazzling Addie Leon, quite cutting out Levi and Miriam

Hyams, and Raphael awkwardly twisted the Widow Finkelstein to the evident delight of Sugarman the Shadchan, who had effected the introduction. It was wonderful how agile they all were, and how dexterously they avoided treading on her brother Benjamin, who lay unconcernedly in the centre of the floor taking assiduous notes in a little copy-book for incorporation in a great novel, while Mrs. Henry Goldsmith stooped down to pat his brown hair patronisingly.

Esther thought it very proper of the grateful *Greeners* to go about offering the dancers rum from Dutch Debby's tea-kettle, and very selfish of Sidney to stand in a corner refusing to join in the dance and making cynical remarks about the whole thing for the amusement of the earnest little figure she had met on the stairs.

CHAPTER XIII

THE DEAD MONKEY AGAIN

ESTHER woke early, little refreshed. The mattress was hard, and in her restricted allowance of space she had to deny herself the luxury of tossing and turning lest she should arouse Debby. To open one's eyes on a new day is not pleasant when situations have to be faced. Esther felt this disagreeable duty could no longer be shirked. Malka's words rang in her ears. How, indeed, could she earn a living? Literature had failed her; with journalism she had no point of contact save the *Flag of Judah*, and that journal was out of the question. Teaching—the last resort of the hopeless—alone remained. Maybe even in the Ghetto there were parents who wanted their children to learn the piano ; and who would find Esther's mediocre digital ability good enough. She might teach as of old in an elementary school. But she would not go back to her own—all the human nature in her revolted at the thought of exposing herself to the sympathy of her former colleagues. Nothing was to be gained by lying sleepless in bed, gazing at the discoloured wall-paper and the forlorn furniture. She slipped out gently and dressed herself, the absence of any apparatus for a bath making her heart heavier with reminders of the realities of poverty. It was not easy to avert her thoughts from her dainty bedroom of yesterday. But she succeeded ; the cheerlessness of the little chamber turned her thoughts backwards to the years of girlhood, and when she had finished dressing she almost mechanically lit the fire and put the kettle to boil. Her childish dexterity returned, unimpaired by disuse. When Debby awoke, she awoke to a cup of tea ready for her to drink in bed— an unprecedented luxury which she received with infinite consternation and pleasure.

'Why, it's like the duchesses who have lady's-maids,' she said, 'and read French novels before getting up.' To complete the picture, her hand dived underneath the bed and extracted a *London Journal* at the risk of upsetting the tea. 'But it's you who ought to be in bed, not me.'

'I've been a sluggard too often,' laughed Esther, catching the contagion of good spirits from Debby's radiant delight. Perhaps the capacity for simple pleasures would come back to her, too.

At breakfast they discussed the situation.

'I'm afraid the bed's too small,' said Esther, when Debby kindly suggested a continuance of hospitality.

'Perhaps I took up too much room,' said the hostess.

'No, dear; you took up too little. We should have to have a wider bed, and, as it is, the bed is almost as big as the room.'

'There's the back-garret overhead! It's bigger, and it looks on the back-yard just as well. I wouldn't mind moving there,' said Debby, 'though I wouldn't let old Guggenheim know that I value the view of the back-yard, or else he'd raise the rent.'

'You forget the *Greeners* who moved in yesterday.'

'Oh, so I do!' answered Debby with a sigh.

'Strange,' said Esther musingly, 'that I should have shut myself out of my old home.'

The postman's knuckles rapping at the door interrupted her reflections. In Royal Street the poor postmen had to mount to each room separately; fortunately the tenants got few letters. Debby was intensely surprised to get one.

'It isn't for me at all,' she cried at last, after a protracted examination of the envelope; 'it's for you, care of me.'

'But that's stranger still,' said Esther. 'Nobody in the world knows my address.'

The mystery was not lessened by the contents. There was simply a blank sheet of paper, and when this was unfolded a half-sovereign rolled out. The postmark was Houndsditch. After puzzling herself in vain, and examining at length the beautiful copy-book penmanship of the address, Esther gave up the enigma. But it reminded her that it would be advisable to apprise her publishers of her departure from the old address, and to ask them to keep any chance letter till she called. She betook herself to their office, walking. The day was bright, but Esther walked in gloom, scarcely daring to think of her position. She entered the office, apathetically hopeless. The junior partner welcomed her heartily.

'I suppose you've come about your account,' he said. 'I have been intending to send it you for some months, but we are so busy bringing out new things before the dead summer season comes on.' He consulted his books. 'Perhaps you would rather not be bothered,' he said, with a formal statement. I have it all clearly here—the book's been doing fairly well—let me write you a cheque at once!'

She murmured assent, her cheeks blanching, her heart throbbing with excitement and surprise.

'There you are—sixty-two pounds ten,' he said. 'Our profits are just one hundred and twenty-five. If you'll endorse it, I'll send a clerk to the bank round the corner and get it cashed for you at once.'

The pen scrawled an agitated autograph that would not have been accepted at the foot of a cheque, if Esther had had a banking account of her own.

'But I thought you said the book was a failure,' she said.

'So it was,' he answered cheerfully, 'so it was at first. But gradually, as its nature leaked out, the demand increased. I understand from Mudie's that it was greatly asked for by their Jewish clients. You see, when there's a run on a three-volume book, the profits are pretty fair. I believed in it myself, or I should never have given you such good terms nor printed five hundred copies. I shouldn't be surprised if we find ourselves able to bring it out in one-volume form in the autumn. We shall always be happy to consider any further work of yours; something on the same lines I should recommend.'

The recommendation did not convey any definite meaning to her at the moment. Still in a pleasant haze, she stuffed the twelve five-pound notes and the three gold-pieces into her purse, scribbled a receipt, and departed. Afterwards the recommendation rang mockingly in her ears. She felt herself sterile, written out already. As for writing again on the same lines, she wondered what Raphael would think if he knew of the profits she had reaped by bespattering his people. But there! Raphael was a prig like the rest. It was no use worrying about *his* opinions. Affluence had come to her—that was the one important and exhilarating fact. Besides, had not the hypocrites really enjoyed her book? A new wave of emotion swept over her—again she felt strong enough to defy the whole world.

When she got 'home,' Debby said, 'Hannah Jacobs called to see you.'

'Oh, indeed; what did she want?'

'I don't know, but from something she said I believe I can guess who sent the half-sovereign.'

'Not Reb Shemuel?' said Esther, astonished.

'No, your cousin Malka. It seems that she saw Hannah leaving Zachariah Square with you, and so went to her house last night to get your address.'

Esther did not know whether to laugh or be angry; she compromised by crying. People were not so bad, after all, nor the fates so hard to her. It was only a little April shower of tears, and soon she was smiling and running upstairs to give the half-sovereign to the *Greeners*. It would have been ungracious to return it to Malka, and she purchased all the luxury of doing good, including the effusive benedictions of the whole family, on terms usually obtainable only by professional almoners.

Then she told Debby of her luck with the publishers. Profound was Debby's awe at the revelation that Esther was able to write stories equal to those in the *London Journal*. After that Debby gave up the idea of Esther living or sleeping with her ; she would as soon have thought of offering a share of her bed to the authoresses of the tales under it. Debby suffered scarce any pang when her one-night companion transferred herself to Reb Shemuel's.

For it was to suggest this that Hannah had called. The idea was her father's ; it came to him when she told him of Esther's strange position. But Esther said she was going to America forthwith, and she only consented on condition of being allowed to pay for her keep during her stay. The haggling was hard, but Esther won. Hannah gave up her room to Esther, and removed her own belongings to Levi's bedroom, which, except at Festival seasons, had been unused for years, though the bed was always kept ready for him. Latterly the women had had to make the bed from time to time, and air the room, when Reb Shemuel was at synagogue. Esther sent her new address to her brothers and sisters, and made inquiries as to the prospects of educated girls in the States. In reply she learnt that Rachel was engaged to be married. Her correspondents were too taken up with this gigantic fact to pay satisfactory attention to her inquiries. The old sense of protecting motherhood came back to Esther when she learnt the news. Rachel was only eighteen, but at once Esther felt middle-aged. It seemed of the fitness of things that she should go to America and resume her interrupted maternal duties. Isaac and Sarah were still little more than children, perhaps they had not yet ceased bickering about their birthdays. She knew her little ones would jump for joy, and Isaac still volunteer sleeping accommodation in his new bed, even though the necessity for it had ceased. She cried when she received the cutting from the American Jewish paper ; under other circumstances she would have laughed. It was one of a batch headed ' Personals,' and ran : ' Sam Wiseberg, the handsome young drummer of Cincinnati, has become engaged to Rachel Ansell, the fair eighteen-year-old type-writer and daughter of Moses Ansell, a well-known Chicago Hebrew. Life's sweetest blessings on the pair ! The marriage will take place in the Fall.' Esther dried her eyes and determined to be present at the ceremony. It is so grateful to the hesitant soul to be presented with a landmark. There was nothing to be gained now by arriving before the marriage ; nay, her arrival just in time for it would clench the festivities. Meantime she attached herself to Hannah's charitable leading-strings, alternately attracted to the Children of the Ghetto by their misery, and repulsed by their failings. She seemed to see them now in their true perspective, correcting the vivid impressions of childhood by the insight

born of wider knowledge of life. The accretion of pagan superstition was greater than she had recollected. Mothers averted
fever by a murmured charm and an expectoration, children in new
raiment carried bits of coal or salt in their pockets to ward off the
evil-eye. On the other hand, there was more resourcefulness,
more pride of independence. Her knowledge of Moses Ansell
had misled her into too sweeping a generalisation. And she was
surprised to realise afresh how much illogical happiness flourished
amid penury, ugliness, and pain. After school-hours the muggy
air vibrated with the joyous laughter of little children, tossing their
shuttlecocks, spinning their tops, turning their skipping-ropes,
dancing to barrel-organs or circling hand-in-hand in rings to the
sound of the merry traditional chants of childhood. Esther often
purchased a pennyworth of exquisite pleasure by enriching some
sad-eyed urchin. Hannah (whose own scanty surplus was fortunately augmented by an anonymous West-End Reform Jew who
employed her as his agent) had no prepossessions to correct ; no
pendulum-oscillations to distract her, no sentimental illusions to
sustain her. She knew the Ghetto as it was ; neither expected
gratitude from the poor, nor feared she might 'pauperise them,'
knowing that the poor Jew never exchanges his self-respect for
respect for his benefactor, but takes by way of rightful supplement
to his income. She did not drive families into trickery, like the
ladies of the West, by being horrified to find them eating meat.
If she presided at a stall at a charitable sale of clothing, she was
not disheartened if articles were snatched from under her hand,
nor did she refuse loans because borrowers sometimes merely used
them to evade the tallyman by getting their jewellery at cash
prices. She not only gave alms to the poor, but made them givers,
organising their own farthings into a powerful auxiliary of the institutions which helped them. Hannah's sweet patience soothed
Esther, who had no natural aptitude for personal philanthropy ;
the primitive ordered pieties of the Reb's household helping to
give her calm. Though she accepted the inevitable, and had
laughed in melancholy mockery at the exaggerated importance
given to love by the novelists (including her cruder self), she
dreaded meeting Raphael Leon. It was very unlikely her whereabouts would penetrate to the West ; and she rarely went outside
the Ghetto by day, or even walked within it in the evening. In
the twilight, unless prostrated by headache, she played on Hannah's
disused old-fashioned grand piano. It had one cracked note
which nearly always spoiled the melody ; she would not have the
note repaired, taking a morbid pleasure in a fantastic analogy between the instrument and herself. On Friday nights after the
Sabbath-hymns she read the *Flag of Judah*. She was not surprised to find Reb Shemuel beginning to look askance at his
favourite paper. She noted a growing tendency in it to insist
mainly on the ethical side of Judaism, salvation by works being
contrasted with the salvation by spasm of popular Christianity.

Once Kingsley's line, ' Do noble things, not dream them all day
long,' was put forth as ' Judaism *versus* Christianity in a nutshell ';
and the writer added, ' for so thy dreams shall become noble, too.'
Sometimes she fancied phrases and lines of argument were aimed
at her.   Was it the editor's way of keeping in touch with her,
using his leaders as a medium of communication—a subtly sweet
secret known only to him and her?   Was it fair to his readers?
Then she would remember his joke about the paper being started
merely to convert her, and she would laugh.   Sometimes he repeated what he had already said to her privately, so that she
seemed to hear him talking.

Then she would shake her head, and say, ' I love you for your
blindness, but I have the terrible gift of vision.'

CHAPTER XIV

SIDNEY SETTLES DOWN

Mrs. Henry Goldsmith's newest seaside resort had the artistic charm which characterised everything she selected.   It was a
straggling, hilly, leafy village, full of archaic relics—human as
well as architectural—sloping down to a gracefully curved bay,
where the blue waves broke in whispers, for on summer days a
halcyon calm overhung this magic spot, and the great sea stretched
away, unwrinkled, ever young.   There were no neutral tones in
the colours of this divine picture—the sea was sapphire, the sky
amethyst.   There were dark-red houses nestling amid foliage, and
green-haired monsters of gray stone squatted about on the yellow
sand, which was strewn with quaint shells and mimic earth-worms,
cunningly wrought by the waves.   Half a mile to the east a blue
river rippled into the bay.   The white bathing-tents which Mrs.
Goldsmith had pitched stood out picturesquely, in harmonious
contrast with the rich boscage that began to climb the hills in the
background.

Mrs. Goldsmith's party lived in the manse ; it was pretty
numerous, and gradually overflowed into the bedrooms of the
neighbouring cottages.   Mr. Goldsmith only came down on Saturday, returning on Monday.   One Friday Mr. Percy Saville, who
had been staying for the week, left suddenly for London, and next
day the beautiful hostess poured into her husband's projecting ears
a tale that made him gnash his projecting teeth, and cut the
handsome stockbroker off his visiting-list for ever.   It was only an
indiscreet word that the susceptible stockbroker had spoken—
under the poetic influences of the scene.   His bedroom came in
handy for Sidney, unexpectedly dropped down from Norway, *viâ*
London, on the very Friday.   The poetic influences of the scene

soon infected the new-comer, too. On the Saturday he was lost for hours, and came up smiling, with Addie on his arm. On the Sunday afternoon the party went boating up the river—a pictur-esque medley of flannels and parasols. Once landed, Sidney and Addie did not return for tea, prior to re-embarking. While Mr. Montagu Samuels was gallantly handing round the sugar, they were sitting somewhere along the bank, half covered with leaves like babes in the wood. The sunset burnt behind the willows—a fiery rhapsody of crimson and orange. The gay laughter of the picnic-party just reached their ears, otherwise an almost solemn calm prevailed—not a bird twittered, not a leaf stirred.

'It'll be all over London to-morrow,' said Sidney in a despon-dent tone.

'I'm afraid so,' said Addie with a delicious laugh.

The sweet English meadows over which her humid eyes wandered were studded with simple wild-flowers. Addie vaguely felt the angels had planted such in Eden. Sidney could not take his eyes off his terrestrial angel clad in appropriate white. Con-fessed love had given the last touch to her intoxicating beauty. She gratified his artistic sense almost completely. But she seemed to satisfy deeper instincts, too. As he looked into her limpid, trustful eyes, he felt he had been a weak fool. An irresistible yearning to tell her all his past and crave forgiveness swept over him.

'Addie,' he said, 'isn't it funny I should be marrying a Jewish girl, after all?'

He wanted to work round to it like that, to tell her of his en-gagement to Miss Hannibal at least, and how, on discovering with whom he was really in love, he had got out of it simply by writing to the Wesleyan M.P. that he was a Jew—a fact sufficient to dis-gust the disciple of Dissent and the clamant champion of religious liberty. But Addie only smiled at the question.

'You smile,' he said; 'I see you do think it funny.'

'That's not why I am smiling.'

'Then why are you smiling?' The lovely face piqued him; he kissed the lips quickly with a bird-like peck.

'Oh—I—no, you wouldn't understand.'

'That means *you* don't understand. But, there! I suppose, when a girl is in love, she's not accountable for her expression. All the same, it is strange. You know, Addie dear, I have come to the conclusion that Judaism exercises a strange centrifugal and centripetal effect on its sons—sometimes it repulses them, some-times it draws them; only it never leaves them neutral. Now, here had I deliberately made up my mind not to marry a Jewess.'

'Oh! Why not?' said Addie, pouting.

'Merely because she would be a Jewess. It's a fact.'

'And why have you broken your resolution?' she said, looking up naïvely into his face, so that the scent of her hair thrilled him.

'I don't know,' he said frankly, scarcely giving the answer to be expected. '*C'est plus fort que moi.* I've struggled hard, but I'm beaten. Isn't there something of the kind in Esther—in Miss Ansell's book? I know I've read it somewhere—and anything that's beastly subtle I always connect with her.'

'Poor Esther!' murmured Addie.

Sidney patted her soft warm hand, and smoothed the finely-curved arm, and did not seem disposed to let the shadow of Esther mar the moment, though he would ever remain grateful to her for the hint which had simultaneously opened his eyes to Addie's affection for him, and to his own answering affection so imperceptibly grown up. The river glided on softly, glorified by the sunset.

'It makes one believe in a dogged destiny,' he grumbled, 'shaping the ends of the race, and keeping it together, despite all human volition. To think that I should be doomed to fall in love, not only with a Jewess but with a pious Jewess! But clever men always fall in love with conventional women. I wonder what makes you so conventional, Addie.'

Addie, still smiling, pressed his hand in silence, and gazed at him in fond admiration.

'Ah, well, since you are so conventional, you may as well kiss me.'

Addie's blush deepened, her eyes sparkled ere she lowered them, and subtly fascinating waves of expression passed across the lovely face.

'They'll be wondering what on earth has become of us,' she said.

'It shall be nothing on earth—something in heaven,' he answered. 'Kiss me, or I shall call you unconventional.'

She touched his cheek hurriedly with her soft lips.

'A very crude and amateur kiss,' he said critically. 'However, after all, I have an excuse for marrying you—which all clever Jews who marry conventional Jewesses haven't got—you're a fine model. That is another of the many advantages of my profession. I suppose you'll be a model wife, in the ordinary sense, too. Do you know, my darling, I begin to understand that I could not love you so much if you were not so religious, if you were not so curiously like a Festival Prayer-Book, with gilt edges and a beautiful binding.'

'Ah, I am so glad, dear, to hear you say that,' said Addie, with the faintest suspicion of implied past disapproval.

'Yes,' he said musingly; 'it adds the last artistic touch to your relation to me.'

'But you will reform!' said Addie with girlish confidence.

'Do you think so? I might commence by becoming a vegetarian—that would prevent me eating forbidden flesh. Have I ever told you my idea that vegetarianism is the first step in a great secret conspiracy for gradually converting the world to

Judaism? But I'm afraid I can't be caught as easily as the Gentiles, Addie dear. You see, a Jewish sceptic beats all others. *Corruptio optimi pessima*, probably. Perhaps you would like me to marry in a synagogue?'

'Why, of course! Where else?'

'Heavens!' said Sidney, in comic despair. 'I feared it would come to that. I shall become a pillar of the synagogue when I am married, I suppose.'

'Well, you'll have to take a seat,' said Addie seriously, 'because otherwise you can't get buried.'

'Gracious, what ghoulish thoughts for an embryo bride! Personally, I have no objection to haunting the Council of the United Synagogue till they give me a decently comfortable grave. But I see what it will be! I shall be whitewashed by the Jewish press, eulogised by platform orators as a shining light in Israel, the brilliant impressionist painter, and all that. I shall pay my synagogue bill and never go. In short, I shall be converted to Philistinism, and die in the odour of respectability. And Judaism will continue to flourish. Oh, Addie, Addie, if I had thought of all that, I should never have asked you to be my wife.'

'I am glad you didn't think of it,' laughed Addie ingenuously.

'There! You never will take me seriously!' he grumbled. 'Nobody ever takes me seriously—I suppose because I speak the truth. The only time you ever took me seriously in my life was a few minutes ago. So you actually think I'm going to submit to the benedictions of a Rabbi.'

'You must,' said Addie.

'I'll be blest if I do,' he said.

'Of course you will,' said Addie, laughing merrily.

'Thanks—I'm glad you appreciate my joke. You perhaps fancy it's yours. However, I'm in earnest. I won't be a respectable high-hatted member of the community—not even for your sake, dear. Why, I might as well go back to my ugly real name, Samuel Abrahams, at once.'

'So you might, dear,' said Addie boldly; and smiled into his eyes to temper her audacity.

'Ah, well, I think it'll be quite enough if *you* change your name,' he said, smiling back.

'It's just as easy for me to change it to Abrahams as to Graham,' she said with charming obstinacy.

He contemplated her for some moments in silence, with a whimsical look on his face. Then he looked up at the sky—the brilliant colour harmonies were deepening into a more sober magnificence.

'I'll tell you what I will do. I'll join the Asmoneans. There! that's a great concession to your absurd prejudices. But you must make a concession to mine. You know how I hate the Jewish canvassing of engagements. Let us keep ours entirely *entre nous* a fortnight—so that the gossips shall at least get their material stale, and we shall be hardened. I wonder why you're so conventional,' he said again, when she had consented without enthusiasm. 'You had the advantage of Esther—of Miss Ansell's society.'

'Call her Esther if you like ; *I* don't mind,' said Addie.

'I wonder Esther didn't convert you,' he went on musingly. 'But I suppose you had Raphael on your right hand, as some prayer or other says. And so you really don't know what's become of her ? '

Nothing beyond what I wrote to you. Mrs. Goldsmith discovered she had written the nasty book, and sent her packing. I have never liked to broach the subject myself to Mrs. Goldsmith, knowing how unpleasant it must be to her. Raphael's version is that Esther went away of her own accord ; but I can't see what grounds he has for judging.'

'I would rather trust Raphael's version,' said Sydney, with an adumbration of a wink in his left eyelid. 'But didn't you look for her ? '

'Where ? If she's in London, she's swallowed up. If she's gone to another place, it's still more difficult to find her.'

'There's the Agony Column ! '

'If Esther wanted us to know her address, what can prevent her sending it ? ' asked Addie with dignity.

'I'd find her soon enough, if I wanted to,' murmured Sidney.

'Yes ; but I'm not sure we want to. After all, she cannot be so nice as I thought. She certainly behaved very ungratefully to Mrs. Goldsmith. You see what comes of wild opinions.'

'Addie ! Addie !' said Sidney reproachfully, 'how *can* you be so conventional ? '

'I'm *not* conventional,' protested Addie, provoked at last. 'I always liked Esther very much. Even now, nothing would give me greater pleasure than to have her for a bridesmaid. But I can't help feeling she deceived us all.'

'Stuff and nonsense !' said Sidney warmly. 'An author has a right to be anonymous. Don't you think I'd paint anonymously if I dared ? Only, if I didn't put my name to my things, no one would buy them. That's another of the advantages of my profession. Once make your name as an artist, and you can get a colossal income by giving up art.'

'It was a vulgar book !' persisted Addie, sticking to the point.

'Fiddlesticks ! It was an artistic book—bungled.'

'Oh, well !' said Addie, as the tears welled from her eyes, 'if you're so fond of unconventional girls, you'd better marry them.'

'I would,' said Sidney, 'but for the absurd restriction against polygamy.'

Addie got up with an indignant jerk. 'You think I'm a child to be played with ! '

She turned her back upon him. His face changed instantly ;

he stood still a moment, admiring the magnificent pose. Then he recaptured her reluctant hand.

'Don't be jealous already, Addie,' he said. It's a healthy sign of affection, is a storm-cloud ; but don't you think it's just a wee, tiny, weeny bit too previous ?'

A pressure of the hand accompanied each of the little adjectives. Addie sat down again, feeling deliciously happy. She seemed to be lapped in a great drowsy ecstasy of bliss.

The sunset was fading into sombre grays before Sidney broke the silence ; then his train of thought revealed itself.

'If you're so down on Esther, I wonder how you can put up with me ! How is it ?'

Addie did not hear the question.

'You think I'm a very wicked, blasphemous boy,' he insisted. 'Isn't that the thought deep down in your heart of hearts ?'

'I'm sure tea must be over long ago,' said Addie anxiously.

'Answer me,' said Sidney inexorably.

'Don't bother. Aren't they cooeying for us ?'

'Answer me.'

'I do believe that was a water-rat. Look ! the water is still eddying.'

'I'm a very wicked, blasphemous boy. Isn't that the thought deep down in your heart of hearts ?'

'You are there, too,' she breathed at last, and then Sidney forgot her beauty for an instant, and lost himself in unaccustomed humility. It seemed passing wonderful to him—that he should be the deity of such a spotless shrine. Could any man deserve the trust of this celestial soul ?

Suddenly the thought that he had not told her about Miss Hannibal, after all, gave him a chilling shock. But he rallied quickly. Was it really worth while to trouble the clear depths of her spirit with his turbid past ? No ; wiser to inhale the odour of the rose at her bosom, sweeter to surrender himself to the intoxicating perfume of her personality, to the magic of a moment that must fade like the sunset, already grown gray.

So Addie never knew.

CHAPTER XV

FROM SOUL TO SOUL

ON the Friday that Percy Saville returned to town, Raphael, in a state of mental prostration modified by tobacco, was sitting in the editorial chair. He was engaged in his pleasing weekly occupation of discovering, from a comparison with the great rival organ, the deficiencies of the *Flag of Judah* in the matter of news, his organisation for the collection of which partook of the happy-go-lucky character of Little Sampson. Fortunately to-day there were no flagrant omissions, no palpable shortcomings such as had once and again thrown the office of the *Flag* into mourning when communal pillars were found dead in the opposition paper.

The arrival of a visitor put an end to the invidious comparison.

'Ah, Strelitski!' cried Raphael, jumping up in glad surprise. 'What an age it is since I've seen you!' He shook the black-gloved hand of the fashionable minister heartily; then his face grew rueful with a sudden recollection. 'I suppose you have come to scold me for not answering the invitation to speak at the distribution of prizes to your religion class?' he said; 'but I *have* been so busy. My conscience has kept up a dull pricking on the subject, though, for ever so many weeks. You're such an epitome of all the virtues that you can't understand the sensation, and even I can't understand why one submits to this undercurrent of reproach rather than take the simple step it exhorts one to. But I suppose it's human nature.' He puffed at his pipe in humorous sadness.

'I suppose it is,' said Strelitski wearily.

'But of course I'll come. You know that, my dear fellow. When my conscience was noisy, the *advocatus diaboli* used to silence it by saying, "Oh, Strelitski 'll take it for granted." You can never catch the *advocatus diaboli* asleep,' concluded Raphael, laughing.

'No,' assented Strelitski. But he did not laugh.

'Oh!' said Raphael, his laugh ceasing suddenly and his face growing long. 'Perhaps the prize-distribution is over?'

Strelitski's expression seemed so stern that for a second it really occurred to Raphael that he might have missed the great event. But before the words were well out of his mouth he remembered that it was an event that made 'copy,' and Little Sampson would have arranged with him as to the reporting thereof.

'No; it's Sunday week. But I didn't come to talk about my religion class at all,' he said pettishly, while a shudder traversed his form. 'I came to ask if you know anything about Miss Ansell.'

Raphael's heart stood still, then began to beat furiously. The sound of her name always affected him incomprehensibly. He began to stammer, then took his pipe out of his mouth and said more calmly:

'How should I know anything about Miss Ansell?'

'I thought you would,' said Strelitski, without much disappointment in his tone.

'Why?'

'Wasn't she your art-critic?'

'Who told you that?'

'Mrs. Henry Goldsmith.'

'Oh!' said Raphael.

'I thought she might possibly be writing for you still, and so as I was passing, I thought I'd drop in and inquire. Hasn't anything been heard of her? Where is she? Perhaps one could help her.'

'I'm sorry, I really know nothing, nothing at all,' said Raphael gravely. 'I wish I did. Is there any particular reason why you want to know?'

As he spoke a strange suspicion that was half an apprehension came into his head. He had been looking the whole time at Strelitski's face with his usual unobservant gaze, just seeing it was gloomy. Now, as in a sudden flash, he saw it sallow and care-worn to the last degree. The eyes were almost feverish, the black curl on the brow was unkempt, and there was a streak or two of gray easily visible against the intense sable. What change had come over him? Why this new-born interest in Esther? Raphael felt a vague unreasoning resentment rising in him, mingled with distress at Strelitski's discomposure.

'No; I don't know that there is any *particular* reason why I want to know,' answered his friend slowly. 'She was a member of my congregation. I always had a certain interest in her, which has naturally not been diminished by her sudden departure from our midst, and by the knowledge that she was the author of that sensational novel. I think it was cruel of Mrs. Henry Goldsmith to turn her adrift; one must allow for the effervescence of genius.'

'Who told you Mrs. Henry Goldsmith turned her adrift?' asked Raphael hotly.

'Mrs. Henry Goldsmith,' said Strelitski with a slight accent of wonder.

'Then it's a lie!' Raphael exclaimed, thrusting out his arms in intense agitation. 'A mean, cowardly lie! I shall never go to see that woman again, unless it is to let her know what I think of her,'

'Ah, then, you do know something about Miss Ansell?' said Strelitski, with growing surprise. Raphael in a rage was a new experience. There were those who asserted that anger was not among his gifts.

'Nothing about her life since she left Mrs. Goldsmith; but I saw her before, and she told me it was her intention to cut herself adrift. Nobody knew about her authorship of the book; nobody would have known to this day if she had not chosen to reveal it.'

The minister was trembling.

'She cut herself adrift?' he repeated interrogatively. 'But why?'

'I will tell you,' said Raphael in low tones. 'I don't think it will be betraying her confidence to say that she found her position of dependence extremely irksome; it seemed to cripple her soul. Now I see what Mrs. Goldsmith is, I can understand better what life in her society meant for a girl like that.'

'And what has become of her?' asked the Russian. His face was agitated, the lips were almost white.

'I do not know,' said Raphael, almost in a whisper, his voice failing in a sudden upwelling of tumultuous feeling. The ever-whirling wheel of journalism—that modern realisation of the labour of Sisyphus—had carried him round and round without giving him even time to remember that time was flying. Day had slipped into week and week into month without his moving an inch from his groove in search of the girl whose unhappiness was yet always at the back of his thoughts. Now he was shaken with astonished self-reproach at his having allowed her to drift perhaps irretrievably beyond his ken.

'She is quite alone in the world, poor thing!' he said after a pause. 'She must be earning her own living, somehow. By journalism, perhaps. But she prefers to live her own life. I am afraid it will be a hard one.' His voice trembled again. The minister's breast, too, was labouring with emotion that checked his speech, but after a moment utterance came to him—a strange choked utterance, almost blasphemous from those clerical lips.

'By God!' he gasped. 'That little girl!'

He turned his back upon his friend and covered his face with his hands, and Raphael saw his shoulders quivering. Then his own vision grew dim. Conjecture, resentment, wonder, self-reproach, were lost in a new and absorbing sense of the pathos of the poor girl's position.

Presently the minister turned round, showing a face that made no pretence of calm.

'That was bravely done,' he said brokenly. 'To cut herself adrift! She will not sink; strength will be given her even as she gives others strength. If I could only see her and tell her! But she never liked me; she always distrusted me. I was a hollow windbag in her eyes—a thing of shams and cant—she shuddered to look at me. Was it not so? You are a friend of hers, you know what she felt.'

'I don't think it was you she disliked,' said Raphael in wondering pity. 'Only your office.'

'Then, by God, she was right!' cried the Russian hoarsely. 'It was this—this that made me the target of her scorn!' He tore off his white tie madly as he spoke, threw it on the ground, and trampled upon it. 'She and I were kindred in suffering; I read it in her eyes, averted as they were at the sight of this accursed thing! You stare at me—you think I have gone mad. Leon, you are not as other men. Can you not guess that this damnable white tie has been choking the life and manhood out of me? But it is over now. Take your pen, Leon, as you are my friend, and write what I shall dictate.'

Silenced by the stress of a great soul, half dazed by the strange, unexpected revelation, Raphael seated himself, took his pen, and wrote:

'We understand that the Rev. Joseph Strelitski has resigned his position in the Kensington Synagogue.'

Not till he had written it did the full force of the paragraph overwhelm his soul.

'But you will not do this?' he said, looking up almost incredulously at the popular minister.

'I will; the position has become impossible. Leon, do you not understand? I am not what I was when I took it. I have lived, and life is change. Stagnation is death. Surely you can understand, for you, too, have changed. Cannot I read between the lines of your leaders?'

'Cannot you read in them?' said Raphael with a wan smile. 'I have modified some opinions, it is true, and developed others; but I have disguised none.'

'Not consciously, perhaps, but you do not speak all your thought.'

'Perhaps I do not listen to it,' said Raphael, half to himself.

'But you—whatever your change—you have not lost faith in primaries?'

'No; not in what I consider such.'

'Then why give up your platform, your housetop, whence you may do so much good? You are loved, venerated.'

Strelitski placed his palms over his ears.

'Don't! don't! he cried. 'Don't you be the *advocatus diaboli*! Do you think I have not told myself all these things a thousand times? Do you think I have not tried every kind of opiate? No, no; be silent, if you can say nothing to strengthen me in my resolution: am I not weak enough already? Promise me, give me your hand, swear to me that you will put that paragraph in the paper. Saturday, Sunday, Monday, Tuesday, Wednesday, Thursday—in six days I shall change a hundred times. Swear to me, so that I may leave this room at peace, the long conflict ended. Promise me you will insert it, though I myself should ask you to cancel it.'

'But——' began Raphael.

Strelitski turned away impatiently and groaned.

'My God!' he cried hoarsely. 'Leon, listen to me,' he said, turning round suddenly. 'Do you realise what sort of a position you are asking me to keep? Do you realise how it makes me the fief of a Rabbinate, that is an anachronism, the bondman of outworn forms, the slave of the *Shulchan Aruch* (a book the Rabbinate would not dare publish in English), the professional panegyrist of the rich? Ours is a generation of whited sepulchres.' He had no difficulty about utterance now; the words flowed in a torrent. 'How can Judaism—and it alone—escape going through the fire of modern scepticism, from which, if religion emerge at all, it will emerge without its dross? Are not we Jews always the first prey of new ideas, with our alert intellect, our swift receptiveness, our keen critical sense? And if we are not hypocrites, we are indifferent—which is almost worse. Indifference is the only infidelity I recognise, and it is unfortunately as conservative as zeal.

Indifference and hypocrisy between them keep orthodoxy alive—while they kill Judaism.'

'Oh, I can't quite admit that,' said Raphael. 'I admit that scepticism is better than stagnation, but I cannot see why orthodoxy is the antithesis to Judaism. Purified—and your own sermons are doing something to purify it—orthodoxy——'

'Orthodoxy cannot be purified unless by juggling with words,' interrupted Strelitski vehemently. 'Orthodoxy is inextricably entangled with ritual observance ; and ceremonial religion is of the ancient world, not the modern.'

'But our ceremonialism is pregnant with sublime symbolism, and its discipline is most salutary. Ceremony is the casket of religion.'

'More often its coffin,' said Strelitski drily. 'Ceremonial religion is so apt to stiffen in a *rigor mortis*. It is too dangerous an element ; it creates hypocrites and Pharisees. All cast-iron laws and dogmas do. Not that I share the Christian sneer at Jewish legalism. Add the Statute Book to the New Testament, and think of the network of laws hampering the feet of the Christian. No ; much of our so-called ceremonialism is merely the primitive mix-up of everything with religion in a theocracy. The Mosaic code has been largely embodied in civil law, and superseded by it.'

'That is just the flaw of the modern world, to keep life and religion apart,' protested Raphael ; ' to have one set of principles for week-days and another for Sundays ; to grind the inexorable mechanism of supply and demand on pagan principles, and make it up out of the poor-box.'

Strelitski shook his head.

'We must make broad our platform, not our phylacteries. It is because I am with you in admiring the Rabbis that I would undo much of their work. Theirs was a wonderful statesmanship, and they built wiser than they knew : just as the patient labours of the superstitious zealots who counted every letter of the Law preserved the text unimpaired for the benefit of modern scholarship. The Rabbis constructed a casket, if you will, which kept the jewel safe, though at the cost of concealing its lustre. But the hour has come now to wear the jewel on our breasts before all the world. The Rabbis worked for their time—we must work for ours. Judaism was before the Rabbis. Scientific criticism shows its thoughts widening with the process of the suns—even as its God, Yahweh, broadened from a local patriotic Deity to the ineffable Name. For Judaism was worked out from within—Abraham asked, "Shall not the Judge of all the earth do right?"—the thunders of Sinai were but the righteous indignation of the developed moral consciousness. In every age our great men have modified and developed Judaism. Why should it not be trimmed into concordance with the culture of the time? Especially when the alternative is death. Yes, death ! We babble about petty minutiæ of ritual while Judaism is dying ! We are like the crew of a sinking ship, holy-stoning the deck instead of being at the pumps. No, I must speak out; I cannot go on salving my conscience by unsigned letters to the press. Away with all this anonymous apostleship!'

He moved about restlessly with animated gestures, as he delivered his harangue at tornado speed, speech bursting from him like some dynamic energy which had been accumulating for years, and could no longer be kept in. It was an upheaval of the whole man under the stress of pent forces. Raphael was deeply moved. He scarcely knew how to act in this unique crisis. Dimly he foresaw the stir and bother there would be in the community. Conservative by instinct, apt to see the elements of good in attacked institutions—perhaps, too, a little timid when it came to take action in the tremendous realm of realities—he was loth to help Strelitski to so decisive a step, though his whole heart went out to him in brotherly sympathy.

'Do not act so hastily,' he pleaded. 'Things are not so black as you see them—you are almost as bad as Miss Ansell. Don't think that I see them rosy; I might have done that three months ago. But don't you—don't all idealists—overlook the quieter phenomena? Is orthodoxy either so inefficacious or so moribund as you fancy? Is there not a steady, perhaps semi-conscious, stream of healthy life, thousands of cheerful, well-ordered households, of people neither perfect nor cultured, but more good than bad? You cannot expect saints and heroes to grow like blackberries.'

'Yes; but look what Jews set up to be—God's witnesses!' interrupted Strelitski. 'This mediocrity may pass in the rest of the world.'

'And does lack of modern lights constitute ignorance?' went on Raphael, disregarding the interruption. He began walking up and down, and thrashing the air with his arms. Hitherto he had remained comparatively quiet, dominated by Strelitski's superior restlessness. 'I cannot help thinking there is a profound lesson in the Bible story of the oxen who, unguided, bore safely the Ark of the Covenant. Intellect obscures more than it illumines.'

'Oh, Leon, Leon, you'll turn Catholic soon!' said Strelitski reprovingly.

'Not with a capital C,' said Raphael, laughing a little. 'But I am so sick of hearing about culture, I say more than I mean. Judaism is so human—that's why I like it. No abstract metaphysics, but a lovable way of living the common life, sanctified by the centuries. Culture is all very well—doesn't the Talmud say the world stands on the breath of the school-children?—but it has become a cant. Too often it saps the moral fibre.'

'You have all the old Jewish narrowness,' said Strelitski.

'I'd rather have that than the new Parisian narrowness—the cant of decadence. Look at my cousin Sidney. He talks as if the Jew only introduced moral headache into the world—in face of the corruptions of paganism which are still flagrant all over

Asia and Africa and Polynesia—the idol worship, the abominations, the disregard of human life, of truth, of justice.'

'But is the civilised world any better? Think of the dishonesty of business, the self-seeking of public life, the infamies and hypocrisies of society, the prostitutions of soul and body! No, the Jew has yet to play a part in history. Supplement his Hebraism by what Hellenic ideals you will, but the Jew's ideals must ever remain the indispensable ones,' said Strelitski, becoming exalted again. 'Without righteousness a kingdom cannot stand. The world is longing for a broad simple faith that shall look on science as its friend and reason as its inspirer. People are turning in their despair even to table-rappings and Mahatmas. Now, for the first time in history, is the hour of Judaism. Only it must enlarge itself; its platform must be all-inclusive. Judaism is but a specialised form of Hebraism; even if Jews stick to their own special historical and ritual ceremonies, it is only Hebraism—the pure spiritual kernel—that they can offer the world.'

'But that is quite the orthodox Jewish idea on the subject,' said Raphael.

'Yes, but orthodox ideas have a way of remaining ideas,' retorted Strelitski. 'Where I am heterodox is in thinking the time has come to work them out. Also in thinking that the monotheism is not the element that needs the most accentuation. The formula of the religion of the future will be a Jewish formula—Character, not Creed. The provincial period of Judaism is over, though even its Dark Ages are still lingering on in England. It must become cosmic, universal. Judaism is too timid, too apologetic, too deferential. Doubtless this is the result of persecution, but it does not tend to diminish persecution. We may as well try the other attitude. It is the world the Jewish preacher should address, not a Kensington congregation. Perhaps, when the Kensington congregation sees the world is listening, it will listen, too,' he said, with a touch of bitterness.

'But it listens to you now,' said Raphael.

'A pleasing illusion which has kept me too long in my false position. With all its love and reverence, do you think it forgets I am its hireling? I may perhaps have a little more prestige than the bulk of my fellows—though even that is partly due to my congregants being rich and fashionable—but at bottom everybody knows I am taken like a house—on a three years' agreement. And I dare not speak, I cannot, while I wear the badge of office; it would be disloyal; my own congregation would take alarm. The position of a minister is like that of a judicious editor—which by the way you are not; he is led, rather than leads. He has to feel his way, to let in light wherever he sees a chink, a cranny. But let them get another man to preach to them the echo of their own voices; there will be no lack of candidates for the salary. For my part, I am sick of this petty Jesuitry; in vain I tell myself it is spiritual statesmanship like that of so many Christian clergymen who are silently bringing Christianity back to Judaism.'

'But it *is* spiritual statesmanship,' asserted Raphael.

'Perhaps. You are wiser, deeper, calmer than I. You are an Englishman, I am a Russian. I am all for action, action, action ! In Russia I should have been a Nihilist, not a philosopher. I can only go by my feelings, and I feel choking. When I first came to England, before the horror of Russia wore off, I used to go about breathing in deep breaths of air, exulting in the sense of freedom. Now I am stifling again. Do you not understand ? Have you never guessed it ? And yet I have often said things to you that should have opened your eyes. I must escape from the house of bondage—must be master of myself, of my word and thought. Oh, the world is so wide, so wide—and we are so narrow ! Only gradually did the web mesh itself about me. At first my fetters were flowery bands, for I believed all I taught and could teach all I believed. Insensibly the flowers changed to iron chains, because I was changing as I probed deeper into life and thought, and saw my dreams of influencing English Judaism fading in the harsh daylight of fact. And yet at moments the iron links would soften to flowers again. Do you think there is no sweetness in adulation, in prosperity—no subtle cajolery that soothes the conscience and coaxes the soul to take its pleasure in a world of make-believe ? Spiritual statesmanship forsooth !' He made a gesture of resolution. 'No, the Judaism of you English weighs upon my spirits. It is so parochial. Everything turns on finance ; the United Synagogue keeps your community orthodox because it has the funds and owns the burying-grounds. Truly a dismal allegory— a creed whose strength lies in its cemeteries. Money is the sole avenue to distinction and to authority ; it has its coarse thumb over education, worship, society. In my country—even in your own Ghetto—the Jews do not despise money, but at least piety and learning are the titles to position and honour. Here the scholar is classed with the *Schnorrer* ; if an artist or an author is admired, it is for his success. You are right ; it is oxen that carry your Ark of the Covenant—fat oxen. You admire them, Leon ; you are an Englishman, and cannot stand outside it all. But I am stifling under this weight of moneyed mediocrity, this *régime* of dull respectability. I want the atmosphere of ideas and ideals.'

He tore at his high clerical collar as though suffocating literally.

Raphael was too moved to defend English Judaism. Besides, he was used to these jeremiads now—had he not often heard them from Sidney ? Had he not read them in Esther's book ? Nor was it the first time he had listened to the Russian's tirades, though he had lacked the key to the internal conflict that embittered them.

'But how will you live ?' he asked, tacitly accepting the situation. 'You will not, I suppose, go over to the Reform Synagogue ?'

'That fossil, so proud of its petty reforms half a century ago that it has stood still ever since to admire them ! It is a synagogue for snobs—who never go there.'

Raphael smiled faintly. It was obvious that Strelitski on the war-path did not pause to weigh his utterances.

'I am glad you are not going over, anyhow. Your congregation would——'

'Crucify me between two money-lenders ?'

'Never mind. But how will you live ?'

'How does Miss Ansell live ? I can always travel with cigars— I know the line thoroughly.' He smiled mournfully. 'But probably I shall go to America—the idea has been floating in my mind for months. There Judaism is grander, larger, nobler. There is room for all parties. The dead bones are not worshipped as relics. Free-thought has its vent-holes—it is not repressed into hypocrisy as among us. There is care for literature, for national ideals. And one deals with millions, not petty thousands. This English community, with its squabbles about rituals, its four Chief Rabbis all in love with one another, its stupid Sephardim, its narrow-minded Reformers, its fatuous self-importance, its invincible ignorance, is but an ant-hill, a negligible quantity in the future of the faith. Westward the course of Judaism, as of empire, take its way—from the Euphrates and Tigris it emigrated to Cordova and Toledo, and the year that saw its expulsion from Spain was the year of the discovery of America. *Ex Oriente lux.* Perhaps it will return to you here by way of the Occident. Russia and America are the two strongholds of the race, and Russia is pouring her streams into America, where they will be made free men and free thinkers. It is in America, then, that the last great battle of Judaism will be fought out ; amid the temples of the New World it will make its last struggle to survive. It is there that the men who have faith in its necessity must be, so that the psychical force conserved at such a cost may not radiate uselessly away. Though Israel has sunk low, like a tree once green and living, and has become petrified and blackened, there is stored-up sunlight in him. Our racial isolation is a mere superstition unless turned to great purposes. We have done nothing *as Jews* for centuries, though our Old Testament has always been an arsenal of texts for the European champions of civil and religious liberty. We have been unconsciously pioneers of modern commerce, diffusers of folk-lore and what not. Cannot we be a conscious force, making for nobler ends ? Could we not, for instance, be the link of federation among the nations, acting everywhere in favour of Peace ? Could we not be the centres of new sociologic movements in each country, as a few American Jews have been the centre of the Ethical Culture movement ?'

'You forget,' said Raphael, 'that, wherever the old Judaism has not been overlaid by the veneer of Philistine civilisation, we are already sociological object-lessons in good fellowship, unpretentious charity, domestic poetry, respect for learning, disrespect for respectability. Our social system is a bequest from the ancient world by which the modern may yet benefit. The demerits you censure in English Judaism are all departures from the old way of living. Why should we not revive or strengthen that, rather than waste ourselves on impracticable novelties? And in your prognostications of the future of the Jews have you not forgotten the all-important factor of Palestine?'

'No; I simply leave it out of count. You know how I have persuaded the Holy Land League to co-operate with the movements for directing the streams of the persecuted towards America. I have alleged with truth that Palestine is impracticable for the moment. I have not said what I have gradually come to think—that the salvation of Judaism is not in the national idea at all. That is the dream of visionaries—and young men,' he added with a melancholy smile. ' May we not dream nobler dreams than political independence? For, after all, political independence is only a means to an end, not an end in itself, as it might easily become, and as it appears to other nations. To be merely one among the nations—that is not, despite George Eliot, so satisfactory an ideal. The restoration to Palestine, or the acquisition of a national centre, may be a political solution, but it is not a spiritual idea. We must abandon it—it cannot be held consistently with our professed attachment to the countries in which our lot is cast—and we have abandoned it. We have fought and slain one another in the Franco-German War, and in the war of the North and the South. Your whole difficulty with your pauper immigrants arises from your effort to keep two contradictory ideals going at once. As Englishmen, you may have a right to shelter the exile; but not as Jews. Certainly, if the nations cast us out, we could draw together and form a nation as of yore. But persecution, expulsion, is never simultaneous; our dispersal has saved Judaism, and it may yet save the world. For I prefer the dream that we are divinely dispersed to bless it, wind-sown seeds to fertilise its waste places. To be a nation without a fatherland, yet with a mother-tongue, Hebrew—there is the spiritual originality, the miracle of history. Such has been the real kingdom of Israel in the past—we have been 'sons of the Law' as other men have been sons of France, of Italy, of Germany. Such may our fatherland continue, with 'the higher life' substituted for 'the Law'—a kingdom not of space, not measured by the vulgar meteyard of an Alexander, but a great spiritual Republic, as devoid of material form as Israel's God, and congruous with his conception of the Divine. And the conquest of this kingdom needs no violent movement—if Jews only practised what they preach, it would be achieved to-morrow; for all expressions of Judaism, even to the lowest, have common sublimities. And this kingdom—as it has no space, so it has no limits; it must grow till all mankind are its subjects. The brotherhood of Israel will be the nucleus of the brotherhood of man.'

'It is magnificent,' said Raphael; 'but it is not Judaism. If the Jews have the future you dream of, the future will have no Jews. America is already decimating them with Sunday-Sabbaths and English Prayer-Books. Your Judaism is as eviscerated as the Christianity I found in vogue when I was at Oxford, which might be summed up : There is no God, but Jesus Christ is His Son. George Eliot was right. Men are men, not pure spirit. A fatherland focusses a people. Without it we are but the gipsies of religion. All over the world, at every prayer, every Jew turns towards Jerusalem. We must not give up the dream. The countries we live in can never be more than " step-fatherlands " to us. Why, if your visions were realised, the prophecy of Genesis, already practically fulfilled, " Thou shalt spread abroad to the west and to the east, and to the north and to the south ; and in thee and in thy seed shall all the families of the earth be blessed," would be so remarkably consummated that we might reasonably hope to come to our own again according to the promises.'

'Well, well,' said Strelitski good-humouredly, 'so long as you admit it is not within the range of practical politics now.'

'It is your own dream that is premature,' retorted Raphael; 'at any rate, the cosmic part of it. You are thinking of throwing open the citizenship of your Republic to the world. But to-day's task is to make its citizens by blood worthier of their privilege.'

'You will never do it with the old generation,' said Strelitski. 'My hope is in the new. Moses led the Jews forty years through the wilderness merely to eliminate the old. Give me young men, and I will move the world.'

'You will do nothing by attempting too much,' said Raphael ; 'you will only dissipate your strength. For my part, I shall be content to raise Judea an inch.'

'Go on, then,' said Strelitski. 'That will give me a barley-corn. But I've wasted too much of your time, I fear. Good-bye. Remember your promise.'

He held out his hand. He had grown quite calm, now his decision was taken.

'Good-bye,' said Raphael, shaking it warmly. 'I think I shall cable to America, " Behold, Joseph the dreamer cometh."'

'Dreams are our life,' replied Strelitski. 'Lessing was right— aspiration is everything.'

'And yet you would rob the orthodox Jew of his dream of Jerusalem ! Well, if you must go, don't go without your tie,' said Raphael, picking it up, and feeling a stolid, practical Englishman in presence of this enthusiast. 'It is dreadfully dirty, but you must wear it a little longer.'

'Only till the New Year, which is bearing down upon us,' said Strelitski, thrusting it into his pocket. 'Cost what it may, I shall no longer countenance the ritual and ceremonial of the season of

Repentance. Good-bye again. If you should be writing to Miss Ansell, I should like her to know how much I owe her.'

'But I tell you I don't know her address,' said Raphael, his uneasiness reawakening.

'Surely you can write to her publishers ?

And the door closed upon the Russian dreamer, leaving the practical Englishman dumfounded at his never having thought of this simple expedient. But before he could adopt it the door was thrown open again by Pinchas, who had got out of the habit of knocking through Raphael being too polite to reprimand him. The poet tottered in, dropped wearily into a chair, and buried his face in his hands, letting an extinct cigar-stump slip through his fingers on to the literature that carpeted the floor.

'What is the matter?' inquired Raphael in alarm.

'I am miserable—vairy miserable.'

'Has anything happened?'

'Nothing. But I have been thinking vat have I come to after all these years, all these vanderings. Nothing ! Vat vill be my end ? Oh, I am so unhappy.'

'But you are better off than you ever were in your life. You no longer live amid the squalor of the Ghetto ; you are clean and well dressed ; you yourself admit that you can afford to give charity now. That looks as if you'd come to something—not nothing.'

'Yes,' said the poet, looking up eagerly, 'and I am famous through the world. *Metatoron's Flames*" will shine eternally.' His head drooped again. 'I have all I vant, and you are the best man in the vorld. But I am the most miserable.'

'Nonsense ! cheer up,' said Raphael.

'I can never cheer up any more. I vill shoot myself. I have realised the emptiness of life. Fame, money, love—all is Dead Sea fruit.'

His shoulders heaved convulsively ; he was sobbing. Raphael stood by helpless, his respect for Pinchas as a poet and for himself as a practical Englishman returning. He pondered over the strange fate that had thrown him among three geniuses—a male idealist, a female pessimist, and a poet who seemed to belong to both sexes and categories. And yet there was not one of the three to whom he seemed able to be of real service. A letter brought in by the office-boy rudely snapped the thread of reflection. It contained three enclosures. The first was an epistle ; the hand was the hand of Mr. Goldsmith, but the voice was the voice of his beautiful spouse.

'DEAR MR. LEON,
                'I have perceived many symptoms lately of your growing divergency from the ideas with which the *Flag of Judah* was started. It is obvious that you find yourself unable to em-phasise the olden features of our faith—the questions of *kosher* meat, etc.—as forcibly as our readers desire. You no doubt

cherish ideals which are neither practical nor within the grasp of the masses to whom we appeal. I fully appreciate the delicacy that makes you reluctant—in the dearth of genius and Hebrew learning—to saddle me with the task of finding a substitute, but I feel it is time for me to restore your peace of mind even at the expense of my own. I have been thinking that, with your kind occasional supervision, it might be possible for Mr. Pinchas, of whom you have always spoken so highly, to undertake the duties of editorship, Mr. Sampson remaining sub-editor as before. Of course I count on you to continue your purely scholarly articles, and to impress upon the two gentlemen who will now have direct relations with me my wish to remain in the background.

'Yours sincerely,

'Henry Goldsmith.

'*P.S.*—On second thoughts I beg to enclose a cheque for four guineas, which will serve instead of a formal month's notice, and will enable you to accept at once my wife's invitation, likewise enclosed herewith. Your sister seconds Mrs. Goldsmith in the hope that you will do so. Our tenancy of the Manse only lasts a a few weeks longer, for of course we return for the New Year holidays.'

This was the last straw. It was not so much the dismissal that staggered him, but to be called a genius and an idealist himself— to have his own orthodoxy impugned—just at this moment, was a rough shock.

'Pinchas!' he said, recovering himself. Pinchas would not look up. His face was still hidden in his hands. 'Pinchas, listen! You are appointed editor of the paper instead of me. You are to edit the next number.'

Pinchas's head shot up like a catapult. He bounded to his feet, then bent down again to Raphael's coat-tail and kissed it passionately.

'Ah, my benefactor, my benefactor!' he cried in a joyous frenzy. 'Now vill I give it to English Judaism. She is in my power. Oh, my benefactor!'

'No, no,' said Raphael, disengaging himself. 'I have nothing to do with it.'

'But de paper—she is yours!' said the poet, forgetting his English in his excitement.

'No, I am only the editor. I have been dismissed, and you are appointed instead of me.'

Pinchas dropped back into his chair like a lump of lead. He hung his head again and folded his arms.

'Then they get not me for editor,' he said moodily.

'Nonsense, why not?' said Raphael, flushing.

'Vat you think me?' Pinchas asked indignantly. 'Do you think I have a stone for a heart like Gideon, M.P., or your English stockbrokers and Rabbis. No, you shall go on being editor. They think you are not able enough, not orthodox enough—they vant me—but do not fear. I shall not accept.'

'But then what will become of the next number?' remonstrated Raphael, touched. 'I must not edit it.'

'Vat you care? Let her die!' cried Pinchas in gloomy complacency. 'You have made her; vy should she survive you? It is not right another should valk in your shoes—least of all, I.'

'But I don't mind—I don't mind a bit,' Raphael assured him. Pinchas shook his head obstinately. 'If the paper dies, Sampson will have nothing to live upon,' Raphael reminded him.

'True, vairy true,' said the poet, patently beginning to yield. 'That alters things. Ve cannot let Sampson starve.'

'No, you see!' said Raphael. 'So you must keep it alive.'

'Yes, but,' said Pinchas, getting up thoughtfully, 'Sampson is going off soon on tour vith his comic opera. He vill not need the *Flag.*'

'Oh, well, edit it till then.'

'Be it so,' said the poet resignedly. 'Till Sampson's comic opera tour.'

'Till Sampson's comic opera tour,' repeated Raphael contentedly.

CHAPTER XVI

LOVE'S TEMPTATION

RAPHAEL walked out of the office, a free man. Mountains of responsibility seemed to roll off his shoulders. His Messianic emotions were conscious of no laceration at the failure of this episode of his life; they were merged in greater. What a fool he had been to waste so much time, to make no effort to find the lonely girl! Surely, Esther must have expected him, if only as a friend, to give some sign that he did not share in the popular execration. Perchance she had already left London or the country, only to be found again by protracted knightly quest! He felt grateful to Providence for setting him free for her salvation. He made at once for the publishers and asked for her address. The junior partner knew of no such person. In vain Raphael reminded him that they had published *Mordecai Josephs.* That was by Mr. Edward Armitage. Raphael accepted the convention, and demanded this gentleman's address instead. That, too, was refused, but all letters would be forwarded. Was Mr. Armitage in England? All letters would be forwarded. Upon that the junior partner stood, inexpugnable.

Raphael went out, not uncomforted. He would write to her at once. He got letter-paper at the nearest restaurant and wrote, 'Dear Miss Ansell.' The rest was a blank. He had not the least idea how to renew the relationship after what seemed an eternity of silence. He stared helplessly round the mirrored walls, seeing mainly his only helpless stare. The placard 'Smoking not permitted till 8 P.M.' gave him a sudden shock. He felt for his pipe, and ultimately found it stuck, half-full of charred bird's-eye, in his breast-pocket. He had apparently not been smoking for some hours. That completed his perturbation. He felt he had undergone too much that day to be in a fit state to write a judicious letter. He would go home and rest a bit, and write the letter—very diplomatically—in the evening. When he got home, he found to his astonishment it was Friday evening, when letter-writing is of the devil. Habit carried him to synagogue, where he sang the Sabbath hymn, 'Come, my beloved, to meet the bride,' with strange sweet tears and a complete indifference to its sacred allegorical signification. Next afternoon he haunted the publishers' doorstep with the brilliant idea that Mr. Armitage sometimes crossed it. In this hope, he did *not* write the letter ; his phrases, he felt, would be better for the inspiration of that gentleman's presence.

Meanwhile he had ample time to mature them, to review the situation in every possible light, to figure Esther under the most poetical images, to see his future alternately radiant and sombre. Four long summer days of espionage only left him with a heart-ache, and a specialist knowledge of the sort of persons who visit publishers. A temptation to bribe the office-boy he resisted as unworthy.

Not only had he not written that letter, but Mr. Henry Goldsmith's edict and Mrs. Henry Goldsmith's invitation were still unacknowledged. On Thursday morning a letter from Addie indirectly reminded him both of his remissness to her hostess, and of the existence of the *Flag of Judah*. He remembered it was the day of going to press ; a vision of the difficulties of the day flashed vividly upon his consciousness ; he wondered if his ex-lieutenants were finding new ones. The smell of the machine-room was in his nostrils ; it co-operated with the appeal of his good-nature to draw him to his successor's help. Virtue proved its own reward. Arriving at eleven o'clock, he found Little Sampson in great excitement, with the fountain of melody dried up on his lips.

'Thank God !' he cried. 'I thought you 'd come when you heard the news.'

'What news ?'

'Gideon the member for Whitechapel 's dead. Died suddenly, early this morning.'

'How shocking !' said Raphael, growing white.

'Yes, isn't it ?' said Little Sampson. 'If he had died yesterday, I shouldn't have minded it so much, while to-morrow would have given us a clear week. He hasn't even been ill,' he grumbled. 'I 've had to send Pinchas to the Museum in a deuce of a hurry, to find out about his early life. I 'm awfully upset about it, and what makes it worse is a wire from Goldsmith, ordering a page obituary at least with black rules, besides a leader. It's simply sickening. The proofs are awful enough as it is—my blessed editor has been writing four columns of his autobiography in his most original English, and he wants to leave out all the news pars to make room for 'em. In one way Gideon's death is a boon; even Pinchas'll see his stuff must be crowded out. It's frightful having to edit your editor. Why wasn't he made sub?'

'That would have been just as trying for you,' said Raphael with a melancholy smile. He took up a galley-proof and began to correct it. To his surprise he came upon his own paragraph about Strelitski's resignation: it caused him fresh emotion. This great spiritual crisis had quite slipped his memory, so egoistic are the best of us at times. 'Please be careful that Pinchas's autobiography does not crowd that out,' he said.

Pinchas arrived late, when Little Sampson was almost in despair. 'It is all right,' he shouted, waving a roll of manuscript. 'I have him from the cradle—the stupid stockbroker, the Man-of-the-Earth, who sent me back my poesie, and vould not let me teach his boy Judaism. And vhile I had the inspiration I wrote the leader also in the Museum—it is here—oh, vairy beaudiful! Listen to the first sentence. "The Angel of Death has passed again over Judea; he has flown off vith our visest and our best, but the black shadow of his ving vill long rest upon the House of Israel!" And the end is vordy of the beginning. "He is dead; but he lives for ever enshrined in the noble tribute to his genius in *Metatoron's Flames.*"'

Little Sampson seized the 'copy' and darted with it to the composing-room, where Raphael was busy giving directions. By his joyful face Raphael saw the crisis was over. Little Sampson handed the manuscript to the foreman, then, drawing a deep breath of relief, he began to hum a sprightly march.

'I say, you're a nice chap!' he grumbled, cutting himself short with a staccato that was not in the music.

'What have I done?' asked Raphael.

'Done? You've got me into a nice mess. The guvnor—the new guvnor; the old guvnor, it seems—called the other day to fix things with me and Pinchas. He asked me if I was satisfied to go on at the same screw. I said he might make it two pound ten. "What, more than double?" says he. "No, only nine shillings extra," says I, "and for that I'll throw in some foreign telegrams the late editor never cared for." And then it came out that he only knew of a sovereign, and fancied I was trying it on.'

'Oh, I'm so sorry,' said Raphael, in deep scarlet distress.

'You must have been paying a guinea out of your own pocket!' said Little Sampson sharply.

Raphael's confusion increased. 'I—I—didn't want it myself,' he faltered. 'You see, it was paid me just for form, and you really did the work. Which reminds me I have a cheque of yours now,' he ended boldly. 'That'll make it right for the coming month, anyhow.'

He hunted out Goldsmith's final cheque, and tendered it sheepishly.

'Oh no, I can't take it now,' said Little Sampson. He folded his arms, and drew his cloak around him like a toga. No August sun ever divested Little Sampson of his cloak.

'Has Goldsmith agreed to your terms, then?' inquired Raphael timidly.

'Oh no, not he. But——'

'Then I must go on paying the difference,' said Raphael decisively. 'I am responsible to you that you get the salary you're used to ; it's my fault that things are changed, and I must pay the penalty.' He crammed the cheque forcibly into the pocket of the toga.

'Well, if you put it in that way,' said Little Sampson, 'I won't say I couldn't do with it. But only as a loan, mind.'

'All right,' murmured Raphael.

'And you'll take it back when my comic opera goes on tour. You won't back out?'

'No.'

'Give us your hand on it,' said Little Sampson huskily. Raphael gave him his hand, and Little Sampson swung it up and down like a baton.

'Hang it all! and that man calls himself a Jew!' he thought. Aloud he said : 'When my comic opera goes on tour.'

They returned to the editorial den, where they found Pinchas raging, a telegram in his hand.

'Ah, the Man-of-the-Earth!' he cried, 'All my beautiful peroration he spoils.' He crumpled up the telegram and threw it pettishly at Little Sampson, then greeted Raphael with effusive joy and hilarity. Little Sampson read the wire. It ran as follows :

'Last sentence of Gideon Leader. It is too early yet in this moment of grief to speculate as to his successor in the constituency. But, difficult as it will be to replace him, we may find some solace in the thought that it will not be impossible. The spirit of the illustrious dead would itself rejoice to acknowledge the special qualifications of one whose name will at once rise to every lip as that of a brother Jew whose sincere piety and genuine public spirit mark him out as the one worthy substitute in the representation of a district embracing so many of our poor Jewish brethren. Is it too much to hope that he will be induced to stand?— Goldsmith.'

'That's a cut above Henry,' murmured Little Sampson, who knew nearly everything, save the facts he had to supply to the public. 'He wired to the wife, and it's hers. Well, it saves him from writing his own puffs, anyhow. I suppose Goldsmith's only the signature, not intended to be the last word on the subject. Wants touching up, though ; can't have "spirit" twice within four lines. How lucky for him Leon is just off the box-seat! That queer beggar would never have submitted to any dictation any more than the boss would have dared show his hand so openly.'

While the sub-editor mused thus, a remark dropped from the editor's lips, which turned Raphael whiter than the news of the death of Gideon had done.

'Yes, and in the middle of writing I look up and see the maiden—oh, vairy beaudiful! How she gives it to English Judaism sharp in that book—the stupid-heads, the Men-of-the-Earth! I could kiss her for it, only I have never been introduced. Gideon, he is there! Ho! ho!' he sniggered, with purely intellectual appreciation of the pungency.

'What maiden? What are you talking about?' asked Raphael, his breath coming painfully.

'Your maiden,' said Pinchas, surveying him with affectionate roguishness. 'The maiden that came to see you here. She vas reading; I valk by and see it is about America.'

'At the British Museum?' gasped Raphael. A thousand hammers beat 'Fool!' upon his brain. Why had he not thought of so likely a place for a *littérateur*?

He rushed out of the office and into a hansom. He put his pipe out in anticipation. In seven minutes he was at the gates, just in time—heaven be thanked!—to meet her abstractedly descending the steps. His heart gave a great leap of joy. He studied the pensive little countenance for an instant before it became aware of him; its sadness shot a pang of reproach through him. Then a great light, as of wonder and joy, came into the dark eyes, and glorified the pale, passionate face. But it was only a flash that faded, leaving the cheeks more pallid than before, the lips quivering.

'Mr. Leon!' she muttered.

He raised his hat, then held out a trembling hand, that closed upon hers with a grip that hurt her.

'I'm so glad to see you again!' he said, with unconcealed enthusiasm. 'I have been meaning to write to you for days—care of your publishers. I wonder if you will ever forgive me!'

'You had nothing to write to me,' she said, striving to speak coldly.

'Oh yes, I had!' he protested.

She shook her head.

'Our journalistic relations are over—there were no others.'

'Oh!' he exclaimed reproachfully, feeling his heart grow chill. 'Surely we were friends?'

She did not answer.

'I wanted to write and tell you how much,' he began desperately, then stammered, and ended—'how much I liked *Mordecai Josephs*.'

This time the reproachful 'Oh!' came from her lips. 'I thought better of you,' she said. 'You didn't say that in the *Flag of Judah*; writing it privately to me wouldn't do me any good in any case.'

He felt miserable ; from the crude standpoint of facts there was no answer to give.   He gave none.

'I suppose it is all about now?' she went on, seeing him silent.

'Pretty well,' he answered, understanding the question.   Then, with an indignant accent, he said, 'Mrs. Goldsmith tells everybody she found it out, and sent you away.'

'I am glad she says that,' she remarked enigmatically.   'And, naturally, everybody detests me?'

'Not everybody,' he began threateningly.

'Don't let us stand on the steps,' she interrupted.   'People will be looking at us.'   They moved slowly downwards, and into the hot, bustling streets.   'Why are you not at the *Flag*?   I thought this was your busy day.'   She did not add, 'And so I ventured to the Museum, knowing there was no chance of your turning up' ; but such was the fact.

'I am not the editor any longer,' he replied.

'Not?'   She almost came to a stop.   'So much for my critical faculty ; I could have sworn to your hand in every number.'

'Your critical faculty equals your creative,' he began.

'Journalism has taught you sarcasm.'

'No, no ! please do not be so unkind.   I spoke in earnestness. I have only just been dismissed.'

'Dismissed!' she echoed incredulously.   'I thought the *Flag* was your own?'

He grew troubled.   'I bought it—but for another.   We—he— has dispensed with my services.'

'Oh how shameful !'

The latent sympathy of her indignation cheered him again.

'I am not sorry,' he said.   'I'm afraid I really was outgrowing its original platform.'

'What?' she asked, with a note of mockery in her voice.   'You have left off being orthodox?'

'I don't say that.   It seems to me, rather, that I have come to understand I never was orthodox in the sense that the orthodox understand the word.   I had never come into contact with them before.   I never realised how unfair orthodox writers are to Judaism.   But I do not abate one word of what I have ever said or written, except, of course, on questions of scholarship, which are always open to revision.'

'But what is to become of me—of my conversion?' she said with mock piteousness.

'You need no conversion !' he answered passionately, abandoning without a twinge all those criteria of Judaism for which he had fought with Strelitski.   'You are a Jewess not only in blood, but in spirit.   Deny it as you may, you have all the Jewish ideals —they are implied in your attack on our society.'

She shook her head obstinately.

'You read all that into me, as you read your modern thought into the old naïve books.'

' I read what is in you. Your soul is in the right, whatever your
brains says.' He went on, almost to echo Strelitski's words,
'Selfishness is the only real atheism ; aspiration, unselfishness,
the only real religion. In the language of our Hillel, this is the
text of the Law ; the rest is commentary. You and I are at one
in believing that, despite all and after all, the world turns on
righteousness, on justice '—his voice became a whisper—' on love.'

The old thrill went through her, as when first they met. Once
again the universe seemed bathed in holy joy. But she shook off
the spell almost angrily. Her face was definitely set towards the
life of the New World. Why should he disturb her anew ? '

' Ah well, I 'm glad you allow me a little goodness,' she said
sarcastically. ' It is quite evident how you have drifted from
orthodoxy. Strange result of the *Flag of Judah* ! Started to convert me, it has ended by alienating you—its editor—from the true
faith. Oh, the irony of circumstance ! But don't look so glum.
It has fulfilled its mission all the same : it *has* converted me—I
will confess it to you.' Her face grew grave, her tones earnest.
' So I haven't an atom of sympathy with your broader attitude. I
am full of longing for the old impossible Judaism.

His face took on a look of anxious solicitude. He was uncertain
whether she spoke ironically or seriously. Only one thing was
certain—that she was slipping from him again. She seemed so
complex, paradoxical, elusive—and yet growing every moment
more dear and desirable.

' Where are you living ? ' he asked abruptly.

' It doesn't matter where,' she answered. ' I sail for America in
three weeks.'

The world seemed suddenly empty. It was hopeless, then—
she was almost in his grasp yet he could not hold her. Some
greater force was sweeping her into strange alien solitudes. A
storm of protest raged in his heart—all he had meant to say to
her rose to his lips, but he only said ' Must you go ?'

' I must. My little sister marries. I have timed my visit so
as to arrive just for the wedding—like a fairy godmother.' She
smiled wistfully.

' Then you will live with your people, I suppose ?'

' I suppose so. I dare say I shall become quite good again.
Ah, your new Judaisms will never appeal like the old, with all its
imperfections. They will never keep the race together through
shine and shade as that did. They do but stave off the inevitable
dissolution. It is beautiful—that old childlike faith in the pillar
of cloud by day and the pillar of fire by night, that patient waiting
through the centuries for the Messiah who even to you, I dare say,
is a mere symbol.' Again the wistful look lit up her eyes. ' That's
what you rich people will never understand—it doesn't seem to go
with dinners in seven courses, somehow.'

' Oh, but I do understand,' he protested. ' It 's what I told
Strelitski, who is all for intellect in religion. He is going to

America, too,' he said, with a sudden pang of jealous apprehension.

'On a holiday?'

'No ; he is going to resign his ministry here.'

'What ! Has he got a better offer in America?'

'Still so cruel to him,' he said reprovingly. 'He is resigning for conscience' sake.'

'After all these years?' she queried sarcastically.

'Miss Ansell, you wrong him ! He was not happy in his position. You were right so far. But he cannot endure his shackles any longer. And it is you who have inspired him to break them.'

'I ?' she exclaimed, startled.

'Yes, I told him why you had left Mrs. Henry Goldsmith's—it seemed to act like an electrical stimulus. Then and there he made me write a paragraph announcing his resignation. It will appear to-morrow.'

Esther's eyes filled with soft light. She walked on in silence ; then, noticing she had automatically walked too much in the direction of her place of concealment, she came to an abrupt stop.'

'We must part here,' she said. 'If I ever come across my old shepherd in America, I will be nicer to him. It is really quite heroic of him—you must have exaggerated my own petty sacrifice alarmingly if it really supplied him with inspiration. What is he going to do in America?'

'To preach a universal Judaism. He is a born idealist; his ideas have always such a magnificent sweep. Years ago he wanted all the Jews to return to Palestine.'

Esther smiled faintly, not at Strelitski, but at Raphael's calling another man an idealist. She had never yet done justice to the strain of common-sense that saved him from being a great man ; he and the new Strelitski were of one breed to her.

'He will make Jews no happier, and Christians no wiser,' she said sceptically. 'The great populations will sweep on, as affected by the Jews as this crowd by you and me. The world will not go back on itself—rather will Christianity transform itself and take the credit. We are such a handful of outsiders. Judaism—old or new—is a forlorn hope.'

'The forlorn hope will yet save the world, he answered quietly, 'but it has first to be saved to the world.'

'Be happy in your hope,' she said gently. 'Good-bye.' She held out her little hand. He had no option but to take it.'

'But we are not going to part like this,' he said desperately. 'I shall see you again before you go to America?'

'No, why should you?'

'Because I love you,' rose to his lips. But the avowal seemed too plump. He prevaricated by retorting, 'Why should I not?'

'Because I fear you,' was in her heart, but nothing rose to her lips. He looked into her eyes to read an answer there, but she dropped them. He saw his opportunity.

'Why should I not?' he repeated.

'Your time is valuable,' she said faintly.

'I could not spend it better than with you,' he answered boldly.

'Please don't insist,' she said in distress.

'But I shall; I am your friend. So far as I know, you are lonely. If you are bent upon going away, why deny me the pleasure of the society I am about to lose for ever?'

'Oh, how can you call it a pleasure—such poor melancholy company as I am!'

'Such poor melancholy company that I came expressly to seek it, for some one told me you were at the Museum. Such poor melancholy company that if I am robbed of it life will be a blank.'

He had not let go her hand; his tones were low and passionate; the heedless traffic of the sultry London street was all about them.

Esther trembled from head to foot; she could not look at him. There was no mistaking his meaning now; her breast was a whirl of delicious pain. But in proportion as the happiness at her beck and call dazzled her, so she recoiled from it. Bent on self-effacement, attuned to the peace of despair, she almost resented the solicitation to be happy; she had suffered so much that she had grown to think suffering her natural element, out of which she could not breathe; she was almost in love with misery. And in so sad a world was there not something ignoble about happiness, a selfish aloofness from the life of humanity? And, illogically blent with this questioning, and strengthening her recoil, was an obstinate conviction that there could never be happiness for her, a being of ignominious birth, without roots in life, futile, shadowy, out of relation to the tangible solidities of ordinary existence. To offer her a warm fireside seemed to be to tempt her to be false to something—she knew not what. Perhaps it was because the warm fireside was in the circle she had quitted, and her heart was yet bitter against it, finding no palliative even in the thought of a triumphant return. She did not belong to it; she was not of Raphael's world. But she felt grateful to the point of tears for his incomprehensible love for a plain, penniless, low-born girl. Surely it was only his chivalry. Other men had not found her attractive. Sidney had not; Levi only fancied himself in love. And yet beneath all her humility was a sense of being loved for the best in her, for the hidden qualities Raphael alone had the insight to divine. She could never think so meanly of herself or of humanity again. He had helped and strengthened her for her lonely future; the remembrance of him would always be an inspiration, and a reminder of the nobler side of human nature.

All this contradictory medley of thought and feeling occupied but a few seconds of consciousness. She answered him without any perceptible pause, lightly enough.

'Really, Mr. Leon, I don't expect *you* to say such things. Why should we be so conventional, you and I? How can your life be a blank, with Judaism yet to be saved?'

'Who am I to save Judaism? I want to save you,' he said passionately.

'What a descent! For heaven's sake stick to your earlier ambition!'

'No, the two are one to me. Somehow you seem to stand for Judaism, too. I cannot disentwine my hopes; I have come to conceive your life as an allegory of Judaism, the offspring of a great and tragic past with the germs of a rich blossoming, yet wasting with an inward canker. I have grown to think of its future as somehow bound up with yours. I want to see your eyes laughing, the shadows lifted from your brow; I want to see you face life courageously, not in passionate revolt nor in passionless despair, but in faith and hope and the joy that springs from them. I want you to seek peace, not in a despairing surrender of the intellect to the faith of childhood, but in that faith intellectually justified. And while I want to help you, and to fill your life with the sunshine it needs, I want you to help me, to inspire me when I falter, to complete my life, to make me happier than I had ever dreamed. Be my wife, Esther. Let me save you from yourself.'

'Let me save you from yourself, Raphael. Is it wise to wed with the gray spirit of the Ghetto that doubts itself?'

And like a spirit she glided from his grasp and disappeared in the crowd.

CHAPTER XVII

THE PRODIGAL SON

THE New Year dawned upon the Ghetto, heralded by a month of special matins and the long-sustained note of the ram's horn. It was in the midst of the Ten Days of Repentance which find their awful climax in the Day of Atonement that a strange letter for Hannah came to startle the breakfast-table at Reb Shemuel's. Hannah read it with growing pallor and perturbation.

'What is the matter, my dear?' asked the Reb anxiously.

'Oh, father,' she cried, 'read this! Bad news of Levi.'

A spasm of pain contorted the old man's furrowed countenance. 'Mention not his name!' he said harshly. 'He is dead.'

'He may be by now!' Hannah exclaimed agitatedly. 'You were right, Esther. He did join a strolling company, and now he is laid up with typhoid in the hospital in Stockbridge. One of his friends writes to tell us. He must have caught it in one of those insanitary dressing-rooms we were reading about.'

Esther trembled all over. The scene in the garret when the fatal telegram came announcing Benjamin's illness had never faded from her mind. She had an instant conviction that it was all over with poor Levi.

'My poor lamb!' cried the Rebbitzin, the coffee cup dropping from her nerveless hand.

'Simcha,' said Reb Shemuel sternly, 'calm thyself; we have no son to lose. The Holy One—blessed be He!—hath taken him from us. The Lord giveth, and the Lord taketh. Blessed be the name of the Lord.'

Hannah rose. Her face was white and resolute. She moved towards the door.

'Whither goest thou?' inquired her father in German.

'I am going to my room, to put on my hat and jacket,' replied Hannah quietly.

'Whither goest thou?' repeated Reb Shemuel.

'To Stockbridge. Mother, you and I must go at once.'

The Reb sprang to his feet. His brow was dark; his eyes gleamed with anger and pain.

'Sit down and finish thy breakfast,' he said.

'How can I eat? Levi is dying,' said Hannah, in low, firm tones. 'Will you come, mother, or must I go alone?'

The Rebbitzin began to wring her hands and weep. Esther stole gently to Hannah's side and pressed the poor girl's hand. 'You and I will go,' her clasp said.

'Hannah!' said Reb Shemuel. 'What madness is this? Dost thou think thy mother will obey thee rather than her husband?'

'Levi is dying. It is our duty to go to him.' Hannah's gentle face was rigid. But there was exultation rather than defiance in the eyes.

'It is not the duty of women,' said Reb Shemuel harshly. 'I will go to Stockbridge. If he dies (God have mercy upon his soul!), I will see that he is buried among his own people. Thou knowest women go not to funerals.' He reseated himself at the table, pushing aside his scarcely touched meal, and began saying the grace. Dominated by his will and by old habit, the three trembling women remained in reverential silence.

'The Lord will give strength to His people; the Lord will bless His people with peace,' concluded the old man in unfaltering accents. He rose from the table and strode to the door, stern and erect. 'Thou wilt remain here, Hannah, and thou, Simcha,' he said. In the passage his shoulders relaxed their stiffness, so that the long snow-white beard drooped upon his breast. The three women looked at one another.

'Mother,' said Hannah, passionately breaking the silence, 'are you going to stay here while Levi is dying in a strange town!'

'My husband wills it,' said the Rebbitzin, sobbing. 'Levi is a sinner in Israel. Thy father will not see him; he will not go to him till he is dead.'

'Oh yes, surely he will,' said Esther. 'But be comforted. Levi is young and strong. Let us hope he will pull through.'

'No, no,' moaned the Rebbitzin. 'He will die, and my husband will but read the psalms at his death-bed. He will not forgive him ; he will not speak to him of his mother and sister.'

'Let *me* go. I will give him your messages,' said Esther.

'No, no,' interrupted Hannah. 'What are you to him? Why should you risk infection for our sakes?'

'Go, Hannah, but secretly,' said the Rebbitzin in a wailing whisper. 'Let not thy father see thee till thou arrive ; then he will not send thee back. Tell Levi that I—oh, my poor child, my poor lamb !' Sobs overpowered her speech.

'No, mother,' said Hannah quietly, 'thou and I shall go. I will tell father we are accompanying him.'

She left the room, while the Rebbitzin fell weeping and terrified into a chair, and Esther vainly endeavoured to soothe her. The Reb was changing his coat when Hannah knocked at the door, and called 'Father.'

'Speak not to me, Hannah,' answered the Reb roughly. 'It is useless.' Then, as if repentant of his tone, he threw open the door, and passed his great trembling hand lovingly over her hair. 'Thou art a good daughter,' he said tenderly. 'Forget that thou hast had a brother.'

'But how can I forget?' she answered him in his own idiom. 'Why should I forget? What hath he done?'

He ceased to smooth her hair—his voice grew sad and stern.

'He hath profaned the Name. He hath lived like a heathen ; he dieth like a heathen now. His blasphemy was a byword in the congregation. I alone knew it not till last Passover. He hath brought down my gray hairs in sorrow to the grave.'

'Yes, father, I know,' said Hannah, more gently. 'But he is not all to blame !'

'Thou meanest that I am not guiltless ; that I should have kept him at my side?' said the Reb, his voice faltering a little.

'No, father, not that! Levi could not always be a baby. He had to walk alone some day.'

'Yes, and did I not teach him to walk alone?' asked the Reb eagerly. 'My God, thou canst not say I did not teach him Thy Law, day and night.' He uplifted his eyes in anguished appeal.

'Yes, but he is not all to blame,' she repeated. 'Thy teaching did not reach his soul ; he is of another generation, the air is different, his life was cast amid conditions for which the Law doth not allow.'

'Hannah !' Reb Shemuel's accents became harsh and chiding again. 'What sayest thou? The Law of Moses is eternal ; it will never be changed. Levi knew God's commandments, but he followed the desire of his own heart and his own eyes. If God's Word were obeyed, he should have been stoned with stones. But Heaven itself hath punished him ; he will die, for it is ordained that whosoever is stubborn and disobedient, that soul shall surely be cut off from among his people. "Keep My commandments, that thy days may be long in the land," God Himself hath said it. Is it not written : "Rejoice, O young man, in thy youth, and let thy heart cheer thee in the days of thy youth, and walk in the ways of thine heart and in the sight of thine eyes ; but know thou that for all these things the Lord will bring thee into judgment"? But thou, my Hannah,' he started caressing her hair again, ' art a good Jewish maiden. Between Levi and thee there is naught in common. His touch would profane thee. Sadden not thy innocent eyes with the sight of his end. Think of him as one who died in boyhood. My God ! why didst thou not take him then?' He turned away, stifling a sob.

'Father,' she put her hand on his shoulder, ' we will go with thee to Stockbridge—I and the mother.'

He faced her again, stern and rigid.

'Cease thy entreaties. I will go alone.'

'No, we will all go.'

'Hannah,' he said, his voice tremulous with pain and astonishment, ' dost thou, too, set light by thy father?'

'Yes,' she cried, and there was no answering tremor in her voice. 'Now thou knowest ! I am not a good Jewish maiden. Levi and I are brother and sister. His touch profane me forsooth !' She laughed bitterly.

'Thou wilt take this journey though I forbid thee?' he cried in acrid accents, still mingled with surprise.

'Yes ; would I had taken the journey thou wouldst have forbidden ten years ago !'

'What journey? thou talkest madness.'

'I talk truth. Thou hast forgotten David Brandon ; I have not. Ten years last Passover I arranged to fly with him, to marry him, in defiance of the Law and thee.'

A new pallor overspread the Reb's countenance, already ashen. He trembled and almost fell backwards.

'But thou didst not?' he whispered hoarsely.

'I did not, I know not why,' she said sullenly ; ' else thou wouldst never have seen me again. It may be I respected thy religion, although thou didst not dream what was in my mind. But thy religion shall not keep me from this journey.'

The Reb had hidden his face in his hands. His lips were moving : was it in grateful prayer, in self-reproach, or merely in nervous trembling? Hannah never knew. Presently the Reb's arms dropped, great tears rolled down towards the white beard. When he spoke, his tones were hushed as with awe.

'This man—tell me, my daughter, thou lovest him still ?'

She shrugged her shoulders with a gesture of reckless despair.

'What does it matter? My life is but a shadow.'

The Reb took her to his breast, though she remained stony to his touch, and laid his wet face against her burning cheeks.

'My child, my poor Hannah! I thought God had sent thee peace ten years ago, that He had rewarded thee for thy obedience to His Law.'

She drew her face away from his.

'It was not His Law; it was a miserable juggling with texts. Thou alone interpretedst God's Law thus. No one knew of the matter.'

He could not argue; the breast against which he held her was shaken by a tempest of grief, which swept away all save human remorse, human love.

'My daughter,' he sobbed, 'I have ruined thy life!' After an agonised pause he said: 'Tell me, Hannah, is there nothing I can do to make atonement to thee?'

'Only one thing, father,' she articulated chokingly; 'forgive Levi.'

There was a moment of solemn silence. Then the Reb spake.

'Tell thy mother to put on her things and take what she needs for the journey. Perchance we may be away for days.'

They mingled their tears in sweet reconciliation. Presently the Reb said:

'Go now to thy mother, and see also that the boy's room be made ready as of old. Perchance God will hear my prayer, and he will yet be restored to us.'

A new peace fell upon Hannah's soul. 'My sacrifice was not in vain after all,' she thought with a throb of happiness that was almost exultation.

But Levi never came back. The news of his death arrived on the eve of *Yom Kippur*, the Day of Atonement, in a letter to Esther who had been left in charge of the house.

'He died quietly at the end,' Hannah wrote, 'happy in the consciousness of father's forgiveness, and leaning trustfully upon his interposition with Heaven; but he had delirious moments, during which he raved painfully. The poor boy was in great fear of death, moaning prayers that he might be spared till after *Yom Kippur* when he would be cleansed of sin, and babbling about serpents that would twine themselves round his arm and brow, like the phylacteries he had not worn. He made father repeat his "Verse" to him over and over again, so that he might remember his name when the angel of the grave asked it; and borrowed father's phylacteries, the headpiece of which was much too large for him with his shaven crown. When he had them on, and the *Talith* round him, he grew easier, and began murmuring the death-bed prayers with father. One of them runs: "O may my death be an atonement for all the sins, iniquities and transgressions of which I have been guilty against Thee!" I trust it may be so indeed. It seems so hard for a young man full of life and high spirits to be cut down, while the wretched are left alive. Your name was often on his lips. I was glad to learn he thought so much of you. "Be sure to give Esther my love," he said almost with his last breath, "and

ask her to forgive me." I know not if you have anything to forgive, or whether this was delirium. He looks quite calm now—
but oh! so worn. They have closed the eyes. The beard he
shocked father so by shaving off, has sprouted scrubbily during
his illness. On the dead face it seems a mockery, like the *Talith*
and phylacteries that have not been removed.'

A phrase of Leonard James vibrated in Esther's ears : ' If the
chappies could see me !'

CHAPTER XVIII

HOPES AND DREAMS

THE morning of the Great White Fast broke bleak and gray.
Esther, alone in the house save for the servant, wandered from
room to room in dull misery. The day before had been almost a
feast-day in the Ghetto—everybody providing for the morrow.
Esther had scarcely eaten anything. Nevertheless she was fasting, and would fast for over twenty-four hours, till the night fell.
She knew not why. Her record was unbroken, and instinct
resented a breach now. She had always fasted—even the
Henry Goldsmiths fasted, and greater than the Henry Goldsmiths !
Q.C.'s fasted, and peers, and prize-fighters, and actors. And yet
Esther, like many far more pious persons, did not think of her sins
for a moment. She thought of everything but them—of the bereaved family in that strange provincial town ; of her own family
in that strange distant land. Well, she would soon be with them
now. Her passage was booked—a steerage passage it was, not
because she could not afford cabin fare, but from her morbid impulse to identify herself with poverty. The same impulse led her
to choose a vessel in which a party of Jewish pauper immigrants
was being shipped farther West. She thought also of Dutch
Debby, with whom she had spent the previous evening ; and of
Raphael Leon, who had sent her, *via* the publishers, a letter
which she could not trust herself to answer cruelly, and which she
deemed it most prudent to leave unanswered. Uncertain of her
powers of resistance, she scarcely ventured outside the house for
fear of his stumbling across her. Happily every day diminished
the chance of her whereabouts leaking out through some unsuspected channel.

About noon her restlessness carried her into the streets. There
was a festal solemnity about the air. Women and children, not
at synagogue, showed themselves at the doors, pranked in their
best. Indifferently pious young men sought relief from the ennui
of the day-long service in lounging about for a breath of fresh air ;
some even strolled towards the Strand, and turned into the
National Gallery, satisfied to reappear for the twilight service.

On all sides came the fervent roar of prayer which indicated a synagogue or a *Chevrah*, the number of places of worship having been indefinitely increased to accommodate those who made their appearance for this occasion only.

Everywhere friends and neighbours were asking one another how they were bearing the fast, exhibiting their white tongues and generally comparing symptoms, the physical aspects of the Day of Atonement more or less completely diverting attention from the spiritual. Smelling-salts passed from hand to hand, and men explained to one another that, but for the deprivation of their cigars, they could endure *Yom Kippur* with complacency.

Esther passed the Ghetto school, within which free services were going on even in the playground, poor Russians and Poles, fanatically observant, foregathering with lax fishmongers and welshers ; and without which hulking young men hovered uneasily, feeling too out of tune with religion to go in, too conscious of the terrors of the day to stay entirely away. From the interior came from sunrise to nightfall a throbbing thunder of supplication, now pealing in passionate outcry, now subsiding to a low rumble. The sounds of prayer that pervaded the Ghetto, and burst upon her at every turn, wrought upon Esther strangely ; all her soul went out in sympathy with these yearning outbursts ; she stopped every now and then to listen, as in those far-off days when the Sons of the Covenant drew her with their melancholy cadences.

At last, moved by an irresistible instinct, she crossed the threshold of a large *Chevrah* she had known in her girlhood, mounted the stairs and entered the female compartment without hostile challenge. The reek of many breaths and candles nearly drove her back, but she pressed forwards towards a remembered window, through a crowd of bewigged women, shaking their bodies fervently to and fro.

This room had no connection with the men's ; it was simply the room above part of theirs, and the declamation of the unseen cantor came but faintly through the flooring, though the clamour of the general masculine chorus kept the pious *au courant* with their husbands. When weather or the whims of the more important ladies permitted, the window at the end was opened ; it gave upon a little balcony, below which the men's chamber projected considerably, having been built out into the back-yard. When this window was opened simultaneously with the skylight in the men's synagogue, the fervid roulades of the cantor were as audible to the women as to their masters.

Esther had always affected the balcony ; there the air was comparatively fresh, and on fine days there was a glimpse of blue sky, and a perspective of sunny red tiles, where brown birds fluttered and cats lounged and little episodes arose to temper the tedium of endless invocation ; and farther off there was a back view of a nunnery, with visions of placid black-hooded faces at windows ; and from the distance came a pleasant drone of monosyllabic

spelling from fresh young voices to relieve the ear from the monotony of long stretches of meaningless mumbling.

Here, lost in a sweet melancholy, Esther dreamed away the long
gray day, only vaguely conscious of the stages of the service—
morning dovetailing into afternoon service, and afternoon into
evening ; of the heavy-jowled woman behind her reciting a Jargon-
version of the Atonement liturgy to a devout coterie ; of the pro-
strations full-length on the floor, and the series of impassioned
sermons ; of the interminably rhyming poems, and the acrostics
with their recurring burdens shouted in devotional frenzy, voice
rising above voice as in emulation, with special staccato phrases
flung heavenwards ; of the wailing confessions of communal sin,
with their accompaniment of sobs and tears and howls and grimaces
and clenchings of palms and beatings of the breast. She was lapped
in a great ocean of sound that broke upon her consciousness like
the waves upon a beach, now with a cooing murmur, now with a
majestic crash, followed by a long receding moan. She lost herself
in the roar, in its barren sensuousness, while the leaden sky grew
duskier and the twilight crept on, and the awful hour drew
nigh when God would seal what He had written, and the annual
scrolls of destiny would be closed, immutable. She saw them loom-
ing mystically through the skylight, the swaying forms below, in
their white grave-clothes, oscillating weirdly backwards and forwards, bowed as by a mighty wind.

Suddenly there fell a vast silence ; even from without no sound
came to break the awful stillness. It was as if all creation paused
to hear a pregnant word.

' " Hear, O Israel, the Lord our God, the Lord is One ! " ' sang
the cantor frenziedly.

And all the ghostly congregation answered with a great cry,
closing their eyes and rocking frantically to and fro :

' " Hear, O Israel, the Lord our God, the Lord is One ! " '

They seemed like a great army of the sheeted dead risen to
testify to the Unity. The magnetic tremor that ran through the
synagogue thrilled the lonely girl to the core ; once again her dead
self woke, her dead ancestors that would not be shaken off lived
and moved in her. She was sucked up into the great wave of passionate faith, and from her lips came in rapturous surrender to an
overmastering impulse the half-hysterical protestation :

' " Hear, O Israel, the Lord our God, the Lord is one ! " '

And then in the brief instant while the congregation, with ever-
ascending rhapsody, blessed God till the climax came with the
sevenfold declaration, ' The Lord, He is God,' the whole history of
her strange, unhappy race flashed through her mind in a whirl of
resistless emotion. She was overwhelmed by the thought of its
sons in every corner of the earth proclaiming to the sombre twilight sky the belief for which its generations had lived and died—
the Jews of Russia sobbing it forth in their pale of enclosure, the
Jews of Morocco in their *mellah*, and of South Africa in their

tents by the diamond mines ; the Jews of the New World in great
free cities, in Canadian backwoods, in South American savannahs;
the Australian Jews on the sheep-farms and the gold-fields and in
the mushroom cities ; the Jews of Asia in their reeking quarters
begirt by barbarian populations. The shadow of a large mysterious destiny seemed to hang over these poor superstitious zealots,
whose lives she knew so well in all their everyday prose, and to
invest the unconscious shuffling sons of the Ghetto with something
of tragic grandeur. The gray dusk palpitated with floating shapes
of prophets and martyrs, scholars and sages and poets, full of a
yearning love and pity, lifting hands of benediction. By what
great highroads and queer byways of history had they travelled
hither, these wandering Jews, 'sated with contempt,' these shrewd
eager fanatics, these sensual ascetics, these human paradoxes,
adaptive to every environment, energising in every field of
activity, omnipresent like some great natural force, indestructible
and almost inconvertible, surviving—with the incurable optimism
that overlay all their poetic sadness—Babylon and Carthage,
Greece and Rome ; involuntarily financing the Crusades, outliv-
ing the Inquisition, illusive of all baits, unshaken by all persecu-
tions—at once the greatest and meanest of races ? Had the Jew
come so far only to break down at last, sinking in morasses of
modern doubt, and irresistibly dragging down with him the Christian
and the Moslem ; or was he yet fated to outlast them both, in
continuous testimony to a hand moulding incomprehensibly the
the life of humanity ? Would Israel develop into the sacred
phalanx, the nobler brotherhood that Raphael Leon had dreamed
of, or would the race that had first proclaimed—through Moses
for the ancient world, through Spinoza for the modern—

'One God, one Law, one Element,'

become, in the larger, wilder dream of the Russian idealist, the
main factor in

' One far-off divine event
To which the whole Creation moves ? '

The roar dwindled to a solemn silence, as though in answer to her
questionings. Then the ram's horn shrilled—a stern long-drawn-
out note, that rose at last into a mighty peal of sacred jubilation.
The Atonement was complete.

The crowd bore Esther downstairs and into the blank indifferent
street. But the long exhausting fast, the fetid atmosphere, the
strain upon her emotions, had overtaxed her beyond endurance.
Up to now the frenzy of the service had sustained her, but as she
stepped across the threshold on to the pavement she staggered and
fell. One of the men pouring out from the lower synagogue caught
her in his arms. It was Strelitski.

*   *   *   *   *   *

A group of three stood on the saloon deck of an outward-bound
steamer. Raphael Leon was bidding farewell to the man he

reverenced without discipleship, and the woman he loved without blindness.

'Look !' he said, pointing compassionately to the wretched throng of Jewish emigrants huddling on the lower deck and scattered about the gangway amid jostling sailors and stevedores and bales and coils of rope ; the men in peaked or fur caps, the women with shawls and babies, some gazing upwards with lacklustre eyes, the majority brooding, despondent, apathetic. 'How could either of you have borne the sights and smells of the steerage ? You are a pair of visionaries. You could not have breathed a day in that society. Look !'

Strelitski looked at Esther instead ; perhaps he was thinking he could have breathed anywhere in her society—nay, breathed even more freely in the steerage than in the cabin if he had sailed away without telling Raphael that he had found her.

'You forget a common impulse took us into such society on the Day of Atonement,' he answered after a moment. 'You forget we are both Children of the Ghetto.'

'I can never forget that,' said Raphael fervently, 'else Esther would at this moment be lost amid the human flotsam and jetsam below, sailing away without you to protect her, without me to look forward to her return, without Addie's bouquet to assure her of a sister's love.'

He took Esther's little hand once more. It lingered confidingly in his own. There was no ring of betrothal upon it, nor would be, till Rachel Ansell in America, and Addie Leon in England, should have passed under the wedding canopy, and Raphael, whose breast-pocket was bulging with a new meerschaum too sacred to smoke, should startle the West End with his eccentric choice, and confirm its impression of his insanity. The trio had said and resaid all they had to tell one another, all the reminders and the recommendations. They stood without speaking now, wrapt in that loving silence which is sweeter than speech.

The sun, which had been shining intermittently, flooded the serried shipping with a burst of golden light, that coaxed the turbid waves to brightness, and cheered the wan emigrants, and made little children leap joyously in their mother's arms. The knell of parting sounded insistent.

'Your allegory seems turning in your favour, Raphael,' said Esther, with a sudden memory.

The pensive smile that made her face beautiful lit up the dark eyes.

'What allegory is that of Raphael's ?' said Strelitski, reflecting her smile on his graver visage. 'The long one in his prize poem ?'

'No,' said Raphael, catching the contagious smile. 'It is our little secret.'

Strelitski turned suddenly to look at the emigrants. The smile faded from his quivering mouth.

The last moment had come. Raphael stooped down towards

the gentle softly-flashing face, which was raised unhesitatingly to meet his, and their lips met in a first kiss, diviner than it is given most mortals to know—a kiss, sad and sweet, troth and parting in one : *Ave et vale*,—'hail and farewell.'

'Good-bye, Strelitski,' said Raphael huskily. 'Success to your dreams.'

The idealist turned round with a start. His face was bright and resolute ; the black curl streamed buoyantly on the breeze.

'Good-bye,' he responded, with a giant's grip of the hand. 'Success to your hopes.'

Raphael darted away with his long stride. The sun was still bright, but for a moment everything seemed chill and dim to Esther Ansell's vision. With a sudden fit of nervous foreboding she stretched out her arms towards the vanishing figure of her lover. But she saw him once again in the tender, waving his handkerchief towards the throbbing vessel that glided with its freight of hopes and dreams across the great waters towards the New World.

GLOSSARY

Achi-Nebbich (*Etymology obscure*), Alas, poor thing (s.).

Afikoman (*Hebraicised Gk.*), portion of a Passover cake taken at the end of Seder-meal (*q.v.*).

Amidah (*H.*), series of Benedictions said standing.

Arbah Kanfus (*H.*), lit. four corners ; a garment consisting of two shoulder-straps supporting a front and back piece with fringes at each corner (Numbers xv. 37-41).

Avirah (*H.*), Sin.

Ashkenazim (*H.*), German, hence also Russian and Polish Jews.

Badchan (*H.*), professional jester.

Bensh (?), say grace.

Beth Din (*H.*), Court of Judgment.

Beth Medrash (*H.*), College.

Bube (*G.*), grandmother.

Cabbalah (*H.*)., **Cabbulah** (*c.*), lit. tradition; mystic lore.

Calloh (*H.*), bride, *fiancée*.

Chazan (*H.*), cantor.

Chevrah (*H.*), small congregation ; a society.

Chine (*H.*), playful humour ; humorous anecdote.

Chocham (*H.*), wise man.

Chomutz (*H.*), leaven.

Chosan (*H.*), bridegroom, *fiancé*.

Chuppah (*H.*), wedding canopy.

Cohen (*H.*), priest.

Dayan (*H.*), Rabbi who renders decisions.

Din (*H.*), law, decision.

Droshes (*H.*) sermons.

Epikouros (*H. from Gk.*), heretic, scoffer ; Epicurean.

Froom (*c. G.*), pious.

Gelt (*c. G.*), money.

Gematriyah (*Hebraicised Gk.*), mystic, numerical interpretation of Scripture.

Gemorah (*H.*), part of the Talmud.

Gonof (*H.*), thief.

Goyah (*H.*), non-Jewess.

Hagadah (*H.*), narrative portion of the Talmud ; Passover-eve ritual.

Halachah (*H.*), legal portion of the Talmud.

Havdalah (*H.*), ceremony separating conclusion of Sabbath or Festival from the subsequent days of toil.

Imbeshreer (*c. G. ohne beschreien*), without bewitching ; unbeshrewn.

Kaddish (*H.*), prayer in praise of God ; specially recited by male mourners.

Kehillah (*H.*), congregation.

Kind, Kinder (*G.*), child, children.

Kosher (*H.*), ritually clean.

Kotzon (*H.*), rich man.

Link (*G.*), lit. left, *i.e.* not right ; hence lax, not pious.

Longe Verachum (*G. and c. H.*), lit. The long 'and He being merciful.' A long extra prayer, said on Mondays and Thursdays.

Lulov (*H.*), palm-branch dressed with myrtle and willow, and used at the Feast of Tabernacles.

Maaseh (*H.*), story, tale.

Machzor (*H.*), Festival prayer-book.

Maggid (*H.*), preacher.

Mazzoltov (*H.*), Good luck, congratulations.

Megillah (*H.*), lit. scroll. The Book of Esther.

Meshuggah, Meshuggene (*H.*), mad.

Meshumad (*H.*), apostate.

Metsiah (*H.*), lit. finding, cp. Fr. *trouvaille* ; bargain.

Mezuzah (*H.*), case containing a scroll, with Heb. verses (Deut. vi. 4-9, 13-21) affixed to every door-post.

Midrash (*H.*), Biblical exposition.

Minchah (*H.*), afternoon prayer.

Minyan (*H.*) quorum of ten males over thirteen necessary for public worship.

Mishpochah (*H.*), family.

Mishnah, Mishnayis (*H.*), collection of the Oral Law.

Missheberach (*H.*), synagogual benediction.

Mitzvah (*H.*), a commandment, *i.e.* a good deed.

Mizrach (*H.*), East ; a sacred picture hung on the east wall in the direction of Jerusalem, to which the face is turned in praying.

Narrischkeit (*c. G.*), foolishness.

Nash (*c. G.*), pilfer (dainties).

Niddah (*H.*), Talmudical tractate on the purification of women.

Nu (*R.*), Well?

Olov Hasholom (*H.*), Peace be upon him ! (loosely applied to deceased females also).

Omer (*H.*), the seven weeks between Passover and Pentecost.

Parnass (*H.*), President of the Congregation.

Pesachdik (*H.*), proper for Passover.

Pidyun Haben (*H.*), redemption of the first-born son.

Piyut (*Hebraicised Gk.*), liturgical poem.

Potch (*c. G.*), slap.

Pullack (*c. G.*), Polish Jew.

Rashi (*H.*), Rabbi Solomon ben Isaac, whose Commentary is often printed under the Hebrew text of the Bible.

Schlemihl (*H.*), unlucky, awkward person.

Schmuck (*c. G.*), lubberly person.

Schmull (*c. G. schmollen*), pout, sulk.

Schnecks (? *G. Schnake*, gay nonsense), affectations.

Schnorrer (*c. G.*), beggar.

Seder (*H.*), Passover-eve ceremony.

Selaim (*H.*), old Jewish coins.

Sephardim (*H.*), Spanish and Portuguese Jews.

Shaaloth u-Teshuvoth (*H.*), questions and answers ; casuistical treatise.

Shabbas (*H.*), Sabbath.

Shadchan (*H.*), professional match-maker.

Shaitel (*c. G.*), wig worn by married women.

Shammos (*c. H.*), beadle.

Shass (*H. abbreviation*), the six sections of the Talmud.

Shechitah (*H.*), slaughter.

Shemah beni (*H.*), Hear, my son ! = Dear me

Shemang (*H.*), Confession of the Unity of God.

Shidduch (*H.*), match.

Shiksah (*H.*), non-Jewish girl,

Shnodar (*H.*), offer money to the synagogue. (An extraordinary instance of Jewish jargon—a compound Hebrew word meaning ' who vows ' — being turned into an English verb and conjugated accordingly in -*ed* and *ing*).

Shochet (*H.*), official slaughterer.

Shofar (*H.*), trumpet of ram's horn, blown during the Penitential season.

Shool (*c. G.*), synagogue.

Shulchan Aruch (*H.*), a sixteenth-century compilation, codifying Jewish law.

Simchath Torah (*H.*), festival of the rejoicing of the Law.

Snoga (*Sp.*), Sephardic synagogue.

Spiel (*G.*), play.

Takif (*H.*), rich man ; swell.

Talith (*H.*), a shawl with fringes, worn by men during prayer.

Tanaim (*H.*), betrothal contract or ceremony.

Térah, Torah (*H.*), Law of Moses.

Tephillin (*H.*), phylacteries.

Tripha (*H.*), ritually unclean.

Wurst (*G.*), sausage.

Yiddish, Yiddishkeit (*c. G.*), Jewish, Judaism.

Yigdal (*H.*), hymn summarising the thirteen creeds drawn up by Maimonides.

Yom Kippur (*H.*), Day of Atonement.

Yom Tov (*H.*), lit. good day ; Festival.

Yontovdik (*hybrid H.*), pertaining to the Festival.

Yosher-Kowach (*c. H.*), May your strength increase ! = Thank you ; a formula to express gratitude—especially at the end of a reading.